I0785114

Clarence Mulford

The Bar-20 Trilogy
(Complete Wild West Series)

OK Publishing 2021

Clarence Mulford

The Bar-20 Trilogy

(Complete Wild West Series)

Wild Adventures of Cassidy and His Gang of Friends: Bar-20, Bar-20 Days & The Bar-20 Three

Published by

MUSAICUM

Books

- Advanced Digital Solutions & High-Quality book Formatting -

musaicumbooks@okpublishing.info

2021 OK Publishing

ISBN 978-80-272-7637-0

Contents

Bar-20

Chapter I
Buckskin

The town lay sprawled over half a square mile of alkali plain, its main Street depressing in its width, for those who were responsible for its inception had worked with a generosity born of the knowledge that they had at their immediate and unchallenged disposal the broad lands of Texas and New Mexico on which to assemble a grand total of twenty buildings, four of which were of wood. As this material was scarce, and had to be brought from where the waters of the Gulf lapped against the flat coast, the last-mentioned buildings were a matter of local pride, as indicating the progressiveness of their owners.

These creations of hammer and saw were of one story, crude and unpainted; their cheap weather sheathing, warped and shrunken by the pitiless sun, curled back on itself and allowed unrestricted entrance to alkali dust and air. The other shacks were of adobe, and reposed in that magnificent squalor dear to their owners, Indians and Mexicans.

It was an incident of the Cattle Trail, that most unique and stupendous of all modern migrations, and its founders must have been inspired with a malicious desire to perpetrate a crime against geography, or else they reveled in a perverse cussedness, for within a mile on every side lay broad prairies, and two miles to the east flowed the indolent waters of the Rio Pecos itself. The distance separating the town from the river was excusable, for at certain seasons of the year the placid stream swelled mightily and swept down in a broad expanse of turbulent, yellow flood.

Buckskin was a town of one hundred inhabitants, located in the valley of the Rio Pecos fifty miles south of the Texas-New Mexico line. The census claimed two hundred, but it was a well-known fact that it was exaggerated. One instance of this is shown by the name of Tom Flynn. Those who once knew Tom Flynn, alias Johnny Redmond, alias Bill Sweeney, alias Chuck Mullen, by all four names, could find them in the census list. Furthermore, he had been shot and killed in the March of the year preceding the census, and now occupied a grave in the young but flourishing cemetery. Perry's Bend, twenty miles up the river, was cognizant of this and other facts, and, laughing in open derision at the padded list, claimed to be the better town in all ways, including marksmanship.

One year before this tale opens, Buck Peters, an example for the more recent Billy the Kid, had paid Perry's Bend a short but busy visit. He had ridden in at the north end of Main Street and out at the south. As he came in he was fired at by a group of ugly cowboys from a ranch known as the C 80. He was hit twice, but he unlimbered his artillery, and before his horse had carried him, half dead, out on the prairie, he had killed one of the group. Several citizens had joined the cowboys and added their bullets against Buck. The deceased had been the best bartender in the country, and the rage of the suffering citizens can well be imagined. They swore vengeance on Buck, his ranch, and his stamping ground.

The difference between Buck and Billy the Kid is that the former never shot a man who was not trying to shoot him, or who had not been warned by some action against Buck that would call for it. He minded his own business, never picked a quarrel, and was quiet and pacific up to a certain point. After that had been passed he became like a raging cyclone in a tenement house, and storm-cellars were much in demand.

"Fanning" is the name of a certain style of gun play not unknown among the bad men of the West. While Buck was not a bad man, he had to rub elbows with them frequently, and he believed that the sauce for the goose was the sauce for the gander. So be bad removed the trigger of his revolver and worked the hammer with the thumb of the "gun hand" or the heel of the unencumbered hand. The speed thus acquired was greater than that of the more modern double-action weapon. Six shots in a few seconds was his average speed when that number was required, and when it is thoroughly understood that at least some of them found their intended bullets it is not difficult to realize that fanning was an operation of danger when Buck was doing it.

He was a good rider, as all cowboys are, and was not afraid of anything that lived. At one time he and his chums, Red Connors and Hopalong Cassidy, had successfully routed a band of fifteen Apaches who wanted their scalps. Of these, twelve never hunted scalps again, nor anything else on this earth, and the other three returned to their tribe with the report that three evil Spirits had chased them with "wheel guns" (cannons).

So now, since his visit to Perry's Bend, the rivalry of the two towns had turned to hatred and an alert and eager readiness to increase the inhabitants of each other's graveyard. A state of war existed, which for a time resulted in nothing worse than acrimonious suggestions. But the time came when the score was settled to the satisfaction of one side, at least.

Four ranches were also concerned in the trouble. Buckskin was surrounded by two, the Bar 20 and the Three Triangle. Perry's Bend was the common point for the C 80 and the Double Arrow. Each of the two ranch contingents accepted the feud as a matter of course, and as a matter of course took sides with their respective towns. As no better class of fighters ever lived, the trouble assumed Homeric proportions and insured a danger zone well worth watching.

Bar-20's northern line was C 80's southern one, and Skinny Thompson took his turn at outriding one morning after the season's round-up. He was to follow the boundary and turn back stray cattle. When he had covered the greater part of his journey he saw Shorty Jones riding toward him on a course parallel to his own and about long revolver range away. Shorty and he had "crossed trails" the year before and the best of feelings did not exist between them.

Shorty stopped and stared at Skinny, who did likewise at Shorty. Shorty turned his mount around and applied the spurs, thereby causing his indignant horse to raise both heels at Skinny. The latter took it all in gravely and, as Shorty faced him again, placed his left thumb to his nose, wiggling his fingers suggestively. Shorty took no apparent notice of this but began to shout:

"Yu wants to keep yore busted-down cows on yore own side. They was all over us day afore yisterday. I'm goin' to salt any more what comes over, and don't yu fergit it, neither."

Thompson wigwagged with his fingers again and shouted in reply: "Yu c'n salt all yu wants to, but if I ketch yu adoin' it yu won't have to work no more. An' I kin say right here thet they's more C 80 cows over here than they's Bar-20's over there."

Shorty reached for his revolver and yelled, "Yore a liar!"

Among the cowboys in particular and the Westerners in general at that time, the three suicidal terms, unless one was an expert in drawing quick and shooting straight with one movement, were the words "liar," "coward," and "thief." Any man who was called one of these in earnest, and he was the judge, was expected to shoot if he could and save his life, for the words were seldom used without a gun coming with them. The movement of Shorty's hand toward his belt before the appellation reached him was enough for Skinny, who let go at long range-and missed.

The two reports were as one. Both urged their horses nearer and fired again. This time Skinny's sombrero gave a sharp jerk and a hole appeared in the crown. The third shot of Skinny's sent the horse of the other to its knees and then over on its side. Shorty very promptly crawled behind it and, as he did so, Skinny began a wide circle, firing at intervals as Shorty's smoke cleared away.

Shorty had the best position for defense, as he was in a shallow coule, but he knew that he could not leave it until his opponent had either grown tired of the affair or had used up his ammunition. Skinny knew it, too. Skinny also knew that he could get back to the ranch house and lay in a supply of food and ammunition and return before Shorty could cover the twelve miles he had to go on foot.

Finally Thompson began to head for home. He had carried the matter as far as he could without it being murder. Too much time had elapsed now, and, besides, it was before breakfast and he was hungry. He would go away and settle the score at some time when they would be on equal terms.

He rode along the line for a mile and chanced to look back. Two C 80 punchers were riding after him, and as they saw him turn and discover them they fired at him and yelled. He rode on for some distance and cautiously drew his rifle out of its long holster at his right leg. Suddenly he turned around in the saddle and fired twice. One of his pursuers fell forward on the neck of his horse, and his comrade turned to help him. Thompson wig-wagged again and rode on, reaching the ranch as the others were finishing their breakfast.

At the table Red Connors remarked that the tardy one had a hole in his sombrero, and asked its owner how and where he had received it.

"Had a argument with C 80 out'n th' line."

"Go 'way! Ventilate enny?"

"One."

"Good boy, sonny! Hey, Hopalong, Skinny perforated C 80 this mawnin'!"

Hopalong Cassidy was struggling with a mouthful of beef. He turned his eyes toward Red without ceasing, and grinning as well as he could under the circumstances managed to grunt out "Gu —," which was as near to "Good" as the beef would allow.

Lanky Smith now chimed in as he repeatedly stuck his knife into a reluctant boiled potato, "How'd yu do it, Skinny?"

"Bet he sneaked up on him," joshed Buck Peters; "did yu ask his pardin, Skinny?"

"Ask nuthin'," remarked Red, "he jest nachurly walks up to C 80 an' sez, 'Kin I have the pleasure of ventilatin' yu?' an' C So he sez, 'If yu do it easy like,' sez he. Didn't he, Thompson?"

"They'll be some ventilatin' under th' table if yu fellows don't lemme alone; I'm hungry," complained Skinny.

"Say, Hopalong, I bets yu I kin clean up C 80 all by my lonesome," announced Buck, winking at Red.

"Yah! Yu onct tried to clean up the Bend, Buckie, an' if Pete an' Billy hadn't afound yu when they come by Eagle Pass that night yu wouldn't be here eatin' beef by th' pound," glancing at the hard-working Hopalong. "It was plum lucky fer yu that they was acourtin' that time, wasn't it, Hopalong?" suddenly asked Red. Hopalong nearly strangled in his efforts to speak. He gave it up and nodded his head.

"Why can't yu git it straight, Connors? I wasn't doin' no courtin', it was Pete. I runned into him on th' other side o' th' pass. I'd look fine acourtin', wouldn't I?" asked the downtrodden Williams.

Pete Wilson skillfully flipped a potato into that worthy's coffee, spilling the beverage of the questionable name over a large expanse of blue flannel shirt. "Yu's all right, yu are. Why, when I meets yu, yu was lost in th' arms of yore ladylove. All I could see was yore feet. Go an' git tangled up with a two hundred and forty pound half-breed squaw an' then try to lay it onter me! When I proposed drownin' yore troubles over at Cowan's, yu went an' got mad over what yu called th' insinooation. An' yu shore didn't look any too blamed fine, neither."

"All th' same," volunteered Thompson, who had taken the edge from his appetite, "we better go over an' pay C 80 a call. I don't like what Shorty said about saltin' our cattle. He'll shore do it, unless I camps on th' line, which same I hain't hankerin' after."

"Oh, he wouldn't stop th' cows that way, Skinny; he was only afoolin'," exclaimed Connors meekly.

"Foolin' yore gran'mother! That there bunch'll do anything if we wasn't lookin'," hotly replied Skinny.

"That's shore nuff gospel, Thomp. They's sore fer mor'n one thing. They got aplenty when Buck went on th' warpath, an they's hankerin' to git square," remarked Johnny Nelson, stealing the pie, a rare treat, of his neighbor when that unfortunate individual was not looking. He had it halfway to his mouth when its former owner, Jimmy Price, a boy of eighteen, turned his head and saw it going.

"Hi-yi! Yu clay-bank coyote, drap thet pie! Did yu ever see such a son-of-a-gun fer pie?" he plaintively asked Red Connors, as he grabbed a mighty handful of apples and crust. "Pie'll kill yu some day, yu bob-tailed jack! I had an uncle that died onct. He et too much pie an' he went an' turned green, an so'll yu if yu don't let it alone."

"Yu ought'r seed th' pie Johnny had down in Eagle Flat," murmured Lanky Smith reminiscently. "She had feet that'd stop a stampede. Johnny was shore loco about her. Swore she was the finest blossom that ever growed." Here he choked and tears of laughter coursed down his weather-beaten face as he pictured her. "She was a dainty Mexican, about fifteen han's high an' about sixteen han's around. Johnny used to chalk off when he hugged her, usen't yu, Johnny? One night when he had got purty well around on th' second lap he run inter a feller jest startin' out on his fust. They hain't caught that Mexican yet."

Nelson was pelted with everything in sight. He slowly wiped off the pie crust and bread and potatoes. "Anybody'd think I was a busted grub wagon," he grumbled. When he had fished the last piece of beef out of his ear he went out and offered to stand treat. As the round-up was over, they slid into their saddles and raced for Cowan's saloon at Buckskin.

Chapter II
The Rashness of Shorty

Buckskin was very hot; in fact it was never anything else. Few people were on the streets and the town was quiet. Over in the Houston hotel a crowd of cowboys was lounging in the barroom. They were very quiet —a condition as rare as it was ominous. Their mounts, twelve in all, were switching flies from their quivering skins in the corral at the rear. Eight of these had a large C 80 branded on their flanks; the other four, a Double Arrow.

In the barroom a slim, wiry man was looking out of the dirty window up the street at Cowan's saloon. Shorty was complaining, "They shore oughter be here now. They rounded up last week." The man nearest assured him that they would come. The man at the window turned and said, "They's yer now."

In front of Cowan's a crowd of nine happy-go-lucky, daredevil riders were sliding from their saddles. They threw their reins over the heads of their mounts and filed in to the bar. Laughter issued from the open door and the clink of glasses could be heard. They stood in picturesque groups, strong, self-reliant, humorous, virile. Their expensive sombreros were pushed far back on their heads and their hairy chaps were covered with the alkali dust from their ride.

Cowan, bottle in hand, pushed out several more glasses. He kicked a dog from under his feet and looked at Buck. "Rounded up yet?" he inquired.

"Shore, day afore yesterday," came the reply. The rest were busy removing the dust from their throats, and gradually drifted into groups of two or three. One of these groups strolled over to the solitary card table, and found Jimmy Price resting in a cheap chair, his legs on the table.

"I wisht yu'd extricate yore delicate feet from off'n this hyar table, James," humbly requested Lanky Smith, morally backed up by those with him.

"Ya-as, they shore is delicate, Mr. Smith," responded Jimmy without moving.

"We wants to play draw, Jimmy," explained Pete.

"Yore shore welcome to play if yu wants to. Didn't I tell yu when yu growed that mustache that yu didn't have to ask me any more?" queried the placid James, paternally.

"Call 'em off, sonny. Pete sez he kin clean me out. Anyhow, yu kin have the fust deal," compromised Lanky.

"I'm shore sorry fer Pete if he cayn't. Yu don't reckon I has to have fust deal to beat yu fellers, do yu? Go way an' lemme alone; I never seed such a bunch fer buttin' in as yu fellers."

Billy Williams returned to the bar. Then he walked along it until he was behind the recalcitrant possessor of the table. While his aggrieved friends shuffled their feet uneasily to cover his approach, he tiptoed up behind Jimmy and, with a nod, grasped that indignant individual firmly by the neck while the others grabbed his feet. They carried him, twisting and bucking, to the middle of the street and deposited him in the dust, returning to the now vacant table.

Jimmy rested quietly for a few seconds and then slowly arose, dusting the alkali from him.

"Th' wall-eyed piruts," he muttered, and then scratched his head for a way to "play hunk." As he gazed sorrowfully at the saloon he heard a snicker from behind him. He, thinking it was one of his late tormentors, paid no attention to it. Then a cynical, biting laugh stung him. He wheeled, to see Shorty leaning against a tree, a sneering leer on his flushed face. Shorty's right hand was suspended above his holster, hooked to his belt by the thumb—a favorite position of his when expecting trouble.

"One of yore reg'lar habits?" he drawled.

Jimmy began to dust himself in silence, but his lips were compressed to a thin white line.

"Does they hurt yu?" pursued the onlooker.

Jimmy looked up. "I heard tell that they make glue outen cayuses, sometimes," he remarked.

Shorty's eyes flashed. The loss of the horse had been rankling in his heart all day.

"Does they git yu frequent?" he asked. His voice sounded hard.

"Oh, 'bout as frequent as yu lose a cayuse, I reckon," replied Jimmy hotly.

Shorty's hand streaked to his holster and Jimmy followed his lead. Jimmy's Colt was caught. He had bucked too much. As he fell Shorty ran for the Houston House.

Pistol shots were common, for they were the universal method of expressing emotions. The poker players grinned, thinking their victim was letting off his indignation. Lanky sized up his hand and remarked half audibly, "He's a shore good kid."

The bartender, fearing for his new beveled, gilt-framed mirror, gave a hasty glance out the window. He turned around, made change and remarked to Buck, "Yore kid, Jimmy, is plugged." Several of the more credulous craned their necks to see, Buck being the first. "Judas!" he shouted, and ran out to where Jimmy lay coughing, his toes twitching. The saloon was deserted and a crowd of angry cowboys surrounded their chum-aboy. Buck had seen Shorty enter the door of the Houston House and he swore. "Chase them C 80 and Arrow cayuses behind the saloon, Pete, an' git under cover."

Jimmy was choking and he coughed up blood. "He's shore-got me. My-gun stuck," he added apologetically. He tried to sit up, but was not able and he looked surprised. "It's purty-damn hot-out here," he suggested. Johnny and Billy carried him in the saloon and placed him by the table, in the chair he had previously vacated. As they stood up he fell across the table and died.

Billy placed the dead boy's sombrero on his head and laid the refractory six-shooter on the table. "I wonder who th' dirty killer was." He looked at the slim figure and started to go out, followed by Johnny. As he reached the threshold a bullet zipped past him and thudded into the frame of the door. He backed away and looked surprised. "That's Shorty's shootin'—he allus misses 'bout that much." He looked out and saw Buck standing behind the live oak that Shorty had leaned against, firing at the hotel. Turning around he made for the rear, remarking to Johnny that "they's in th' Houston." Johnny looked at the quiet figure in the chair and swore softly. He followed Billy. Cowan, closing the door and taking a buffalo gun from under the bar, went out also and slammed the rear door forcibly.

Chapter III
The Argument

Up the street two hundred yards from the Houston House Skinny and Pete lay hidden behind a bowlder. Three hundred yards on the other side of the hotel Johnny and Billy were stretched out in an arroyo. Buck was lying down now, and Hopalong, from his position in the barn belonging to the hotel, was methodically dropping the horses of the besieged, a job he hated as much as he hated poison. The corral was their death trap. Red and Lanky were emitting clouds of smoke from behind the store, immediately across the street from the barroom. A buffalo gun roared down by the plaza and several Sharps cracked a protest from different points. The town had awakened and the shots were dropping steadily.

Strange noises filled the air. They grew in tone and volume and then dwindled away to nothing. The hum of the buffalo gun and the sobbing pi-in-in-ing of the Winchesters were liberally mixed with the sharp whines of the revolvers.

There were no windows in the hotel now. Raw furrows in the bleached wood showed yellow, and splinters mysteriously sprang from the casings. The panels of the door were producing cracks and the cheap door handle flew many ways at once. An empty whisky keg on the stoop boomed out mournfully at intervals and finally rolled down the steps with a rumbling protest. Wisps of smoke slowly climbed up the walls and seemed to be waving defiance to the curling wisps in the open.

Pete raised his shoulder to refill the magazine of his smoking rifle and dropped the cartridges all over his lap. He looked sheepishly at Skinny and began to load with his other hand.

"Yore plum loco, yu are. Don't yu reckon they kin hit a blue shirt at two hundred?" Skinny cynically inquired. "Got one that time," he announced a second later.

"I wonder who's got th' buffalo," grunted Pete. "Mus' be Cowan," he replied to his own question and settled himself to use his left hand.

"Don't yu git Shorty; he's my meat," suggested Skinny.

"Yu better tell Buck-he ain't got no love fer Shorty," replied Pete, aiming carefully.

The panic in the corral ceased and Hopalong was now sending his regrets against the panels of the rear door. He had cut his last initial in the near panel and was starting a wobbly "H" in its neighbor. He was in a good position. There were no windows in the rear wall, and as the door was a very dangerous place he was not fired at.

He began to get tired of this one-sided business and crawled up on the window ledge, dangling his feet on the outside. He occasionally sent a bullet at a different part of the door, but amused himself by annoying Buck.

"Plenty hot down there?" he pleasantly inquired, and as he received no answer he tried again. "Better save some of them cartridges fer some other time, Buck."

Buck was sending 45-70's into the shattered window with a precision that presaged evil to any of the defenders who were rash enough to try to gain the other end of the room.

Hopalong bit off a chew of tobacco and drowned a green fly that was crawling up the side of the barn. The yellow liquid streaked downward a short distance and was eagerly sucked up by the warped boards.

A spurt of smoke leaped from the battered door and the bored Hopalong promptly tumbled back inside. He felt of his arm, and then, delighted at the notice taken of his artistic efforts, shot several times from a crack on his right. "This yer's shore gittin' like home," he gravely remarked to the splinter that whizzed past his head. He shot again at the door and it sagged outward, accompanied by the thud of a falling body. "Pies like mother used to make," he announced to the loft as he slipped the magazine full of .45-70's. "An' pills like popper used to take," he continued when he had lowered the level of the water in his flask.

He rolled a cigarette and tossed the match into the air, extinguishing it by a shot from his Colt.

"Got any cigarettes, Hoppy?" said a voice from below.

"Shore," replied the joyous puncher, recognizing Pete; "how'd yu git here?"

"Like a cow. Busy?"

"None whatever. Comin' up?"

"Nope. Skinny wants a smoke too."

Hopalong handed tobacco and papers down the hole. "So long."

"So long," replied the daring Pete, who risked death twice for a smoke.

The hot afternoon dragged along and about three o'clock Buck held up an empty cartridge belt to the gaze of the curious Hopalong. That observant worthy nodded and threw a double handful of cartridges, one by one, to the patient and unrelenting Buck, who filled his gun and piled the few remaining ones up at his side. "Th' lives of mice and men gang aft all wrong," he remarked at random.

"Th' son-of-a-gun's talkin' Shakespeare," marveled Hopalong. "Satiate any, Buck?" he asked as that worthy settled down to await his chance.

"Two," he replied, "Shorty an' another. Plenty damn hot down here," he complained. A spurt of alkali dust stung his face, but the hand that made it never made another. "Three," he called. "How many, Hoppy?"

"One. That's four. Wonder if th' others got any?"

"Pete said Skinny got one," replied the intent Buck.

"Th' son-of-a-gun, he never said nothin' about it, an' me a fillin' his ornery paws with smokin'." Hopalong was indignant.

"Bet yu ten we don't git 'em afore dark," he announced.

"Got yu. Go yu ten more I gits another," promptly responded Buck.

"That's a shore cinch. Make her twenty."

"She is."

"Yu'll have to square it with Skinny, he shore wanted Shorty plum' bad," Hopalong informed the unerring marksman.

"Why didn't he say suthin' about it? Anyhow, Jimmy was my bunkie."

Hopalong's cigarette disintegrated and the board at his left received a hole. He promptly disappeared and Buck laughed. He sat up in the loft and angrily spat the soaked paper out from between his lips.

"All that trouble fer nothin', th' white-eyed coyote," he muttered. Then he crawled around to one side and fired at the center of his "C." Another shot hurtled at him and his left arm fell to his side. "That's funny-wonder where th' damn pirut is?" He looked out cautiously and saw a cloud of smoke over a knothole which was situated close up under the eaves of the barroom; and it was being agitated. Some one was blowing at it to make it disappear. He aimed very carefully at the knot and fired. He heard a sound between a curse and a squawk and was not molested any further from that point.

"I knowed he'd git hurt," he explained to the bandage, torn from the edge of his kerchief, which he carefully bound around his last wound.

Down in the arroyo Johnny was complaining.

"This yer's a no good bunk," he plaintively remarked.

"It shore ain't —but it's th' best we kin find," apologized Billy.

"That's th' sixth that feller sent up there. He's a damn poor shot," observed Johnny; "must be Shorty."

"Shorty kin shoot plum' good-tain't him," contradicted Billy.

"Yas-with a six-shooter. He's off'n his feed with a rifle," explained Johnny.

"Yu wants to stay down from up there, yu ijit," warned Billy as the disgusted Johnny crawled up the bank. He slid down again with a welt on his neck.

"That's somebody else now. He oughter a done better'n that," he said.

Billy had fired as Johnny started to slide and he smoothed his aggrieved chum. "He could onct, yu means."

"Did yu git him?" asked the anxious Johnny, rubbing his welt. "Plum' center," responded the business-like Billy. "Go up agin, mebby I kin git another," he suggested tentatively.

"Mebby you kin go to blazes. I ain't no gallery," grinned the now exuberant owner of the welt.

"Who's got the buffalo?" he inquired as the great gun roared.

"Mus' be Cowan. He's shore all right. Sounds like a bloomin' cannon," replied Billy. "Lemme alone with yore fool questions, I'm busy," he complained as his talkative partner started to ask another. "Go an' git me some water —I'm alkalied. An' git some .45's, mine's purty near gone."

Johnny crawled down the arroyo and reappeared at Hopalong's barn.

As he entered the door a handful of empty shells fell on his hat and dropped to the floor. He shook his head and remarked, "That mus' be that fool Hopalong."

"Yore shore right. How's business?" inquired the festive Cassidy.

"Purty fair. Billy's got one. How many's gone?"

"Buck's got three, I got two and Skinny's got one. That's six, an' Billy is seven. They's five more," he replied.

"How'd yu know?" queried Johnny as he filled his flask at the horse trough.

"Because they's twelve cayuses behind the hotel. That's why."

"They might git away on 'em," suggested the practical Johnny.

"Can't. They's all cashed in."

"Yu said that they's five left," ejaculated the puzzled water carrier.

"Yah; yore a smart cuss, ain't yu?"

Johnny grinned and then said, "Got any smokin'?" Hopalong looked grieved. "I ain't no store. Why don't yu git generous and buy some?"

He partially filled Johnny's hand, and as he put the sadly depleted bag away he inquired, "Got any papers?"

"Nope."

"Got any matches?" he asked cynically.

"Nope."

"Kin yu smoke 'em?" he yelled, indignantly.

"Shore nuff," placidly replied the unruffled Johnny. "Billy wants some .45-70's."

Hopalong gasped. "Don't he want my gun, too?"

"Nope. Got a better one. Hurry up, he'll git mad." Hopalong was a very methodical person. He was the only one of his crowd to carry a second cartridge strap. It hung over his right shoulder and rested on his left hip. His waist belt held thirty cartridges for the revolvers. He extracted twenty from that part of the shoulder strap hardest to get at, the back, by simply pulling it over his shoulder and plucking out the bullets as they came into reach.

"That's all yu kin have. I'm Buck's ammernition jackass," he explained. "Bet yu ten we gits 'em afore dark" —he was hedging.

"Any fool knows that. I'll take yu if yu bets th' other way," responded Johnny, grinning. He knew Hopalong's weak spot.

"Yore on," promptly responded Hopalong, who would bet on anything.

"Well, so long," said Johnny as he crawled away.

"Hey, yu, Johnny!" called out Hopalong, "don't yu go an' tell anybody I got any pills left. I ain't no ars'nal."

Johnny replied by elevating one foot and waving it. Then he disappeared.

Behind the store, the most precarious position among the besiegers, Red Connors and Lanky Smith were ensconced and commanded a view of the entire length of the barroom. They could see the dark mass they knew to be the rear door and derived a great amount of amusement from the spots of light which were appearing in it.

They watched the "C" (reversed to them) appear and be completed. When the wobbly "H" grew to completion they laughed heartily. Then the hardwood bar had been dragged across the field of vision and up to the front windows, and they could only see the indiscriminate holes which appeared in the upper panels at frequent intervals.

Every time they fired they had to expose a part of themselves to a return shot, with the result that Lanky's forearm was seared its entire length. Red had been more fortunate and only had a bruised ear.

They laboriously rolled several large rocks out in the open, pushing them beyond the shelter of the store with their rifles. When they had crawled behind them they each had another wound. From their new position they could see Hopalong sitting in his window. He promptly waved his sombrero and grinned.

They were the most experienced fighters of all except Buck, and were saving their shots. When they did shoot they always had some portion of a man's body to aim at, and the damage they inflicted was considerable. They said nothing, being older than the rest and more taciturn, and they were not reckless. Although Hopalong's antics made them laugh, they grumbled at his recklessness and were not tempted to emulate him. It was noticeable, too, that they shoved their rifles out simultaneously and, although both were aiming, only one fired. Lanky's gun cracked so close to the enemy's that the whirr of the bullet over Red's head was merged in the crack of his partner's reply.

When Hopalong saw the rocks roll out from behind the store he grew very curious. Then he saw a flash, followed instantly by another from the second rifle. He saw several of these follow shots and could sit in silence no longer. He waved his hat to attract attention and then shouted, "How many?" A shot was sent straight up in the air and he notified Buck that there were only four left.

The fire of these four grew less rapid-they were saving their ammunition. A pot shot at Hopalong sent that gentleman's rifle hurtling to the ground. Another tore through his hat, removing a neat amount of skin and hair and giving him a lifelong part. He fell back inside and proceeded to shoot fast and straight with his revolvers, his head burning as though on fire. When he had vented the dangerous pressure of his anger he went below and tried to fish the rifle in with a long stick. It was obdurate, so he sent three more shots into the door, and, receiving no reply, ran out around the corner of his shelter and grasped the weapon. When half way back he sank to the ground. Before another shot could be fired at him with any judgment a ripping, spitting rifle was being frantically worked from the barn. The bullets tore the door into seams and gaps; the lowest panel, the one having the "H" in it, fell inward in chunks. Johnny had returned for another smoke.

Hopalong, still grasping the rifle, rolled rapidly around the corner of the barn. He endeavored to stand, but could not. Johnny, hearing rapid and fluent swearing, came out.

"Where'd they git yu?" he asked.

"In th' off leg. Hurts like blazes. Did yu git him?"

"Nope. I jest come fer another cig; got any left?"

"Up above. Yore gall is shore apallin'. Help me in, yu two-laigged jackass."

"Shore. We'll shore pay our 'tentions to that door. She'll go purty soon-she's as full of holes as th' Bad Lan's," replied Johnny. "Git aholt an' hop along, Hopalong."

He helped the swearing Hopalong inside, and then the lead they pumped into the wrecked door was scandalous. Another panel fell in and Hopalong's "C" was destroyed. A wide crack appeared in the one above it and grew rapidly. Its mate began to gape and finally both were driven in. The increase in the light caused by these openings allowed Red and Lanky to secure better aim and soon the fire of the defenders died out.

Johnny dropped his rifle and, drawing his six-shooter, ran out and dashed for the dilapidated door, while Hopalong covered that opening with a fusilade.

As Johnny's shoulder sent the framework flying inward he narrowly missed sudden death. As it was he staggered to the side, out of range, and dropped full length to the ground, flat on his face. Hopalong's rifle cracked incessantly, but to no avail. The man who had fired the shot was dead. Buck got him immediately after he had shot Johnny.

Calling to Skinny and Red to cover him, Buck sprinted to where Johnny lay gasping. The bullet had struck his shoulder. Buck, Colt in hand, leaped through the door, but met with no resistance. He signaled to Hopalong, who yelled, "They's none left."

The trees and rocks and gullies and buildings yielded men who soon crowded around the hotel. A young doctor, lately graduated, appeared. It was his first case, but he eased Johnny. Then he went over to Hopalong, who was now raving, and attended to him. The others were patched up as well as possible and the struggling young physician had his pockets crammed full of gold and silver coins.

The scene of the wrecked barroom was indescribable. Holes, furrows, shattered glass and bottles, the liquor oozing down the walls of the shelves and running over the floor; the ruined furniture, a wrecked bar, seared and shattered and covered with blood; bodies as they had been piled in the corners; ropes, shells, hats; and liquor everywhere, over everything, met the gaze of those who had caused the chaos.

Perry's Bend had failed to wipe out the score.

Chapter IV
The Vagrant Sioux

Buckskin gradually readjusted itself to the conditions which had existed before its sudden leap into the limelight as a town which did things. The soiree at the Houston House had drifted into the past, and was now substantially established as an epoch in the history of the town. Exuberant joy gave way to dignity and deprecation, and to solid satisfaction; and the conversations across the bar brought forth parallels of the affair to be judged impartially-and the impartial judgment was, unanimously, that while there had undoubtedly been good fights before Perry's Bend had disturbed the local quiet, they were not quite up to the new standard of strenuous hospitality. Finally the heat blistered everything back into the old state, and the shadows continued to be in demand.

One afternoon, a month after the reception of the honorable delegation from Perry's Bend, the town of Buckskin seemed desolated, and the earth and the buildings thereon were as huge furnaces radiating a visible heat, but when the blazing sun had begun to settle in the west it awoke with a clamor which might have been laid to the efforts of a zealous Satan. At this time it became the Mecca of two score or more joyous cowboys from the neighboring ranches, who livened things as those knights of the saddle could.

In the scant but heavy shadow of Cowan's saloon sat a picturesque figure from whom came guttural, resonant rumblings which mingled in a spirit of loneliness with the fretful sighs of a flea-tormented dog. Both dog and master were vagrants, and they were tolerated because it was a matter of supreme indifference as to who came or how long they stayed as long as the ethics and the unwritten law of the cow country were inviolate. And the breaking of these caused no unnecessary anxiety, for justice was both speedy and sure.

When the outcast Sioux and his yellow dog had drifted into town some few months before they had caused neither expostulation nor inquiry, as the cardinal virtue of that whole broad land was to ask a man no questions which might prove embarrassing to all concerned; judgment was of observation, not of history, and a man's past would reveal itself through actions. It mattered little whether he was an embezzler or the wild chip from some prosperous eastern block, as men came to the range to forget and to lose touch with the pampered East; and the range absorbed them as its own.

A man was only a man as his skin contained the qualities necessary; and the illiterate who could ride and shoot and live to himself was far more esteemed than the educated who could not do those things. The more a man depends upon himself and the closer is his contact to a quick judgment the more laconic and even-poised he becomes. And the knowledge that he is himself a judge tends to create caution and judgment. He has no court to uphold his honor and to offer him protection, so he must be quick to protect himself and to maintain his own standing. His nature saved him, or it executed; and the range absolved him of all unpaid penalties of a careless past.

He became a man born again and he took up his burden, the exactions of a new environment, and he lived as long as those exactions gave him the right to live. He must tolerate no restrictions of his natural rights, and he must not restrict; for the one would proclaim him a coward, the other a bully; and both received short shrifts in that land of the self-protected. The basic law of nature is the survival of the fittest.

So, when the wanderers found their level in Buckskin they were not even asked by what name men knew them. Not caring to hear a name which might not harmonize with their idea of the fitness of things, the cowboys of the Bar-20 had, with a freedom born of excellent livers and fearless temperaments, bestowed names befitting their sense of humor and adaptability. The official title of the Sioux was By-and-by; the dog was known as Fleas. Never had names more clearly described the objects to be represented, for they were excellent examples of cowboy discernment and aptitude.

In their eyes By-and-by was a man. He could feel and he could resent insults. They did not class him as one of themselves, because he did not have energy enough to demand and justify such classification. With them he had a right to enjoy his life as he saw fit so long as he did not trespass on or restrict the rights of others. They were not analytic in temperament, neither were they moralists. He was not a menace to society, because society had superb defenses. So they vaguely recognized his many poor qualities and clearly saw his few good ones. He could shoot, when permitted, with the best; no horse, however refractory, had ever been known to throw him; he was an adept at following the trails left by rustlers, and that was an asset; he became of value to the community; he was an economic factor.

His ability to consume liquor with indifferent effects raised him another notch in their estimation. He was not always talking when some one else wished to-another count. There remained about him that stoical indifference to the petty; that observant nonchalance of the Indian; and there was a suggestion, faint, it was true, of a dignity common to chieftains. He was a log of grave deference which tossed on their sea of mischievous hilarity.

He wore a pair of corduroy trousers, known to the care-free as "pants," which were held together by numerous patches of what had once been brilliantly colored calico. A pair of suspenders, torn into two separate straps, made a belt for himself and a collar for his dog. The trousers had probably been secured during a fit of absent-mindedness on his part when their former owner had not been looking. Tucked at intervals in the top of the corduroys (the exceptions making convenient shelves for alkali dust) was what at one time had been a stiff-bosomed shirt. This was open down the front and back, the weight of the trousers on the belt holding it firmly on the square shoulders of the wearer, thus precluding the necessity of collar buttons. A pair of moccasins, beautifully worked with wampum, protected his feet from the onslaughts of cacti and the inquisitive and pugnacious sand flies; and lying across his lap was a repeating Winchester rifle, not dangerous because it was empty, a condition due to the wisdom of the citizens in forbidding any one to sell, trade or give to him those tubes of concentrated trouble, because he could get drunk.

The two were contented and happy. They had no cares nor duties, and their pleasures were simple and easily secured, as they consisted of sleep and a proneness to avoid moving. Like the untrammeled coyote, their bed was where sleep overtook them; their food, what the night wrapped in a sense of security, or the generosity of the cowboys of the Bar-20. No tub-ridden Diogenes ever knew so little of responsibility or as much unadulterated content. There is a penalty even to civilization and ambition.

When the sun had cast its shadows beyond By-and-by's feet the air became charged with noise; shouts, shots and the rolling thunder of madly pounding hoofs echoed flatly throughout the town. By-and-by yawned, stretched and leaned back, reveling in the semi-conscious ecstasy of the knowledge that he did not have to immediately get up. Fleas opened one eye and cocked an ear in inquiry, and then rolled over on his back, squirmed and sighed contentedly and long. The outfit of the Bar-20 had come to town.

The noise came rapidly nearer and increased in volume as the riders turned the corner and drew rein suddenly, causing their mounts to slide on their haunches in ankle-deep dust.

"Hullo, old Buck-with-th'-pants, how's yore liver?"

"Come up an irrigate, old tank!"

"Chase th' flea ranch an' trail along!"

These were a few of the salutations discernible among the medley of playful yells, the safety valves of supercharged good-nature.

"Skr-e-e!" yelled Hopalong Cassidy, letting off a fusillade of shots in the vicinity of Fleas, who rapidly retreated around the corner, where he wagged his tail in eager expectation. He was not disappointed, for a cow pony tore around in pursuit and Hopalong leaned over and scratched the yellow back, thumping it heartily, and, tossing a chunk of beef into the open jaws of the delighted dog, departed as he had come. The advent of the outfit meant a square meal, and the dog knew it.

In Cowan's, lined up against the bar, the others were earnestly and assiduously endeavoring, with a promise of success, to get By-and-by drunk, which endeavors coincided perfectly with By-and-by's idea of the fitness of things. The fellowship and the liquor combined to thaw out his reserve and to loosen his tongue. After gazing with an air of injured surprise at the genial loosening of his knees he gravely handed his rifle with an exaggerated sweep of his arm, to the cowboy nearest him, and wrapped his arms around the recipient to insure his balance. The rifle was passed from hand to hand until it came to Buck Peters, who gravely presented it to its owner as a new gun.

By-and-by threw out his stomach in an endeavor to keep his head in line with his heels, and grasping the weapon with both hands turned to Cowan, to whom he gave it.

"Yu hab this un. Me got two. Me keep new un, mebby so." Then he loosened his belt and drank long and deep.

A shadow darkened the doorway and Hopalong limped in. Spying By-and-by pushing the bottle into his mouth, while Red Connors propped him, he grinned and took out five silver dollars, which he jingled under By-and-by's eyes, causing that worthy to lay aside the liquor and erratically grab for the tantalizing fortune.

"Not yet, sabe?" said Hopalong, changing the position of the money. "If yu wants to corral this here herd of simoleons yu has to ride a cayuse what Red bet me yu can't ride. Yu has got to grow on that there saddle and stayed growed for five whole minutes by Buck's ticker. I ain't a-goin' to tell yu he's any saw-horse, for yu'd know better, as yu reckons Red wouldn't bet on no losin' proposition if he knowed better, which same he don't. Yu straddles that four-laigged cloudburst an' yu gets these, sabe? I ain't seen th' cayuse yet that yu couldn't freeze to, an' I'm backin' my opinions with my moral support an' one month's pay."

By-and-by's eyes began to glitter as the meaning of the words sifted through his befuddled mind. Ride a horse-five dollars-ride a five-dollars horse-horses ride dollars-then he straightened up and began to speak in an incoherent jumble of Sioux and bad English. He, the mighty rider of the Sioux; he, the bravest warrior and the greatest hunter; could he ride a horse for five dollars? Well, he rather thought he could. Grasping Red by the shoulder, he tacked for the door and narrowly missed hitting the bottom step first, landing, as it happened, in the soft dust with Red's leg around his neck. Somewhat sobered by the jar, he stood up and apologized to the crowd for Red getting in the way, declaring that Red was a "Heap good un," and that he didn't mean to do it.

The outfit of the Bar-20 was, perhaps, the most famous of all from Canada to the Rio Grande. The foreman, Buck Peters, controlled a crowd of men (who had all the instincts of boys) that had shown no quarter to many rustlers, and who, while always carefree and easy-going (even fighting with great good humor and carelessness), had established the reputation of being the most reckless gang of daredevil gun-fighters that ever pounded leather. Crooked gaming houses, from El Paso to Cheyenne and from Phoenix to Leavenworth, unanimously and enthusiastically damned them from their boots to their sombreros, and the sheriffs and marshals of many localities had received from their hands most timely assistance-and some trouble. Wiry, indomitable, boyish and generous, they were splendid examples of virile manhood; and, surrounded as they were with great dangers and a unique civilization, they should not, in justice, be judged by opinions born of the commonplace.

They were real cowboys, which means, public opinion to the contrary notwithstanding, that they were not lawless, nor drunken, shooting bullies who held life cheaply, as their kin has been unjustly pictured; but while these men were naturally peaceable they had to continually rub elbows with men who were not. Gamblers, criminals, bullies and the riffraff that fled from the protected East had drifted among them in great numbers, and it was this class that caused the trouble.

The hardworking "cow-punchers" lived according to the law of the land, and they obeyed that greatest of all laws, that of self-preservation. Their fun was boisterous, but they paid for all the damage they inflicted; their work was one continual hardship, and the reaction of one extreme swings far toward the limit of its antithesis. Go back to the Apple if you would trace the beginning of self-preservation and the need.

Buck Peters was a man of mild appearance, somewhat slow of speech and correspondingly quick of action, who never became flurried. His was the master hand that controlled, and his Colts enjoyed the reputation of never missing when a hit could have been expected with reason. Many floods, stampedes and blizzards had assailed his nerves, but he yet could pour a glass of liquor, held at arm's length, through a knothole in the floor without wetting the wood.

Next in age came Lanky Smith, a small, undersized man of retiring disposition. Then came Skinny Thompson, six feet four on his bared soles, and true to his name; Hopalong described him as "th' shadow of a chalk mark." Pete Wilson, the slow-witted and very taciturn, and Billy Williams, the wavering pessimist, were of ordinary height and appearance. Red Connors, with hair that shamed the name, was the possessor of a temper which was as dry as tinder; his greatest weakness was his regard for the rifle as a means of preserving peace. Johnny Nelson was the protege, and he could do no wrong.

The last, Hopalong Cassidy, was a combination of irresponsibility, humor, good nature, love of fighting, and nonchalance when face to face with danger. His most prominent attribute was that of always getting into trouble without any intention of so doing; in fact, he was much aggrieved and surprised when it came. It seemed as though when any "bad man" desired to add to his reputation he invariably selected Hopalong as the means (a fact due, perhaps, to the perversity of things in general). Bad men became scarce soon after Hopalong became a fixture in any locality. He had been crippled some years before in a successful attempt to prevent the assassination of a friend, Sheriff Harris, of Albuquerque, and he still possessed a limp.

When Red had relieved his feelings and had dug the alkali out of his ears and eyes, he led the Sioux to the rear of the saloon, where a "pinto" was busily engaged in endeavoring to pitch a saddle from his back, employing the intervals in trying to see how much of the picket rope he could wrap around his legs.

When By-and-by saw what he was expected to ride he felt somewhat relieved, for the pony did not appear to have more than the ordinary amount of cussedness. He waved his hand, and Johnny and Red bandaged the animal's eyes, which quieted him at once, and then they untangled the rope from around his legs and saw that the cinches were secure. Motioning to By-and-by that all was ready, they jerked the bandage off as the Indian settled himself in the saddle.

Had By-and-by been really sober he would have taken the conceit out of that pony in chunks, and as it was he experienced no great difficulty in holding his seat; but in his addled state of mind he grasped the end of the cinch strap in such a way that when the pony jumped forward in its last desperate effort the buckle slipped and the cinch became unfastened; and By-and-by, still seated in the saddle, flew head foremost into the horse trough, where he spilled much water.

As this happened Cowan turned the corner, and when he saw the wasted water (which he had to carry, bucketful at a time, from the wells a good quarter of a mile away) his anger blazed forth, and yelling, he ran for the drenched Sioux, who was just crawling out of his bath. When the unfortunate saw the irate man bearing down on him he sputtered in rage and fear, and, turning, he ran down the street, with Cowan thundering flatfootedly behind on a fat man's gallop, to the hysterical cheers of the delighted outfit, who saw in it nothing but a good joke.

When Cowan returned from his hopeless task, blowing and wheezing, he heard sundry remarks, sotto voce, which were not calculated to increase his opinion of his physical condition.

"Seems to me," remarked the irrepressible Hopalong, "that one of those cayuses has got th' heaves."

"It shore sounds like it," acquiesced Johnny, red in the face from holding in his laughter, "an' say, somebody interferes."

"All knock-kneed animals do, yu heathen," supplied Red.

"Hey, yu, let up on that and have a drink on th' house," invited Cowan. "If I gits that durn war whoop I'll make yu think there's been a cyclone. I'll see how long that bum hangs around this here burg, I will."

Red's eyes narrowed and his temper got the upper hand. "He ain't no bum when yu gives him rotgut at a quarter of a dollar a glass, is he? Any time that 'bum' gits razzled out for nothin' more'n this, why, I goes too; an' I ain't sayin' nothin' about goin' peaceable-like, neither."

"I knowed somethin' like this 'ud happen," dolefully sang out Billy Williams, strong on the side of his pessimism.

"For th' Lord's sake, have you broke out?" asked Red, disgustedly. "I'm goin' to hit the trail-but just keep this afore yore mind: if By-and-by gits in any accidents or ain't in sight when I comes to town again, this here climate'll be a heep sight hotter'n it is now. No hard feelings, sabe? It's just a casual bit of advice. Come on, fellows, let's amble —I'm hungry."

As they raced across the plain toward the ranch a pair of beady eyes, snapping with a drunken rage, watched them from an arroyo; and when Cowan entered the saloon the next morning he could not find By-and-by's rifle, which he had placed behind the bar. He also missed a handful of cartridges from the box near the cash drawer; and had he looked closely at his bottled whisky he would have noticed a loss there. A horse was missing from a Mexican's corral and there were rumors that several Indians had been seen far out on the plain.

Chapter V
The Law of the Range

"Phew! I'm shore hungry," said Hopalong, as he and Red dismounted at the ranch the next morning for breakfast. "Wonder what's good for it?"

"They's three things that's good for famine," said Red, leading the way to the bunk house. "Yu can pull in yore belt, yu can drink, an yu can eat. Yore getting as bad as Johnny-but he's young yet."

The others met their entrance with a volley of good-humored banter, some of which was so personal and evoked such responses that it sounded like the preliminary skirmish to a fight. But under all was that soft accent, that drawl of humorous appreciation and eyes twinkling in suppressed merriment. Here they were thoroughly at home and the spirit of comradeship manifested itself in many subtle ways; the wit became more daring and sharp, Billy lost some of his pessimism, and the alertness disappeared from their manner.

Skinny left off romping with Red and yawned. "I wish that cook'ud wake up an' git breakfast. He's the cussedest hombre I ever saw-he kin go to sleep standin' up an' not know it. Johnny's th' boy that worries him-th' kid comes in an' whoops things up till he's gorged himself."

"Johnny's got th' most appallin' feel for grub of anybody I knows," added Red. "I wonder what's keepin' him-he's usually hangin' around here bawlin' for his grub like a spoiled calf, long afore cookie's got th' fire goin'."

"Mebby he rustled some grub out with him —I saw him tip-toein' out of th' gallery this mornin' when I come back for my cigs," remarked Hopalong, glancing at Billy.

Billy groaned and made for the gallery. Emerging half a minute later he blurted out his tale of woe: "Every time I blows myself an' don't drink it all in town some slab-sided maverick freezes to it. It's gone," he added, dismally.

"Too bad, Billy-but what is it?" asked Skinny.

"What is it? Wha'd yu think it was, you emaciated match? Jewelry? Cayuses? It's whisky-two simoleons' worth. Some-thin's allus wrong. This here whole yearth's wrong, just like that cross-eyed sky pilot said over to —"

"Will yu let up?" Yelled Red, throwing a sombrero at the grumbling unfortunate. "Yu ask Buck where yore tanglefoot is.

"I'd shore look nice askin' th' boss if he'd rustled my whisky, wouldn't I? An' would yu mind throwin' somebody else's hat? I paid twenty wheels for that eight years ago, and I don't want it mussed none."

"Gee, yore easy! Why, Ah Sing, over at Albuquerque, gives them away every time yu gits yore shirt washed," gravely interposed Hopalong as he went out to cuss the cook.

"Well, what'd yu think of that?" Exclaimed Billy in an injured tone.

"Oh, yu needn't be hikin' for Albuquerque-Washee Washee'ud charge yu double for washin' yore shirt. Yu ought to fall in di' river some day-then he might talk business," called Hopalong over his shoulder as he heaved an old boot into the gallery. "Hey, yu hibernatin' son of morphine, if yu don't git them flapjacks in here pretty sudden-like I'll scatter yu all over di' landscape, sabe? Yu just wait till Johnny comes!"

"Wonder where th' kid is?" asked Lanky, rolling a cigarette. "Off somewhere lookin' at di' sun through di' bottom of my bottle," grumbled Billy.

Hopalong started to go out, but halted on the sill and looked steadily off toward the northwest. "That's funny. Hey, fellows, here comes Buck an' Johnny ridin' double-on a walk, too!" he exclaimed. "Wonder what th'—thunder! Red, Buck's carryun' him! Somethin's busted!" he yelled, as he dashed for his pony and made for the newcomers.

"I told yu he was hittin' my bottle," pertly remarked Billy, as he followed the rest outside.

"Did yu ever see Johnny drunk? Did yu ever see him drink more'n two glasses? Shut yore wailin' face-they's somethin' worse'n that in this here," said Red, his temper rising. "Hopalong an' me took yore cheap liquor-it's under Pete's bunk," he added.

The trio approached on a walk and Johnny, delirious and covered with blood, was carried into the bunk house. Buck waited until all had assembled again and then, his face dark with anger, spoke sharply and without the usual drawl: "Skragged from behind, blast them! Get some grub an' water an' be quick. We'll see who the gent with th' grudge is."

At this point the expostulations of the indignant cook, who, not understanding the cause, regarded the invasion of china shop bulls as sacrilegious, came to his ears. Striding quickly to the door, he grabbed the pan the Mexican was about to throw and, turning the now frightened man around, thundered, "Keep quiet an' get 'em some grub."

When rifles and ammunition had been secured they mounted and followed him at a hard gallop along the back trail. No words were spoken, for none were necessary. All knew that they would not return until they had found the man for whom they were looking, even if the chase led to Canada. They did not ask Buck for any of the particulars, for the foreman was not in the humor to talk, and all, save Hopalong, whose curiosity was always on edge, recognized only two facts and cared for nothing else: Johnny had been ambushed and they were going to get the one who was responsible.

They did not even conjecture as to who it might be, because the trail would lead them to the man himself, and it mattered nothing who or what he was-there was only one course to take with an assassin. So they said nothing, but rode on with squared jaws and set lips, the seven ponies breast to breast in a close arc.

Soon they came to an arroyo which they took at a leap. As they approached it they saw signs in the dust which told them that a body had lain there huddled up; and there were brown spots on the baked alkali. The trail they followed was now single, Buck having ridden along the bank of the arroyo when hunting for Johnny, for whom he had orders. This trail was very irregular, as if the horse had wandered at will. Suddenly they came upon five tracks, all pointing one way, and four of these turned abruptly and disappeared in the northwest. Half a mile beyond the point of separation was a chaparral, which was an important factor to them.

Each man knew just what had taken place as if he had been an eyewitness, for the trail was plain. The assassins had waited in the chaparral for Johnny to pass, probably having seen him riding that way. When he had passed and his back had been turned to them they had fired and wounded him severely at the first volley, for Johnny was of the stuff that fights back and his revolvers had showed full chambers and clean barrels when Red had examined them in the bunk house. Then they had given chase for a short distance and, from some inexplicable motive, probably fear, they had turned and ridden off without knowing how bad he was hit. It was this trail that led to the northwest, and it was this trail that they followed without pausing.

When they had covered fifty miles they sighted the Cross Bar O ranch where they hoped to secure fresh mounts. As they rode up to the ranch house the owner, Bud Wallace, came around the corner and saw them.

"Hullo, boys! What deviltry are yu up to now?" he asked. Buck leaped from his mount, followed by the others, and shoved his sombrero back on his head as he started to remove the saddle.

"We're trailin' a bunch of murderers. They ambushed Johnny an' blame near killed him. I stopped here to get fresh cayuses."

"Yu did right!" replied Wallace heartily. Then raising his voice he shouted to some of his men who were near the corral to bring up the seven best horses they could rope. Then he told the cook to bring out plenty of food and drink.

"I got four punchers what ain't doin' nothin' but eat," he suggested.

"Much obliged, Wallace, but there's only four of 'em, an' we'd rather get 'em ourselves-Johnny'ud feel better," replied Buck, throwing his saddle on the horse that was led up to him.

"How's yore cartridges-got plenty?" Persisted Wallace.

"Two hundred apiece," responded Buck, springing into his saddle and riding off. "So long," he called.

"So long, an' plug blazes out of them," shouted Wallace as the dust swept over him.

At five in the afternoon they forded the Black River at a point where it crossed the state line from New Mexico, and at dusk camped at the base of the Guadalupe Mountains. At daybreak they took up the chase, grim and merciless, and shortly afterward they passed the smoldering remains of a camp fire, showing that the pursued had been in a great hurry, for it should have been put out and masked. At noon they left the mountains to the rear and sighted the Barred Horeshoe, which they approached.

The owner of the ranch saw them coming, and from their appearance surmised that something was wrong.

"What is it?" He shouted. "Rustlers?"

"Nope. Murderers. I wants to swap cayuses quick," answered Buck.

"There they are. Th' boys just brought 'em in. Anything else I can let yu have?"

"Nope," shouted Buck as they galloped off.

"Somebody's goin' to get plugged full of holes," murmured the ranch owner as he watched them kicking up the dust in huge clouds.

After they had forded a tributary of the Rio Penasco near the Sacramento Mountains and had surmounted the opposite bank, Hopalong spurred his horse to the top of a hummock and swept the plain with Pete's field glasses, which he had borrowed for the occasion, and returned to the rest, who had kept on without slacking the pace. As he took up his former position he grunted, "War-whoops," and unslung his rifle, an example followed by the others.

The ponies were now running at top speed, and as they shot over a rise their riders saw their quarry a mile and a half in advance. One of the Indians looked back and discharged his rifle in defiance, and it now became a race worthy of the name-Death fled from Death. The fresher mounts of the cowboys steadily cut down the distance and, as the rifles of the pursuers began to speak, the hard-pressed Indians made for the smaller of two knolls, the plain leading to the larger one being too heavily strewn with bowlders to permit speed.

As the fugitives settled down behind the rocks which fringed the edge of their elevation a shot from one of them disabled Billy's arm, but had no other effect than to increase the score to be settled. The pursuers rode behind a rise and dismounted, from where, leaving their mounts protected, they scattered out to surround the knoll.

Hopalong, true to his curiosity, finally turned up on the highest point of the other knoll, a spur of the range in the west, for he always wanted to see all he could. Skinny, due to his fighting instinct, settled one hundred yards to the north and on the same spur. Buck lay hidden behind an enormous bowlder eight hundred yards to the northeast of Skinny, and the same distance southeast of Buck was Red Connors, who was crawling up the bed of an arroyo. Billy, nursing his arm, lay in front of the horses, and Pete, from his position between Billy and Hopalong, was crawling from rock to rock in an endeavor to get near enough to use his Colts, his favorite and most effective weapons. Intermittent puffs of smoke arising from a point between Skinny and Buck showed where Lanky Smith was improving each shining hour.

There had been no directions given, each man choosing his own position, yet each was of strategic worth. Billy protected the horses, Hopalong and Skinny swept the knoll with a plunging fire, and Lanky and Buck lay in the course the besieged would most likely take if they tried a dash. Off to the east Red barred them from creeping down the arroyo, and from where Pete was he could creep up to within sixty yards if he chose the right rocks. The ranges varied from four hundred yards for Buck to sixty for Pete, and the others averaged close to three hundred, which allowed very good shooting on both sides.

Hopalong and Skinny gradually moved nearer to each other for companionship, and as the former raised his head to see what the others were doing he received a graze on the ear.

"Wow!" he yelled, rubbing the tingling member.

Two puffs of smoke floated up from the knoll, and Skinny swore.

"Where'd he get yu, Fat?" asked Hopalong.

"G'wan, don't get funny, son," replied Skinny.

Jets of smoke arose from the north and east, where Buck and Red were stationed, and Pete was half way to the knoll. So far he hadn't been hit as he dodged in and out, and, emboldened by his luck, he made a run of five yards and his sombrero was shot from his head. Another dash and his empty holster was ripped from its support. As he crouched behind a rock he heard a yell from Hopalong, and saw that interested individual waving his sombrero to cheer him on. An angry pang! from the knoll caused that enthusiastic rooter to drop for safety.

"Locoed son-of-a-gun," complained Pete. "He'll shore git potted." Then he glanced at Billy, who was the center of several successive spurts of dust.

"How's business, Billy?" he called pleasantly.

"Oh, they'll git me yet," responded the pessimist. "Yu needn't git anxious. If that off buck wasn't so green he'd 'a' had me long ago."

"Ya-hoo! Pete! Oh, Pete!" called Hopalong, sticking his head out at one side and grinning as the wondering object of his hail craned his neck to see what the matter was.

"Huh?" grunted Pete, and then remembering the distance he shouted, "What's th' matter?"

"Got any cigarettes?" asked Hopalong.

"Yu poor sheep!" said Pete, and turning back to work he drove a .45 into a yellow moccasin.

Hopalong began to itch and he saw that he was near an ant hill. Then the cactus at his right boomed out mournfully and a hole appeared in it. He fired at the smoke and a yell informed him that he had made a hit. "Go 'way!" he complained as a green fly buzzed past his nose. Then he scratched each leg with the foot of the other and squirmed incessantly, kicking out with both feet at once. A warning metallic whir-r-r! on his left caused to yank them in again, and turning his head quickly he the pleasure of lopping off the head of a rattlesnake with his Colt's.

"Glad yu wasn't a copperhead," he exclaimed. "Somebody had ought 'a' shot that fool Noah. Blast the ants!" He drowned with a jet of tobacco juice a Gila monster that was staring at him and took a savage delight in its frantic efforts to bury itself.

Soon he heard Skinny swear and he sung out: "What's the matter, Skinny? Git plugged again?"

"Naw, bugs-ain't they mean?" Plaintively asked his friend. "They ain't none over here. What kind of bugs?"

"Sufferin' Moses, I ain't no bugologist! All kinds!"

But Hopalong got it at last. He had found tobacco and rolled a cigarette, and in reaching for a match exposed his shoulder to a shot that broke his collar bone. Skinny's rifle cracked in reply and the offending brave rolled out from behind a rock. From the fuss emanating from Hopalong's direction Skinny knew that his neighbor had been hit.

"Don't yu care, Hoppy. I got th' cuss," he said consolingly. "Where'd he git yu?" he asked.

"In di' heart, yu pie-faced nuisance. Come over here an' corral this cussed bandage an' gimme some water," snapped the injured man.

Skinny wormed his way through the thorny chaparral and bound up the shoulder. "Anything else?" he asked.

"Yes. Shoot that bunch of warts an' blow that tobacco-eyed Gila to Cheyenne. This here's worse than the time we cleaned out th' C 80 outfit!" Then he kicked the dead toad and swore at the sun.

"Close yore yap; yore worse than a kid! Anybody'd think yu never got plugged afore," said Skinny indignantly.

"I can cuss all I wants," replied Hopalong, proving his assertion as he grabbed his gun and fired at the dead Indian. A bullet whined above his head and Skinny fired at the smoke. He peeped out and saw that his friends were getting nearer to the knoll.

"They's closin' in now. We'll soon be gittin' home," he reported.

Hopalong looked out in time to see Buck make a dash for a bowlder that lay ten yards in front of him, which he reached in safety. Lanky also ran in and Pete added five more yards to his advance. Buck made another dash, but leaped into the air, and, coming down as if from an intentional high jump, staggered and stumbled for a few paces and then fell flat, rolling over and over toward the shelter of a split rock, where he lay quiet. A leering red face peered over the rocks on the knoll, but the whoop of exultation was cut short, for Red's rifle cracked and the warrior rolled down the steep bank, where another shot from the same gun settled him beyond question.

Hopalong choked and, turning his face away, angrily dashed his knuckles into his eyes. "Blast 'em! Blast 'em! They've got Buck! They've got Buck, blast 'em! They've got Buck, Skinny! Good old Buck! They've got him! Jimmy's gone, Johnny's plugged, and now Buck's gone! Come on!" he sobbed in a frenzy of vengeance. "Come on, Skinny! We'll tear their cussed hides into a deeper red than they are now! Oh, blast it, I can't see-where's my gun?" He groped for the rifle and fought Skinny when the latter, red-eyed but cool, endeavored to restrain him. "Lemme go, curse yu! Don't yu know they got Buck? Lemme go!"

"Down! Red's got di' skunk. Yu can't do nothin' —they'd drop yu afore yu took five steps. Red's got him, I tell yu! Do yu want me to lick yu? We'll pay 'em back with interest if yu'll keep yore head!" exclaimed Skinny, throwing the crazed man heavily.

Musical tones, rising and falling in weird octaves, whining pityingly, diabolically, sobbing in a fascinating monotone and slobbering in ragged chords, calling as they swept over the plain, always calling and exhorting, they mingled in barbaric discord with the defiant barks of the six-shooters and the inquiring cracks of the Winchesters. High up in the air several specks sailed and drifted, more coming up rapidly from all directions. Buzzards know well where food can be found.

As Hopalong leaned back against a rock he was hit in the thigh by a ricochet that tore its way out, whirling like a circular saw, a span above where it entered. The wound was very nasty, being ripped twice the size made by an ordinary shot, and it bled profusely. Skinny crawled over and attended to it, making a tourniquet of his neckerchief and clumsily bandaging it with a strip torn from his shirt.

"Yore shore lucky, yu are," he grumbled as he made his way back to his post, where he vented his rancor by emptying the semi-depleted magazine of his Winchester at the knoll.

Hopalong began to sing and shout and he talked of Jimmy and his childhood, interspersing the broken narrative with choice selections as sung in the music halls of Leavenworth and Abilene. He wound up by yelling and struggling, and Skinny had his hands full in holding him.

"Hopalong! Cassidy! Come out of that! Keep quiet-yu'll shore git plugged if yu don't stop that plungin'. For gosh sake, did yu hear that?" A bullet viciously hissed between them and flattened out on a near-by rock; others cut their way through the chaparral to the sound of falling twigs, and Skinny threw himself on the struggling man and strapped Hopalong with his belt to the base of a honey mesquite that grew at his side.

"Hold still, now, and let that bandage alone. Yu allus goes off di' range when yu gets plugged," he complained. He cut down a cactus and poured the sap over the wounded man's face, causing him to gurgle and look around. His eyes had a sane look now and Skinny slid off his chest.

"Git that-belt loose; I ain't —no cow," brokenly blazed out the picketed Hopalong. Skinny did so, handed the irate man his Colts and returned to his own post, from where he fired twice, reporting the shots.

"I'm tryin' to get him on th' glance' first one went high an' th' other fell flat," he explained.

Hopalong listened eagerly, for this was shooting that he could appreciate. "Lemme see," he commanded. Skinny dragged him over to a crack and settled down for another try.

"Where is he, Skinny?" Asked Hopalong.

"Behind that second big one. No, over on this here side. See that smooth granite? If I can get her there on th' right spot he'll shore know it." He aimed carefully and fired.

Through Pete's glasses Hopalong saw a leaden splotch appear on the rock and he notified the marksman that he was shooting high. "Put her on that bump closer down," he suggested. Skinny did so and another yell reached their ears.

"That's a dandy. Yore shore all right, yu old cuss," complimented Hopalong, elated at the success of the experiment.

Skinny fired again and a brown arm flopped out into sight. Another shot struck it and it jerked as though it were lifeless.

"He's cashed. See how she jumped? Like a rope," remarked Skinny with a grin. The arm lay quiet.

Pete had gained his last cover and was all eyes and Colts. Lanky was also very close in and was intently watching one particular rock. Several shots echoed from the far side of the knoll and they knew that Red was all right. Billy was covering a cluster of rocks that protruded above the others and, as they looked, his rifle rang out and the last defender leaped down and disappeared in the chaparral. He wore yellow trousers and an old boiled shirt.

"By an'-by, by all that's bad!" yelled Hopalong. "Th' measly coyote! An' me a-fillin' his ornery hide with liquor. Well, they'll have to find him all over again now," he complained, astounded by the revelation. He fired into the chaparral to express his pugnacious disgust and scared out a huge tarantula, which alighted on Skinny's chaps, crawling rapidly toward the unconscious man's neck. Hopalong's face hardened and he slowly covered the insect and fired, driving it into the sand, torn and lifeless. The bullet touched the leathern garment and Skinny remonstrated, knowing that Hopalong was in no condition for fancy shooting.

"Huh!" exclaimed Hopalong. "That was a tarantula what I plugged. He was headin' for yore neck," he explained, watching the chaparral with apprehension.

"Go 'way, was it? Bully for yu!" exclaimed Skinny, tarantulas being placed at par with rattlesnakes, and he considered that he had been saved from a horrible death. "Thought yu said they wasn't no bugs over here," he added in an aggrieved tone.

"They wasn't none. Yu brought 'em. I only had th' main show-Gilas, rattlers an' toads," he replied, and then added, "Ain't it cussed hot up here?"

"She is. Yu won't have no cinch ridin' home with that leg. Yu better take my cayuse-he's busted more'n yourn," responded Skinny.

"Yore cayuse is at th' Cross Bar O, yu wall-eyed pirute."

"Shore 'nuff. Funny how a feller forgets sometimes. Lemme alone now, they's goin' to git By-an'-by. Pete an' Lanky has just went in after him."

That was what had occurred. The two impatient punchers, had grown tired of waiting, and risked what might easily have been death in order to hasten matters. The others kept up a rapid fire, directed at the far end of the chaparral on the knoll, in order to mask the movements of their venturesome friends, intending also to drive By-and-by toward them so that he would be the one to get picked off as he advanced.

Several shots rang out in quick succession on the knoll and the chaparral became agitated. Several more shots sounded from the depth of the thicket and a mounted Indian dashed out of the northern edge and headed in Buck's direction. His course would take him close to Buck, whom he had seen fall, and would let him escape at a point midway between Red and Skinny, as Lanky was on the knoll and the range was very far to allow effective shooting by these two.

Red saw him leave the chaparral and in his haste to reload jammed the cartridge, and By-and-by swept on toward temporary safety, with Red dancing in a paroxysm of rage, swelling his vocabulary with words he had forgotten existed.

By-and-by, rising to his full height in the saddle, turned and wiggled his fingers at the frenzied Red and made several other signs that the cowboy was in the humor to appreciate to the fullest extent. Then he turned and shook his rifle at the marksmen on the larger knoll, whose best shots kicked up the dust fully fifty yards too short. The pony was sweeping toward the reservation and friends only fifteen miles away, and By-and-by knew that once among the mountains he would be on equal footing at least with his enemies.

As he passed the rock behind which Buck lay sprawled on his face he uttered a piercing whoop of triumph and leaned forward on his pony's neck. Twenty leaps farther and the spiteful crack of a rifle echoed from where the foreman was painfully supporting himself on his elbows. The pony swept on in a spurt of nerve-racking speed, but alone. By-and-by shrieked again and crashed heavily to the ground, where he rolled inertly and then lay still. Men like Buck are dangerous until their hearts have ceased to beat.

Chapter VI
Trials of the Convalescent

The days at the ranch passed in irritating idleness for those who had obstructed the flight of hostile lead, and worse than any of the patients was Hopalong, who fretted and fumed at his helplessness, which retarded his recovery. But at last the day came when he was fit for the saddle again, and he gave notice of his joy in whoops and forthwith announced that he was entitled to a holiday; and Buck had not the heart to refuse him.

So he started forth in his quest of peace and pleasure, but instead had found only trouble and had been forced to leave his card at almost every place he had visited.

There was that affair in Red Hot Gulch, Colorado, where, under pressure, he had invested sundry pieces of lead in the persons of several obstreperous citizens and then had paced the zealous and excitable sheriff to the state line.

He next was noticed in Cheyenne, where his deformity was vividly dwelt upon, to the extent of six words, by one Tarantula Charley, the aforesaid Charley not being able to proceed to greater length on account of heart failure. As Charley had been a ubiquitous nuisance, those present availed themselves of the opportunity offered by Hopalong to indulge in a free drink.

Laramie was his next stopping place, and shortly after his arrival he was requested to sing and dance by a local terror, who informed all present that he was the only seventeen-buttoned rattlesnake in the cow country. Hopalong, hurt and indignant at being treated like a common tenderfoot, promptly knocked the terror down. After he had irrigated several square feet of parched throats belonging to the audience he again took up his journey and spent a day at Denver, where he managed to avoid any further trouble.

Santa Fe loomed up before him several days later and he entered it shortly before noon. At this time the old Spanish city was a bundle of high-strung nerves, and certain parts of it were calculated to furnish any and all kinds of excitement except revival meetings and church fairs. Hopalong straddled a lively nerve before he had been in the city an hour. Two local bad men,

Slim Travennes and Tex Ewalt, desiring to establish the fact that they were roaring prairie fires, attempted to consume the placid and innocent stranger as he limped across the plaza in search of a game of draw poker at the Black Hills Emporium, with the result that they needed repairs, to the chagrin and disgust of their immediate acquaintances, who endeavored to drown their mortification and sorrow in rapid but somewhat wild gun play, and soon remembered that they had pressing engagements elsewhere.

Hopalong reloaded his guns and proceeded to the Emporium, where he found a game all prepared for him in every sense of the word. On the third deal he objected to the way in which the dealer manipulated the cards, and when the smoke cleared away he was the only occupant of the room, except a dog belonging to the bartender that had intercepted a stray bullet.

Hunting up the owner of the hound, he apologized for being the indirect cause of the animal's death, deposited a sum of Mexican dollars in that gentleman's palm and went on his way to Alameda, which he entered shortly after dark, and where an insult, simmering in its uncalled-for venom, met him as he limped across the floor of the local dispensary on his way to the bar. There was no time for verbal argument and precedent had established the manner of his reply, and his repartee was as quick as light and most effective. Having resented the epithets he gave his attention to the occupants of the room.

Smoke drifted over the table in an agitated cloud and dribbled lazily upward from the muzzle of his six-shooter, while he looked searchingly at those around him. Strained and eager faces peered at his opponent, who was sliding slowly forward in his chair, and for the length of a minute no sound but the guarded breathing of the onlookers could be heard. This was broken by a nervous cough from the rear of the room, and the faces assumed their ordinary nonchalant expressions, their rugged lines heavily shadowed in the light of the flickering oil lamps, while the shuffling of cards and the clink of silver became audible. Hopalong Cassidy had objected to insulting remarks about his affliction.

Hopalong was very sensitive about his crippled leg and was always prompt to resent any scorn or curiosity directed at it, especially when emanating from strangers. A young man of twenty-three years, when surrounded by nearly perfect specimens of physical manhood, is apt to be painfully self-conscious of any such defect, and it reacted on his nature at times, even though he was well-known for his happy-go-lucky disposition and playfulness. He consoled himself with the knowledge that what he lost in symmetry was more than balanced by the celerity and certainty of his gun hand, which was right or left, or both, as the occasion demanded.

Several hours later, as his luck was vacillating, he felt a heavy hand on his shoulder, and was overjoyed at seeing Buck and Red, the latter grinning as only Red could grin, and he withdrew from the game to enjoy his good fortune.

While Hopalong had been wandering over the country the two friends had been hunting for him and had traced him successfully, that being due to the trail he had blazed with his six-shooters. This they had accomplished without harm to themselves, as those of whom they inquired thought that they must want Hopalong "bad," and cheerfully gave the information required.

They had started out more for the purpose of accompanying him for pleasure, but that had changed to an urgent necessity in the following manner:

While on the way from Denver to Santa Fe they had met Pete Willis of the Three Triangle, a ranch that adjoined their own, and they paused to pass the compliments of the season.

"Purty far from th' grub wagon, Pie," remarked Buck.

"Oh, I'm only goin' to Denver," responded Pie.

"Purty hot," suggested Red.

"She shore is. Seen anybody yu knows?" Pie asked.

"One or two-Billy of th' Star Crescent an' Panhandle Lukins," answered Buck.

"That so? Panhandle's goin' to punch for us next year. I'll hunt him up. I heard down south of Albuquerque that Thirsty Jones an' his brothers are lookin' for trouble," offered Pie.

"Yah! They ain't lookin' for no trouble-they just goes around blowin' off. Trouble? Why, they don't know what she is," remarked Red contemptuously.

"Well, they's been dodgin' th' sheriff purty lively lately, an' if that ain't trouble I don't know what is," said Pie.

"It shore is, an' hard to dodge," acquiesced Buck.

"Well, I has to amble. Is Panhandle in Denver? Yes? I calculates as how me an' him'll buck th' tiger for a whirl-he's shore lucky. Well, so long," said Pie as he moved on.

"So long," responded the two.

"Hey, wait a minute," yelled Pie after he had ridden a hundred yards. "If yu sees Hopalong yu might tell him that th' Joneses are goin' to hunt him up when they gits to Albuquerque. They's shore sore on him. 'Tain't none of my funeral, only they ain't always a-carin' how they goes after a feller. So long," and soon he was a cloud of dust on the horizon.

"Trouble!" snorted Red; "well, between dodgin' Harris an' huntin' Hopalong I reckons they'll shore find her." Then to himself he murmured, "Funny how everythin' comes his way."

"That's gospel shore enough, but, as Pie said, they ain't a whole lot particular as how they deal th' cards. We better get a move on an' find that ornery little cuss," replied Buck.

"O. K., only I ain't losin' no sleep about Hoppy. His gun's too lively for me to do any worryin'," asserted Red.

"They'll get lynched some time, shore," declared Buck.

"Not if they find Hoppy," grimly replied Red.

They tore through Santa Fe, only stopping long enough to wet their throats, and after several hours of hard riding entered Alameda, where they found Hopalong in the manner narrated.

After some time the three left the room and headed for Albuquerque, twelve miles to the south. At ten o'clock they dismounted before the Nugget and Rope, an unpainted wooden building supposed to be a clever combination of barroom, dance and gambling hall and hotel. The cleverness lay in the man who could find the hotel part.

Chapter VII
The Open Door

The proprietor of the Nugget and Rope, a German named Baum, not being troubled with police rules, kept the door wide open for the purpose of inviting trade, a proceeding not to the liking of his patrons for obvious reasons. Probably not one man in ten was fortunate enough to have no one "looking for him," and the lighted interior assured good hunting to any one in the dark street. He was continually opening the door, which every newcomer promptly and forcibly slammed shut. When he saw men walk across the room for the express purpose of slamming it he began to cherish the idea that there was a conspiracy on foot to anger him and thus force him to bring about his own death.

After the door had been slammed three times in one evening by one man, the last slam being so forcible as to shake two bottles from the shelf and to crack the door itself, he became positive that his suspicions were correct, and so was very careful to smile and take it as a joke. Finally, wearied by his vain efforts to keep it open and fearing for the door, he hit upon a scheme, the brilliancy of which inflated his chest and gave him the appearance of a prize-winning bantam. When his patrons strolled in that night there was no door to slam, as it lay behind the bar.

When Buck and Red entered, closely followed by Hopalong, they elbowed their way to the rear of the room, where they could see before being seen. As yet they had said nothing to Hopalong about Pie's warning and were debating in their minds whether they should do so or not, when Hopalong interrupted their thoughts by laughing. They looked up and he nodded toward the front, where they saw that anxious eyes from all parts of the room were focused on the open door. Then they noticed that it had been removed.

The air of semi-hostile, semi-anxious inquiry of the patrons and the smile of satisfaction covering the face of Baum appealed to them as the most ludicrous sight their eyes had seen for months, and they leaned back and roared with laughter, thus calling forth sundry looks of disapproval from the innocent causes of their merriment. But they were too well known in Albuquerque to allow the disapproval to approach a serious end, and finally, as the humorous side of the situation dawned on the crowd, they joined in the laugh and all went merrily.

At the psychologic moment some one shouted for a dance and the suggestion met with uproarious approval. At that moment Harris, the sheriff, came in and volunteered to supply the necessary music if the crowd would pay the fine against a straying fiddler he had corraled the day before. A hat was quickly passed and a sum was realized which would pay several fines to come and Harris departed for the music.

A chair was placed on the bar for the musician and, to the tune of "Old Dan Tucker" and an assortment of similar airs, the board floor shook and trembled. It was a comical sight and Hopalong, the only wallflower besides Baum and the sheriff, laughed until he became weak. Cow punchers play as they work, hard and earnestly, and there was plenty of action. Sombreros flapped like huge wings and the baggy chaps looked like small, distorted balloons.

The Virginia reel was a marvel of supple, exaggerated grace and the quadrille looked like a free-for-all for unbroken colts. The honor of prompter was conferred upon the sheriff, and he gravely called the changes as they were usually called in that section of the country:

> "Oh, th' ladies trail in
> An' th' gents trail out,
> An' all stampede down th' middle.
> If yu ain't got th' tin
> Yu can dance an' shout,
> But yu must keep up with th' fiddle."

As the dance waxed faster and the dancers grew hotter Hopalong, feeling lonesome because he wouldn't face ridicule, even if it was not expressed, went over and stood by the sheriff. He and Harris were good friends, for he had received the wound that crippled him in saving the sheriff from assassination. Harris killed the man who had fired that shot, and from this episode on the burning desert grew a friendship that was as strong as their own natures.

Harris was very well liked by the majority and feared by the rest, for he was a square man and the best sheriff the county had ever known. Quiet and unassuming, small of stature and with a kind word for every one, he was a universal favorite among the better class of citizens. Quick as a flash and unerring in his shooting, he was a nightmare to the "bad men." No profane word had ever been known to leave his lips, and he was the possessor of a widespread reputation for generosity. His face was naturally frank and open; but when his eyes narrowed with determination it became blank and cold. When he saw his young friend sidle over to him he smiled and nodded a hearty welcome.

"They's shore cuttin' her loose," remarked Hopalong.

"First two pairs forward an' back! —they shore is," responded the prompter.

"Who's th' gent playin' lady to Buck?" Queried Hopalong.

"Forward again an' ladies change! —Billy Jordan."

Hopalong watched the couple until they swung around and then he laughed silently. "Buck's got too many feet," he seriously remarked to his friend.

"Swing th' girl yu loves th' best! —he ain't lonesome, look at that —"

Two shots rang out in quick succession and Harris stumbled, wheeled and pitched forward on his face as Hopalong's sombrero spun across his body. For a second there was an intense silence, heavy, strained and sickening. Then a roar broke forth and the crowd of frenzied merry-makers, headed by Hopalong, poured out into the street and spread out to search the town. As daylight dawned the searchers began to straggle back with the same report of failure. Buck and Red met on the street near the door and each looked questioningly at the other. Each shook his head and looked around, their fingers toying absentmindedly at their belts. Finally Buck cleared his throat and remarked casually,

"Mebby he's following 'em."

Red nodded and they went over toward their horses. As they were hesitating which route to take, Billy Jordan came up.

"Mebby yu'd like to see yore pardner-he's out by Buzzard's Spring. We'll take care of him," jerking his thumb over his shoulder toward the saloon where Harris's body lay. "And we'll all git th' others later. They cain't git away for long."

Buck and Red nodded and headed for Buzzard's Spring. As they neared the water hole they saw Hopalong sitting on a rock, his head resting in one hand while the other hung loosely from his knee. He did not notice them when they arrived, and with a ready tact they sat quietly on their horses and looked in every direction except toward him. The sun became a ball of molten fire and the sand flies annoyed them incessantly, but still they sat and waited, silent and apologetic.

Hopalong finally arose, reached for his sombrero, and, finding it gone, swore long and earnestly at the scene its loss brought before him. He walked over to his horse and, leaping into the saddle, turned and faced his friends. "Yu old sons-of-guns," he said. They looked sheepish and nodded negatively in answer to the look of inquiry in his eyes. "They ain't got 'em yet," remarked Red slowly. Hopalong straightened up, his eyes narrowed and his face became hard and resolute as he led the way back toward the town.

Buck rode up beside him and, wiping his face with his shirt sleeve, began to speak to Red. "We might look up th' Joneses, Red. They had been dodgin' th' sheriff purty lively lately, an' they was huntin' Hopalong. Ever since we had to kill their brother in Buckskin they has been yappin' as how they was goin' to wipe us out. Hopalong an' Harris was standin' clost together an' they tried for both. They shot twice, one for Harris an' one for Hopalong, an' what more do yu want?"

"It shore looks thataway, Buck," replied Red, biting into a huge plug of tobacco which he produced from his chaps. "Anyhow, they wouldn't be no loss if they didn't. Member what Pie said?"

Hopalong looked straight ahead, and when he spoke the words sounded as though he had bitten them off: "Yore right, Buck, but I gits first try at Thirsty. He's my meat an' I'll plug th' fellow what says he ain't. Damn him!"

The others replied by applying their spurs, and in a short time they dismounted before the Nugget and Rope. Thirsty wouldn't have a chance to not care how he dealt the cards.

Buck and Red moved quickly through the crowd, speaking fast and earnestly. When they returned to where they had left their friend they saw him half a block away and they followed slowly, one on either side of the street. There would be no bullets in his back if they knew what they were about, and they usually did.

As Hopalong neared the corner, Thirsty and his two brothers turned it and saw him. Thirsty said something in a low voice, and the other two walked across the street and disappeared behind the store. When assured that they were secure, Thirsty walked up to a huge boulder on the side of the street farthest from the store and turned and faced his enemy, who approached rapidly until about five paces away, when he slowed up and finally stopped.

For a number of seconds they sized each other up, Hopalong quiet and deliberate with a deadly hatred; Thirsty pale and furtive with a sensation hitherto unknown to him. It was Right meeting Wrong, and Wrong lost confidence. Often had Thirsty Jones looked death in the face and laughed, but there was something in Hopalong's eyes that made his flesh creep.

He glanced quickly past his foe and took in the scene with one flash of his eyes. There was the crowd, eager, expectant, scowling. There were Buck and Red, each lounging against a boulder, Buck on his right, Red on his left. Before him stood the only man he had ever feared.

Hopalong shifted his feet and Thirsty, coming to himself with a start, smiled. His nerve had been shaken, but he was master of himself once more.

"Well!" he snarled, scowling.

Hopalong made no response, but stared him in the eyes.

Thirsty expected action, and the deadly quiet of his enemy oppressed him. He stared in turn, but the insistent searching of his opponent's eyes scorched him and he shifted his gaze to Hopalong's neck.

"Well!" he repeated uneasily.

"Did yu have a nice time at th' dance last night?" Asked Hopalong, still searching the face before him.

"Was there a dance? I was over in Alameda," replied Thirsty shortly.

"Ya-as, there was a dance, an' yu can shoot purty durn far if yu was in Alameda," responded Hopalong, his voice low and monotonous.

Thirsty shifted his feet and glanced around. Buck and Red were still lounging against their bowlders and apparently were not paying any attention to the proceedings. His fickle nerve came back again, for he knew he would receive fair play. So he faced Hopalong once more and regarded him with a cynical smile.

"Yu seems to worry a whole lot about me. Is it because yu has a tender feelin', or because it's none of yore blame business?" He asked aggressively.

Hopalong paled with sudden anger, but controlled himself.

"It's because yu murdered Harris," he replied.

"Shoo! An' how does yu figger it out?" Asked Thirsty, jauntily.

"He was huntin' yu hard an' yu thought yu'd stop it, so yu came in to lay for him. When yu saw me an' him together yu saw di' chance to wipe out another score. That's how I figger it out," replied Hopalong quietly.

"Yore a reg'lar 'tective, ain't yu?" Thirsty asked ironically.

"I've got common sense," responded Hopalong.

"Yu has? Yu better tell th' rest that, too," replied Thirsty.

"I know yu shot Harris, an' yu can't get out of it by makin' funny remarks. Anyhow, yu won't be much loss, an' th' stage company'll feel better, too."

"Shoo! An' suppose I did shoot him, I done a good job, didn't I?"

"Yu did the worst job yu could do, yu highway robber," softly said Hopalong, at the same time moving nearer. "Harris knew yu stopped th' stage last month, an' that's why yu've been dodgin' him."

"Yore a liar!" shouted Thirsty, reaching for his gun.

The movement was fatal, for before he could draw, the Colt in Hopalong's holster leaped out and flashed from its owner's hip and Thirsty fell sideways, face down in the dust of the street.

Hopalong started toward the fallen man, but as he did so a shot rang out from behind the store and he pitched forward, stumbled and rolled behind the bowlder. As he stumbled his left hand streaked to his hip, and when he fell he had a gun in each hand.

As he disappeared from sight Goodeye and Bill Jones stepped from behind the store and started to run away. Not able to resist the temptation to look again, they stopped and turned and Bill laughed.

"Easy as sin," he said.

"Run, yu fool-Red an' Buck'll be here. Want to git plugged?" shouted Goodeye angrily.

They turned and started for a group of ponies twenty yards away, and as they leaped into the saddles two shots were fired from the street. As the reports died away Buck and Red turned the corner of the store, Colts in hand, and, checking their rush as they saw the saddles emptied, they turned toward the street and saw Hopalong, with blood oozing from an abrasion on his cheek, sitting up cross-legged, with each hand holding a gun, from which came thin wisps of smoke.

"Th' son-of-a-gun!" cried Buck, proud and delighted.

"Th' son-of-a-gun!" echoed Red, grinning.

Chapter VIII
Hopalong Keeps His Word

The waters of the Rio Grande slid placidly toward the Gulf, the hot sun branding the sleepy waters with streaks of molten fire. To the north arose from the gray sandy plain the Quitman Mountains, and beyond them lay Bass Ca on. From the latter emerged a solitary figure astride a broncho, and as he ascended the topmost rise he glanced below him at the placid stream and beyond it into Mexico. As he sat quietly in his saddle he smiled and laughed gently to himself. The trail he had just followed had been replete with trouble which had suited the state of his mind and he now felt humorous, having cleaned up a pressing debt with his six-shooter. Surely there ought to be a mild sort of excitement in the land he faced, something picturesque and out of the ordinary. This was to be the finishing touch to his trip, and he had left his two companions at Albuquerque in order that he might have to himself all that he could find.

Not many miles to the south of him lay the town which had been the rendezvous of Tamale Jose, whose weakness had been a liking for other people's cattle. Well he remembered his first man hunt: the discovery of the theft, the trail and pursuit and-the ending. He was scarcely eighteen years of age when that event took place, and the wisdom he had absorbed then had stood him in good stead many times since. He had even now a touch of pride at the recollection how, when his older companions had failed to get Tamale Jose, he with his undeveloped strategy had gained that end. The fight would never be forgotten, as it was his first, and no sight of wounds would ever affect him as did those of Red Connors as he lay huddled up in the dark corner of that old adobe hut.

He came to himself and laughed again as he thought of Carmencita, the first girl he had ever known-and the last. With a boy's impetuosity he had wooed her in a manner far different from that of the peons who sang beneath her window and talked to her mother. He had boldly scaled the wall and did his courting in her house, trusting to luck and to his own ability to avoid being seen. No hidden meaning lay in his words; he spoke from his heart and with no concealment. And he remembered the treachery that had forced him, fighting, to the camp of his outfit; and when he had returned with his friends she had disappeared.

To this day he hated that mud-walled convent and those sisters who so easily forgot how to talk. The fragrance of the old days wrapped themselves around him, and although he had ceased to pine for his black-eyed Carmencita-well, it would be nice if he chanced to see her again. Spurring his mount into an easy canter he swept down to and across the river, fording it where he had crossed it when pursuing Tamale Jose.

The town lay indolent under the Mexican night, and the strumming of guitars and the tinkle of spurs and tiny bells softly echoed from several houses. The convent of St. Maria lay indistinct in its heavy shadows and the little church farther up the dusty street showed dim lights in its stained windows. Off to the north became audible the rhythmic beat of a horse and soon a cowboy swept past the convent with a mocking bow.

He clattered across the stone-paved plaza and threw his mount back on its haunches as he stopped before a house. Glancing around and determining to find out a few facts as soon as possible, he rode up to the low door and pounded upon it with the butt of his Colt. After waiting for possibly half a minute and receiving no response he hammered a tune upon it with two Colts and had the satisfaction of seeing half a score of heads protrude from the windows in the nearby houses.

"If I could scare up another gun I might get th' whole blamed town up," he grumbled whimsically, and fell on the door with another tune.

"Who is it?" came from within. The voice was distinctly feminine and Hopalong winked to himself in congratulation.

"Me," he replied, twirling his fingers from his nose at the curious, forgetting that the darkness hid his actions from sight.

"Yes, I know; but who is 'me'?" Came from the house.

"Ain't I a fool!" he complained to himself, and raising his voice he replied coaxingly, "Open th' door a bit an' see. Are yu Carmencita?"

"O-o-o! but you must tell me who it is first."

"Mr. Cassidy," he replied, flushing at the 'mister,' "an' I wants to see Carmencita."

"Carmencita who?" teasingly came from behind the door. Hopalong scratched his head. "Gee, yu've roped me —I suppose she has got another handle. Oh, yu know-she used to live here about seven years back. She had great big black eyes, pretty cheeks an' a mouth that 'ud stampede anybody. Don't yu know now? She was about so high," holding out his hands in the darkness.

The door opened a trifle on a chain and Hopalong peered eagerly forward.

"Ah, it is you, the brave Americano! You must go away quick or you will meet with harm. Manuel is awfully jealous and he will kill you! Go at once, please!"

Hopalong pulled at the half-hearted down upon his lip and laughed softly. Then he slid the guns back in their holsters and felt for his sombrero.

"Manuel wants to see me first, Star Eyes."

"No! no!" she replied, stamping upon the floor vehemently. "You must go now-at once!"

"I'd shore look nice hittin' th' trail because Manuel Somebody wants to get hurt, wouldn't I? Don't yu remember how I used to shinny up this here wall an' skin th' cat gettin' through that hole up there what yu said was a window? Ah, come on an' open th' door —I'd shore like to see yu again!" pleaded the irrepressible.

"No! no! Go away. Oh, won't you please go away!"

Hopalong sighed audibly and turned his horse. As he did so he heard the door open and a sigh reached his ears. He wheeled like a flash and found the door closed again on its chain. A laugh of delight came from behind it.

"Come out, please! —just for a minute," he begged, wishing that he was brave enough to smash the door to splinters and grab her.

"If I do, will you go away?" Asked the girl. "Oh, what will Manuel say if he comes? And all those people, they'll tell him!"

"Hey, yu!" shouted Hopalong, brandishing his Colts at the protruding heads. "Git scarce! I'll shore plug th' last one in!" Then he laughed at the sudden vanishing.

The door slowly opened and Carmencita, fat and drowsy, wobbled out to him. Hopalong's feelings were interfering with his breathing as he surveyed her. "Oh, yu shore are mistaken, Mrs. Carmencita. I wants to see yore daughter!"

"Ah, you have forgotten the little Carmencita who used to look for you. Like all the men, you have forgotten," she cooed reproachfully. Then her fear predominated again and she cried, "Oh, if my husband should see me now!"

Hopalong mastered his astonishment and bowed. He had a desire to ride madly into the Rio Grande and collect his senses.

"Yu are right-this is too dangerous —I'll amble on some," he replied hastily. Under his breath he prayed that the outfit would never learn of this. He turned his horse and rode slowly up the street as the door closed.

Rounding the corner he heard a soft footfall, and swerving in his saddle he turned and struck with all his might in the face of a man who leaped at him, at the same time grasping the uplifted wrist with his other hand. A curse and the tinkle of thin steel on the pavement accompanied the fall of his opponent. Bending down from his saddle he picked up the weapon and the next minute the enraged assassin was staring into the unwavering and, to him, growing muzzle of a Colt's .45.

"Yu shore had a bum teacher. Don't yu know better'n to push it in? An' me a cowpuncher, too! I'm most grieved at yore conduct-it shows you don't appreciate cow-wrastlers. This is safer," he remarked, throwing the stiletto through the air and into a door, where it rang out angrily and quivered. "I don't know as I wants to ventilate yu; we mostly poisons coyotes up my way," he added. Then a thought struck him. "Yu must be that dear Manuel I've been hearin' so much about?"

A snarl was the only reply and Hopalong grinned.

"Yu shore ain't got no call to go loco that way, none whatever. I don't want yore Carmencita. I only called to say hulloo," responded Hopalong, his sympathies being aroused for the wounded man before him from his vivid recollection of the woman who had opened the door.

"Yah!" snarled Manuel. "You wants to poison my little bird. You with your fair hair and your cursed swagger!"

The six-shooter tentatively expanded and stopped six inches from the Mexican's nose. "Yu wants to ride easy, hombre. I ain't no angel, but I don't poison no woman; an' don't yu amble off with th' idea in yore head that she wants to be poisoned. Why, she near stuck a knife in me!" he lied.

The Mexican's face brightened somewhat, but it would take more than that to wipe out the insult of the blow. The horse became restless, and when Hopalong had effectively quieted it he spoke again.

"Did yu ever hear of Tamale Jose?"

"Yes."

"Well, I'm th' fellow that stopped him in th' 'dobe hut by th' arroyo. I'm tellin' yu this so yu won't do nothin' rash an' leave Carmencita a widow. Sabe?"

The hate on the Mexican's face redoubled and he took a short step forward, but stopped when the muzzle of the Colt kissed his nose. He was the brother of Tamale Jose. As he backed away from the cool touch of the weapon he thought out swiftly his revenge. Some of his brother's old companions were at that moment drinking mescal in a saloon down the street, and they would be glad to see this Americano die. He glanced past his house at the saloon and Hopalong misconstrued his thoughts.

"Shore, go home. I'll just circulate around some for exercise. No hard feelings, only yu better throw it next time," he said as he backed away and rode off. Manuel went down the street and then ran into the saloon, where he caused an uproar.

Hopalong rode to the end of the plaza and tried to sing, but it was a dismal failure. Then he felt thirsty and wondered why he hadn't thought of it before. Turning his horse and seeing the saloon he rode up to it and in, lying flat on the animal's neck to avoid being swept off by the door frame. His entrance scared white some half a dozen loungers, who immediately sprang up in a decidedly hostile manner. Hopalong's Colts peeped over the ears of his horse and he backed into a corner near the bar.

"One, two, three-now, altogether, breathe! Yu acts like yu never saw a real puncher afore. All th' same," he remarked, nodding at several of the crowd, "I've seen yu afore. Yu are th' gents with th' hot-foot get-a-way that vamoosed when we got Tamale."

Curses were flung at him and only the humorous mood he was in saved trouble. One, bolder than the rest, spoke up: "The senor will not see any 'hot-foot get-a-way,' as he calls it, now! The senor was not wise to go so far away from his friends!'"

Hopalong looked at the speaker and a quizzical grin slowly spread over his face. "They'll shore feel glad when I tells them yu was askin' for 'em. But didn't yu see too much of 'em once, or was yu poundin' leather in the other direction? Yu don't want to worry none about me-an' if yu don't get yore hands closter to yore neck they'll be heck to pay! There, that's more like home," he remarked, nodding assurance.

Reaching over he grasped a bottle and poured out a drink, his Colt slipping from his hand and dangling from his wrist by a thong. As the weapon started to fall several of the audience involuntarily moved as if to pick it up. Hopalong noticed this and paused with the glass half way to his lips. "Don't bother yoreselves none; I can git it again," he said, tossing off the liquor.

"Wow! Holy smoke!" he yelled. "This ain't drink! Sufferin' coyotes, nobody can accuse yu of sellin' liquor! Did yu make this all by yoreself?" He asked incredulously of the proprietor, who didn't know whether to run or to pray. Then he noticed that the crowd was spreading out and his Colts again became the center of interest.

"Yu with th' lovely face, sit down!" he ordered as the person addressed was gliding toward the door. "I ain't a-goin' to let yu pot me from th' street. Th' first man who tries to get scarce will stop somethin' hot. An' yu all better sit down," he suggested, sweeping them with his guns. One man, more obdurate than the rest, was slow in complying and Hopalong sent a bullet through the top of his high sombrero, which had a most gratifying effect.

"You'll regret this!" hissed a man in the rear, and a murmur of assent arose. Some one stirred slightly in searching for a weapon and immediately a blazing Colt froze him into a statue.

"Yu shore looks funny; eeny, meeny, miny, mo," counted off the daring horseman; "move a bit an' off yu go," he finished. Then his face broke out in another grin as he thought of more enjoyment.

"That there gent on th' left," he said, pointing out with a gun the man he meant. "Yu sing us a song. Sing a nice little song."

As the object of his remarks remained mute he let his thumb ostentatiously slide back with the hammer of the gun under it. "Sing! Quick!" The man sang.

As Hopalong leaned forward to say something a stiletto flashed past his neck and crashed into the bottle beside him. The echo of the crash was merged into a report as Hopalong fired from his waist. Then he backed out into the Street and, wheeling, galloped across the plaza and again faced the saloon. A flash split the darkness and a bullet hummed over his head and thudded into an adobe wall at his back. Another shot and he replied, aiming at the flash.

From down the Street came the sound of a window opening and he promptly caused it to close again. Several more windows opened and hastily closed, and he rode slowly toward the far end of the plaza. As he faced the saloon once more he heard a command to throw up his hands and saw the glint of a gun, held by a man who wore the insignia of sheriff. Hopalong complied, but as his hands went up two spurts of fire shot forth and the sheriff dropped his weapon, reeled and sat down. Hopalong rode over to him and swinging down, picked up the gun and looked the officer over.

"Shoo, yu'll be all right soon-yore only plugged in th' arms," he remarked as he glanced up the street. Shadowy forms were gliding from cover to cover and he immediately caused consternation among them by his accuracy. "Ain't it sad?" He complained to the wounded man. "I never starts out but what somebody makes me shoot 'em. Came down here to see a girl an' find she's married. Then when I moves on peaceable-like her husband makes me hit him. Then I wants a drink an' he goes an' fans a knife at me, an' me just teachin' him how! Then yu has to come along an' make more trouble".

"Now look at them fools over there," he said, pointing at a dark shadow some fifty paces off. "They're pattin' their backs because I don't see 'em, an' if I hurts them they'll git mad. Guess I'll make 'em dust along," he added, shooting into the spot. A howl went up and two men ran away at top speed.

The sheriff nodded his sympathy and spoke. "I reckons you had better give up. You can't get away. Every house, every corner and shadow holds a man. You are a brave man, but, as you say, unfortunate. Better help me up and come with me-they'll tear you to pieces."

"Shore I'll help yu up —I ain't got no grudge against nobody. But my friends know where I am an' they'll come down here an' raise a ruction if I don't show up. So, if it's all th' same to you, I'll be ambling right along," he said as he helped the sheriff to his feet.

"Have you any objections to telling me your name?" Asked the sheriff as he looked himself over.

"None whatever," answered Hopalong heartily. "I'm Hopalong Cassidy of th' Bar 20, Texas."

"You don't surprise me —I've heard of you," replied the sheriff wearily. "You are the man who killed Tamale Jose, whom I hunted for unceasingly. I found him when you had left and I got the reward. Come again some time and I'll divide with you; two hundred and fifty dollars," he added craftily.

"I shore will, but I don't want no money," replied Hopalong as he turned away. "Adios, senor," he called back.

"Adios," replied the sheriff as he kicked a nearby door for assistance.

The cow-pony tied itself up in knots as it pounded down the street toward the trail, and although he was fired on he swung into the dusty trail with a song on his lips. Several hours later he stood dripping wet on the American side of the Rio Grande and shouted advice to a score of Mexican cavalrymen on the opposite bank. Then he slowly picked his way toward El Paso for a game at Faro Dan's.

The sheriff sat in his easy chair one night some three weeks later, gravely engaged in rolling a cigarette. His arms were practically well, the wounds being in the fleshy parts. He was a philosopher and was disposed to take things easy, which accounted for his being in his official position for fifteen years. A gentleman at the core, he was well educated and had visited a goodly portion of the world. A book of Horace lay open on his knees and on the table at his side lay a shining new revolver, Hopalong having carried off his former weapon. He read aloud several lines and in reaching for a light for his cigarette noticed the new six-shooter. His mind leaped from Horace to Hopalong, and he smiled grimly at the latter's promise to call.

Glancing up, his eyes fell on a poster which conveyed the information in Spanish and in English that there was offered

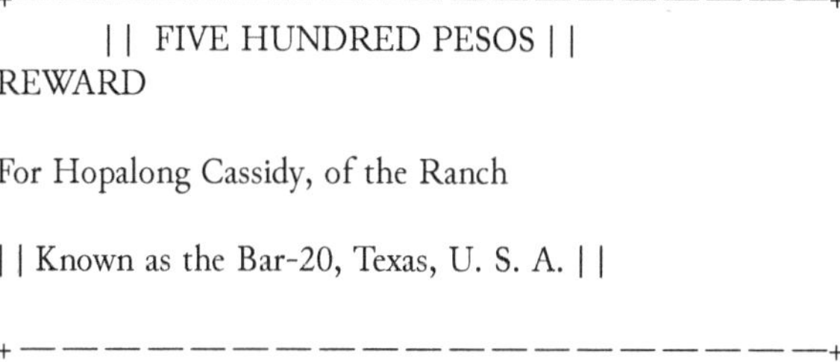

and which gave a good description of that gentleman.

Sighing for the five hundred, he again took up his book and was lost in its pages when he heard a knock, rather low and timid. Wearily laying aside his reading, he strode to the door, expecting to hear a lengthy complaint from one of his townsmen. As he threw the door wide open the light streamed out and lighted up a revolver and behind it the beaming face of a cowboy, who grinned.

"Well, I'll be damned!" ejaculated the sheriff, starting back in amazement.

"Don't say that, sheriff; you've got lots of time to reform," replied a humorous voice. "How's th' wings?"

"Almost well: you were considerate," responded the sheriff. "Let's go in-somebody might see me out here an' get into trouble," suggested the visitor, placing his foot on the sill.

"Certainly-pardon my discourtesy," said the sheriff. "You see, I wasn't expecting you to-night," he explained, thinking of the elaborate preparations that he would have gone to if he had thought the irrepressible would call.

"Well, I was down this way, an' seeing as how I had promised to drop in I just natchurally dropped," replied Hopalong as he took the chair proffered by his host.

After talking awhile on everything and nothing the sheriff coughed and looked uneasily at his guest.

"Mr. Cassidy, I am sorry you called, for I like men of your energy and courage and I very much dislike to arrest you," remarked the sheriff. "Of course you understand that you are under arrest," he added with anxiety.

"Who, me?" Asked Hopalong with a rising inflection.

"Most assuredly," breathed the sheriff.

"Why, this is the first time I ever heard anything about it," replied the astonished cowpuncher. "I'm an American-don't that make any difference?"

"Not in this case, I'm afraid. You see, it's for manslaughter."

"Well, don't that beat th' devil, now?" Said Hopalong. He felt sorry that a citizen of the glorious United States should be prey for troublesome sheriffs, but he was sure that his duty to Texas called upon him never to submit to arrest at the hands of a Mexican. Remembering the Alamo, and still behind his Colt, he reached over and took up the shining weapon from the table and snapped it open on his knee. After placing the cartridges in his pocket he tossed the gun over on the bed and, reaching inside his shirt, drew out another and threw it after the first.

"That's yore gun; I forgot to leave it," he said, apologetically. "Anyhow yu needs two," he added.

Then he glanced around the room, noticed the poster and walked over and read it. A full swift sweep of his gloved hand tore it from its fastenings and crammed it under his belt. The glimmer of anger in his eyes gave way as he realized that his head was worth a definite price, and he smiled at what the boys would say when he showed it to them. Planting his feet far apart and placing his arms akimbo he faced his host in grim defiance.

"Got any more of these?" He inquired, placing his hand on the poster under his belt.

"Several," replied the sheriff.

"Trot 'em out," ordered Hopalong shortly.

The sheriff sighed, stretched and went over to a shelf, from which he took a bundle of the articles in question. Turning slowly he looked at the puncher and handed them to him.

"I reckons they's all over this here town," remarked Hopalong.

"They are, and you may never see Texas again."

"So? Well, yu tell yore most particular friends that the job is worth five thousand, and that it will take so many to do it that when th' mazuma is divided up it won't buy a meal. There's only one man in this country tonight that can earn that money, an' that's me," said the puncher. "An' I don't need it," he added, smiling.

"But you are my prisoner-you are under arrest," enlightened the sheriff, rolling another cigarette. The sheriff spoke as if asking a question. Never before had five hundred dollars been so close at hand and yet so unobtainable. It was like having a check-book but no bank account.

"I'm shore sorry to treat yu mean," remarked Hopalong, "but I was paid a month in advance an' I'll have to go back an' earn it."

"You can-if you say that you will return," replied the sheriff tentatively. The sheriff meant what he said and for the moment had forgotten that he was powerless and was not the one to make terms.

Hopalong was amazed and for a time his ideas of Mexicans staggered under the blow. Then he smiled sympathetically as he realized that he faced a white man.

"Never like to promise nothin'," he replied. "I might get plugged, or something might happen that wouldn't let me." Then his face lighted up as a thought came to him. "Say, I'll cut di' cards with yu to see if I comes back or not."

The sheriff leaned back and gazed at the cool youngster before him. A smile of satisfaction, partly at the self-reliance of his guest and partly at the novelty of his situation, spread over his face. He reached for a pack of Mexican cards and laughed. "Man! You're a cool one —I'll do it. What do you call?"

"Red," answered Hopalong.

The sheriff slowly raised his hand and revealed the ace of hearts. Hopalong leaned back and laughed, at the same time taking from his pocket the six extracted cartridges. Arising and going over to the bed he slipped them in the chambers of the new gun and then placed the loaded weapon at the sheriff's elbow.

"Well, I reckon I'll amble, sheriff," he said as he opened the door. "If yu ever sifts up my way drop in an' see me-th' boys'll give yu a good time."

"Thanks; I will be glad to," replied the sheriff. "You'll take your pitcher to the well once too often some day, my friend. This courtesy," glancing at the restored revolver, "might have cost you dearly."

"Shoo! I did that once an' th' feller tried to use it," replied the cowboy as he backed through the door. "Some people are awfully careless," he added. "So long —"

"So long," replied the sheriff, wondering what sort of a man he had been entertaining.

The door closed softly and soon after a joyous whoop floated in from the Street. The sheriff toyed with the new gun and listened to the low caress of a distant guitar.

"Well, don't that beat all?" He ejaculated.

Chapter IX
The Advent of McAllister

The blazing sun shone pitilessly on an arid plain which was spotted with dust-gray clumps of mesquite and thorny chaparral. Basking in the burning sand and alkali lay several Gila monsters, which raised their heads and hissed with wide-open jaws as several faint, whip-like reports echoed flatly over the desolate plain, showing that even they had learned that danger was associated with such sounds.

Off to the north there became visible a cloud of dust and at intervals something swayed in it, something that rose and fell and then became hidden again. Out of that cloud came sharp, splitting sounds, which were faintly responded to by another and larger cloud in its rear. As it came nearer and finally swept past, the Gilas, to their terror, saw a madly pounding horse, and it carried a man. The latter turned in his saddle and raised a gun to his shoulder and the thunder that issued from it caused the creeping audience to throw up their tails in sudden panic and bury themselves out of sight in the sand.

The horse was only a broncho, its sides covered with hideous yellow spots, and on its near flank was a peculiar scar, the brand. Foam flecked from its crimsoned jaws and found a resting place on its sides and on the hairy chaps of its rider. Sweat rolled and streamed from its heaving flanks and was greedily sucked up by the drought-cursed alkali. Close to the rider's knee a bloody furrow ran forward and one of the broncho's ears was torn and limp. The broncho was doing its best-it could run at that pace until it dropped dead. Every ounce of strength it possessed was put forth to bring those hind hoofs well in front of the forward ones and to send them pushing the sand behind in streaming clouds. The horse had done this same thing many times-when would its master learn sense?

The man was typical in appearance with many of that broad land. Lithe, sinewy and bronzed by hard riding and hot suns, he sat in his Cheyenne saddle like a centaur, all his weight on the heavy, leather-guarded stirrups, his body rising in one magnificent straight line. A bleached moustache hid the thin lips, and a gray sombrero threw a heavy shadow across his eyes. Around his neck and over his open, blue flannel shirt lay loosely a knotted silk kerchief, and on his thighs a pair of open-flapped holsters swung uneasily with their ivory handled burdens. He turned abruptly, raised his gun to his shoulder and fired, then he laughed recklessly and patted his mount, which responded to the confident caress by lying flatter to the earth in a spurt of heart-breaking speed.

"I'll show 'em who they're trailin'. This is th' second time I've started for Muddy Wells, an' I'm goin' to git there, too, for all th' Apaches out of Hades!"

To the south another cloud of dust rapidly approached and the rider scanned it closely, for it was directly in his path. As he watched it he saw something wave and it was a sombrero!

Shortly afterward a real cowboy yell reached his ears. He grinned and slid another cartridge in the greasy, smoking barrel of the Sharp's and fired again at the cloud in his rear. Some few minutes later a whooping, bunched crowd of madly riding cowboys thundered past him and he was recognized.

"Hullo, Frenchy!" yelled the nearest one. "Comin' back?"

"Come on, McAllister!" shouted another; "we'll give 'em blazes!" In response the straining broncho suddenly stiffened, bunched and slid on its haunches, wheeled and retraced its course. The rear cloud suddenly scattered into many smaller ones and all swept off to the east. The rescuing band overtook them and, several hours later, when seated around a table in Tom Lee's saloon, Muddy Wells, a count was taken of them, which was pleasing in its facts.

"We was huntin' coyotes when we saw yu," said a smiling puncher who was known as Salvation Carroll chiefly because he wasn't.

"Yep! They've been stalkin' Tom's chickens," supplied Waffles, the champion poker player of the outfit. Tom Lee's chickens could whip anything of their kind for miles around and were reverenced accordingly.

"Sho! Is that so?" Asked Frenchy with mild incredulity, such a state of affairs being deplorable.

"She shore is!" answered Tex Le Blanc, and then, as an afterthought, he added, "Where'd yu hit th' War-whoops?"

"'Bout four hours back. This here's th' second time I've headed for this place-last time they chased me to Las Cruces."

"That so?" Asked Bigfoot Baker, a giant. "Ain't they allus interferin', now? Anyhow, they're better'n coyotes."

"They was purty well heeled," suggested Tex, glancing at a bunch of repeating Winchesters of late model which lay stacked in a corner. "Charley here said he thought they was from th' way yore cayuse looked, didn't yu, Charley?" Charley nodded and filled his pipe.

"'Pears like a feller can't amble around much nowadays without havin' to fight," grumbled Lefty Allen, who usually went out of his way hunting up trouble.

"We're goin' to th' Hills as soon as our cookie turns up," volunteered Tenspot Davis, looking inquiringly at Frenchy. "Heard any more news?"

"Nope. Same old story-lots of gold. Shucks, I've bit on so many of them rumors that they don't feaze me no more. One man who don't know nothin' about prospectin' goes an' stumbles over a fortune an' those who know it from A to Izzard goes 'round pullin' in their belts."

"We don't pull in no belts-we knows just where to look, don't we, Tenspot?" Remarked Tex, looking very wise.

"Ya-as we do," answered Tenspot, "if yu hasn't dreamed about it, we do."

"Yu wait; I wasn't dreamin', none whatever," assured Tex.

"I saw it!"

"Ya-as, I saw it too onct," replied Frenchy with sarcasm. "Went and lugged fifty pound of it all th' way to th' assay office-took me two days! an' that there four-eyed cuss looks at it and snickers. Then he takes me by di' arm an' leads me to th' window. 'See that pile, my friend? That's all like yourn,' sez he. 'It's worth about one simoleon a ton at th' coast. They use it for ballast.'"

"Aw! But this what I saw was gold!" exploded Tex.

"So was mine, for a while!" laughed Frenchy, nodding to the bartender for another round.

"Well, we're tired of punchin' cows! Ride sixteen hours a day, year in an' year out, an' what do we get? Fifty a month an' no chance to spend it, an' grub that'd make a coyote sniffle! I'm for a vacation, an' if I goes broke, why, I'll punch again!" asserted Waffles, the foreman, thus revealing the real purpose of the trip.

"What'd yore boss say?" Asked Frenchy.

"Whoop! What didn't he say! Honest, I never thought he had it in him. It was fine. He cussed an hour frontways an' then trailed back on a dead gallop, with us a-laughin' fit to bust.

Then he rustles for his gun an' we rustles for town," answered Waffles, laughing at his remembrance of it.

As Frenchy was about to reply his sombrero was snatched from his head and disappeared. If he "got mad" he was to be regarded as not sufficiently well acquainted for banter and he was at once in hot water; if he took it good-naturedly he was one of the crowd in spirit; but in either case he didn't get his hat without begging or fighting for it. This was a recognized custom among the O-Bar-O outfit and was not intended as an insult.

Frenchy grabbed at the empty air and arose. Punching Lefty playfully in the ribs he passed his hands behind that person's back. Not finding the lost head-gear he laughed and, tripping Lefty up, fell with him and, reaching up on the table for his glass, poured the contents down Lefty's back and arose.

"Yu son-of-a-gun!" indignantly wailed that unfortunate. "Gee, it feels funny," he added, grinning as he pulled the wet shirt away from his spine.

"Well, I've got to be amblin'," said Frenchy, totally ignoring the loss of his hat. "Goin' down to Buckskin," he offered, and then asked, "When's yore cook comin'?"

"Day after to-morrow, if he don't get loaded," replied Tex.

"Who is he?"

"A one-eyed Mexican-Quiensabe Antonio."

"I used to know him. He's a heck of a cook. Dished up th' grub one season when I was punchin' for th' Tin-Cup up in Montana," replied Frenchy.

"Oh, he kin cook now, all right." replied Waffles.

"That's about all he can cook. Useter wash his knives in th' coffee pot an' blow on di' tins. I chased him a mile one night for leavin' sand in th' skillet. Yu can have him —I don't envy yu none whatever.

"He don't sand no skillet when little Tenspot's around," assured that person, slapping his holster. "Does he, Lefty?"

"If he does, yu oughter be lynched," consoled Lefty.

"Well, so long," remarked Frenchy, riding off to a small store, where he bought a cheap sombrero.

Frenchy was a jack-of-all-trades, having been cow-puncher, prospector, proprietor of a "hotel" in Albuquerque, foreman of a ranch, sheriff, and at one time had played angel to a venturesome but poor show troupe. Beside his versatility he was well known as the man who took the stage through the Sioux country when no one else volunteered. He could shoot with the best, but his one pride was the brand of poker he handed out. Furthermore, he had never been known to take an unjust advantage over any man and, on the contrary, had frequently voluntarily handicapped himself to make the event more interesting. But he must not be classed as being hampered with self-restraint.

His reasons for making this trip were two-fold: he wished to see Buck Peters, the foreman of the Bar-20 outfit, as he and Buck had punched cows together twenty years before and were firm friends; the other was that he wished to get square with Hopalong Cassidy, who had decisively cleaned him out the year before at poker. Hopalong played either in great good luck or the contrary, while Frenchy played an even, consistent game and usually left off richer than when he began, and this decisive defeat bothered him more than he would admit, even to himself.

The round-up season was at hand and the Bar-20 was short of ropers, the rumors of fresh gold discoveries in the Black Hills having drawn all the more restless men north. The outfit also had a slight touch of the gold fever, and only their peculiar loyalty to the ranch and the assurance of the foreman that when the work was over he would accompany them, kept them from joining the rush of those who desired sudden and much wealth as the necessary preliminary of painting some cow town in all the "bang up" style such an event would call for. Therefore they had been given orders to secure the required assistance, and they intended to do so, and were prepared to kidnap, if necessary, for the glamour of wealth and the hilarity of the vacation made the hours falter in their speed.

As Frenchy leaned back in his chair in Cowan's saloon, Buckskin, early the next morning, planning to get revenge on Hopalong and then to recover his sombrero, he heard a medley of yells and whoops and soon the door flew open before the strenuous and concentrated entry of a mass of twisting and kicking arms and legs, which magically found their respective owners and reverted to the established order of things.

When the alkali dust had thinned he saw seven cow-punchers sitting on the prostrate form of another, who was earnestly engaged in trying to push Johnny Nelson's head out in the street with one foot as he voiced his lucid opinion of things in general and the seven in particular. After Red Connors had been stabbed in the back several times by the victim's energetic elbow he ran out of the room and presently returned with a pleased expression and a sombrero full of water, his finger plugging an old bullet hole in the crown.

"Is he any better, Buck?" Anxiously inquired the man with the reservoir.

"About a dollar's worth," replied the foreman. "Jest put a little right here," he drawled as he pulled back the collar of the unfortunate's shirt.

"Ow! wow! WOW!" wailed the recipient, heaving and straining. The unengaged leg was suddenly wrested loose, and as it shot up and out Billy Williams, with his pessimism aroused to a blue-ribbon pitch, sat down forcibly in an adjacent part of the room, from where he lectured between gasps on the follies of mankind and the attributes of army mules.

Red tiptoed around the squirming bunch, looking for an opening, his pleased expression now having added a grin.

"Seems to be gittin' violent-like," he soliloquized, as he aimed a stream at Hopalong's ear, which showed for a second as Pete Wilson strove for a half-nelson, and he managed to include Johnny and Pete in his effort.

Several minutes later, when the storm had subsided, the woeful crowd enthusiastically urged Hopalong to the bar, where he "bought."

"Of all th' ornery outfits I ever saw —" began the man at the table, grinning from ear to ear at the spectacle he had just witnessed.

"Why, hullo, Frenchy! Glad to see yu, yu old son-of-a-gun! What's th' news from th' Hills?" Shouted Hopalong.

"Rather locoed, an' there's a locoed gang that's headin' that way. Goin' up?" he asked.

"Shore, after round-up. Seen any punchers trailin' around loose?"

"Ya-as," drawled Frenchy, delving into the possibilities suddenly opened to him and determining to utilize to the fullest extent the opportunity that had come to him unsought. "There's nine over to Muddy Wells that yu might git if yu wants them bad enough. They've got a sombrero of mine," he added deprecatingly.

"Nine! Twisted Jerusalem, Buck! Nine whole cow-punchers a-pinin' for work," he shouted, but then added thoughtfully, "Mebby they's engaged," it being one of the courtesies of the land not to take another man's help.

"Nope. They've stampeded for th' Hills an' left their boss all alone," replied Frenchy, well knowing that such desertion would not, in the minds of the Bar-20 men, add any merits to the case of the distant outfit.

"Th' sons-of-guns," said Hopalong, "let's go an' get 'em," he suggested, turning to Buck, who nodded a smiling assent.

"Oh, what's the hurry?" Asked Frenchy, seeing his projected game slipping away into the uncertain future and happy in the thought that he would be avenged on the O-Bar-O outfit.

"They'll be there till to-morrow noon-they's waitin' for their cookie, who's goin' with them."

"A cook! A cook! Oh, joy, a cook!" exulted Johnny, not for one instant doubting Buck's ability to capture the whole outfit and seeing a whirl of excitement in the effort.

"Anybody we knows?" Inquired Skinny Thompson.

"Shore. Tenspot Davis, Waffles, Salvation Carroll, Bigfoot Baker, Charley Lane, Lefty Allen, Kid Morris, Curley Tate an' Tex Le Blanc," responded Frenchy.

"Umm-m. Might as well rope a blizzard," grumbled Billy. "Might as well try to git th' Seventh Cavalry. We'll have a pious time corralling that bunch. Them's th' fellows that hit that bunch of inquirin' Crow braves that time up in th' Bad Lands an' then said by-bye to th' Ninth."

"Aw, shut up! They's only two that's very much, an' Buck an' Hopalong can sing 'em to sleep," interposed Johnny, afraid that the expedition would fall through.

"How about Curley and Tex?" Pugnaciously asked Billy.

"Huh, jest because they buffaloed yu over to Las Vegas yu needn't think they's dangerous. Salvation an' Tenspot are only ones who can shoot," stoutly maintained Johnny.

"Here yu, get mum," ordered Buck to the pair. "When this outfit goes after anything it generally gets it. All in favor of kidnappin' that outfit signify di' same by kickin' Billy," whereupon Bill swore.

"Do yu want yore hat?" Asked Buck, turning to Frenchy.

"I shore do," answered that individual.

"If yu helps us at th' round-up we'll get it for yu. Fifty a month an' grub," offered the foreman.

"O.K." replied Frenchy, anxious to even matters.

Buck looked at his watch. "Seven o'clock-we ought to get there by five if we relays at th' Barred-Horseshoe. Come on."

"How are we goin' to git them?" Asked Billy.

"Yu leave that to me, son. Hopalong an' Frenchy'll tend to that part of it," replied Buck, making for his horse and swinging into the saddle, an example which was followed by the others, including Frenchy.

As they swung off Buck noticed the condition of Frenchy's mount and halted. "Yu take that cayuse back an' get Cowan's," he ordered.

"That cayuse is good for Cheyenne-she eats work, an' besides I wants my own," laughed Frenchy.

"Yu must had a reg'lar picnic from th' looks of that crease," volunteered Hopalong, whose curiosity was mastering him. "Shoo! I had a little argument with some feather dusters-th' O-Bar-O crowd cleaned them up."

"That so?" Asked Buck.

"Yep! They sorter got into th' habit of chasin' me to Las Cruces an' forgot to stop."

"How many'd yu get?" Asked Lanky Smith.

"Twelve. Two got away. I got two before th' crowd showed up-that makes fo'teen."

"Now th' cavalry'll be huntin' yu," croaked Billy.

"Hunt nothin'! They was in war-paint-think I was a target? —Think I was goin' to call off their shots for 'em?"

They relayed at the Barred-Horseshoe and went on their way at the same pace. Shortly after leaving the last-named ranch Buck turned to Frenchy and asked, "Any of that outfit think they can play poker?"

"Shore. Waffles."

"Does th' reverend Mr. Waffles think so very hard?"

"He shore does."

"Do th' rest of them mavericks think so too?"

"They'd bet their shirts on him."

At this juncture all were startled by a sudden eruption from Billy. "Haw! Haw! Haw!" he roared as the drift of Buck's intentions struck him. "Haw! Haw! Haw!"

"Here, yu long-winded coyote," yelled Red, banging him over the head with his quirt, "If yu don't 'Haw! Haw!' away from my ear I'll make it a Wow! Wow! What d'yu mean? Think I am a echo cliff? Yu slabsided doodle-bug, yu!"

"G'way, yu crimson topknot, think my head's a hunk of quartz? Fer a plugged peso I'd strew yu all over th' scenery!" shouted Billy, feigning anger and rubbing his head.

"There ain't no scenery around here," interposed Lanky. "This here be-utiful prospect is a sublime conception of th' devil."

"Easy, boy! Them highfalutin' words'il give yu a cramp some day. Yu talk like a newly-made sergeant," remarked Skinny.

"He learned them words from the sky-pilot over at El Paso," volunteered Hopalong, winking at Red. "He used to amble down th' aisle afore the lights was lit so's he could get a front seat. That was all hunky for a while, but every time he'd go out to irrigate, that female organ-wrastler would seem to call th' music off for his special benefit. So in a month he'd sneak in an' freeze to a chair by th' door, an' after a while he'd shy like blazes every time he got within eye range of th' church."

"Shore. But do yu know what made him get religion all of a sudden? He used to hang around on di' outside after th' joint let out an' trail along behind di' music-slinger, lookin' like he didn't know what to do with his hands. Then when he got woozy one time she up an' told him that she had got a nice long letter from her hubby. Then Mr. Lanky hit th' trail for Santa Fe so hard that there wasn't hardly none of it left. I didn't see him for a whole month," supplied Red innocently.

"Yore shore funny, ain't yu?" sarcastically grunted Lanky. "Why, I can tell things on yu that'd make yu stand treat for a year."

"I wouldn't sneak off to Santa Fe an' cheat yu out of them. Yu ought to be ashamed of yoreself."

"Yah!" snorted the aggrieved little man. "I had business over to Santa Fe!"

"Shore," endorsed Hopalong. "We've all had business over to Santa Fe. Why, about eight years ago I had business —"

"Choke up," interposed Red. "About eight years ago yu was washin' pans for cookie, an' askin' me for cartridges. Buck used to larrup yu about four times a day eight years ago."

To their roars of laughter Hopalong dropped to the rear, where, red-faced and quiet, he bent his thoughts on how to get square.

"We'll have a pleasant time corralling that gang," began Billy for the third time.

"For heaven's sake get off that trail!" replied Lanky. "We aint goin' to hold 'em up. De-plomacy's th' game."

Billy looked dubious and said nothing. If he hadn't proven that he was as nervy as any man in the outfit they might have taken more stock in his grumbling.

"What's the latest from Abilene way?" Asked Buck of Frenchy.

"Nothin' much 'cept th' barb-wire ruction," replied the recruit.

"What's that?" Asked Red, glancing apprehensively back at Hopalong.

"Why, th' settlers put up barb-wire fence so's the cattle wouldn't get on their farms. That would a been all right, for there wasn't much of it. But some Britishers who own a couple of big ranches out there got smart all of a sudden an' strung wire all along their lines. Punchers crossin' th' country would run plumb into a fence an' would have to ride a day an' a half, mebbe, afore they found th' corner. Well, naturally, when a man has been used to ridin' where he blame pleases an' as straight as he pleases he ain't goin' to chase along a five-foot fence to Trisco when he wants to get to Waco. So th' punchers got to totin' wire-snips, an' when they runs up agin a fence they cuts down half a mile or so. Sometimes they'd tie their ropes to a strand an' pull off a couple of miles an' then go back after th' rest. Th' ranch bosses sent out men to watch th' fences an' told 'em to shoot any festive puncher that monkeyed with th' hardware. Well, yu know what happens when a puncher gets shot at."

"When fences grow in Texas there'll be th' devil to pay," said Buck. He hated to think that some day the freedom of the range would be annulled, for he knew that it would be the first blow against the cowboys' occupation. When a man's cattle couldn't spread out all over the land he wouldn't have to keep so many men. Farms would spring up and the sun of the free-and-easy cowboy would slowly set.

"I reckons th' cutters are classed th' same as rustlers," remarked Red with a gleam of temper.

"By th' owners, but not by th' punchers; an' it's th' punchers that count," replied Frenchy.

"Well, we'll give them a fight," interposed Hopalong, riding up. "When it gets so I can't go where I please I'll start on th' warpath. I won't buck the cavalry, but I'll keep it busy huntin' for me an' I'll have time to 'tend to th' wire-fence men, too. Why, we'll be told we can't tote our guns!"

"They're sayin' that now," replied Frenchy. "Up in Buffalo, Smith, who's now marshal, makes yu leave 'em with th' bartenders."

"I'd like to see any two-laigged cuss get my guns If I didn't want him to!" began Hopalong, indignant at the idea.

"Easy, son," cautioned Buck. "Yu would do what th' rest did because yu are a square man. I'm about as hard-headed a puncher as ever straddled leather an' I've had to use my guns purty considerable, but I reckons if any decent marshal asked me to cache them in a decent way, why, I'd do it. An' let me brand somethin' on yore mind —I've heard of Smith of Buffalo, an' he's mighty nifty with his hands. He don't stand off an' tell yu to unload yore lead-ranch, but he ambles up close an' taps yu on yore shirt; if yu makes a gunplay he naturally knocks yu clean across th' room an' unloads yu afore yu gets yore senses back. He weighs about a hundred an' eighty an' he's shore got sand to burn."

"Yah! When I makes a gun play she plays! I'd look nice in Abilene or Paso or Albuquerque without my guns, wouldn't I? Just because I totes them in plain sight I've got to hand 'em over to some liquor-wrastler? I reckons not! Some hip-pocket skunk would plug me afore I could wink. I'd shore look nice loping around a keno layout without my guns, in th' same town with some cuss huntin' me, wouldn't I? A whole lot of good a marshal would a done Jimmy, an' didn't Harris get his from a cur in th' dark?" shouted Hopalong, angered by the prospect.

"We're talkin' about Buffalo, where everybody has to hang up their guns," replied Buck. "An' there's th' law —"

"To blazes with th' law!" whooped Hopalong in Red's ear as he unfastened the cinch of Red's saddle and at the same time stabbing that unfortunate's mount with his spurs, thereby causing a hasty separation of the two. When Red had picked himself up and things had quieted down again the subject was changed, and several hours later they rode into Muddy Wells, a town with a little more excuse for its existence than Buckskin. The wells were in an arid valley west of Guadaloupe Pass, and were not only muddy but more or less alkaline.

Chapter. X
Peace Hath its Victories

As they neared the central group of buildings they heard a hilarious and assertive song which sprang from the door and windows of the main saloon. It was in jig time, rollicking and boisterous, but the words had evidently been improvised for the occasion, as they clashed immediately with those which sprang to the minds of the outfit, although they could not be clearly distinguished. As they approached nearer and finally dismounted, however, the words became recognizable and the visitors were at once placed in harmony with the air of jovial recklessness by the roaring of the verses and the stamping of the time.

>Oh we're red-hot cow-punchers playin' on our luck,
>An' there ain't a proposition that we won't buck:
>From sunrise to sunset we've ridden on the range,
>But now we're oft for a howlin' change.

>CHORUS
>Laugh a little, sing a little, all th' day;

Play a little, drink a little-we can pay;
Ride a little, dig a little an' rich we'll grow.
Oh, we're that bunch from th' O-Bar-O!
Oh, there was a little tenderfoot an' he had a little gun,

An' th' gun an' him went a-trailin' up some fun.
They ambles up to Santa Fe' to find a quiet game,
An' now they're planted with some more of th' same!

As Hopalong, followed by the others, pushed open the door and entered he took up the chorus with all the power of Texan lungs and even Billy joined in. The sight that met their eyes was typical of the men and the mood and the place. Leaning along the walls, lounging on the table and straddling chairs with their forearms crossed on the backs were nine cowboys, ranging from old twenty to young fifty in years, and all were shouting the song and keeping time with their hands and feet.

In the center of the room was a large man dancing a fair buck-and-wing to the time so uproariously set by his companions. Hatless, neck-kerchief loose, holsters flapping, chaps rippling out and close, spurs clinking and perspiration streaming from his tanned face, danced Bigfoot Baker as though his life depended on speed and noise. Bottles shook and the air was fogged with smoke and dust. Suddenly, his belt slipping and letting his chaps fall around his ankles, he tripped and sat down heavily. Gasping for breath, he held out his hand and received a huge plug of tobacco, for Bigfoot had won a contest.

Shouts of greeting were hurled at the newcomers and many questions were fired at them regarding "th' latest from th' Hills." Waffles made a rush for Hopalong, but fell over Big-foot's feet and all three were piled up in a heap. All were beaming with good nature, for they were as so many school boys playing truant. Prosaic cow-punching was relegated to the rear and they looked eagerly forward to their several missions. Frenchy told of the barb-wire fence war and of the new regulations of "Smith of Buffalo" regarding cow-punchers' guns, and from the caustic remarks explosively given it was plain to be seen what a wire fence could expect, should one be met with, and there were many imaginary Smiths put hors de combat.

Kid Morris, after vainly trying to slip a blue-bottle fly inside of Hopalong's shirt, gave it up and slammed his hand on Hopalong's back instead, crying: "Well, I'll be doggoned if here ain't Hopalong! How's th' missus an' th' deacon an' all th' folks to hum? I hears yu an' Frenchy's reg'lar poker fiends!"

"Oh, we plays onct in a while, but we don't want none of yore dust. Yu'll shore need it all afore th' Hills get through with yu," laughingly replied Hopalong.

"Oh, yore shore kind! But I was a sort of reckonin' that we needs some more. Perfesser P. D. Q. Waffles is our poker man an' he shore can clean out anything I ever saw. Mebbe yu fellers feel reckless-like an' would like to make a pool," he cried, addressing the outfit of the Bar-20, "an' back yore boss of th' full house agin ourn?"

Red turned slowly around and took a full minute in which to size the Kid up. Then he snorted and turned his back again.

The Kid stared at him in outraged dignity. "Well, what say!" he softly murmured. Then he leaped forward and walloped Red on the back. "Hey, yore royal highness!" he shouted. "Yu-yu-yu-oh, hang it-yu! Yu slab-sided, ring-boned, saddle-galled shade of a coyote, do yu think I'm only meanderin' in th' misty vales of-of—"

Suggestions intruded from various sources. "Hades?" offered Hopalong. "Cheyenne?" Murmured Johnny. "Misty mistiness of misty?" tentatively supplied Waffles.

Red turned around again. "Better come up an' have somethin'," he sympathetically invited, wiping away an imaginary tear.

"An' he's so young!" sobbed Frenchy.

"An' so fair!" wailed Tex.

"An' so ornery!" howled Lefty, throwing his arms around the discomfited youngster. Other arms went around him, and out of the sobbing mob could be heard earnest and heart-felt cussing, interspersed with imperative commands, which were gradually obeyed.

The Kid straightened up his wearing apparel. "Come on, yu locoed —"

"Angels?" Queried Charley Lane, interrupting him. "Sweet things?" breathed Hopalong in hopeful expectancy.

"Oh, blast it!" yelled the Kid as he ran out into the street to escape the persecution.

"Good Kid, all right," remarked Waffles. "He'll go around an' lick some Mexican an' come back sweet as honey."

"Did somebody say poker?" Asked Bigfoot, digressing from the Kid.

"Oh, yu fellows don't want no poker. Of course yu don't. Poker's mighty uncertain," replied Red.

"Yah!" exclaimed Tex Le Blanc, pushing forward. "I'll just bet yu to a standstill that Waffles an' Salvation'll round up all th' festive simoleons yu can get together! An' I'll throw in Frenchy's hat as an inducement."

"Well, if yore shore set on it make her a pool," replied Red, "an' th' winners divide with their outfit. Here's a starter," he added, tossing a buckskin bag on the table. "Come on, pile 'em up."

The crowd divided as the players seated themselves at the table, the O-Bar-O crowd grouping themselves behind their representatives; the Bar-20 behind theirs. A deck of cards was brought and the game was on.

Red, true to his nature, leaned back in a corner, where, hands on hips, he awaited any hostile demonstration on the part of the O-Bar-O; then, suddenly remembering, he looked half ashamed of his warlike position and became a peaceful citizen again. Buck leaned with his broad back against the bar, talking over his shoulder to the bartender, but watching Tenspot Davis, who was assiduously engaged in juggling a handful of Mexican dollars.

Up by the door Bigfoot Baker, elated at winning the buck-and-wing contest, was endeavoring to learn a new step, while his late rival was drowning his defeat at Buck's elbow. Lefty Allen was softly singing a Mexican love song, humming when the words would not come. At the table could be heard low-spoken card terms and good-natured banter, interspersed with the clink of gold and silver and the soft pat-pat of the onlookers' feet unconsciously keeping time to Lefty's song. Notwithstanding the grim assertiveness of belts full of .45's and the peeping handles of long-barreled Colts, set off with picturesque chaps, sombreros and tinkling spurs, the scene was one of peaceful content and good-fellowship.

"Ugh!" grunted Johnny, walking over to Red and informing that person that he, Red, was a worm-eaten prune and that for half a wink he, Johnny, would prove it. Red grabbed him by the seat of his corduroys and the collar of his shirt and helped him outside, where they strolled about, taking pot shots at whatever their fancy suggested.

Down the street in a cloud of dust rumbled the Las Cruces-El Paso stage and the two punchers went up to meet it. Raw furrows showed in the woodwork, one mule was missing and the driver and guard wore fresh bandages. A tired tenderfoot leaped out with a sigh of relief and hunted for his baggage, which he found to be generously perforated. Swearing at the God-forsaken land where a man had to fight highwaymen and Indians inside of half a day he grumblingly lugged his valise toward a forbidding-looking shack which was called a hotel.

The driver released his teams and then turned to Red. "Hullo, old hoss, how's th' gang?" he asked genially. "We've had a heck of a time this yere trip," he went on without waiting for Red to reply. "Five miles out of Las Cruces we stood off a son-of-a-gun that wanted th' dude's wealth. Then just this side of the San Andre foothills we runs into a bunch of young bucks who turned us off this yere way an' gave us a runnin' fight purty near all th' way. I'm a whole lot farther from Paso now than I was when I started, an seem as I lost a jack I'll be some time gittin' there. Yu don't happen to sabe a jack I can borrow, do yu?"

"I don't know about no jack, but I'll rope yu a bronch," offered Red, winking at Johnny.

"I'll pull her myself before I'll put dynamite in di' traces," replied the driver. "Yu fellers might amble back a ways with me-them buddin' warriors'll be layin' for me."

"We shore will," responded Johnny eagerly. "There's nine of us now an' there'll be nine more an' a cook to-morrow, mebby."

"Gosh, yu grows some," replied the guard. "Eighteen'll be a plenty for them glory hunters."

"We won't be able to," contradicted Red, "for things are peculiar."

At this moment the conversation was interrupted by the tenderfoot, who sported a new and cheap sombrero and also a belt and holster complete.

"Will you gentlemen join me?" He asked, turning to Red and nodding at the saloon. "I am very dry and much averse to drinking alone."

"Why, shore," responded Red heartily, wishing to put the stranger at ease.

The game was running about even as they entered and Lefty Allen was singing "The Insult," the rich tenor softening the harshness of the surroundings.

> I've swum th' Colorado where she's almost lost to view, I've braced
> th' Jaro layouts in Cheyenne;
> I've fought for muddy water with a howlin' bunch of Sioux, An'
> swallowed hot tamales, an' cayenne.
> I've rid a pitchin' broncho 'till th' sky was underneath, I've
>
> tackled every desert in th' land;
> I've sampled XXXX whiskey 'till I couldn't hardly see, An' dallied
> with th' quicksands of the Grande.
> I've argued with th' marshals of a half-a-dozen burgs, I've been
>
> dragged free an' fancy by a cow;
> I've had three years' campaignin' with th' fightin', bitin' Ninth,
> An' never lost my temper 'till right now.
> I've had the yaller fever an I've been shot full of holes, I've
>
> grabbed an army mule plumb by its tail;
> I've never been so snortin', really highfalutin' mad As when y'u up
> an' hands me ginger ale!

Hopalong laughed joyously at a remark made by Waffles and the stranger glanced quickly at him. His merry, boyish face, underlined by a jaw showing great firmness and set with an expression of aggressive self-reliance, impressed the stranger and he remarked to Red, who lounged lazily near him, that he was surprised to see such a face on so young a man and he asked who the player was.

"Oh, his name's Hopalong Cassidy," answered Red. "He's di' cuss that raised that ruction down in Mexico last spring. Rode his cayuse in a saloon and played with the loungers and had to shoot one before he got out. When he did get out he had to fight a whole bunch of Mexicans an' even potted their marshal, who had di' drop on him. Then he returned and visited the marshal about a month later, took his gun away from him an' then cut th' cards to see if he was a prisoner or not. He's a shore funny cuss."

The tenderfoot gasped his amazement. "Are you not fooling with me?" He asked.

"Tell him yu came after that five hundred dollars reward and see," answered Red goodnaturedly.

"Holy smoke!" shouted Waffles as Hopalong won his sixth consecutive pot. "Did yu ever see such luck?" Frenchy grinned and some time later raked in his third. Salvation then staked his last cent against Hopalong's flush and dropped out.

Tenspot flipped to Waffles the money he had been juggling and Lefty searched his clothes for wealth. Buck, still leaning against the bar, grinned and winked at Johnny, who was pouring hair-raising tales into the receptive ears of the stranger. Thereupon Johnny confided to his newly found acquaintance the facts about the game, nearly causing that person to explode with delight.

Waffles pushed back his chair, stood up and stretched. At the finish of a yawn he grinned at his late adversary. "I'm all in, yu old son-of-a-gun. Yu shore can play draw. I'm goin' to try yu again some time. I was beat fair an' square an' I ain't got no kick comin', none whatever," he remarked, as he shook hands with Hopalong.

"Oh, we're that gang from th' O-Bar-O," hummed the Kid as he sauntered in. One cheek was slightly swollen and his clothes shed dust at every step. "Who wins?" he inquired, not having heard Waffles.

"They did, blast it!" exploded Bigfoot.

One of the Kid's peculiarities was revealed in the unreasoning and hasty conclusions he arrived at. From no desire to imply unfairness, but rather because of his bitterness against failure of any kind and his loyalty to Waffles, came his next words:

"Mebby they skinned yu."

Like a flash Waffles sprang before him, his hand held up, palm out. "He don't mean nothin' —he's only a ignorant kid!" he cried.

Buck smiled and wrested the Colt from Johnny's ever-ready hand. "Here's another," he said. Red laughed softly and rolled Johnny on the floor. "Yu jackass," he whispered, "don't yu know better'n to make a gun-play when we needs them all?"

"What are we goin' to do?" Asked Tex, glancing at the bulging pockets of Hopalong's chaps.

"We're goin' to punch cows again, that's what we're to do," answered Bigfoot dismally.

"An' whose are we goin' to punch? We can't go back to the old man," grumbled Tex.

Salvation looked askance at Buck and then at the others. "Mebby," he began, "Mebby we kin git a job on th' Bar-20." Then turning to Buck again he bluntly asked, "Are yu short of punchers?"

"Well, I might use some," answered the foreman, hesitating. "But I ain't got only one cook, an' — —"

"We'll git yu th' cook all O.K.," interrupted Charley Lane vehemently. "Hi, yu cook!" he shouted, "amble in here an' git a rustle on!"

There was no reply, and after waiting for a minute he and Waffles went into the rear room, from which there immediately issued great chunks of profanity and noise. They returned looking pugnacious and disgusted, with a wildly fighting man who was more full of liquor than was the bottle which he belligerently waved.

"This here animated distillery what yu sees is our cook," said Waffles. "We eats his grub, nobody else. If he gits drunk that's our funeral; but he won't get drunk! If yu wants us to punch for yu say so an' we does; if yu don't, we don't."

"Well," replied Buck thoughtfully, "mebby I can use yu." Then with a burst of recklessness he added, "Yes, if I lose my job! But yu might sober that Mexican up if yu let him fall in th' horse trough."

As the procession wended its way on its mission of wet charity, carrying the cook in any manner at all, Frenchy waved his long lost sombrero at Buck, who stood in the door, and shouted, "Yu old son-of-a-gun, I'm proud to know yu!"

Buck smiled and snapped his watch shut "Time to amble," he said.

Chapter XI
Holding the Claim

"Oh, we're that gang from th' O-Bar-O," hummed Waffles, sinking the branding-iron in the flank of a calf. The scene was one of great activity and hilarity. Several fires were burning near the huge corral and in them half a dozen irons were getting hot. Three calves were being held down for the brand of the "Bar-20" and two more were being dragged up on their sides by the ropes of the cowboys, the proud cow-ponies showing off their accomplishments at the expense of the calves' feelings. In the corral the dust arose in steady clouds as calf after calf was "cut out" by the ropers and dragged out to get "tagged." Angry cows fought valiantly for their terrorized offspring, but always to no avail, for the hated rope of some perspiring and dust-grimed rider sent them crashing to earth. Over the plain were herds of cattle and groups of madly riding cowboys, and two cook wagons were stalled a short distance from the corral. The round-up of the Bar-20 was taking place, and each of the two outfits tried to outdo the other and each individual strove for a prize. The man who cut out and dragged to the fire the most calves in three days could leave for the Black Hills at the expiration of that time, the rest to follow as soon as they could.

In this contest Hopalong Cassidy led his nearest rival, Red Connors, both of whom were Bar-20 men, by twenty cut-outs, and there remained but half an hour more in which to compete. As Red disappeared into the sea of tossing horns Hopalong dashed out with a whoop.

"Hi, yu trellis-built rack of bones, come along there! Whoop!" he yelled, turning the prisoner over to the squad by the fire.

"Chalk up this here insignificant wart of cross-eyed perversity: an' how many?" He called as he galloped back to the corral.

"One ninety-eight," announced Buck, blowing the sand from the tally sheet. "That's shore goin' some," he remarked to himself.

When the calf sprang up it was filled with terror, rage and pain, and charged at Billy from the rear as that pessimistic soul was leaning over and poking his finger at a somber horned-toad. "Wow!" he yelled as his feet took huge steps up in the air, each one strictly on its own course. "Woof!" he grunted in the hot sand as he arose on his hands and knees and spat alkali.

"What's s'matter?" He asked dazedly of Johnny Nelson. "Ain't it funny!" he yelled sarcastically as he beheld Johnny holding his sides with laughter. "Ain't it funny!" he repeated belligerently. "Of course that four-laigged, knock-kneed, wobblin' son-of-a-Piute had to cut me out. They wasn't nobody in sight but Billy! Why didn't yu say he was comin'? Think I can see four ways to once? Why didn't —" At this point Red cantered up with a calf, and by a quick maneuver, drew the taut rope against the rear of Billy's knees, causing that unfortunate to sit down heavily. As he arose choking with broken-winded profanity Red dragged the animal to the fire, and Billy forgot his grievances in the press of labor.

"How many, Buck?" Asked Red.

"One-eighty."

"How does she stand?"

"Yore eighteen to th' bad," replied the foreman. "Th' son-of-a-gun!" marveled Red, riding off.

Another whoop interrupted them, and Billy quit watching out of the corner eye for pugnacious calves as he prepared for Hopalong.

"Hey, Buck, this here cuss was with a Barred-Horseshoe cow," he announced as he turned it over to the branding man. Buck made a tally in a separate column and released the animal. "Hullo, Red! Workin'?" Asked Hopalong of his rival.

"Some, yu little cuss," answered Red with all the good nature in the world. Hopalong was his particular "side partner," and he could lose to him with the best of feelings.

"Yu looks so nice an' cool, an' clean, I didn't know," responded Hopalong, eyeing a streak of sweat and dust which ran from Red's eyes to his chin and then on down his neck.

"What yu been doin'? Plowin' with yore nose?" Returned Red, smiling blandly at his friend's appearance.

"Yah!" snorted Hopalong, wheeling toward the corral. "Come on, yu pie-eatin' doodle-bug; I'll beat yu to th' gate!"

The two ponies sent showers of sand all over Billy, who eyed them in pugnacious disgust. "Of all th' locoed imps that ever made life miserable fer a man, them's th' worst! Is there any piece of fool nonsense they hain't harnessed me with?" He beseeched of Buck. "Is there anything they hain't done to me? They hides my liquor; they stuffs th' sweat band of my hat with rope; they ties up my pants; they puts water in. My boots an' toads in my bunk-ain't they never goin' to get sane?"

"Oh, they're only kids-they can't help it," offered Buck. "Didn't they hobble my cayuse when I was on him an' near bust my neck?"

Hopalong interrupted the conversation by driving up another calf, and Buck, glancing at his watch, declared the contest at an end.

"Yu wins," he remarked to the newcomer. "An' now yu get scarce or Billy will shore straddle yore nerves. He said as how he was goin' to get square on yu to-night."

"I didn't, neither, Hoppy!" earnestly contradicted Billy, who bad visions of a night spent in torment as a reprisal for such a threat. "Honest I didn't, did I, Johnny?" He asked appealingly.

"Yu shore did," lied Johnny, winking at Red, who had just ridden up.

"I don't know what yore talkin' about, but yu shore did," replied Red.

"If yu did," grinned Hopalong, "I'll shore make yu hard to find. Come on, fellows," he said; "grub's ready. Where's Frenchy?"

"Over chewin' th' rag with Waffles about his hat-he's lost it again," answered Red. "He needs a guardian fer that bonnet. Th' Kid an' Salvation has jammed it in th' corral fence an' Waffles has to stand fer it."

"Let's put it in th' grub wagon an see him cuss cookie," suggested Hopalong.

"Shore," indorsed Johnny; Cookie'll feed him bum grub for a week to get square.

Hopalong and Johnny ambled over to the corral and after some trouble located the missing sombrero, which they carried to the grub wagon and hid in the flour barrel. Then they went over by the excited owner and dropped a few remarks about how strange the cook was acting and how he was watching Frenchy.

Frenchy jumped at the bait and tore over to the wagon, where he and the cook spent some time in mutual recrimination. Hopalong nosed around and finally dug up the hat, white as new-fallen snow.

"Here's a hat-found it in th' dough barrel," he announced, handing it over to Frenchy, who received it in open-mouthed stupefaction.

"Yu pie-makin' pirate! Yu didn't know where my lid was, did yu! Yu cross-eyed lump of hypocrisy!" yelled Frenchy, dusting off the flour with one full-armed swing on the cook's face, driving it into that unfortunate's nose and eyes and mouth. "Yu white-washed Chink, yu-rub yore face with water an' yu've got pancakes."

"Hey! What you doin'!" yelled the cook, kicking the spot where he had last seen Frenchy. "Don't yu know better'n that!"

"Yu live close to yoreself or I'll throw yu so high th' sun'll duck," replied Frenchy, a smile illuminating his face.

"Hey, cookie," remarked Hopalong confidentially, "I know who put up this joke on yu. Yu ask Billy who hid th' hat," suggested the tease. "Here he comes now-see how queer he looks."

"Th' mournful Piute," ejaculated the cook. "I'll shore make him wish he'd kept on his own trail. I'll flavor his slush [coffee] with year-old dish-rags!"

At this juncture Billy ambled up, keeping his weather eye peeled for trouble. "Who's a dish-rag?" He queried. The cook mumbled something about crazy hens not knowing when to quit cackling and climbed up in his wagon. And that night Billy swore off drinking coffee.

When the dawn of the next day broke, Hopalong was riding toward the Black Hills, leaving Billy to untie himself as best he might.

The trip was uneventful and several weeks later he entered Red Dog, a rambling shanty town, one of those western mushrooms that sprang up in a night. He took up his stand at the Miner's

Rest, and finally secured six claims at the cost of nine hundred hard-earned dollars, a fund subscribed by the outfits, as it was to be a partnership affair.

He rode out to a staked-off piece of hillside and surveyed his purchase, which consisted of a patch of ground, six holes, six piles of dirt and a log hut. The holes showed that the claims bad been tried and found wanting.

He dumped his pack of tools and provisions, which he had bought on the way up, and lugged them into the cabin. After satisfying his curiosity he went outside and sat down for a smoke, figuring up in his mind how much gold he could carry on a horse. Then, as he realized that he could get a pack mule to carry the surplus, he became aware of a strange presence near at hand and looked up into the muzzle of a Sharp's rifle. He grasped the situation in a flash and calmly blew several heavy smoke rings around the frowning barrel.

"Well?" He asked slowly.

"Nice day, stranger," replied the man with the rifle, "but don't yu reckon yu've made a mistake?"

Hopalong glanced at the number burned on a near-by stake and carelessly blew another smoke ring. He was waiting for the gun to waver.

"No, I reckons not," he answered. "Why?"

"Well, I'll jest tell yu since yu asks. This yere claim's mine an' I'm a reg'lar terror, I am. That's why; an' seein' as it is, yu better amble some."

Hopalong glanced down the street and saw an interested group watching him, which only added to his rage for being in such a position. Then he started to say something, faltered and stared with horror at a point several feet behind his opponent. The "terror" sprang to one side in response to Hop-along's expression, as if fearing that a snake or some such danger threatened him. As he alighted in his new position he fell forward and Hopalong slid a smoking Colt in its holster.

Several men left the distant group and ran toward the claim. Hopalong reached his arm inside the door and brought forth his rifle, with which he covered their advance.

"Anything yu want?" he shouted savagely.

The men stopped and two of them started to sidle in front of two others, but Hopalong was not there for the purpose of permitting a move that would screen any gun play and he stopped the game with a warning shout. Then the two held up their hands and advanced.

"We wants to git Dan," called out one of them, nodding at the prostrate figure.

"Come ahead," replied Hopalong, substituting a Colt for the rifle.

They carried their badly wounded and insensible burden back to those whom they had left, and several curses were hurled at the cowboy, who only smiled grimly and entered the hut to place things ready for a siege, should one come. He had one hundred rounds of ammunition and provisions enough for two weeks, with the assurance of reinforcements long before that time would expire. He cut several rough loopholes and laid out his weapons for quick handling. He knew that he could stop any advance during the day and planned only for night attacks. How long he could go without sleep did not bother him, because he gave it no thought, as he was accustomed to short naps and could awaken at will or at the slightest sound.

As dusk merged into dark he crept forth and collected several handfuls of dry twigs, which he scattered around the hut, as the cracking of these would warn him of an approach. Then he went in and went to sleep.

He awoke at daylight after a good night's rest, and feasted on canned beans and peaches. Then he tossed the cans out of the door and shoved his hat out. Receiving no response he walked out and surveyed the town at his feet. A sheepish grin spread over his face as he realized that there was no danger. Several red-shirted men passed by him on their way to town, and one, a grizzled veteran of many gold camps, stopped and sauntered up to him.

"Mornin'," said Hopalong.

"Mornin'," replied the stranger. "I thought I'd drop in an' say that I saw that gun-play of yourn yesterday. Yu ain't got no reason to look fer a rush. This camp is half white men an' half bullies, an' th' white men won't stand fer no play like that. Them fellers that jest passed are neighbors of yourn, an' they won't lay abed if yu needs them. But yu wants to look out fer th' joints in th' town. Guess this business is out of yore line," he finished as he sized Hopalong up.

"She shore is, but I'm here to stay. Got tired of punchin' an' reckoned I'd get rich." Here he smiled and glanced at the hole. "How're yu makin' out?" He asked.

"'Bout five dollars a day apiece, but that ain't nothin' when grub's so high. Got reckless th' other day an' had a egg at fifty cents."

Hopalong whistled and glanced at the empty cans at his feet. "Any marshal in this burg?"

"Yep. But he's one of th' gang. No good, an' drunk half th' time an' half drunk th' rest. Better come down an' have something," invited the miner.

"I'd shore like to, but I can't let no gang get in that door," replied the puncher.

"Oh, that's all right; I'll call my pardner down to keep house till yu gits back. He can hold her all right. Hey, Jake!" he called to a man who was some hundred paces distant; "Come down here an' keep house till we gits back, will yu?"

The man lumbered down to them and took possession as Hopalong and his newly found friend started for the town.

They entered the "Miner's Rest" and Hopalong fixed the room in his mind with one swift glance. Three men-and they looked like the crowd he had stopped before-were playing poker at a table near the window. Hopalong leaned with his back to the bar and talked, with the players always in sight.

Soon the door opened and a bewhiskered, heavy-set man tramped in, and walking up to Hopalong, looked him over.

"Huh," he sneered, "Yu are th' gent with th' festive guns that plugged Dan, ain't yu?"

Hopalong looked at him in the eyes and quietly replied:

"An' who th' deuce are yu?"

The stranger's eyes blazed and his face wrinkled with rage as he aggressively shoved his jaw close to Hopalong's face.

"Yu runt, I'm a better man than yu even if yu do wear hair pants," referring to Hopalong's chaps. "Yu cow-wrastlers make me tired, an' I'm goin' to show yu that this town is too good for you. Yu can say it right now that yu are a ornery, game-leg —"

Hopalong smashed his insulter squarely between the eyes with all the power of his sinewy body behind the blow, knocking him in a heap under the table. Then he quickly glanced at the card players and saw a hostile movement. His gun was out in a flash and he covered the trio as he walked up to them. Never in all his life had he felt such a desire to kill. His eyes were diamond points of accumulated fury, and those whom he faced quailed before him.

"Yu scum! Draw, please draw! Pull yore guns an' gimme my chance! Three to one, an' I'll lay my guns here," he said, placing them on the bar and removing his hands. "'Nearer My God to Thee' is purty appropriate fer yu just now! Yu seem to be a-scared of yore own guns. Git down on yore dirty knees an' say good an' loud that yu eats dirt! Shout out that yu are too currish to live with decent men," he said, even-toned and distinct, his voice vibrant with passion as he took up his Colts. "Get down!" he repeated, shoving the weapons forward and pulling back the hammers.

The trio glanced at each other, and all three dropped to their knees and repeated in venomous hatred the words Hopalong said for them.

"Now git! An' if I sees yu when I leaves I'll send yu after yore friend. I'll shoot on sight now. Git!" He escorted them to the door and kicked the last one out.

His miner friend still leaned against the bar and looked his approval.

"Well done, youngster! But yu wants to look out-that man," pointing to the now groping victim of Hopalong's blow, "is th' marshal of this town. He or his pals will get yu if yu don't watch th' corners."

Hopalong walked over to the marshal, jerked him to his feet and slammed him against the bar. Then he tore the cheap badge from its place and threw it on the floor. Reaching down, he drew the marshal's revolver from its holster and shoved it in its owner's hand.

"Yore th' marshal of this place an' it's too good for me, but yore gain' to pick up that tin lie," pointing at the badge, "an' yore goin' to do it right now. Then yore gain' to get kicked out of that door, an' if yu stops runnin' while I can see yu I'll fill yu so full of holes yu'll catch cold. Yore a sumptious marshal, yu are! Yore th' snortingest ki-yi that ever stuck its tail atween its laigs, yu are. Yu pop-eyed wall flower, yu wants to peep to yoreself or some papoose'll slide yu over th' Divide so fast yu won't have time to grease yore pants. Pick up that license-tag an' let me see you perculate so lively that yore back'll look like a ten-cent piece in five seconds. Flit!"

The marshal, dazed and bewildered, stooped and fumbled for the badge. Then he stood up and glanced at the gun in his hand and at the eager man before him. He slid the weapon in his belt and drew his hand across his fast-closing eyes. Cursing streaks of profanity, he staggered to the door and landed in a heap in the street from the force of Hopalong's kick. Struggling to his feet, he ran unsteadily down the block and disappeared around a corner.

The bartender, cool and unperturbed, pushed out three glasses on his treat: "I've seen yu afore, up in Cheyenne —'member? How's yore friend Red?" He asked as he filled the glasses with the best the house afforded.

"Well, shore 'nuff! Glad to see yu, Jimmy! What yu doin' away off here?" Asked Hopalong, beginning to feel at home.

"Oh, jest filterin' round like. I'm awful glad to see yu-this yere wart of a town needs siftin' out. It was only last week I was wishin' one of yore bunch 'ud show up-that ornament yu jest buffaloed shore raised th' devil in here, an' I wished I had somebody to prospect his anatomy for a lead mine. But he's got a tough gang circulating with him. Ever hear of Dutch Shannon or Blinky Neary? They's with him."

"Dutch Shannon? Nope," he replied.

"Bad eggs, an' not a-carin' how they gits square. Th' feller yu' salted yesterday was a bosom friend of th' marshal's, an' he passed in his chips last night."

"So?"

"Yep. Bought a bottle of ready-made nerve an' went to his own funeral. Aristotle Smith was lookin' fer him up in Cheyenne last year. Aristotle said he'd give a century fer five minutes' palaver with him, but he shied th' town an' didn't come back. Yu know Aristotle, don't yu? He's th' geezer that made fame up to Poison Knob three years ago. He used to go to town ridin' astride a log on th' lumber flume. Made four miles in six minutes with th' promise of a ruction when he stopped. Once when he was loaded he tried to ride back th' same way he came, an' th' first thing he knowed he was three miles farther from his supper an' a-slippin' down that valley like he wanted to go somewhere. He swum out at Potter's Dam an' it took him a day to walk back. But he didn't make that play again, because he was frequently sober, an' when he wasn't he'd only stand off an' swear at th' slide."

"That's Aristotle, all hunk. He's th' chap that used to play checkers with Deacon Rawlins. They used empty an' loaded shells for men, an' when they got a king they'd lay one on its side. Sometimes they'd jar th' board an' they'd all be kings an' then they'd have a cussin' match," replied Hopalong, once more restored to good humor.

"Why," responded Jimmy, "he counted his wealth over twice by mistake an' shore raised a howl when he went to blow it-thought he's been robbed, an' laid behind th' houses fer a week lookin' fer th' feller that done it."

"I've heard of that cuss-he shore was th' limit. What become of him?" Asked the miner.

"He ambled up to Laramie an' stuck his head in th' window of that joint by th' plaza an' hollered 'Fire,' an' they did. He was shore a good feller, all th' same," answered the bartender. Hopalong laughed and started for the door. Turning around he looked at his miner friend and asked: "Comin' along? I'm goin' back now."

"Nope. Reckon I'll hit th' tiger a whirl. I'll stop in when I passes."

"All right. So long," replied Hopalong, slipping out of the door and watching for trouble. There was no opposition shown him, and he arrived at his claim to find Jake in a heated argument with another of the gang.

"Here he comes now," he said as Hopalong walked up. "Tell him what yu said to me."

"I said yu made a mistake," said the other, turning to the cowboy in a half apologetic manner.

"An' what else?" Insisted Jake.

"Why, ain't that all?" Asked the claim-jumper's friend in feigned surprise, wishing that he had kept quiet.

"Well I reckons it is if yu can't back up yore words," responded Jake in open contempt.

Hopalong grabbed the intruder by the collar of his shirt and hauled him off the claim. "Yu keep off this, understand? I just kicked yore marshal out in th' street, an' I'll pay yu th' next call. If yu rambles in range of my guns yu'll shore get in th' way of a slug. Yu an' yore gang wants to browse on th' far side of th' range or yu'll miss a sunrise some mornin'. Scoot!"

Hopalong turned to his companion and smiled. "What'd he say?" He asked genially.

"Oh, he jest shot off his mouth a little. They's all no good. I've collided with lots of them all over this country. They can't face a good man an' keep their nerve. What'd yu say to th' marshal?"

"I told him what he was an' threw him outen th' street," replied Hopalong. "In about two weeks we'll have a new marshal an' he'll shore be a dandy."

"Yes? Why don't yu take th' job yoreself? We're with yu."

"Better man comin'. Ever hear of Buck Peters or Red Connors of th' Bar-20, Texas?"

"Buck Peters? Seems to me I have. Did he punch fer th' Tin-Cup up in Montana, 'bout twenty years back?"

"Shore! Him and Frenchy McAllister punched all over that country an' they used to paint Cheyenne, too," replied Hopalong, eagerly.

"I knows him, then. I used to know Frenchy, too. Are they comin' up here?"

"Yes," responded Hopalong, struggling with another can while waiting for the fire to catch up. "Better have some grub with me-don't like to eat alone," invited the cowboy, the reaction of his late rage swinging him to the other extreme.

When their tobacco had got well started at the close of the meal and content had taken possession of them Hopalong laughed quietly and finally spoke:

"Did yu ever know Aristotle Smith when yu was up in Montana?"

"Did I! Well, me an' Aristotle prospected all through that country till he got so locoed I had to watch him fer fear he'd blow us both up. He greased th' fryin' pan with dynamite one night, an' we shore had to eat jerked meat an' canned stuff all th' rest of that trip. What made yu ask? Is he comin' up too?"

"No, I reckons not. Jimmy, th' bartender, said that he cashed in up at Laramie. Wasn't he th' cuss that built that boat out there on th' Arizona desert because he was scared that a flood might come? Th' sun shore warped that punt till it wasn't even good for a hencoop."

"Nope. That was Sister-Annie Tompkins. He was purty near as bad as Aristotle, though. He roped a puma up on th' Sacramentos, an' didn't punch no more fer three weeks. Well, here comes my pardner an' I reckons I'll amble right along. If yu needs any referee or a side pardner in any ruction yu has only got to warble up my way. So long."

The next ten days passed quietly, and on the afternoon of the eleventh Hopalong's miner friend paid him a visit.

"Jake recommends yore peaches," he laughed as he shook Hopalong's hand. "He says yu boosted another of that crowd. That bein' so I thought I would drop in an' say that they're comin' after yu to-night, shore. Just heard of it from yore friend Jimmy. Yu can count on us when th' rush comes. But why didn't yu say yu was a pard of Buck Peters'? Me an' him used to shoot up Laramie together. From what yore friend James says, yu can handle this gang by yore lonesome, but if yu needs any encouragement yu make some sign an' we'll help th' event along some. They's eight of us that'll be waitin' up to get th' returns an' we're shore goin' to be in range."

"Gee, it's nice to run across a friend of Buck's! Ain't he a son-of-a-gun?" Asked Hopalong, delighted at the news. Then, without waiting for a reply, he went on: "Yore shore square, all right, an' I hates to refuse yore offer, but I got eighteen friends comin' up an' they ought to get here by tomorrow. Yu tell Jimmy to head them this way when they shows up an' I'll have th' claim for them. There ain't no use of yu fellers gettin' mixed up in this. Th' bunch that's comin' can clean out any gang this side of sunup, an' I expects they'll shore be anxious to begin when they finds me eatin' peaches an' wastin' my time shootin' bums. Yu pass th' word along to yore friends, an' tell them to lay low an' see th' Arory Boerallis hit this town with its tail up. Tell Jimmy to do it up good when he speaks about me holdin' th' claim —I likes to see Buck an' Red fight when they're good an' mad."

The miner laughed and slapped Hopalong on the shoulder. "Yore all right, youngster! Yore just like Buck was at yore age. Say now, I reckons he wasn't a reg'lar terror on wheels! Why, I've seen him do more foolish things than any man I knows of, an' I calculate that if Buck pals with yu there ain't no water in yore sand. My name's Tom Halloway," he suggested.

"An' mine's Hopalong Cassidy," was the reply. "I've heard Buck speak of yu."

"Has yu? Well, don't it beat all how little this world is? Somebody allus turnin' up that knows somebody yu knows. I'll just amble along, Mr. Cassidy, an' don't yu be none bashful about callin' if yu needs me. Any pal of Buck's is my friend. Well, so long," said the visitor as he strode off. Then he stopped and turned around. "Hey, mister!" he called. "They are goin' to roll a fire barrel down agin yu from behind," indicating by an outstretched arm the point from where it would start. "If it burns yu out I'm goin' to take a band from up there," pointing to a cluster of rocks well to the rear of where the crowd would work from, "an' I don't care whether yu likes it or not," he added to himself.

Hopalong scratched his head and then laughed. Taking up a pick and shovel, he went out behind the cabin and dug a trench parallel with and about twenty paces away from the rear wall. Heaping the excavated dirt up on the near side of the cut, he stepped back and surveyed his labor with open satisfaction. "Roll yore fire barrel an' be dogged," he muttered. "Mebby she won't make a bully light for pot shots, though," he added, grinning at the execution he would do.

Taking up his tools, he went up to the place from where the gang would roll the barrel, and made half a dozen mounds of twigs, being careful to make them very flimsy. Then he covered them with earth and packed them gently. The mounds looked very tempting from the view-point of a marksman in search of earth-works, and appeared capable of stopping any rifle ball that could be fired against them. Hopalong looked them over critically and stepped back.

"I'd like to see th' look on th' face of th' son-of-a-gun that uses them for cover-won't he be surprised" and he grinned gleefully as he pictured his shots boring through them. Then he placed in the center of each a chip or a pebble or something that he thought would show up well in the firelight.

Returning to the cabin, he banked it up well with dirt and gravel, and tossed a few shovelfuls up on the roof as a safety valve to his exuberance. When he entered the door he had another idea, and fell to work scooping out a shallow cellar, deep enough to shelter him when lying at full length. Then he stuck his head out of the window and grinned at the false covers with their prominent bull's-eyes.

"When that prize-winnin' gang of ossified idiots runs up agin' these fortifications they shore will be disgusted. I'll bet four dollars an' seven cents they'll think their medicine-man's no good. I hopes that puff-eyed marshal will pick out that hump with th' chip on it," and he hugged himself in anticipation.

He then cut down a sapling and fastened it to the roof and on it he tied his neckerchief, which fluttered valiantly and with defiance in the light breeze. "I shore hopes they appreciates that," he remarked whimsically, as he went inside the hut and closed the door.

The early part of the evening passed in peace, and Hopalong, tired of watching in vain, wished for action. Midnight came, and it was not until half an hour before dawn that he was attacked. Then a noise sent him to a loophole, where he fired two shots at skulking figures some distance off. A fusillade of bullets replied; one of them ripped through the door at a weak spot and drilled a hole in a can of the everlasting peaches. Hopalong set the can in the frying pan and then flitted from loophole to loophole, shooting quick and straight. Several curses told him that he had not missed, and he scooped up a finger of peach juice. Shots thudded into the walls of his fort in an unceasing stream, and, as it grew lighter, several whizzed through the loopholes. He kept close to the earth and waited for the rush, and when it came sent it back, minus two of its members.

As he reloaded his Colts a bullet passed through his shirt sleeve and he promptly nailed the marksman. He looked out of a crack in the rear wall and saw the top of an adjoining hill crowned with spectators, all of whom were armed. Some time later he repulsed another attack and heard a faint cheer from his friends on the hill. Then he saw a barrel, blazing from end to end, roll out from the place he had so carefully covered with mounds. It gathered speed and bounded over the rough ground, flashed between two rocks and leaped into the trench, where it crackled and roared in vain.

"Now," said Hopalong, blazing at the mounds as fast as he could fire his rifle, "we'll just see what yu thinks of yore nice little covers."

Yells of consternation and pain rang out in a swelling chorus, and legs and arms jerked and flopped, one man, in his astonishment at the shot that tore open his cheek, sitting up in plain sight of the marksman. Roars of rage floated up from the main body of the besiegers, and the discomfited remnant of barrel-rollers broke for real cover.

Then he stopped another rush from the front, made upon the supposition that he was think-ing only of the second detachment. A hearty cheer arose from Tom Halloway and his friends, ensconced in their rocky position, and it was taken up by those on the hill, who danced and yelled their delight at the battle, to them more humorous than otherwise.

This recognition of his prowess from men of the caliber of his audience made him feel good, and he grinned: "Gee, I'll bet Halloway an' his friends is shore itchin' to get in this," he mur-mured, firing at a head that was shown for an instant. "Wonder what Red'll say when Jimmy tells him-bet he'll plow dust like a cyclone," and Hopalong laughed, picturing to himself the satiation of Red's anger. "Old red-headed son-of-a-gun," murmured the cowboy affectionately, "he shore can fight."

As he squinted over the sights of his rifle his eye caught sight of a moving body of men as they cantered over the flats about two miles away. In his eagerness he forgot to shoot and carefully counted them. "Nine," he grumbled. "Wonder what's th' matter?" Fearing that they were not his friends. Then a second body numbering eight cantered into sight and followed the first.

"Whoop! There's th' Red-head!" he shouted, dancing in his joy. "Now," he shouted at the peach can joyously, "yu wait about thirty minutes an' yu'll shore reckon Hades has busted loose!"

He grabbed up his Colts, which he kept loaded for repelling rushes, and recklessly emptied them into the bushes and between the rocks and trees, searching every likely place for a human target. Then he slipped his rifle in a loophole and waited for good shots, having worked off the dangerous pressure of his exuberance.

Soon he heard a yell from the direction of the "Miner's Rest," and fell to jamming cartridges into his revolvers so that he could sally out and join in the fray by the side of Red.

The thunder of madly pounding hoofs rolled up the trail, and soon a horse and rider shot around the corner and headed for the copse. Three more raced close behind and then a bunch of six, followed by the rest, spread out and searched for trouble.

Red, a Colt in each hand and hatless, stood up in his stirrups and sent shot after shot into the fleeing mob, which he could not follow on account of the nature of the ground. Buck wheeled and dashed down the trail again with Red a close second, the others packed in a solid mass and after them. At the first level stretch the newcomers swept down and hit their enemies, going through them like a knife through cheese. Hopalong danced up and down with rage when he could not find his horse, and had to stand and yell, a spectator.

The fight drifted in among the buildings, where it became a series of isolated duels, and soon Hopalong saw panic-stricken horses carrying their riders out of the other side of the town. Then he went gunning for the man who had rustled his horse. He was unsuccessful and returned to his peaches.

Soon the riders came up, and when they saw Hopalong shove a peach into his powder-grimed mouth they yelled their delight.

"Yu old maverick! Eatin' peaches like yu was afraid we'd git some!" shouted Red indignantly, leaping down and running up to his pal as though to thrash him.

Hopalong grinned pleasantly and fired a peach against Red's eye. "I was savin' that one for yu, Reddie," he remarked, as he avoided Buck's playful kick. "Yu fellers git to work an' dig up some wealth —I'm hungry." Then he turned to Buck: "Yore th' marshal of this town, an' any son-of-a-gun what don't like it had better write. Oh, yes, here comes Tom Halloway —'member him?"

Buck turned and faced the miner and his hand went out with a jerk.

"Well, I'll be locoed if I didn't punch with yu on th' Tin-Cup!" he said.

"Yu shore did an' yu was purty devilish, but that there Cassidy of yourn beats anything I ever seen."

"He's a good kid," replied Buck, glancing to where Red and Hopalong were quarreling as to who had eaten the most pie in a contest held some years before.

Johnny, nosing around, came upon the perforated and partially scattered piles of earth and twigs, and vented his disgust of them by kicking them to pieces. "Hey! Hoppy! Oh, Hoppy!" he called, "what are these things?"

Hopalong jammed Red's hat over that person's eyes and replied: "Oh, them's some loaded dice I fixed for them."

"Yu son-of-a-gun!" sputtered Red, as he wrestled with his friend in the exuberance of his pride. "Yu son-of-a-gun! Yu shore ought to be ashamed to treat 'em that way!"

"Shore," replied Hopalong. "But I ain't!"

Chapter XII
The Hospitality of Travennes

Mr. Buck Peters rode into Alkaline one bright September morning and sought refreshment at the Emporium. Mr. Peters had just finished some business for his employer and felt the satisfaction that comes with the knowledge of work well done. He expected to remain in Alkaline for several days, where he was to be joined by two of his friends and punchers, Mr. Hopalong Cassidy and Mr. Red Connors, both of whom were at Cactus Springs, seventy miles to the east. Mr. Cassidy and his friend had just finished a nocturnal tour of Santa Fe and felt somewhat peevish and dull in consequence, not to mention the sadness occasioned by the expenditure of the greater part of their combined capital on such foolishness as faro, roulette and wet-goods.

Mr. Peters and his friends had sought wealth in the Black Hills, where they had enthusiastically disfigured the earth in the fond expectation of uncovering vast stores of virgin gold. Their hopes were of an optimistic brand and had existed until the last canister of cornmeal flour had been emptied by Mr. Cassidy's burro, which waited not upon it's master's pleasure nor upon the ethics of the case. When Mr. Cassidy had returned from exercising the animal and himself over two miles of rocky hillside in the vain endeavor to give it his opinion of burros and sundry chastisements, he was requested, as owner of the beast, to give his counsel as to the best way of securing eighteen breakfasts. Remembering that the animal was headed north when he last saw it and that it was too old to eat, anyway, he suggested a plan which had worked successfully at other times for other ends, namely, poker. Mr. McAllister, an expert at the great American game, volunteered his service in accordance with the spirit of the occasion and, half an hour later, he and Mr. Cassidy drifted into Pell's poker parlors, which were located in the rear of a Chinese laundry, where they gathered unto themselves the wherewithal for the required breakfasts. An hour spent in the card room of the "Hurrah" convinced its proprietor that they had wasted their talents for the past six weeks in digging for gold. The proof of this permitted the departure of the outfits with their customary elan.

At Santa Fe the various individuals had gone their respective ways, to reassemble at the ranch in the near future, and for several days they had been drifting south in groups of twos and threes and, like chaff upon a stream, had eddied into Alkaline, where Mr. Peters had found them arduously engaged in postponing the final journey. After he had gladdened their hearts and soothed their throats by making several pithy remarks to the bartender, with whom he established their credit, he cautioned them against letting any one harm them and, smiling at the humor of his warning, left abruptly.

Cactus Springs was burdened with a zealous and initiative organization known as vigilantes, whose duty it was to extend the courtesies of the land to cattle thieves and the like. This organization boasted of the name of Travennes' Terrors and of a muster roll of twenty. There was also a boast that no one had ever escaped them which, if true, was in many cases unfortunate. Mr. Slim Travennes, with whom Mr. Cassidy had participated in an extemporaneous exchange of Colt's courtesies in Santa Fe the year before, was the head of the organization and was also chairman of the committee on arrivals, and the two gentlemen of the Bar-20 had not been in town an hour before he knew of it.

Being anxious to show the strangers every attention and having a keen recollection of the brand of gun-play commanded by Mr. Cassidy, he planned a smoother method of procedure and one calculated to permit him to enjoy the pleasures of a good old age. Mr. Travennes knew that horse thieves were regarded as social enemies, that the necessary proof of their guilt was the finding of stolen animals in their possession, that death was the penalty and that every man, whether directly concerned or not, regarded, himself as judge, jury and executioner.

He had several acquaintances who were bound to him by his knowledge of crimes they had committed and would could not refuse his slightest wish. Even if they had been free agents they were not above causing the death of an innocent man. Mr. Travennes, feeling very self-satisfied at his cleverness, arranged to have the proof placed where it would do the most harm and intended to take care of the rest by himself.

Mr. Connors, feeling much refreshed and very hungry, arose at daylight the next morning, and dressing quickly, started off to feed and water the horses. After having several tilts with the landlord about the bucket he took his departure toward the corral at the rear. Peering through the gate, he could hardly believe his eyes. He climbed over it and inspected the animals at close range, and found that those which he and his friend had ridden for the last two months were not to be seen, but in their places were two better animals, which concerned him greatly. Being fair and square himself, he could not understand the change and sought enlightenment of his more imaginative and suspicious friend.

"Hey, Hopalong!" he called, "come out here an' see what th' blazes has happened!"

Mr. Cassidy stuck his auburn head out of the wounded shutter and complacently surveyed his companion. Then he saw the horses and looked hard.

"Quit yore foolin', yu old cuss," he remarked pleasantly, as he groped around behind him with his feet, searching for his boots. "Anybody would think yu was a little boy with yore fool jokes. Ain't yu ever goin' to grow up?"

"They've got our bronch," replied Mr. Connors in an injured tone. "Honest, I ain't kiddin' yu," he added for the sake of peace.

"Who has?" Came from the window, followed immediately by, "Yu've got my boots!"

"I ain't —they're under th' bunk," contradicted and explained Mr. Connors. Then, turning to the matter in his mind he replied, "I don't know who's got them. If I did do yu think I'd be holdin' hands with myself?"

"Nobody'd accuse yu of anything like that," came from the window, accompanied by an overdone snicker.

Mr. Connors flushed under his accumulated tan as he remembered the varied pleasures of Santa Fe, and he regarded the bronchos in anything but a pleasant state of mind.

Mr. Cassidy slid through the window and approached his friend, looking as serious as he could.

"Any tracks?" He inquired, as he glanced quickly over the ground to see for himself.

"Not after that wind we had last night. They might have growed there for all I can see," growled Mr. Connors.

"I reckon we better hold a pow-wow with th' foreman of this shack an' find out what he knows," suggested Mr. Cassidy. "This looks too good to be a swap."

Mr. Connors looked his disgust at the idea and then a light broke in upon him. "Mebby they was hard pushed an' wanted fresh cayuses," he said. "A whole lot of people get hard pushed in this country. Anyhow, we'll prospect th' boss."

They found the proprietor in his stocking feet, getting the breakfast, and Mr. Cassidy regarded the preparations with open approval. He counted the tin plates and found only three, and, thinking that there would be more plates if there were others to feed, glanced into the landlord's room. Not finding signs of other guests, on whom to lay the blame for the loss of his horse, he began to ask questions.

"Much trade?" He inquired solicitously.

"Yep," replied the landlord.

Mr. Cassidy looked at the three tins and wondered if there had ever been any more with which to supply his trade. "Been out this morning?" he pursued.

"Nope."

"Talks purty nigh as much as Buck," thought Mr. Cassidy, and then said aloud, "Anybody else here?"

"Nope."

Mr. Cassidy lapsed into a painful and disgusted silence and his friend tried his hand.

"Who owns a mosaic bronch, Chinee flag on th' near side, Skillet brand?" asked Mr. Connors.

"Quien sabe?"

"Gosh, he can nearly keep still in two lingoes," thought Mr. Cassidy.

"Who owns a bob-tailed pinto, saddle-galled, cast in th' near eye, Star Diamond brand, white stockin' on th' off front prop, with a habit of scratchin' itself every other minute?" went on Mr. Connors.

"Slim Travennes," replied the proprietor, flopping a flapjack. Mr. Cassidy reflectively scratched the back of his hand and looked innocent, but his mind was working overtime.

"Who's Slim Travennes?" Asked Mr. Connors, never having heard of that person, owing to the reticence of his friend.

"Captain of th' vigilantes."

"What does he look like on th' general run?" Blandly inquired Mr. Cassidy, wishing to verify his suspicions. He thought of the trouble he had with Mr. Travennes up in Santa Fe and of the reputation that gentleman possessed. Then the fact that Mr. Travennes was the leader of the local vigilantes came to his assistance and he was sure that the captain had a hand in the change. All these points existed in misty groups in his mind, but the next remark of the landlord caused them to rush together and reveal the plot.

"Good," said the landlord, flopping another flapjack, "and a warnin' to hoss thieves."

"Ahem," coughed Mr. Cassidy and then continued, "is he a tall, lanky, yaller-headed son-of-a-gun, with a big nose an' lots of ears?"

"Mebby so," answered the host.

"Urn, slopping over into bad Sioux," thought Mr. Cassidy, and then said aloud, "How long has he hung around this here layout?" At the same time passing a warning glance at his companion.

The landlord straightened up. "Look here, stranger, if yu hankers after his pedigree so all-fired hard yu had best pump him."

"I told yu this here feller wasn't a man what would give away all he knowed," lied Mr. Connors, turning to his friend and indicating the host. "He ain't got time for that. Anybody can see that he is a powerful busy man. An' then he ain't no child."

Mr. Cassidy thought that the landlord could tell all he knew in about five minutes and then not break any speed records for conversation, but he looked properly awed and impressed. "Well, yu needn't go an' get mad about it! I didn't know, did I?"

"Who's gettin' mad?" Pugnaciously asked Mr. Connors. After his injured feelings had been soothed by Mr. Cassidy's sullen silence he again turned to the landlord.

"What did this Travennes look like when yu saw him last?" Coaxed Mr. Connors.

"Th' same as he does now, as yu can see by lookin' out of th' window. That's him down th' street," enlightened the host, thawing to the pleasant Mr. Connors.

Mr. Cassidy adopted the suggestion and frowned. Mr. Travennes and two companions were walking toward the corral and Mr. Cassidy once again slid out of the window, his friend going by the door.

Chapter XIII
Travennes' Discomfiture

When Mr. Travennes looked over the corral fence he was much chagrined to see a man and a Colt both paying strict attention to his nose.

"Mornin', Duke," said the man with the gun. "Lose anything?"

Mr. Travennes looked back at his friends and saw Mr. Connors sitting on a rock holding two guns. Mr. Travennes' right and left wings were the targets and they pitted their frowns against Mr. Connors' smile.

"Not that I knows of," replied Mr. Travennes, shifting his feet uneasily.

"Find anything?" Came from Mr. Cassidy as he sidled out of the gate.

"Nope," replied the captain of the Terrors, eying the Colt. "Are yu in the habit of payin' early mornin' calls to this here corral?" persisted Mr. Cassidy, playing with the gun.

"Ya-as. That's my business —I'm th' captain of the vigilantes."

"That's too bad," sympathized Mr. Cassidy, moving forward a step.

Mr. Travennes looked put out and backed off. "What yu mean, stickin' me up this-away?" He asked indignantly.

"Yu needn't go an' get mad," responded Mr. Cassidy. "Just business. Yore cayuse an' another shore climbed this corral fence last night an' ate up our bronchs, an' I just nachurly want to know about it."

Mr. Travennes looked his surprise and incredulity and craned his neck to see for himself. When he saw his horse peacefully scratching itself he swore and looked angrily up the street. Mr. Connors, behind the shack, was hidden to the view of those on the street, and when two men ran up at a signal from Mr. Travennes, intending to insert themselves in the misunderstanding, they were promptly lined up with the first two by the man on the rock.

"Sit down," invited Mr. Connors, pushing a chunk of air out of the way with his guns. The last two felt a desire to talk and to argue the case on its merits, but refrained as the black holes in Mr. Connors' guns hinted at eruption. "Every time yu opens yore mouths yu gets closer to th' Great Divide," enlightened that person, and they were childlike in their belief.

Mr. Travennes acted as though he would like to scratch his thigh where his Colt's chafed him, but postponed the event and listened to Mr. Cassidy, who was asking questions.

"Where's our cayuses, General?"

Mr. Travennes replied that he didn't know. He was worried, for he feared that his captor didn't have a secure hold on the hammer of the ubiquitous Colt's.

"Where's my cayuse?" Persisted Mr. Cassidy.

"I don't know, but I wants to ask yu how yu got mine," replied Mr. Travennes.

"Yu tell me how mine got out an' I'll tell yu how yourn got in," countered Mr. Cassidy.

Mr. Connors added another to his collection before the captain replied.

"Out in this country people get in trouble when they're found with other folks' cayuses," Mr. Travennes suggested.

Mr. Cassidy looked interested and replied: "Yu shore ought to borrow some experience, an' there's lots floating around. More than one man has smoked in a powder mill, an' th' number of them planted who looked in th' muzzle of a empty gun is scandalous. If my remarks don't perculate right smart I'll explain."

Mr. Travennes looked down the street again, saw number five added to the line-up, and coughed up chunks of broken profanity, grieving his host by his lack of courtesy.

"Time," announced Mr. Cassidy, interrupting the round. "I wants them cayuses an' I wants 'em right now. Yu an' me will amble off an' get 'em. I won't bore yu with tellin' yu what'll happen if yu gets skittish. Slope along an' don't be scared; I'm with yu," assured Mr. Cassidy as he looked over at Mr. Connors, whose ascetic soul pined for the flapjacks of which his olfactories caught intermittent whiffs.

"Well, Red, I reckons yu has got plenty of room out here for all yu may corral; anyhow there ain't a whole lot more. My friend Slim an' I are shore going to have a devil of a time if we can t find them cussed bronchs. Whew, them flapjacks smell like a plain trail to payday. Just think of th' nice maple juice we used to get up to Cheyenne on them frosty mornings."

"Get out of here an' lemme alone! 'What do yu allus want to go an' make a feller unhappy for? Can't yu keep still about grub when yu knows I ain't had my morning's feed yet?" Asked Mr. Connors, much aggrieved.

"Well, I'll be back directly an' I'll have them cayuses or a scalp. Yu tend to business an' watch th' herd. That shorthorn yearling at th' end of th' line" —pointing to a young man who looked capable of taking risks —"he looks like he might take a chance an' gamble with yu," remarked Mr. Cassidy, placing Mr. Travennes in front of him and pushing back his own sombrero. "Don't put too much maple juice on them flapjacks, Red," he warned as he poked his captive in the back of the neck as a hint to get along. Fortunately Mr. Connors' closing remarks are lost to history.

Observing that Mr. Travennes headed south on the quest, Mr. Cassidy reasoned that the missing bronchos ought to be somewhere in the north, and he postponed the southern trip until such time when they would have more leisure at their disposal. Mr. Travennes showed a strong inclination to shy at this arrangement, but quieted down under persuasion, and they started off toward where Mr. Cassidy firmly believed the North Pole and the cayuses to be.

"Yu has got quite a metropolis here," pleasantly remarked Mr. Cassidy as under his direction they made for a distant corral. "I can see four different types of architecture, two of 'em on one residence," he continued as they passed a wood and adobe hut. "No doubt the railroad will put a branch down here some day an' then yu can hire their old cars for yore public buildings. Then when yu gets a post-office yu will shore make Chicago hustle some to keep her end up. Let's assay that hollow for horse-hide; it looks promisin'."

The hollow was investigated but showed nothing other than cactus and baked alkali. The corral came next, and there too was emptiness. For an hour the search was unavailing, but at the end of that time Mr. Cassidy began to notice signs of nervousness on the part of his guest, which grew less as they proceeded. Then Mr. Cassidy retraced their steps to the place where the nervousness first developed and tried another way and once more returned to the starting point.

"Yu seems to hanker for this fool exercise," quoth Mr. Trayennes with much sarcasm. "If yu reckons I'm fond of this locoed ramblin' yu shore needs enlightenment."

"Sometimes I do get these fits," confessed Mr. Cassidy, "an' when I do I'm dead sore on objections. Let's peek in that there hut," he suggested.

"Huh; yore ideas of cayuses are mighty peculiar. Why don't you look for 'em up on those cactuses or behind that mesquite? I wouldn't be a heap surprised if they was roostin' on th' roof. They are mighty knowing animals, cayuses. I once saw one that could figger like a schoolmarm," remarked Mr. Travennes, beginning sarcastically and toning it down as he proceeded, out of respect for his companion's gun.

"Well, they might be in th' shack," replied Mr. Cassidy. "Cayuses know so much that it takes a month to unlearn them. I wouldn't like to bet they ain't in that hut, though."

Mr. Travennes snickered in a manner decidedly uncomplimentary and began to whistle, softly at first. The gentleman from the Bar-20 noticed that his companion was a musician; that when he came to a strong part he increased the tones until they bid to be heard at several hundred yards. When Mr. Travennes had reached a most passionate part in "Juanita" and was expanding his lungs to do it justice he was rudely stopped by the insistent pressure of his guard's Colt's on the most ticklish part of his ear.

"I shore wish yu wouldn't strain yoreself thataway," said Mr. Cassidy, thinking that Mr. Travennes might be endeavoring to call assistance. "I went an' promised my mother on her deathbed that I wouldn't let nobody whistle out loud like that, an' th' opery is hereby stopped. Besides, somebody might hear them mournful tones an' think that something is th' matter, which it ain't."

Mr. Travennes substituted heartfelt cursing, all of which was heavily accented.

As they approached the hut Mr. Cassidy again tickled his prisoner and insisted that he be very quiet, as his cayuse was very sensitive to noise and it might be there. Mr. Cassidy still thought Mr. Travennes might have friends in the hut and wouldn't for the world disturb them, as he would present a splendid target as he approached the building.

Chapter XIV
The Tale of a Cigarette

The open door revealed three men asleep on the earthen floor, two of whom were Mexicans. Mr. Cassidy then for the first time felt called upon to relieve his companion of the Colt's which so sorely itched that gentleman's thigh and then disarmed the sleeping guards.

"One man an' a half," murmured Mr. Cassidy, it being in his creed that it took four Mexicans to make one Texan.

In the far corner of the room were two bronchos, one of which tried in vain to kick Mr. Cassidy, not realizing that he was ten feet away. The noise awakened the sleepers, who sat up and then sprang to their feet, their hands instinctively streaking to their thighs for the weapons which peeked contentedly from the bosom of Mr. Cassidy's open shirt. One of the Mexicans made a lightning-like grab for the back of his neck for the knife which lay along his spine and was shot in the front of his neck for his trouble. The shot spoiled his aim, as the knife flashed past Mr. Cassidy's arm, wide by two feet, and thudded into the door frame, where it hummed angrily.

"The only man who could do that right was th' man who invented it, Mr. Bowie, of Texas," explained Mr. Cassidy to the other Mexican. Then he glanced at the broncho, that was squealing in rage and fear at the shot, which sounded like a cannon in the small room, and laughed.

"That's my cayuse, all right, an' he wasn't up no cactus nor roostin' on th' roof, neither. He's th' most affectionate beast I ever saw. It took me nigh onto six months afore I could ride him without fighting him to a standstill," said Mr. Cassidy to his guest. Then he turned to the horse and looked it over. "Come here! What d'yu mean, acting thataway? Yu ragged end of nothin' wobbling in space! Yu wall-eyed, ornery, locoed guide to Hades! Yu won't be so frisky when yu've made them seventy hot miles between here an' Alkaline in five hours," he promised, as he made his way toward the animal.

Mr. Travennes walked over to the opposite wall and took down a pouch of tobacco which hung from a peg. He did this in a manner suggesting ownership, and after he had deftly rolled a cigarette with one hand he put the pouch in his pocket and, lighting up, inhaled deeply and with much satisfaction. Mr. Cassidy turned around and glanced the group over, wondering if the tobacco had been left in the hut on a former call.

"Did yu find yore makings?" He asked, with a note of congratulations in his voice.

"Yep. Want one?" Asked Mr. Travennes.

Mr. Cassidy ignored the offer and turned to the guard whom he had found asleep.

"Is that his tobacco?" He asked, and the guard, anxious to make everything run smoothly, told the truth and answered:

"Shore. He left it here last night," whereupon Mr. Travennes swore and Mr. Cassidy smiled grimly.

"Then yu knows how yore cayuse got in an' how mine got out," said the latter. "I wish yu would explain," he added, fondling his Colts.

Mr. Travennes frowned and remained silent.

"I can tell yu, anyhow," continued Mr. Cassidy, still smiling, but his eyes and jaw belied the smile. "Yu took them cayuses out because yu wanted yourn to be found in their places. Yu remembered Santa Fe an' it rankled in yu. Not being man enough to notify me that yu'd shoot on sight an' being afraid my friends would get yu if yu plugged me on th' sly, yu tried to make out that me an' Red rustled yore cayuses. That meant a lynching with me an' Red in th' places of honor. Yu never saw Red afore, but yu didn't care if he went with me. Yu don't deserve fair play, but I'm going to give it to yu because I don't want anybody to say that any of th' Bar-20 ever murdered a man, not even a skunk like yu. My friends have treated me too square for that. Yu can take this gun an yu can do one of three things with it, which are: walk out in th' open a hundred paces an' then turn an walk toward me–after you face me yu can set it a-going whenever yu want to; the second is, put it under yore hat an' I'll put mine an' th' others back by the cayuses. Then we'll toss up an' th' lucky man gets it to use as he wants. Th' third is, shoot yourself."

Mr. Cassidy punctuated the close of his ultimatum by handing the weapon, muzzle first, and, because the other might be an adept at "twirling," he kept its recipient covered during the operation. Then, placing his second Colt's with the captured weapons, he threw them through the door, being very careful not to lose the drop on his now armed prisoner.

Mr. Travennes looked around and wiped the sweat from his forehead, and being an observant gentleman, took the proffered weapon and walked to the east, directly toward the sun, which at this time was halfway to the meridian. The glare of its straight rays and those reflected from the shining sand would, in a measure, bother Mr. Cassidy and interfere with the accuracy of his aim, and he was always thankful for small favors.

Mr. Travennes was the possessor of accurate knowledge regarding the lay of the land, and the thought came to him that there was a small but deep hole out toward the east and that it was about the required distance away. This had been dug by a man who had labored all day in the burning sun to make an oven so that he could cook mesquite root in the manner he had seen the Apaches cook it. Mr. Travennes blessed hobbies, specific and general, stumbled thoughtlessly and disappeared from sight as the surprised Mr. Cassidy started forward to offer his assistance.

Upon emphatic notification from the man in the hole that his help was not needed, Mr. Cassidy wheeled around and in great haste covered the distance separating him from the hut, whereupon Mr. Travennes swore in self-congratulation and regret. Mr. Cassidy's shots barked a cactus which leaned near Mr. Travennes' head and flecked several clouds of alkali near that person's nose, causing him to sneeze, duck, and grin.

"It's his own gun," grumbled Mr. Cassidy as a bullet passed through his sombrero, having in mind the fact that his opponent had a whole belt full of .44's. If it had been Mr. Cassidy's gun that had been handed over he would have enjoyed the joke on Mr. Travennes, who would have had five cartridges between himself and the promised eternity, as he would have been unable to use the .44's in Mr. Cassidy's .45, while the latter would have gladly consented to the change, having as he did an extra .45. Never before had Mr. Cassidy looked with reproach upon his .45 caliber Colt's, and he sighed as he used it to notify Mr. Travennes that arbitration was not to be considered, which that person indorsed, said indorsement passing so close to Mr. Cassidy's ear that he felt the breeze made by it.

"He's been practicin' since I plugged him up in Santa Fe," thought Mr. Cassidy, as he retired around the hut to formulate a plan of campaign.

Mr. Travennes sang "Hi-le, hi-lo," and other selections, principally others, and wondered how Mr. Cassidy could hoist him out. The slack of his belt informed him that he was in the middle of a fast, and suggested starvation as the derrick that his honorable and disgusted adversary might employ.

Mr. Cassidy, while figuring out his method of procedure, absent-mindedly jabbed a finger in his eye, and the ensuing tears floated an idea to him. He had always had great respect for ricochet shots since his friend Skinny Thompson had proved their worth on the hides of Sioux. If he could disturb the sand and convey several grains of it to Mr. Travennes' eyes the game would be much simplified. While planning for the proposed excavation, a la Colt's, he noticed several stones lying near at hand, and a new and better scheme presented itself for his consideration. If Mr. Travennes could be persuaded to get out of-well, it was worth trying.

Mr. Cassidy lined up his gloomy collection and tersely ordered them to turn their backs to him and to stay in that position, the suggestion being that if they looked around they wouldn't be able to dodge quickly enough. He then slipped bits of his lariat over their wrists and an-kles, tying wrists to ankles and each man to his neighbor. That finished to his satisfaction, he dragged them in the hut to save them from the burning rays of the sun.

Having performed this act of kindness, he crept along the hot sand, taking advantage of every bit of cover afforded, and at last he reached a point within a hundred feet of the besieged. During the trip Mr. Travennes sang to his heart's content, some of the words being improvised for the occasion and were not calculated to increase Mr. Cassidy's respect for his own wisdom if he should hear them. Mr. Cassidy heard, however, and several fragments so forcibly intruded on his peace of mind that he determined to put on the last verse himself and to suit himself.

Suddenly Mr. Travennes poked his head up and glanced at the hut. He was down again so quickly that there was no chance for a shot at him and he believed that his enemy was still sojourning in the rear of the building, which caused him to fear that he was expected to live on nothing as long as he could and then give himself up. Just to show his defiance he stretched himself out on his back and sang with all his might, his sombrero over his face to keep the glare of the sun out of his eyes.

He was interrupted, however, forgot to finish a verse as he had intended, and jumped to one side as a stone bounced off his leg. Looking up, he saw another missile curve into his patch of sky and swiftly bear down on him. He avoided it by a hair's breadth and wondered what had happened. Then what Mr. Travennes thought was a balloon, being unsophisticated in matters pertaining to aerial navigation, swooped down upon him and smote him on the shoulder and also bounced off.

Mr. Travennes hastily laid music aside and took up elocution as he dodged another stone and wished that the mesquite-loving crank had put on a roof. In evading the projectile he let his sombrero appear on a level with the desert, and the hum of a bullet as it passed through his head-gear and into the opposite wall made him wish that there had been constructed a cellar, also.

"Hi-le, hi-lo" intruded upon his ear, as Mr. Cassidy got rid of the surplus of his heart's joy. Another stone the size of a man's foot shaved Mr. Travennes' ear and he hugged the side of the hole nearest his enemy.

"Hibernate, blank yu!" derisively shouted the human catapult as he released a chunk of sand-stone the size of a quail. "Draw in yore laigs an' buck," was his God-speed to the missile.

"Hey, yu!" indignantly yowled Mr. Travennes from his defective storm cellar. "Don't yu know any better'n to heave things thataway?"

"Hi-le, hi-lo," sang Mr. Cassidy, as another stone soared aloft in the direction of the complainant. Then he stood erect and awaited results with a Colt's in his hand leveled at the rim of the hole. A hat waved and an excited voice bit off chunks of expostulation and asked for an armistice. Then two hands shot up and Mr. Travennes, sore and disgusted and desperate, popped his head up an blinked at Mr. Cassidy's gun.

"Yu was fillin' th' hole up," remarked Mr. Travennes in an accusing tone, hiding the real reason for his evacuation. "In a little while I'd a been th' top of a pile instead of th' bottom of a hole," he announced, crawling out and rubbing his head.

Mr. Cassidy grinned and ordered his prisoner to one side while be secured the weapon which lay in the hole. Having obtained it as quickly as possible be slid it in his open shirt and clambered out again.

"Yu remind me of a feller I used to know," remarked Mr. Travennes, as he led the way to the hut, trying not to limp. "Only he throwed dynamite. That was th' way he cleared off chaparral-blowed it off. He got so used to heaving away everything he lit that he spoiled three pipes in two days."

Mr. Cassidy laughed at the fiction and then became grave as he pictured Mr. Connors sitting on the rock and facing down a line of men, any one of whom was capable of his destruction if given the interval of a second.

When they arrived at the hut Mr. Cassidy observed that the prisoners had moved considerably. There was a cleanly swepttrail four yards long where they had dragged themselves, and they sat in the end nearer the guns. Mr. Cassidy smiled and fired close to the Mexican's ear, who lost in one frightened jump a little of what he had so laboriously gained.

"Yu'll wear out yore pants," said Mr. Cassidy, and then added grimly, "an' my patience."

Mr. Travennes smiled and thought of the man who so ably seconded Mr. Cassidy's efforts and who was probably shot by this time. The outfit of the Bar-20 was so well known throughout the land that he was aware the name of the other was Red Connors. An unreasoning streak of sarcasm swept over him and he could not resist the opportunity to get in a stab at his captor.

"Mebby yore pard has wore out somebody's patience, too," said Mr. Travennes, suggestively and with venom.

His captor wheeled toward him, his face white with passion, and Mr. Travennes shrank back and regretted the words.

"I ain't shootin' dogs this here trip," said Mr. Cassidy, trembling with scorn and anger, "so yu can pull yourself together. I'll give yu another chance, but yu wants to hope almighty hard that Red is O. K. If he ain't, I'll blow yu so many ways at once that if yu sprouts yu'll make a good acre of weeds. If he is all right yu'd better vamoose this range, for there won't be no hole for yu to crawl into next time. What friends yu have left will have to tote yu off an' plant yu," he finished with emphasis. He drove the horses outside, and, after severing the bonds on his prisoners, lined them up.

"Yu," he began, indicating all but Mr. Travennes, "yu amble right smart toward Canada," pointing to the north. "Keep a-going till yu gets far enough away so a Colt won't find yu." Here he grinned with delight as he saw his Sharp's rifle in its sheath on his saddle and, drawing it forth, he put away his Colts and glanced at the trio, who were already industriously plodding northward. "Hey!" he shouted, and when they sullenly turned to see what new idea he had found he gleefully waved his rifle at them and warned them further: "This is a Sharp's an' it's good for half a mile, so don't stop none too soon."

Having sent them directly away from their friends so they could not have him "potted" on the way back, he mounted his broncho and indicated to Mr. Travennes that he, too, was to ride, watching that that person did not make use of the Winchester which Mr. Connors was foolish enough to carry around on his saddle. Winchesters were Mr. Cassidy's pet aversion and Mr. Connors' most prized possession, this difference of opinion having upon many occasions caused hasty words between them. Mr. Connors, being better with his Winchester than Mr. Cassidy was with his Sharp's, had frequently proved that his choice was the wiser, but Mr. Cassidy was loyal to the Sharp's and refused to be convinced. Now, however, the Winchester became pregnant with possibilities and, therefore, Mr. Travennes rode a few yards to the left and in advance, where the rifle was in plain sight, hanging as it did on the right of Mr. Connors' saddle, which Mr. Travennes graced so well.

The journey back to town was made in good time and when they came to the buildings Mr. Cassidy dismounted and bade his companion do likewise, there being too many corners that a fleeing rider could take advantage of. Mr. Travennes felt of his bumps and did so, wishing hard things about Mr. Cassidy.

Chapter XV
The Penalty

While Mr. Travennes had been entertained in the manner narrated, Mr. Connors had passed the time by relating stale jokes to the uproarious laughter of his extremely bored audience, who had heard the aged efforts many times since they had first seen the light of day, and most of whom earnestly longed for a drink. The landlord, hearing the hilarity, had taken advantage of the opportunity offered to see a free show. Not being able to see what the occasion was for the mirth, he had pulled on his boots and made his way to the show with a flapjack in the skillets which, in his haste, he had forgotten to put down. He felt sure that he would be entertained, and he was not disappointed. He rounded the corner and was enthusiastically welcomed by the hungry Mr. Connors, whose ubiquitous guns coaxed from the skillet its dyspeptic wad.

"Th' saints be praised!" ejaculated Mr. Connors as a matter of form, not having a very clear idea of just what saints were, but he knew what flapjacks were and greedily overcame the heroic resistance of the one provided by chance and his own guns. As he rolled his eyes in ecstatic content the very man Mr. Cassidy had warned him against suddenly arose and in great haste disappeared around the corner of the corral, from which point of vantage he vented his displeasure at the treatment he had received by wasting six shots at the mortified Mr. Connors.

"Steady!" sang out that gentleman as the line-up wavered. "He's a precedent to hell for yu fellers! Don't yu get ambitious, none whatever." Then he wondered how long it would take the fugitive to secure a rifle and return to release the others by drilling him at long range.

His thoughts were interrupted by the vision of a red head that climbed into view over a rise a short distance off and he grinned his delight as Mr. Cassidy loomed up, jaunty and triumphant. Mr. Cassidy was executing calisthenics with a Colt in the rear of Mr. Travennes' neck and was leading the horses.

Mr. Connors waved the skillet and his friend grinned his congratulations at what the token signified.

"I see yu got some more," said Mr. Cassidy, as he went down the line-up from the rear and collected nineteen weapons of various makes and conditions, this number being explained by the fact that all but one of the prisoners wore two. Then he added the five that had kicked against his ribs ever since he had left the hut, and carefully threaded the end of his lariat through the trigger guards.

"Looks like we stuck up a government supply mule, Red," he remarked, as he fastened the whole collection to his saddle. "Fourteen colts, six Merwin-Hulbert's, three Prescott, an' one puzzle," he added, examining the puzzle. "Made in Germany, it says, and it shore looks like it. It's got little pins stickin' out of th' cylinder, like you had to swat it with a hammer or a rock, or somethin' to make it go off. Must be damn dangerous, to most anybody around. Looks more like a cactus than a six-shooter-gosh, it's a ten-shooter! I allus said them Dutchmen was bloody-minded cusses. Think of bein' able to shoot yoreself ten times before th' blame thing stops!" Then looking at the line-up for the owner of the weapon, he laughed at the woeful countenances displayed. "Did they sidle in by companies or squads?" He asked.

"By twos, mostly. Then they parade-rested an' got discharged from duty. I had eleven, but one got homesick, or disgusted, or something, an' deserted. It was that cussed flapjack," confessed and explained Mr. Connors.

"What!" said Mr. Cassidy in a loud voice. "Got away! Well, we'll have to make our get-away plumb sudden or we'll never go."

At this instant the escaped man again began his bombardment from the corner of the corral and Mr. Cassidy paused, indignant at the fusillade which tore up the dust at his feet. He looked reproachfully at Mr. Connors and then circled out on the plain until he caught a glimpse of a fleeing cow-puncher, whose back rapidly grew smaller in the fast-increasing distance.

"That's yore friend, Red," said Mr. Cassidy as he returned from his reconnaissance. "He's that short-horn yearling. Mebby he'll come back again," he added hopefully. "Anyhow, we've got to move. He'll collect reinforcements an' mebby they all won't shoot like him. Get up on yore Clarinda an' hold th' fort for me," he ordered, pushing the farther horse over to his friend. Mr. Connors proved that an agile man can mount a restless horse and not lose the drop, and backed off three hundred yards, deftly substituting his Winchester for the Colts. Then Mr. Cassidy likewise mounted with his attention riveted elsewhere and backed off to the side of his companion.

The bombardment commenced again from the corral, but this time Mr. Connors' rifle slid around in his lap and exploded twice. The bellicose gentleman of the corral yelled in pain and surprise and vanished.

"Purty good for a Winchester," said Mr. Cassidy in doubtful congratulation.

"That's why I got him," snapped Mr. Connors in brief reply, and then he laughed. "Is them th' vigilantes what never let a man get away?" He scornfully asked, backing down the street and patting his Winchester.

"Well, Red, they wasn't all there. They was only twelve all told," excused Mr. Cassidy. "An' then we was two," he explained, as he wished the collection of six-shooters was on Mr. Connors' horse so they wouldn't bark his shin.

"An we still are," corrected Mr. Connors, as they wheeled and galloped for Alkaline.

As the sun sank low on the horizon Mr. Peters finished ordering provisions at the general store, the only one Alkaline boasted, and sauntered to the saloon where he had left his men. He found diem a few dollars richer, as they had borrowed ten dollars from the bartender on their reputations as poker players and had used the money to stake Mr. McAllister in a game against the local poker champion.

"Has Hopalong an' Red showed up yet?" Asked Mr. Peters, frowning at the delay already caused.

"Nope," replied Johnny Nelson, as he paused from tormenting Billy Williams.

At that minute the doorway was darkened and Mr. Cassidy and Mr. Connors entered and called for refreshments. Mr. Cassidy dropped a huge bundle of six-shooters on the floor, making caustic remarks regarding their utility.

"What's th' matter?" Inquired Mr. Peters of Mr. Cassidy. "Yu looks mad an' anxious. An' where in blazes did yu corral them guns?"

Mr. Cassidy drank deep and then reported with much heat what had occurred at Cactus Springs and added that he wanted to go back and wipe out the town, said desire being luridly endorsed by Mr. Connors.

"Why, shore," said Mr. Peters, "we'll all go. Such doings must be stopped instanter." Then he turned to the assembled outfits and asked for a vote, which was unanimous for war.

Shortly afterward eighteen angry cowpunchers rode to the east, two red-haired gentlemen well in front and urging speed. It was 8 P.M. when they left Alkaline, and the cool of the night was so delightful that the feeling of ease which came upon them made them lax and they lost three hours in straying from the dim trail. At eight o'clock the next morning they came in sight of their destination and separated into two squads, Mr. Cassidy leading the northern division and Mr. Connors the one which circled to the south. The intention was to attack from two directions, thus taking the town from front and rear.

Cactus Springs lay gasping in the excessive heat and the vigilantes who had toed Mr. Connors' line the day before were lounging in the shade of the "Palace" saloon, telling what they would do if they ever faced the same man again. Half a dozen sympathizers offered gratuitous condolence and advice and all were positive that they knew where Mr. Cassidy and Mr. Connors would go when they died.

The rolling thunder of madly pounding hoofs disturbed their post-mortem and they arose in a body to flee from half their number, who, guns in hands, charged down upon them through clouds of sickly white smoke. Travennes' Terrors were minus many weapons and they could not be expected to give a glorious account of themselves. Windows rattled and fell in and doors and walls gave off peculiar sounds as they grew full of holes. Above the riot rattled the incessant crack of Colt's and Winchester, emphasized at close intervals by the assertive roar of buffalo guns. Off to the south came another rumble of hoofs and Mr. Connors, leading the second squad, —arrived to participate in the payment of the debt.

Smoke spurted from windows and other points of vantage and hung wavering in the heated air. The shattering of woodwork told of heavy slugs finding their rest, and the whines that grew and diminished in the air sang the course of .45s.

While the fight raged hottest Mr. Nelson sprang from his horse and ran to the "Palace," where he collected and piled a heap of tinder like wood, and soon the building burst out in flames, which, spreading, swept the town from end to end.

Mr. Cassidy fired slowly and seemed to be waiting for something. Mr. Connors laid aside his hot Winchester and devoted his attention to his Colts. A spurt of flame and smoke leaped from the window of a 'dobe hut and Mr. Connors sat down, firing as he went. A howl from the window informed him that he had made a hit, and Mr. Cassidy ran out and dragged him to the shelter of a near-by bowlder and asked how much he was hurt.

"Not much-in the calf," grunted Mr. Connors. "He was a bad shot-must have been the cuss that got away yesterday," speculated the injured man as he slowly arose to his feet. Mr. Cassidy dissented from force of habit and returned to his station. Mr. Travennes, who was sleeping late that morning, coughed and fought for air in his sleep, awakened in smoke, rubbed his eyes to make sure and, scorning trousers and shirt, ran clad in his red woolen undergarments to the corral, where he mounted his scared horse and rode for the desert and safety.

Mr. Cassidy, swearing at the marksmanship of a man who fired at his head and perforated his sombrero, saw a crimson rider sweep down upon him, said rider being heralded by a blazing .44.

"Gosh!" ejaculated Mr. Cassidy, scarcely believing his eyes. "Oh, it's my friend Slim going to hades," he remarked to himself in audible and relieved explanation. Mr. Cassidy's Colts cracked a protest and then he joined Mr. Peters and the others and with them fought his way out of the flame-swept town of Cactus Springs.

An hour later Mr. Connors glanced behind him at the smoke silhouetted on the horizon and pushed his way to where Mr. Cassidy rode in silence. Mr. Connors grinned at his friend of the red hair, who responded in the same manner.

"Did yu see Slim?" Casually inquired Mr. Connors, looking off to the south.

Mr. Cassidy sat upright in his saddle and felt of his Colts. "Yes," he replied, "I saw him."

Mr. Connors thereupon galloped on in silence.

Chapter XVI

Rustlers on the Range

The affair at Cactus Springs had more effect on the life at the Bar-20 than was realized by the foreman. News travels rapidly, and certain men, whose attributes were not of the sweetest, heard of it and swore vengeance, for Slim Travennes had many friends, and the result of his passing began to show itself. Outlaws have as their strongest defense the fear which they inspire, and little time was lost in making reprisals, and these caused Buck Peters to ride into Buckskin one bright October morning and then out the other side of the town. Coming to himself with a start he looked around shamefacedly and retraced his course. He was very much troubled, for, as foreman of the Bar-20, he had many responsibilities, and when things ceased to go aright he was expected not only to find the cause of the evil, but also the remedy. That was what he was paid seventy dollars a month for and that was what he had been endeavoring to do. As yet, however, he had only accomplished what the meanest cook's assistant had done. He knew the cause of his present woes to be rustlers (cattle thieves), and that was all.

Riding down the wide, quiet street, he stopped and dismounted before the ever-open door of a ramshackle, one-story frame building. Tossing the reins over the flattened ears of his vicious pinto he strode into the building and leaned easily against the bar, where he drummed with his fingers and sank into a reverie.

A shining bald pate, bowed over an open box, turned around and revealed a florid face, set with two small, twinkling blue eyes, as the proprietor, wiping his hands on his trousers, made his way to Buck's end of the bar.

"Mornin', Buck. How's things?"

The foreman, lost in his reverie, continued to stare out the door.

"Mornin'," repeated the man behind the bar. "How's things?"

"Oh!" ejaculated the foreman, smiling, "purty cussed."

"Anything flew?"

"Th' C-80 lost another herd last night."

His companion swore and placed a bottle at the foreman's elbow, but the latter shook his head. "Not this mornin' —I'll try one of them vile cigars, however."

"Them cigars are th' very best that —" began the proprietor, executing the order.

"Oh, heck!" exclaimed Buck with weary disgust. "Yu don't have to palaver none: I shore knows all that by heart."

"Them cigars —" repeated the proprietor.

"Yas, yas; them cigars —I know all about them cigars. Yu gets them for twenty dollars a thousand an' hypnotizes us into payin' yu a hundred," replied the foreman, biting off the end 'of his weed. Then he stared moodily and frowned. "I wonder why it is?" He asked. "We punchers like good stuff an' we pays good prices with good money. What do we get? Why, cabbage leaves an' leather for our smokin' an' alcohol an' extract for our drink. Now, up in Kansas City we goes to a sumptious layout, pays less an' gets bang-up stuff. If yu smelled one of them K. C. cigars yu'd shore have to ask what it was, an' as for the liquor, why, yu'd think St. Peter asked yu to have one with him. It's shore wrong somewhere."

"They have more trade in K. C.," suggested the proprietor.

"An' help, an' taxes, an' a license, an' rent, an' brass, cut glass, mahogany an' French mirrors," countered the foreman.

"They have more trade," reiterated the man with the cigars.

"Forty men spend thirty dollars apiece with yu every month." The proprietor busied himself under the bar. "Yu'll feel better to-morrow. Anyway, what do yu care, yu won't lose yore job," he said, emerging.

Buck looked at him and frowned, holding back the words which formed in anger. What was the use, he thought, when every man judged the world in his own way.

"Have yu seen any of th' boys?" He asked, smiling again.

"Nary a boy. Who do yu reckon's doin' all this rustlin'?"

"I'm reckonin', not shoutin'," responded the foreman.

The proprietor looked out the window and grinned: "Here comes one of yourn now."

The newcomer stopped his horse in a cloud of dust, playfully kicked the animal in the ribs and entered, dusting the alkali from him with a huge sombrero. Then he straightened up and sniffed: "What's burnin'?" he asked, simulating alarm. Then he noticed the cigar between the teeth of his foreman and grinned: "Gee, but yore a brave man, Buck."

"Hullo, Hopalong," said the foreman. "Want a smoke?" Waving his hand toward the box on the bar.

Mr. Hopalong Cassidy side-stepped and began to roll a cigarette: "Shore, but I'll burn my own —I know what it is."

"What was yu doin' to my cayuse afore yu come in?" Asked Buck.

"Nothin'," replied the newcomer. "That was mine what I kicked in th' corrugations."

"How is it yore ridin' the calico?" Asked the foreman. "I thought yu was dead stuck on that piebald."

"That piebald's a goat; he's beein livin' off my pants lately," responded Hopalong. "Every time I looks th' other way he ambles over and takes a bite at me. Yu just wait 'til this rustler business is roped, an' branded, an' yu'll see me eddicate that blessed scrapheap into eatin' grass again." He swiped Billy's shirt th' other day-took it right off th' corral wall, where Billy's left it to dry. Then, seeing Buck raise his eyebrows, he explained: "Shore, he washed it again. That makes three times since last fall."

The proprietor laughed and pushed out the ever-ready bottle, but Hopalong shoved it aside and told the reason: "Ever since I was up to K. C. I've been spoiled. I'm drinkin' water an' slush."

"For Pete's sake, has any more of yu fellers been up to K. C.?" queried the proprietor in alarm.

"Shore: Red an' Billy was up there, too." responded Hopalong. "Red's got a few remarks to shout to yu about yore pain-killer. Yu better send for some decent stuff afore he comes to town," he warned.

Buck swung away from the bar and looked at his dead cigar. Then he turned to Hopalong. "What did you find?" He asked.

"Same old story: nice wide trail up to th' Staked Plain-then nothin'."

"It shore beats me," soliloquized the foreman. "It shore beats me."

"Think it was Tamale Jose's old gang?" Asked Hopalong.

"If it was they took th' wrong trail home-that ain't th' way to Mexico."

Hopalong tossed aside his half-smoked cigarette. "Well, come on home; what's th' use stewin' over it? It'll come out all O.K. in th' wash." Then he laughed: "There won't be no piebald waitin' for it."

Evading Buck's playful blow he led the way to the door, and soon they were a cloud of dust on the plain. The proprietor, despairing of customers under the circumstances, absent-mindedly wiped oil on the bar, and sought his chair for a nap, grumbling about the way his trade had fallen off, for there were few customers, and those who did call were heavy with loss of sleep, and with anxiety, and only paused long enough to toss off their drink. On the ranges there were occurrences which tried men's souls.

For several weeks cattle had been disappearing from the ranges and the losses had long since passed the magnitude of those suffered when Tamale Jose and his men had crossed the Rio Grande and repeatedly levied heavy toll on the sleek herds of the Pecos Valley. Tamale Jose had raided once too often, and prosperity and plenty had followed on the ranches and the losses had been forgotten until the fall round-ups clearly showed that rustlers were again at work.

Despite the ingenuity of the ranch owners and the unceasing vigilance and night rides of the cow-punchers, the losses steadily increased until there was promised a shortage which would permit no drive to the western terminals of the railroad that year. For two weeks the banks of the Rio Grande had been patrolled and sharp-eyed men searched daily for trails leading southward, for it was not strange to think that the old raiders were again at work, notwithstanding the fact that they had paid dearly for their former depredations.

The patrols failed to discover anything out of the ordinary and the searchers found no trails. Then it was that the owners and foremen of the four central ranches met in Cowan's saloon and sat closeted together for all of one hot afternoon.

The conference resulted in riders being dispatched from all the ranches represented, and one of the couriers, Mr. Red Connors, rode north, his destination being far-away Montana. All the ranches within a radius of a hundred miles received letters and blanks and one week later the Pecos Valley Cattle-Thief Elimination Association was organized and working, with Buck as Chief Ranger.

One of the outcomes of Buck's appointment was a sudden and marked immigration into the affected territory. Mr. Connors returned from Montana with Mr. Frenchy McAllister, the foreman of the Tin-Cup, who was accompanied by six of his best and most trusted men. Mr. McAllister and party were followed by Mr. You-bet Somes, foreman of the Two-X-Two of Arizona, and five of his punchers, and later on the same day Mr. Pie Willis, accompanied by Mr. Billy Jordan and his two brothers, arrived from the Panhandle. The O-Bar-O, situated close to the town of Muddy Wells, increased its payroll by the addition of nine men, each of whom bore the written recommendation of the foreman of the Bar-20. The C-80, Double Arrow and the Three Triangle also received heavy reinforcements, and even Carter, owner of the Barred Horseshoe, far removed from the zone of the depredations, increased his outfits by half their regular strength.

Buck believed that if a thing was worth doing at all that it was worth doing very well, and his acquaintances were numerous and loyal. The collection of individuals that responded to the call were noteworthy examples of "gun-play" and their aggregate value was at par with twice their numbers in cavalry.

Each ranch had one large ranch-house and numerous line-houses scattered along the boundaries. These latter, while intended as camps for the outriders, had been erected in the days, none too remote, when Apaches, Arrapahoes, and even Cheyennes raided southward, and they had been constructed with the idea of defense paramount. Upon more than one occasion a solitary line-rider had retreated within their adobe walls and had successfully resisted all the cunning and ferocity of a score of paint-bedaubed warriors and, when his outfit had rescued him, emerged none the worse for his ordeal.

On the Bar-20, Buck placed these houses in condition to withstand seige. Twin barrels of water stood in opposite corners, provisions were stored on the hanging shelves and the bunks once again reveled in untidiness. Spare rifles, in pattern ranging from long-range Sharp's and buffalo guns to repeating rifles, leaned against the walls, and unbroken boxes of cartridges were piled above the bunks. Instead of the lonesome outrider, he placed four men to each house, two of whom were to remain at home and hold the house while their companions rode side by side on their multi-mile beat.

There were six of these houses and, instead of returning each night to the same line-house, the outriders kept on and made the circuit, thus keeping every one well informed and breaking the monotony. These measures were expected to cause the rustling operations to cease at once, but the effect was to shift the losses to the Double Arrow, the line-houses of which boasted only one puncher each. Unreasonable economy usually defeats its object.

The Double Arrow was restricted on the north by the Staked Plain, which in itself was considered a superb defense. The White Sand Hills formed its eastern boundary and were thought to be second only to the northern protection. The only reason that could be given for the hitherto comparative immunity from the attacks of the rustlers was that its cattle clung to the southern confines where there were numerous springs, thus making imperative the crossing of its territory to gain the herds.

It was in line-house No. 3, most remote of all, that Johnny Redmond fought his last fight and was found face down in the half ruined house with a hole in the back of his head, which proved that one man was incapable of watching all the loop holes in four walls at once. There must have been some casualties on the other side, for Johnny was reputed to be very painstaking in his "gunplay," and the empty shells which lay scattered on the floor did not stand for as many ciphers, of that his foreman was positive.

He was buried the day he was found, and the news of his death ran quickly from ranch to ranch and made more than one careless puncher arise and pace the floor in anger. More men came to the Double Arrow and its sentries were doubled. The depredations continued, however, and one night a week later Frank Swift reeled into the ranch-house and fell exhausted across the supper table. Rolling hoof-beats echoed flatly and died away on the plain, but the men who pursued them returned empty handed. The wounds of the unfortunate were roughly dressed and in his delirium he recounted the fight. His companion was found literally shot to pieces twenty paces from the door. One wall was found blown in, and this episode, when coupled with the use of dynamite, was more than could be tolerated.

When Buck had been informed of this he called to him Hopalong Cassidy, Red Connors and Frenchy McAllister, and the next day the three men rode north and the contingents of the ranches represented in the Association were divided into two squads, one of which was to remain at home and guard the ranches; the other, to sleep fully dressed and armed and never to stray far from their ranch-houses and horses. These latter would be called upon to ride swiftly and far when the word came.

Chapter XVII
Mr. Trendley Assumes Added Importance

That the rustlers were working under a well organized system was evident. That they were directed by a master of the game was ceaselessly beaten into the consciousness of the Association by the diversity, dash and success of their raids. No one, save the three men whom they had destroyed, had ever seen them. But, like Tamale Jose, they had raided once too often.

Mr. Trendley, more familiarly known to men as "Slippery," was the possessor of a biased conscience, if any at all. Tall, gaunt and weather-beaten and with coal-black eyes set deep beneath hairless eyebrows, he was sinister and forbidding. Into his forty-five years of existence he had crowded a century of experience, and unsavory rumors about him existed in all parts of the great West. From Canada to Mexico and from Sacramento to Westport his name stood for brigandage. His operations had been conducted with such consummate cleverness that in all the accusations there was lacking proof.

Only once had he erred, and then in the spirit of pure deviltry and in the days of youthful folly, and his mistake was a written note. He was even thought by some to have been concerned in the Mountain Meadow Massacre; others thought him to have been the leader of the band of outlaws that had plundered along the Santa Fe Trail in the late '60's. In Montana and Wyoming he was held responsible for the outrages of the band that had descended from the Hole-in-the-Wall territory and for over a hundred miles carried murder and theft that shamed as being weak the most assiduous efforts of zealous Cheyennes. It was in this last raid that he had made the mistake and it was in this raid that Frenchy McAllister had lost his wife.

When Frenchy had first been approached by Buck as to his going in search of the rustlers he had asked to go alone. This had been denied by the foreman of the Bar-20 because the men whom he had selected to accompany the scout were of such caliber that their presence could not possibly form a hindrance. Besides being his most trusted friends they were regarded by him as being the two best exponents of "gun-play" that the West afforded. Each was a specialist: Hopalong, expert beyond belief with his Colt's six-shooters, was only approached by Red, whose Winchester was renowned for its accuracy. The three made a perfect combination, as the rashness of the two younger men would be under the controlling influence of a man who could retain his coolness of mind under all circumstances.

When Buck and Frenchy looked into each other's eyes there sprang into the mind of each the same name–Slippery Trendley. Both had spent the greater part of a year in fruitless search for that person, the foreman of the Tin-Cup in vengeance for the murder of his wife, the blasting of his prospects and the loss of his herds; Buck, out of sympathy for his friend and also because they had been partners in the Double Y. Now that the years had passed and the long-sought-for opportunity was believed to be at hand, there was promised either a cessation of the outrages or that Buck would never again see his friends.

When the three mounted and came to him for final instructions Buck forced himself to be almost repellent in order to be capable of coherent speech. Hopalong glanced sharply at him and then understood, Red was all attention and eagerness and remarked nothing but the words.

"Have yu ever heard of Slippery Trendley?" Harshly inquired the foreman.

They nodded, and on the faces of the younger men a glint of hatred showed itself, but Frenchy wore his poker countenance.

Buck continued: "Th' reason I asked yu was because I don't want yu to think yore goin' on no picnic. I ain't shore it's him, but I've had some hopeful information. Besides, he is th' only man I knows of who's capable of th' plays that have been made. It's hardly necessary for me to tell yu to sleep with one eye open and never to get away from yore guns. Now I'm goin' to tell yu th' hardest part: yu are goin' to search th' Staked Plain from one end to th' other, an' that's what no white man's ever done to my knowledge.

"Now, listen to this an' don't forget it. Twenty miles north from Last Stand Rock is a spring; ten miles south of that bend in Hell Arroyo is another. If yu gets lost within two days from th' time yu enters th' Plain, put yore left hand on a cactus sometime between sun-up an' noon, move around until yu are over its shadow an' then ride straight ahead-that's south. If you goes loco beyond Last Stand Rock, follow th' shadows made before noon-that's th' quickest way to th' Pecos. Yu all knows what to do in a sand-storm, so I won't bore you with that. Repeat all I've told yu," he ordered and they complied.

"I'm tellin' yu this," continued the foreman, indicating the two auxiliaries, "because yu might get separated from Frenchy. Now I suggests that yu look around near the' Devils Rocks: I've heard that there are several water holes among them, an' besides, they might be turned into fair corrals. Mind yu, I know what I've said sounds damned idiotic for anybody that has had as much experience with th' Staked Plain as I have, but I've had every other place searched for miles around. Th' men of all th' ranches have been scoutin' an' th' Plain is th' only place left. Them rustlers has got to be found if we have to dig to hell for them. They've taken th' pot so many times that they reckons they owns it, an' we've got to at least make a bluff at drawin' cards. Mebby they're at th' bottom of th' Pecos," here he smiled faintly, "but wherever they are, we've got to find them. I want to holler 'Keno."

"If you finds where they hangs out come away instanter," here his face hardened and his eyes narrowed, "for it'll take more than yu three to deal with them th' way I'm a-hankerin' for. Come right back to th' Double Arrow, send me word by one of their punchers an' get all the rest you can afore I gets there. It'll take me a day to get th' men together an' to reach yu. I'm goin' to use smoke signals to call th' other ranches, so there won't be no time lost. Carry all th' water yu can pack when yu leaves th' Double Arrow an' don't depend none on cactus juice. Yu better take a pack horse to carry it, an' yore grub-yu can shoot it if yu have to hit th' trail real hard."

The three riders felt of their accouterments, said "So long," and cantered off for the pack horse and extra ammunition. Then they rode toward the Double Arrow, stopping at Cowan's long enough to spend some money, and reached the Double Arrow at nightfall. Early the next morning they passed the last line-house and, with the profane well-wishes of its occupants ringing in their ears, passed onto one of Nature's worst blunders-the Staked Plain.

Chapter XVIII

The Search Begins

As the sun arose it revealed three punchers riding away from civilization. On all sides, stretching to the evil-appearing horizon, lay vast blotches of dirty-white and faded yellow alkali and sand. Occasionally a dwarfed mesquite raised its prickly leaves and rustled mournfully. With the exception of the riders and an occasional Gila monster, no life was discernible. Cacti of all shapes and sizes reared aloft their forbidding spines or spread out along the sand. All was dead, ghastly; all was oppressive, startlingly repellent in its sinister promise; all was the vastness of desolation.

Hopalong knew this portion of the desert for ten miles inward-he had rescued straying cattle along its southern rim-but once beyond that limit they would have to trust to chance and their own abilities. There were water holes on this skillet, but nine out of ten were death traps, reeking with mineral poisons, colored and alkaline. The two mentioned by Buck could not be depended on, for they came and went, and more than one luckless wanderer had depended on them to allay his thirst, and had died for his trust.

So the scouts rode on in silence, noting the half-buried skeletons of cattle which were strewn plentifully on all sides. Nearly three per cent, of the cattle belonging to the Double Arrow yearly found death on this tableland, and the herds of that ranch numbered many thousand heads. It was this which made the Double Arrow the poorest of the ranches, and it was this which allowed insufficient sentries in its line-houses. The skeletons were not all of cattle, for at rare intervals lay the sand-worn frames of men.

On the morning of the second day the oppression increased with the wind and Red heaved a sigh of restlessness. The sand began to skip across the plain, in grains at first and hardly noticeable. Hopalong turned in his saddle and regarded the desert with apprehension. As he looked he saw that where grains had shifted handfuls were now moving. His mount evinced signs of uneasiness and was hard to control.

A gust of wind, stronger than the others, pricked his face and grains of sand rolled down his neck. The leather of his saddle emitted strange noises as if a fairy tattoo was being beaten upon it and he raised his hand and pointed off toward the east. The others looked and saw what had appeared to be a fog rise out of the desert and intervene between them and the sun. As far as eye could reach small whirlwinds formed and broke and one swept down and covered them with stinging sand. The day became darkened and their horses whinnied in terror and the clumps of mesquite twisted and turned to the gusts.

Each man knew what was to come upon them and they dismounted, hobbled their horses and threw them bodily to the earth, wrapping a blanket around the head of each. A rustling as of paper rubbing together became noticeable and they threw themselves flat upon the earth, their heads wrapped in their coats and buried in the necks of their mounts. For an hour they endured the tortures of hell and then, when the storm had passed, raised their heads and cursed Creation. Their bodies burned as though they had been shot with fine needles and their clothes were meshes where once was tough cloth. Even their shoes were perforated and the throat of each ached with thirst.

Hopalong fumbled at the canteen resting on his hip and gargled his mouth and throat, washing down the sand which wouldn't come up. His friends did likewise and then looked around. After some time had elapsed the loss of their pack horse was noticed and they swore again. Hopalong took the lead in getting his horse ready for service and then rode around in a circle half a mile in diameter, but returned empty handed. The horse was gone and with it went their main supply of food and drink.

Frenchy scowled at the shadow of a cactus and slowly rode toward the northeast, followed closely by his friends. His hand reached for his depleted canteen, but refrained-water was to be saved until the last minute.

"I'm goin' to build a shack out here an' live in it, I am!" exploded Hopalong in withering irony as he dug the sand out of his ears and also from his sixshooter. "I just nachurally dotes on this, I do!"

The others were too miserable to even grunt and he neatly severed the head of a Gila monster from its scaly body as it opened it venomous jaws in rage at this invasion of its territory. "Lovely place!" he sneered.

"You better save them cartridges, Hoppy," interposed Red as his companion fired again, feeling that he must say something.

"An' what for?" blazed his friend. "To plug sand storms? Anybody what we find on this God-forsaken lay-out won't have to be shot-they will commit suicide an' think it's fun! Tell yu what, if them rustlers hangs out on this sand range they're better men than I reckons they are. Anybody what hides up here shore earns all he steals." Hopalong grumbled from force of habit and because no one else would. His companions understood this and paid no attention to him, which increased his disgust.

"What are we up here for?" He asked, belligerently. "Why, because them Double Arrow idiots can't even watch a desert! We have to do their work for them an' they hangs around home an' gets slaughtered! Yes, sir!" he shouted, "they can't even take care of themselves when they're in line-houses what are forts. Why, that time we cleaned out them an' th' C-80 over at Buckskin they couldn't help runnin' into singin' lead!"

"Yes," drawled Red, whose recollection of that fight was vivid. "Yas, an' why?" He asked, and then replied to his own question. "Because yu sat up in a barn behind them, Buck played his gun on th' side window, Pete an' Skinny lay behind a rock to one side of Buck, me an' Lanky was across th' Street in front of them, an' Billy an' Johnny was in th' arroyo on th' other side. Cowan laid on his stummick on th' roof of his place with a buffalo gun, an' the whole blamed town was agin them. There wasn't five seconds passed that lead wasn't rippin' through th' walls of their shack. Th' Houston House wasn't made for no fort, an' besides, they wasn't like th' gang that's punchin' now. That's why."

Hopalong became cheerful again, for here was a chance to differ from his friend. The two loved each other the better the more they squabbled.

"Yas!" responded Hopalong with sarcasm. "Yas!" he reiterated, drawling it out. "Yu was in front of them, an' with what? Why, an' old, white-haired, interfering Winchester, that's what! Me an' my Sharp's —"

"Yu and yore Sharp's!" exploded Red, whose dislike for that rifle was very pronounced. "Yu and yore Sharp's."

"Me an' my Sharp's, as I was palaverin' before bein' interrupted," continued Hopalong, "did more damage in five min —"

"Says yu!" snapped Red with heat. "All yu an yore Sharp's could do was to cut yore initials in th' back door of their shack, an' — —"

"Did more damage in five minutes," continued Hopalong, "than all th' blasted Winchesters in th' whole damned town. Why —"

"An' then they was cut blamed poor. Every time that cannon of yourn exploded I shore thought th' —"

"Why, Cowan an' his buffalo did more damage (Cowan was reputed to be a very poor shot) than yu an —"

"I thought th' artillery was comin' into th' disturbance. I could see yore red head —"

"MY red head!" exclaimed Hopalong, sizing up the crimson warlock of his companion. "MY red head!" he repeated, and then turned to Frenchy: "Hey, Frenchy, who's got th' reddest hair, me or Red?"

Frenchy slowly turned in his saddle and gravely scrutinized them. Being strictly impartial and truthful, he gave up the effort of differentiating and smiled. "Why, if the tops of yore heads were poked through two holes in a board an' I didn't know which was which, I'd shore make a mistake if I tried to name 'em"

But Red had the last word. "Anyhow, you didn't have a Sharp's in that fight-you had a .45-70 Winchester, just like mine!"

Thereupon the discussion was directed at the judge, and the forenoon passed very pleasantly, Frenchy even smiling in his misery.

Chapter XIX
Hopalong's Decision

Shortly after noon, Hopalong, who had ridden with his head bowed low in meditation, looked up and slapped his thigh. Then he looked at Red and grinned.

"Look ahere, Red," he began, "there ain't no rustlers with their headquarters on this God-forsaken sand heap, an' there never was. They have to have water an' lots of it, too, an' th' nearest of any account is th' Pecos, or some of them streams over in th' Panhandle. Th' Panhandle is th' best place. There are lots of streams an' lakes over there an' they're right in a good grass country. Why, an' army could hide over there an' never be found unless it was hunted for blamed good. Then, again, it's close to the railroad. Up north aways is th' south branch of th' Santa Fe Trail an' it's far enough away not to bother anybody in th' middle Panhandle. Then there's Fort Worth purty near, an' other trails. Didn't Buck say he had all th' rest of th' country searched? He meant th' Pecos Valley an th' Davis Mountains country. All th' rustlers would have to do if they were in th' Panhandle would be to cross th' Canadian an th' Cimarron an' hit th' trail for th' railroad. Good fords, good grass an' water all th' way, cattle fat when they are delivered an plenty of room. Th' more I thinks about it th' more I cottons to the Panhandle."

"Well, it shore does sound good," replied Red, reflectively.

"Do yu mean th' Cunningham Lake region or farther north?"

"Just th' other side of this blasted desert: anywhere where there's water," responded Hopalong, enthusiastically. "I've been doin' some hot reckonin' for th' last two hours an' this is th' way it looks to me: they drives th' cows up on this skillet for a ways, then turns east an' hits th' trail for home an' water. They can get around th' ca on near Thatcher's Lake by a swing of th' north. I tell yu that's th' only way out'n this. Who could tell where they turned with th' wind raisin' th' deuce with the trail? Didn't we follow a trail for a ways, an' then what? Why, there wasn't none to follow. We can ride north 'till we walk behind ourselves an' never get a peek at them. I am in favor of headin' for th' Sulphur Spring Creek district. We can spend a couple of weeks, if we has to, an' prospect that whole region without havin' to cut our' water down to a smell an' a taste an live on jerked beef. If we investigates that country we'll find something else than sand storms, poisoned water holes an' blisters."

"Ain't th' Panhandle full of nesters (farmers)?" Inquired Red, doubtfully.

"Along th' Canadian an' th' edges, yas; in th' middle, no," explained Hopalong. "They hang close together on account of th' war-whoops, an' they like th' trails purty well because of there allus bein' somebody passin'."

"Buck ought to send some of th' Panhandle boys up there," suggested Red. "There's Pie Willis an' th' Jordans-they knows th' Panhandle like yu knows poker."

Frenchy had paid no apparent attention to the conversation up to this point, but now he declared himself. "Yu heard what Buck said, didn't yu?" He asked. "We were told to search th' Staked Plains from one end to th' other an' I'm goin' to do it if I can hold out long enough. I ain't goin' to palaver with yu because what yu say can't be denied as far as wisdom is concerned. Yu may have hit it plumb center, but I knows what I was ordered to do, an' yu can't get me to go over there if you shouts all night. When Buck says anything, she goes. He wants to know where th' cards are stacked an' why he can't holler 'Keno,' an' I'm goin' to find out if I can. Yu can go to Patagonia if yu wants to, but yu go alone as far as I am concerned."

"Well, it's better if yu don't go with us," replied Hopalong, taking it for granted that Red would accompany him. "Yu can prospect this end of th' game an' we'll be takin' care of th' other. It's two chances now where we only had one afore."

"Yu go east an' I'll hunt around as ordered," responded Frenchy.

"East nothin'," replied Hopalong. "Yu don't get me to wallow in hot alkali an' lose time ridin' in ankle-deep sand when I can hit th' south trail, skirt th' White Sand Hills an' be in God's country again. I ain't goin' to wrastle with no ca on this here trip, none whatever. I'm goin' to travel in style, get to Big Spring by ridin' two miles to where I could only make one on this stove. Then I'll head north along Sulpher Spring Creek an' have water an' grass all th' way, barrin' a few stretches. While you are bein' fricasseed I'll be streakin' through cottonwood groves an' ridin' in the creek."

"Yu'll have to go alone, then," said Red, resolutely. "Frenchy ain't a-goin' to die of lonesomeness on this desert if I knows what I'm about, an' I reckon I do, some. Me an' him'll follow out what Buck said, hunt around for a while an' then Frenchy can go back to th' ranch to tell Buck what's up an' I'll take th' trail yu are a-scared of an' meet yu at th' east end of Cunningham Lake three days from now."

"Yu better come with me," coaxed Hopalong, not liking what his friend had said about being afraid of the trail past the ca on and wishing to have some one with whom to talk on his trip. "I'm goin' to have a nice long swim to-morrow night," he added, trying bribery.

"An' I'm goin' to try to keep from hittin' my blisters," responded Red. "I don't want to go swimmin' in no creek full of moccasins —I'd rather sleep with rattlers or copperheads. Every time I sees a cotton-mouth I feels like I had just sit down on one.

"I'll flip a coin to see whether yu comes or not," proposed Hopalong.

"If yu wants to gamble so bad I'll flip yu to see who draws our pay next month, but not for what you said," responded Red, choking down the desire to try his luck.

Hopalong grinned and turned toward the south. "If I sees Buck afore yu do, I'll tell him yu an' Frenchy are growin' watermelons up near Last Stand Rock an' are waitin' for rain. Well, so long," he said.

"Yu tell Buck we're obeyin' orders!" shouted Red, sorry that he was not going with his bunkie.

Frenchy and Red rode on in silence, the latter feeling strangely lonesome, for he and the departed man had seldom been separated when journeys like this were to be taken. And when in search of pleasure they were nearly always together. Frenchy, while being very friendly with Hopalong, a friendship that would have placed them side by side against any odds, was not accustomed to his company and did not notice his absence.

Red looked off toward the south for the tenth time and for the tenth time thought that his friend might return. "He's a son-of-a-gun," he soliloquized.

His companion looked up: "He shore is, an' he's right about this rustler business, too. But we'll look around for a day or so an' then yu raise dust for th' Lake. I'll go back to th' ranch an' get things primed, so there'll be no time lost when we get th' word."

"I'm sorry I went an' said what I did about me takin' th' trail he was a-scared of," confessed Red, after a pause. "Why, he ain't a-scared of nothin'."

"He got back at yu about them watermelons, so what's th' difference?" Asked Frenchy. "He don't owe yu nothin'."

An hour later they searched the Devil's Rocks, but found no rustlers. Filling their canteens at a tiny spring and allowing their mounts to drink the remainder of the water, they turned toward Hell Arroyo, which they reached at nightfall. Here, also, their search availed them nothing and they paused in indecision. Then Frenchy turned toward his companion and advised him to ride toward the Lake in the night when it was comparatively cool.

Red considered and then decided that the advice was good. He rolled a cigarette, wheeled and faced the east and spurred forward: "So long," he called.

"So long," replied Frenchy, who turned toward the south and departed for the ranch.

The foreman of the Bar-20 was cleaning his rifle when he heard the hoof-beats of a galloping horse and he ran around the corner of the house to meet the newcomer, whom he thought to be a courier from the Double Arrow. Frenchy dismounted and explained why he returned alone.

Buck listened to the report and then, noting the fire which gleamed in his friend's eyes, nodded his approval to the course. "I reckon it's Trendley, Frenchy —I've heard a few things since yu left. An' yu can bet that if Hopalong an' Red have gone for him he'll be found. I expect action any time now, so we'll light th' signal fire." Then he hesitated; "Yu light it-yu've been waiting a long time for this."

The balls of smoke which rolled upward were replied to by other balls at different points on the plain, and the Bar-20 prepared to feed the numbers of hungry punchers who would arrive within the next twenty-four hours.

Two hours had not passed when eleven men rode up from the Three Triangle, followed eight hours later by ten from the O-Bar-O. The outfits of the Star Circle and the Barred Horseshoe, eighteen in all, came next and had scarcely dismounted when those of the C-80 and the Double Arrow, fretting at the delay, rode up. With the sixteen from the Bar-20 the force numbered seventy-five resolute and pugnacious cowpunchers, all aching to wipe out the indignities suffered.

Chapter XX
A Problem Solved

Hopalong worried his way out of the desert on a straight line, thus cutting in half the distance he had traveled when going into it. He camped that night on the sand and early the next morning took up his journey. It was noon when he began to notice familiar sights, and an hour later he passed within a mile of line-house No. 3, Double Arrow. Half an hour later he espied a cow-puncher riding like mad. Thinking that an investigation would not be out of place, he rode after the rider and overtook him, when that person paused and retraced his course.

"Hullo, Hopalong!" shouted the puncher and he came near enough to recognize his pursuer. "Thought yu was farmin' up on th' Staked Plain?"

"Hullo, Pie," replied Hopalong, recognizing Pie Willis. "What was yu chasin' so hard?"

"Coyote-damn 'em, but can't they go some? They're gettin' so thick we'll shore have to try strichnine an' thin 'em out."

"I thought anybody that had been raised in th' Panhandle would know better'n to chase greased lightnin'," rebuked Hopalong. "Yu has got about as much show catchin' one of them as a tenderfoot has of bustin' an outlawed cayuse."

"Shore; I know it," responded Pie, grinning. "But it's fun seem' them hunt th' horizon. What are yu doin' down here an' where are yore pardners?"

Thereupon Hopalong enlightened his inquisitive companion as to what had occurred and as to his reasons for riding south.

Pie immediately became enthusiastic and announced his intention of accompanying Hopalong on his quest, which intention struck that gentleman as highly proper and wise. Then Pie hastily turned and played at chasing coyotes in the direction of the line-house, where he announced that his absence would be accounted for by the fact that he and Hopalong were going on a journey of investigation into the Panhandle. Billy Jordan who shared with Pie the accommodations of the house, objected and showed, very clearly, why he was eminently better qualified to take up the proposed labors than his companions. The suggestions were fast getting tangled up with the remarks, when Pie, grabbing a chunk of jerked beef, leaped into his saddle and absolutely refused to heed the calls of his former companion and return. He rode to where Hopalong was awaiting him as if he was afraid he wasn't going to live long enough to get there. Confiding to his companion that Billy was a "locoed sage hen," he led the way along the base of the White Sand Hills and asked many questions. Then they turned toward the east and galloped hard.

It had been Hopalong's intention to carry out what he had told Red and to go to Big Spring first and thence north along Sulphur Spring Creek, but to this his guide strongly dissented. There was a short cut, or several of them for that matter, was Pie's contention, and any one of them would save a day's hard riding. Hopalong made no objection to allowing his companion to lead the way over any trail he saw fit, for he knew that Pie had been born and brought up in the Panhandle, the Cunningham Lake district having been his back yard, as it were. So they followed the short cut having the most water and grass, and pounded out a lively tattoo as they raced over the stretches of sand which seemed to slide beneath them.

"What do yu know about this here business?" Inquired Pie, as they raced past a chaparral and onto the edge of a grassy plain.

"Nothin' more'n yu do, only Buck said he thought Slippery Trendley is at th' bottom of it."

"What!" ejaculated Pie in surprise. "Him!"

"Yore on. An' between yu an' me an' th' Devil, I wouldn't be a heap surprised if Deacon Rankin is with him, neither."

Pie whistled: "Are him an' th' Deacon pals?"

"Shore," replied Hopalong, buttoning up his vest and rolling a cigarette. "Didn't they allus hang out together! One watched that th' other didn't get plugged from behind. It was a sort of yu-scratch-my-back-an'-I'll-scratch-yourn arrangement."

"Well, if they still hangs out together, I know where to hunt for our cows," responded Pie. "Th' Deacon used to range along th' headwaters of th' Colorado-it ain't far from Cunningham Lake. Thunderation!" he shouted, "I knows th' very ground they're on —I can take yu to th' very shack!" Then to himself he muttered: "An' that doodlebug Billy Jordan thinkin' he knowed more about th' Panhandle than me!"

Hopalong showed his elation in an appropriate manner and his companion drank deeply from the proffered flask; Thereupon they treated their mounts to liberal doses of strap-oil and covered the ground with great speed.

They camped early, for Hopalong was almost worn out from the exertions of the past few days and the loss of sleep he had sustained. Pie, too excited to sleep and having had unbroken rest for a long period, volunteered to keep guard, and his companion eagerly consented.

Early the next morning they broke camp and the evening of the same day found them fording Sulphur Spring Creek, and their quarry lay only an hour beyond, according to Pie. Then they forded one of the streams which form the headwaters of the Colorado, and two hours later they dismounted in a cottonwood grove. Picketing their horses, they carefully made their way through the timber, which was heavily grown with brush, and, after half an hour's maneuvering, came within sight of the further edge.

Dropping down on all fours, they crawled to the last line of brush and looked out over an extensive bottoms. At their feet lay a small river, and in a clearing on the farther side was a rough camp, consisting of about a dozen leanto shacks and log cabins in the main collection, and a few scattered cabins along the edge. A huge fire was blazing before the main collection of huts, and to the rear of these was an indistinct black mass, which they knew to be the corral.

At a rude table before the fire more than a score of men were eating supper and others could be heard moving about and talking at different points in the background. While the two scouts were learning the lay of the land, they saw Mr. Trendley and Deacon Rankin walk out of the cabin most distant from the fire, and the latter limped. Then they saw two men lying on rude cots, and they wore bandages. Evidently Johnny Redmond had scored in his fight.

The odor of burning cowhide came from the corral, accompanied by the squeals of cattle, and informed them that brands were being blotted out. Hopalong longed to charge down and do some blotting out of another kind, but a heavy hand was placed on his shoulder and he silently wormed his way after Pie as that person led the way back to the horses. Mounting, they picked their way out of the grove and rode over the plain at a walk. When far enough away to insure that the noise made by their horses would not reach the ears of those in the camp they cantered toward the ford they had taken on the way up.

After emerging from the waters of the last forded stream, Pie raised his hand and pointed off toward the northwest, telling his companion to take that course to reach Cunningham Lake. He himself would ride south, taking, for the saving of time, a yet shorter trail to the Double Arrow, from where he would ride to Buck. He and the others would meet Hopalong and Red at the split rock they had noticed on their way up.

Hopalong shook hands with his guide and watched him disappear into the night. He imagined he could still catch whiffs of burning cowhide and again the picture of the camp came to his mind. Glancing again at the point where Pie had disappeared, he stuffed his sombrero under a strap on his saddle and slowly rode toward the lake. A coyote slunk past him on a time-destroying lope and an owl hooted at the foolishness of men. He camped at the base of a cottonwood and at daylight took up his journey after a scanty breakfast from his saddle-bags.

Shortly before noon he came in sight of the lake and looked for his friend. He had just ridden around a clump of cotton-woods when he was hit on the back with something large and soft. Turning in his saddle, with his Colts ready, he saw Red sitting on a stump, a huge grin extending over his features. He replaced the weapon, said something about fools and dismounted, kicking aside the bundle of grass his friend had thrown.

"Yore shore easy," remarked Red, tossing aside his cold cigarette. "Suppose I was Trendley, where would yu be now?"

"Diggin' a hole to put yu in," pleasantly replied Hopalong. "If I didn't know he wasn't around this part of the country I wouldn't a rode as I did."

The man on the stump laughed and rolled a fresh cigarette. Lighting it, he inquired where Mr. Trendley was, intimating by his words that the rustler had not been found.

"About thirty miles to th' southeast," responded the other. "He's figurin' up how much dust he'll have when he gets our cows on th' market. Deacon Rankin is with him, too."

"Th' deuce!" exclaimed Red, in profound astonishment.

"Yore right," replied his companion. Then he explained all the arrangements and told of the camp.

Red was for riding to the rendezvous at once, but his friend thought otherwise and proposed a swim, which met with approval. After enjoying themselves in the lake they dressed and rode along the trail Hopalong had made in coming for his companion, it being the intention of the former to learn more thoroughly the lay of the land immediately surrounding the camp. Red was pleased with this, and while they rode he narrated all that had taken place since the separation on the Plain, adding that he had found the trail left by the rustlers after they had quitted the desert and that he had followed it for the last two hours of his journey. It was well beaten and an eighth of a mile wide.

At dark they came within sight of the grove and picketed their horses at the place used by Pie and Hopalong. Then they moved forward and the same sight greeted their eyes that had been seen the night before. Keeping well within the edge of the grove and looking carefully for sentries, they went entirely around the camp and picked out several places which would be of strategic value later on. They noticed that the cabin used by Slippery Trendley was a hundred paces from the main collection of huts and that the woods came to within a tenth part of that distance of its door. It was heavily built, had no windows and faced the wrong direction.

Moving on, they discovered the storehouse of the enemy, another tempting place. It was just possible, if a siege became necessary, for several of the attacking force to slip up to it and either destroy it by fire or take it and hold it against all comers. This suggested a look at the enemy's water supply, which was the river. A hundred paces separated it from the nearest cabin and any rustler who could cross that zone under the fire of the besiegers would be welcome to his drink.

It was very evident that the rustlers had no thought of defense, thinking, perhaps, that they were immune from attack with such a well covered trail between them and their foes. Hopalong mentally accused them of harboring suicidal inclinations and returned with his companion to the horses. They mounted and sat quietly for a while, and then rode slowly away and at dawn reached the split rock, where they awaited the arrival of their friends, one sleeping while the other kept guard. Then they drew a rough map of the camp, using the sand for paper, and laid out the plan of attack.

As the evening of the next day came on they saw Pie, followed by many punchers, ride over a rise a mile to the south and they rode out to meet him.

When the force arrived at the camp of the two scouts they were shown the plan prepared for them. Buck made a few changes in the disposition of the men and then each member was shown where he was to go and was told why. Weapons were put in a high state of efficiency, canteens were refilled and haversacks were somewhat depleted. Then the newcomers turned in and slept while Hopalong and Red kept guard.

Chapter XXI
The Call

At three o'clock the next morning a long line of men slowly filed into the cottonwood grove, being silently swallowed up by the dark. Dismounting, they left their horses in the care of three of their number and disappeared into the brush. Ten minutes later forty of the force were distributed along the edge of the grove fringing on the bank of the river and twenty more minutes gave ample time for a detachment of twenty to cross the stream and find concealment in the edge of the woods which ran from the river to where the corral made an effective barrier on the south.

Eight crept down on the western side of the camp and worked their way close to Mr. Trendley's cabin door, and the seven who followed this detachment continued and took up their positions at the rear of the corral, where, it was hoped, some of the rustlers would endeavor to escape into the woods by working their way through the cattle in the corral and then scaling the stockade wall. These seven were from the Three Triangle and the Double Arrow, and they were positive that any such attempt would not be a success from the view-point of the rustlers.

Two of those who awaited the pleasure of Mr. Trendley crept forward, and a rope swished through the air and settled over the stump which lay most convenient on the other side of the cabin door. Then the slack moved toward the woods, raised from the ground as it grew taut and, with the stump for its axis, swung toward the door, where it rubbed gently against the rough logs. It was made of braided horsehair, was half an inch in diameter and was stretched eight inches above the ground.

As it touched the door, Lanky Smith, Hopalong and Red stepped out of the shelter of the woods and took up their positions behind the cabin, Lanky behind the northeast corner where he would be permitted to swing his right arm. In his gloved right hand he held the carefully arranged coils of a fifty-foot lariat, and should the chief of the rustlers escape tripping he would have to avoid the cast of the best roper in the southwest.

The two others took the northwest corner and one of them leaned slightly forward and gently twitched the tripping-rope. The man at the other end felt the signal and whispered to a companion, who quietly disappeared in the direction of the river and shortly afterward the mournful cry of a whip-poor-will dirged out on the early morning air. It had hardly died away when the quiet was broken by one terrific crash of rifles, and the two camp guards asleep at the fire awoke in another world.

Mr. Trendley, sleeping unusually well for the unjust, leaped from his bed to the middle of the floor and alighted on his feet and wide awake. Fearing that a plot was being consummated to deprive him of his leadership, he grasped the Winchester which leaned at the head of his bed and, tearing open the door, crashed headlong to the earth. As he touched the ground, two shadows sped out from the shelter of the cabin wall and pounced upon him. Men who can rope, throw and tie a wild steer in thirty seconds flat do not waste time in trussing operations, and before a minute had elapsed he was being carried into the woods, bound and helpless. Lanky sighed, threw the rope over one shoulder and departed after his friends.

When Mr. Trendley came to his senses he found himself bound to a tree in the grove near the horses. A man sat on a stump not far from him, three others were seated around a small fire some distance to the north, and four others, one of whom carried a rope, made their way into the brush. He strained at his bonds, decided that the effort was useless and watched the man on the stump, who struck a match and lit a pipe. The prisoner watched the light flicker up and go out and there was left in his mind a picture that he could never forget. The face which had been so cruelly, so grotesquely revealed was that of Frenchy McAllister, and across his knees lay a heavy caliber Winchester. A curse escaped from the lips of the outlaw; the man on the stump spat at a firefly and smiled.

From the south came the crack of rifles, incessant and sharp. The reports rolled from one end of the clearing to the other and seemed to sweep in waves from the center of the line to the ends. Faintly in the infrequent lulls in the firing came an occasional report from the rear of the corral, where some desperate rustler paid for his venture.

Buck went along the line and spoke to the riflemen, and after some time had passed and the light had become stronger, he collected the men into groups of five and six. Taking one group and watching it closely, it could be seen that there was a world of meaning in this maneuver. One man started firing at a particular window in an opposite hut and then laid aside his empty gun and waited. When the muzzle of his enemy's gun came into sight and lowered until it had nearly gained its sight level, the rifles of the remainder of the group crashed out in a volley and usually one of the bullets, at least, found its intended billet. This volley firing became universal among the besiegers and the effect was marked.

Two men sprinted from the edge of the woods near Mr. Trendley's cabin and gained the shelter of the storehouse, which soon broke out in flames. The burning brands fell over the main collection of huts, where there was much confusion and swearing. The early hour at which the attack had been delivered at first led the besieged to believe that it was an Indian affair, but this impression was soon corrected by the volley firing, which turned hope into despair. It was no great matter to fight Indians, that they had done many times and found more or less enjoyment in it; but there was a vast difference between brave and puncher, and the chances of their salvation became very small. They surmised that it was the work of the cow-men on whom they had preyed and that vengeful punchers lay hidden behind that death-fringe of green willow and hazel.

Red, assisted by his inseparable companion, Hopalong, laboriously climbed up among the branches of a black walnut and hooked one leg over a convenient limb. Then he lowered his rope and drew up the Winchester which his accommodating friend fastened to it. Settling himself in a comfortable position and sheltering his body somewhat by the tree, he shaded his eyes by a hand and peered into the windows of the distant cabins.

"How is she, Red?" Anxiously inquired the man on the ground.

"Bully: want to come up?"

"Nope. I'm goin' to catch yu when yu lets go," replied Hopalong with a grin.

"Which same I ain't goin' to," responded the man in the tree.

He swung his rifle out over a forked limb and let it settle in the crotch. Then he slew his head around until he gained the bead he wished. Five minutes passed before he caught sight of his man and then he fired. Jerking out the empty shell he smiled and called out to his friend: "One."

Hopalong grinned and went off to tell Buck to put all the men in trees.

Night came on and still the firing continued. Then an explosion shook the woods. The storehouse had blown up and a sky full of burning timber fell on the cabins and soon three were half consumed, their occupants dropping as they gained the open air. One hundred paces makes fine pot-shooting, as Deacon Rankin discovered when evacuation was the choice necessary to avoid cremation. He never moved after he touched the ground and Red called out: "Two," not knowing that his companion had departed.

The morning of the next day found a wearied and hopeless garrison, and shortly before noon a soiled white shirt was flung from a window in the nearest cabin. Buck ran along the line and ordered the firing to cease and caused to be raised an answering flag of truce. A full minute passed and then the door slowly opened and a leg protruded, more slowly followed by the rest of the man, and Cheyenne Charley strode out to the bank of the river and sat down. His example was followed by several others and then an unexpected event occurred. Those in the cabins who preferred to die fighting, angered at this desertion, opened fire on their former comrades, who barely escaped by rolling down the slightly inclined bank into the river. Red fired again and laughed to himself. Then the fugitives swam down the river and landed under the guns of the last squad. They were taken to the rear and, after being bound, were placed under a guard. There were seven in the party and they looked worn out.

When the huts were burning the fiercest the uproar in the corral arose to such a pitch as to drown all other sounds. There were left within its walls a few hundred cattle whose brands had not yet been blotted out, and these, maddened to frenzy by the shooting and the flames, tore from one end of the enclosure to the other, crashing against the alternate walls with a noise which could be heard far out on the plain. Scores were trampled to death on each charge and finally the uproar subsided in sheer want of cattle left with energy enough to continue. When the corral was investigated the next day there were found the bodies of four rustlers, but recognition was impossible.

Several of the defenders were housed in cabins having windows in the rear walls, which the occupants considered fortunate. This opinion was revised, however, after several had endeavored to escape by these openings. The first thing that occurred when a man put his head out was the hum of a bullet, and in two cases the experimenters lost all need of escape.

The volley firing had the desired effect, and at dusk there remained only one cabin from which came opposition. Such a fire was concentrated on it that before an hour had passed the door fell in and the firing ceased. There was a rush from the side, and the Barred Horseshoe men who swarmed through the cabins emerged without firing a shot. The organization that had stirred up the Pecos Valley ranches had ceased to exist.

Chapter XXII
The Showdown

A fire burned briskly in front of Mr. Trendley's cabin that night and several punchers sat around it occupied in various ways. Two men leaned against the wall and sang softly of the joys of the trail and the range. One of them, Lefty Allen, of the O-Bar-O, sang in his sweet tenor, and other men gradually strolled up and seated themselves on the ground, where the fitful gleam of responsive pipes and cigarettes showed like fireflies. The songs followed one after another, first a lover's plea in soft Spanish and then a rollicking tale of the cow-towns and men. Supper had long since been enjoyed and all felt that life was, indeed, well worth living.

A shadow loomed against the cabin wall and a procession slowly made its way toward the open door. The leader, Hopalong, disappeared within and was followed by Mr. Trendley, bound and hobbled and tied to Red, the rear being brought up by Frenchy, whose rifle lolled easily in the crotch of his elbow. The singing went on uninterrupted and the hum of voices between the selections remained unchanged. Buck left the crowd around the fire and went into the cabin, where his voice was heard assenting to something. Hopalong emerged and took a seat at the fire, sending two punchers to take his place. He was joined by Frenchy and Red, the former very quiet.

In the center of a distant group were seven men who were not armed. Their belts, half full of cartridges, supported empty holsters. They sat and talked to the men around them, swapping notes and experiences, and in several instances found former friends and acquaintances. These men were not bound and were apparently members of Buck's force. Then one of them broke down, but quickly regained his nerve and proposed a game of cards. A fire was started and several games were immediately in progress. These seven men were to die at daybreak.

As the night grew older man after man rolled himself in his blanket and lay down where he sat, sinking off to sleep with a swiftness that bespoke tired muscles and weariness. All through the night, however, there were twelve men on guard, of whom three were in the cabin.

At daybreak a shot from one of the guards awakened every man within hearing, and soon they romped and scampered down to the river's edge to indulge in the luxury of a morning plunge. After an hour's horseplay they trooped back to the cabin and soon had breakfast out of the way.

Waffles, foreman of the O-Bar-O, and You-bet Somes strolled over to the seven unfortunates who had just completed a choking breakfast and nodded a hearty "Good morning." Then others came up and finally all moved off toward the river. Crossing it, they disappeared into the grove and all sounds of their advance grew into silence.

Mr. Trendley, escorted outside for the air, saw the procession as it became lost to sight in the brush. He sneered and asked for a smoke, which was granted. Then his guards were changed and the men began to straggle back from the grove.

Mr. Trendley, with his back to the cabin, scowled defiantly at the crowd that hemmed him in. The coolest, most damnable murderer in the West was not now going to beg for mercy. When he had taken up crime as a means of livelihood he had decided that if the price to be paid for his course was death, he would pay like a man. He glanced at the cottonwood grove, wherein were many ghastly secrets, and smiled. His hairless eyebrows looked like livid scars and his lips quivered in scorn and anger.

As he sneered at Buck there was a movement in the crowd before him and a pathway opened for Frenchy, who stepped forward slowly and deliberately, as if on his way to some bar for a drink. There was something different about the man who had searched the Staked Plain with Hopalong and Red: he was not the same puncher who had arrived from Montana three weeks before. There was lacking a certain air of carelessness and he chilled his friends, who looked upon him as if they had never really known him. He walked up to Mr. Trendley and gazed deeply into the evil eyes.

Twenty years before, Frenchy McAllister had changed his identity from a happy-go-lucky, devil-may-care cow-puncher and became a machine. The grief that had torn his soul was not of the kind which seeks its outlet in tears and wailing; it had turned and struck inward, and now his deliberate ferocity was icy and devilish. Only a glint in his eyes told of exultation, and his words were sharp and incisive; one could well imagine one heard the click of his teeth as they bit off the consonants: every letter was clear-cut, every syllable startling in its clearness.

"Twenty years and two months ago to-day," he began, "you arrived at the ranchhouse of the Double Y, up near the Montana-Wyoming line. Everything was quiet, except, perhaps, a woman's voice, singing. You entered, and before you left you pinned a note to that woman's dress. I found it, and it is due."

The air of carelessness disappeared from the members of the crowd and the silence became oppressive. Most of those present knew parts of Frenchy's story, and all were in hearty accord with anything he might do. He reached within his vest and brought forth a deerskin bag. Opening it, he drew out a package of oiled silk and from that he took a paper. Carefully replacing the silk and the bag, he slowly unfolded the sheet in his hand and handed it to Buck, whose face hardened. Two decades had passed since the foreman of the Bar-20 had seen that precious sheet, but the scene of its finding would never fade from his memory. He stood as if carved from stone, with a look on his face that made the crowd shift uneasily and glance at Trendley.

Frenchy turned to the rustler and regarded him evilly. "You are the hellish brute that wrote that note," pointing to the paper in the hand of his friend. Then, turning again, he spoke: "Buck, read that paper."

The foreman cleared his throat and read distinctly:

"McAllister: Yore wife is too blame good to live.

TRENDLEY."

There was a shuffling sound, but Buck and Frenchy, silently backed up by Hopalong and Red, intervened, and the crowd fell back, where it surged in indecision.

"Gentlemen," said Frenchy, "I want you to vote on whether any man here has more right to do with Slippery Trendley as he sees fit than myself. Any one who thinks so, or that he should be treated like the others, step forward. Majority rules."

There was no advance and he spoke again: "Is there any one here who objects to this man dying?"

Hopalong and Red awkwardly bumped their knuckles against their guns and there was no response.

The prisoner was bound with cowhide to the wall of the cabin and four men sat near and facing him. The noonday meal was eaten in silence, and the punchers rode off to see about rounding up the cattle that grazed over the plain as far as eye could see. Supper-time came and passed, and busy men rode away in all directions. Others came and relieved the guards, and at midnight another squad took up the vigil.

Day broke and the thunder of hoofs as the punchers rounded up the cattle became very noticeable. One herd swept past toward the south, guarded and guided by fifteen men. Two hours later and another followed, taking a slightly different trail so as to avoid the close-cropped grass left by the first. At irregular intervals during the day other herds swept by, until six had passed and denuded the plain of cattle.

Buck, perspiring and dusty, accompanied by Hopalong and Red, rode up to where the guards smoked and joked. Frenchy came out of the cabin and smiled at his friends. Swinging in his left hand was a newly filled Colt's .45, which was recognized by his friends as the one found in the cabin and it bore a rough "T" gouged in the butt.

Buck looked around and cleared his throat: "We've got th' cows on th' home trail, Frenchy," he suggested.

"Yas?" Inquired Frenchy. "Are there many?"

"Yas," replied Buck, waving his hand at the guards, ordering them to follow their friends. "It's a good deal for us: we've done right smart this hand. An' it's a good thing we've got so many punchers: we got a lot of cattle to drive."

"About five times th' size of th' herd that blamed near made angels out'en me an' yu," responded Frenchy with a smile.

"I hope almighty hard that we don't have no stampedes on this here drive. If th' last herds go wild they'll pick up th' others, an' then there'll be th' devil to pay."

Frenchy smiled again and shot a glance at where Mr. Trendley was bound to the cabin wall.

Buck looked steadily southward for some time and then flecked a foam-sud from the flank of his horse. "We are goin' south along th' Creek until we gets to Big Spring, where we'll turn right smart to th' west. We won't be able to average more'n twelve miles a day, 'though I'm goin' to drive them hard. How's yore grub?"

"Grub to burn."

"Got yore rope?" Asked the foreman of the Bar-20, speaking as if the question had no especial meaning.

Frenchy smiled: "Yes."

Hopalong absent-mindedly jabbed his spurs into his mount with the result that when the storm had subsided the spell was broken and he said "So long," and rode south, followed by Buck and Red. As they swept out of sight behind a grove Red turned in his saddle and waved his hat. Buck discussed with assiduity the prospects of a rainfall and was very cheerful about the recovery of the stolen cattle. Red could see a tall, broad-shouldered man standing with his feet spread far apart, swinging a Colt's .45, and Hopalong swore at everything under the sun. Dust arose in streaming clouds far to the south and they spurred forward to overtake the outfits.

Buck Peters, riding over the starlit plain, in his desire to reach the first herd, which slept somewhere to the west of him under the care of Waffles, thought of the events of the past few weeks and gradually became lost in the memories of twenty years before, which crowded up before his mind like the notes of a half-forgotten song. His nature, tempered by two decades of a harsh existence, softened as he lived again the years that had passed and as he thought of the things which had been. He was so completely lost in his reverie that he failed to hear the muffled hoofbeats of a horse that steadily gained upon him, and when Frenchy McAllister placed a friendly hand on his shoulder he started as if from a deep sleep.

The two looked at each other and their hands met. The question which sprang into Buck's eyes found a silent answer in those of his friend. They rode on side by side through the clear night and together drifted back to the days of the Double Y.

After an hour had passed, the foreman of the Bar-20 turned to his companion and then hesitated:

"Did, did-was he a cur?"

Frenchy looked off toward the south and, after an interval, replied: "Yas." Then, as an after thought, he added, "Yu see, he never reckoned it would be that way."

Buck nodded, although he did not fully understand, and the subject was forever closed.

Chapter XXIII
Mr. Cassidy Meets a Woman

The work of separating the cattle into herds of the different brands was not a big contract, and with so many men it took but a comparatively short time, and in two days all signs of the rustlers had faded. It was then that good news went the rounds and the men looked forward to a week of pleasure, which was all the sharper accentuated by the grim mercilessness of the expedition into the Panhandle. Here was a chance for unlimited hilarity and a whole week in which to give strict attention to celebrating the recent victory.

So one day Mr. Hopalong Cassidy rode rapidly over the plain, thinking about the joys and excitement promised by the carnival to be held at Muddy Wells. With that rivalry so common to Western towns the inhabitants maintained that the carnival was to break all records, this because it was to be held in their town. Perry's Bend and Buckskin had each promoted a similar affair, and if this year's festivities were to be an improvement on those which had gone before, they would most certainly be worth riding miles to see. Perry's Bend had been unfortunate m being the first to hold a carnival, inasmuch as it only set a mark to be improved upon, and Buckskin had taken advantage of this and had added a brass band, and now in turn was to be eclipsed.

The events slated were numerous and varied, the most important being those which dealt directly with the everyday occupations of the inhabitants of that section of the country. Broncho busting, steer-roping and tying, rifle and revolver shooting, trick riding and fancy roping made up the main features of the programme and were to be set off by horse and foot racing and other county fair necessities. Altogether, the proud citizens of the town looked forward with keen anticipation to the coming excitements, and were prone to swagger a bit and to rub their hands in condescending egoism, while the crowded gambling halls and saloons, and the three-card-monte men on the street corners enriched themselves at the cost of venturesome know-it-ails.

Hopalong was firmly convinced that his day of hard riding was well worth while, for the Bar-20 was to be represented in strength. Probably a clearer insight into his idea of a carnival can be gained by his definition, grouchily expressed to Red Connors on the day following the last affair: "Raise cain, go broke, wake up an' begin punching cows all over again." But that was the day after and the day after is always filled with remorse.

Hopalong and Red, having twice in succession won the revolver and rifle competitions, re-spectively, hoped to make it 'Three straight.' Lanky Smith, the Bar-20 rope expert, had taken first prize in the only contest he had entered. Skinny Thompson had lost and drawn with Lefty Allen, of the O-Bar-O, in the broncho-busting event, but as Skinny had improved greatly in the interval, his friends confidently expected him to "yank first place" for the honor of his ranch. These expectations were backed with all the available Bar-20 money, and, if they were not re-alized, something in the nature of a calamity would swoop down upon and wrap that ranch in gloom. Since the O-Bar-O was aggressively optimistic the betting was at even money, hats and guns, and the losers would begin life anew so far as earthly possessions were concerned. No other competitors were considered in this event, as Skinny and Lefty had so far outclassed all others that the honor was believed to lie between these two.

Hopalong, blissfully figuring out the chances of the different contestants, galloped around a clump of mesquite only fifteen miles from Muddy Wells and stiffened in his saddle, for twenty rods ahead of him on the trail was a woman. As she heard him approach she turned and waited for him to overtake her, and when she smiled he raised his sombrero and bowed.

"Will you please tell me where I am?" She asked.

"Yu are fifteen miles southeast of Muddy Wells," he replied.

"But which is southeast?"

"Right behind yu," he answered. "Th' town lies right ahead."

"Are you going there?" She asked.

"Yes, ma'am."

"Then you will not care if I ride with you?" She asked. "I am a trifle frightened."

"Why, I'd be some pleased if yu do, 'though there ain't nothing out here to be afraid of now."

"I had no intention of getting lost," she assured him, "but I dismounted to pick flowers and cactus leaves and after a while I had no conception of where I was."

"How is it yu are out here?" He asked. "Yu shouldn't get so far from town."

"Why, papa is an invalid and doesn't like to leave his room, and the town is so dull, although the carnival is waking it up somewhat. Having nothing to do I procured a horse and determined to explore the country. Why, this is like Stanley and Livingstone, isn't it? You rescued the explorer!" And she laughed heartily. He wondered who in thunder Stanley and Livingstone were, but said nothing.

"I like the West, it is so big and free," she continued. "But it is very monotonous at times, especially when compared with New York. Papa swears dreadfully at the hotel and declares that the food will drive him insane, but I notice that he eats much more heartily than he did when in the city. And the service! —it is awful. But when one leaves the town behind it is splendid, and I can appreciate it because I had such a hard season in the city last winter-so many balls, parties and theaters that I simply wore myself out."

"I never hankered much for them things," Hopalong replied. "An' I don't like th' towns much, either. Once or twice a year I gets as far as Kansas City, but I soon tires of it an' hits th' back trail. Yu see, I don't like a fence country —I wants lots of room an' air."

She regarded him intently: "I know that you will think me very forward."

He smiled and slowly replied: "I think yu are all O. K."

"There do not appear to be many women in this country," she suggested.

"No, there ain't many," he replied, thinking of the kind to be found in all of the cow-towns. "They don't seem to hanker for this kind of life-they wants parties an' lots of dancin' an' them kind of things. I reckon there ain't a whole lot to tempt em to come.

"You evidently regard women as being very frivolous," she replied.

"Well, I'm speakin' from there not being any out here," he responded, "although I don't know much about them, to tell th' truth. Them what are out here can't be counted." Then he flushed and looked away.

She ignored the remark and placed her hand to her hair:

"Goodness! My hair must look terrible!"

He turned and looked: "Yore hair is pretty —I allus did like brown hair."

She laughed and put back the straggling locks: "It is terrible! Just look at it! Isn't it awful?"

"Why, no: I reckons not," he replied critically. "It looks sort of free an' easy thataway."

"Well, it's no matter, it cannot be helped," she laughed. "Let's race!" she cried and was off like a shot.

He humored her until he saw that her mount was getting unmanageable, when he quietly overtook her and closed her pony's nostrils with his hand, the operation having a most gratifying effect.

"Joe hadn't oughter let yu had this cayuse," he said.

"Why, how do you know of whom I procured it?" She asked. "By th' brand: it's a O-Bar-O, canceled, with J. H. over it. He buys all of his cayuses from th' O-Bar-O."

She found out his name, and, after an interval of silence, she turned to him with eyes full of inquiry: "What is that thorny shrub just ahead?" She asked.

"That's mesquite," he replied eagerly.

"Tell me all about it," she commanded.

"Why, there ain't much to tell," he replied, "only it's a valuable tree out here. Th' Apaches use it a whole lot of ways. They get honey from th' blossoms an' glue an' gum, an' they use th' bark for tannin' hide. Th' dried pods an' leaves are used to feed their cattle, an' th' wood makes corrals to keep 'em in. They use th' wood for making other things, too, an' it is of two colors. Th' sap makes a dye what won't wash out, an' th' beans make a bread what won't sour or get hard. Then it makes a barrier that shore is a dandy-coyotes an' men can't get through it, an' it protects a whole lot of birds an' things. Th' snakes hate it like poison, for th' thorns get under their scales an' whoops things up for 'em. It keeps th' sand from shiftin', too. Down South where there is plenty of water, it often grows forty feet high, but up here it squats close to th' ground so it can save th' moisture. In th' night th' temperature sometimes falls thirty degrees, an' that helps it, too."

"How can it live without water?" She asked.

"It gets all th' water it wants," he replied, smiling. "Th' tap roots go straight down 'til they find it, sometimes fifty feet. That's why it don't shrivel up in th' sun. Then there are a lot of little roots right under it an' they protects th' tap roots. Th' shade it gives is th' coolest out here, for th' leaves turn with th' wind an' lets th' breeze through-they're hung on little stems."

"How splendid!" she exclaimed. "Oh! Look there!" she cried, pointing ahead of them. A chaparral cock strutted from its decapitated enemy, a rattlesnake, and disappeared in the chaparral.

Hopalong laughed: "Mr. Scissors-bill Road-runner has great fun with snakes. He runs along th' sand-an' he can run, too-an' sees a snake takin' a siesta. Snip! goes his bill an' th' snake slides over th' Divide. Our fighting friend may stop some coyote's appetite before morning, though, unless he stays where he is."

Just then a gray wolf blundered in sight a few rods ahead of them, and Hopalong fired instantly. His companion shrunk from him and looked at him reproachfully.

"Why did you do that!" she demanded.

"Why, because they costs us big money every year," he replied. "There's a bounty on them because they pull down calves, an' sometimes full grown cows. I'm shore wonderin' why he got so close-they're usually just out of range, where they stays."

"Promise me that you will shoot no more while I am with you.

"Why, shore: I didn't think yu'd care," he replied. "Yu are like that sky-pilot over to Las Cruces-he preached agin killin' things, which is all right for him, who didn't have no cows."

"Do you go to the missions?" She asked.

He replied that he did, sometimes, but forgot to add that it was usually for the purpose of hilarity, for he regarded sky-pilots with humorous toleration.

"Tell me all about yourself-what you do for enjoyment and all about your work," she requested.

He explained in minute detail the art of punching cows, and told her more of the West in half an hour than she could have learned from a year's experience. She showed such keen interest in his words that it was a pleasure to talk to her, and he monopolized the conversation until the town intruded its sprawling collection of unpainted shacks and adobe huts in their field of vision.

Chapter XXIV

The Strategy of Mr. Peters

Hopalong and his companion rode into Muddy Wells at noon, and Red Connors, who leaned with Buck Peters against the side of Tom Lee's saloon, gasped his astonishment. Buck looked twice to be sure, and then muttered incredulously: "What th' heck!" Red repeated the phrase and retreated within the saloon, while Buck stood his ground, having had much experience with women, inasmuch as he had narrowly escaped marrying. He thought that he might as well get all the information possible, and waited for an introduction. It was in vain, however, for the two rode past without noticing him.

Buck watched them turn the corner and then called for Red to come out, but that person, fearing an ordeal, made no reply and the foreman went in after him. The timorous one was corraling bracers at the bar and nearly swallowed down the wrong channel when Buck placed a heavy hand on his broad shoulder.

"G'way!" remarked Red. "I don't want no introduction, none whatever," he asserted. "G'way!" he repeated, backing off suspiciously.

"Better wait 'til yu are asked," suggested Buck. "Better wait 'til yu sees th' rope afore yu duck." Then he laughed: "Yu bashful fellers make me plumb disgusted. Why, I've seen yu face a bunch of guns an never turn a hair, an' here yore all in because yu fear yu'll have to stand around an' hide yore hands. She won't bite yu. Anyway, from what I saw, Hopalong is due to be her grub-he never saw me at all, th' chump."

"He shore didn't see me, none," replied Red with distinct relief. "Are they gone?"

"Shore," answered Buck. "An' if they wasn't they wouldn't see us, not if we stood in front of them an' yelled. She's a hummer-stands two hands under him an' is a whole lot prettier than that picture Cowan has got over his bar. There's nothing th' matter with his eyesight, but he's plumb locoed, all th' same. He'll go an' get stuck on her an' then she'll hit th' trail for home an' mamma, an' he won't be worth his feed for a year." Then he paused in consternation: "Thunder, Red: he's got to shoot to-morrow!"

"Well, suppose he has?" Responded Red. "I don't reckon she'll stampede his gun-play none.

"Yu don't reckon, eh?" Queried Buck with much irony. "No, an' that's what's th' matter with yu. Why, do yu expect to see him to-morrow? Yu won't if I knows him an' I reckon I do. Nope, he'll be follerin' her all around."

"He's got sand to burn," remarked Red in awe. "Wonder how he got to know her?"

"Yu can gamble she did th' introducing part-he ain't got th' nerve to do it himself. He saved her life, or she thinks he did, or some romantic nonsense like that. So yu better go around an' get him away, an' keep him away, too."

"Who, me?" Inquired Red in indignation. "Me go around an' tote him off? I ain't no wagon: yu go, or send Johnny."

"Johnny would say something real pert an' get knocked into th' middle of next week for it. He won't do, so I reckon yu better go yoreself," responded Buck, smiling broadly and moving off.

"Hey, yu! Wait a minute!" cried Red in consternation. Buck paused and Red groped for an excuse: "Why don't you send Billy?" He blurted in desperation.

The foreman's smile assumed alarming proportions and he slapped his thigh in joy: "Good boy!" he laughed. "Billy's th' man-good Lord, but won't he give Cupid cold feet! Rustle around an' send th' pessimistic soul to me."

Red, grinning and happy, rapidly visited door after door, shouted, "Hey, Billy!" and proceeded to the next one. He was getting pugnacious at his lack of success when he espied Mr. Billy Williams tacking along the accidental street as if he owned it. Mr. Williams was executing fancy steps and was trying to sing many songs at once.

Red stopped and grabbed his bibulous friend as that person veered to starboard: "Yore a peach of a life-preserver, yu are!" he exclaimed.

Billy balanced himself, swayed back and forth and frowned his displeasure at this unwarranted action: "I ain't no wife-deserter!" he shouted. "Unrope me an' give me th' trail! No tenderfoot can ride me!" Then he recognized his friend and grinned joyously: "Shore I will, but only one. Jus' one more, jus' one more. Yu see, m'friend, it was all Jimmy's fault. He —"

Red secured a chancery hold and dragged his wailing and remonstrating friend to Buck, who frowned with displeasure.

"This yere," said Red in belligerent disgust, "is th' dod-blasted hero what's a-goin' to save Hopalong from a mournful future. What are we a-goin' to do?"

Buck slipped the Colt's from Billy's holster and yanked the erring one to his feet: "Fill him full of sweet oil, source him in th' trough, walk him around for awhile an' see what it does," he ordered.

Two hours later Billy walked up to his foreman and weakly asked what was wanted. He looked as though he had just been released from a six-months' stay in a hospital.

"Yu go over to th' hotel an' find Hopalong," said the foreman sternly. "Stay with him all th' time, for there is a plot on foot to wing him on th' sly. If yu ain't mighty spry he'll be dead by night."

Having delivered the above instructions and prevarications, Buck throttled the laugh which threatened to injure him and scowled at Red, who again fled into the saloon for fear of spoiling it all with revealed mirth.

The convalescent stared in open-mouthed astonishment:

"What's he doin' in th' hotel, an' who's goin' to plug him?" He asked.

"Yu leave that to me," replied Buck, "All yu has to do is to get on th' job with yore gun," handing the weapon to him, "an' freeze to him like a flea on a cow. Mebby there'll be a woman in th' game, but that ain't none of yore funeral-yu do what I said."

"Blast th' women!" exploded Billy, moving off. When he had entered the hotel Buck went in to Red.

"For Pete's sake!" moaned that person in senseless reiteration. "Th' Lord help Billy! Holy Mackinaw!" he shouted. "Gimme a drink an' let me tell th' boys."

The members of the outfit were told of the plot and they gave their uproarious sanction, all needing bracers to sustain them.

Billy found the clerk swapping lies with the bartender and, procuring the desired information, climbed the stairs and hunted for room No. 6. Discovering it, he dispensed with formality, pushed open the door and entered.

He found his friend engaged in conversation with a pretty young woman, and on a couch at the far side of the room lay an elderly white-whiskered gentleman who was reading a magazine. Billy felt like a criminal for a few seconds and then there came to him the thought that his was a mission of great import and he braced himself to face any ordeal. "Anyway," he thought, "th' prettier they are th' more dust they can raise."

"What are yu doing here?" Cried Hopalong in amazement.

"That's all right," averred the protector, confidentially.

"What's all right?"

"Why, everything," replied Billy, feeling uncomfortable.

The elderly man hastily sat up and dropped his magazine when he saw the armed intruder, his eyes as wide open as his mouth. He felt for his spectacles, but did not need them, for he could see nothing but the Colt's which Billy jabbed at him.

"None of that!" snapped Billy. "'ands up!" he ordered, and the hands went up so quick that when they stopped the jerk shook the room. Peering over the gentleman's leg, Billy saw the spectacles and backed to the wall as he apologized: "It's shore on me, Stranger —I reckoned yu was contemplatin' some gun-play."

Hopalong, blazing with wrath, arose and shoved Billy toward the hail, when Mr. Johnny Nelson, oozing fight and importance, intruded his person into the zone of action.

"Lord!" ejaculated the newcomer, staring at the vision of female loveliness which so suddenly greeted him. "Mamma," he added under his breath. Then he tore off his sombrero: "Come out of this, Billy, yu chump!" he exploded, backing toward the door, being followed by the protector.

Hopalong slammed the door and turned to his hostess, apologizing for the disturbance.

"Who are they?" Palpitated Miss Deane.

"What the deuce are they doing up here!" blazed her father. Hopalong disclaimed any knowledge of them and just then Billy opened the door and looked in.

"There he is again!" cried Miss Deane, and her father gasped. Hopalong ran out into the hall and narrowly missed kicking Billy into Kingdom Come as that person slid down the stairs, surprised and indignant.

Mr. Billy Williams, who sat at the top of the stairs, was feeling hungry and thirsty when he saw his friend, Mr. Pete Wilson, the slow witted, approaching.

"Hey, Pete," he called, "come up here an' watch this door while I rustles some grub. Keep yore eyes open," he cautioned.

As Pete began to feel restless the door opened and a dignified gentleman with white whiskers came out into the hall and then retreated with great haste and no dignity. Pete got the drop on the door and waited. Hopalong yanked it open and kissed the muzzle of the weapon before he could stop, and Pete grinned.

"Coming to th' fight?" He loudly asked. "It's going to be a shore 'nough sumptious scrap-just th' kind yu allus like. Come on, th' boys are waitin' for yu."

"Keep quiet!" hissed Hopalong.

"What for?" Asked Pete in surprise. "Didn't yu say yu shore wanted to see that scrap?"

"Shut yore face an' get scarce, or yu'll go home in cans!"

As Hopalong seated himself once more Red strolled up to the door and knocked. Hopalong ripped it open and Red, looking as fierce and worried as he could, asked Hopalong if he was all right. Upon being assured by smoking adjectives that he was, the caller looked relieved and turned thoughtfully away.

"Hey, yu! Come here!" called Hopalong.

Red waved his hand and said that he had to meet a man and clattered down the stairs. Hopalong thought that he, also, had to meet a man and, excusing himself, hastened after his friend and overtook him in the Street, where he forced a confession. Returning to his hostess he told her of the whole outrage, and she was angry at first, but seeing the humorous side of it, she became convulsed with laughter. Her father re-read his paragraph for the thirteenth time and then, slamming the magazine on the floor, asked how many times he was expected to read ten lines before he knew what was in them, and went down to the bar.

Miss Deane regarded her companion with laughing eyes and then became suddenly sober as he came toward her.

"Go to your foreman and tell him that you will shoot to-morrow, for I will see that you do, and I will bring luck to the Bar-20. Be sure to call for me at one o'clock: I will be ready."

He hesitated, bowed, and slowly departed, making his way to Tom Lee's, where his entrance hushed the hilarity which had reigned. Striding to where Buck stood, he placed his hands on his hips and searched the foreman's eyes.

Buck smiled: "Yu ain't mad, are yu?" He asked.

Hopalong relaxed: "No, but blame near it."

Red and the others grabbed him from the rear, and when he had been "buffaloed" into good humor he threw them from him, laughed and waved his hand toward the bar:

"Come up, yu sons-of-guns. Yore a cussed nuisance sometimes, but yore a bully gang all th' same."

Chapter XXV

Mr. Ewalt Draws Cards

Tex Ewalt, cow-puncher, prospector, sometimes a rustler, but always a dude, rode from El Paso in deep disgust at his steady losses at faro and monte. The pecuniary side of these caused him no worry, for he was flush. This pleasing opulence was due to his business ability, for he had recently sold a claim for several thousand dollars. The first operation was simple, being known in Western phraseology as "jumping"; and the second, somewhat more complicated, was known as "salting."

The first of the money spent went for a complete new outfit, and he had parted with just three hundred and seventy dollars to feed his vanity. He desired something contrasty and he procured it. His sombrero, of gray felt a quarter of an inch thick, flaunted a band of black leather, on which was conspicuously displayed a solid silver buckle. His neck was protected by a crimson kerchief of the finest, heaviest silk. His shirt, in pattern the same as those commonly worn in the cow country, was of buckskin, soft as a baby's cheek and impervious to water, and the Angora goatskin chaps, with the long silken hair worn outside, were as white as snow. Around his waist ran loosely a broad, black leather belt supporting a heavy black holster, in which lay its walnut-handled burden, a .44 caliber six-shooter; and thirty center-fire cartridges peeked from their loops, fifteen on a side. His boots, the soles thin and narrow and the heels high, were black and of the finest leather. Huge spurs, having two-inch rowels, were held in place by buckskin straps, on which, also, were silver buckles. Protecting his hands were heavy buckskin gloves, also waterproof, having wide, black gauntlets.

Each dainty hock of his dainty eight-hundred-pound buckskin pony was black, and a black star graced its forehead. Well groomed, with flowing mane and tail, and with the brand on its flank being almost imperceptible, the animal was far different in appearance from most of the cow-ponies. Vicious and high-spirited, it cavorted just enough to show its lines to the best advantage.

The saddle, a famous Cheyenne and forty pounds in weight, was black, richly embossed, and decorated with bits of beaten silver which flashed back the sunlight. At the pommel hung a thirty-foot coil of braided horsehair rope, and at the rear was a Sharp's .50-caliber, breech-loading rifle, its owner having small use for any other make. The color of the bridle was the same as the saddle and it supported a heavy U bit which was capable of a leverage sufficient to break the animal's jaw.

Tex was proud of his outfit, but his face wore a frown-not there only on acount of his losses, but also by reason of his mission, for under all his finery beat a heart as black as any in the cow country. For months he had smothered hot hatred and he was now on his way to ease himself of it.

He and Slim Travennes had once exchanged shots with Hopalong in Santa Fe, and the month which he had spent in bed was not pleasing, and from that encounter had sprung the hatred. That he had been in the wrong made no difference with him. Some months later he had learned of the death of Slim, and it was due to the same man. That Slim had again been in the wrong also made no difference, for he realized the fact and nothing else.

Lately he had been told of the death of Slippery Trendley and Deacon Rankin, and he accepted their passing as a personal affront. That they had been caught red-handed in cattle stealing of huge proportions and received only what was customary under the conditions formed no excuse in his mind for their passing. He was now on his way to attend the carnival at Muddy Wells, knowing that his enemy would be sure to be there.

While passing through Las Cruces he met Porous Johnson and Silent Somes, who were thirsty and who proclaimed that fact, whereupon he relieved them of their torment and, looking forward to more treatment of a similar nature, they gladly accompanied him without asking why or where.

As they left the town in their rear Tex turned in his saddle and surveyed them with a cynical smile.

"Have yu heard anything of Trendley?" He asked.

They shook their heads.

"Him an' th' Deacon was killed over in th' Panhandle," he said.

"What!" chorused the pair.

"Jack Dorman, Shorty Danvers, Charley Teale, Stiffhat Bailey, Billy Jackson, Terry Nolan an' Sailor Carson was lynched."

"What!" they shouted.

"Fish O'Brien, Pinochle Schmidt, Tom Wilkins, Apache Gordon, Charley of th' Bar Y, Penobscot Hughes an' about twenty others died fightin'."

Porous looked his astonishment: "Cavalry?"

"An' I'm going after th' dogs who did it," he continued, ignoring the question. "Are yu with me? —Yu used to pal with some of them, didn't yu?"

"We did, an' we're shore with yu!" cried Porous.

"Yore right," endorsed Silent. "But who done it?"

"That gang what's punchin' for th' Bar-20-Hopalong Cassidy is th' one I'm pining for. Yu fellers can take care of Peters an' Connors."

The two stiffened and exchanged glances of uncertainty and apprehension. The outfit of the Bar-20 was too well known to cause exuberant joy to spring from the idea of war with it, and well in the center of all the tales concerning it were the persons Tex had named. To deliberately set forth with the avowed intention of planting these was not at all calculated to induce sweet dreams.

Tex sneered his contempt.

"Yore shore uneasy: yu ain't a-scared, are yu?" He drawled. Porous relaxed and made a show of subduing his horse: "I reckon I ain't scared plumb to death. Yu can deal me a hand," he asserted.

"I'll draw cards too," hastily announced Silent, buttoning his vest. "Tell us about that jamboree over in th' Panhandle."

Tex repeated the story as he had heard it from a bibulous member of the Barred Horseshoe, and then added a little of torture as a sauce to whet their appetites for revenge.

"How did Trendley cash in?" Asked Porous.

"Nobody knows except that bum from th' Tin-Cup. I'll get him later. I'd a got Cassidy up in Santa Fe, too, if it wasn't for th' sun in my eyes. Me an' Slim loosened up on him in th' Plaza, but we couldn't see nothing with him a-standin' against th' sun."

"Where's Slim now?" Asked Porous. "I ain't seen him for some time."

"Slim's with Trendley," replied Tex. "Cassidy handed him over to St. Pete at Cactus Springs. Him an' Connors sicked their outfit on him an' his vigilantes, bein helped some by th' O-Bar-O. They wiped th' town plumb off th' earth, an' now I'm going to do some wipin' of my own account. I'll prune that gang of some of its blossoms afore long. It's cost me seventeen friends so far, an' I'm going to stop th' leak, or make another."

They entered Muddy Wells at sunrise on the day of the carnival and, eating a hearty breakfast, sallied forth to do their share toward making the festivities a success.

The first step considered necessary for the acquirement of case and polish was begun at the nearest bar, and Tex, being the host, was so liberal that his friends had reached a most auspicious state when they followed him to Tom Lee's.

Tex was too wise to lose his head through drink and had taken only enough to make him careless of consequences. Porous was determined to sing "Annie Laurie," although he hung on the last word of the first line until out of breath and then began anew. Silent, not wishing to be outdone, bawled at the top of his lungs a medley of music-hall words to the air of a hymn.

Tex, walking as awkwardly as any cow-puncher, approached Tom Lee's, his two friends trailing erratically, arm in arm, in his rear. Swinging his arm he struck the door a resounding blow and entered, hand on gun, as it crashed back. Porous and Silent stood in the doorway and quarreled as to what each should drink and, compromising, lurched in and seated themselves on a table and resumed their vocal perpetrations.

Tex swaggered over to the bar and tossed a quarter upon it: "Corn juice," he laconically exclaimed. Tossing off the liquor and glancing at his howling friends, he shrugged his shoulders and strode out by the rear door, slamming it after him. Porous and Silent, recounting friends who had "cashed in" fell to weeping and they were thus occupied when Hopalong and Buck entered, closely followed by the rest of the outfit.

Buck walked to the bar and was followed by Hopalong, who declined his foreman's offer to treat. Tom Lee set a bottle at Buck's elbow and placed his hands against the bar.

"Friend of yourn just hit the back trail," he remarked to Hopalong. "He was primed some for trouble, too," he added.

"Yaas?" Drawled Hopalong with little interest.

The proprietor restacked the few glasses and wiped off the bar. "Them's his pardners," he said, indicating the pair on the table.

Hopalong turned his head and gravely scrutinized them. Porous was bemoaning the death of Slim Travennes and Hopalong frowned.

"Don't reckon he's no relation of mine," he grunted.

"Well, he ain't yore sister," replied Tom Lee, grinning.

"What's his brand?" Asked the puncher.

"I reckon he's a maverick, 'though yu put yore brand on him up to Santa Fe a couple of years back. Since he's throwed back on yore range I reckon he's yourn if yu wants him."

"I reckon Tex is some sore," remarked Hopalong, rolling a cigarette.

"I reckon he is," replied the proprietor, tossing Buck's quarter in the cash box. "But, say, you should oughter see his rig."

"Yaas?"

"He's shore a cow-punch dude-my, but he's some sumptious an' highfalutin'. An' bad? Why, he reckons th' Lord never brewed a more high-toned brand of cussedness than his'n. He shore reckons he's the baddest man that ever simmered."

"How'd he look as th' leadin' man in a necktie festival?" Blazed Johnny from across the room, feeling called upon to help the conversation.

"He'd be a howlin' success, son," replied Skinny Thompson, "judgin' by his friends what we elevated over in th' Panhandle."

Lanky Smith leaned forward with his elbow on the table, resting his chin in the palm of his hand: "Is Ewalt still a-layin' for yu, Hopalong?" He asked.

Hopalong turned wearily and tossed his half-consumed cigarette into the box of sand which did duty as a cuspidore: "I reckon so; an' he shore can hatch whenever he gets good an ready, too."

"He's probably a-broodin' over past grievances," offered Johnny, as he suddenly pushed Lanky's elbow from the table, nearly causing a catastrophe.

"Yu'll be broodin' over present grievances if yu don't look out, yu everlastin' nuisance yu," growled Lanky, planting his elbow in its former position with an emphasis which conveyed a warning.

"These bantams ruffle my feathers," remarked Red. "They go around braggin' about th' egg they're goin' to lay an' do enough cacklin' to furnish music for a dozen. Then when th' affair comes off yu'll generally find they's been settin' on a door-knob."

"Did yu ever see a hen leave th' walks of peace an' bugs an' rustle hell-bent across th' trail plumb in front of a cayuse?" Asked Buck. "They'll leave off rustlin' grub an' become candidates for th' graveyard just for cussedness. Well, a whole lot of men are th' same way. How many times have I seen them swagger into a gin shop an' try to run things sudden an' hard, an' that with half a dozen better men in th' same room? There's shore a-plenty of trouble a-comin' to every man without rustlin' around for more.

"'Member that time yu an' Frenchy tried to run th' little town of Frozen Nose, up in Montana?" Asked Johnny, winking at the rest.

"An' we did run it, for a while," responded Buck. "But that only goes to show that most young men are chumps-we were just about yore age then."

Red laughed at the youngster's discomfiture: "That little squib of yourn shore touched her off—I reckon we irrigates on yu this time, don't we?"

"Th' more th' Kid talks, th' more money he needs," remarked Lanky, placing his glass on the bar. "He had to blow me an' Skinny twice last night."

"I got two more after yu left," added Skinny "He shore oughter practice keeping still."

At one o'clock sharp Hopalong walked up to the clerk of the hotel and grinned. The clerk looked up:

"Hullo, Cassidy?" He exclaimed, genially. "What was all that fuss about this mornin' when I was away? I haven't seen you for a long time, have I? How are you?"

"That fuss was a fool joke of Buck's, an' I wish they had been throwed out," Hopalong replied. "What I want to know is if Miss Deane is in her room. Yu see, I have a date with her."

The clerk grinned:

"So she's roped you, too, has she?"

"What do yu mean?" Asked Hopalong in surprise. "Well, well," laughed the clerk. "You punchers are easy. Any third-rate actress that looks good to eat can rope you fellows, all right. Now look here, Laura, you keep shy of her corral, or you'll be broke so quick you won't believe you ever had a cent: that's straight. This is the third year that she's been here and I know what I'm talking about. How did you come to meet her?"

Hopalong explained the meeting and his friend laughed again:

"Why, she knows this country like a book. She can't get lost anywhere around here. But she's blame clever at catching punchers."

"Well, I reckon I'd better take her, go broke or not," replied Hopalong. "Is she in her room?"

"She is, but she is not alone," responded the clerk. "There is a dude puncher up there with her and she left word here that she was indisposed, which means that you are outlawed."

"Who is he?" Asked Hopalong, having his suspicions. "That friend of yours: Ewalt. He sported a wad this morning when she passed him, and she let him make her acquaintance. He's another easy mark. He'll be busted wide open to-night."

"I reckon I'll see Tex," suggested Hopalong, starting for the stairs.

"Come back, you chump!" cried the clerk. "I don't want any shooting here. What do you care about it? Let her have him, for it's an easy way out of it for you. Let him think he's cut you out, for he'll spend all the more freely. Get your crowd and enlighten them-it'll be better than a circus. This may sound like a steer, but it's straight."

Hopalong thought for a minute and then leaned on the cigar case:

"I reckon I'll take about a dozen of yore very best cigars, Charley. Got any real high-toned brands?"

"Cortez panatella-two for a simoleon," Chancy replied. "But, seein' that it's you, I'll throw off a dollar on a dozen. They're a fool notion of the old man, for we can't sell one in a month."

Hopalong dug up a handful and threw one on the counter, lighting another: "Yu light a Cortez panatella with me," he said, pocketing the remainder. "That's five simoleons she didn't get. So long."

He journeyed to Tom Lee's and found his outfit making merry. Passing around his cigars he leaned against the bar and delighted in the first really good smoke he had since he came home from Kansas City.

Johnny Nelson blew a cloud of smoke at the ceiling and paused with a pleased expression on his face:

"This is a lalapoloosa of a cigar," he cried. "Where'd yu get it, an' how many's left?"

"I got it from Charley, an' there's more than yu can buy at fifty a shot."

"Well, I'll just take a few for luck," Johnny responded, running out into the street. Returning in five minutes with both hands full of cigars he passed them around and grinned: "They're birds, all right!"

Hopalong smiled, turned to Buck and related his conversation with Chancy. "What do yu think of that?" He asked as he finished.

"I think Charley oughter be yore guardian," replied the foreman.

"He was," replied Hopalong.

"If we sees Tex we'll all grin hard," laughed Red, making for the door. "Come on to th' contests-Lanky's gone already."

Muddy Wells streamed to the carnival grounds and relieved itself of its enthusiasm and money at the booths on the way. Cow-punchers rubbed elbows with Indians and Mexicans, and the few tourists that were present were delighted with the picturesque scene. The town was full of fakirs and before one of them stood a group of cow-punchers, apparently drinking in the words of a barker.

"Right this way, gents, and see the woman who don't eat. Lived for two years without food, gents. Right this way, gents. Only a quarter of a dollar. Get your tickets, gents, and see —"

Red pushed forward:

"What did yu say, pard?" He asked. "I'm a little off in my near ear. What's that about eatin' a woman for two years?"

"The greatest wonder of the age, gents. The wom —"

"Any discount for th' gang?" Asked Buck, gawking.

"Why don't yu quit smokin' an' buy th' lady a meal?" Asked Johnny from the center of the group.

"Th' cane yu ring th' cane yu get!" came from the other side of the street and Hopalong purchased rings for the outfit. Twenty-four rings got one cane, and it was divided between them as they wended their way toward the grounds.

"That makes six wheels she didn't get," murmured Hopalong. As they passed the snake charmer's booth they saw Tex and his companion ahead of them in the crowd, and they grinned broadly. "I like th' front row in th' balcony," remarked Johnny, who had been to Kansas City. "Don't cry in th' second act-it ain't real," laughed Red. "We'll hang John Brown on a sour appletree-in th' Panhandle," sang Skinny as they passed them.

Arriving at the grounds they hunted up the registration committee and entered in the contests. As Hopalong signed for the revolver competition he was rudely pushed aside and Tex wrote his name under that of his enemy. Hopalong was about to show quick resentment for the insult, but thought of what Charley had said, and he grinned sympathetically. The seats were filling rapidly, and the outfit went along the ground looking for friends. A bugle sounded and a hush swept over the crowd as the announcement was made for the first event.

"Broncho-busting-Red Devil, never ridden: Frenchy McAllister, Tin-Cup, Montana; Meteor, killed his man: Skinny Thompson, Bar-20, Texas; Vixen, never ridden: Lefty Allen, O-Bar-O, Texas."

All eyes were focused on the plain where the horse was being led out for the first trial. After the usual preliminaries had been gone through Frenchy walked over to it, vaulted in the saddle and the bandage was torn from the animal's eyes. For ten minutes the onlookers were held spellbound by the fight before them, and then the horse kicked and galloped away and Frenchy was picked up and carried from the field.

"Too bad!" cried Buck, running from the outfit.

"Did yu see it?" asked Johnny excitedly, "Th' cinch busted." Another horse was led out and Skinny Thompson vaulted to the saddle, and after a fight of half an hour rode the animal from the enclosure to the clamorous shouts of his friends. Lefty Allen also rode his mount from the same gate, but took ten minutes more in which to do it.

The announcer conferred with the timekeepers and then stepped forward: "First, Skinny Thompson, Bar-20, thirty minutes and ten seconds; second, Lefty Allen, O-Bar-O, forty minutes and seven seconds."

Skinny returned to his friends shamefacedly and did not look as if he had just won a championship. They made way for him, and Johnny, who could not restrain his enthusiasm pounded him on the back and cried: "Yu old son-of-a-gun!"

The announcer again came forward and gave out the competitors for the next contest, steer-roping and tying. Lanky Smith arose and, coiling his rope carefully, disappeared into the crowd. The fun was not so great in this, but when he returned to his outfit with the phenomenal time of six minutes and eight seconds for his string of ten steers, with twenty-two seconds for one of them, they gave him vociferous greeting. Three of his steers had gotten up after he had leaped from his saddle to tie them, but his horse had taken care of that. His nearest rival was one minute over him and Lanky retained the championship.

Red Connors shot with such accuracy in the rifle contest as to run his points twenty per cent higher than Waffles, of the O-Bar-O, and won the new rifle.

The main interest centered in the revolver contest, for it was known that the present champion was to defend his title against an enemy and fears were expressed in the crowd that there would be an "accident." Buck Peters and Red stood just behind the firing line with their hands on hips, and Tex, seeing the precautions, smiled grimly as he advanced to the line.

Six bottles, with their necks an inch above a board, stood twenty paces from him, and he broke them all in as many shots, taking twelve seconds in which to do it. Hopalong followed him and tied the score. Three tin balls rolling erratically in a blanket supported by two men were sent flying into the air in four shots, Tex taking six seconds. His competitor sent them from the blanket in three shots and in the same time. In slow shooting from sights Tex passed his rival in points and stood to win. There was but one more event to be contested and in it Hopalong found his joy.

Shooting from the hip when the draw is timed is not the sport of even good shots, and when Tex made sixty points out of a possible hundred, he felt that he had shot well. When Hopalong went to the line his friends knew that they would now see shooting such as would be almost unbelievable, that the best draw-and-shoot marksman in their State was the man who limped slightly as he advanced and who chewed reflectively on his fifty-cent cigar. He wore two guns and he stepped with confidence before the marshal of the town, who was also judge of the contest.

The iron ball which lay on the ground was small enough for the use of a rifle and could hardly be seen from the rear seats of the amphitheater. There was a word spoken by the timekeeper, and a gloved hand flashed down and up, and the ball danced and spun and leaped and rolled as shot after shot followed it with a precision and speed which brought the audience to a heavy silence. Taking the gun which Buck tossed to him and throwing it into the empty holster, he awaited the signal, and then smoke poured from his hips and the ball jumped continuously. Both guns emptied in the two-hand shooting, he wheeled and jerked loose the guns which the marshal wore, spinning around without a pause, the target hardly ceasing in its rolling. Under his arms he shot, backward and between his legs; leaping from side to side, ducking and dodging, following the ball wherever it went. Reloading the weapons quickly, he stepped forward and followed the ball until once more his guns were empty. Then he turned and walked back to the side of the marshal, smiling a little. His friends, and there were many in the crowd, torn from their affected nonchalance by shooting the like of which they had not attributed even to him, roared and shouted and danced in a frenzy of delight.

Red also threw his guns to Hopalong, who caught them in the air and turning, faced Tex, who stood white of face and completely lost in the forgetfulness of admiration and amazement. The guns jerked again and a button flew from the buckskin shirt of his enemy; another tore a flower from his breast and another drove it into the ground at his feet as others stirred his hair and cut the buckle off his pretty sombrero. Tex, dazed, but wise enough to stand quiet, felt his belt tear loose and drop to his feet, felt a spur rip from its strap and saw his cigarette leap from his lips. Throwing the guns to Red, Hopalong laughed and abruptly turned and was lost in the crowd.

For several seconds there was silence, but when the dazed minds realized what their eyes had seen, there arose a roar which shook the houses in the town. Roar after roar thundered forth and was sent crashing back again by the distant walls, sweeping down on the discomfited dude and causing him to slink into the crowd to find a place less conspicuous. He was white yet and keen fear gripped his heart as he realized that he had come to the carnival with the expressed purpose of killing his enemy in fair combat. The whole town knew it, for he had taken pains to spread the news.

The woman he had been with knew it from words which she had overheard while on her way to the grounds with him. His friends knew it and would laugh him into forgetfulness as the fool who boasted. Now he understood why he had lost so many friends: they had attempted what he had sworn to attempt. Look where he would he could see only a smoke-wrapped demon who moved and shot with a speed incredible. There was reason why Slim had died. There was reason why Porous and Silent had paled when they learned of their mission.

He hated his conspicuous clothes and his pretty broncho, and the woman who had gotten him to squander his money, and who was doubtless convulsed with laughter at his expense. He worked himself into a passion which knew no fear and he ran for the streets of the town, there to make good his boast or to die. When he found his enemy he felt himself grasped with a grip of steel and Buck Peters swung him around and grinned maliciously in his face:

"You plaything!" hoarsely whispered the foreman. "Why don't yu get away while yu can? Why do yu want to throw yoreself against certain death? I don't want my pleasure marred by a murder, an' that is what it will be if yu makes a gun-play at Hopalong. He'll shoot yu as he did yore buttons. Take yore pretty clothes an' yore pretty cayuse an' go where this is not known, an' if ever again yu feels like killing Hopalong, get drunk an' forget it."

Bar-20 Days

Chapter I
On a Strange Range

Two tired but happy punchers rode into the coast town and dismounted in front of the best hotel. Putting up their horses as quickly as possible they made arrangements for sleeping quarters and then hastened out to attend to business. Buck had been kind to delegate this mission to them and they would feel free to enjoy what pleasures the town might afford. While at that time the city was not what it is now, nevertheless it was capable of satisfying what demands might be made upon it by two very active and zealous cow-punchers. Their first experience began as they left the hotel.

"Hey, you cow-wrastlers!" said a not unpleasant voice, and they turned suspiciously as it continued: "You've shore got to hang up them guns with the hotel clerk while you cavorts around on this range. This is *fence* country."

They regarded the speaker's smiling face and twinkling eyes and laughed. "Well, yo're the foreman if you owns that badge," grinned Hopalong, cheerfully. "We don't need no guns, no-how, in this town, we don't. Plumb forgot we was toting them. But mebby you can tell us where lawyer Jeremiah T. Jones grazes in daylight?"

"Right over yonder, second floor," replied the marshal. "An' come to think of it, mebby you better leave most of yore cash with the guns-somebody'll take it away from you if you don't. It'd be an awful temptation, an' flesh is weak."

"Huh!" laughed Johnny, moving back into the hotel to leave his gun, closely followed by Hopalong. "Anybody that can turn that little trick on me an' Hoppy will shore earn every red cent; why, we've been to Kansas City!"

As they emerged again Johnny slapped his pocket, from which sounded a musical jingling. "If them weak people try anything on us, we may come between them and *their* money!" he boasted.

"From the bottom of my heart I pity you," called the marshal, watching them depart, a broad smile illuminating his face. "In about twenty-four hours they'll put up a holler for me to go git it back for 'em," he muttered. "An' I almost believe I'll do it, too. I ain't never seen none of that breed what ever left a town without empty pockets an' aching heads-an' the smarter they think they are the easier they fall." A fleeting expression of discontent clouded the smile, for the lure of the open range is hard to resist when once a man has ridden free under its sky and watched its stars. "An' I wish I was one of 'em again," he muttered, sauntering on.

Jeremiah T. Jones, Esq., was busy when his door opened, but he leaned back in his chair and smiled pleasantly at their bow-legged entry, waving them towards two chairs. Hopalong hung his sombrero on a letter press and tipped his chair back against the wall; Johnny hung grimly to his hat, sat stiffly upright until he noticed his companion's pose, and then, deciding that everything was all right, and that Hopalong was better up in etiquette than himself, pitched his sombrero dexterously over the water pitcher and also leaned against the wall. Nobody could lose him when it came to doing the right thing.

"Well, gentlemen, you look tired and thirsty. This is considered good for all human ailments of whatsoever nature, degree, or wheresoever located, in part or entirety, *ab initio*," Mr. Jones remarked, filling glasses. There was no argument and when the glasses were empty, he continued: "Now what can I do for you? From the Bar-20? Ah, yes; I was expecting you. We'll get right at it," and they did. Half an hour later they emerged on the street, free to take in the town, or to have the town take them in, —which was usually the case.

"What was that he said for us to keep away from?" asked Johnny with keen interest.

"Sh! Not so loud," chuckled Hopalong, winking prodigiously.

Johnny pulled tentatively at his upper lip but before he could reply his companion had accosted a stranger.

"Friend, we're pilgrims in a strange land, an' we don't know the trails. Can you tell us where the docks are?"

"Certainly; glad to. You'll find them at the end of this street," and he smilingly waved them towards the section of the town which Jeremiah T. Jones had specifically and earnestly warned them to avoid.

"Wonder if you're as thirsty as me?" solicitously inquired Hopalong of his companion.

"I was just wondering the same," replied Johnny. "Say," he confided in a lower voice, "blamed if I don't feel sort of lost without that Colt. Every time I lifts my right laig she goes too high-don't feel natural, nohow."

"Same here; I'm allus feeling to see if I lost it," Hopalong responded. "There ain't no rubbing, no weight, nor nothing."

"Wish I had something to put in its place, blamed if I don't."

"Why, now yo're talking-mebby we can buy something," grinned Hopalong, happily. "Here's a hardware store-come on in."

The clerk looked up and laid aside his novel. "Good-morning, gentlemen; what can I do for you? We've just got in some fine new rifles," he suggested.

The customers exchanged looks and it was Hopalong who first found his voice. "Nope, don't want no rifles," he replied, glancing around. "To tell the truth, I don't know just what we do want, but we want something, all right-got to have it. It's a funny thing, come to think of it; I can't never pass a hardware store without going in an' buying something. I've been told my father was the same way, so I must inherit it. It's the same with my pardner, here, only he gets his weakness from his whole family, and it's different from mine. He can't pass a saloon without going in an' buying something."

"Yo're a cheerful liar, an' you know it," retorted Johnny. "You know the reason why I goes in saloons so much-you'd never leave 'em if I didn't drag you out. He inherits that weakness from his grandfather, twice removed," he confided to the astonished clerk, whose expression didn't know what to express.

"Let's see: a saw?" soliloquized Hopalong. "Nope; got lots of 'em, an' they're all genuine Colts," he mused thoughtfully. "Axe? Nails? Augurs? Corkscrews? Can we use a corkscrew, Johnny? Ah, thought I'd wake you up. Now, what was it Cookie said for us to bring him? Bacon? Got any bacon? Too bad-oh, don't apologize; it's all right. Cold chisels-that's the thing if you ain't got no bacon. Let me see a three-pound cold chisel about as big as that," — extending a huge and crooked forefinger, —"an' with a big bulge at one end. Straight in the middle, circling off into a three-cornered wavy edge on the other side. What? Look here! You can't tell us nothing about saloons that we don't know. I want a three-pound cold chisel, any kind, so it's cold."

Johnny nudged him. "How about them wedges?"

"Twenty-five cents a pound," explained the clerk, groping for his bearings.

"They might do," Hopalong muttered, forcing the article mentioned into his holster. "Why, they're quite hocus-pocus. You take the brother to mine, Johnny."

"Feels good, but I dunno," his companion muttered. "Little wide at the sharp end. Hey, got any loose shot?" he suddenly asked, whereat Hopalong beamed and the clerk gasped. It didn't seem to matter whether they bought bacon, cold chisels, wedges, or shot; yet they looked sober.

"Yes, sir; what size?"

"Three pounds of shot, I said!" Johnny rumbled in his throat. "Never mind what size."

"We never care about size when we buy shot," Hopalong smiled. "But, Johnny, wouldn't them little screws be better?" he asked, pointing eagerly.

"Mebby; reckon we better get 'em mixed-half of each," Johnny gravely replied. "Anyhow, there ain't much difference."

The clerk had been behind that counter for four years, and executing and filling orders had become a habit with him; else he would have given them six pounds of cold chisels and corkscrews, mixed. His mouth was still open when he weighed out the screws.

"Mix 'em! Mix 'em!" roared Hopalong, and the stunned clerk complied, and charged them for the whole purchase at the rate set down for screws.

Hopalong started to pour his purchase into the holster which, being open at the bottom, gayly passed the first instalment through to the floor. He stopped and looked appealingly at Johnny, and Johnny, in pain from holding back screams of laughter, looked at him indignantly. Then a guileless smile crept over Hopalong's face and he stopped the opening with a wad of wrapping paper and disposed of the shot and screws, Johnny following his laudable example. After haggling a moment over the bill they paid it and walked out, to the apparent joy of the clerk.

"Don't laugh, Kid; you'll spoil it all," warned Hopalong, as he noted signs of distress on his companion's face. "Now, then; what was it we said about thirst? Come on; I see one already."

Having entered the saloon and ordered, Hopalong beamed upon the bartender and shoved his glass back again. "One more, kind stranger; it's good stuff."

"Yes, feels like a shore-enough gun," remarked Johnny, combining two thoughts in one expression, which is brevity.

The bartender looked at him quickly and then stood quite still and listened, a puzzled expression on his face.

Tic-tickety-tick-tic-tic, came strange sounds from the other side of the bar. Hopalong was intently studying a chromo on the wall and Johnny gazed vacantly out of the window.

"What's that? What in the deuce is that?" quickly demanded the man with the apron, swiftly reaching for his bung-starter.

Tickety-tic-tic-tic-tic-tic, the noise went on, and Hopalong, slowly rolling his eyes, looked at the floor. A screw rebounded and struck his foot, while shot were rolling recklessly.

"Them's making the noise," Johnny explained after critical survey.

"Hang it! I knowed we ought to 'a' got them wedges!" Hopalong exclaimed, petulantly, closing the bottom of the sheath. "Why, I won't have no gun left soon 'less I holds it in." The complaint was plaintive.

"Must be filtering through the stopper," Johnny remarked. "But don't it sound nice, especially when it hits that brass cuspidor!"

The bartender, grasping the mallet even more firmly, arose on his toes and peered over the bar, not quite sure of what he might discover. He had read of infernal machines although he had never seen one. "What the blazes!" he exclaimed in almost a whisper; and then his face went hard. "You get out of here, quick! You've had too much already! I've seen drunks, but —G'wan! Get out!"

"But we ain't begun yet," Hopalong interposed hastily. "You see —"

"Never mind what I see! I'd hate to see what you'll be seeing before long. God help you when you finish!" rather impolitely interrupted the bartender. He waved the mallet and made for the end of the counter with no hesitancy and lots of purpose in his stride. "G'wan, now! Get out!"

"Come on, Johnny; I'd shoot him only we didn't put no powder with the shot," Hopalong remarked sadly, leading the way out of the saloon and towards the hardware store.

"You better get out!" shouted the man with the mallet, waving the weapon defiantly. "An' don't you never come back again, neither," he warned.

"Hey, it leaked," Hopalong said pleasantly as he closed the door of the hardware store behind him, whereupon the clerk jumped and reached for the sawed-off shotgun behind the counter. Sawed-off shotguns are great institutions for arguing at short range, almost as effective as dynamite in clearing away obstacles.

"Don't you come no nearer!" he cried, white of face. "You git out, or I'll let *this* leak, an' give you *all* shot, an' more than you can carry!"

"Easy! Easy there, pardner; we want them wedges," Hopalong replied, somewhat hurriedly. "The others ain't no good; I choked on the very first screw. Why, I wouldn't hurt you for the world," Hopalong assured him, gazing interestedly down the twin tunnels.

Johnny leaned over a nail keg and loosed the shot and screws into it, smiling with childlike simplicity as he listened to the tintinnabulation of the metal shower among the nails. "It *does* drop when you let go of it," he observed.

"Didn't I tell you it would? I allus said so," replied Hopalong, looking back to the clerk and the shotgun. "Didn't I, stranger?"

The clerk's reply was a guttural rumbling, ninety per cent profanity, and Hopalong, nodding wisely, picked up two wedges. "Johnny, here's yore gun. If this man will stop talking to hisself and drop that lead-sprayer long enough to take our good money, we'll wear em."

He tossed a gold coin on the table, and the clerk, still holding tightly to the shotgun, tossed the coin into the cash box and cautiously slid the change across the counter. Hopalong picked up the money and, emptying his holster into the nail keg, followed his companion to the street, in turn followed slowly by the suspicious clerk. The door slammed shut behind them, the bolt shot home, and the clerk sat down on a box and cogitated.

Hopalong hooked his arm through Johnny's and started down the street. "I wonder what that feller thinks about us, anyhow. I'm glad Buck sent Red over to El Paso instead of us. Won't he be mad when we tell him all the fun we've had?" he asked, grinning broadly.

They were to meet Red at Dent's store on the way back and ride home together.

They were strangely clad for their surroundings, the chaps glaringly out of place in the Seaman's Port, and winks were exchanged by the regular *habitues* when the two punchers entered the room and called for drinks. They were very tired and a little under the weather, for they had made the most of their time and spent almost all of their money; but any one counting on robbing them would have found them sober enough to look out for themselves. Night had found them ready to go to the hotel, but on the way they felt that they must have one more bracer, and finish their exploration of Jeremiah T. Jones' tabooed section. The town had begun to grow wearisome and they were vastly relieved when they realized that the rising sun would see them in the saddle and homeward bound, headed for God's country, which was the only place for cow-punchers after all.

"Long way from the home port, ain't you, mates?" queried a tar of Hopalong. Another seaman went to the bar to hold a short, whispered consultation with the bartender, who at first frowned and then finally nodded assent.

"Too far from home, if that's what yo're driving at," Hopalong replied. "Blast these hard trails-my feet are shore on the prod. Ever meet my side pardner? Johnny, here's a friend of mine, a salt-water puncher, an' he's welcome to the job, too."

Johnny turned his head ponderously and nodded. "Pleased to meet you, stranger. An' what'll you all have?"

"Old Holland, mate," replied the other, joining them.

"All up!" invited Hopalong, waving them forward. "Might as well do things right or not at all. Them's my sentiments, which I holds as proper. Plain rye, general, if you means me," he replied to the bartender's look of inquiry.

He drained the glass and then made a grimace. "Tastes a little off-reckon it's my mouth; nothing tastes right in this cussed town. Now, up on our —" He stopped and caught at the bar. "Holy smoke! That's shore alcohol!"

Johnny was relaxing and vainly trying to command his will power. "Something's wrong; what's the matter?" he muttered sleepily.

"Guess you meant beer; you ain't used to drinking whiskey," grinned the bartender, derisively, and watching him closely.

"I can-drink as much whiskey as —" and, muttering, Johnny slipped to the floor.

"That wasn't whiskey!" cried Hopalong, sleepily, "that liquor was *fixed*!" he shouted, sudden anger bracing him. "An' I'm going to fix *you*, too!" he added, reaching for his gun, and drawing forth a wedge. His sailor friend leaped at him, to go down like a log, and Hopalong, seething with rage, wheeled and threw the weapon at the man behind the bar, who also went down. The wedge, glancing from his skull, swept a row of bottles and glasses from the shelf and, caroming, went through the window.

In an instant Hopalong was the vortex of a mass of struggling men and, handicapped as he was, fought valiantly, his rage for the time neutralizing the effects of the drug. But at last, too sleepy to stand or think, he, too, went down.

"By the Lord, that man's a fighter!" enthusiastically remarked the leader, gently touching his swollen eye. "George must 'a' put an awful dose in that grog."

"Lucky for us he didn't have no gun-the wedge was bad enough," groaned a man on the floor, slowly sitting up. "Whoever swapped him that wedge for his gun did us a good turn, all right."

A companion tentatively readjusted his lip. "I don't envy Wilkins his job breaking in that man when he gets awake."

"Don't waste no time, mates," came the order. "Up with 'em an' aboard. We've done our share; let the mate do his, an' be hanged. Hullo, Portsmouth; coming around, eh?" he asked the man who had first felt the wedge. "I was scared you was done for that time."

"No more shanghaiing hair pants for me, no more!" thickly replied Portsmouth. "Oh, my head, it's bust open!"

"Never mind about the bartender-let him alone; we can't waste no time with him now!" commanded the leader sharply. "Get these fellers on board before we're caught with 'em. We want our money after that."

"All clear!" came a low call from the lookout at the door, and soon a shadowy mass surged across the street and along a wharf. There was a short pause as a boat emerged out of the gloom, some whispered orders, and then the squeaking of oars grew steadily fainter in the direction of a ship which lay indistinct in the darkness.

Chapter II
The Rebound

A man moaned and stirred restlessly in a bunk, muttering incoherently. A stampeded herd was thundering over him, the grinding hoofs beating him slowly to death. He saw one mad steer stop and lower its head to gore him and just as the sharp horns touched his skin, he awakened. Slowly opening his bloodshot eyes he squinted about him, sick, weak, racking with pain where heavy shoes had struck him in the melee, his head reverberating with roars which seemed almost to split it open. Slowly he regained his full senses and began to make out his surroundings. He was in a bunk which moved up and down, from side to side, and was never still. There was a small, round window near his feet-thank heaven it was open, for he was almost suffocated by the foul air and the heat. Where was he? What had happened? Was there a salty odor in the air, or was he still dreaming? Painfully raising himself on one elbow he looked around and caught sight of a man in the bunk across. It was Johnny Nelson! Then, bit by bit, the whole thing came to him and he cursed heartily as he reviewed it and reached the only possible conclusion. He was at sea! He, Hopalong Cassidy, the best fighting unit of a good fighting outfit, shanghaied and at sea! Drugged, beaten, and stolen to labor on a ship.

Johnny was muttering and moaning and Hopalong slowly climbed out of the narrow bunk, unsteadily crossed the moving floor, and shook him. "Reckon he's in a stampede, too!" he growled. "They shore raised h —l with us. Oh, what a beating we got! But we'll pass it along with trimmings."

Johnny's eyes opened and he looked around in confusion. "Wha', Hopalong!"

"Yes; it's me, the prize idiot of a blamed good pair of 'em. How'd you feel?"

"Sleepy an' sick. My eyes ache an' my head's splitting. Where's Buck an' the rest?"

Hopalong sat down on the edge of the bunk and sore luridly, eloquently, beautifully, with a fervor and polish which left nothing to be desired in that line, and caused his companion to gaze at him in astonishment.

"I had a mighty bad dream, but you must 'a' had one a whole lot worse, to listen to you," Johnny remarked. "Gee, you're going some! What's the matter with you. You sick, too?"

Thereupon Hopalong unfolded the tale of woe and when Johnny had grasped its import and knew that his dream had been a stern reality, he straightway loosed his vocabulary and earned a draw. "Well, I'm going back again," he finished, with great decision, arising to make good his assertion.

"Swim or walk?" asked Hopalong nonchalantly.

"Huh! Oh, Lord!"

"Well, I ain't going to either swim or walk," Hopalong soliloquized. "I'm just going to stay right here in this one-by-nothing cellar an' spoil the health an' good looks of any pirate that comes down that ladder to get me out." He looked around, interested in life once more, and his trained eye grasped the strategic worth of their position. "Only one at a time, an' down that ladder," he mused, thoughtfully. "Why, Johnny, we owns this range as long as we wants to. They can't get us out. But, say, if only we had our guns!" he sighed, regretfully.

"You're right as far as you go; but you don't go to the eating part. We'll starve, an' we ain't got no water. I can drink about a bucketful right now," moodily replied his companion.

"Well, yo're right; but mebby we can find food an' water."

"Don't see no signs of none. Hey!" Johnny exclaimed, smiling faintly in his misery. "Let's get busy an' burn the cussed thing up! Got any matches?"

"First you want to drown yoreself swimming, an' now you want to roast the pair of us to death," Hopalong retorted, eyeing the rear wall of the room. "Wonder what's on the other side of that partition?"

Johnny looked. "Why, water; an' lots of it, too."

"Naw; the water is on the other sides."

"Then how do I know? —sh! I hear somebody coming on the roof."

"Tumble back in yore bunk-quick!" Hopalong hurriedly whispered. "Be asleep-if he comes down here it'll be our deal."

The steps overhead stopped at the companionway and a shadow appeared across the small patch of sunlight on the floor of the forecastle. "Tumble up here, you blasted loafers!" roared a deep voice.

No reply came from the forecastle-the silence was unbroken.

"If I have to come down there I'll —" the first mate made promises in no uncertain tones and in very impolite language. He listened for a moment, and having very good ears and hearing nothing, made more promises and came down the ladder quickly and nimbly.

"*I'll* bring you to," he muttered, reaching a brawny hand for Hopalong's nose, and missing. But he made contact with his own face, which stopped a short-arm blow from the owner of the aforesaid nose, a jolt full of enthusiasm and purpose. Beautiful and dazzling flashes of fire filled the air and just then something landed behind his ear and prolonged the pyrotechnic display. When the skyrockets went up he lost interest in the proceedings and dropped to the floor like a bag of meal.

Hopalong cut another piece from the rope in his hand and watched his companion's busy fingers. "Tie him good, Johnny; he's the only ace we've drawn in this game so far, an' we mustn't lose him."

Johnny tied an extra knot for luck and leaned forward, his eyes riveted on the bump under the victim's coat. His darting hand brought into sight that which pleased him greatly. "Oh, joy! Here, Hoppy; you take it."

Hopalong turned the weapon over in his hand, spun the cylinder and gloated, the clicking sweet music to his ears. "Plumb full, too! I never reckoned I'd ever be so tickled over a snub-nosed gun like this-but I feel like singing!"

"An' I feel like dying," grunted Johnny, grabbing at his stomach. "If the blamed shack would only stand still!" he groaned, gazing at the floor with strong disgust. "I don't reckon I've ever been so blamed sick in all my —" the sentence was unfinished, for the open porthole caught his eye and he leaped forward to use it for a collar.

Hopalong gazed at him in astonishment and sudden pity took possession of him as his pallid companion left the porthole and faced him.

"You ought to have something to eat, Kid —I'm purty hungry myself-what the blazes!" he exclaimed, for Johnny's protesting wail was finished outside the port. Then a light broke upon him and he wondered how soon it would be his turn to pay tribute to Neptune.

"Mr. Wilkins!" shouted a voice from the deck, and Hopalong moved back a step. "Mr. Wilkins!" After a short silence the voice soliloquized: "Guess he changed his mind about it; I'll get 'em up for him," and feet came into view. When halfway down the ladder the second mate turned his head and looked blankly down a gun barrel while a quiet but angry voice urged him further: "Keep a-coming, keep a-coming!" The second mate complained, but complied.

"Stick 'em up higher-now, Johnny, wobble around behind the nice man an' take *his* gun-you shut yore yap! I'm bossing this trick, not you. Got it, Kid? There's the rope-that's right. Nobody'd think you sick to see you work. Well, that's a good draw; but it's only a pair of aces against a full, at that. Wonder who'll be the next. Hope it's the foreman."

Johnny, keeping up by sheer grit, pointed to the rear wall. "What about that?"

For reply his companion walked over to it, put his shoulder to it and pushed. He stepped back and hurled his weight against it, but it was firm despite its squeaking protest. Then he examined it foot by foot and found a large knot, which he drove in by a blow of the gun. Bending, he squinted through the opening for a full minute and then reported:

"Purty black in there at this end, but up at the other there's a light from a hole in the roof, an' I could see boxes an' things like that. I reckon it's the main cellar."

"If we could get out at the other end with that gun you've got we could raise blazes for a while," suggested Johnny. "Anyhow, mebby they can come at us that way when they find out what we've gone an' done."

"Yo're right," Hopalong replied, looking around. Seeing an iron bar he procured it and, pushing it through the knot hole in the partition, pulled. The board, splitting and cracking under the attack, finally broke from its fastenings with a sharp report, and Hopalong, pulling it aside, stepped out of sight of his companion. Johnny was grinning at the success of his plan when he was interrupted.

"Ahoy, down there!" yelled a stentorian voice from above. "Mr. Wilkins! What the devil are you doing so long?" and after a very short wait other feet came into sight. Just then the second mate, having managed to slip off the gag, shouted warning:

"Look out, Captain! They've got us and our guns! One of them has —" but Johnny's knee thudded into his chest and ended the sentence as a bullet sent a splinter flying from under the captain's foot.

"Hang these guns!" Johnny swore, and quickly turned to secure the gag in the mouth of the offending second mate. "You make any more yaps like that an' I'll wing you for keeps with yore own gun!" he snapped. "We're caught in yore trap an' we'll fight to a finish. You'll be the first to go under if you gets any smart."

"Ahoy, men!" roared the captain in a towering rage, dancing frantically about on the deck and shouting for the crew to join him. He filled the air with picturesque profanity and stamped and yelled in passion at such rank mutiny.

"Hand grenades! Hand grenades!" he cried. Then he remembered that his two mates were also below and would share in the mutineers' fate, and his rage increased at his galling helplessness. When he had calmed sufficiently to think clearly he realized that it was certain death for any one to attempt going down the ladder, and that his must be a waiting game. He glanced at his crew, thirteen good men, all armed with windlass bars and belaying pins, and gave them orders. Two were to watch the hatch and break the first head to appear, while the others returned to work. Hunger and thirst would do the rest. And what joy would be his when they were forced to surrender!

Hopalong groped his way slowly towards the patch of light, barking his shins, stumbling and falling over the barrels and crates and finally, losing his footing at a critical moment, tumbled down upon a box marked "Cotton." There was a splintering crash and the very faint clink of metal. Dazed and bruised, he sat up and felt of himself-and found that he had lost his gun in the fall.

"Now, where in blazes did it fly to?" he muttered angrily, peering about anxiously. His eyes suddenly opened their widest and he stared in surprise at a field gun which covered him; and then he saw parts of two more.

"Good Lord! Is this a gunboat?" he cried. "Are we up against bluejackets an' Uncle Sam?" He glanced quickly back the way he had come when he heard Johnny's shot, but he could see nothing. He figured that Johnny had sense enough to call for help if he needed it, and put that possibility out of his mind. "Naw, this ain't no gunboat-the Government don't steal men; it enlists 'em. But it's a funny pile of junk, all the same. Where in blazes is that toy gun? *Well*, I'll be hanged!" and he plunged toward the "Cotton" box he had burst in his descent, and worked at it frantically.

"Winchesters! Winchesters!" he cried, dragging out two of them. "Whoop! Now for the cartridges-there shore must be some to go with these guns!" He saw a keg marked "Nails," and managed to open it after great labor-and found it full of army Colts. Forcing down the desire to turn a handspring, he slipped one of the six-shooters in his empty holster and patted it lovingly. "Old friend, I'm shore glad to see you, all right. You've been used, but that don't make no difference." Searching further, he opened a full box of *machetes*, and soon after found cartridges of many kinds and calibres. It took him but a few minutes to make his selection and cram his pockets with them. Then he filled two Colts and two Winchesters-and executed a short jig to work off the dangerous pressure of his exuberance.

"But what an unholy lot of weapons," he soliloquized on his way back to Johnny. "An' they're all second-hand. Cannons, too-an' *machetes*!" he exclaimed, suddenly understanding. "Jumping Jerusalem! —a filibustering expedition bound for Cuba, or one of them wildcat republics down south! Oh, ho, my friends; I see where you have bit off more'n you can chew." In his haste to impart the joyous news to his companion, he barked his shins shamefully.

" 'Way down south in the land o' cotton, cinnamon seed an" —whoa, blast you!" and Hopalong stuck his head through the opening in the partition and grinned. "Heard you shoot, Kid; I reckoned you might need me-an' these!" he finished, looking fondly upon the weapons as he shoved them into the forecastle.

Johnny groaned and held his stomach, but his eyes lighted up when he saw the guns, and he eagerly took one of each kind, a faint smile wreathing his lips. "Now we'll show these water snakes what kind of men they stole," he threatened.

Up on the deck the choleric captain still stamped and swore, and his crew, with well-concealed mirth, went about their various duties as if they were accustomed to have shanghaied men act this way. They sympathized with the unfortunate pair, realizing how they themselves would feel if shanghaied to break broncos.

Hogan, A. B., stated the feelings of his companions very well in his remarks to the men who worked alongside: "In me hear-rt I'm dommed glad av it, Yensen. I hope they bate the old man at his own game. 'T is a shame in these days for honest men to be took in that unlawful way. I've heard me father tell of the press gangs on the other side, an' 't is small business."

Yensen looked up to reply, chanced to glance aft, and dropped his calking iron in his astonishment. "Yumping Yimminy! Luk at dat fallar!"

Hogan looked. "The deuce! That's a man after me own heat-rt! Kape yore pagan mouth shut! If ye take a hand agin 'em I'll swab up the deck wid yez. G'wan wor-rking like a sane man, ye ijit!"

"Ay ent ban fight wit dat fallar! Luk at the gun!"

A man had climbed out of the after hatch and was walking rapidly towards them, a rifle in his hands, while at his thigh swung a Colt. He watched the two seamen closely and caught sight of Hogan's twinkling blue eyes, and a smile quivered about his mouth. Hogan shut and opened one eye and went on working.

As soon as Hopalong caught sight of the captain, the rifle went up and he announced his presence without loss of time. "Throw up yore hands, you pole-cat! I'm running this ranch from now on!"

The captain wheeled with a jerk and his mouth opened, and then clicked shut as he started forward, his rage acting galvanically. But he stopped quickly enough when he looked down the barrel of the Winchester and glared at the cool man behind it.

"What the blank are you doing?" he yelled.

"Well, I ain't kidnapping cow-punchers to steal my boat," replied Hopalong. "An' you fellers stand still or I'll drop you cold!" he ordered to the assembled and restless crew. "Johnny!" he shouted, and his companion popped up through the hatch like a jack-in-the-box. "Good boy, Johnny. Tie this coyote foreman like you did the others," he ordered. While Johnny obeyed, Hopalong looked around the circle, and his eyes rested on Hogan's face, studying it, and found something there which warmed his heart. "Friend, do you know the back trail? Can you find that runt of a town we left?"

"Aye, aye."

"Shore, you; who'd you think I was talking to? Can you find the way back, the way we came?"

"Shure an' I can that, if I'm made to."

"You'll swing for mutiny if you do, you bilge-wallering pirate!" roared the trussed captain. "Take that gun away from him, d'ye hear!" he yelled at the crew. "I'm captain of this ship, an' I'll hang every last one of you if you don't obey orders! This is mutiny!"

"You won't do no hanging with that load of weapons below!" retorted Hopalong. "Uncle Sam is looking for filibusters-this here gun is 'cotton,'" he said, grinning. He turned to the crew. "But you fellers are due to get shot if you sees her through," he added.

"I'm captain of this ship —" began the helpless autocrat.

"You shore look like it, all right," Hopalong replied, smiling. "If yo're the captain you order her turned around and headed over the back trail, or I'll drop you overboard off yore own ship!" Then fierce anger at the thought of the indignities and injuries he and his companion had suffered swept over him and prompted a one-minute speech which left no doubt as to what he would do if his demand was not complied with. Johnny, now free to watch the crew, added a word or two of endorsement, and he acted a little as if he rather hoped it would not be complied with: he itched for an excuse.

The captain did some quick thinking; the true situation could not be disguised, and with a final oath of rage he gave in. "'Bout ship, Hogan; nor' by nor'west," he growled, and the seaman started away to execute the command, but was quickly stopped by Hopalong.

"Hogan, is that right?" he demanded. "No funny business, or we'll clean up the whole bunch, an' blamed quick, too!"

"That's the course, sor. That's the way back to town. I can navigate, an' me orders are plain. Ye're Irish, by the way av ye, and 't is back to town ye go, sor!" He turned to the crew: "Stand by, me boys." And in a short time the course was nor' by nor'west.

The return journey was uneventful and at nightfall the ship lay at anchor off the low Texas coast, and a boat loaded with men grounded on the sandy beach. Four of them arose and leaped out into the mild surf and dragged the boat as high up on the sand as it would go. Then the two cow-punchers followed and one of them gave a low-spoken order to the Irishman at his side.

"Yes, sor," replied Hogan, and hastened to help the captain out onto the sand and to cut the ropes which bound him. "Do ye want the mates, too, sor?" he asked, glancing at the trussed men in the boat.

"No; the foreman's enough," Hopalong responded, handing his weapons to Johnny and turning to face the captain, who was looking into Johnny's gun as he rubbed his arms to restore perfect circulation.

"Now, you flat-faced coyote, yo're going to get the beating of yore life, an' I'm going to give it to you!" Hopalong cried, warily advancing upon the man whom he held to be responsible for the miseries of the past twenty-four hours. "You didn't give me a square deal, but I'm man enough to give you one! When you drug an' steal any more cow-punchers —" action stopped his words.

It was a great fight. A filibustering sea captain is no more peaceful than a wild boar and about as dangerous; and while this one was not at his best, neither was Hopalong. The latter luckily had acquired some knowledge of the rudiments of the game and had the vigor of youth to oppose to the captain's experience and his infuriated but well-timed rushes. The seamen, for the honor of their calling and perhaps with a mind to the future, cheered on the captain and danced up and down in their delight and excitement. They had a lot of respect for the prowess of their master, and for the man who could stand up against him in a fair and square fist fight. To give assistance to either in a fair fight was not to be thought of, and Johnny's gun was sufficient after-excuse for non-interference.

The *sop! sop!* of the punishing blows as they got home and the steady circling of Hopalong in avoiding the dangerous attacks, went on minute after minute. Slowly the captain's strength was giving out, and he resorted to trickery as his last chance. Retreating, he half raised his arms and lowered them as if weary, ready as a cat to strike with all his weight if the other gave an opening. It ought to have worked-it had worked before-but Hopalong was there to win, and without the momentary hesitation of the suspicious fighter he followed the retreat and his hard hand flashed in over the captain's guard a fraction of a second sooner than that surprised gentleman anticipated. The ferocious frown gave way to placid peace and the captain reclined at the feet of the battered victor, who stood waiting for him to get up and fight. The captain lay without a sign of movement and as Hopalong wondered, Hogan was the first to speak.

"Fer the love av hiven, let him be! Ye needn't wait-he's done; I know by the sound av it!" he exclaimed, stepping forward. "'T was a purty blow, an' 't was a gr-rand foight ye put up, sor! A gr-rand foight, but any more av that is murder! 'T is an Irishman's game, sor, an' ye did yersilf proud. But now let him be-no man, least av all a Dootchman, iver tuk more than that an' lived!"

Hopalong looked at him and slowly replied between swollen lips, "Yo're right, Hogan; we're square now, I reckon."

"That's right, sor," Hogan replied, and turned to his companions. "Put him in the boat; an' mind ye handle him gintly-we'll be sailing under him soon. Now, sor, if it's yer pleasure, I'll be after saying good-bye to ye, sor; an' to ye, too," he said, shaking hands with both punches. "Fer a sick la-ad ye're a wonder, ye are that," he smiled at Johnny, "but ye want to kape away from the water fronts. Good-bye to ye both, an' a pleasant journey home. The town is tin miles to me right, over beyant them hills."

"Good-bye, Hogan," mumbled Hopalong gratefully. "Yo're square all the way through; an' if you ever get out of a job or in any kind of trouble that I can help you out of, come up to the Bar-20 an' you won't have to ask twice. Good luck!" And the two sore and aching punchers, wiser in the ways of the world, plodded doggedly towards the town, ten miles away.

The next morning found them in the saddle, bound for Dent's hotel and store near the San Miguel Canyon. When they arrived at their destination and Johnny found there was some hours to wait for Red, his restlessness sent him roaming about the country, not so much "seeking what he might devour" as hoping something might seek to devour him. He was so sore over his recent kidnapping that he longed to find a salve. He faithfully promised Hopalong that he would return at noon.

Chapter III
Dick Martin Starts Something

Dick Martin slowly turned, leaned his back against the bar, and languidly regarded a group of Mexicans at the other end of the room. Singly, or in combinations of two or more, each was imparting all he knew, or thought he knew about the ghost of San Miguel Canyon. Their fellow-countryman, new to the locality, seemed properly impressed. That it was the ghost of

Carlos Martinez, murdered nearly one hundred years before at the big bend in the canyon, was conceded by all; but there was a dispute as to why it showed itself only on Friday nights, and why it was never seen by any but a Mexican. Never had a Gringo seen it. The Mexican stranger was appealed to: Did this not prove that the murder had been committed by a Mexican? The stranger affected to consider the question.

Martin surveyed them with outward impassiveness and inward contempt. A realist, a cynic, and an absolute genius with a Colt .45, he was well known along the border for his dare-devil exploits and reckless courage. The brainiest men in the Secret Service, Lewis, Thomas, Sayre, and even old Jim Lane, the local chief, whose fingers at El Paso felt every vibration along the Rio Grande, were not as well known-except to those who had seen the inside of Government penitentiaries-and they were quite satisfied to be so eclipsed. But the Service knew of the ghost, as it knew everything pertaining to the border, and gave it no serious thought; if it took interest in all the ghosts and superstitions peculiar to the Mexican temperament it would have no time for serious work. Martin once, in a spirit of savage denial, had wasted the better part of several successive Friday nights in the San Miguel, but to no avail. When told that the ghost showed itself only to Mexicans he had shrugged his shoulders eloquently and laughed, also eloquently.

"A Greaser," he replied, "is one-half fear and superstition, an' the other half imagination. There ain't no ghosts, but I know the *Greasers* have seen 'em, all right. A Greaser can see anything scary if he makes up his mind to. If *I* ever see one an' he keeps on being one after I shoot, I'll either believe in ghosts, or quit drinking." His eyes twinkled as he added: "An' of the two, I think I'd *prefer* to see ghosts!"

He was flushed and restless with deviltry. His fifth glass always made him so; and to-night there was an added stimulus. He believed the strange Mexican to be Juan Alvarez, who was so clever that the Government had never been able to convict him. Alvarez was fearless to recklessness and Martin, eager to test him, addressed the group with the blunt terseness for which he was famed, and hated.

"Greasers are cowards," he asserted quietly, and with a smile which invited excitement. He took a keen delight in analyzing the expressions on the faces of those hit. It was one of his favorite pastimes when feeling coltish.

The group was shocked into silence, quickly followed by great unrest and hot, muttered words. Martin did not move a muscle, the smile was set, but between the half-closed eyelids crouched Combat, on its toes. The Mexicans knew it was there without looking for it-the tone of his voice, the caressing purr of his words, and his unnatural languor were signs well known to them. Not a criminal sneaking back from voluntary banishment in Mexico who had seen those signs ever forgot them, if he lived. Martin watched the group cat-like, keenly scrutinizing each face, reading the changing emotions in every shifting expression; he had this art down so well that he could tell when a man was debating the pull of a gun, and beat him on the draw by a fraction of a second.

"De senor ees meestak," came the reply, as quiet and caressing as the words which provoked it. The strange Mexican was standing proudly and looking into the squinting eyes with only a grayness of face and a tigerish litheness to tell what he felt.

"None go through the canyon after dark on Fridays," purred Martin.

"*I* go tro' de canyon nex' Friday night. Eef I do, then you mak apology to me?"

"I'll limit my remark to all but one Greaser."

The Mexican stepped forward. "I tak' thees gloove an' leave eet at de Beeg Ben', for you to fin' in daylight," he said, tapping one of Martin's gauntlets which lay on the bar. "You geev' me eet befo' I go?"

"Yes; at nine o'clock to-morrow night," Martin replied, hiding his elation. He was sure that he knew the man now.

The Mexican, cool and smiling, bowed and left the room, his companions hastening after him.

"Well, I'll bet twenty-five dollars he flunks!" breathed the bartender, straightening up.

Martin turned languidly and smiled at him. "I'll take that, Charley," he replied.

Johnny Nelson was always late, and on this occasion he was later than usual. He was to have joined Hopalong and Red, if Red had arrived, at Dent's at noon the day before, and now it was after nine o'clock at night as he rode through San Felippe without pausing and struck east for the canyon. The dropping trail down the canyon was serious enough in broad daylight, but at night to attempt its passage was foolhardy, unless one knew every turn and slant by heart, which Johnny did not. He was thirty-three hours late now, and he was determined to make up what he could in the next three.

When Johnny left Hopalong at Dent's he had given his word to be back on time and not to keep his companions waiting, for Red might be on time and he would chafe if he were delayed. But, alas for Johnny's good intentions, his course took him through a small Mexican hamlet in which lived a senorita of remarkable beauty and rebellious eyes; and Johnny tarried in the town most of the day, riding up and down the streets, practising the nice things he would say if he met her. She watched him from the heavily draped window, and sighed as she wondered if her dashing Americano would storm the house and carry her off like the knights of old. Finally he had to turn away with heavy and reluctant heart, promising himself that he would return when no petulant and sarcastic companions were waiting for him. Then-ah! what dreams youth knows.

Half an hour ahead of him on another trail rode Juan, smiling with satisfaction. He had come to San Felippe to get a look at the canyon on Friday nights, and Martin had given him an excuse entirely unexpected. For this he was truly grateful, even while he knew that the American had tried to pick a quarrel with him and thus rid the border of a man entirely too clever for the good of customs receipts; and failing in that, had hoped the treacherous canyon trail would gain that end in another manner. Old Jim Lane's fingers touched wires not one whit more sensitive than those which had sent Juan Alvarez to look over the San Miguel-and Lane's wires had been slow this time. When Juan had left the saloon the night before and had seen Manuel slip away from the group and ride off into the north, he had known that the ghost would show itself the following night.

But Juan was to be disappointed. He was still some distance from the canyon when a snarling bulk landed on the haunches of his horse. He jerked loose his gun and fired twice and then knew nothing. When he opened his eyes he lay quietly, trying to figure it out with a head throbbing with pain from his fall. The cougar must have been desperate for food to attack a man. He moved his foot and struck something soft and heavy. His shots had been lucky, but they had not saved him his horse and a sprained arm and leg. There would be no gauntlet found at the Big Bend at daylight.

When Johnny Nelson reached the twin boulders marking the beginning of the sloping run where the trail pitched down, he grinned happily at sight of the moon rising over the low hills and then grabbed at his holster, while every hair in his head stood up curiously. A wild, haunting, feminine scream arose to a quavering soprano and sobbed away into silence. No words can adequately describe the unearthly wail in that cry and it took a full half-minute for Johnny to become himself again and to understand what it was. Once more it arose, nearer, and Johnny peered into the shadows along a rough backbone of rock, his Colt balanced in his half-raised hand.

"You come 'round me an' you'll get hurt," he muttered, straining his eyes to peer into the blackness of the shadows. "Come on out, Soft-foot; the moon's yore finish. You an' me will have it out right here an' now —I don't want no cougar trailing me through that ink-black canyon on a two-foot ledge —" he thought he saw a shadow glide across a dim patch of moonlight, but when his smoke rifted he knew he had missed. "Damn it! You've got a mate 'round here somewhere," he complained. "Well, I'll have to chance it, anyhow. Come on, bronc! Yo're shaking like a leaf-get out of this!"

When he began to descend into the canyon he allowed his horse to pick its own way without any guidance from him, and gave all of his attention to the trail behind him. The horse could get along better by itself in the dark, and it was more than possible that one or two lithe cougars might be slinking behind him on velvet paws. The horse scraped along gingerly, feeling its way step by step, and sending stones rattling and clattering down the precipice at his left to tinkle into the stream at the bottom.

"Gee, but I wish I'd not wasted so much time," muttered the rider uneasily. "This here canyon-cougar combination is the worst *I* ever butted up against. I'll never be late again, not never; not for all the girls in the world. Easy, bronc," he cautioned, as he felt the animal slip and quiver. "Won't this trail ever start going up again?" he growled petulantly, taking his eyes off the black back trail, where no amount of scrutiny showed him anything, and turned in the saddle to peer ahead-and a yell of surprise and fear burst from him, while chills ran up and down his spine. An unearthly, piercing shriek suddenly rang out and filled the canyon with ear-splitting uproar and a glowing, sheeted half-figure of a man floated and danced twenty feet from him and over the chasm. He jerked his gun and fired, but only once, for his mount had its own ideas about some things and this particular one easily headed the list. The startled rider grabbed reins and pommel, his blood congealed with fear of the precipice less than a foot from his side, and he gave all his attention to the horse. But scared as he was he heard, or thought that he heard, a peculiar sound when he fired, and he would have sworn that he hit the mark-the striking of the bullet was not drowned in the uproar and he would never forget the sound of that impact. He rounded Big Bend as if he were coming up to the judge's stand, and when he struck the upslant of the emerging trail he had made a record. Cold sweat beaded his forehead and he was trembling from head to foot when he again rode into the moonlight on the level plain, where he tried to break another record.

Chapter IV
Johnny Arrives

Meanwhile Hopalong and Red quarrelled petulantly and damned the erring Johnny with enthusiastic abandon, while Dent smiled at them and joked; but his efforts at levity made little impression on the irate pair. Red, true to his word, had turned up at the time set, in fact, he was half an hour ahead of time, for which miracle he endeavored to take great and disproportionate credit. Dent was secretly glad about the delay, for he found his place lonesome. He thoroughly enjoyed the company of the two gentlemen from the Bar-20, whose actions seemed to be governed by whims and who appeared to lack all regard for consequences; and they squabbled so refreshingly, and spent their money cheerfully. Now, if they would only wind up the day by fighting! Such a finish would be joy indeed. And speaking of fights, Dent was certain that Mr. Cassidy had been in one recently, for his face bore marks that could only be acquired in that way.

After supper the two guests had relapsed into a silence which endured only as long as the pleasing fulness. Then the squabbling began again, growing worse until they fell silent from lack of adequate expression. Finally Red once again spoke of their absent friend.

"We oughtn't get peevish, Hoppy-he's only thirty-six hours late," suggested Red. "An' he might be a week," he added thoughtfully, as his mind ran back over a long list of Johnny's misdeeds.

"Yes, he might. An' won't he have a fine cock-an'-bull tale to explain it," growled Hopalong, reminiscently. "His excuses are the worst part of it generally."

"Eh, does he-make excuses?" asked Dent, mildly surprised.

"He does to *us*," retorted Red savagely. "He's worse than a woman; take him all in all an' you've got the toughest proposition that ever wore pants. But he's a good feller, at that."

"Well, you've got a lot of nerve, you have!" retorted Hopalong. "You don't want to say anything about the Kid-if there's anybody that can beat him in being late an' acting the fool generally, it's you. An' what's more, you know it!"

Red wheeled to reply, but was interrupted by a sudden uproar outside, fluent swearing coming towards the house. The door opened with a bang, admitting a white-faced, big-eyed man with one leg jammed through the box he had landed on in dismounting.

"Gimme a drink, quick!" he shouted wildly, dragging the box over to the bar with a cheerful disregard for chairs and other temporary obstructions. "Gimme a drink!" he reiterated.

"Give you six hops in the neck!" yelled Red, missing and almost sitting down because of the enthusiasm he had put into his effort. Johnny side-stepped and ducked, and as he straightened up to ask for whys and wherefores, Red's eyes opened wide and he paused in his further intentions to stare at the apparition.

"Sick?" queried Hopalong, who was frightened.

"Gimme that drink!" demanded Johnny feverishly, and when he had it he leaned against the bar and mopped his face with a trembling hand.

"What's the matter with you, anyhow?" asked Red, with deep anxiety.

"Yes; for God's sake, what's happened to you?" demanded Hopalong.

Johnny breathed deeply and threw back his shoulders as if to shake off a weight. "Fellers, I had a cougar soft-footing after me in that dark canyon, my cayuse ran away on a two-foot ledge up the wall, —*an'*—*I*—*saw*—*a*—*ghost!*"

There was a respectful silence. Johnny, waiting a reasonable length of time for replies and exclamations, flushed a bit and repeated his frank and candid statement, adding a few adjectives to it. "*A real, screeching, flying ghost!* An' I'm going *home*, an' I'm going to *stay* there. I ain't never coming back no more, not for anything. Damn this border country, *anyhow!*"

The silence continued, whereupon Johnny grew properly indignant. "You act like I told you it was going to rain! Why don't you say something? Didn't you hear what I said, you fools!" he asked pugnaciously. "Are you in the habit of having a thing like that told you? Why don't you show some interest, you dod-blasted, thick-skulled wooden-heads?"

Red looked at Hopalong, Hopalong looked at Red, and then they both looked at Dent, whose eyes were fixed in a stare on Johnny.

"Huh!" snorted Hopalong, warily arising. "Was that all?" he asked, nodding at Red, who also arose and began to move cautiously toward their erring friend. "Didn't you see no more'n one ghost? Anybody that can see one ghost, an' no more, is wrong somewhere. Now, stop, an' think; didn't you see *two?*" He was advancing carefully while he talked, and Red was now behind the man who saw one ghost.

"Why, you—" there was a sudden flurry and Johnny's words were cut short in the melee.

"Good, Red! Ouch!" shouted Hopalong. "Look out! Got any rope, Dent? Well, hurry up: there ain't no telling what he'll do if he's loose. The mescal they sells down in this country ain't liquor-it's poison," he panted. "An' he can't even stand whiskey!"

Finding the rope was easier than finding a place to put it, and the unequal battle raged across the room and into the next, where it sounded as if the house were falling down. Johnny's voice was shrill and full of vexation and his words were extremely impolite and lacked censoring. His feet appeared to be numerous and growing rapidly, judging from the amount of territory they covered and defended, and Red joyfully kicked Hopalong in the melee, which in this instance also stands for stomach; Red always took great pains to do more than his share in a scrimmage. Dent hovered on the flanks, his hands full of rope, and begged with great earnestness to be allowed to apply it to parts of Johnny's thrashing anatomy. But as the flanks continued to change with bewildering swiftness he begged in vain, and began to make suggestions and give advice pleasing to the three combatants. Dent knew just how it should be done, and was generous with the knowledge until Johnny zealously planted five knuckles on his one good eye, when the engagement became general.

The table skidded through the door on one leg and caromed off the bar at a graceful angle, collecting three chairs and one sand-box cuspidor on the way. The box on Johnny's leg had long since departed, as Hopalong's shin could testify. One chair dissolved unity and distributed itself lavishly over the room, while the bed shrunk silently and folded itself on top of Dent, who bucked it up and down with burning zeal and finally had sense enough to crawl from under it. He immediately celebrated his liberation by getting a strangle hold on two legs, one of which happened to be the personal property of Hopalong Cassidy; and the battle raged on a lower plane. Red raised one hand as he carefully traced a neck to its own proper head and then his steel fingers opened and swooped down and shut off the dialect. Hopalong pushed Dent off him and managed to catch Johnny's flaying arm on the third attempt, while Dent made tentative sorties against Johnny's spurred boots.

"Phew! Can he fight like that when he's sober?" reverently asked Dent, seeing how close his fingers could come to his gaudy eye without touching it. "I won't be able to see at all in an hour," he added, gloomily.

Hopalong, seated on Johnny's chest, soberly made reply as he tenderly flirted with a raw shin. "It's the mescal. I'm going to slip some of that stuff into Pete's cayuse some of these days," he promised, happy with a new idea. Pete Wilson had no sense of humor.

"That ghost was plumb lucky," grunted Red, "an' so was the sea-captain," he finished as an afterthought, limping off toward the bar, slowly and painfully followed by his disfigured companions. "One drink; then to bed."

After Red had departed, Hopalong and Dent smoked a while and then, knocking the ashes out of his pipe, Hopalong arose. "An' yet, Dent, there are people that believe in ghosts," he remarked, with a vast and settled contempt.

Dent gave critical scrutiny to the scratched bar for a moment. "Well, the Greasers all say there *is* a ghost in the San Miguel, though I never saw it. But some of them have seen it, an' no Greasers ride that trail no more."

"Huh!" snorted Hopalong. "Some Greasers must have filled the Kid up on ghosts while he was filling hisself up on mescal. Ghosts? R-a-t-s!"

"It shows itself only to Greasers, an' then only on Friday nights," explained Dent, thoughtfully. This was Friday night. Others had seen that ghost, but they were all Mexicans; now that a "white" man of Johnny's undisputed calibre had been so honored Dent's skepticism wavered and he had something to think about for days to come. True, Johnny was not a Greaser; but even ghosts might make mistakes once in a while.

Hopalong laughed, dismissing the subject from his mind as being beneath further comment. "Well, we won't argue —I'm too tired. An' I'm sorry you got that eye, Dent."

"Oh, that's all right," hastily assured the store-keeper, smiling faintly. "I was just spoiling for a fight, an' now I've had it. Feels sort of good. Yes, first thing in the morning-breakfast'll be ready soon as you are. Good-night."

But the proprietor couldn't sleep. Finally he arose and tiptoed into the room where Johnny lay wrapped in the sleep of the exhausted. After cautious and critical inspection, which was made hard because of his damaged eye, he tiptoed back to his bunk, shaking his head slowly. "He wasn't drunk," he muttered. "He saw that ghost all right; an' I'll bet everything I've got on it!"

At daybreak three quarrelling punchers rode homeward and after a monotonous journey arrived at the bunk house and reported. It took them two nights adequately to describe their experiences to an envious audience. The morning after the telling of the ghost story things began to happen. Red starting it by erecting a sign.

NOTISE-NO GHOSTS ALOWED

An exuberant handful of the outfit watched him drive the last nail and step back to admire his work, and the running fire of comment covered all degrees of humor, and promised much hilarity in the future at the expense of the only man on the Bar-20 who had seen a ghost.

In a week Johnny and his acute vision had become a bye-word in that part of the country and his friends had made it a practice to stop him and gravely discuss spirit manifestations of all kinds. He had thrashed Wood Wright and been thrashed by Sandy Lucas in two beautiful and memorable fights and was only waiting to recover from the last affair before having the matter out with Rich Finn. These facts were beginning to have the effect he strove for; though Cowan still sold a new concoction of gin, brandy, and whiskey which he called "Flying Ghost," and which he proudly guaranteed would show more ghosts per drink than any liquor south of the Rio Grande-and some of his patrons were eager to back up his claims with real money.

This was the condition of affairs when Hopalong Cassidy strolled into Cowan's and forgot his thirst in the story being told by a strange Mexican. It was Johnny's ghost, without a doubt, and when he had carelessly asked a few questions he was convinced that Johnny had really seen something. On the way home he cogitated upon it and two points challenged his intelligence with renewed insistence: the ghost showed itself only on Friday, and then only to "Greasers." His suspicious mind would not rest until he had reviewed the question from all sides, and his opinion was that there was something more than spiritual about the ghost of the San Miguel-and a cold, practical reason for it.

When he rode into the corral at the ranch he saw that another sign had been put on the corral wall. He had destroyed the first, speaking his mind in full at the time. He swept his gloved hand upward with a rush, tore the flimsy board from its fastenings, broke it to pieces across his saddle, and tossed the fragments from him. He was angry, for he had warned the outfit that they were carrying the joke too far, that Johnny was giving way to hysterical rage more frequently, and might easily do something that they all would regret. And he felt sorry for the Kid; he knew what Johnny's feelings were and he made up his mind to start a few fights himself if the persecution did not cease. When he stepped into the bunk house and faced his friends they listened to a three-minute speech that made them squirm, and as he finished talking the deep voice of the foreman endorsed the promises he had just heard made, for Buck had entered the gallery without being noticed. The joke had come to an end.

When Johnny rode in that evening he was surprised to find Hopalong waiting for him a short distance from the corral and he replied to his friend's gesture by riding over to him. "What's up now?" he asked.

"Come along with me. I want to talk to you for a few minutes," and Hopalong led the way toward the open, followed by Johnny, who was more or less suspicious. Finally Hopalong stopped, turned, and looked his companion squarely in the eyes. "Kid, I'm in dead earnest. This ain't no fool joke-now you tell me what that ghost looked like, how he acted, an' all about it. I mean what I say, because now I know that you saw *something*. If it wasn't a ghost it was made to look like one, anyhow. Now go ahead."

"I've told you a dozen times already," retorted Johnny, his face flushing. "I've begged you to believe me an' told you that I wasn't fooling. How do I know you ain't now? I'm not going to tell —"

"Hold on; yes, you are. Yo're going to tell it slow, an' just like you saw it," Hopalong interrupted hastily. "I know I've doubted it, but who wouldn't! Wait a minute —I've done a heap of thinking in the past few days an' I know that you saw a ghost. Now, everybody knows that there ain't no such thing as ghosts; then what was it you saw? There's a game on, Kid, an' it's a dandy; an' you an' me are going to bust it up an' get the laugh on the whole blasted crowd, from Buck to Cowan."

Johnny's suspicions left him with a rush, for his old Hoppy was one man in a thousand, and when he spoke like that, with such sharp decision, Johnny knew what it meant. Hopalong listened intently and when the short account was finished he put out his hand and smiled.

"We're the fools, Kid; not you. There's something crooked going on in that canyon, an' I know it! But keep mum about what we think."

Johnny lost his grouch so suddenly and beamed upon his friends with such a superior air that they began to worry about what was in the wind. The suspense wore on them, for with Hopalong's assistance, Johnny might spring some game on them all that would more than pay up for the fun they had enjoyed at his expense; and the longer the suspense lasted the worse it became. They never lost sight of him while he was around and Hopalong had to endure the same surveillance; and it was no uncommon thing to see small groups of the anxious men engaged in deep discussion. When they found that Buck must have been told and noticed his smile was as fixed as Hopalong's or Johnny's, they were certain that trouble of some nature was in store for them.

Several weeks later Buck Peters drew rein and waited for a stranger to join him.

"Howdy. Is yore name Peters?" asked the newcomer, sizing him up in one trained glance.

"Well, who are you, an' what do you want?"

"I want to see Peters, Buck Peters. That yore name?"

"Yes; what of it?"

"My name's Fox. Old Jim Lane gave me a message for you," and the stranger spoke earnestly to some length. "There; that's the situation. We've got to have shrewd men that they don't know an' won't suspect. Lane wants to pay a couple of yore men their wages for a month or two. He said he was shore he could count on you to help him out."

"He's right; he can. I don't forget favors. I've got a couple of men that-there's one of 'em now. Hey, Hoppy! Whoop-e, Hoppy!"

Mr. Cassidy arrived quickly, listened eagerly, named Red and Johnny to accompany him, overruled his companions by insisting that if Johnny didn't go the whole thing was off, carried his point, and galloped off to find the lucky two, his eyes gleaming with anticipation and joy. Fox laughed, thanked the foreman, and rode on his way north; and that night three cow-punchers rode south, all strangely elated. And the friends who watched them go heaved signs of relief, for the reprisals evidently were to be postponed for a while.

Chapter V
The Ghost of the San Miguel

Juan Alvarez had not been in San Felippe since Dick Martin left, which meant for over a month. Martin was down the river looking for a man who did not wish to be found; and some said that Martin cared nothing about international boundaries when he wanted any one real bad. And there was that geologist who wore blue glasses and was always puttering around in the canyon and hammering chips of rock off the steep walls; he must have slipped one noon, because his body was found on a flat boulder at the edge of the stream. Manuel had found it and wanted to be paid for his trouble in bringing it to town-but Manuel was a fool. Who, indeed, would pay good money for a dead Gringo, especially after he was dead? And there were three cow-punchers holding a herd of 6-X cattle up north, an hour or so from the town. They wanted to buy steers from Senor Rodriguez, but said that he was a robber and threatened to cut his ears off. Cannot a man name his own price? These cow-punchers liked to get drunk and gallop through San Felippe, shooting like crazy men. They got drunk one Friday night and went shouting and singing to the Big Bend in the canyon to see the flying ghost, and they called it names and fired off their pistols and sang loudly; and for a week they insulted all the Mexicans in town by calling them liars and cowards. Was it the fault of any one that the ghost would show itself only to Mexicans? Oh, these Gringos-might the good God punish them for their sins!

Thus the peons complained to the padre while they kept one eye open for the advent of the rowdy cow-punchers, who always wanted to drink, and then to fight with some one, either with fists or pistols. Why should any one fight with them, especially with such things as fists?

"Let them fight among themselves. What have you to do with heretics?" reproved the good padre, who ostracized himself from the pleasant parts of the wide world that he might make easier the life and struggles of his ignorant flock. "God is not hasty-He will punish in His own way when it best suits Him. And perhaps you will profit much if you are more regular to mass instead of wasting the cool hours of the morning in bed. Think well of what I have said, my children."

But the cow-punchers were not punished and they swore they would not leave the vicinity until they had all the steers they wanted, and at their own price. And one night their herd stampeded and was checked only in time to save it from going over the canyon's edge. And for some reason Sanchez kept out of the padre's way and did not go to confess when he should, for the padre spoke plainly and set hard obligations for penance.

The cow-punchers swore that it had been done by some Mexican and said that they would come to town some day soon and kill three Mexicans unless the guilty one was found and brought to them. Then the padre mounted his donkey and went out to them to argue and they finally told him they would wait for two weeks. But the padre was too smart for them-he sent a messenger to find Senor Dick Martin, and in one week Senor Martin came to town. There was no fight. The Gringo rowdies were cowards at heart and Martin could not shoot them down in cold blood, and he could not arrest them, because he was not a policeman or even a sheriff, but only a revenue officer, which was a most foolish law. But he watched them all the time and wanted them to fight-there was no more shooting or drunkenness in town. Nobody wanted to fight Senor Martin, for he was a great man. He even went so far as to talk with them about it and wave his arms, but they were as frightened at him as little children might be.

So the Mexicans gossiped and exulted, some of the bolder of them even swaggering out to the Gringo camp; but Martin drove them back again, saying he would not allow them to bully men who could not retaliate, which was right and fair. Then, afraid to go away and leave the mad cow-punchers so close to town, he ordered them to drive their herd farther east, nearer to Dent's store, and never to return to San Felippe unless they needed the padre; and they obeyed him after a long talk. After seeing them settled in their new camp, which was on Monday morning, Martin returned to San Felippe and told the padre where he could be found and then rode away again. San Felippe celebrated for a whole day and two Mexican babies were christened after Senor Dick Martin, which was honor all around.

Friday, when Manuel went over to spy upon the cow-punchers in their new camp, he found them so drunk that they could not stand, and before he crept away at dusk two of them were sleeping like gorged snakes and the third was firing off his revolver at random, which diversion had not a little to do with Manuel's departure.

When Manuel crept away he headed straight for a crevice near the wall of the canyon at the Big Bend and, reaching it, looked all around and then dropped into it. Not long thereafter another Mexican appeared, this one from San Felippe, and also disappeared into the crevice. As darkness fell Manuel reappeared with something under his jacket and a moment later a light gleamed at the base of a slender sapling which grew on the edge of the canyon wall and leaned out over the abyss. It was cleverly placed, for only at one spot on the Mexican side of the distant Rio Grande could it be seen-the high canyon walls farther down screened it from any one who might be riding on the north bank of the river. In a moment there came an answering twinkle and Manuel, covering the lantern with a blanket, was swallowed up in the darkness of the crevice.

Without a trace of emotion, Dick Martin, from his place of concealment, caught the answering gleam, and he watched Manuel disappear. "Cassidy was right in every point; Lewis or Sayre couldn't 'a' done this better. I hope he won't be late," he muttered, and settled himself more comfortably to wait for the cue for action, smiling as the moon poked its rim over the low hills to his right. "This means promotion for me, or I've very much mistaken," he chuckled.

Hopalong was not late and as soon as it was dark he and his companions stole into the canyon on foot. They felt their way down the east end of the trail, not far from Dent's, toward the Big Bend, which they gained without a mishap. Johnny was sent up to a place they had noticed and marked in their memories at the time they had rioted down to defy the ghost. He was to stop any one trying to escape up the San Felippe end of the canyon trail, and his confidence in his ability to do this was exuberant. Hopalong and Red slowly and laboriously worked their way down the perilous path leading to the bottom, forded the stream, and crept up the other side, where they found cover not far from a wide crack in the canyon wall. Upon the occasion of their hilarious visit to the Big Bend they had observed that a faint trail led to the crack and had cogitated deeply upon this fact.

Three hours passed before the watchers in and above the canyon were rewarded by anything further; and then a light flickered far down the canyon and close to the edge of the stream. Immediately strange noises were heard and suddenly the ghost swung out of the opening in the rock wall near Hopalong and Red and danced above their heads, while the shrieking which had so frightened Johnny and his horse filled the canyon with uproar and sent Martin wriggling nearer to the crevice which he had watched so closely. The noise soon ceased, but the ghost danced on, and the sound of men stumbling along the rocky ledge bordering the stream became more and more audible. Four were in the party and they all carried bulky loads on their backs and grunted with pleasure and relief as they entered the entrance in the wall. When the last man had disappeared and the noise of their passing had died out, Johnny's rope sailed up and out, and the ghost swayed violently and then began to sag in an unaccountable manner towards the trail as the owner of the rope hitched its free end around a spur of rock and made it fast. Then he feverishly scrambled down the steep path to join his friends.

Hopalong and Red, wriggling on their stomachs towards the crack in the wall, paused in amazement and stared across the canyon; and then the former chuckled and whispered something in his companion's ear. "That was why he lugged his rope along! He's just idiot enough to want a souveneer an' plaything at the risk of losing the game. Come on! —they'll tumble to what's up an' get away if we don't hustle."

When the two punchers cautiously and noiselessly entered the crack and felt their way along its rock walls they heard fluent swearing in Spanish by the man who worked the ghost, and who could not understand its sudden ambition to take root. It was made painfully clear to him a moment later when a pair of brawny hands reached out of the darkness behind him and encircled his throat a hand's width below his gleaming cigarette. Another pair used cords with deftness and despatch and he was left by himself to browse upon the gag when all his senses returned.

Hopalong, with Red inconsiderately stepping on his heels, felt his way along the wall of the crevice, alert and silent, his Colt nestling comfortably in his right hand, while the left was pushed out ahead feeling for trouble. As they worked farther away from the canyon distant voices could be heard and they forthwith proceeded even more cautiously. When Hopalong came to the second bend in the narrow passage he peered around it and stopped so abruptly that Red's nose almost spread itself over the back of his head. Red's indignation was all the harder to bear because it must bloom unheard.

In a huge, irregular room, whose roof could not be discerned in the dim light of the few candles, five men were resting in various attitudes of ease as they discussed the events of the night and tried to compute their profits. They were secure, for Manuel, having by this time put away the ghost and megaphone, was on duty at the mouth of the crevice, and he was as sensitive to danger as a hound.

"The risk is not much and the profits are large," remarked Pedro, in Spanish. "We must burn a candle for the repose of the soul of Carlos Martinez. It is he that made our plans safe. And a candle is not much when we —"

"Hands up!" said a quiet voice, followed by grim commands. The Mexicans jumped as if stung by a scorpion, and could just discern two of the rowdy gringo cow-punchers in the heavy shadows of the opposite wall, but the candle light glinted in rings on the muzzles of their six-shooters. Had Manuel betrayed them? But they had little time or inclination for cogitation regarding Manuel.

"Easy there!" shouted Red, and Pedro's hand stopped when half way to his chest. Pedro was a gambler by nature, but the odds were too heavy and he sullenly obeyed the command.

"Stick 'em up! Stick 'em up! Higher yet, an' hold 'em there," purred a soft voice from the other end of the room, where Dick Martin smiled pleasantly upon them and wondered if there was anything on earth harder to pound good common sense into than a "Greaser's" head. His gun was blue, but it was, nevertheless, the most prominent part of his make-up, even if the light was poor.

One of the Mexicans reached involuntarily for his gun, for he was a gun-man by training; while his companions felt for their knives, deadly weapons in a melee. Martin, crying, "Watch 'em, Cassidy!" side-stepped and lunged forward with the speed and skill of a boxer, and his hard left hand landed on the point of Juan Alvarez' jaw with a force and precision not to be withstood. But to make more certain that the Mexican would not take part in any possible demonstration of resistance, Martin's right circled up in a short half-hook and stopped against Juan's short ribs. Martin weighed one hundred and eighty pounds and packed no fat on his well-knit frame.

At this moment a two-legged cyclone burst upon the scene in the person of Johnny Nelson, whose rage had been worked up almost to the weeping point because he had lost so much time hunting for the crevice where it was not. Seeing Juan fall, and the glint of knives, he started in to clean things up, yelling, "I'm a ghost! I'm a ghost! Take 'em alive! Take 'em alive!"

Hopalong and Red felt that they were in his way, and taking care of one Mexican between them, while Martin knocked out another, they watched the exits, —for anything was possible in such a chaotic mix-up, —and gave Johnny plenty of room. The latter paused, triumphant, looked around to see if he had missed any, and then advanced upon his friends and shoved his jaw up close to Hopalong's face. "Tried to lose me, didn't you! Wouldn't wait for me! For seven cents an' a toothbrush I'd give you what's left!"

Red grabbed him by trousers and collar and heaved him into the passageway. "Go out an' play with yore souveneer or we'll step on you!"

Johnny sat up, rubbed certain portions of his anatomy, and grinned. "Oh, I've got it, all right! I'm shore going to take that ghost home an' make some of them fools *eat* it!"

Martin smiled as he finished tying the last prisoner. "That's right, Nelson; you've got it on 'em this time. Make 'em chew it."

Chapter VI
Hopalong Loses a Horse

For a month after their return from the San Miguel, Hopalong and his companions worked with renewed zest, and told and retold the other members of the outfit of their unusual experiences near the Mexican border. Word had come up to them that Martin had secured the conviction of the smugglers and was in line for immediate advancement. No one on the range had the heart to meet Johnny Nelson, for Johnny carried with him a piece of the ghost, and became pugnacious if his once-jeering friends and acquaintances refused to nibble on it. Cowan still sold his remarkable drink, but he had yielded to Johnny's persuasive methods and now called it "Nelson's Pet."

One bright day the outfit started rounding up a small herd of three-year-olds, which Buck had sold, and by the end of the week the herd was complete and ready for the drive. This took two weeks and when Hopalong led his drive outfit through Hoyt's Corners on its homeward journey he felt the pull of the town of Grant, some miles distant, and it was too strong to be resisted. Flinging a word of explanation to the nearest puncher, he turned to lope away, when Red's voice checked him. Red wanted to delay his home-coming for a day or two and attend to a purely personal matter at a ranch lying to the west. Hopalong, knowing the reason for Red's wish, grinned and told him to go, and not to propose until he had thought the matter over very carefully. Red's reply was characteristic, and after arranging a rendezvous and naming the time, the two separated and rode toward their destinations, while the rest of the outfit kept on towards their ranch.

"A man owes something to *all* his friends," Hopalong mused. In this case he owed a return game of draw poker to certain of Grant's leading citizens, and he liked to pay his obligations when opportunity offered.

It was mid-afternoon when he topped a rise and saw below him the handful of shacks making up the town. A look of pleased interest flickered across his face as he noticed a patched and dirty tent pitched close up to the nearest shack. "Show!" he exclaimed. "Now, ain't that luck! I'll shore take it in. If it's a circus, mebby it has a trick mule to ride —I'll never forget that one up in Kansas City," he grinned. But almost instantly a doubt arose and tempered the grin. "Huh! Mebby it's the branding chute of some gospel sharp." As he drew near he focussed his eyes on the canvas and found that his fears were justified.

"All Are Welcome," he spelled out slowly. "Shore they are!" he muttered. "I never nowhere saw such hard-working, all-embracing rustlers as them fellers. They'll stick their iron on anything from a wobbly calf or dying dogie to a staggering-with-age mosshead, an' shout 'tally one' with the same joy. Well, not for mine, *this* trip. I'm going to graze loose an' buck-jump all I wants. Anyhow, if I did let him brand me I'd only backslide in a week," and Hopalong pressed his pony to a more rapid gait as two men emerged from the tent. "There's the sky-pilot now," he muttered —"an' there's Dave!" he shouted, waving his arm. "Oh, Dave! Dave!"

Dave Wilkes looked up, and his grin of delight threatened to engulf his ears. "Hullo, Cassidy! Glad to see you! Keep right on for the store —I'll be with you in a minute." When David told his companion the visitor's name the evangelist held up his hand eloquently and spoke.

"I know all about him!" he exclaimed sorrowfully. "If I can lead him out of his wickedness I will rest content though I save no more souls this fortnight. Is it all true?"

"Huh! What true?"

"All that I have heard about him."

"Well, I dunno what you've heard," replied Dave, with grave caution, "but I reckon it might be if it didn't cover lying, stealing, cowardice, an' such coyote traits. He's shore a holy terror with a short gun, all right, but lemme tell you something mebby you *ain't* heard: There ain't a square man in this part of the country that won't feel some honored an' proud to be called a friend of Hopalong Cassidy. Them's the sentiments rampaging hereabouts. I ain't denying that he's gone an' killed off a lot of men first an' last-but the only trouble there is that he didn't get 'em soon enough. They all had lived too blamed long when they went an' stacked up agin him an' that lightning short gun of hissn. But, say, if yo're calculating to tackle him at yore game, lead him gentle-don't push none. He comes to life real sudden when he's shoved. So long; see you later, mebby."

The revivalist looked after him and mused, "I hope I was informed wrong, but this much I have to be thankful for: The wickedness of most of these men, these over-grown children, is manly, stalwart, and open; few of them are vicious or contemptible. Their one great curse is drink."

When Hopalong entered the store he was vociferously welcomed by two men, and the proprietor joining them, the circle was complete. When the conversation threatened to repeat itself cards were brought and the next two hours passed very rapidly. They were expensive hours to the Bar-20 puncher, who finally arose with an apologetic grin and slapped his thigh significantly.

"Well, you've got it all; I'm busted wide open, except for a measly dollar, an' I shore hopes you don't want that," he laughed. "You play a whole lot better than you did the last time I was here. I've got to move along. I'm going east an' see Wallace an' from there I've got to meet Red an' ride home with him. But you come an' see us when you can-it's *me* that wants revenge this time."

"Huh; you'll be wanting it worse than ever if we do," smiled Dave.

"Say, Hoppy," advised Tom Lawrence, "better drop in an' hear the sky-pilot's palaver before you go. It'll do you a whole lot of good, an' it can't do you no harm, anyhow."

"You going?" asked Hopalong suspiciously.

"Can't —got too much work to do," quickly responded Tom, his brother Art nodding happy confirmation.

"Huh; I reckoned so!" snorted Hopalong sarcastically, as he shook hands all around. "You all know where to find us-drop in an' see us when you get down our way," he invited.

"Sorry you can't stay longer, Cassidy," remarked Dave, as his friend mounted. "But come up again soon-an' be shore to tell all the boys we was asking for 'em," he called.

Considering the speed with which Hopalong started for Wallace's, he might have been expecting a relay of "quarter" horses to keep it going, but he pulled up short at the tent. Such inconsistency is trying to the temper of the best-mannered horse, and this particular animal was not in the least good-mannered, wherefore its rider was obliged to soothe its resentment in his own peculiar way, listening meanwhile to the loud and impassioned voice of the evangelist haranguing his small audience.

"I wonder," said Hopalong, glancing through the door, "if them friends of mine reckon I'm any ascared to go in that tent? Huh, I'll just show 'em anyhow!" whereupon he dismounted, flung the reins over his horse's head, and strode through the doorway.

The nearest seat, a bench made by placing a bottom board of the evangelist's wagon across two up-ended boxes, was close enough to the exhorter and he dropped into it and glanced carelessly at his nearest neighbor. The carelessness went out of his bearing as his eyes fastened themselves in a stare on the man's neck-kerchief. Hopalong was hardened to awful sights and at his best was not an artistic soul, but the villainous riot of fiery crimson, gaudy yellow, and pugnacious and domineering green which flaunted defiance and insolence from the stranger's neck caused his breath to hang over one count and then come double strong at the next exhalation. "Gee whiz!" he whispered.

The stranger slowly turned his head and looked coldly upon the impudent disturber of his reverent reflections. "Meaning?" he questioned, with an upward slant in his voice. The neck-kerchief seemed to grow suddenly malignant and about to spring. "Meaning?" repeated the other with great insolence, while his eyes looked a challenge.

While Hopalong's eyes left the scrambled color-insult and tried to banish the horrible after-image, his mind groped for the rules of etiquette governing free fist fights in gospel tents, and while he hesitated as to whether he should dent the classic profile of the color-bearer or just twist his nose as a sign of displeasure, the voice of the evangelist arose to a roar and thundered out. Hopalong ducked instinctively.

" —Stop! Stop before it is too late, before death takes you in the wallow of your sins! Repent and gain salvation —"

Hopalong felt relieved, but his face retained its expression of childlike innocence even after he realized that he was not being personally addressed; and he glanced around. It took him ninety-seven seconds to see everything there was to be seen, and his eyes were drawn irresistibly back to the stranger's kerchief. "Awful! Awful thing for a drinking man to wear, or run up against unexpectedly!" he muttered, blinking. "Worse than snakes," he added thoughtfully.

"Look ahere, you —" began the owner of the offensive decoration, if it might be called such, but the evangelist drowned his voice in another flight of eloquence.

" —*Peace*! *Peace* is the message of the Lord to His children," roared the voice from the upturned soap box, and when the speaker turned and looked in the direction of the two men-with-a-difference he found them sitting up very straight and apparently drinking in his words with great relish; whereupon he felt that he was making gratifying progress toward the salvation of their spotted souls. He was very glad, indeed, that he had been so grievously misinformed about the personal attributes of one Hopalong Cassidy, —glad and thankful.

"Death cometh as a thief in the night," the voice went on. "Think of the friends who have gone before; who were well one minute and gone the next! And it must come to all of us, to all of us, to me and to you —"

The man with the afflicted neck started rocking the bench.

"Something is coming to somebody purty soon," murmured Hopalong. He began to sidle over towards his neighbor, his near hand doubled up into a huge knot of protuberant knuckles and white-streaked fingers; but as he was about to deliver his hint that he was greatly displeased at the antics of the bench, a sob came to his ears. Turning his head swiftly, he caught sight of the stranger's face, and sorrow was marked so strongly upon it that the sight made Hopalong gape. His hand opened slowly and he cautiously sidled back again, disgruntled, puzzled, and vexed at himself for having strayed into a game where he was so hopelessly at sea. He thought it all over carefully and then gave it up as being too deep for him to solve. But he determined one thing: He was not going to leave before the other man did, anyhow.

"An' if I catch that howling kerchief outside," he muttered, smacking his lips with satisfaction at what was in store for it. His visit to Wallace was not very important, anyway, and it could wait on more important events.

"There sits a sinner!" thundered out the exhorter, and Hopalong looked stealthily around for a sight of a villain. "God only has the right to punish. 'Vengeance is mine,' saith the Lord, and whosoever takes the law into his own hands, whosoever takes human life, defies the Creator. There sits a man who has killed his fellow-men, his brothers! Are you not a sinner, *Cassidy*?"

Cassidy jumped clear of the bench as he jerked his head around and stared over the suddenly outstretched arm and pointing finger of the speaker and into his accusing eyes.

"Answer me! Are you not a sinner?"

Hopalong stood up, confused, bewildered, and then his suspended thoughts stirred and formed. "Guilty, I reckon, an' in the first degree. But they didn't get no more'n what was coming to 'em, no more'n they earned. An' that's straight!"

"How do you know they didn't? How do you know they earned it? How do you *know*?" demanded the evangelist, who was delighted with the chance to argue with a sinner. He had great faith in "personal contact," and his was the assurance of training, of the man well rehearsed and fully prepared. And he knew that if he should be pinned into a corner by logic and asked for *his* proofs, that he could squirm out easily and take the offensive again by appealing to faith, the last word in sophistry, and a greater and more powerful weapon than intelligence. *This* was his game, and it was fixed; he could not lose if he could arouse enough interest in a man to hold him to the end of the argument. He continued to drive, to crowd. "What right have you to think so? What right have you to judge them? Have you divine insight? Are you inspired? 'Judge not lest ye be judged,' saith the Lord, and you *dare* to fly in the face of that great command!"

"You've got me picking the pea in *this* game, all right," responded Hopalong, dropping back on the bench. "But lemme tell you one thing; Command or no command, devine or not devine, I know when a man has lived too long, an' when he's going to try to get me. An' all the gospel sharps south of heaven can't stop me from handing a thief what he's earned. Go on with the show, but count me out."

While the evangelist warmed to the attack, vaguely realizing that he had made a mistake in not heeding Dave Wilkes' tip, Hopalong became conscious of a sense of relief stealing over him and he looked around wonderingly for the cause. The man with the kerchief had "folded his tents" and departed; and Hopalong, heaving a sigh of satisfaction, settled himself more comfortably and gave real attention to the discourse, although he did not reply to the warm and eloquent man on the soap box. Suddenly he sat up with a start as he remembered that he had a long and hard ride before him if he wished to see Wallace, and arising, strode towards the exit, his chest up and his chin thrust out. The only reply he made to the excited and personal remarks of the revivalist was to stop at the door and drop his last dollar into the yeast box before passing out.

For a moment he stood still and pondered, his head too full of what he had heard to notice that anything out of the ordinary had happened. Although the evangelist had adopted the wrong method he had gained more than he knew and Hopalong had something to take home with him and wrestle out for himself in spare moments; that is, he would have had but for one thing: As he slowly looked around for his horse he came to himself with a sharp jerk, and hot profanity routed the germ of religion incubating in his soul. His horse was missing! Here was a pretty mess, he thought savagely; and then his expression of anger and perplexity gave way to a flickering grin as the probable solution came to his mind.

"By the Lord, I never saw such a bunch to play jokes," he laughed. "Won't they never grow up? They was watching me when I went inside an' sneaked up and rustled my cayuse. Well, I'll get back again without much trouble, all right. They ought to know me better by this time."

"Hey, stranger!" he called to a man who was riding past, "have you seen anything of a skinny roan cayuse fifteen han's high, white stocking on the near foreleg, an' a bandage on the off fetlock, Bar-20 being the brand?"

The stranger, knowing the grinning inquisitor by sight, suspected that a joke was being played: he also knew Dave Wilkes and that gentleman's friends. He chuckled and determined to help it along a little. "Shore did, pardner; saw a man leading him real cautious. Was he yourn?"

"Oh, no; not at all. He belonged to my great-great-grandfather, who left him to my second cousin. You see, I borrowed it," he grinned, making his way leisurely towards the general store, kept by his friend Dave, the joker. "Funny how everybody likes a joke," he muttered, opening the door of the store. "Hey, Dave," he called.

Mr. Wilkes wheeled suddenly and stared. "Why, I thought you was half-way to Wallace's by now!" he exclaimed. "Did you come back to lose that lone dollar?"

"Oh, I lost that too. But yo're a real smart cuss, now ain't you?" queried Hopalong, his eyes twinkling and his face wreathed with good humor. "An' how innocent you act, too. Thought you could scare me, didn't you? Thought I'd go tearing 'round this fool town like a house afire, hey? Well, I reckon you can guess again. Now, I'm owning up that the joke's on me, so you hand over my cayuse, an' I'll make up for lost time."

Dave Wilkes' face expressed several things, but surprise was dominant. "Why, I ain't even seen yore ol' cayuse, you chump! Last time I saw it you was on him, going like the devil. Did somebody pull you off it an' take it away from you?" he demanded with great sarcasm. "Is somebody abusing you?"

Hopalong bit into a generous handful of dried apricots, chewed complacently for a moment, and replied: "'At's aw right; I want my cayuse." Swallowing hastily, he continued: "I want it, an' I've come to the right place for it, too. Hand it over, David."

"Dod blast it, I tell you I ain't got it!" retorted Dave, beginning to suspect that something was radically wrong. "I ain't seen it, an' I don't know nothing about it."

Hopalong wiped his mouth with his sleeve. "Well, then, Tom or Art does, all right."

"No, they don't, neither; I watched 'em leave an' they rode straight out of town, an' went the other way, same as they allus do." Dave was getting irritated. "Look here, you; are you joking or drunk, or both, or is that animule of yourn really missing?"

"Huh!" snorted Hopalong, trying some new prunes. "Ese prunes er purty good," he mumbled, in grave congratulation. "I don' get prunes like 'ese very of'n."

"I reckon you don't! They ought to be good! Cost me thirty cents a half-pound," Dave retorted with asperity, anxiously shifting his feet. It didn't take much of a loss to wipe out a day's profits with him.

"An' I don't reckon you paid none too much for 'em, at that," Mr. Cassidy responded, nodding his head in comprehension. "Ain't no worms in 'em, is there?"

"Shore there is!" exploded Dave. "Plumb full of 'em!"

"You don't say! Hardly know whether to take a chance with the worms or try the apricots. Ain't no worms in them, anyhow. But when am I going to get my cayuse? I've got a long way to go, an' delay is costly-how much did you say these yaller fellers cost?" he asked significantly, trying another handful of apricots.

"On the dead level, cross my heart an' hope to die, but I ain't seen yore cayuse since you left here," earnestly replied Dave. "If you don't know where it is, then somebody went an' lifted it. It looks like it's up to you to do some hunting, 'stead of cultivating a belly-ache at *my* expense. *I* ain't trying to keep you, God knows!"

Hopalong glanced out of the window as he considered, and saw, entering the saloon, the same puncher who had confessed to seeing his horse. "Hey Dave; wait a minute!" and he dashed out of the store and made good time towards the liquid refreshment parlor. Dave promptly nailed the covers on the boxes of prunes and apricots and leaned innocently against the cracker box to await results, thinking hard all the while. It looked like a plain case of horse-stealing to him.

"Stranger," cried Hopalong, bouncing into the bar-room, "where did you see that cayuse of mine?"

"The ancient relic of yore family was aheading towards Hoyt's Corners," the stranger replied, grinning broadly. "It's a long walk. Have something before you starts?"

"Damn the walk! Who was riding him?"

"Nobody at all."

"What do you mean?"

"He wasn't being rid when I saw him."

"Hang it, man; that cayuse was stole from me!"

"Somewhat in the nature of a calamity, now ain't it?" smiled the stranger, enjoying his contributions to the success of the joke.

"You bet yore life it is!" shouted Hopalong, growing red and then pale. "You tell me who was leading him, understand?"

"Well, I couldn't see his face, honest I couldn't," replied the stranger. "Every time I tried it I was shore blinded by the most awful an' horrible neck-kerchief I've ever had the hard luck to lay my eyes on. Of all the drunks I ever met, them there colors was-Hey! Wait a minute!" he shouted at Hopalong's back.

"Dave, gimme yore cayuse an' a rifle-quick!" cried Hopalong from the middle of the street as he ran towards the store. "Hypocrite son-of-a-hoss-thief went an' run mine off. Might 'a' knowed nobody but a thief could wear such a kerchief!"

"I'm with you!" shouted Dave, leading the way on the run towards the corral in the rear of his store.

"No, you ain't with me, neither!" replied Hopalong, deftly saddling. "This ain't no plain hoss-thief case-it's a private grudge. See you later, mebby," and he was pacing a cloud of dust towards the outskirts of the town.

Dave looked after him. "Well, that feller has shore got a big start on you, but he can't keep ahead of that Doll of mine for very long. She can out-run anything in these parts. 'Sides, Cassidy's cayuse looked sort of done up, while mine's as fresh as a bird. That thief will get what's coming to him, all right."

Chapter VII
Mr. Cassidy Cogitates

While Hopalong tried to find his horse, Ben Ferris pushed forward, circling steadily to the east and away from the direction of Hoyt's corners, which was as much a menace to his health and happiness as the town of Grant, twenty miles to his rear. If he could have been certain that no danger was nearer to him than these two towns, he would have felt vastly relieved, even if his horse was not fresh. During the last hour he had not urged it as hard as he had in the beginning of his flight and it had dropped to a walk for minutes at a stretch. This was not because he felt that he had plenty of time, but for the reason that he understood horses and could not afford to exhaust his mount so early in the chase. He glanced back from time to time as if fearing what might be on his trail, and well he might fear. According to all the traditions and customs of the range, both of which he knew well, somewhere between him and Grant was a posse of hard-riding cow-punchers, all anxious and eager for a glance at him over their sights. In his mind's eye he could see them, silent, grim, tenacious, reeling off the miles on that distance-eating lope. He had stolen a horse, and that meant death if they caught him. He loosened his gaudy kerchief and gulped in fear, not of what pursued, but of what was miles before him. His own saddle, strapped behind the one he sat in, bumped against him with each reach of the horse and had already made his back sore-but he must endure it for a time. Never in all his life had minutes been so precious.

Another hour passed and the horse seemed to be doing well, much better than he had hoped-he would rest it for a few minutes at the next water while he drank his fill and changed the bumping saddle. As he rounded a turn and entered a heavily grassed valley he saw a stream close at hand and, leaping off, fixed the saddle first. As he knelt to drink he caught a movement and jumped up to catch his mount. Time after time he almost touched it, but it evaded him and kept up the game, cropping a mouthful of grass during each respite.

"All right!" he muttered as he let it eat. "I'll get my drink while you eat an' then I'll get you!"

He knelt by the stream again and drank long and deep. As he paused for breath something made him leap up and to one side, reaching for his Colt at the same instant. His fingers found only leather and he swore fiercely as he remembered-he had sold the Colt for food and kept the rifle for defence. As he faced the rear a horseman rounded the turn and the fugitive, wheeling, dashed for the stolen horse forty yards away, where his rifle lay in its saddle sheath. But an angry command and the sharp hum of a bullet fired in front of him checked his flight and he stopped short and swore.

"I reckon the jig's up," remarked Mr. Cassidy, balancing the up-raised Colt with nicety and indifference.

"Yea; I reckon so," sullenly replied the other, tears running into his eyes.

"Well, I'm damned!" snorted Hopalong with cutting contempt. "Crying like a li'l baby! Got nerve enough to steal my cayuse, an' then go an' beller like a lost calf when I catch you. Yo're a fine specimen of a hoss-thief, I don't think!"

"Yo're a liar!" retorted the other, clenching his fists and growing red.

Mr. Cassidy's mouth opened and then clicked shut as his Colt swung down. But he did not shoot; something inside of him held his trigger finger and he swore instead. The idea of a man stealing his horse, being caught red-handed and unarmed, and still possessed of sufficient courage to call his captor a name never tolerated or overlooked in that country! And the idea that he, Hopalong Cassidy, of the Bar-20, could not shoot such a thief! "Damn that sky pilot! He's shore gone an' made me loco," he muttered, savagely, and then addressed his prisoner. "Oh, you ain't crying? Wind got in yore eyes, I reckon, an' sort of made 'em leak a little-that it? Or mebby them unholy green roses an' yaller grass on that blasted fool neck-kerchief of yourn are too much for *your* eyes, too!"

"Look ahere!" snapped the man on the ground, stepping forward, one fist upraised. "I came nigh onto licking you this noon in that gospel sharp's tent for making fun of that scarf, an' I'll do it yet if you get any smart about it! You mind yore own business an' close yore fool eyes if you don't like my clothes!"

"Say! You ain't no cry-baby after all. Hanged if I even think yo're a real genuine hoss-thief!" enthused Mr. Cassidy. "You act like a twin brother; but what the devil ever made you steal that cayuse, anyhow?"

"An' that's none of yore business, neither; but I'll tell you, just the same," replied the thief. "I had to have it; that's why. I'll fight you rough-an'-tumble to see if I keep it, or if you take the cayuse an' shoot me besides: is it a go?"

Hopalong stared at him and then a grin struggled for life, got it, and spread slowly over his tanned countenance. "Yore gall is refreshing! Damned if it ain't worse than the scarf. Here, you tell me what made you take a chance like stealing a cayuse this noon —I'm getting to like you, bad as you are, hanged if I ain't!"

"Oh, what's the use?" demanded the other, tears again coming into his eyes. "You'll think I'm lying an' trying to crawl out-an' I won't do neither."

"*I* didn't say *you* was a liar," replied Hopalong. "It was the other way about. Reckon you can try me, anyhow; can't you?"

"Yes; I s'pose so," responded the other, slowly, and in a milder tone of voice. "An' when I called you that I was mad and desperate. I was hasty-you see, my wife's dying, or dead, over in Winchester. I was riding hard to get to her before it was too late when my cayuse stepped into a hole just the other side of Grant-you know what happened. I shot the animal, stripped off my saddle an' hoofed it to town, an' dropped into that gospel dealer's layout to see if he could make me feel any better-which he could not. I just couldn't stand his palaver about death an' slipped out. I was going to lay for you an' lick you for the way you acted about this scarf-had to do something or go loco. But when I got outside there was yore cayuse, all saddled an' ready to go. I just up an' threw my saddle on it, followed suit with myself an' was ten miles out of town before I realized just what I'd done. But the realizing part of it didn't make no difference to me —I'd 'a' done it just the same if I had stopped to think it over. That's flat, an' straight. I've got to get to that li'l woman as quick as I can, an' I'd steal all the cayuses in the whole damned country if they'd do me any good. That's all of it-take it or leave it. I put it up to you. That's yore cayuse, but you ain't going to get it without fighting me for it! If you shoot me down without giving me a chance, all right! I'll cut a throat for that wore-out bronc!"

Hopalong was buried in thought and came to himself just in time to cover the other and stop him not six feet away. "Just a minute, before you make me shoot you! I want to think about it."

"Damn that gun!" swore the fugitive, nervously shifting his feet and preparing to spring. "We'd 'a' been fighting by this time if it wasn't for that!"

"You stand still or I'll blow you apart," retorted Hopalong, grimly. "A man's got a right to think, ain't he? An' if I had somebody here to mind these guns so you couldn't sneak 'em on me I'd fight you so blamed quick that you'd be licked before you knew you was at it. But we ain't going to fight —*stand still*! You ain't got no show at all when yo're dead!"

"Then you gimme that cayuse-my God, man! Do you know the hell I've been through for the last two days? Got the word up at Daly's Crossing an' ain't slept since. I'll go loco if the strain lasts much longer! She asking for me, begging to see me: an' me, like a damned idiot, wasting time out here talking to another. Ride with me, behind me-it's only forty miles more-tie me to the saddle an' blow me to pieces if you find I'm lying-do anything you wants; but let me get to Winchester before dark!"

Hopalong was watching him closely and at the end of the other's outburst threw back his head. "I reckon I'm a plain fool, a jackass; but I don't care. I'll rope that cayuse for you. You come along to save time," Hopalong ordered, spurring forward. His borrowed rope sailed out, tightened, and in a moment he was working at the saddle. "Here, you; I'm going to swamp mounts with you-this one is fresher an' faster." He had his own saddle off and the other on in record time, and stepped back. "There; don't stand there like a fool-wake up an' hustle! I might change my mind-that's the way to move! Gimme that neck-kerchief for a souveneer, an' get out. Send that cayuse back to Dave Wilkes, at Grant-it's hissn. Don't thank me; just gimme that scarf an' ride like the devil."

The other, already mounted, tore the kerchief from his throat and handed it quickly to his benefactor. "If you ever want a man to take you out of hell, send to Winchester for Ben Ferris-that's me. So long!"

Mr. Cassidy sat on his saddle where he had dropped it after making the exchange and looked after the galloping horseman, and when a distant rise had shut him from sight, turned his eyes on the scarf in his hand and cogitated. Finally, with a long-drawn sigh he arose, and, placing the scarf on the ground, caught and saddled his horse. Riding gloomily back to where the riot of color fluttered on the grass he drew his Colt and sent six bullets through it with a great amount of satisfaction. Not content with the damage he had inflicted, he leaned over and swooped it up. Riding further he also swooped up a stone and tied the kerchief around it, and then stood up in his stirrups and drew back his arm with critical judgment. He sat quietly for a time after the gaudy missile had disappeared into the stream and then, wheeling, cantered away. But he did not return to the town of Grant-he lacked the nerve to face Dave Wilkes and tell his childish and improbable story. He would ride on and meet Red as they had agreed; a letter would do for Mr. Wilkes, and after he had broken the shock in that manner he could pay him a personal visit sometime soon. Dave would never believe the story and when it was told Hopalong wanted to have the value of the horse in his trousers pocket. Of course, Ben Ferris *might* have told the truth and he might return the horse according to directions. Hopalong emerged from his reverie long enough to appeal to his mount:

"Bronc, I've been thinking: am I or am I not a jackass?"

Chapter VIII
Red Brings Trouble

After a night spent on the plain and a cigarette for his breakfast, Hopalong, grouchy and hungry, rode slowly to the place appointed for his meeting with Red, but Mr. Connors was over two hours late. It was now mid-forenoon and Hopalong occupied his time for a while by riding out fancy designs on the sand; but he soon tired of this makeshift diversion and grew petulant. Red's tardiness was all the worse because the erring party to the agreement had turned in his saddle at Hoyt's Corners and loosed a flippant and entirely uncalled-for remark about his friend's ideas regarding appointments.

"Well, that red-headed Romeo is shore late this time," Hopalong muttered. "Why don't he find a girl closer to home, anyhow? Thank the Lord I ain't got no use for shell games of any kind. Here I am, without anything to eat an' no prospects of anything, sitting up on this locoed layout like a sore thumb, an' can't move without hitting myself! An' it'll be late to-day before I can get any grub, too. Oh, well," he sighed, "I ain't in love, so things might be a whole lot worse with me. An' he ain't in love, neither, only he won't listen to reason. He gets mad an' calls me a sage hen an' says I'm stuck on myself because some fool told me I had brains."

He laughed as he pictured the object of his friend's affections. "Huh; anybody that got one good, square look at her wouldn't ever accuse him of having brains. But he'll forget her in a month. That was the life of his last hobbling fit an' it was the worst he ever had."

Grinning at his friend's peculiarly human characteristics he leaned back in the saddle and felt for tobacco and papers. As he finished pouring the chopped alfalfa into the paper he glanced up and saw a mounted man top the sky-line of the distant hills and shoot down the slope at full speed.

"I knowed it: started three hours late an' now he's trying to make it up in the last mile," Hopalong muttered, dexterously spreading the tobacco along the groove and quickly rolling the cigarette. Lighting it he looked up again and saw that the horseman was wildly waving a sombrero.

"Huh! Wigwagging for forgiveness," laughed the man who waited. "Old son-of-a-gun, I'd wait a week if I had some grub, an' he knows it. Couldn't get mad at him if I tried."

Mr. Connors' antics now became frantic and he shouted something at the top of his voice. His friend spurred his mount. "Come on, bronc; wake up. His girl said 'yes' an' now he wants me to get him out of his trouble." Whereupon he jogged forward. "What's that?" he shouted, sitting up very straight. "What's that?"

Red energetically swept the sombrero behind him and pointed to the rear. "War-whoops! W-a-r w-h-o-o-p-s! Injuns, you chump!" Mr. Connors appeared to be mildly exasperated.

"Yes?" sarcastically rejoined Mr. Cassidy in his throat, and then shouted in reply: "Love an' liquor don't mix very well in you. Wake up! Come out of it!"

"That's straight —I mean it!" cried Mr. Connors, close enough now to save the remainder of his lungs. "It's a bunch of young bucks on their first war-trail, I reckon. 'T ain't Geronimo, all right; I wouldn't be here now if it was. Three of 'em chased me an' the two that are left are coming hot-foot somewhere the other side of them hills. They act sort of mad, too."

"Mebby they ain't acting at all," cheerily replied his companion. "An' then that's the way you got that graze?" pointing to a bloody furrow on Mr. Connors' cheek. "But just the same it looks like the trail left by a woman's finger nail."

"Finger nail nothing," retorted Mr. Connors, flushing a little. "But, for God's sake, are you going to sit here like a wart on a dead dog an' wait for 'em?" he demanded with a rising inflection. "Do you reckon yo're running a dance, or a party, or something like that?"

"How many?" placidly inquired Mr. Cassidy, gazing intently towards the high sky-line of the distant hills.

"Two-an' I won't tell you again, neither!" snapped the owner of the furrowed cheek. "The others are 'way behind now-but we're standing *still!*"

"Why didn't you say there was others?" reproved Hopalong. "Naturally I didn't see no use of getting all het up just because two sprouted papooses feel like crowding us a bit; it wouldn't be none of *our* funeral, would it?" and the indignant Mr. Cassidy hurriedly dismounted and hid his horse in a nearby chaparral and returned to his companion at a run.

"Red, gimme yore Winchester an' then hustle on for a ways, have an accident, fall off yore cayuse, an' act scared to death, if you know how. It's that little trick Buck told us about, an' it shore ought to work fine here. We'll see if two infant feather-dusters can lick the Bar-20. Get a-going!"

They traded rifles, Hopalong taking the repeater in place of the single-shot gun he carried, and Red departed as bidden, his face gradually breaking into an enthusiastic grin as he ruminated upon the plan. "Level-headed old cuss; he's a wonder when it comes to planning or fighting. An' lucky, —well, I reckon!"

Hopalong ran forward for a short distance and slid down the steep bank of a narrow arroyo and waited, the repeater thrust out through the dense fringe of grass and shrubs which bordered the edge. When settled to his complete satisfaction and certain that he was effectually screened from the sight of any one in front of him, he arose on his toes and looked around for his companion, and laughed. Mr. Connors was bending very dejectedly apparently over his prostrate horse, but in reality was swearing heartily at the ignorant quadruped because it strove with might and main to get its master's foot off its head so it could arise. The man in the arroyo turned again and watched the hills and it was not long before he saw two Indians burst into view over the crest and gallop towards his friend. They were not to be blamed because they did not know the pursued had joined a friend, for the second trail was yet some distance in front of them.

"Pair of budding warriors, all right; an' awful important. Somebody must 'a' told *them* they had brains," Mr. Cassidy muttered. "They're just at the age when they knows it all an' have to go 'round raising hell all the time. Wonder when they jumped the reservation."

The Indians, seeing Mr. Connors arguing with his prostrate horse, and taking it for granted that he was not stopping for pleasure or to view the scenery, let out a yell and dashed ahead at grater speed, at the same time separating so as to encircle him and attack him front and rear at the same time. They had a great amount of respect for cowboys.

This manoeuvre was entirely unexpected and clashed violently with Mr. Cassidy's plan of procedure, so two irate punchers swore heartily at their rank stupidity in not counting on it. Of course everybody that knew anything at all about such warfare knew that they would do just such a thing, which made it all the more bitter. But Red had cultivated the habit of thinking quickly and he saw at once that the remedy lay with him; he astonished the exultant savages by straddling his disgruntled horse as it scrambled to its feet and galloping away from them, bearing slightly to the south, because he wished to lure his pursuers to ride closer to his anxious and eager friend.

This action was a success, for the yelling warriors, slowing perceptibly because of their natural astonishment at the resurrection and speed of an animal regarded as dead or useless, spurred on again, drawing closer together, and along the chord of the arc made by Mr. Connors' trail. Evidently the fool white man was either crazy or had original and startling ideas about the way to rest a horse when hard pressed, which pleased them much, since he had lost so much time. The pleasures of the war-trail would be vastly greater if all white men had similar ideas.

Hopalong, the light of fighting burning strong in his eyes, watched them sweep nearer and nearer, splendid examples of their type and seeming to be a part of their mounts. Then two shots rang out in quick succession and a cloud of pungent smoke arose lazily from the edge of the arroyo as the warriors fell from their mounts not sixty yards from the hidden marksman.

Mr. Connors' rifle spat fire once to make assurance doubly sure and he hastily rejoined his friend as that person climbed out of the arroyo.

"Huh! They must have been half-breeds!" snorted Red in great disgust, watching his friend shed sand from his clothes. "I allus opined that 'Paches was too blamed slick to bite on a game like that."

"Well, they are purty 'lusive animals, 'Paches; but there are exceptions," replied Hopalong, smiling at the success of their scheme. "Them two ain't 'Paches-they're the exceptions. But let me tell you that's a good game, just the same. It is as long as they don't see the second trail in time. Didn't Buck and Skinny get two that way?"

"Yes, I reckon so. But what'll we do now? What's the next play?" asked Red, hurriedly, his eyes searching the sky-line of the hills. "The rest of the coyotes will be here purty soon, an' they'll be madder than ever now. An' you better gimme back that gun, too."

"Take yore old gun-who wants the blamed thing, anyhow?" Hopalong demanded, throwing the weapon at his friend as he ran to bring up the hidden horse. When he returned he grinned pleasantly. "Why, we'll go on like we was greased for calamity, that's what we'll do. Did you reckon we was going to play leap-frog around here an' wait for the rest of them paint-shops, like a blamed fool pair of idiots?"

"I didn't know what *you* might do, remembering how you acted when I met you," retorted Red, shifting his cartridge belt so the empty loops were behind and out of the way. "But I shore knowed what we ought to do, all right."

"Well, mebby you also know how many's headed this way; do you?"

"You've got me stumped there; but there's a round dozen, anyway," Red replied. "You see, the three that chased me were out scouting ahead of the main bunch; an' I didn't have no time to take no blasted census."

"Then we've got to hit the home trail, an' hit it hard. Wind up that four-laigged excuse of yourn, an' take my dust," Hopalong responded, leading the way. "If we can get home there'll be a lot of disgusted braves hitting the high spots on the back trail trying to find a way out. Buck an' the rest of the boys will be a whole lot pleased, too. We can muster thirty men in two hours if we gets to Buckskin, an' that's twenty more than we'll need."

"Tell you one thing, Hoppy; we can get as far as Powers' old ranch house, an' that's shore," replied Red, thoughtfully.

"Yes!" exploded his companion in scorn and pity. "That old sieve of a shack ain't good enough for *me* to die in, no matter what you think about it. Why, it's as full of holes as a stiff hat in a melee. Yo're on the wrong trail; think again."

Mr. Cassidy objected not because he believed that Powers' old ranch house was unworthy of serious consideration as a place of refuge and defence, but for the reason that he wished to reach Buckskin so his friends might all get in on the treat. Times were very dull on the ranch, and this was an occasion far too precious to let slip by. Besides, he then would have the pleasure of leading his friends against the enemy and battling on even terms. If he sought shelter he and Red would have to fight on the defensive, which was a game he hated cordially because it put him in a relatively subordinate position and thereby hurt his pride.

"Let me tell you that it's a whole lot better than thin air with a hard-working circle around us-an' you know what that means," retorted Mr. Connors. "But if you don't want to take a chance in the shack, why mebby we can make Wallace's, or the Cross-O-Cross. That is, if we don't get turned out of our way."

"We don't head for no Cross-O-Cross or Wallace's," rejoined his friend with emphasis, "an' we won't waste no time in Powers' shack, neither; we'll push right through as hard as we can go for Buckskin. Let them fellers find their own hunting-our outfit comes first. An' besides that'll mean a detour in a country fine for ambushes. We'd never get through."

"Well, have it yore own way, then!" snapped Red. "You allus was a hard-headed old mule, anyhow." In his heart Red knew that Hopalong was right about Wallace's and the Cross-O-Cross.

Some time after the two punchers had quitted the scene of their trap, several Apaches loped up, read the story of the tragedy at a glance, and galloped on in pursuit. They had left the reservation a fortnight before under the able leadership of that veteran of many war-trails — Black Bear. Their leader, chafing at inaction and sick of the monotony of reservation life, had yielded to the entreaties of a score of restless young men and slipped away at their head, eager for the joys of raiding and plundering. But instead of stealing horses and murdering isolated whites as they had expected, they met with heavy repulses and were now without the mind of their leader. They had fled from one defeat to another and twice had barely eluded the cavalry which pursued them. Now two more of their dwindling force were dead and another had been found but an hour before. Rage and ferocity seethed in each savage heart and they determined to get the puncher they had chased, and that other whose trail they now saw for the first time. They would place at least one victory against the string of their defeats, and at any cost. Whips rose and fell and the war-party shot forward in a compact group, two scouts thrown ahead to feel the way.

Red and Hopalong rode on rejoicing, for there were three less Apaches loose in the Southwest for the inhabitants to swear about and fear, and there was an excellent chance of more to follow. The Southwest had no toleration for the Government's policy of dealing with Indians and derived a great amount of satisfaction every time an Apache was killed. It still clung to the time-honored belief that the only good Indian was a dead one. Mr. Cassidy voiced his elation and then rubbed an empty stomach in vain regret, —when a bullet shrilled past his head, so unexpectedly as to cause him to duck instinctively and then glance apologetically at his red-haired friend; and both spurred their mounts to greater speed. Next Mr. Connors grabbed frantically at his perforated sombrero and grew petulant and loquacious.

"Both them shots was lucky, Hoppy; the feller that fired at me did it on the dead run; but that won't help us none if one of 'em connects with us. You gimme that Sharps-got to show 'em that they're taking big chances crowding us this way." He took the heavy rifle and turned in the saddle. "It's an even thousand, if it's a yard. He don't look very big, can't hardly tell him from his cayuse; an' the wind's puffy. Why don't you dirty or rust this gun? The sun glitters all along the barrel. Well, here goes."

"Missed by a mile," reproved Hopalong, who would have been stunned by such a thing as a hit under the circumstances, even if his good-shooting friend had made it.

"Yes! Missed the coyote I aimed for, but I got the cayuse of his off pardner; see it?"

"Talk about luck!"

"That's all right: it takes blamed good shooting to miss that close in this case. Look! It's slowed 'em up a bit, an' that's about all I hoped to do. Bet they think I'm a real, shore-'nuff medicine-man. Now gimme another cartridge."

"I will not; no use wasting lead at this range. We'll need all the cartridges we got before we get out of this hole. You can't do nothing without stopping-an' that takes time."

"Then I'll stop! The blazes with the time! Gimme another, d'ye hear?"

Mr. Cassidy heard, complied, and stopped beside his companion, who was very intent upon the matter at hand. It took some figuring to make a hit when the range was so great and the sun so blinding and the wind so capricious. He lowered the rifle and peered through the smoke at the confusion he had caused by dropping the nearest warrior. He was said to be the best rifle shot in the Southwest, which means a great deal, and his enemies did not deny it. But since the Sharps shot a special cartridge and was reliable up to the limit of its sight gauge, a matter of eighteen hundred yards, he did not regard the hit as anything worthy of especial mention. Not so his friend, who grinned joyously and loosed his admiration.

"Yo're a shore wonder with that gun, Red! Why don't you lose that repeater an' get a gun like mine? Lord, if I could use a rifle like you, I wouldn't have that gun of yourn for a gift. Just look at what you did with it! Please get one like it."

"I'm plumb satisfied with the repeater," replied Red. "I don't miss very often at eight hundred with it, an' that's long enough range for most anybody. An' if I do miss, I can send another that won't, an' right on the tail of the first, too."

"Ah, the devil! You make me disgusted with yore fool talk about that carbine!" snapped his companion, and the subject was dropped.

The merits of their respective rifles had always been a bone of contention between them and one well chewed, at that. Red was very well satisfied with his Winchester, and he was a good judge.

"You did stop 'em a little," asserted Mr. Cassidy some time later when he looked back. "You stopped 'em coming straight, but they're spreading out to work up around us. Now, if we had good cayuses instead of these wooden wonders, we could run away from 'em dead easy, draw their best mounted warriors to the front an' then close with 'em. Good thing their cayuses are well tired out, for as it is we've got to make a stand purty soon. Gee! They don't like you, Red; they're calling you names in the sign language. Just look at 'em cuss you!"

"How much water have you got?" inquired his friend with anxiety.

"Canteen plumb full. How're you fixed?"

"I got the same, less one drink. That gives us enough for a couple of days with some to spare, if we're careful," Mr. Connors replied. New Mexican canteens are built on generous lines and are known as life-preservers.

"Look at that glory-hunter go!" exclaimed Red, watching a brave who was riding half a mile to their right and rapidly coming abreast of them. "Wonder how he got over there without us seeing him."

"Here; stop him!" suggested Hopalong, holding out his Sharps. "We can't let him get ahead of us and lay in ambush-that's what he's playing to do."

"My gun's good, and better, for me, at this range; but you know, I can't hit a jack-rabbit going over rough country as fast as that feller is," replied his companion, standing up in his stirrups and firing.

"Huh! Never touched him! But he's edging off a-plenty. See him cuss you. What's he calling you, anyhow?"

"Aw, shut up! How the devil do *I* know? I don't talk with my arms."

"Are you superstitious, Red?"

"No! Shut up!"

"Well, I am. See that feller over there? If he gets in front of us it's a shore sign that somebody's going to get hurt. He'll have plenty of time to get cover an' pick us off as we come up."

"Don't you worry-his cayuse is deader'n ours. They must 'a' been pushing on purty hard the last few days. See it stumble? —what'd I tell you!"

"Yes; but they're gaining on us slow but shore. We've got to make a stand purty soon-how much further do you reckon that infernal shack is, anyhow?" Hopalong asked sharply.

"'T ain't fur off-see it any minute now."

"Here," remarked Hopalong, holding out his rifle, "stencil yore mark on his hide; catch him just as he strikes the top of that little rise."

"Ain't got time-that shack can't be much further."

And it wasn't, for as they galloped over a rise they saw, half a mile ahead of them, an adobe building in poor state of preservation. It was Powers' old ranch house, and as they neared it, they saw that there was no doubt about the holes.

"Told you it was a sieve," grunted Hopalong, swinging in on the tail of his companion. "Not worth a hang for anything," he added bitterly.

"It'll answer, all right," retorted Red grimly.

Chapter IX
Mr. Holden Drops In

Mr. Cassidy dismounted and viewed the building with open disgust, walking around it to see what held it up, and when he finally realized that it was self-supporting his astonishment was profound. Undoubtedly there were shacks in the United States in worse condition, but he hoped their number was small. Of course he knew that the building was small. Of course he knew that the building would make a very good place of defence, but for the sake of argument he called to his companion and urged that they be satisfied with what defence they could extemporize in the open. Mr. Connors hotly and hastily dissented as he led the horses into the building, and straightway the subject was arbitrated with much feeling and snappy eloquence. Finally Hopalong thought that Red was a chump, and said so out loud, whereat Red said unpleasant things about his good friend's pedigree, attributes, intelligence, et al., even going so far as to prognosticate his friend's place of eternal abode. The remarks were fast getting to be somewhat personal in tenor when a whine in the air swept up the scale to a vicious shriek as it passed between them, dropped rapidly to a whine again and quickly died out in the distance, a flat report coming to their ears a few seconds later. Invisible bees seemed to be winging through the air, the angry and venomous droning becoming more pronounced each passing moment, and the irregular cracking of rifles grew louder rapidly. An angry *s-p-a-t!* told of where a stone behind them had launched the ricochet which hurled skyward with a wheezing scream. A handful of 'dobe dust sprang from the corner of the building and sifted down upon them, causing Red to cough.

"That ricochet was a Sharps!" exclaimed Hopalong, and they lost no time in getting into the building, where the discussion was renewed as they prepared for the final struggle. Red grunted his cheerful approval, for now he was out of the blazing sun and where he could better appreciate the musical tones of the flying bullets; but his companion, slamming shut the door and propping it with a fallen roof-beam, grumbled and finally gave rein to his rancor by sneering at the Winchester.

"It shore gets me that after all I have said about that gun you will tote it around with you and force yoreself into a suicide's grave," quoth Mr. Cassidy, with exuberant pugnacity. "I ain't in no way objecting to the suicide part of it, but I can't see that it's at all fair to drag *me* onto the edge of everlasting eternity with you. If you ain't got no regard for yore own life you shore ought to think a little about yore friend's. Now you'll waste all yore cartridges an' then come snooping around me to borrow my gun. Why don't you lose the damned thing?"

"What I pack ain't none of yore business, which same I'll uphold," retorted Mr. Connors, at last able to make himself heard. "You get over on yore own side an' use yore Colt; I've wondered a whole lot where you ever got the sense to use a Colt —*I* wouldn't be a heap surprised to see you toting a pearl-handled .22, like the kids use. Now you 'tend to yore grave-yard aspirants, an' lemme do the same with mine."

"The Lord knows I've stood a whole lot from you because you just can't help being foolish, but I've got plumb weary and sick of it. It stops right here or you won't get no 'Paches," snorted Hopalong, peering intently through a hole in the shack. The more they squabbled the better they liked it, —controversies had become so common that they were merely a habit; and they served to take the grimness out of desperate situations.

"Aw, you can't lick one side of me," averred Red loftily. "You never did stop anybody that was anything," he jeered as he fired from his window. "Why, you couldn't even hit the bottom of the Grand Canyon if you leaned over the edge."

"You could, if you leaned too far, you red-headed wart of a half-breed," snapped Hopalong. "But how about the Joneses, Tarantula Charley, Slim Travennes, an' all the rest? How about them, hey?"

"Huh! You couldn't 'a' got any of 'em if they had been sober," and Mr. Connors shook so with mirth that the Indian at whom he had fired got away with a whole skin and cheerfully derided the marksman. "That 'Pache shore reckons it was you shooting at him, I missed him so far. Now, you shut up — I want to get some so we can go home. I don't want to stay out here all night an' the next day as well," Red grumbled, his words dying slowly in his throat as he voiced other thoughts.

Hopalong caught sight of an Apache who moved cautiously through a chaparral lying about nine hundred yards away. As long as the distant enemy lay quietly he could not be discerned, but he was not content with assured safety and took a chance. Hopalong raised his rifle to his shoulder as the Indian fired and the latter's bullet, striking the edge of the hole through which Mr. Cassidy peered, kicked up a generous handful of dust, some of which found lodgment in that individual's eyes.

"Oh! Oh! Oh! Wow!" yelled the unfortunate, dancing blindly around the room in rage and pain, and dropping his rifle to grab at his eyes. "Oh! Oh! Oh!"

His companion wheeled like a flash and grabbed him as he stumbled past. "Are you plugged bad, Hoppy? Where did they get you? Are you hit bad?" and Red's heart was in his voice.

"No, I ain't plugged bad!" mimicked Hopalong. "I ain't plugged at all!" he blazed, kicking enthusiastically at his solicitous friend. "Get me some water, you jackass! Don't stand there like a fool! I ain't going to fall down. Don't you know my eyes are full of 'dobe?"

Red, avoiding another kick, hastily complied, and as hastily left Mr. Cassidy to wash out the dirt while he returned to his post by the window. "Anybody'd think you was full of red-eye, the way you act," muttered Red peevishly.

Hopalong, rubbing his eyes of the dirt, went back to the hole in the wall and looked out. "Hey, Red! Come over here an' spill that brave's conceit. I can't keep my eyes open long enough to aim, an' it's a nice shot, too. It'd serve him right if you got him!"

Mr. Connors obeyed the summons and peered out cautiously. "I can't see him, nohow; where is the coyote?"

"Over there in that little chaparral; see him now? *There!* See him moving. Do you mean to tell me —"

"Yep; I see him, all right. You watch," was the reply. "He's just over nine hundred-where's yore Sharps?" He took the weapon, glanced at the Buffington sight, which he found to be set right, and aimed carefully.

Hopalong blinked through another hole as his friend fired and saw the Indian flop down and crawl aimlessly about on hands and knees. "What's he doing now, Red?"

"Playing marbles, you chump; an' here goes for his agate," replied the man with the Sharps, firing again. "There! Gee!" he exclaimed, as a bullet hummed in through the window he had quitted for the moment, and thudded into the wall, making the dry adobe fly. It had missed him by only a few inches and he now crept along the floor to the rear of the room and shoved his rifle out among the branches of a stunted mesquite which grew before a fissure in the wall. "You keep away from that windy for a minute, Hoppy," he warned as he waited.

A terror-stricken lizard flashed out of the fissure and along the wall where the roof had fallen in and flitted into a hole, while a fly buzzed loudly and hovered persistently around Red's head, to the rage of that individual. "Ah, ha!" he grunted, lowering the rifle and peering through the smoke. A yell reached his ears and he forthwith returned to his window, whistling softly.

Evidently Mr. Cassidy's eyes were better and his temper sweeter, for he hummed "Dixie" and then jumped to "Yankee Doodle," mixing the two airs with careless impartiality, which was a sign that he was thinking deeply. "Wonder what ever became of Powers, Red. Peculiar feller, he was."

"In jail, I reckon, if drink hasn't killed him."

"Yes; I reckon so," and Mr. Cassidy continued his medley, which prompted his friend quickly to announce his unqualified disapproval.

"You can make more of a mess of them two songs than anybody I ever heard murder 'em! *Shut up!*" —and the concert stopped, the vocalist venting his feelings at an Indian, and killing the horse instead.

"Did you get him?" queried Red.

"Nope; but I got his cayuse," Hopalong replied, shoving a fresh cartridge into the foul, greasy breech of the Sharps. "An' here's where I get him-got to square up for my eyes some way," he muttered, firing. "Missed! Now what do you think of that!" he exclaimed.

"Better take my Winchester," suggested Red, in a matter-of-fact way, but he chuckled softly and listened for the reply.

"Aw, you go to the devil!" snapped Mr. Cassidy, firing again. "Whoop! Got him that time!"

"Where?" asked his companion, with strong suspicion.

"None of yore business!"

"Aw, darn it! Who spilled the water?" yelled Red, staring blankly at the overturned canteen.

"Pshaw! Reckon I did, Red," apologized his friend ruefully. "Now of all the cussed luck!"

"Oh, well; we've got another, an' you had to wash out yore eyes. Lucky we each had one — *Holy smoke!* It's most all gone! The top is loose!"

Heartfelt profanity filled the room and the two disgusted punchers went sullenly back to their posts. It was a calamity of no small magnitude, for, while food could be dispensed with for a long time if necessary, going without water was another question. It was as necessary as cartridges.

Then Hopalong laughed at the ludicrous side of the whole affair, thereby revealing one of the characteristics which endeared him to his friends. No matter how desperate a situation might be, he could always find in it something at which to laugh. He laughed going into danger and coming out of it, with a joke or a pleasantry always trembling on the end of his tongue.

"Red, did it ever strike you how cussed thirsty a feller gets just as soon as he knows he can't have no drink? But it don't make much difference, nohow. We'll get out of this little scrape just as we've allus got out of trouble. There's some mad war-whoops outside that are worse off than we are, because they are at the wrong end of yore gun. I feel sort of sorry for 'em."

"Yo're shore a happy idiot," grinned Red. "Hey! Listen!"

Galloping was heard and Hopalong, running to the door, looked out through a crack as sudden firing broke out around the rear of the shack, and fell to pulling away the props, crying, "It's a puncher, Red; he's riding this way! Come on an' help him in!"

"He's a blamed fool to ride this way! I'm with you!" replied Red, running to his side.

Half a mile from the house, coming across the open space as fast as he could urge his horse, rode a cowboy, and not far behind him raced about a dozen Apaches, yelling and firing.

Red picked up his companion's rifle, and steadying it against the jamb of the door, fired, dropping one of the foremost of the pursuers. Quickly reloading again, he fired and missed. The third shot struck another horse, and then taking up his own gun he began to fire rapidly, as rapidly as he could work the lever and yet make his shots tell. Hopalong drew his Colt and ran back to watch the rear of the house, and it was well that he did so, for an Apache in that direction, believing that the trapped punchers were so busily engaged with the new developments as to forget for the moment, sprinted towards the back window; and he had gotten within twenty paces of the goal when Hopalong's Colt cracked a protest. Seeing that the warrior was no longer a combatant, Mr. Cassidy ran back to the door just as the stranger fell from his horse and crawled past Red. The door slammed shut, the props fell against it, and the two friends turned to the work of driving back the second band, which, however, had given up all hope of rushing the house in the face of Red's telling fire, and had sought cover instead.

The stranger dragged himself to the canteens and drank what little water remained, and then turned to watch the two men moving from place to place, firing coolly and methodically. He thought he recognized one of them from the descriptions he had heard, but he was not sure.

"My name's Holden," he whispered hoarsely, but the cracking of the rifles drowned his voice. During a lull he tried again. "My name's Holden," he repeated weakly. "I'm from the Cross-O-Cross, an' can't get back there again."

"Mine's Cassidy, an' that's Connors, of the Bar-20. Are you hurt very bad?"

"No; not very bad," lied Holden, trying to smile. "Gee, but I'm glad I fell in with you two fellers," he exclaimed. He was but little more than a boy, and to him Hopalong Cassidy and Red Connors were names with which to conjure. "But I'm plumb sorry I went an' brought you more trouble," he added regretfully.

"Oh, pshaw! We had it before you came-you needn't do no worrying about that, Holden; besides, I reckon you couldn't help it," Hopalong grinned facetiously. "But tell us how you came to mix up with that bunch," he continued.

Holden shuddered and hesitated a moment, his companions alertly shifting from crack to crack, window to window, their rifles cracking at intervals. They appeared to him to act as if they had done nothing else all their lives but fight Indians from that shack, and he braced up a little at their example of coolness.

"It's an awful story, awful!" he began. "I was riding towards Hoyt's Corners an' when I got about half way there I topped a rise an' saw a nester's house about half a mile away. It wasn't there the last time I rode that way, an' it looked so peaceful an' home-like that I stopped an' looked at it a few minutes. I was just going to start again when that war-party rode out of a barranca close to the house an' went straight for it at top speed. It seemed like a dream, 'cause I thought Apaches never got so far east. They don't, do they? I thought not-these must 'a' got turned out of their way an' had to hustle for safety. Well, it was all over purty quick. I saw 'em drag out two women an' —an' —purty soon a man. He was fighting like fury, but he didn't last long. Then they set fire to the house an' threw the man's body up on the roof. I couldn't seem to move till the flames shot up, but then I must 'a' went sort of loco, because I emptied my gun at 'em, which was plumb foolish at that distance, for me. The next thing I knowed was that half of 'em was coming my way as hard as they could ride, an' I lit out instanter; an' here I am. I can't get that sight outen my head nohow-it'll drive me loco!" he screamed, sobbing like a child from the horror of it all.

His auditors still moved around the room, growing more and more vindictive all the while and more zealously endeavoring to create a still greater deficit in one Apache war-party. They knew what he had looked upon, for they themselves had become familiar with the work of Apaches in Arizona. They could picture it vividly in all its devilish horror. Neither of them paid any apparent attention to their companion, for they could not spare the time, and, also, they believed it best to let him fight out his own battles unassisted.

Holden sobbed and muttered as the minutes dragged along, at times acting so strangely as to draw a covert side-glance from one or both of the Bar-20 punchers. Then Mr. Connors saw his boon companion suddenly lean out of a window and immediately become the target for the hard-working enemy. He swore angrily at the criminal recklessness of it. "Hey, you! Come in out of that! Ain't you got no brains at all, you blasted idiot! Don't you know that we need every gun?"

"Yes; that's right. I sort of forgot," grinned the reckless one, obeying with alacrity and looking sheepish. "But you know there's two thundering big tarantulas out there fighting like blazes. You ought to see 'em jump! It's a sort of a leap-frog fight, Red."

"Fool!" snorted Mr. Connors belligerently. "*You'd* 'a' jumped if one of them slugs had 'a' got you! Yo're the damnedest fool that ever walked on two laigs, you blasted sage-hen!" Mr. Connors was beginning to lose his temper and talk in his throat.

"Well, they didn't get me, did they? What you yelling about, anyhow?" growled Hopalong, trying to brazen it out.

"An' *you* talking about suicide to me!" snapped Mr. Connors, determined to rub it in and have the last word.

Mr. Holden stared, open-mouthed, at the man who could enjoy a miserable spider fight under such distressing circumstances, and his shaken nerves became steadier as he gave thought to the fact that he was a companion of the two men about whose exploits he had heard so much. Evidently the stories had not been exaggerated. What must they think of him for giving way as he had? He rose to his feet in time to see a horse blunder into the open on Red's side of the house, and after it blundered its owner, who immediately lost all need of earthly conveyances. Holden laughed from the joy of being with a man who could shoot like that, and he took up his rifle and turned to a crack in the wall, filled with the determination to let his companions know that he was built of the right kind of timber after all, wounded as he was.

Red's only comment, as he pumped a fresh cartridge into the barrel, was, "He must 'a' thought he saw a spider fight, too."

"Hey, Red," called Hopalong. "The big one is dead."

"What big one?"

"Why, don't you remember? That big tarantula I was watching. One was bigger than the other, but the little feller shore waded into him an'—"

"Go to the devil!" shouted Red, who had to grin, despite his anger.

"Presently, presently," replied Hopalong, laughing.

So the day passed, and when darkness came upon them all of the defenders were wounded, Holden desperately so.

"Red, one of us has got to try to make the ranch," Hopalong suddenly announced, and his friend knew he was right. Since Holden had appeared upon the scene they had known that they could not try a dash; one of them had to stay.

"We'll toss for it; heads, I go," Red suggested, flipping a coin.

"Tails!" cried Hopalong. "It's only thirty miles to Buckskin, an' if I can get away from here I'm good to make it by eleven to-night. I'll stop at Cowan's an' have him send word to Lucas an' Bartlett, so there'll be enough in case any of our boys are out on the range in some line house. We can pick 'em up on the way back, so there won't be no time lost. If I get through you can expect excitement on the outside of this sieve by daylight. You an' Holden can hold her till then, because they never attack at night. It's the only way out of this for us-we ain't got cartridges or water enough to last another day."

Red, knowing that Hopalong was taking a desperate chance in working through the cordon of Indians which surrounded them, and that the house was safe when compared to running such a gantlet, offered to go through the danger line with him. For several minutes a wordy war raged and finally Red accepted a compromise; he was to help, but not to work through the line.

"But what's the use of all this argument?" feebly demanded Holden. "Why don't you both go? I ain't a-going to live nohow, so there ain't no use of anybody staying here with me, to die with me. Put a bullet through me so them devils can't play with me like they do with others, an' then get away while you've got a chance. Two men can get through as easy as one." He sank back, exhausted by the effort.

"No more of that!" cried Red, trying to be stern. "I'm going to stay with you an' see things through. I'd be a fine sort of a coyote to sneak off an' leave you for them fiends. An', besides, I can't get away; my cayuse is hit too hard an' yourn is dead," he lied cheerfully. "An' yo're going to get well, all right. I've seen fellers hit harder than you are pull through."

Hopalong walked over to the prostrate man and shook hands with him. "I'm awful glad I met you, Holden. Yo're pure grit all the way through, an' I like to tie to that kind of a man. Don't you worry about nothing; Red can handle this proposition, an' we'll have you in Buckskin by to-morrow night; you'll be riding again in two weeks. So long."

He turned to Red and shook hands silently, led his horse out of the building and mounted, glad that the moon had not yet come up, for in the darkness he had a chance.

"Good luck, Hoppy!" cried Red, running to the door. "Good luck!"

"You bet-an' lots of it, too," groaned Holden, but he was gone. Then Red wheeled. "Holden, keep yore eyes an' ears open. I'm going out to see that he gets off. He may run into a —" and he, too, was gone.

Holden watched the doors and windows, striving to resist the weak, giddy feeling in his head, and ten minutes later he heard a shot and then several more in quick succession. Shortly afterward Red called out, and almost immediately the Bar-20 puncher crawled in through a window.

"Well?" anxiously cried the man on the floor. "Did he make it?"

"I reckon so. He got away from the first crowd, anyhow. I wasn't very far behind him, an' by the time they woke up to what was going on he was through an' riding like blazes. I heard him call 'em half-breeds a moment later an' it sounded far off. They hit me, —fired at my flash, like I drilled one of them. But it ain't much, anyhow. How are you feeling now?"

"Fine!" lied the other. "That Cassidy is shore a wonder-he's all right, an' so are you. I'll never see him again, but I shore hope he gets through!"

"Don't be foolish. Here, you finish the water in yore canteen —I picked it up outside by yore cayuse. Then go to sleep," ordered Red. "I'll do all the watching that's necessary."

"I will if you'll call me when you get sleepy."

"Why, shore I will. But don't you want the rest of the water? I ain't a bit thirsty —I had all I could hold just before you came," Red remarked as his companion pushed the canteen against him in the dark. He was choking with thirst. "Well, then; all right," and Red pretended to drink. "Now, then, you go to sleep; a good snooze will do you a world of good-it's just what you need."

Chapter X
Buck Takes a Hand

Cowan's saloon, club, and place of general assembly for the town of Buckskin and the nearby ranches, held a merry crowd, for it was pay-day on the range and laughter and liquor ran a close race. Buck Peters, his hands full of cigars, passed through the happy-go-lucky, do-as-you-please crowd and invited everybody to smoke, which nobody refused to do. Wood Wright, of the C-80, tuned his fiddle anew and swung into a rousing quick-step. Partners were chosen, the "women" wearing handkerchiefs on their arms to indicate the fact, and the room shook and quivered as the scraping of heavy boots filled the air with a cloud of dust. "Allaman left!" cried the prompter, and then the dance stopped as if by magic. The door had crashed open and a blood-stained man staggered in and towards the bar, crying, "Buck! Red's hemmed in by 'Paches!"

"Good God!" roared the foreman of the Bar-20, leaping forward, the cigars falling to the floor to be crushed and ground into powder by careless feet. He grasped his puncher and steadied him while Cowan slid an extra generous glassful of brandy across the bar for the wounded man. The room was in an uproar, men grabbing rifles and running out to get their horses, for it was plain to be seen that there was hard work to be done, and quickly. Questions, threats, curses filled the air, those who remained inside to get the story listening intently to the jerky narrative; those outside, caring less for the facts of an action past than for the action to come, shouted impatiently for a start to be made, even threatening to go on and tackle the proposition by themselves if there were not more haste. Hopalong told in a graphic, terse manner all that was necessary, while Buck and Cowan hurriedly bandaged his wounds.

"Come on! Come on!" shouted the mounted crowd outside, angry, and impatient for a start, the prancing of horses and the clinking of metal adding to the noise. "Get a move on! *Will you hurry up!*"

"Listen, Hoppy!" pleaded Buck, in a furore. "Shut up, you outside!" he yelled. "You say they know that you got away, Hoppy?" he asked. "All right —*Lanky!*" he shouted. "*Lanky!*"

"All right, Buck!" and Lanky Smith roughly pushed his way through the crowd to his foreman's side. "Here I am."

"Take Skinny and Pete with you, an' a lead horse apiece. Strike straight for Powers' old ranch house. Them Injuns'll have pickets out looking for Hoppy's friends. You three get the pickets nearest the old trail through that arroyo to the southeast, an' then wait for us. We'll come along the high bank on the left. Don't make no noise doing it, neither, if you can help it. Understand? Good! Now ride like the devil!"

Lanky grabbed Pete and Skinny on his way out and disappeared into the corral; and very soon thereafter hoof-beats thudded softly in the sandy street and pounded into the darkness of the north, soon lost to the ear. An uproar of advice and good wishes crashed after them, for the game had begun.

"It's Powers' old shack, boys!" shouted a man in the door to the restless force outside, which immediately became more restless. "Hey! Don't go yet!" he begged. "Wait for me an' the rest. Don't be a lot of idiots!"

Excited and impatient voices replied from the darkness, vexed, grouchy, and querulous. "Then get a move on —*whoa!* —it'll be light before we get there if you don't hustle!" roared one voice above the confusion. "You know what *that* means!"

"Come on! Come on! For God's sake, are you tied to the bar?"

"Yo're a lot of old grandmothers! Come on!"

Hopalong appeared in the door. "I'll show you the way, boys!" he shouted. "Cowan, put my saddle on yore cayuse —*pronto!*"

"Good for you, Hoppy!" came from the street. "We'll wait!"

"You stay here; yo're hurt too much!" cried Buck to his puncher, as he grabbed up a box of cartridges from a shelf behind the bar. "Ain't you got no sense? There's enough of us to take care of this without you!"

Hopalong wheeled and looked his foreman squarely in the eyes. "Red's out there, waiting for me —I'm going! I'd be a fine sort of a coyote to leave him in that hell hole an' not go back, wouldn't I!" he said, with quiet determination.

"Good for you, Cassidy!" cried a man who hastened out to mount.

"Well, then, come on," replied Buck. "There's blamed few like you," he muttered, following Hopalong outside.

"Here's the cayuse, Cassidy," cried Cowan, turning the animal over to him. "*Wait*, Buck!" and he leaped into the building and ran out again, shoving a bottle of brandy and a package of food into the impatient foreman's hand. "Mebby Red or Hoppy'll need it-so long, an' good luck!" and he was alone in a choking cloud of dust, peering through the darkness along the river trail after a black mass that was swallowed up almost instantly. Then, as he watched, the moon pushed its rim up over the hills and he laughed joyously as he realized what its light would mean to the crowd. "There'll be great doings when *that* gang cuts loose," he muttered with savage elation. "Wish I was with 'em. Damn Injuns, anyhow!"

Far ahead of the main fighting force rode the three special-duty men, reeling off the miles at top speed and constantly distancing their friends, for they changed mounts at need, thanks to the lead horses provided by Mr. Peters' cool-headed foresight. It was a race against dawn, and every effort was made to win-the life of Red Connors hung in the balance and a minute might turn the scale.

In Powers' old ranch house the night dragged along slowly to the grim watcher, and the man huddled in the corner stirred uneasily and babbled, ofttimes crying out in horror at the vivid dreams of his disordered mind. Pacing ceaselessly from window to window, crack to crack, when the moon came up, Mr. Connors scanned the bare, level plain with anxious eyes, searching out the few covers and looking for dark spots on the dull gray sand. They never attacked at night, but still —. Through the void came the quavering call of a coyote, and he listened for the reply, which soon came from the black chaparral across the clearing. He knew where two of them were hiding, anyhow. Holden was muttering and tried to answer the calls, and Red looked at him for the hundredth time that night. He glanced out of the window again and noticed that there was a glow in the eastern sky, and shortly afterwards dawn swiftly developed.

Pouring the last few drops of the precious water between the wounded man's parched and swollen lips, he tossed the empty canteen from him and stood erect.

"Pore devil," he muttered, shaking his head sorrowfully, as he realized that Holden's delirium was getting worse all the time. "If you was all right we could give them wolves hell to dance to. Well, you won't know nothing about it if we go under, an' that's some consolation." He examined his rifle and saw that the Colt at his thigh was fully loaded and in good working order. "An' they'll pay us for their victory, by God! They'll pay for it!" He stepped closer to the window, throwing the rifle into the hollow of his arm. "It's about time for the rush; about time for the game —"

There was movement by that small chaparral to the south! To the east something stirred into bounding life and action; a coyote called twice-and then they came, on foot and silently as fleeting shadows, leaning forward to bring into play every ounce of energy in the slim, red legs. Smoke filled the room with its acrid sting. The crashing of the Winchester, worked with wonderful speed and deadly accuracy by the best rifle shot in the Southwest, brought the prostrate man to his feet in an instinctive response to the call to action, the necessity of defence. He grasped his Colt and stumbled blindly to a window to help the man who had stayed with him.

On Red's side of the house one warrior threw up his arms and fell forward, sprawling with arms and legs extended; another pitched to one side and rolled over twice before he lay still; the legs of the third collapsed and threw him headlong, bunched up in a grotesque pile of lifeless flesh; the fourth leaped high into the air and turned a somersault before he struck the sand, badly wounded, and out of the fight. Holden, steadying himself against the wall, leaned in a window on the other side of the shack and emptied his Colt in a dazed manner-doing his very best. Then the man with the rifle staggered back with a muttered curse, his right arm useless, and dropped the weapon to draw his Colt with the other hand.

Holden shrieked once and sank down, wagging his head slowly from side to side, blood oozing from his mouth and nostrils; and his companion, goaded into a frenzy of blood-lust and insane rage at the sight, threw himself against the door and out into the open, to die under the clear sky, to go like the man he was if he must die. "Damn you! It'll cost you more yet!" he screamed, wheeling to place his back against the wall.

The triumphant yells of the exultant savages were cut short and turned to howls of dismay by a fusillade which thundered from the south where a crowd of hard-riding, hard-shooting cow-punchers tore out of the thicket like an avalanche and swept over the open sand, yelling and cursing, and then separated to go in hot pursuit of the sprinting Apaches. Some stood up in their stirrups and fired down at a slant, making a short, chopping motion with their heavy Colts; others leaned forward, far over the necks of their horses, and shot with stationary guns; while yet others, with reins dangling free, worked the levers of blue Winchesters so rapidly that the flashes seemed to merge into a continuous flame.

"Thank God! Thank God-an' Hoppy!" groaned the man at the door of the shack, staggering forward to meet the two men who had lost no time in pursuit of the enemy, but had ridden straight to him.

"I was scared stiff you was done fer!" cried Hopalong, leaping off his horse and shaking hands with his friend, whose hand-clasp was not as strong as usual. "How's Holden?" he demanded, anxiously.

"He passed. It was a close —" began Red, weakly, but his foreman interposed.

"Shut up, an' drink this!" ordered Buck, kindly but sternly. "We'll do the talking for a while; you can tell us all about it later on. Why, *hullo!*" he cried as Lanky Smith and his two happy companions rode up. "Reckon you must 'a' got them pickets."

"Shore we did! Stalked 'em on our bellies, didn't we, Skinny?" modestly replied Mr. Smith, the roping expert of the Bar-20. "Ropes an' clubbed guns did the rest. Anyhow, there was only two anywhere near the trail."

"We didn't see you," responded the foreman, tying the knot of a bandage on Mr. Connors' arm. "An' we looked sharp, too."

"Reckon we was hunting for more; we sort of forgot what you said about waiting for you," Mr. Smith replied, grinning broadly.

"An' you've got a good memory now," smiled Mr. Peters.

"We didn't find no more, though," offered Mr. Pete Wilson, with grave regret. "An' we looked good, too. But we got Red, an' that's the whole game. Red, you old son-of-a-gun, you can lick yore weight in powder!"

"It's too bad about Holden," muttered Red, sullenly.

Chapter XI
Hopalong Nurses a Grouch

After the excitement incident to the affair at Powers' shack had died down and the Bar-20 outfit worked over its range in the old, placid way, there began to be heard low mutterings, and an air of peevish discontent began to be manifested in various childish ways. And it was all caused by the fact that Hopalong Cassidy had a grouch, and a big one. It was two months old and growing worse daily, and the signs threatened contagion. His foreman, tired and sick of the snarling, fidgety, petulant atmosphere that Hopalong had created on the ranch, and driven to desperation, eagerly sought some chance to get rid of the "sore-thumb" temporarily and give him an opportunity to shed his generous mantle of the blues. And at last it came.

No one knew the cause for Hoppy's unusual state of mind, although there were many conjectures, and they covered the field rather thoroughly; but they did not strike on the cause. Even Red Connors, now well over all ill effects of the wounds acquired in the old ranch house, was forced to guess; and when Red had to do that about anything concerning Hopalong he was well warranted in believing the matter to be very serious.

Johnny Nelson made no secret of his opinion and derived from it a great amount of satisfaction, which he admitted with a grin to his foreman.

"Buck," he said, "Hoppy told me he went broke playing poker over in Grant with Dave Wilkes and them two Lawrence boys, an' that shore explains it all. He's got pack sores from carrying his unholy licking. It was due to come for him, an' Dave Wilkes is just the boy to deliver it. That's the whole trouble, an' I know it, an' I'm damned glad they trimmed him. But he ain't got no right of making *us* miserable because he lost a few measly dollars."

"Yo're wrong, son; dead, dead wrong," Buck replied. "He takes his beatings with a grin, an' money never did bother him. No poker game that ever was played could leave a welt on him like the one we all mourn, an' cuss. He's been doing something that he don't want us to know-made a fool of hisself some way, most likely, an' feels so ashamed that he's sore. I've knowed him too long an' well to believe that gambling had anything to do with it. But this little trip he's taking will fix him up all right, an' I couldn't 'a' picked a better man-or one that I'd rather get rid of just now."

"Well, lemme tell you it's blamed lucky for him that you picked him to go," rejoined Johnny, who thought more of the woeful absentee than he did of his own skin. "I was going to lick him, shore, if it went on much longer. Me an' Red an' Billy was going to beat him up good till he forgot his dead injuries an' took more interest in his friends."

Buck laughed heartily. "Well, the three of you might 'a' done it if you worked hard an' didn't get careless, but I have my doubts. Now look here-you've been hanging around the bunk house too blamed much lately. Henceforth an' hereafter you've got to earn your grub. Get out on that west line an' hustle."

"You know I've had a toothache!" snorted Johnny with a show of indignation, his face as sober as that of a judge.

"An' you'll have a stomach ache from lack of grub if you don't earn yore right to eat purty soon," retorted Buck. "You ain't had a toothache in yore whole life, an' you don't know what one is. G'wan, now, or I'll give you a backache that'll ache!"

"Huh! Devil of a way to treat a sick man!" Johnny retorted, but he departed exultantly, whistling with much noise and no music. But he was sorry for one thing: he sincerely regretted that he had not been present when Hopalong met his Waterloo. It would have been pleasing to look upon.

While the outfit blessed the proposed lease of range that took him out of their small circle for a time, Hopalong rode farther and farther into the northwest, frequently lost in abstraction which, judging by its effect upon him, must have been caused by something serious. He had not heard from Dave Wilkes about that individual's good horse which had been loaned to Ben Ferris, of Winchester. Did Dave think he had been killed or was still pursuing the man whose neck-kerchief had aroused such animosity in Hopalong's heart? Or had the horse actually been returned? The animal was a good one, a successful contender in all distances from one to five miles, and had earned its owner and backers much money-and Hopalong had parted with it as easily as he would have borrowed five dollars from Red. The story, as he had often reflected since, was as old as lying —a broken-legged horse, a wife dying forty miles away, and a horse all saddled which needed only to be mounted and ridden.

These thoughts kept him company for a day and when he dismounted before Stevenson's "Hotel" in Hoyt's Corners he summed up his feelings for the enlightenment of his horse.

"Damn it, bronc! I'd give ten dollars right now to know if I was a jackass or not," he growled. "But he was an awful slick talker if he lied. An' I've got to go up an' face Dave Wilkes to find out about it!"

Mr. Cassidy was not known by sight to the citizens of Hoyt's Corners, however well versed they might be in his numerous exploits of wisdom and folly. Therefore the habitues of Stevenson's Hotel did not recognize him in the gloomy and morose individual who dropped his saddle on the floor with a crash and stamped over to the three-legged table at dusk and surlily demanded shelter for the night.

"Gimme a bed an' something to eat," he demanded, eyeing the three men seated with their chairs tilted against the wall. "Do I get 'em?" he asked, impatiently.

"You do," replied a one-eyed man, lazily arising and approaching him. "One dollar, now."

"An' take the rocks outen that bed —I want to sleep."

"A dollar per for every rock you find," grinned Stevenson, pleasantly. "There ain't no rocks in *my* beds," he added.

"Some folks likes to be rocked to sleep," facetiously remarked one of the pair by the wall, laughing contentedly at his own pun. He bore all the ear-marks of being regarded as the wit of the locality-every hamlet has one; I have seen some myself.

"Hee, hee, hee! Yo're a droll feller, Charley," chuckled Old John Ferris, rubbing his ear with unconcealed delight. "That's a good un."

"One drink, now," growled Hopalong, mimicking the proprietor, and glaring savagely at the "droll feller" and his companion. "An' mind that it's a good one," he admonished the host.

"It's better," smiled Stevenson, whereat Old John crossed his legs and chuckled again. Stevenson winked.

"Riding long?" he asked.

"Since I started."

"Going fur?"

"Till I stop."

"Where do you belong?" Stevenson's pique was urging him against the ethics of the range, which forbade personal questions.

Hopalong looked at him with a light in his eye that told the host he had gone too far. "Under my sombrero!" he snapped.

"Hee, hee, hee!" chortled Old John, rubbing his ear again and nudging Charley. "He ain't no fool, hey?"

"Why, I don't know, John; he won't tell," replied Charley.

Hopalong wheeled and glared at him, and Charley, smiling uneasily, made an appeal: "Ain't mad, are you?"

"Not yet," and Hopalong turned to the bar again, took up his liquor and tossed it off. Considering a moment he shoved the glass back again, while Old John tongued his lips in anticipation of a treat. "It is good-fill it again."

The third was even better and by the time the fourth and fifth had joined their predecessors Hopalong began to feel a little more cheerful. But even the liquor and an exceptionally well-cooked supper could not separate him from his persistent and set grouch. And of liquor he had already taken more than his limit. He had always boasted, with truth, that he had never been drunk, although there had been two occasions when he was not far from it. That was one doubtful luxury which he could not afford for the reason that there were men who would have been glad to see him, if only for a few seconds, when liquor had dulled his brain and slowed his speed of hand. He could never tell when and where he might meet one of these.

He dropped into a chair by a card table and, baffling all attempts to engage him in conversation, reviewed his troubles in a mumbled soliloquy, the liquor gradually making him careless. But of all the jumbled words his companions' diligent ears heard they recognized and retained only the bare term "Winchester"; and their conjectures were limited only by their imaginations.

Hopalong stirred and looked up, shaking off the hand which had aroused him. "Better go to bed, stranger," the proprietor was saying. "You an' me are the last two up. It's after twelve, an' you look tired and sleepy."

"Said his wife was sick," muttered the puncher. "Oh, what you saying?"

"You'll find a bed better'n this table, stranger-it's after twelve an' I want to close up an' get some sleep. I'm tired myself."

"Oh, that all? Shore I'll go to bed-like to see anybody stop me! Ain't no rocks in it, hey?"

"Nary a rock," laughingly reassured the host, picking up Hopalong's saddle and leading the way to a small room off the "office," his guest stumbling after him and growling about the rocks that lived in Winchester. When Stevenson had dropped the saddle by the window and departed, Hopalong sat on the edge of the bed to close his eyes for just a moment before tackling the labor of removing his clothes. A crash and a jar awakened him and he found himself on the floor with his back to the bed. He was hot and his head ached, and his back was skinned a little-and how hot and stuffy and choking the room had become! He thought he had blown out the light, but it still burned, and three-quarters of the chimney was thickly covered with soot. He was stifling and could not endure it any longer. After three attempts he put out the light, stumbled against his saddle and, opening the window, leaned out to breathe the pure air. As his lungs filled he chuckled wisely and, picking up the saddle, managed to get it and himself through the window and on the ground without serious mishap. He would ride for an hour, give the room time to freshen and cool off, and come back feeling much better. Not a star could be seen as he groped his way unsteadily towards the rear of the building, where he vaguely remembered having seen the corral as he rode up.

"Huh! Said he lived in Winchester an' his name was Bill-no, Ben Ferris," he muttered, stumbling towards a noise he knew was made by a horse rubbing against the corral fence. Then his feet got tangled up in the cinch of his saddle, which he had kicked before him, and after great labor he arose, muttering savagely, and continued on his wobbly way. "Goo' Lord, it's darker'n cats in —*oof*!" he grunted, recoiling from forcible contact with the fence he sought. Growling words unholy he felt his way along it and finally his arm slipped through an opening and he bumped his head solidly against the top bar of the gate. As he righted himself his hand struck the nose of a horse and closed mechanically over it. Cow-ponies look alike in the dark and he grinned jubilantly as he complimented himself upon finding his own so unerringly.

"Anything is easy, when you know how. Can't fool me, ol' cayuse," he beamed, fumbling at the bars with his free hand and getting them down with a fool's luck. "You can't do it —I got you firs', las', an' always; an' I got you good. Yessir, I got you good. Quit that rearing, you ol' fool! Stan' still, can't you?" The pony sidled as the saddle hit its back and evoked profane abuse from the indignant puncher as he risked his balance in picking it up to try again, this time successfully. He began to fasten the girth, and then paused in wonder and thought deeply, for the pin in the buckle would slide to no hole but the first. "Huh! Getting fat, ain't you, piebald?" he demanded with withering sarcasm. "You blow yoreself up any more'n I'll bust you wide open!" heaving up with all his might on the free end of the strap, one knee pushing against the animal's side. The "fat" disappeared and Hopalong laughed. "Been learnin' new tricks, ain't you? Got smart since you been travellin', hey?" He fumbled with the bars again and got two of them back in place and then, throwing himself across the saddle as the horse started forward as hard as it could go, slipped off, but managed to save himself by hopping along the ground. As soon as he had secured the grip he wished he mounted with the ease of habit and felt for the reins. "G'wan now, an' easy-it's plumb dark an' my head's bustin'."

When he saddled his mount at the corral he was not aware that two of the three remaining horses had taken advantage of their opportunity and had walked out and made off in the darkness before he replaced the bars, and he was too drunk to care if he had known it.

The night air felt so good that it moved him to song, but it was not long before the words faltered more and more and soon ceased altogether and a subdued snore rasped from him. He awakened from time to time, but only for a moment, for he was tired and sleepy.

His mount very quickly learned that something was wrong and that it was being given its head. As long as it could go where it pleased it could do nothing better than head for home, and it quickened its pace towards Winchester. Some time after daylight it pricked up its ears and broke into a canter, which soon developed signs of irritation in its rider. Finally Hopalong opened his heavy eyes and looked around for his bearings. Not knowing where he was and too tired and miserable to give much thought to a matter of such slight importance, he glanced around for a place to finish his sleep. A tree some distance ahead of him looked inviting and towards it he rode. Habit made him picket the horse before he lay down and as he fell asleep he had vague recollections of handling a strange picket rope some time recently. The horse slowly turned and stared at the already snoring figure, glanced over the landscape, back the to queerest man it had ever met, and then fell to grazing in quiet content. A slinking coyote topped a rise a short distance away and stopped instantly, regarding the sleeping man with grave curiosity and strong suspicion. Deciding that there was nothing good to eat in that vicinity and that the man was carrying out a fell plot for the death of coyotes, it backed away out of sight and loped on to other hunting grounds.

Chapter XII
A Friend in Need

Stevenson, having started the fire for breakfast, took a pail and departed towards the spring; but he got no farther than the corral gate, where he dropped the pail and stared. There was only one horse in the enclosure where the night before there had been four. He wasted no time in surmises, but wheeled and dashed back towards the hotel, and his vigorous shouts brought Old John to the door, sleepy and peevish. Old John's mouth dropped open as he beheld his habitually indolent host marking off long distances on the sand with each falling foot.

"What's got inter you?" demanded Old John.

"Our broncs are gone! Our broncs are gone!" yelled Stevenson, shoving Old John roughly to one side as he dashed through the doorway and on into the room he had assigned to the sullen and bibulous stranger. "I knowed it! I knowed it!" he wailed, popping out again as if on springs. "He's gone, an' he's took our broncs with him, the measly, low-down dog! I knowed he wasn't no good! I could see it in his eye; an' he wasn't drunk, not by a darn sight. Go out an' see for yoreself if they ain't gone!" he snapped in reply to Old John's look. "Go on out, while I throw some cold grub on the table-won't have no time this morning to do no cooking. He's got five hours' start on us, an' it'll take some right smart riding to get him before dark; but we'll do it, an' hang him, too!"

"What's all this here rumpus?" demanded a sleepy voice from upstairs. "Who's hanged?" and Charley entered the room, very much interested. His interest increased remarkably when the calamity was made known and he lost no time in joining Old John in the corral to verify the news.

Old John waved his hands over the scene and carefully explained what he had read in the tracks, to his companion's great irritation, for Charley's keen eyes and good training had already told him all there was to learn; and his reading did not exactly agree with that of his companion.

"Charley, he's gone and took our cayuses; an' that's the very way he came —'round the corner of the hotel. He got all tangled up an' fell over there, an' here he bumped inter the palisade, an' dropped his saddle. When he opened the bars he took my roan gelding because it was the best an' fastest, an' then he let out the others to mix us up on the tracks. See how he went? Had to hop four times on one foot afore he could get inter the saddle. An' that proves he was sober, for no drunk could hop four times like that without falling down an' being drug to death. An' he left his own critter behind because he knowed it wasn't no good. It's all as plain as the nose on your face, Charley," and Old John proudly rubbed his ear. "Hee, hee, hee! You can't fool Old John, even if he is getting old. No, sir, b' gum."

Charley had just returned from inside the corral, where he had looked at the brand on the far side of the one horse left, and he waited impatiently for his companion to cease talking. He took quick advantage of the first pause Old John made and spoke crisply.

"I don't care what corner he came 'round, or what he bumped inter; an' any fool can see that. An' if he left that cayuse behind because he thought it wasn't no good, he *was* drunk. That's a Bar-20 cayuse, an' no hoss-thief ever worked for that ranch. He left it behind because he stole it; that's why. An' he didn't let them others out because he wanted to mix us up, neither. How'd he know if we couldn't tell the tracks of our own animals? He did that to make us lose time; that's what he did it for. An' he couldn't tell what bronc he took last night-it was too dark. He must 'a' struck a match an' seen where that Bar-20 cayuse was an' then took the first one nearest that wasn't it. An' now you tell me how the devil he knowed yourn was the fastest, which it ain't," he finished, sarcastically, gloating over a chance to rub it into the man he had always regarded as a windy old nuisance.

"Well, mebby what you said is —"

"Mebby nothing!" snapped Charley. "If he wanted to mix the tracks would he 'a' hopped like that so we couldn't help telling what cayuse he rode? He knowed we'd pick his trail quick, an' he knowed that every minute counted; that's why he hopped-why, yore roan was going like the wind afore he got in the saddle. If you don't believe it, look at them toe-prints!"

"H'm; reckon yo're right, Charley. My eyes ain't nigh as good as they once was. But I heard him say something 'bout Winchester," replied Old John, glad to change the subject. "Bet he's going over there, too. He won't get through that town on no critter wearing my brand. Everybody knows that roan, an' —"

"Quit guessing!" snapped Charley, beginning to lose some of the tattered remnant of his respect for old age. "He's a whole lot likely to head for a town on a stolen cayuse, now ain't he! But we don't care where he's heading; we'll foller the trail."

"Grub pile!" shouted Stevenson, and the two made haste to obey.

"Charley, gimme a chaw of yore tobacker," and Old John, biting off a generous chunk, quietly slipped it into his pocket, there to lay until after he had eaten his breakfast.

All talk was tabled while the three men gulped down a cold and uninviting meal. Ten minutes later they had finished and separated to find horses and spread the news; in fifteen more they had them and were riding along the plain trail at top speed, with three other men close at their heels. Three hundred yards from the corral they pounded out of an arroyo, and Charley, who was leading, stood up in his stirrups and looked keenly ahead. Another trail joined the one they were following and ran with and on top of it. This, he reasoned, had been made by one of the strays and would turn away soon. He kept his eyes looking well ahead and soon saw that he was right in his surmise, and without checking the speed of his horse in the slightest degree he went ahead on the trail of the smaller hoof-prints. In a moment Old John spurred forward and gained his side and began to argue hot-headedly.

"Hey! Charley!" he cried. "Why are you follering this track?" he demanded.

"Because it's his; that's why."

"Well, here, wait a minute!" and Old John was getting red from excitement. "How do you know it is? Mebby he took the other!"

"He started out on the cayuse that made these little tracks," retorted Charley, "an' I don't see no reason to think he swapped animules. Don't you know the prints of yore own cayuse?"

"Lawd, no!" answered Old John. "Why, I don't hardly ride the same cayuse the second day, straight hand-running. I tell you we ought to foller that other trail. He's just cute enough to play some trick on us."

"Well, you better do that for us," Charley replied, hoping against hope that the old man would chase off on the other and give his companions a rest.

"He ain't got sand enough to tackle a thing like that single-handed," laughed Jed White, winking to the others.

Old John wheeled. "Ain't, hey! I am going to do that same thing an' prove that you are a pack of fools. I'm too old to be fooled by a common trick like that. An' I don't need no help — I'll ketch him all by myself, an' hang him, too!" And he wheeled to follow the other trail, angry and outraged. "Young fools," he muttered. "Why, I was fighting all around these parts afore any of 'em knowed the difference between day an' night!"

"Hard-headed old fool," remarked Charley, frowning, as he led the way again.

"He's gittin' old an' childish," excused Stevenson. "They say warn't nobody in these parts could hold a candle to him in his prime."

Hopalong muttered and stirred and opened his eyes to gaze blankly into those of one of the men who were tugging at his hands, and as he stared he started his stupefied brain sluggishly to work in an endeavor to explain the unusual experience. There were five men around him and the two who hauled at his hands stepped back and kicked him. A look of pained indignation slowly spread over his countenance as he realized beyond doubt that they were really kicking him, and with sturdy vigor. He considered a moment and then decided that such treatment was most unwarranted and outrageous and, furthermore, that he must defend himself and chastise the perpetrators.

"Hey!" he snorted, "what do you reckon yo're doing, anyhow? If you want to do any kicking, why kick each other, an' I'll help you! But I'll lick the whole bunch of you if you don't quite mauling me. Ain't you got no manners? Don't you know anything? Come 'round waking a feller up an' man-handling —"

"Get up!" snapped Stevenson, angrily.

"Why, ain't I seen you before? Somewhere? Sometime?" queried Hopalong, his brow wrinkling from intense concentration of thought. "I ain't dreaming; I've seen a one-eyed coyote som'ers, lately, ain't I?" he appealed, anxiously, to the others.

"Get up!" ordered Charley, shortly.

"An' I've seen you, too. Funny, all right."

"You've seen me, all right," retorted Stevenson. "Get up, damn you! Get up!"

"Why, I can't—my han's are tied!" exclaimed Hopalong in great wonder, pausing in his exertions to cogitate deeply upon this most remarkable phenomenon. "Tied up! Now what the devil do you think—"

"Use yore feet, you thief!" rejoined Stevenson roughly, stepping forward and delivering another kick. "Use yore feet!" he reiterated.

"Thief! Me a thief! Shore I'll use my feet, you yaller dog!" yelled the prostrate man, and his boot heel sank into the stomach of the offending Mr. Stevenson with sickening force and laudable precision. He drew it back slowly, as if debating shoving it farther. "Call me a thief, hey! Come poking 'round kicking honest punchers an' calling 'em names! Anybody want the other boot?" he inquired with grave solicitation.

Stevenson sat down forcibly and rocked to and fro, doubled up and gasping for breath, and Hopalong squinted at him and grinned with happiness. "Hear him sing! Reg'lar ol' brass band. Sounds like a cow pulling its hoofs outen the mud. Called me a thief, he did, just now. An' I won't let nobody kick me an' call me names. He's a liar, just a plain, squaw's dog liar, he—"

Two men grabbed him and raised him up, holding him tightly, and they were not over careful to handle him gently, which he naturally resented. Charley stepped in front of him to go to the aid of Stevenson and caught the other boot in his groin, dropping as if he had been shot. The man on the prisoner's left emitted a yell and loosed his hold to sympathize with a bruised shinbone, and his companion promptly knocked the bound and still intoxicated man down. Bill Thomas swore and eyed the prostrate figure with resentment and regret. "Hate to hit a man who can fight like that when he's loaded an' tied. I'm glad, all the same, that he ain't sober an' loose."

"An' you ain't going to hit him no more!" snapped Jed White, reddening with anger. "I'm ready to hang him, 'cause that's what he deserves, an' what we're here for, but I'm damned if I'll stand for any more mauling. I don't blame him for fighting, an' they didn't have no right to kick him in the beginning."

"Didn't kick him in the beginning," grinned Bill. "Kicked him in the ending. Anyhow," he continued seriously, "I didn't hit him hard-didn't have to. Just let him go an' shoved him quick."

"I'm just naturally going to clean house," muttered the prisoner, sitting up and glaring around. "Untie my han's an' gimme a gun or a club or anything, an' watch yoreselves get licked. Called me a thief! What are you fellers, then?—sticking me up an' busting me for a few measly dollars. Why didn't you take my money an' lemme sleep, 'stead of waking me up an' kicking me? I wouldn't 'a' cared then."

"Come on, now; get up. We ain't through with you yet, not by a whole lot," growled Bill, helping him to his feet and steadying him. "I'm plumb glad you kicked 'em; it was coming to 'em."

"No, you ain't; you can't fool me," gravely assured Hopalong. "Yo're lying, an' you know it. What you going to do now? Ain't I got money enough? Wish I had an even break with you fellers! Wish my outfit was here!"

Stevenson, on his feet again, walked painfully up and shook his fist at the captive, from the side. "You'll find out what we want of you, you damned hoss-thief!" he cried. "We're going to tie you to that there limb so yore feet'll swing above the grass, that's what we're going to do."

Bill and Jed had their hands full for a moment and as they finally mastered the puncher, Charley came up with a rope. "Hurry up-no use dragging it out this way. I want to get back to the ranch some time before next week."

"Why I ain't no hoss-thief, you liar!" Hopalong yelled. "My name's Hopalong Cassidy of the Bar-20, an' when I tell my friends about what you've gone an' done they'll make you hard to find! You gimme any kind of a chance an' I'll do it all by myself, sick as I am, you yaller dogs!"

"Is that yore cayuse?" demanded Charley, pointing.

Hopalong squinted towards the animal indicated. "Which one?"

"There's only one there, you fool!"

"That so?" replied Hopalong, surprised. "Well, I never seen it afore. My cayuse is-is-where the devil *is* it?" he asked, looking around anxiously.

"How'd you get that one, then, if it ain't yours?"

"Never had it — 't ain't mine, nohow," replied Hopalong, with strong conviction. "Mine was a *hoss*."

"You stole that cayuse last night outen Stevenson's corral," continued Charley, merely as a matter of form. Charley believed that a man had the right to be heard before he died-it wouldn't change the result and so could not do any harm.

"Did I? Why —" his forehead became furrowed again, but the events of the night before were vague in his memory and he only stumbled in his soliloquy. "But *I* wouldn't swap my cayuse for that spavined, saddle-galled, ring-boned bone-yard! Why, it interferes, an' it's got the heaves something awful!" he finished triumphantly, as if an appeal to common sense would clinch things. But he made no headway against them, for the rope went around his neck almost before he had finished talking and a flurry of excitement ensued. When the dust settled he was on his back again and the rope was being tossed over the limb.

The crowd had been too busily occupied to notice anything away from the scene of their strife and were greatly surprised when they heard a hail and saw a stranger sliding to a stand not twenty feet from them. "What's this?" demanded the newcomer, angrily.

Charley's gun glinted as it swung up and the stranger swore again. "What you doing?" he shouted. "Take that gun off'n me or I'll blow you apart!"

"Mind yore business an' sit still!" Charley snapped. "You ain't in no position to blow anything apart. We've got a hoss-thief an' we're shore going to hang him regardless."

"An' if there's any trouble about it we can hang two as well as we can one," suggested Stevenson, placidly. "You sit tight an' mind yore own affairs, stranger," he warned.

Hopalong turned his head slowly. "He's a liar, stranger; just a plain, squaw's dog of a liar. An' I'll be much obliged if you'll lick hell outen 'em an' let —*why, hullo, hoss-thief*!" he shouted, at once recognizing the other. It was the man he had met in the gospel tent, the man he had chased for a horse-thief and then swapped mounts with. "Stole any more cayuses?" he asked, grinning, believing that everything was all right now. "Did you take that cayuse back to Grant?" he finished.

"Han's up!" roared Stevenson, also covering the stranger. "So yo're another one of 'em, hey? We're in luck to-day. Watch him, boys, till I get his gun. If he moves, drop him quick."

"You damned fool!" cried Ferris, white with rage. "He ain't no thief, an' neither am I! My name's Ben Ferris an' I live in Winchester. Why, that man you've got is Hopalong Cassidy-Cassidy, of the Bar-20!"

"Sit still-you can talk later, mebby," replied Stevenson, warily approaching him. "Watch him, boys!"

"Hold on!" shouted Ferris, murder in his eyes. "Don't you try that on me! I'll get one of you before I go; I'll shore get one! You can listen a minute, an' I can't get away."

"All right; talk quick."

Ferris pleaded as hard as he knew how and called attention to the condition of the prisoner. "If he did take the wrong cayuse he was too blind drunk to know it! Can't you *see* he was!" he cried.

"Yep; through yet?" asked Stevenson, quietly.

"No! I ain't started yet!" Ferris yelled. "He did me a good turn once, one that I can't never repay, an' I'm going to stop this murder or go with him. If I go I'll take one of you with me, an' my friends an' outfit'll get the rest."

"Wait till Old John gets here," suggested Jed to Charley. "He ought to know this feller."

"For the Lord's sake!" snorted Charley. "He won't show up for a week. Did you hear that, fellers?" he laughed, turning to the others.

"Stranger," began Stevenson, moving slowly ahead again. "You give us yore guns an' sit quiet till we gets this feller out of the way. We'll wait till Old John Ferris comes before doing anything with you. He ought to know you."

"He knows me all right; an' he'd like to see me hung," replied the stranger. "I won't give up my guns, an' you won't lynch Hopalong Cassidy while I can pull a trigger. That's flat!" He began to talk feverishly to gain time and his eyes lighted suddenly. Seeing that Jed White was wavering, Stevenson ordered them to go on with the work they had come to perform, and he watched Ferris as a cat watches a mouse, knowing that he would be the first man hit if the stranger got a chance to shoot. But Ferris stood up very slowly in his stirrups so as not to alarm the five with any quick movement, and shouted at the top of his voice, grabbing off his sombrero and waving it frantically. A faint cheer reached his ears and made the lynchers turn quickly and look behind them. Nine men were tearing towards them at a dead gallop and had already begun to forsake their bunched-up formation in favor of an extended line. They were due to arrive in a very few minutes and caused Mr. Ferris' heart to overflow with joy.

"Me an' my outfit," he said, laughing softly and waving his hand towards the newcomers, "started out this morning to round up a bunch of cows, an' we got jackasses instead. Now lynch him, damn you!"

The nine swept up in skirmish order, guns out and ready for anything in the nature of trouble that might zephyr up. "What's the matter, Ben?" asked Tom Murphy ominously. As under-foreman of the ranch he regarded himself as spokesman. And at that instant catching sight of the rope, he swore savagely under his breath.

"Nothing, Tom; nothing now," responded Mr. Ferris. "They was going to hang my friend there, Mr. Hopalong Cassidy, of the Bar-20. He's the feller that lent me his cayuse to get home on when Molly was sick. I'm going to take him back to the ranch when he gets sober an' introduce him to some very good friends of hissn that he ain't never seen. Ain't I, Cassidy?" he demanded with a laugh.

But Mr. Cassidy made no reply. He was sound asleep, as he had been since the advent of his very good and capable friend, Mr. Ben Ferris, of Winchester.

Chapter XIII
Mr. Townsend, Marshal

Mr. Cassidy went to the ranch and lived like a lord until shame drove him away. He had no business to live on cake and pie and wonderful dishes that Mrs. Ferris and her sister literally forced on him, and let Buck's mission wait on his convenience. So he tore himself away and made up for lost time as he continued his journey on his own horse, for which Tom Murphy and three men had faced down the scowling population of Hoyt's Corners. The rest of his journey was without incident until, on his return home along another route, he rode into Rawhide and heard about the marshal, Mr. Townsend.

This individual was unanimously regarded as an affliction upon society and there had been objections to his continued existence, which had been overruled by the object himself. Then word had gone forth that a substantial reward and the undying gratitude of a considerable number of people awaited the man who would rid the community of the pest who seemed to be ubiquitous. Several had come in response to the call, one had returned in a wagon, and the others were now looked upon as martyrs, and as examples of asinine foolhardiness. Then it had been decided to elect a marshal, or perhaps two or three, to preserve the peace of the town; but this was a flat failure. In the first place, Mr. Townsend had dispersed the meeting with no date set for a new one; in the second, no man wanted the office; and as a finish to the comedy, Mr. Townsend cheerfully announced that hereafter and henceforth he was the marshal, self-appointed and self-sustained. Those who did not like it could easily move to other localities.

With this touch of office-holding came ambition, and of stern stuff. The marshal asked himself why he could not be more officers than one and found no reason. Thereupon he announced that he was marshal, town council, mayor, justice, and pound-keeper. He did not go to the trouble of incorporating himself as the Town of Rawhide, because he knew nothing of such immaterial things; but he was the town, and that sufficed.

He had been grievously troubled about finances in the past, and he firmly believed that genius such as his should be above such petty annoyances as being "broke." That was why he constituted himself the keeper of the public pound, which contented him for a short time, but later, feeling that he needed more money than the pound was giving him, he decided that the spirit of the times demanded public improvements, and therefore, as the executive head of the town, he levied taxes and improved the town by improving his wardrobe and the manner of his living. Each saloon must pay into the town treasury the sum of one hundred dollars per year, which entitled it to police protection and assured it that no new competitors would be allowed to do business in Rawhide.

Needless to say he was not furiously popular, and the crowds congregated where he was not. His tyranny was based upon his uncanny faculty of anticipating the other man's draw. The citizens were not unaccustomed to seeing swift death result to the slower man from misplaced confidence in his speed of hand-that was in the game-an even break; but to oppose an individual who *always* knew what you were going to do before you knew it yourself-this was very discouraging. Therefore, he flourished and waxed fat.

Of late, however, he had been very low in finances and could expect no taxes to be paid for three months. Even the pound had yielded him nothing for over a week, the old patrons of Rawhide's stores and saloons preferring to ride twenty miles farther in another direction than to redeem impounded horses. Perhaps his prices had been too high, he thought; so he assembled the town council, the mayor, the marshal, and the keeper of the public pound to consult upon the matter. He decided that the prices were too high and at once posted a new notice announcing the cut. It was hard to fall from a dollar to "two bits," but the treasury was low-the times were panicky.

As soon as he had changed the notice he strolled up to the Paradise to inform the bartender that impounding fines had been cut to bargain prices and to ask him to make the fact generally known through his patrons. As he came within sight of the building he jumped with pleasure, for a horse was standing dejectedly before the door. Joy of joys, trade was picking up —a stranger had come to town! Hastening back to the corral, he added a cipher to the posted figure, added a decimal point, and changed the cents sign to that of a dollar. Two dollars and fifty cents was now the price prescribed by law. Returning hastily to the Paradise, he led the animal away, impounded it, and then sat down in front of the corral gate with his Winchester across his knees. Two dollars and fifty cents! Prosperity had indeed returned!

"Where the CG ranch is I dunno, but I do know where one of their cayuses is," he mused, glancing between two of the corral posts at the sleepy animal. "If I has to auction it off to pay for its keep and the fine, the saddle will bring a good, round sum. I allus knowed that a dollar wasn't enough, nohow."

Nat Fisher, punching cows for the CG and tired of his job, leaned comfortably back in his chair in the Paradise and swapped lies with the all-wise bartender. After a while he realized that he was hopelessly outclassed at this diversion and he dug down into his pocket and brought to light some loose silver and regarded it thoughtfully. It was all the money he had and was beginning to grow interesting.

"Say, was you ever broke?" he asked suddenly, a trace of sadness in his voice.

The bartender glanced at him quickly, but remained judiciously silent, smelling the preamble of an attempt to "touch."

"Well, I have been, am now, an' allus will be, more or less," continued Fisher, in soliloquy, not waiting for an answer to his question. "Money an' me don't ride the same range, not any. Here I am fifty miles away from my ranch, with four dollars and ninety-five cents between me an' starvation an' thirst, an' me not going home for three days yet. I was going to quit the CG this month, but now I gotta go on working for it till another pay-day. I don't even own a cayuse. Now, just to show you what kind of a prickly pear I am, I'll cut the cards with you to see who owns this," he suggested, smiling brightly at his companion.

The bartender laughed, treated on the house, and shuffled out from behind the bar with a pack of greasy playing cards. "All at once, or a dollar a shot?" he asked, shuffling deftly.

"Any way it suits you," responded Fisher, nonchalantly. He knew how a sport should talk; and once he had cut the cards to see who should own his full month's pay. He hoped he would be more successful this time.

"Don't make no difference to me," rejoined the bartender.

"All right; all at once, an' have it over with. It's a kid's game, at that."

"High wins, of course?"

"High wins."

The bartender pushed the cards across the table for his companion to cut. Nat did so, and turned up a deuce. "Oh, don't bother," he said, sliding the four dollars and ninety-five cents across the table.

"Wait," grinned the bartender, who was a stickler for rules. He reached over and turned up a card, and then laughed. "Matched, by George!"

"Try again," grinned Fisher, his face clearing with hope.

The bartender shuffled, and Fisher turned a five, which proved to be just one point shy when his companion had shown his card.

"Now," remarked Fisher, watching his money disappear into the bartender's pocket, "I'll put up my gun agin ten of yore dollars if yo're game. How about it?"

"Done-that's a good weapon."

"None better. Ah, a jack!"

"I say queen-nope, *king*!" exulted the dispenser of liquids. "Say, mebby you can get a job around here when you quit the CG," he suggested.

"That's a good idea," replied Fisher. "But let's finish this while we're at it. I got a good saddle outside on my cayuse-go look it over an' tell me how much you'll put up agin it. If you win it an' can't use it, you can sell it. It's first class."

The bartender walked to the door, looked carefully around for a moment, his eyes fastening upon a trail in the sandy street. Then he laughed. "There ain't no saddle out here," he reported, well knowing where it could be found.

"What! Has that ornery piebald-well, what do you think of that!" exclaimed Fisher, looking up and down the street. "This is the first time that ever happened to me. Why, some coyote stole it! Look at the tracks!"

"No; it ain't stolen," the bartender responded. He considered a moment and then made a suggestion. "Mebby the marshal can tell you where it is-he knows everything like that. Nobody can take a cayuse out of this town while the marshal is up an' well."

"Lucky town, all right," chirped Fisher. "An' where is the marshal?"

"You'll find him down the back way a couple of hundred yards; can't miss him. He allus hangs out there when there are cayuses in town."

"Good for him! I'll chase right down an' see him; an' when I get that piebald — —!"

The bartender watched him go around the corner and shook his head sadly. "Yes; hell of a lucky town," he snorted bitterly, listening for the riot to begin.

The marshal still sat against the corral gate and stroked the Winchester in beatific contemplation. He had a fine job and he was happy. Suddenly leaning forward to look up the road, he smiled derisively and shifted the gun. A cow-puncher was coming his way rapidly, and on foot.

"Are you the marshal of this flea of a town?" politely inquired the newcomer.

"I am the same," replied the man with the rifle. "Anything I kin do for you?"

"Yes; have you seen a piebald cayuse straying around loose-like, or anybody leading one-CG being the brand?"

"I did; it was straying."

"An' which way did it go?"

"Into the town pound."

"What! Pond! What'n blazes is it doing with a pond? Couldn't it drink without getting in? Where's the pond?"

"Right here. It's eating its fool head off. I said pound, not pond. P-o-u-n-d; which means that it's pawned, in hock, for destroying the vegetation of Rawhide, an' disturbing the public peace."

"Good joke on the piebald, all right; it was never locked up before," laughed Fisher, trying to read a sign that faced away from him at a slight angle. "Get it out for me an' I'll disturb *its* peace. Sorry it put you to all that trouble," he sympathized.

"Two dollars an' four bits, an' a dollar initiation fee-it wasn't never in the pound before. That makes three an' a half. Got the money with you?"

"What!" yelled Fisher, emerging from his trance. "What!" he yelled again.

"I ain't none deaf," placidly replied the marshal. "Got the money, the three an' a half?"

"If you think yo're going to skin me outen three-fifty, one-fifty, or one measly cent, you need some medicine, an' I'll give it to you in pill form! You'd make a bum-looking angel, so get up an' hand over that cayuse, *an' do it damned quick*!"

"Three-fifty, an' two bits extry for feed. It'll cost you 'bout a dollar a day for feed. At the end of the week I'll sell that cayuse at auction to pay its bills if you don't cough up. Got the money?"

"I've got a lead slug for you if I can borrow my gun for five minutes!" retorted Fisher, seething double from anger.

"Five dollars more for contempt of court," pleasantly responded Mr. Townsend. "As Justice of the Peace of this community I must allow no disrespect, no contempt of the sovereign law of this town to go unpunished. That makes it eight-seventy-five."

"An' to think I lost my gun!" shouted Fisher, dancing with rage. "I'll get that cayuse out an' I won't pay a cent, not a damned cent! An' I'll get you at the same time!"

"Now you dust around for fifteen dollars even an' stop yore contempt of court an' threats or I'll drill you just for luck!" rejoined Mr. Townsend, angrily. "If you keep on working yore mouth like that there won't be nothing coming to you when I sell that cayuse of yourn. Turn around an' strike out or I'll put you with yore ancestors!"

Chapter XIV
The Stranger's Plan

Fisher, wild with rage, returned to the Paradise and profanely unfolded the tale of his burning wrongs to the bartender and demanded the loan of his gun, which the bartender promptly refused. The present owner of the gun liked Fisher very much for being such a sport and sympathized with him deeply, but he did not want to have such a pleasing acquaintance killed.

"Now, see here: you cool down an' I'll lend you fifteen dollars on that saddle of yourn. You go up an' get that cayuse out before the price goes up any higher-you don't know that man like I do," remarked the man behind the bar earnestly. "That feller Townsend can shoot the eyes out of a small dog at ten miles, purty nigh. Do you savvy my drift?"

"I won't pay him a cussed cent, an' when he goes to sell that piebald at auction, I'll be on hand with a gun; I'll get one somewhere, all right, even if I have to steal it. Then I'll shoot out *his* eyes at ten paces. Why, he's a two-laigged hold-up! That man would —" he stopped as a stranger entered the room. "Hey, stranger! Don't you leave that cayuse of yourn outside all alone or that coyote of a marshal will steal it, shore. He's the biggest thief I ever knowed. He'll lift yore animal quick as a wink!" Fisher warned, excitedly.

The stranger looked at him in surprise and then smiled. "Is it usual for a marshal to steal cayuses? Somewhat out of line, ain't it?" he asked Fisher, glancing at the bartender for light.

"I don't care what's the rule-that marshal just stole my cayuse; an' he'll take yourn, too, if you ain't careful," Fisher replied.

"Well," drawled the stranger, smiling still more, "I reckon I ain't going to stay out there an' watch it, an' I can't bring it in here. But I reckon it'll be all right. You see, I carry 'big medicine' agin hoss-thieves," he replied, tapping his holster and smiling as he remembered the time, not long past, when he himself had been accused of being one. "I'll take a chance if he will-what'll you all have?"

"Little whiskey," replied Fisher, uneasily, worrying because he could not stand for a return treat. "But, say; you keep yore eye on that animal, just the same," he added, and then hurriedly gave his reasons. "An' the worst part of the whole thing is that I ain't got no gun, an' can't seem to borrow none, neither," he added, wistfully eyeing the stranger's Colt. "I gambled mine away to the bartender here an' he won't lemme borrow it for five minutes!"

"Why, I never heard tell of such a thing before!" exclaimed the stranger, hardly believing his ears, and aghast at the thought that such conditions could exist. "Friend," he said, addressing the bartender, "how is it that this sort of thing can go on in this town?" When the bartender had explained at some length, his interested listener smote the bar with a heavy fist and voiced his outraged feelings. "I'll shore be plumb happy to spread that coyote marshal all over his cussed pound! Say, come with me; I'm going down there right now an' get that cayuse, an' if the marshal opens his mouth to peep I'll get him, too. I'm itching for a chance to tunnel a man like him. Come on an' see the show!"

"Not much!" retorted Fisher. "While I am some pleased to meet a white man, an' have a deep an' abiding gratitude for yore noble offer, I can't let you do it. He put it over on me, an' I'm the one that's got to shoot him up. He's mine, my pudding; an' I'm hogging him all to myself. That is one luxury I can indulge in even if I am broke; an' I'm sorry, but I can't give you cards. Seeing, however, as you are so friendly to the cause of liberty an' justice, suppose you lend me yore gun for about three minutes by the watch. From what I've been told about this town such an act will win for you the eternal love an' gratitude of a down-trodden people; yore gun will blaze the way to liberty an' light, freedom an' the right to own yore own property, an' keep it. All I ask is that I be the undeserving medium."

"A-men," sighed the bartender. "Deacon Jones will now pass down the aisle an' collect the buttons an' tin money."

"Stranger," continued Fisher, warming up, when he saw that his words had not produced the desired result, "King James the Twelfth, on the memorable an' blood-soaked field of Trafalgar, gave men their rights. On that great day he signed the Magnet Charter, and proved himself as great a liberator as the sainted Lincoln. You, on this most auspicious occasion, hold in yore strong hand the destiny of this town-the women an' children in this cursed community will rise up an' bless you forever an' pass yore name down to their ancestors as a man of deeds an' honor! Let us pause to consider this —"

"Hold that pause!" interrupted the astounded bartender hurriedly, and with shaking voice. "String it out till I get untangled! I ain't up much on history, so I won't take no chance with that; but I want to tell our eloquent guest that there ain't no women *or* children in this town. An' if there was, I sort of reckon their ancestors would be born first. What do you think about it —"

"Let us pause to consider the shameful an' burning *indignity* perpetrated upon us to-day!" continued Fisher, unheeding the bartender's words. "I, a peaceful, law-abiding *citizen* of this *glorious* Commonwealth, a free an' *equal* member of a liberty-loving nation, a nation whose standard is, *now* and forever, 'Gimme liberty or gimme det', a *nation* that stands for all the conceivable benefits that mankind may enjoy, a *nation* that scintillates pyrotechnically over the prostitution of power —"

Bang! went the bartender's fist on the counter. "Hey! Pause again! Wait a minute! Go back to 'shameful an' burning,' and gimme a chance!"

"—that stands for an even break, I, Nathaniel G. Fisher, have been deprived of one of my inalienable rights, the right of locomotion to distant an' other parts. *An"* I say, right here an' now, that I won't allow no spavined individual with thieving prehensils to —"

"Has that pound-keeper got a rifle?" calmly interrupted the stranger, without a pang of remorse.

"He has. Thus has it allus been with tyrants-well armed, fortified by habit an' tradition —"

"Then you won't get my gun, savvy? We'll find another way to get that cayuse as long as you feel that the marshal is yore hunting. Besides, this man's gall deserves some respect; it is genius, an' to pump genius full of cold lead is to act rash. Now, suppose you tell me when this auction is due to come off."

"Oh, not for a week; he wants to run up the board an' keep expenses. Tyrants, such as him —"

"Shore," interposed the bartender, "he'll make the expenses equal what he gets for the cayuse, no matter what it comes to. An' he's the whole town, an' the justice of the peace, besides. What he says goes."

"Well, I'm the Governor of the State an' I've got the Supreme Court right here in my holster, so I reckon I can reverse his official acts an' fill his legal opinions full of holes," the stranger replied, laughing heartily. "Bartender, will you help me play a little joke on His Honore, the Town, —just a little harmless joke?"

"Well, that all depends whether the joke is harmless on *me*. You see, he can shoot like the devil-he allus knows when a man is going to draw, an' gets his gun out first. I ain't got no respect for him, but I take off my hat to his gunplay, all right."

The stranger smiled. "Well, I can shoot a bit myself. But I shore wish he'd hold that auction quick —I've got to go on home without losing any more time. Fisher, suppose you go down to the pound and dare that tumble-bug to hold the auction this afternoon. Tell him that you'll shoot him full of holes if he goes pulling off any auction to-day, an' dare him to try it. I want it to come off before night, an' I reckon that'll hustle it along."

"I'll do anything to get the edge on that thief," replied Fisher, quickly, "but don't you reckon I'd better tote a gun, going down an' bearding such a thief in his own den? You know I allus like to shoot when I'm being shot at."

"Well, I don't blame you; it's only a petty weakness," grinned the stranger, hanging onto his Colt as if fearing that the other would snatch it and run. "But you'll do better without any gun-me an' the bartender don't want to have to go down there an' bring you back on a plank."

"All right, then," sighed Fisher, reluctantly, "but he'll jump the price again. He'll fine me for contempt of court an' make me pay money I ain't got for disturbing him. But I'm game-so long."

When he had gained the street, the stranger turned to the bartender. "Now, friend, you tell me if this man of gall, this Mr. Townsend, has got many friends in town-anybody that'll be likely to pot shoot from the back when things get warm. I can't watch both ends unless I know what I'm up against."

"*No!* Every man in town hates him," answered the bartender, hastily, and with emphasis.

"Ah, that's good. Now, I wonder if you could see 'most everybody that's in town now an' get 'em to promise to help me by letting me run this all by myself. All I want them to do is not to say a word. It ain't hard to keep still when you want to."

"Why, I reckon I might see 'em-there ain't many here this time of day," responded the bartender. "But what's yore game, anyhow?" he asked, suddenly growing suspicious.

"It's just a little scheme I figgered out," the stranger replied, and then he confided in the bartender, who jigged a few fancy steps to show his appreciation of the other's genius. His suspicions left him at once, and he hastened out to tell the inhabitants of the town to follow his instructions to the letter, and he knew they would obey, and be glad, hilariously glad, to do so. While he was hurrying around giving his instructions, the CG puncher returned to the hotel and reported.

"Well, it worked, all right," Fisher growled. "I told him what I'd do to him if he tried to auction that cayuse off an' he retorted that if I didn't shut up an' mind my own business, that he'd sell the horse this noon, at twelve o'clock, in the public square, wherever that is. I told him he was a coyote and dared him to do it. Told him I'd pump him full of air ducts if he didn't wait till next week. Said I had the promise of a gun an' that it'd give me great pleasure to use it on him if he tried any auctioneering at my expense this noon. Then he fined me five dollars more, swore that he'd show me what it meant to dare the marshal of Rawhide an' insult the dignity of the court an' town council, an' also that he'd shoot my liver all through my system if I didn't leave him to his reflections. Now, look here, stranger; noon is only two hours away an' I'm due to lose my outfit: what are *you* going to do to get me out of this mess?" he finished anxiously, hands on hips.

"You did real well, very fine, indeed," replied the stranger, smiling with content. "An' don't you worry about that outfit —I'm going to get it back for you an' a little bit more. So, as long as you don't lose nothing, you ain't got no kick coming, have you? An' you ain't got no interest in what I'm going to do. Just sit tight an' keep yore eyes an' ears open at noon. Meantime, if you want something to do to keep you busy, practise making speeches-you ought to be ashamed to be punching cows an' working for a living when you could use yore talents an' get a lot of graft besides. Any man who can say as much on nothing as you can ought to be in the Senate representing some railroad company or waterpower steal-you don't have to work there, just loaf an' take easy money for cheating the people what put you there. Now, don't get mad —I'm only stringing you: I wouldn't be mean enough to call you a senator. To tell the truth, I think yo're too honest to even think of such a thing. But go ahead an' practise —I don't mind it a bit."

"Huh! I couldn't go to Congress," laughed Fisher. "I'd have to practise by getting elected mayor of some town an' then go to the Legislature for the finishing touches."

"Mr. Townsend would beat you out," murmured the stranger, looking out of the window and wishing for noon. He sauntered over to a chair, placed it where he could see his horse, and took things easy. The bartender returned with several men at his heels, and all were grinning and joking. They took up their places against the bar and indulged in frequent fits of chuckling, not letting their eyes stray from the man in the chair and the open street through the door, where the auction was to be held. They regarded the stranger in the light of a would-be public benefactor, a martyr, who was to provide the town with a little excitement before he followed his predecessors into the grave. Perhaps he would *not* be killed, perhaps he would shoot the pound-keeper and general public nuisance-but ah, this was the stuff of which dreams were made: the marshal would never be killed, he would thrive and outlive his fellow-townsmen, and die in bed at a ripe old age.

One of the citizens, dangling his legs from the card table, again looked closely at the man with the plan, and then turned to a companion beside him. "I've seen that there feller som'ers, sometime," he whispered. "I *know* I have. But I'll be teetotally dod-blasted if I can place him."

"Well, Jim; I never saw him afore, an' I don't know who he is," replied the other, refilling his pipe with elaborate care, "but if he can kill Townsend to-day, I'll be so plumb joyous I won't know what to do with m'self."

"I'm afraid he won't, though," remarked another, lolling back against the bar. "The marshal was born to hang-nobody can beat him on the draw. But, anyhow, we're going to see some fun."

The first speaker, still straining his memory for a clue to the stranger's identity, pulled out a handful of silver and placed it on the table. "I'll bet that he makes good," he offered, but there were no takers.

The stranger now lazily arose and stepped into the doorway, leaning against the jamb and shaking his holster sharply to loosen the gun for action. He glanced quickly behind him and spoke curtly: "Remember, now —*I* am to do all the talking at this auction; you fellers just look on."

A mumble of assent replied to him, and the townsmen craned their necks to look out. A procession slowly wended its way up the street, led by the marshal, astride a piebald horse bearing the crude brand of the CG. Three men followed him and numerous dogs of several colors, sizes, and ages roamed at will, in a listless, bored way, between the horse and the men. The dust arose sluggishly and slowly dissipated in the hot, shimmering air, and a fly buzzed with wearying persistence against the dirty glass in the front window.

The marshal, peering out from under the pulled-down brim of his Stetson, looked critically at the sleepy horse standing near the open door of the Paradise and sought its brand, but in vain, for it was standing with the wrong side towards him. Then he glanced at the man in the door, a puzzled expression stealing over his face. He had known that man once, but time and events had wiped him nearly out of his memory and he could not place him. He decided that the other horse could wait until he had sold the one he was on, and, stopping before the door of the Paradise, he raised his left arm, his right arm lying close to his side, not far from the holster on his thigh.

"Gentlemen an' feller-citizens," he began: "As marshal of this booming city, I am about to offer for sale to the highest bidder this A Number 1 piebald, pursooant to the decree of the local court an' with the sanction of the town council an' the mayor. This same sale is for to pay the town for the board an' keep of this animal, an' to square the fine in such cases made an' provided. It's sound in wind an' limb, fourteen han's high, an' in all ways a beautiful piece of hoss-flesh. Now, gentlemen, how much am I bid for this cayuse? Remember, before you make me any offer, that this animal is broke to punching cows an' is a first-class cayuse."

The crowd in the Paradise had flocked out into the street and oozed along the front of the building, while the stranger now leaned carelessly against his own horse, critically looking over the one on sale. Fisher, uneasy and worried, squirmed close at hand and glanced covertly from his horse and saddle to the guns in the belts on the members of the crowd.

It was the stranger who broke the silence: "Two bits I bid-two bits," he said, very quietly, whereat the crowd indulged in a faint snicker and a few nudges.

The marshal looked at him and then ignored him. "How much, gentlemen?" he asked, facing the crowd again.

"Two bits," repeated the stranger, as the crowd remained silent.

"Two bits!" yelled the marshal, glaring at him angrily: "*Two bits!* Why, the *look* in this cayuse's eyes is worth four! Look at the spirit in them eyes, look at the intelligence! The saddle alone is worth a clean forty dollars of any man's money. I am out here to sell this animal to the highest bidder; the sale's begun, an' I want bids, not jokes. Now, who'll start it off?" he demanded, glancing around; but no one had anything to say except the terse stranger, who appeared to be getting irritated.

"You've got a starter —I've given you a bid. I bid two bits —t-w-o b-i-t-s, twenty-five cents. Now go ahead with yore auction."

The marshal thought he saw an attempt at humor, and since he was feeling quite happy, and since he knew that good humor is conducive to good bidding, he smiled, all the time, however, racking his memory for the name of the humorist. So he accepted the bid: "All right, this gentleman bids two bits. Two bits I am bid-two bits. Twenty-five cents. Who'll make it twenty-five dollars? Two bits-who says twenty-five dollars? Ah, did *you* say twenty-five dollars?" he snapped, leveling an accusing and threatening fore-finger at the man nearest him, who squirmed restlessly and glanced at the stranger. "*Did you say twenty-five dollars?*" he shouted.

The stranger came to the rescue. "He did not. He hasn't opened his mouth. But *I* said twenty-five *cents*," quietly observed the humorist.

"Who'll gimme thirty? Who'll gimme thirty dollars? Did I hear thirty dollars? Did I hear twenty-five dollars bid? Who said thirty dollars? Did *you* say twenty-five dollars?"

"How could he when he was talking politics to the man behind him?" asked the stranger. "I said two bits," he added complacently, as he watched the auctioneer closely.

"I want twenty-five dollars-an' you shut yore blasted mouth!" snapped the marshal at the persistent twenty-five-cent man. He did not see the fire smouldering in the squinting eyes so alertly watching him. "Twenty-five dollars-not a cent less takes the cayuse. Why, gentlemen, he's worth twenty in *cans*! Gimme twenty-five dollars, somebody. *I* bid twenty-five. I want thirty. I want thirty, gentlemen; you must gimme thirty. *I* bid twenty-five dollars-who's going to make it thirty?"

"Show us yore twenty-five an' she's yourn," remarked the stranger, with exasperating assurance, while Fisher grew pale with excitement. The stranger was standing clear of his horse now, and alert readiness was stamped all over him. "You accepted my bid-show yore twenty-five dollars or take my two bits."

"You close that face of yourn!" exploded the marshal, angrily. "I don't mind a little fun, but you've got altogether too damned much to say. You've queered the bidding, an' now you shut up!"

"I said two bits an' I mean just that. You show yore twenty-five or gimme that cayuse on my bid," retorted the stranger.

"By the pans of Julius Caesar!" shouted the marshal. "I'll put you to sleep so you'll never wake up if I hears any more about you an' yore two bits!"

"Show me, Rednose," snapped the other, his gun out in a flash. "I want that cayuse, an' I want it quick. You show me twenty-five dollars or I'll take it out from under you on my bid, you yaller dog! *Stop it!* Shut up! That's suicide, that is. Others have tried it an' failed, an' yo're no sleight-of-hand gun-man. This is the first time I ever paid a hoss-thief in *silver*, or bought stolen goods, but everything has to have a beginning. You get nervous with that hand of yourn an' I'll cure you of it! Git off that piebald, an' quick!"

The marshal felt stunned and groped for a way out, but the gun under his nose was as steady as a rock. He sat there stupidly, not knowing enough to obey orders.

"Come, get off that cayuse," sharply commanded the stranger. "An' I'll take yore Winchester as a fine for this high-handed business you've been carrying on. You may be the local court an' all the town officials, but I'm the Governor, an' here's my Supreme Court, as I was saying to the boys a little while ago. Yo're overruled. Get off that cayuse, an' don't waste no more time about it, neither!"

The marshal glared into the muzzle of the weapon and felt a sinking in the pit of his stomach. Never before had he failed to anticipate the pull of a gun. As the stranger said, there must always be a beginning, a first time. He was thinking quickly now; he was master of himself again, but he realized that he was in a tight place unless he obeyed the man with the drop. Not a man in town would help him; on the other hand, they were all against him, and hugely enjoying his discomfiture. With some men he could afford to take chances and jerk at his gun even when at such a disadvantage, but —

"Stranger," he said slowly, "what's yore name?"

The crowd listened eagerly.

"My *friends* call me Hopalong Cassidy; other people, other things-you gimme that cayuse an' that Winchester. Here! Hand the gun to Fisher, so there won't be no lamentable accidents: I don't want to shoot you, 'less I have to."

"They're both yourn," sighed Mr. Townsend, remembering a certain day over near Alameda, when he had seen Mr. Cassidy at gun-play. He dismounted slowly and sorrowfully. "Do I —do I get my two bits?" he asked.

"You shore do-yore gall is worth it," said Mr. Cassidy, turning the piebald over to its overjoyed owner, who was already arranging further gambling with his friend, the bartender.

Mr. Townsend pocketed the one bid, surveyed glumly the hilarious crowd flocking in to the bar to drink to their joy in his defeat, and wandered disconsolately back to the pound. He was never again seen in that locality, or by any of the citizens of Rawhide, for between dark and dawn he resumed his travels, bound for some locality far removed from limping, red-headed drawbacks.

Chapter XV

Johnny Learns Something

For several weeks after Hopalong got back to the ranch, full of interesting stories and minus the grouch, things went on in a way placid enough for the most peacefully inclined individual that ever sat a saddle. And then trouble drifted down from the north and caused a look of anxiety to spoil Buck Peters' pleasant expression, and began to show on the faces of his men. When one finds the carcasses of two cows on the same day, and both are skinned, there can be only one conclusion. The killing and skinning of two cows out of herds that are numbered by thousands need not, in themselves, bring lines of worry to any foreman's brow; but there is the sting of being cheated, the possibility of the losses going higher unless a sharp lesson be given upon the folly of fooling with a very keen and active buzz-saw, —and it was the determination of the outfit of the Bar-20 to teach that lesson, and as quickly as circumstances would permit.

It was common knowledge that there was a more or less organized band of shiftless malcontents making its headquarters in and near Perry's Bend, some distance up the river, and the deduction in this case was easy. The Bar-20 cared very little about what went on at Perry's Bend-that was a matter which concerned only the ranches near that town-as long as no vexatious happenings sifted too far south. But they had so sifted, and Perry's Bend, or rather the undesirable class hanging out there, was due to receive a shock before long.

About a week after the finding of the first skinned cows, Pete Wilson tornadoed up to the bunk house with a perforated arm. Pete was on foot, having lost his horse at the first exchange of shots, which accounts for the expression describing his arrival. Pete hated to walk, he hated still more to get shot, and most of all he hated to have to admit that his rifle-shooting was so far below par. He had seen the thief at work and, too eager to work up close to the cattle skinner before announcing his displeasure, had missed the first shot. When he dragged himself out from under his deceased horse the scenery was undisturbed save for a small cloud of dust hovering over a distant rise to the north of him. After delivering a short and bitter monologue he struck out for the ranch and arrived in a very hot and wrathful condition. It was contagious, that condition, and before long the entire outfit was in the saddle and pounding north, Pete overjoyed because his wound was so slight as not to bar him from the chase. The shock was on the way, and as events proved, was to be one long to linger in the minds of the inhabitants of Perry's Bend and the surrounding range.

The patrons of the Oasis liked their tobacco strong. The pungent smoke drifted in sluggish clouds along the low, black ceiling, following its upward slant toward the east wall and away from the high bar at the other end. This bar, rough and strong, ran from the north wall to within a scant two feet of the south wall, the opening bridged by a hinged board which served as an extension to the counter. Behind the bar was a rear door, low and double, the upper part barred securely-the lower part was used most. In front of and near the bar was a large round table, at which four men played cards silently, while two smaller tables were located along the north wall. Besides dilapidated chairs there were half a dozen low wooden boxes partly filled with sand, and attention was directed to the existence and purpose of these by a roughly lettered sign on the wall, reading: "Gents will look for a box first," which the "gents" sometimes did. The majority of the "gents" preferred to aim at various knotholes in the floor and bet on the result, chancing the outpouring of the proprietor's wrath if they missed.

On the wall behind the bar was a smaller and neater request: "Leave your guns with the bartender. —Edwards." This, although a month old, still called forth caustic and profane remarks from the regular frequenters of the saloon, for hitherto restraint in the matter of carrying weapons had been unknown. They forthwith evaded the order in a manner consistent with their characteristics-by carrying smaller guns where they could not be seen. The majority had simply sawed off a generous part of the long barrels of their Colts and Remingtons, which did not improve their accuracy.

Edwards, the new marshal of Perry's Bend, had come direct from Kansas and his reputation as a fighter had preceded him. When he took up his first day's work he was kept busy proving that he was the rightful owner of it and that it had not been exaggerated in any manner or degree. With the exception of one instance the proof had been bloodless, for he reasoned that gun-play should give way, whenever possible, to a crushing "right" or "left" to the point of the jaw or the pit of the stomach. His proficiency in the manly art was polished and thorough and bespoke earnest application. The last doubting Thomas to be convinced came to five minutes after his diaphragm had been rudely and suddenly raised several inches by a low right hook, and as he groped for his bearings and got his wind back again he asked, very feebly, where "Kansas" was; and the name stuck.

When Harlan heard the nickname for the first time he stopped pulling the cork out of a whiskey bottle long enough to remark, casually, "I allus reckoned Kansas was purty close to hell," and said no more about it. Harlan was the proprietor and bartender of the Oasis and catered to the excessive and uncritical thirsts of the ruck of range society, and he had objected vigorously to the placing of the second sign in his place of business; but at the close of an incisive if inelegant reply from the marshal, the sign went up, and stayed up. Edwards' language and delivery were as convincing as his fists.

The marshal did not like the Oasis; indeed, he went further and cordially hated it. Harlan's saloon was a thorn in his side and he was only waiting for a good excuse to wipe it off the local map. He was the Law, and behind him were the range riders, who would be only too glad to have the nest of rustlers wiped out and its gang of ne'er-do-wells scattered to the four winds. Indeed, he had been given to understand in a most polite and diplomatic way that if this were not done lawfully they would try to do it themselves, and they had great faith in their ability to handle the situation in a thorough and workmanlike manner. This would not do in a law-abiding community, as he called the town, and so he had replied that the work was his, and that it would be performed as soon as he believed himself justified to act. Harlan and his friends were fully conversant with the feeling against them and had become a little more cautious, alertly watching out for trouble.

On the evening of the day which saw Pete Wilson's discomfiture most of the habitues had assembled in the Oasis where, besides the card-players already mentioned, eight men lounged against the bar. There was some laughter, much subdued talking, and a little whispering. More whispering went on under that roof than in all the other places in town put together; for here rustling was planned, wayfaring strangers were "trimmed" in "frame-ups" at cards, and a hunted man was certain to find assistance. Harlan had once boasted that no fugitive had ever been taken from his saloon, and he was behind the bar and standing on the trap door which led to the six-by-six cellar when he made the assertion. It was true, for only those in his confidence knew of the place of refuge under the floor; it had been dug at night and the dirt carefully disposed of.

It had not been dark very long before talking ceased and card-playing was suspended while all looked up as the front door crashed open and two punchers entered, looking the crowd over with critical care.

"Stay here, Johnny," Hopalong told his youthful companion, and then walked forward, scrutinizing each scowling face in turn, while Johnny stood with his back to the door, keenly alert, his right hand resting lightly on his belt not far from the holster.

Harlan's thick neck grew crimson and his eyes hard. "Looking fer something?" he asked with bitter sarcasm, his hands under the bar. Johnny grinned hopefully and a sudden tenseness took possession of him as he watched for the first hostile move.

"Yes," Hopalong replied coolly, appraising Harlan's attitude and look in one swift glance, "but it ain't here, now. Johnny, get out," he ordered, backing after his companion, and safely outside, the two walked towards Jackson's store, Johnny complaining about the little time spent in the Oasis.

As they entered the store they saw Edwards, whose eye asked a question.

"No; he ain't in there yet," Hopalong replied.

"Did you look all over? Behind the bar?" Edwards asked, slowly. "He can't get out of town through that cordon you've got strung around it, an' he ain't nowhere else. Leastwise, I couldn't find him."

"Come on back!" excitedly exclaimed Johnny, turning towards the door. "You didn't look behind the bar! Come on-bet you ten dollars that's where he is!"

"Mebby yo're right, Kid," replied Hopalong, and the marshal's nodding head decided it.

In the saloon there was strong language, and Jack Quinn, expert skinner of other men's cows, looked inquiringly at the proprietor. "What's up now, Harlan?"

The proprietor laughed harshly but said nothing-taciturnity was his one redeeming trait. "Did you say cigars?" he asked, pushing a box across the bar to an impatient customer. Another beckoned to him and he leaned over to hear the whispered request, a frown struggling to show itself on his face. "Nix; you know my rule. No trust in here."

But the man at the far end of the line was unlike the proprietor and he prefaced his remarks with a curse. "*I* know what's up! They want Jerry Brown, that's what! An' I hopes they don't get him, the bullies!"

"What did he do? Why do they want him?" asked the man who had wanted trust.

"Skinning. He was careless or crazy, working so close to their ranch houses. Nobody that had any sense would take a chance like that," replied Boston, adept at sleight-of-hand with cards and very much in demand when a frame-up was to be rung in on some unsuspecting stranger. His one great fault in the eyes of his partners was that he hated to divvy his winnings and at times had to be coerced into sharing equally.

"Aw, them big ranches make me mad," announced the first speaker. "Ten years ago there was a lot of little ranchers, an' every one of 'em had his own herd, an' plenty of free grass an' water for it. Where are the little herds now? Where are the cows that *we* used to own?" he cried, hotly. "What happens to a maverick-hunter now-a-days? By God, if a man helps hisself to a pore, sick dogie he's hunted down! It can't go on much longer, an' that's shore."

Cries of approbation arose on all sides, for his auditors ignored the fact that their kind, by avarice and thievery, had forever killed the occupation of maverick-hunting. That belonged to the old days, before the demand for cows and their easy and cheap transportation had boosted the prices and made them valuable.

Slivers Lowe leaped up from his chair. "Yo're right, Harper! Dead right! *I* was a little cattle owner once, so was you, an' Jerry, an' most of us!" Slivers found it convenient to forget that fully half of his small herd had perished in the bitter and long winter of five years before, and that the remainder had either flowed down his parched throat or been lost across the big round table near the bar. Not a few of his cows were banked in the east under Harlan's name.

The rear door opened slightly and one of the loungers looked up and nodded. "It's all right, Jerry. But get a move on!"

"Here, *you*!" called Harlan, quickly bending over the trap door, "*Lively!*"

Jerry was half way to the proprietor when the front door swung open and Hopalong, closely followed by the marshal, leaped into the room, and immediately thereafter the back door banged open and admitted Johnny. Jerry's right hand was in his side coat pocket and Johnny, young and self-confident, and with a lot to learn, was certain that he could beat the fugitive on the draw.

"I reckon you won't blot no more brands!" he cried, triumphantly, watching both Jerry and Harlan.

The card-players had leaped to their feet and at a signal from Harlan they surged forward to the bar and formed a barrier between Johnny and his friends; and as they did so that puncher jerked at his gun, twisting to half face the crowd. At that instant fire and smoke spurted from Jerry's side coat pocket and the odor of burning cloth arose. As Johnny fell, the rustler ducked low and sprang for the door. A gun roared twice in the front of the room and Jerry staggered a little and cursed as he gained the opening, but he plunged into the darkness and threw himself into the saddle on the first horse he found in the small corral.

When the crowd massed, Hopalong leaped at it and strove to tear his way to the opening at the end of the bar, while the marshal covered Harlan and the others. Finding that he could not get through. Hopalong sprang on the shoulder of the nearest man and succeeded in winging the fugitive at the first shot, the other going wild. Then, frantic with rage and anxiety, he beat his way through the crowd, hammering mercilessly at heads with the butt of his Colt, and knelt at his friend's side.

Edwards, angered almost to the point of killing, ordered the crowd to stand against the wall, and laughed viciously when he saw two men senseless on the floor. "Hope he beat in yore heads!" he gritted, savagely. "Harlan, put yore paws up in sight or I'll drill you clean! Now climb over an' get in line-quick!"

Johnny moaned and opened his eyes. "Did-did I —get him?"

"No; but he gimleted you, all right," Hopalong replied. "You'll come 'round if you keep quiet." He arose, his face hard with the desire to kill. "I'm coming back for *you*, Harlan, after I get yore friend! An' all the rest of you pups, too!"

"Get me out of here," whispered Johnny.

"Shore enough, Kid; but keep quiet," replied Hopalong, picking him up in his arms and moving carefully towards the door. "We'll get him, Johnny; an' all the rest, too, when ——" The voice died out in the direction of Jackson's and the marshal, backing to the front door, slipped out and to one side, running backward, his eyes on the saloon.

"Yore day's about over, Harlan," he muttered. "There's going to be some few funerals around here before many hours pass."

When he reached the store he found the owner and two Double-Arrow punchers taking care of Johnny. "Where's Hopalong?" he asked.

"Gone to tell his foreman," replied Jackson. "Hey, youngster, you let them bandages alone! Hear me?"

"Hullo, Kansas," remarked John Bartlett, foreman of the Double-Arrow. "I come nigh getting yore man; somebody rode past me like a streak in the dark, so I just ups an' lets drive for luck, an' so did he. I heard him cuss an' I emptied my gun after him."

"The rest was a-passing the word along to ride in when I left the line," remarked one of the other punchers. "How you feeling now, Johnny?"

Chapter XVI
The End of the Trail

The rain slanted down in sheets and the broken plain, thoroughly saturated, held the water in pools or sent it down the steep sides of the arroyo, to feed the turbulent flood which swept along the bottom, foam-flecked and covered with swiftly moving driftwood. Around a bend in the arroyo, where the angry water flung itself against the ragged bulwark of rock and flashed away in a gleaming line of foam, a horseman appeared bending low in the saddle for better protection against the storm. He rode along the edge of the stream on the farther bank, opposite the steep bluff on the northern side, forcing his wounded and jaded horse to keep fetlock deep in the water which swirled and sucked about its legs. He was trying his hardest to hide his trail. Lower down the hard, rocky ground extended to the water's edge, and if he could delay his pursuers for an hour or so, he felt that, even with his tired horse, he would have more than an even chance.

But they had gained more than he knew. Suddenly above him on the top of the steep bluff across the torrent a man loomed up against the clouds, peered intently into the arroyo, and then waved his sombrero to an unseen companion. A puff of smoke flashed from his shoulder and streaked away, the report of the shot lost in the gale. The fugitive's horse reared and plunged into the deep water and with its rider was swept rapidly towards the bend, the way they had come.

"That makes the fourth time I've missed that coyote!" angrily exclaimed Hopalong as Red Connors joined him.

The other quickly raised his rifle and fired; and the horse, spilling its rider out of the saddle, floated away tail first. The fugitive, gripping his rifle, bobbed and whirled at the whim of the greedy water as shots struck near him. Making a desperate effort, he staggered up the bank and fell exhausted behind a boulder.

"Well, the coyote is afoot, anyhow," said Red, with great satisfaction.

"Yes; but how are we going to get to him?" asked Hopalong. "We can't get the cayuses down here, an' we can't swim *that* water without them. An' if we could, he'd pot us easy."

"There's a way out of it somewhere," Red replied, disappearing over the edge of the bluff to gamble with Fate.

"Hey! Come back here, you chump!" cried Hopalong, running forward. "He'll get you, shore!"

"That's a chance I've got to take if I get him," was the reply.

A puff of smoke sailed from behind the boulder on the other bank and Hopalong, kneeling for steadier aim, fired and then followed his friend. Red was downstream casting at a rock across the torrent but the wind toyed with the heavy, water-soaked *reata* as though it were a string. As Hopalong reached his side a piece of driftwood ducked under the water and an angry humming sound died away downstream. As the report reached their ears a jet of water spurted up into Red's face and he stepped back involuntarily.

"He's so shaky," Hopalong remarked, looking back at the wreath of smoke above the boulder. "I reckon I must have hit him harder than I thought in Harlan's. Gee! He's wild as blazes!" he yelled as a bullet hummed high above his head and struck sharply against the rock wall.

"Yes," Red replied, coiling the rope. "I was trying to rope that rock over there. If I could anchor to that, the current would push us over quick. But it's too far with this wind blowing."

"We can't do nothing here 'cept get plugged. He'll be getting steadier as he rests from his fight with the water," Hopalong remarked, and added quickly, "Say, remember that meadow back there a ways? We can make her from there, all right."

"Yo're right; that's what we've got to do. He's sending 'em nearer every shot-Gee! I could 'most feel the wind of that one. An' blamed if it ain't stopped raining. Come on."

They clambered up the slippery, muddy bank to where they had left their horses, and cantered back over their trail. Minute after minute passed before the cautious skulker among the rocks across the stream could believe in his good fortune. When he at last decided that he was alone again he left his shelter and started away, with slowly weakening stride, over cleanly washed rock where he left no trail.

It was late in the afternoon before the two irate punchers appeared upon the scene, and their comments, as they hunted slowly over the hard ground, were numerous and bitter. Deciding that it was hopeless in that vicinity, they began casting in great circles on the chance of crossing the trail further back from the river. But they had little faith in their success. As Red remarked, snorting like a horse in his disgust, "I'll bet four dollars an' a match he's swum down the river clean to hell just to have the laugh on us." Red had long since given it up as a bad job, though continuing to search, when a shout from the distant Hopalong sent him forward on a run.

"Hey, Red!" cried Hopalong, pointing ahead of them. "Look there! Ain't that a house?"

"Naw; course not! It's a —it's a ship!" Red snorted sarcastically. "What did you think it might be?"

"G'wan!" retorted his companion. "It's a mission."

"Ah, g'wan yoreself! What's a mission doing up here?" Red snapped.

"What do you think they do? What do they do anywhere?" hotly rejoined Hopalong, thinking about Johnny. "There! See the cross?"

"Shore enough!"

"An' there's tracks at last-mighty wobbly, but tracks just the same. Them rocks couldn't go on forever. Red, I'll bet he's cashed in by this time."

"Cashed nothing! Them fellers don't."

"Well, if he's in that joint we might as well go back home. We won't get him, not nohow," declared Hopalong.

"Huh! You wait an' see!" replied Red, pugnaciously.

"Reckon you never run up agin a mission real hard," Hopalong responded, his memory harking back to the time he had disagreed with a convent, and they both meant about the same to him as far as winning out was concerned.

"Think I'm a fool kid?" snapped Red, aggressively.

"Well, you ain't no *kid*."

"You let *me* do the talking; *I'll* get him."

"All right; an' I'll do the laughing," snickered Hopalong, at the door. "Sic 'em, Red!"

The other boldly stepped into a small vestibule, Hopalong close at his heels. Red hitched his holster and walked heavily into a room at his left. With the exception of a bench, a table, and a small altar, the room was devoid of furnishings, and the effect of these was lost in the dim light from the narrow windows. The peculiar, not unpleasant odor of burning incense and the dim light awakened a latent reverence and awe in Hopalong, and he sneaked off his sombrero, an inexplicable feeling of guilt stealing over him. There were three doors in the walls, deeply shrouded in the dusk of the room, and it was very hard to watch all three at once.

Red was peering into the dark corners, his hand on the butt of his Colt, and hardly knew what he was looking for. "This joint must 'a' looked plumb good to that coyote, all right. He had a hell of a lot of luck, but he won't keep it for long, damn him!" he remarked.

"Quit cussing!" tersely ordered Hopalong. "An' for God's sake, throw out that damned cigarette! Ain't you got no manners?"

Red listened intently and then grinned. "Hear that? They're playing dominoes in there—come on!"

"Aw, you chump! 'Dominee' means 'mother' in Latin, which is what they speaks."

"How do you know?"

"Hanged if I can tell —I've heard it somewhere, that's all."

"Well, I don't care what it means. This is a frame-up so that coyote can get away. I'll bet they gave him a cayuse an' started him off while we've been losing time in here. I'm going inside an' ask some questions."

Before he could put his plan into execution, Hopalong nudged him and he turned to see his friend staring at one of the doors. There had been no sound, but he would swear that a monk stood gravely regarding them, and he rubbed his eyes. He stepped back suspiciously and then started forward again.

"Look here, stranger," he remarked, with quiet emphasis, "we're after that cow-lifter, an' we mean to get him. Savvy?"

The monk did not appear to hear him, so he tried another tack. "*Habla Espanola?*" he asked, experimentally.

"You have ridden far?" replied the monk in perfect English.

"All the way from the Bend," Red replied, relieved. "We're after Jerry Brown. He tried to kill Johnny, an' near made good. An' I reckon we've treed him, judging from the tracks."

"And if you capture him?"

"He won't have no more use for no side pocket shooting."

"I see; you will kill him."

"Shore's it's wet outside."

"I'm afraid you are doomed to disappointment."

"Ya-as?" asked Red with a rising inflection.

"You will not want him now," replied the monk.

Red laughed sarcastically and Hopalong smiled.

"There ain't a-going to be no argument about it. Trot him out," ordered Red, grimly.

The monk turned to Hopalong. "Do you, too, want him?"

Hopalong nodded.

"My friends, he is safe from your punishment."

Red wheeled instantly and ran outside, returning in a few moments, smiling triumphantly. "There are tracks coming in, but there ain't none going away. He's here. If you don't lead us to him we'll shore have to rummage around an' poke him out for ourselves: which is it?"

"You are right-he is here, and he is not here."

"We're waiting," Red replied, grinning.

"When I tell you that you will not want him, do you still insist on seeing him?"

"We'll see him, an' we'll want him, too."

As the rain poured down again the sound of approaching horses was heard, and Hopalong ran to the door in time to see Buck Peters swing off his mount and step forward to enter the building. Hopalong stopped him and briefly outlined the situation, begging him to keep the men outside. The monk met his return with a grateful smile and, stepping forward, opened the chapel door, saying, "Follow me."

The unpretentious chapel was small and nearly dark, for the usual dimness was increased by the lowering clouds outside. The deep, narrow window openings, fitted with stained glass, ran almost to the rough-hewn rafters supporting the steep-pitched roof, upon which the heavy rain beat again with a sound like that of distant drums. Gusts of rain and the water from the roof beat against the south windows, while the wailing wind played its mournful cadences about the eaves, and the stanch timbers added their creaking notes to swell the dirge-like chorus.

At the farther end of the room two figures knelt and moved before the white altar, the soft light of flickering candles playing fitfully upon them and glinting from the altar ornaments, while before a rough coffin, which rested upon two pedestals, stood a third, whose rich, sonorous Latin filled the chapel with impressive sadness. "Give eternal rest to them, O Lord," —the words seeming to become a part of the room. The ineffably sad, haunting melody of the mass whispered back from the room between the assaults of the enraged wind, while from the altar came the responses in a low, Gregorian chant, and through it all the clinking of the censer chains added intermittent notes. Aloft streamed the vapor of the incense, wavering with the air currents, now lost in the deep twilight of the sanctuary, and now faintly revealed by the glow of the candles, perfuming the air with its aromatic odor.

As the last deep-toned words died away the celebrant moved slowly around the coffin, swinging the censer over it and then, sprinkling the body and making the sign of the cross above its head, solemnly withdrew.

From the shadows along the side walls other figures silently emerged and grouped around the coffin. Raising it they turned it slowly around and carried it down the dim aisle in measured tread, moving silently as ghosts.

"He is with God, Who will punish according to his sins," said a low voice, and Hopalong started, for he had forgotten the presence of the guide. "God be with you, and may you die as he died-repentant and in peace."

Buck chafed impatiently before the chapel door leading to a small, well-kept graveyard, wondering what it was that kept quiet for so long a time his two most assertive men, when he had momentarily expected to hear more or less turmoil and confusion.

C-r-e-a-k! He glanced up, gun in hand and raised as the door swung slowly open. His hand dropped suddenly and he took a short step forward; six black-robed figures shouldering a long box stepped slowly past him, and his nostrils were assailed by the pungent odor of the incense. Behind them came his fighting punchers, humble, awed, reverent, their sombreros in their hands, and their heads bowed.

"What in blazes!" exclaimed Buck, wonder and surprise struggling for the mastery as the others cantered up.

"He's cashed," Red replied, putting on his sombrero and nodding toward the procession.

Buck turned like a flash and spoke sharply: "Skinny! Lanky! Follow that glory-outfit, an' see what's in that box!"

Billy Williams grinned at Red. "Yo're shore pious, Red."

"Shut up!" snapped Red, anger glinting in his eyes, and Billy subsided.

Lanky and Skinny soon returned from accompanying the procession.

"I had to look twice to be shore it was him. His face was plumb happy, like a baby. But he's gone, all right," Lanky reported.

"Deader'n hell," remarked Skinny, looking around curiously. "This here is some shack, ain't it?" he finished.

"All right-he knowed how he'd finish when he began. Now for that dear Mr. Harlan," Buck replied, vaulting into the saddle. He turned and looked at Hopalong, and his wonder grew. "Hey, *you!* Yes, *you!* Come out of that an' put on yore lid! Straddle leather-we can't stay here all night."

Hopalong started, looked at his sombrero and silently obeyed. As they rode down the trail and around a corner he turned in his saddle and looked back; and then rode on, buried in thought.

Billy, grinning, turned and playfully punched him in the ribs. "Getting glory, Hoppy?"

Hopalong raised his head and looked him steadily in the eyes; and Billy, losing his curiosity and the grin at the same instant, looked ahead, whistling softly.

Chapter XVII
Edwards' Ultimatum

Edwards slid off the counter in Jackson's store and glowered at the pelting rain outside, perturbed and grouchy. The wounded man in the corner stirred and looked at him without interest and forthwith renewed his profane monologue, while the proprietor, finishing his task, leaned back against the shelves and swore softly. It was a lovely atmosphere.

"Seems to me they've been gone a long time," grumbled the wounded man. "Reckon he led 'em a long chase-had six hours' start, the toad." He paused and then as an afterthought said with conviction: "But they'll get him-they allus do when they make up their minds to it."

Edwards nodded moodily and Jackson replied with a monosyllable.

"Wish I could 'a' gone with 'em," Johnny growled. "I like to square my own accounts. It's allus that way. I get plugged an' my friends clean the slate. There was that time Bye-an'-Bye went an' ambushed me-ah, the devil! But I tell you one thing: when I get well I'm going down to Harlan's an' clean house proper."

"Yo're in hard luck again: that'll be done as soon as yore friends get back," Jackson replied, carefully selecting a dried apricot from a box on the counter and glancing at the marshal to see how he took the remark.

"That'll be done before then," Edwards said crisply, with the air of a man who has just settled a doubt. "They won't be back much before to-morrow if he headed for the country I think he did. I'm going down to the Oasis an' tell that gang to clear out of this town. They've been here too long now. I never had 'em dead to rights before, but I've got it on 'em this time. I'd 'a' sent 'em packing yesterday only I sort of hated to take a man's business away from him an' make him lose his belongings. But I've wrastled it all out an' they've got to go." He buttoned his coat about him and pulled his sombrero more firmly on his head, starting for the door. "I'll be back soon," he said over his shoulder as he grasped the handle.

"You better wait till you get help-there's too many down there for one man to watch an' handle," Jackson hastily remarked. "Here, I'll go with you," he offered, looking for his hat.

Edwards laughed shortly. "You stay here. I do my own work by myself when I can-that's what I'm here for, an' I can do this, all right. If I took any help they'd reckon I was scared," and the door slammed shut behind him.

"He's got sand a plenty," Jackson remarked. "He'd try to push back a stampede by main strength if he reckoned it was his duty. It's his good luck that he wasn't killed long ago — I'd 'a' been."

"They're a bunch of cowards," replied Johnny. "As long as you ain't afraid of 'em, none of 'em wants to start anything. Bunch of sheep!" he snorted. "Didn't Jerry shoot me through his pocket?"

"Yes; an' yo're another lucky dog," Jackson responded, having in mind that at first Johnny had been thought to be desperately wounded. "Why, yore friends have got the worst of this game; they're worse off than you are-out all day an' night in this cussed storm."

While they talked Edwards made his way through the cold downpour to Harlan's saloon, alone and unafraid, and greatly pleased by the order he would give. At last he had proof enough to work on, to satisfy his conscience, for the inevitable had come as the culmination of continued and clever defiance of law and order.

He deliberately approached the front door of the Oasis and, opening it, stepped inside, his hands resting on his guns-he had packed two Colts for the last twenty-four hours. His appearance caused a ripple of excitement to run around the room. After what had taken place, a visit from him could mean only one thing-trouble. And it was entirely possible that he had others within call to help him out if necessary.

Harlan knew that he would be the one held responsible and he ceased wiping a glass and held the cloth suspended in one hand and the glass in the other. "Well?" he snapped, angrily, his eyes smouldering with fixed hatred.

"Mebby you think it's well, but it's going to be a blamed sight better before sundown to-morrow night," evenly replied the marshal. "I just dropped in sort of free-like to tell you to pack up an' get out of town before dark-load yore wagon an' vamoose; an' take yore friends with you, too. If you don't —" he did not finish in words, for his tightening lips made them unnecessary.

"*What!*" yelled Harlan, red with anger. He placed his hands on the bar and leaned over it as if to give emphasis to his words. "*Me* pack up an' git! *Me* leave this shack! Who's going to pay me for it, hey? *Me* leave town! You drop out again an' go back to Kansas where you come from-they're easier back there!"

"Well, so far I ain't found nothing very craggy 'round here," retorted Edwards, closely watching the muttering crowd by the bar. "Takes more than a loud voice an' a pack of sneaking coyotes to send me looking for something easier. An' let me tell you this: *You* stay away from Kansas-they hangs people like you back there. That's whatever. You pack up an' git out of this town or I'll start a burying plot with you on yore own land."

The low, angry buzz of Harlan's friends and their savage, scowling faces would have deterred a less determined man; but Edwards knew they were afraid of him, and the men on whom he could call to back him up. And he knew that there must always be a start, there must be one man to show the way; and each of the men he faced was waiting for some one else to lead.

"You all slip over the horizon before dark to-night, an' it's dark early these days," he continued. "*Don't get restless with yore hands!*" he snapped ominously at the crowd. "I means what I say-you shake the mud from this town off yore boots before dark-before that Bar-20 outfit gets back," he finished meaningly.

Questions, imprecations, and threats filled the room, and the crowd began to spread out slowly. His guns came out like a flash and he laughed with the elation that comes with impending battle. "The first man to start it'll drop," he said evenly. "Who's going to be the martyr?"

"I *won't* leave town!" shouted Harlan. "I'll stay here if I'm killed for it!"

"I admire yore loyalty to principle, but you've got damned little sense," retorted the marshal. "You ain't no practical man. *Keep yore hands where they are!*" —his vibrant voice turned the shifting crowd to stone-like rigidity and he backed slowly toward the door, the poor light gleaming dully from the polished blue steel of his Colts. Rugged, lion-like, charged to the finger tips with reckless courage and dare-devil self-confidence, his personality overflowed and dominated the room, almost hypnotic in its effect. He was but one against many, but he was the master, and they knew it; they had known it long enough to accept it without question, and the training now stood him in good stead.

For a moment he stood in the open doorway, keenly scrutinizing them for signs of danger, his unwavering guns charged with certain death and his strong face made stronger by the shadows in its hollows. "Before dark!" —and he was gone.

He left behind him deep silence, which endured for several moments.

"By the Lord, I *won't!*" cried Harlan, still staring at the door.

The spell was broken and a babel of voices filled the room, threats mingling with excuses, hot, vibrant, profane. These men were not cowards all the way through, but only when face to face with the master. They had flourished in a way by their wits alone on the same range with the outfits of the C-80 and the Double-Arrow, for individually they were "bad," and collectively they made a force of no mean strength. Edwards had landed among them like a thunderbolt and had proved his prowess, and they still held him in awesome respect. His reckless audacity and grim singleness of purpose had saved him on more than one occasion, for had he wavered once he would have been shot down without mercy. But gradually his enforcement of hampering laws became more and more intolerable, and their subordinated spirits were nearly on the point of revolt. When he faced them they resumed their former positions in relation to him-but once out of his sight they plotted to destroy him. Here was the crisis: it was now or never. They could not evade his ultimatum-it was obey or fight.

Submission was not to be thought of, for to flee would be to lose caste, and the story of such an act would follow them wherever they went, and brand them as cowards. Here they had lived, and here they would stay if possible, and to this end they discussed ways and means.

"Harlan's right!" emphatically announced Laramie Joe. "We can't pull out and have this foller us."

"We should have started it with a rush when he was in here," remarked Boston, regretfully.

Harlan stopped his pacing and faced them, shoving out a bottle of whiskey as an aid to his logic.

"That chance is past, an' I don't know but what it is a good thing," he began. "He was primed an' looking fer trouble, an' he'd shore got a few of us afore he went under. What we want is strategy-that's the game. You fellers have got as much brains as him, an' if we thrash this thing out we can find a way to call his play-an' get him! No use of any of us getting plugged 'less we have to. But whatever we do we've got to start it right quick an' have it over before that Bar-20 gang comes back. Harper, you an' Quinn go scouting-an' don't take no guns with you, neither. Act like you was hitting the long trail out, an' work back here on a circle. See how many of his friends are in town. While you are gone the rest of us will hold a pow-wow an' take the kinks out of this game. Chase along, an' don't waste no time."

"Good!" cried Slivers Lowe emphatically. "There's blamed few fellers in town now that have any use for him, for most of them are off on the ranges. Bet we won't have more than six to fight, an' there's that many of us here."

The scouts departed at once and the remaining four drew close in consultation.

"One more drink around and then no more till this trouble is over," Harlan said, passing the bottle. The drinks, in view of the coming drought and the thirsty work ahead, were long and deep, and new courage and vindictiveness crept through their veins.

"Now here's the way it looks to me," Harlan continued, placing the bottle, untasted by himself, on the floor behind him. "We've got to work a surprise an' take Edwards an' his friends off their guard. That'll be easy if we're careful, because they think we ain't looking for fight. When we get them out of the way we can take Jackson's store an' use one of the other shacks and wait for the Bar-20 to ride in. They'll canter right in, like they allus do, an' when they get close enough we'll open the game with a volley an' make every shot tell. 'T won't last long, 'cause every one of us will have his man named before they get here. Then the few straddlers in town, seeing how easy we've gone an' handled it'll join us. We've got four men to come in yet, an' by the time the C-80 an' Double-Arrow hears about it we'll be fixed to drive 'em back home. We ought to be over a dozen strong by dark."

"That sounds good, all right," remarked Slivers, thoughtfully, "but can we do it that easy?"

"Course we can! We ain't fools, an' we all can shoot as well as them," snapped Laramie Joe, the most courageous of the lot. Laramie had taken only one drink, and that a small one, for he was wise enough to realize that he needed his wits as keen as he could have them.

"We can do it easy, if Edwards goes under first," hastily replied Harlan. "An' me an' Laramie will see to that part of it. If we don't get him, you all can hit the trail an' we won't be sore about it. That is, unless you are made of the stuff that stands up an' fights 'stead of running away. I reckon I ain't none mistaken in any of you. You'll all be there when things get hot."

"You can bet the shack *I* won't do no trail-hitting," growled Boston, glancing at Slivers, who squirmed a little under the hint.

"Well, I'm glued to the crowd; you can't lose me, fellers," Slivers remarked, re-crossing his legs uneasily. "Are we going to begin it from here?"

"We ought to spread out cautions and surround Jackson's, or wherever Edwards is," Laramie Joe suggested. "That's my —"

"Yo're right! Now you've hit it plumb on the head!" interrupted Harlan, slapping Laramie heartily across the back. "What did I tell you about our brains?" he cried, enthusiastically. He had been on the point of suggesting that plan of operations when Laramie took the words out of his mouth. "I'd never thought of that, Laramie," he lied, his face beaming. "Why, we've got 'em licked to a finish right now!"

"This *is* a hummer of a game," laughed Slivers. "But how about the Bar-20 crowd?"

"I've told you that already," replied the proprietor.

"You bet it's a hummer," cried Boston, reaching for the whiskey bottle under cover of the excitement and enthusiasm.

Harlan pushed it away with his foot and raised his clenched fist. "Do you wonder I didn't think of that plan?" he demanded. "Ain't I been too mad to think at all? Hain't I seen my friends treated like dogs, an' made to swaller insults when I couldn't raise my hand to stop it? Didn't I see Jerry Brown chased out of my place like a wild beast? If we are what we've been called, then we'll sneak out of town with our tails atween our laigs; but if we're men we'll stay right here an' cram the insults down the throats of them that made 'em! If we're *men* let's prove it an' make them liars swaller our lead."

"My sentiments an' allus was!" roared Slivers, slapping Harlan's shoulder.

"We're men, all right, an' we'll show 'em it, too!"

At that instant the door opened and four guns covered it before it had swung a foot.

"Put 'em down–it's Quinn!" exclaimed the man in the doorway, flinching a bit. "All right, Jed," he called over his shoulder to the man who crowded him. After Quinn came Big Jed and Harper brought up the rear. They had no more than shaken the water from their sombreros when the back door let in Charley Rich and his two companions, Frank and Tom Nolan. While greetings were being exchanged and the existing conditions explained to the newcomers, Harper and Quinn led Harlan to one side and reported, the proprietor smiling and nodding his head wisely. And while he listened, Slivers surreptitiously corralled the whiskey bottle and when the last man finished with it there was nothing in it but air.

"Well, boys," exclaimed Harlan, "things are our way. Quinn, here, met Joe Barr, of the C-80, who said Converse an' four other fellers, all friends of Edwards, stopped at the ranch an' won't be back home till the storm stops. Harper saw Fred Neil going back to his ranch, so all we've got to figger on is the marshal, Barr, an' Jackson, an' they're all in Jackson's store. Lacey might cut in, since he'd sell more liquor if I went under, but he can't do very much if he does take a hand. Now we'll get right at it." The whole thing was gone over thoroughly and in detail, positions assigned and a signal agreed upon. Seeing that weapons were in good condition after their long storage in the cellar, and that cartridge belts were full, the ten men left the room one at a time or in pairs, Harlan and Laramie Joe being the last. And both Harlan and Laramie delayed long enough to take the precaution of placing horses where they would be handy in case of need.

Chapter XVIII
Harlan Strikes

Joe Barr laughingly replied to Johnny Nelson's growled remarks about the condition of things in general and tried to soothe him, but Johnny was unsoothable.

"An' I've been telling him right along that he's got the best of it," complained Jackson in a weary voice. "Got a measly hole through his shoulder-good Lord! if it had gone a little lower!" he finished with a show of exasperation.

"An' ain't I been telling you all along that it ain't the measly hole in my shoulder that's got me on the prod?" retorted Johnny, with more earnestness than politeness. "But why couldn't I go with my friends after Jerry an' get shot later if I had to get it at all? Look what I'm missing, roped an' throwed in this cussed ten-by-ten shack while they're having a little excitement."

"Yo're missing some blamed nasty weather, Kid," replied the marshal. "You ain't got no kick coming at all. Why, I got soaked clean through just going down to the Oasis."

"Well, I'm kicking, just the same," snapped Johnny. "An' furthermore, I don't see nobody big enough to stop me, neither-did you all get that?"

The rear door opened and Fred Neal looked in. "Hey, Barr; come out an' gimme a hand in the corral. Busted my cinch all to pieces half a mile out-an' how the devil it ever busted like that is —" the door slammed shut and softened his monologue.

"Would you listen to that!" snorted Barr in an injured tone. "Didn't I go an' tell him near a month ago that his cussed cinch wouldn't hold no better'n a piece of wet paper?" His complaint added materially to the atmosphere of sullen discontent pervading the room. "An' now I gotter go out in this rain an' —" the slam of the door surpassed anything yet attempted in that line of endeavor. Jackson grabbed a can of corn as it jarred off the shelf behind him and directed a pleasing phrase after the peevish Barr.

"Say, won't somebody please smile?" gravely asked Edwards. "I never saw such a happy, cheerful bunch before."

"I might smile if I wasn't so blamed hungry," retorted Johnny. "Doesn't anybody ever eat in this town?" he asked in great sarcasm. "Mebby a good feed won't do me no good, but I'm going to fill myself regardless. An' after that, if the grub don't shock me to death, I'm shore going to trim somebody at Ol' Sledge-for two bits a hand."

"If I could play you enough hands at that price I could sell out an' live high without working," grinned Jackson, preparing to give the reckless invalid all he could eat. "That's purty high, Kid; but I just feel real devilish, an' I'm coming in."

"An' I'll go over to my shack, get some money, an' bust the pair of you," laughed Edwards, again buttoning his coat and going towards the door. "Holy Cats! A log must 'a' got jammed in the sluice-gate up there," he muttered, scowling at the black sky. "It's coming down harder'n ever, but here goes," and he stepped quickly into the storm.

Jackson paused with a frying pan in his hands and looked through the window after the departing marshal, and saw him stagger, stumble forward, then jerk out his guns and begin firing. Hard firing now burst out in front and Jackson, cursing angrily, dropped the pan and reached for his rifle-to drop it also and sink down, struck by the bullet which drilled through the window. Johnny let out a yell of rage, grabbed his Colt, and ran to the door in time to see Edwards slowly raise up on one elbow, fire his last shot, and fall back riddled by bullets.

Jackson crawled to his rifle and then to the side window, where he propped his back against a box and prepared to do his best. "It was shore a surprise," he swore. "An' they went an' got Edwards before he could do anything."

"They did not!" retorted Johnny. "He —" the glass in the door vibrated sharply and the speaker, stepping to one side out of sight, with a new and superficial wound, opened fire on the building down the street. Two men were lying on the ground across the street-these Edwards had shot-and another was trying to drag himself to the shelter of a building. A man sprinted from an old corral close by in a brave and foolhardy attempt to save his friend, and Johnny swore because he had to fire twice at the same mark.

The rear door crashed open and shut as Barr, closely followed by Neal, ran in. They had been caught in the corral but, thanks to Harlan's whiskey, had managed to hold their own until they had a chance to make a rush for the store.

"Where's the marshal?" cried Barr, catching sight of Jackson. "Are you plugged bad?" he asked, anxiously.

"Well, I ain't plugged a whole lot *good*!" snapped Jackson. "An' Edwards is dead. They shot him down without warning. We're going to get ours, too-these walls don't stop them bullets. How many out there?"

"Must be a dozen," hastily replied Neal, who had not remained idle. Both he and Barr were working like mad men moving boxes and barrels against the walls to make a breastwork capable of stopping the bullets which came through the boards.

"I reckon —I'm bleeding inside," Jackson muttered, wearily and without hope. "Wonder how-long we-can hold out?"

"We'll hold out till we're good an' dead!" replied Johnny, hotly. "They ain't got us yet an' they'll pay for it before they do. If we can hold 'em off till Buck an' the rest come back we'll have the pleasure of seeing 'em buried."

"Oh, I'll get you next time!" assured Barr to an enemy, slipping a fresh cartridge into the Sharps and peering intently at a slight rise on the muddy plain. "You shoot like yo're drunk," he mumbled.

"But what is it all about, anyhow?" asked Neal, finding time for an immaterial question. "Who are they? —can't see nothing but blurs through this rain!"

"Yes; what's the game?" asked Barr, mildly surprised that he had not thought of it before.

"It's that Oasis gang," Johnny responded. He fired, and growled with disappointment. "Harlan's at the head of it," he added.

"Edwards-told Harlan to-get out of-town," Jackson began.

"An' to take his gang with him," Johnny interposed quickly to save Jackson from the strain. "They had till dark. Guess the rest. Oh, you *coyote*!" he shouted, staggering back. There was a report farther down the barricade and Neal called out, "I got him, Nelson; he's done. How are you?"

"Mad! Mad!" yelled Johnny, touching his twice-wounded shoulder and dancing with rage and pain. "Right in the same place! Oh, wait! *Wait!* Hey, gimme a rifle —I can't do nothing with a Colt at this range; my name ain't Hopalong," and he went slamming around the room in hot search of what he wanted.

"There ain't —no more-Johnny," feebly called Jackson, raising slightly to ease himself. "You can have-my gun purty-soon. I won't be able-to use it-much longer."

"Why don't Buck an' Hoppy hurry up!" snarled Johnny.

"Be a long time-mebby," mumbled Jackson, his trembling hands trying to steady the rifle. "They're all-around us. *Ah*, missed!" he intoned hoarsely, trying to pump the lever with un-obeying hands. "I can't last-much —" the words ceased abruptly and the clatter of the rifle on the floor told the story.

Johnny stumbled over to him and dragged him aside, covering the upturned face with his own sombrero, and picked up the rifle. Rolling a barrel of flour against the wall below the window he fixed himself as comfortably as possible and threw a shell into the chamber.

"Now, you coyotes; you pay *me* for *that*!" he gritted, resting the gun on the window sill and holding it so he could work it with one hand and shoulder.

"Wonder how them pups ever pumped up enough courage to cut loose like this?" queried Neal from behind his flour barrel.

"Whiskey," hazarded Barr. "Harlan must 'a' got 'em drunk. An' that's three times I've missed that snake. Wish it would stop raining so I could see better."

"Why don't you wish they'd all drop dead? Wish good when you wish at all: got as much chance of having it come true," responded Neal, sarcastically. He smothered a curse and looked curiously at his left arm, and from it to the new, yellow-splintered hole in the wall, which was already turning dark from the water soaking into it. "Hey, Joe; we need some more boxes!" he exclaimed, again looking at his arm.

"Yes," came Johnny's voice. "Three of 'em-five of 'em, an' about six feet long an' a foot deep. But if my outfit gets here in time we'll want more'n a dozen."

"Say! Lacey's firing now!" suddenly cried Barr. "He's shooting out of his windy. That'll stop 'em from rushing us! Good boy, Lacey!" he shouted, but Lacey did not hear him in the uproar.

"An' he's worse off than we are, being alone," commented Neal. "Hey! One of us better make a break for help-my ranch's the nearest. What d'ye say?"

"It's suicide; they'll get you before you get ten feet," Barr replied with conviction.

"No; they won't —the corral hides the back door, an' all the firing is on this side. I can sneak along the back wall an' by keeping the buildings atween me an' them, get a long ways off before they know anything about it. Then it's a dash-an' they can't catch me. But can you fellers hold out if I do?"

"Two can hold out as good as three-go ahead," Johnny replied. "Leave me some of yore Colt cartridges, though. You can't use 'em all before you get home."

"Don't stop fer that; there's a shelfful of all kinds behind the counter," Barr interposed.

"Well, so long an' good luck," and the rear door closed, and softly this time.

"Two hours is some wait under the present circumstances," Barr muttered, shifting his position behind his barricade. "He can't do it in less, nohow."

Johnny ducked and looked foolish. "Missed me by a foot," he explained. "He can't do it in two-not there an' back," he replied. "The trail is mud over the fetlocks. Give him three at the least."

"They ain't shooting as much as they was before."

"Waiting till they gets sober, I reckon," Johnny replied.

"If we don't hear no ruction in a few minutes we'll know he got away all right," Barr soliloquized. "An' he's got a fine cayuse for mud, too."

"Hey, why can't you do the same thing if he makes it?" Johnny suddenly asked. "I can hold her alone, all right."

"Yo're a cheerful liar, you are," laughed Barr. "But can *you* ride?"

"Reckon so, but I ain't a-going to."

"Why, we *both* can go-it's a cinch!" Barr cried. "Come on!"

"Lord! —an' I never even thought of that! Reckon I was too mad," Johnny replied. "But I sort of hates to leave Jackson an' Edwards," he added, sullenly.

"But they're gone! You can't do them no good by staying."

"Yes; I know. An' how about Lacey chipping in on our fight?" demanded Johnny. "I ain't a-going to leave him to take it all. You go, Barr; it wasn't yore fight, nohow. You didn't even know what you was fighting for!"

"Huh! When anybody shoots at me it's my fight, all right," replied Barr, seating himself on the floor behind the breastwork. "I forgot all about Lacey," he apologized. At that instant a tomato can went *spang!* and fell off the shelf. "An' it's too late, anyhow; they ain't a-going to let nobody else get away on that side."

"An' they're tuning up again, too," Johnny replied, preparing for trouble. "Look out for a rush, Barr."

Chapter XIX
The Bar-20 Returns

Hopalong Cassidy stopped swearing at the weather and looked up and along the trail in front of him, seeing a hard-riding man approach. He turned his head and spoke to Buck Peters, who rode close behind him. "Somebody's shore in a hurry-why, it's Fred Neal."

It was. Mr. Neal was making his arms move and was also shouting something at the top of his voice. The noise of the rain and of the horses' hoofs splashing in the mud and water at first made his words unintelligible, but it was not long before Hopalong heard something which made him sit up even straighter. In a moment Neal was near enough to be heard distinctly and the outfit shook itself out of its weariness and physical misery and followed its leader at reckless speed. As they rode, bunched close together, Neal briefly and graphically outlined the relative positions of the combatants, and while Buck's more cautious mind was debating the best way to proceed against the enemy, Hopalong cried out the plan to be followed. There would be no strategy-Johnny, wounded and desperate, was fighting for his life. The simplest way was the best —a dash regardless of consequences to those making it, for time was a big factor to the two men in Jackson's store.

"Ride right at 'em!" Hopalong cried. "I know that bunch. They'll be too scared to shoot straight. Paralyze 'em! Three or four are gone now-an' the whole crowd wasn't worth one of the men they went out to get. The quicker it's over the better."

"Right you are," came from the rear.

"Ride up the arroyo as close as we can get, an' then over the edge an' straight at 'em," Buck ordered. "Their shooting an' the rain will cover what noise we make on the soft ground. An' boys, *no quarter*!"

"Reckon *not*!" gritted Red, savagely. "Not with Edwards an' Jackson dead, an' the Kid fighting for his life!"

"They're still at it!" cried Lanky Smith, as the faint and intermittent sound of firing was heard; the driving wind was blowing from the town, and this, also, would deaden the noise of their approach.

"Thank the Lord! That means that there's somebody left to fight 'em," exclaimed Red. "Hope it's the Kid," he muttered.

"They can't rush the store till they get Lacey, an' they can't rush him till they get the store," shouted Neal over his shoulder. "They'd be in a cross fire if they tried either-an' that's what licks 'em."

"They'll be in a cross fire purty soon," promised Pete, grimly.

Hopalong and Red reached the edge of the arroyo first and plunged over the bank into the yellow storm-water swirling along the bottom like a miniature flood. After them came Buck, Neal, and the others, the water shooting up in sheets as each successive horse plunged in. Out again on the farther side they strung out into single file along the narrow foot-hold between water and bank and raced towards the sharp bend some hundreds of yards ahead, the point in the arroyo's course nearest the town. The dripping horses scrambled up the slippery incline and then, under the goading of spurs and quirts, leaped forward as fast as they could go across the level, soggy plain.

A quarter of a mile ahead of them lay the scattered shacks of the town, and as they drew nearer to it the riders could see the flashes of guns and the smoke-fog lying close to the ground. Fire spat from Jackson's store and a cloud of smoke still lingered around a window in Lacey's saloon. Then a yell reached their ears, a yell of rage, consternation and warning. Figures scurried to seek cover and the firing from Jackson's and Lacey's grew more rapid.

A mounted man emerged from a corral and tore away, others following his example, and the outfit separated to take up the chase individually. Harlan, wounded hard, was trying to run to where he had left his horse, and after him fled Slivers Lowe. Hopalong was gaining on them when he saw Slivers raise his arm and fire deliberately into the back of the proprietor of the Oasis, leap over the falling body, vault into the saddle of Harlan's horse and gallop for safety. Hopalong's shots went wide and the last view any one had of Slivers in that part of the country was when he dropped into an arroyo to follow it for safety. Laramie Joe fled before Red Connors and Red's rage was so great that it spoiled his accuracy, and he had the sorrow of seeing the pursued grow faint in the mist and fog. Pursuit was tried until the pursuers realized that their mounts were too worn out to stand a show against the fresh animals ridden by the survivors of the Oasis crowd.

Red circled and joined Hopalong. "Blasted coyotes," he growled. "Killed Jackson an' Edwards, an' wanted the Kid! He's shore showed 'em what fighting is, all right. But I wonder what got into 'em all at once to give 'em nerve enough to start things?"

"Edwards paid his way, all right," replied Hopalong. "If I do as well when my time comes I won't do no kicking."

"Yore time ain't coming that way," responded Red, grinning. "You'll die a natural death in bed, unless you gets to cussing me."

"Shore there ain't no more, Buck?" Hopalong called.

"Yes. There was only five, I reckon, an' they was purty well shot up when we took a hand. You know, Johnny was in it all the time," replied the foreman, smiling. "This town's had the cleaning up it's needed for some time," he added.

They were at Jackson's store now, and hurriedly dismounted and ran in to see Johnny. They found him lying across some boxes, which brought him almost to the level of a window sill. He was too weak to stand, while near him in similar condition lay Barr, too weak from loss of blood to do more than look his welcome.

"How are you, Kid?" cried Buck anxiously, bending over him, while others looked to Barr's injuries.

"Tired, Buck, awful tired; an' all shot up," Johnny slowly replied. "When I saw you fellers-streak past this windy —I sort of went flat-something seemed to break inside me," he said, faintly and with an effort, and the foreman ordered him not to talk. Deft fingers, schooled by practice in rough and ready surgery, were busy over him and in half an hour he lay on Jackson's cot, covered with bandages.

"Why, hullo, Lacey!" exclaimed Hopalong, leaping forward to shake hands with the man Red and Billy had gone to help. "Purty well scratched up, but lively yet, hey?"

"I'm able to hobble over here an' shake han's with these scrappers-they're shore wonders," Lacey replied. "Fought like a whole regiment! Hullo, Johnny!" and his hand-clasp told much.

"Yore cross fire did it, Lacey; that was the whole thing," Johnny smiled. "Yo're all right!"

Red turned and looked out of the window toward the Oasis and then glanced at Buck. "Reckon we better burn Harlan's place-it's all that's left of that gang now," he suggested.

"Why, yes; I reckon so," replied the foreman. "That's as —"

"No, we won't!" Hopalong interposed quickly. "That stands till Johnny sets it off. It's the Kid's celebration-he was shot in it."

Johnny smiled.

Chapter XX
Barb Wire

After the flurry at Perry's Bend the Bar-20 settled down to the calm routine work and sent several drive herds to their destination without any unusual incidents. Buck thought that the last herd had been driven when, late in the summer, he received an order that he made haste to fill. The outfit was told to get busy and soon rounded up the necessary number of three-year-olds. Then came the road branding, the final step except inspection, and this was done not far from the ranch house, where the facilities were best for speedy work.

Entirely recovered from all ill effects of his afternoon in Jackson's store up in Perry's bend, Johnny Nelson waited with Red Connors on the platform of the branding chute and growled petulantly at the sun, the dust, but most of all at the choking, smarting odor of burned hair which filled their throats and caused them to rub the backs of grimy hands across their eyes. Chute-branding robbed them of the excitement, the leaven of fun and frolic, which they always took from open or corral branding-and the work of a day in the corral or open was condensed into an hour or two by the chute. This was one cow wide, narrow at the bottom and flared out as it went up, so the animal could not turn, and when filled was, to use Johnny's graphic phrase, "like a chain of cows in a ditch." Eight of the wondering and crowded animals, guided into the pen by men who knew their work to the smallest detail and lost no time in its performance, filed into the pen after those branded had filed out. As the first to enter reached the farther end a stout bar dropped into place, just missing the animal's nose; and as the last cow discovered that it could go no farther and made up its mind to back out, it was stopped by another bar, which fell behind it. The iron heaters tossed a hot iron each to Red and Johnny and the eight were marked in short order, making about two hundred and fifty they had branded in three hours. This number compared very favorably with that of the second chute where Lanky Smith and Frenchy McAlister waved cold irons and sarcastically asked their iron men if the sun was supposed to provide the heat; whereat the down-trodden heaters provided heat with great generosity in their caustic retorts.

"Oh, Susanna, don't you cry for me," sang Billy Williams, one of the feeders. "But why in Jericho don't you fellers get a move on you? You ain't no good on the platform-you ought to be mixing biscuits for Cookie. Frenchy and Lanky are the boys to turn 'em out," he offered, gratis.

Red's weary air bespoke a vast and settled contempt for such inanities and his iron descended against the side of the victim below him-he would not deign to reply. Not so with Johnny, who could not refrain from hot retort.

"Don't be a fool *all* the time," snapped Johnny. "Mind yore own business, you shorthorn. Big-mouthed old woman, that's what —" his tone dropped and the words sank into vague mutterings which a strangling cough cut short. "Blasted idiot," he whispered, tears coming into his eyes at the effort. Burning hair is bad for throat and temper alike.

Red deftly knocked his companion's iron up and spoke sharply. "You mind yourn better-that makes the third you've tried to brand twice. Why don't you look what yo're doing? Hot iron! Hot iron! What're you fellers doing?" he shouted down at the heaters. "This ain't no time to go to sleep. How d'ye expect us to do any work when you ain't doing any yoreselves!" Red's temper was also on the ragged edge.

"You've got one in yore other hand, you sheep!" snorted one of the iron heaters with restless pugnacity. "Go tearing into us when you —" he growled the rest and kicked viciously at the fire.

"Lovely bunch," grinned Billy who, followed by Pete Wilson, mounted the platform to relieve the branders. "Chase yoreselves-me an' Pete are shore going to show you cranky bugs how to do a hundred an hour. Ain't we, Pete? An' look here, you," he remarked to the heaters, "don't you fellers keep *us* waiting for hot irons!"

"That's right! Make a fool out of yoreself first thing!" snapped one of the pair on the ground.

"Billy, I never loved you as much as I do this minute," grinned Johnny wearily. "Wish you'd 'a' come along to show us how to do it an hour ago."

"I would, only —"

"Quit chinning an' get busy," remarked Red, climbing down. "The chute's full; an' it's all yourn."

Billy caught the iron, gave it a preliminary flourish, and started to work with a speed that would not endure for long. He branded five out of the eight and jeered at his companion for being so slow.

"Have yore fun now, Billy," Pete replied with placid good nature. "Before we're through with this job you'll be lucky if you can do two of the string, if you keep up that pace."

"He'll be missing every other one," growled his heater with overflowing malice. "That iron ain't cold, you Chinaman!"

"Too cold for me-don't miss none," chuckled Billy sweetly. "Fill the chute! Fill the chute! Don't keep us waiting!" he cried to the guiders, hopping around with feigned eagerness and impatience.

Hopalong Cassidy rode up and stopped as Red returned to take the place of one of the iron heaters. "How they coming, Red?" he inquired.

"Fast. You can sic that inspector on 'em the first thing to-morrow morning, if he gets here on time. Bet he's off som'ers getting full of redeye. Who're going with you on this drive?"

"The inspector is all right-he's here now an' is going to spend the night with us so as to be on hand the first thing to-morrow," replied Hopalong, grinning at the hard-working pair on the platform. "Why, I reckon I'll take you, Johnny, Lanky, Billy, Pete, an' Skinny, an' we'll have two hoss-wranglers an' a cook, of course. We'll drive up the right-hand trail through West Valley this time. It's longer, but there'll be more water that way at this time of the year. Besides, I don't want no more foot-sore cattle to nurse along. Even the West Valley trail will be dry enough before we strike Bennett's Creek."

"Yes; we'll have to drive 'em purty hard till we reach the creek," replied Red, thoughtfully. "Say; we're going to have three thousand of the finest three-year-old steers ever sent north out of these parts. An' we ought to do it in a month an' deliver 'em fat an' frisky. We can feed 'em good for the last week."

"I just sent some of the boys out to drive in the cayuses," Hopalong remarked, "an' when they get here you fellers match for choice an' pick yore remuda. No use taking too few. About eight apiece'll do us nice. I shore like a good cavvieyeh."

"Hullo, Hoppy!" came from the platform as Billy grinned his welcome through the dust on his face. "Want a job?"

"Hullo yoreself," growled Pete. "Stick yore iron on that fourth steer before he gets out, an' talk less with yore mouth."

"Pete's still rabid," called Billy, performing the duty Pete suggested.

"That may be the polite name for it," snorted one of the iron heaters, testing an iron, "but that ain't what I'd say. Might as well cover the subject thoroughly while yo're on it."

"Yes, verily," endorsed his companion.

"Here comes the last of 'em," smiled Pete, watching several cattle being driven towards the chute. "We'll have to brand 'em on the move, Billy; there ain't enough to fill the chute."

"All right; hot iron, you!"

Early the next morning the inspector looked them over and made his count, the herd was started north and at nightfall had covered twelve miles. For the next week everything went smoothly, but after that, water began to be scarce and the herd was pushed harder, and became harder to handle.

On the night of the twelfth day out four men sat around the fire in West Valley at a point a dozen miles south of Bennett's Creek, and ate heartily. The night was black-not a star could be seen and the south wind hardly stirred the trampled and burned grass. They were thoroughly tired out and their tempers were not in the sweetest state imaginable, for the heat during the last four days had been almost unbearable even to them and they had had their hands full with the cranky herd. They ate silently, hungrily-there would be time enough for the few words they had to say when the pipes were going for a short smoke before turning in.

"I feel like hell," growled Red, reaching for another cup of coffee, but there was no reply; he had voiced the feelings of all.

Hopalong listened intently and looked up, staring into the darkness, and soon a horseman was seen approaching the fire. Hopalong nodded welcome and waved his hand towards the food, and the stranger, dismounting, picketed his horse and joined the circle. When the pipes were lighted he sighed with satisfaction and looked around the group. "Driving north, I see."

"Yes; an' blamed glad to get off this dry range," Hopalong replied. "The herd's getting cranky an' hard to hold-but when we pass the creek everything'll be all right again. An' ain't it hot! When you hear us kick about the heat it means something."

"I'm going yore way," remarked the stranger. "I came down this trail about two weeks ago. Reckon I was the last to ride through before the fence went up. Damned outrage, says I, an' I told 'em so, too. They couldn't see it that way an' we had a little disagreement about it. They said as how they was going to patrol it."

"Fence! What fence?" exclaimed Red.

"Where's there any fence?" demanded Hopalong sharply.

"Twenty mile north of the creek," replied the stranger, carefully packing his pipe.

"What? Twenty miles north of the creek?" cried Hopalong. "What creek?"

"Bennett's. The 4X has strung three strands of barb wire from Coyote Pass to the North Arm. Thirty mile long, without a gate, so they says."

"But it don't close this trail!" cried Hopalong in blank astonishment.

"It shore does. They say they owns that range an' can fence it in all they wants. I told 'em different, but naturally they didn't listen to me. An' they'll fight about it, too."

"But they *can't* shut off this trail!" exclaimed Billy, with angry emphasis. "They don't own it no more'n we do!"

"I know all about that-you heard me tell you what they said."

"But how can we get past it?" demanded Hopalong.

"Around it, over the hills. You'll lose about three days doing it, too."

"I can't take no sand-range herd over them rocks, an' I ain't going to drive 'round no North Arm or Coyote Pass if I could," Hopalong replied with quiet emphasis. "There's poison springs on the east an' nothing but rocks on the west. We go straight through."

"I'm afraid that you'll have to fight if you do," remarked the stranger.

"Then we'll fight!" cried Johnny, leaning forward. "Blasted coyotes! What right have they got to block a drive trail that's as old as cattle-raising in these parts! That trail was here before I was born, it's allus been open, an' it's going to stay open! You watch us go through!"

"Yo're dead right, Kid; we'll cut that fence an' stick to this trail, an' fight if we has to," endorsed Red. "The Bar-20 ain't crawling out of no hole that it can walk out of. They're bluffing; that's all."

"I don't think they are; an' there's twelve men in that outfit," suggested the stranger, offhand.

"We ain't got time to count odds; we never do down our way when we know we're right. An' we're right enough in this game," retorted Hopalong, quickly. "For the last twelve days we've had good luck, barring the few on this dry range; an' now we're in for the other kind. By the Lord, I wish we was here without the cows to take care of-we'd show 'em something about blocking drive trails that ain't in their little book!"

"Blast it all! Wire fences coming down this way now," mused Johnny, sullenly. He hated them by training as much as he hated horse-thieves and sheep; and his companions had been brought up in the same school. Barb wire, the death-knell to the old-time punching, the bar to riding at will, a steel insult to fire the blood-it had come at last.

"We've shore got to cut it, Red, —" began Hopalong, but the cook had to rid himself of some of his indignation and interrupted with heat.

"Shore we have!" came explosively from the tail board of the chuck wagon. "Got to lay it agin my li'l axe an' swat it with my big ol' monkey wrench! An' won't them posts save me a lot of trouble hunting chips an' firewood!"

"We've shore got to cut it, Red," Hopalong repeated slowly. "You an' Johnny an' me'll ride ahead after we cross the creek to-morrow an' do it. I don't hanker after no fight with all these cows on my han's, but we've got to risk one."

"Shore!" cried Johnny, hotly. "I can't get over the gall of them fellers closing up the West Valley drive trail. Why, I never heard tell of such a thing afore!"

"We're short-handed; we ought to have more'n we have to guard the herd if there's a fight. If it stampedes-oh, well, that'll work out to-morrow. The creek's only about twelve miles away an' we'll start at daylight, so tumble in," Hopalong said as he arose. "Red, I'm going out to take my shift —I'll send Pete in. Stranger," he added, turning, "I'm much obliged to you for the warning. They might 'a' caught us with our hands tied."

"Oh, that's all right," hastily replied the stranger, who was in hearty accord with the plans, such as they were. "My name's Hawkins, an' I don't like range fences no more'n you do. I used to hunt buffalo all over this part of the country before they was all killed off, an' I allus rode where I pleased. I'm purty old, but I can still see an' shoot; an' I'm going to stick right along with you fellers an' see it through. Every man counts in this game."

"Well, that's blamed white of you," Hopalong replied, greatly pleased by the other's offer. "But I can't let you do it. I don't want to drag you into no trouble, an' —"

"You ain't dragging me none; I'm doing it myself. I'm about as mad as you are over it. I ain't good for much no more, an' if I shuffles off fighting barb wire I'll be doing my duty. First it was nesters, then railroads an' more nesters, then sheep, an' now it's wire-won't it never stop? By the Lord, it's got to stop, or this country will go to the devil an' won't be fit to live in. Besides, I've heard of your fellers before —I'll tie to the Bar-20 any day."

"Well, I reckon you must if you must; yo're welcome enough," laughed Hopalong, and he strode off to his picketed horse, leaving the others to discuss the fence, with the assistance of the cook, until Pete rode in.

Chapter XXI
The Fence

When Hopalong rode in at midnight to arouse the others and send them out to relieve Skinny and his two companions, the cattle were quieter than he had expected to leave them, and he could see no change of weather threatening. He was asleep when the others turned in, or he would have been further assured in that direction.

Out on the plain where the herd was being held, Red and the three other guards had been optimistic until half of their shift was over and it was only then that they began to worry. The knowledge that running water was only twelve miles away had the opposite effect than the one expected, for instead of making them cheerful, it caused them to be beset with worry and fear. Water was all right, and they could not have got along without it for another day; but it was, in this case, filled with the possibility of grave danger.

Johnny was thinking hard about it as he rode around the now restless herd, and then pulled up suddenly, peered into the darkness and went on again. "Damn that disreputable li'l rounder! Why the devil can't he behave, 'stead of stirring things up when they're ticklish?" he muttered, but he had to grin despite himself. A lumbering form had blundered past him from the direction of the camp and was swallowed up by the night as it sought the herd, annoying and arousing the thirsty and irritable cattle along its trail, throwing challenges right and left and stirring up trouble as it passed. The fact that the challenges were bluffs made no difference to the pawing steers, for they were anxious to have things out with the rounder.

This frisky disturber of bovine peace was a yearling that had slipped into the herd before it left the ranch and had kept quiet and respectable and out of sight in the middle of the mass for the first few days and nights. But keeping quiet and respectable had been an awful strain, and his mischievous deviltry grew constantly harder to hold in check. Finally he could stand the repression no longer, and when he gave way to his accumulated energy it had the snap and ginger of a tightly stretched rubber band recoiling on itself. On the fourth night out he had thrown off his mask and announced his presence in his true light by butting a sleepy steer out of its bed, which bed he straightway proceeded to appropriate for himself. This was folly, for the ground was not cold and he had no excuse for stealing a body-warmed place to lie down; it was pure cussedness, and retribution followed hard upon the act. In about half a minute he had discovered the great difference between bullying poor, miserable, defenceless dogies and trying to bully a healthy, fully developed, and pugnacious steer. After assimilating the preliminary punishment of what promised to be the most thorough and workmanlike thrashing he had ever known, the indignant and frightened bummer wheeled and fled incontinently with the aroused steer in angry pursuit. The best way out was the most puzzling to the vengeful steer, so the bummer cavorted recklessly through the herd, turning and twisting and doubling, stepping on any steer that happened to be lying down in his path, butting others, and leavening things with great success. Under other conditions he would have relished the effect of his efforts, for the herd had arisen as one animal and seemed to be debating the advisability of stampeding; but he was in no mood to relish anything and thought only of getting away. Finally escaping from his pursuer, that had paused to fight with a belligerent brother, he rambled off into the darkness to figure it all out and to maintain a sullen and chastened demeanor for the rest of the night. This was the first time a brick had been under the hat.

But the spirits of youth recover quickly-his recovered so quickly that he was banished from the herd the very next night, which banishment, not being at all to his liking, was enforced only by rigid watchfulness and hard riding; and he was roundly cursed from dark to dawn by the worried men, most of whom disliked the bumming youngster less than they pretended. He was only a cub, a wild youth having his fling, and there was something irresistibly likable and comical in his awkward antics and eternal persistence, even though he was a pest. Johnny saw more in him than his companions could find, and had quite a little sport with him: he made fine practice for roping, for he was about as elusive as a grasshopper and uncertain as a flea. Johnny was in the same general class and he could sympathize with the irrepressible nuisance in its efforts to stir up a little life and excitement in so dull a crowd; Johnny hoped to be as successful in his mischievous deviltry when he reached the town at the end of the drive.

But to-night it was dark, and the bummer gained his coveted goal with ridiculous ease, after which he started right in to work off the high pressure of the energy he had accumulated during the last two nights. He had desisted in his efforts to gain the herd early in the evening and had rambled off and rested during the first part of the night, and the herders breathed softly lest they should stir him to renewed trials. But now he had succeeded, and although only Johnny had seen him lumber past, the other three guards were aware of it immediately by the results and swore in their throats, for the cattle were now on their feet, snorting and moving about restlessly, and the rattling of horns grew slowly louder.

"Ain't he having a devil of a good time!" grinned Johnny. But it was not long before he realized the possibilities of the bummer's efforts and he lost his grin. "If we get through the night without trouble I'll see that you are picketed if it takes me all day to get you," he muttered. "Fun is fun, but it's getting a little too serious for comfort."

Sometime after the middle of the second shift the herd, already irritable, nervous, and cranky because of the thirst they were enduring, and worked up to the fever pitch by the devilish manoeuvres of the exuberant and hard-working bummer, wanted only the flimsiest kind of an excuse to stampede, and they might go without an excuse. A flash of lightning, a crash of thunder, a wind-blown paper, a flapping wagon cover, the sudden and unheralded approach of a careless rider, the cracking and flare of a match, or the scent of a wolf or coyote-or water, would send an avalanche of three thousand crazed steers crashing its irresistible way over a pitch-black plain.

Red had warned Pete and Billy, and now he rode to find Johnny and send him to camp for the others. As he got halfway around the circle he heard Johnny singing a mournful lay, and soon a black bulk loomed up in the dark ahead of him. "That you, Kid?" he asked. "That you, Johnny?" he repeated, a little louder.

The song stopped abruptly. "Shore," replied Johnny. "We're going to have trouble aplenty to-night. Glad daylight ain't so very far off. That cussed li'l rake of a bummer got by me an' into the herd. He's shore raising Ned to-night, the li'l monkey: it's getting serious, Red."

"I'll shoot that yearling at daylight, damn him!" retorted Red. "I should 'a' done it a week ago. He's picked the worst time for his cussed devilment! You ride right in an' get the boys, an' get 'em out here quick. The whole herd's on its toes waiting for the signal; an' the wink of an eye'll send 'em off. God only knows what'll happen between now and daylight! If the wind should change an' blow down from the north, they'll be off as shore as shooting. One whiff of Bennett's Creek is all that's needed, Kid; an' —"

"Oh, pshaw!" interposed Johnny. "There ain't no wind at all now. It's been quiet for an hour."

"Yes; an' that's one of the things that's worrying me. It means a change, shore."

"Not always; we'll come out of this all right," assured Johnny, but he spoke without his usual confidence. "There ain't no use —" he paused as he felt the air stir, and he was conscious of Red's heavy breathing. There was a peculiar hush in the air that he did not like, a closeness that sent his heart up in his throat, and as he was about to continue a sudden gust snapped his neck-kerchief out straight. He felt that refreshing coolness which so often precedes a storm and as he weighed it in his mind a low rumble of thunder rolled in the north and sent a chill down his back.

"Good God! Get the boys!" cried Red, wheeling. "It's *changed*! An' Pete an' Billy out there in front of—*there they go*!" he shouted as a sudden tremor shook the earth and a roaring sound filled the air. He was instantly lost to ear and eye, swallowed by the oppressive darkness as he spurred and quirted into a great, choking cloud of dust which swept down from the north, unseen in the night. The deep thunder of hoofs and the faint and occasional flash of a six-shooter told him the direction, and he hurled his mount after the uproar with no thought of the death which lurked in every hole and rock and gully on the uneven and unseen plain beneath him. His mouth and nose were lined with dust, his throat choked with it, and he opened his burning eyes only at intervals, and then only to a slit, to catch a fleeting glance of-nothing. He realized vaguely that he was riding north, because the cattle would head for water, but that was all, save that he was animated by a desperate eagerness to gain the firing line, to join Pete and Billy, the two men who rode before that crazed mass of horns and hoofs and who were pleading and swearing and yelling in vain only a few feet ahead of annihilation-if they were still alive. A stumble, a moment's indecision, and the avalanche would roll over them as if they were straws and trample them flat beneath the pounding hoofs, a modern Juggernaut. If he, or they, managed to escape with life, it would make a good tale for the bunk house some night; if they were killed it was in doing their duty-it was all in a day's work.

Johnny shouted after him and then wheeled and raced towards the camp, emptying his Colt in the air as a warning. He saw figures scurrying across the lighted place, and before he had gained it his friends raced past him and gave him hard work catching up to them. And just behind him rode the stranger, to do what he could for his new friends, and as reckless of consequences as they.

It seemed an age before they caught up to the stragglers, and when they realized how true they had ridden in the dark they believed that at last their luck was turning for the better, and pushed on with renewed hope. Hopalong shouted to those nearest him that Bennett's Creek could not be far away and hazarded the belief that the steers would slow up and stop when they found the water they craved; but his words were lost to all but himself.

Suddenly the punchers were almost trapped and their escape made miraculous, for without warning the herd swerved and turned sharply to the right, crossing the path of the riders and forcing them to the east, showing Hopalong their silhouettes against the streak of pale gray low down in the eastern sky. When free from the sudden press of cattle they slowed perceptibly, and Hopalong did likewise to avoid running them down. At that instant the uproar took on a new note and increased threefold. He could hear the shock of impact, whip-like reports, the bellowing of cattle in pain, and he arose in his stirrups to peer ahead for the reason, seeing, as he did so, the silhouettes of his friends arise and then drop from his sight. Without additional warning his horse pitched forward and crashed to the earth, sending him over its head. Slight as was the warning it served to ease his fall, for instinct freed his feet from the stirrups, and when he struck the ground it was feet first, and although he fell flat at the next instant, the shock had been broken. Even as it was, he was partly stunned, and groped as he arose on his hands and knees. Arising painfully he took a short step forward, tripped and fell again; and felt a sharp pain shoot through his hand as it went first to break the fall. Perhaps it was ten seconds before he knew what it was that had thrown him, and when he learned that he also learned the reason for the whole calamity-in his torn and bleeding hand he held a piece of barb wire.

"Barb wire!" he muttered, amazed. "Barb wire! Why, what the —*Damn that ranch!*" he shouted, sudden rage sweeping over him as the situation flashed through his mind and banished all the mental effects of the fall. "They've gone an' strung it south of the creek as well! Red! Johnny! Lanky!" he shouted at the top of his voice, hoping to be heard over the groaning of injured cattle and the general confusion. "Good Lord! *are they killed*!"

They were not, thanks to the forced slowing up, and to the pool of water and mud which formed an arm of the creek, a back-water away from the pull of the current. They had pitched into the mud and water up to their waists, some head first, some feet first, and others as they would go into a chair. Those who had been fortunate enough to strike feet first pulled out the divers, and the others gained their feet as best they might and with varying degrees of haste, but all mixed profanity and thankfulness equally well; and were equally and effectually disguised.

Hopalong, expecting the silence of death or at least the groaning of injured and dying, was taken aback by the fluent stream of profanity which greeted his ears. But all efforts in that line were eclipsed when the drive foreman tersely explained about the wire, and the providential mud bath was forgotten in the new idea. They forthwith clamored for war, and the sooner it came the better they would like it.

"Not now, boys; we've got work to do first," replied Hopalong, who, nevertheless, was troubled grievously by the same itching trigger finger. They subsided-as a steel spring subsides when held down by a weight-and went off in search of their mounts. Daylight had won the skirmish in the east and was now attacking in force, and revealed a sight which, stilling the profanity for the moment, caused it to flow again with renewed energy. The plain was a shambles near the creek, and dead and dying steers showed where the fence had stood. The rest of the herd had passed over these. The wounded cattle and three horses were put out of their misery as the first duty. The horse that Hopalong had ridden had a broken back; the other two, broken legs. When this work was out of the way the bruised and shaken men gave their attention to the scattered cattle on the other side of the creek, and when Hawkins rode up after wasting time in hunting for the trail in the dark, he saw four men with the herd, which was still scattered; four others near the creek, of whom only Johnny was mounted, and a group of six strangers riding towards them from the west and along the fence, or what was left of that portion of it.

"That's awful!" he cried, stopping his limping horse near Hopalong. "An' here come the fools that done it."

"Yes," replied Johnny, his voice breaking from rage, "but they won't go back again! I don't care if I'm killed if I can get one or two of that crowd —"

"Shut up, Kid!" snapped Hopalong as the 4X outfit drew near. "I know just how you feel about it; feel that way myself. But there ain't a-going to be no fighting while I've got these cows on my han's. That gang'll be here when we come back, all right."

"Mebby one or two of 'em won't," remarked Hawkins, as he looked again over the carnage along the fence. "I never did much pot-shooting, 'cept agin Injuns; but I dunno —" He did not finish, for the strangers were almost at his elbow.

Cranky Joe led the 4X contingent and he did the talking for it without waste of time. "Who the hell busted that fence?" he demanded, belligerently, looking around savagely. Johnny's hand twitched at the words and the way they were spoken.

"I did; did you think somebody leaned agin it?" replied Hopalong, very calmly, —so calmly that it was about one step short of an explosion.

"Well, why didn't you go around?"

"Three thousand stampeding cattle don't go 'round wire fences in the dark."

"Well, that's not our fault. Reckon you better dig down an' settle up for the damages, an' half a cent a head for water; an' then go 'round. You can't stampede through the other fence."

"That so?" asked Hopalong.

"Reckon it is."

"Yo're real shore it is?"

"Well there's only six of us here, but there's six more that we can get blamed quick if we need 'em. It's so, all right."

"Well, coming down to figures, there's eight here, with two hoss-wranglers an' a cook to come," retorted Hopalong, kicking the belligerent Johnny on the shins. "We're just about mad enough to tackle anything: ever feel that way?"

"Oh, no use getting all het up," rejoined Cranky Joe. "We ain't a-going to fight 'less we has to. Better pay up."

"Send yore bills to the ranch-if they're O. K., Buck'll pay 'em."

"Nix; I take it when I can get it."

"I ain't got no money with me that I can spare."

"Then you can leave enough cows to buy back again."

"I'm not going to pay you one damned cent, an' the only cows I'll leave are the dead ones-an' if I could take them with me I'd do it. An' I'm not going around the fence, neither."

"Oh, yes; you are. An' yo're going to pay," snapped Cranky Joe.

"Take it out of the price of two hundred dead cows an' gimme what's left," Hopalong retorted. "It'll cost you nine of them twelve men to pry it out'n me."

"You won't pay?" demanded the other, coldly.

"Not a plugged peso."

"Well, as I said before, I don't want to fight nobody 'less I has to," replied Cranky Joe. "I'll give you a chance to change yore mind. We'll be out here after it to-morrow, cash or cows. That'll give you twenty-four hours to rest yore herd an' get ready to drive. Then you pay, an' go back, 'round the fence."

"All right; to-morrow suits me," responded Hopalong, who was boiling with rage and felt constrained to hold it back. If it wasn't for the cows —!

Red and three companions swept up and stopped in a swirl of dust and asked questions until Hopalong shut them up. Their arrival and the manner of their speech riled Cranky Joe, who turned around and loosed one more remark; and he never knew how near to death he was at that moment.

"You fellers must own the earth, the way you act," he said to Red and his three companions.

"We ain't fencing it in to prove it," rejoined Hopalong, his hand on Red's arm.

Cranky Joe wheeled to rejoin his friends. "To-morrow," he said, significantly.

Hopalong and his men watched the six ride away, too enraged to speak for a moment. Then the drive foreman mastered himself and turned to Hawkins. "Where's their ranch house?" he demanded, sharply. "There must be some way out of this, an' we've got to find it; an' before to-morrow."

"West; three hours' ride along the fence. I could find 'em the darkest night what ever happened; I was out there once," Hawkins replied.

"Describe 'em as exact as you can," demanded Hopalong, and when Hawkins had done so the Bar-20 drive foreman slapped his thigh and laughed nastily. "One house with one door an' only two windows-are you shore? Good! Where's the corrals? Good again! So they'll take pay for their blasted fence, eh? Cash or cows, hey! Don't want no fight 'less it's necessary, but they're going to make us pay for the fence that killed two hundred head, an' blamed nigh got us, too. An' half a cent a head for drinking water! I've paid that more'n once-some of the poor devils squatting on the range ain't got nothing to sell but water, but I don't buy none out of Bennett's Creek! Pete, you mounted fellers round up a little-bunch the herd a little closer, an' drive straight along the trail towards that other fence. We'll all help you as soon as the wranglers bring us up something to ride. Push 'em hard, limp or no limp, till dark. They'll be too tired to go crow-hopping 'round any in the dark to-night. An' say! When you see that bummer, if he wasn't got by the fence, drop him clean. So they've got twelve men, hey! Huh!"

"What you going to do?" asked Red, beginning to cool down, and very curious.

"Yes; tell us," urged Johnny.

"Why, I'm going to cut that fence, an' cut it all to hell. Then I'm going to push the herd through it as far out of danger as I can. When they're all right Cookie an' the hoss-wranglers will have to hold 'em during the night while we do the rest."

"What's the rest?" demanded Johnny.

"Oh, I'll tell you that later; it can wait," replied Hopalong. "Meanwhile, you get out there with Pete an' help get the herd in shape. We'll be with you soon-here comes the wranglers an' the cavvieyeh. 'Bout time, too."

Chapter XXII
Mr. Boggs is Disgusted

The herd gained twelve miles by dark and would pass through the northern fence by noon of the next day, for Cook's axe and monkey wrench had been put to good use. For quite a distance there was no fence: about a mile of barb wire had been pulled loose and was tangled up into several large piles, while rings of burned grass and ashes surrounded what was left of the posts. The cook had embraced this opportunity to lay in a good supply of firewood and was the happiest man in the outfit.

At ten o'clock that night eight figures loped westward along the southern fence and three hours later dismounted near the first corral of the 4X ranch. They put their horses in a depression on the plain and then hastened to seek cover, being careful to make no noise.

At dawn the door of the bunk house opened quickly and as quickly slammed shut again, three bullets in it being the reason. An uproar ensued and guns spat from the two windows in the general direction of the unseen besiegers, who did not bother about replying; they had given notification of their presence and until it was necessary to shoot there was no earthly use of wasting ammunition. Besides, the drive outfit had cooled down rapidly when it found that its herd was in no immediate danger and was not anxious to kill any one unless there was need. The situation was conducive to humor rather than anger. But every time the door moved it collected more lead, and it finally remained shut.

The noise in the bunk house continued and finally a sombrero was waved frantically at the south window and a moment later Nat Boggs, foreman of the incarcerated 4X outfit, stuck his head out very cautiously and yelled questions which bore directly on the situation and were to the point. He appeared to be excited and unduly heated, if one might judge from his words and voice. There was no reply, which still further added to his heat and excitement. Becoming bolder and a little angrier he allowed his impetuous nature to get the upper hand and forthwith attempted the feat of getting through that same window; but a sharp *pat!* sounded on a board not a foot from him, and he reconsidered hastily. His sombrero again waved to insist on a truce, and collected two holes, causing him much mental anguish and threatening the loss of his worthy soul. He danced up and down with great agility and no grace and made remarks, thereby leading a full-voiced chorus.

"Ain't that a hell of a note?" he demanded plaintively as he paused for breath. "Stick *yore* hat out, Cranky, an' see what *you* can do," he suggested, irritably.

Cranky Joe regarded him with pity and reproach, and moved back towards the other end of the room, muttering softly to himself. "I know it ain't much of a bonnet, but he needn't rub it in," he growled, peevishly.

"Try again; mebby they didn't see you," suggested Jim Larkin, who had a reputation for never making a joke. He escaped with his life and checked himself at the side of Cranky Joe, with whom he conferred on the harshness of the world towards unfortunates.

The rest of the morning was spent in snipe-shooting at random, trusting to luck to hit some one, and trusting in vain. At noon Cranky Joe could stand the strain no longer and opened the door just a little to relive the monotony. He succeeded, being blessed with a smashed shoulder, and immediately became a general nuisance, adding greatly to the prevailing atmosphere. Boggs called him a few kinds of fools and hastened to nail the door shut; he hit his thumb and his heart became filled with venom.

"*Now* look at what they went an' done!" he yelled, running around in a circle. "Damned outrage!"

"Huh!" snorted Cranky Joe with maddening superiority. "That ain't nothing-just look at me!"

Boggs looked, very fixedly, and showed signs of apoplexy, and Cranky Joe returned to his end of the room to resume his soliloquy.

"Why don't you come out an' take them cows!" inquired an unkind voice from without. "Ain't changed yore mind, have you?"

"We'll give you a drink for half a cent a head-that's the regular price for watering cows," called another.

The faint ripple of mirth which ran around the plain was lost in opinions loudly expressed within the room; and Boggs, tears of rage in his eyes, flung himself down on a chair and invented new terms for describing human beings.

John Terry was observing. He had been fluttering around the north window, constantly getting bolder, and had not been disturbed. When he withdrew his sombrero and found that it was intact he smiled to himself and leaned his elbows on the sill, looking carefully around the plain. The discovery that there was no cover on the north side cheered him greatly and he called to Boggs, outlining a plan of action.

Boggs listened intently and then smiled for the first time since dawn. "Bully for you, Terry!" he enthused. "Wait till dark-we'll fool 'em."

A bullet chipped the 'dobe at Terry's side and he ducked as he leaped back. "From an angle-what did I tell you?" he laughed. "We'll drop out here an' sneak behind the house after dark. They'll be watching the door-an' they won't be able to see us, anyhow."

Boggs sucked his thumb tenderly and grinned. "After which —," he elated.

"After which —," gravely repeated Terry, the others echoing it with unrestrained joy.

"Then, mebby, I can get a drink," chuckled Larkin, brightening under the thought.

"The moon comes up at ten," warned a voice. "It'll be full to-night —an' there ain't many clouds in sight."

"*Ol' King Cole was a merry ol' soul*," hummed McQuade, lightly.

"An' —a —merry-ol' —soul-was-he! —was-he!" thundered the chorus, deep-toned and strong. "*He had a wife for every toe, an' some toes counted three!*"

"Listen!" cried Meade, holding up his hand.

"*An' every wife had sixteen dogs, an' every dog a flea!*" shouted a voice from the besiegers, followed by a roar of laughter.

The hilarity continued until dark, only stopping when John Terry slipped out of the window, dropped to all-fours and stuck his head around the corner of the rear wall. He saw many stars and was silently handed to Pete Wilson.

"What was that noise?" exclaimed Boggs in a low tone. "Are you all right, Terry?" he asked, anxiously.

Three knocks on the wall replied to his question and then McQuade went out, and three more knocks were heard.

"Wonder why they make that funny noise," muttered Boggs.

"Bumped inter something, I reckon," replied Jim Larkin. "Get out of my way —I'm next."

Boggs listened intently and then pushed Duke Lane back. "Don't like that-sounds like a crack on the head. Hey, Jim! *Say* something!" he called softly. The three knocks were repeated, but Boggs was suspicious and he shook his head decisively. "To 'ell with the knocking —*say* something!"

"Still got them twelve men?" asked a strange voice, pleasantly.

"*An' every dog a flea*," hummed another around the corner.

"Hell!" shouted Boggs. "To the door, fellers! To the door-quick!"

A whistle shrilled from behind the house and a leaden tattoo began on the door. "Other window!" whispered O'Neill. The foreman got there before him and, shoving his Colt out first to clear the way, yelled with rage and pain as a pole hit his wrist and knocked the weapon out of his hand. He was still commenting when Duke Lane pried open the door and, dropping quickly on his stomach, wriggled out, followed closely by Charley Beal and Tim. At that instant the tattoo drummed with greater vigor and such a hail of lead poured in through the opening that the door was promptly closed, leaving the three men outside to shift for themselves with the darkness their only cover.

Duke and his companions whispered together as they lay flat and agreed upon a plan of action. Going around the ends of the house was suicide and no better than waiting for the rising moon to show them to the enemy; but there was no reason why the roof could not be utilized. Tim and Charley boosted Duke up, then Tim followed, and the pair on the roof pulled Charley to their side. Flat roofs were great institutions they decided as they crawled cautiously towards the other side. This roof was of hard, sun-baked adobe, over two feet thick, and they did not care if their friends shot up on a gamble.

"Fine place, all right," thought Charley, grinning broadly. Then he turned an agonized face to Tim, his chest rising. "*Hitch! Hitch!*" he choked, fighting with all his will to master it. "*Hitch-chew! Hitch-chew! Hitch-chew!*" he sneezed, loudly. There was a scramble below and a ripple of mirth floated up to them.

"*Hitch-chew?*" jeered a voice. "What do we want to hit you for?"

"Look us over, children," invited another.

"Wait until the moon comes up," chuckled the third. "Be like knocking the nigger baby down for Red an' the others. Ladies and gents: We'll now have a little sketch entitled 'Shooting snipe by moonlight.'"

"Jack-snipe, too," laughed Pete. "Will somebody please hold the bag?"

The silence on the roof was profound and the three on the ground tried again.

"Let me call yore attention to the trained coyotes, ladies an' gents," remarked Johnny in a deep, solemn voice. "Coyotes are not birds; they do not roost on roofs as a general thing; but they are some intelligent an' can be trained to do lots of foolish tricks. These ani-mules were —"

"Step this way, people; on-ly ten cents, two nickels," interrupted Pete. "They bark like dogs, an' howl like hell."

"Shut up!" snapped Tim, angrily.

"After the moon comes up," said Hopalong, "when you fellers get tired dodging, you can chuck us yore guns an' come down. An' don't forget that this side of the house is much the safest," he warned.

"Go to hell!" snarled Duke, bitterly.

"Won't; they're laying for me down there."

Johnny crawled to the north end of the wall and, looking cautiously around the corner, funnelled his hands: "On the roof, Red! On the roof!"

"Yes, dear," was the reply, followed by gun-shots.

"Hey! Move over!" snapped Tim, working towards the edge furthest from the cheerful Red, whose bullets were not as accurate in the dark as they promised to become in a few minutes when the moon should come up.

"Want to shove me off?" snarled Charley, angrily. "For heaven's sake, Duke, do you want the whole earth?" he demanded of his second companion.

"You just bet yore shirt I do! An' I want a hole in it, too!"

"Ain't you got no sense?"

"Would I be up here if I had?"

"It's going to be hot as blazes up here when the sun gets high," cheerfully prophesied Tim: "an' dry, too," he added for a finishing touch.

"We'll be lucky if we're live enough to worry about the sun's heat —*say*, that was a *close* one!" exclaimed Duke, frantically trying to flatten a little more. "Ah, thought so-there's that blamed moon!"

"Wish I'd gone out the window instead," growled Charley, worming behind Duke, to the latter's prompt displeasure.

"You fellers better come down, one at a time," came from below. "Send yore guns down first, too. Red's a blamed good shot."

"Hope he croaks," muttered Duke. "*That's* closer yet!"

Tim's hand raised and a flash of fire singed Charley's hair. "Got to do something, anyhow," he explained, lowering the Colt and peering across the plain.

"You damned near succeeded!" shouted Charley, grabbing at his head. "Why, they're three hundred, an' you trying for 'em with a —*oh!*" he moaned, writhing.

"Locoed fool!" swore Duke, "showing 'em where we are! They're doing good enough as it is! You ought-got *you*, too!"

"*I'm* going down-that blamed fool out there ain't caring what he hits," mumbled Charley, clenching his hands from pain. He slid over the edge and Pete grabbed him.

"Next," suggested Pete, expectantly.

Tim tossed his Colt over the edge. "Here's another," he swore, following the weapon. He was grabbed and bound in a trice.

"When may we expect you, Mr. Duke?" asked Johnny, looking up.

"Presently, friend, presently. I want to —*wow!*" he finished, and lost no time in his descent, which was meteoric. "That feller'll *kill* somebody if he ain't careful!" he complained as Pete tied his hands behind his back.

"You wait till daylight an' see," cheerily replied Pete as the three were led off to join their friends in the corral.

There was no further action until the sun arose and then Hopalong hailed the house and demanded a parley, and soon he and Boggs met midway between the shack and the line.

"What d'you want?" asked Boggs, sullenly.

"Want you to stop this farce so I can go on with my drive."

"Well, I ain't holding you!" exploded the 4X foreman.

"Oh, yes; but you are. I can't let you an' yore men out to hang on our flanks an' worry us; an' I don't want to hold you in that shack till you all die of thirst, or come out to be all shot up. Besides, I can't fool around here for a week; I got business to look after."

"Don't you worry about us dying with thirst; that ain't worrying us none."

"I heard different," replied Hopalong, smiling. "Them fellers in the corral drank a quart apiece. See here, Boggs; you can't win, an' you know it. Yo're not bucking me, but the whole range, the whole country. It's a fight between conditions-the fence idea agin the open range idea, an' open trails. The fence will lose. You closed a drive trail that's 'most as old as cow-raising. Will the punchers of this part of the country stand for it? Suppose you lick us, —which you won't —can you lick all the rest of us, the JD, Wallace's, Double-Arrow, C-80, Cross-O-Cross, an' the others! That's just what it amounts to, an' you better stop right now, before somebody gets killed. You know what that means in this section. Yo're six to our eight, you ain't got a drink in that shack, an' you dasn't try to get one. You can't do a thing agin us, an' you know it."

Boggs rested his hands on his hips and considered, Hopalong waiting for him to reply. He knew that the Bar-20 man was right but he hated to admit it, he hated to say he was whipped.

"Are any of them six hurt?" he finally asked.

"Only scratches an' sore heads," responded Hopalong, smiling. "We ain't tried to kill anybody, yet. I'm putting that up to you."

Boggs made no reply and Hopalong continued: "I got six of yore twelve men prisoners, an' all yore cayuses are in my han's. I'll shoot every animal before I'll leave 'em for you to use against me, an' I'll take enough of yore cows to make up for what I lost by that fence. You've got to pay for them dead cows, anyhow. If I do let you out you'll have to road-brand me two hundred, or pay cash. My herd ain't worrying me-it's moving all the time. It's through that other fence by now. An' if I have to keep my outfit here to pen you in or shoot you off I can send to the JD for a gang to push the herd. Don't make no mistake: yo're getting off easy. Suppose one of my men had been killed at the fence-what then?"

"Well, what do you want me to do?"

"Stop this foolishness an' take down them fences for a mile each side of the trail. If Buck has to come up here the whole thing'll go down. Road-brand me two hundred of yore three-year-olds. Now as soon as you agree, an' say that the fight's over, it will be. You can't win out; an' what's the use of having yore men killed off?"

"I hate to quit," replied the other, gloomily.

"I know how that is; but yo're wrong on this question, dead wrong. You don't own this range or the trail. You ain't got no right to close that old drive trail. Honest, now; have you?"

"You say them six ain't hurt?"

"No more'n I said."

"An' if I give in will you treat my men right?"

"Shore."

"When will you leave."

"Just as soon as I get them two hundred three-year-olds."

"Well, I hate a quitter; but I can't do nothing, nohow," mused the 4X foreman. He cleared his throat and turned to look at the house. "All right; when you get them cows you get out of here, an' don't never come back!"

Hopalong flung his arm with a shout to his men and the other kicked savagely at an inoffensive stick and slouched back to his bunk house, a beaten man.

Chapter XXIII
Tex Ewalt Hunts Trouble

Not more than a few weeks after the Bar-20 drive outfit returned to the ranch a solitary horseman pushed on towards the trail they had followed, bound for Buckskin and the Bar-20 range. His name was Tex Ewalt and he cordially hated all of the Bar-20 outfit and Hopalong in particular. He had nursed a grudge for several years and now, as he rode south to rid himself of it and to pay a long-standing debt, it grew stronger until he thrilled with anticipation and the sauce of danger. This grudge had been acquired when he and Slim Travennes had enjoyed a duel with Hopalong Cassidy up in Santa Fe, and had been worsted; it had increased when he learned of Slim's death at Cactus Springs at the hands of Hopalong; and, some time later, hearing that two friends of his, "Slippery" Trendley and "Deacon" Rankin, with their gang, had "gone out" in the Panhandle with the same man and his friends responsible for it, Tex hastened to Muddy Wells to even the score and clean his slate. Even now his face burned when he remembered his experiences on that never-to-be-forgotten occasion. He had been played with, ridiculed, and shamed, until he fled from the town as a place accursed, hating everything and everybody. It galled him to think that he had allowed Buck Peters' momentary sympathy to turn him from his purpose, even though he was convinced that the foreman's action had saved his life. And now Tex was returning, not to Muddy Wells, but to the range where the Bar-20 outfit held sway.

Several years of clean living had improved Tex, morally and physically. The liquor he had once been in the habit of consuming had been reduced to a negligible quantity; he spent the money on cartridges instead, and his pistol work showed the results of careful and dogged practice, particularly in the quickness of the draw. Punching cows on a remote northern range had repaid him in health far more than his old game of living on his wits and other people's lack of them, as proved by his clear eye and the pink showing through the tan above his beard; while his somber, steady gaze, due to long-held fixity of purpose, indicated the resourcefulness of a perfectly reliable set of nerves. His low-hung holster tied securely to his trousers leg to assure smoothness in drawing, the restrained swing of his right hand, never far from the well-worn scabbard which sheathed a triggerless Colt's "Frontier" —these showed the confident and ready gun-man, the man who seldom missed. "Frontiers" left the factory with triggers attached, but the absence of that part did not always incapacitate a weapon. Some men found that the regular method was too slow, and painstakingly cultivated the art of thumbing the hammer. "Thumbing" was believed to save the split second so valuable to a man in argument with his peers. Tex was riding with the set purpose of picking a fair fight with the best six-shooter expert it had ever been his misfortune to meet, and he needed that split second. He knew that he needed it and the knowledge thrilled him with a peculiar elation; he had changed greatly in the past year and now he wanted an "even break" where once he would have called all his wits into play to avoid it. He had found himself and now he acknowledged no superior in anything.

On his way south he met and talked with men who had known him, the old Tex, in the days when he had made his living precariously. They did not recognize him behind his beard, and he was content to let the oversight pass. But from these few he learned what he wished to know, and he was glad that Hopalong Cassidy was where he had always been, and that his gun-work had improved rather than depreciated with the passing of time. He wished to prove himself master of The Master, and to be hailed as such by those who had jeered and laughed at his ignominy several years before. So he rode on day after day, smiling and content, neither under-rating nor over-rating his enemy's ability with one weapon, but trying to think of him as he really was. He knew that if there was any difference between Hopalong Cassidy and himself that it must be very slight-perhaps so slight as to result fatally to both; but if that were so then it would have to work out as it saw fit-he at least would have accomplished what many, many others had failed in.

In the little town of Buckskin, known hardly more than locally, and never thought of by outsiders except as the place where the Bar-20 spent their spare time and money, and neutral ground for the surrounding ranches, was Cowan's saloon, in the dozen years of its existence the scene of good stories, boisterous fun, and quick deaths. Put together roughly, of crude materials, sticking up in inartistic prominence on the dusty edge of a dustier street; warped, bleached by the sun, and patched with boards ripped from packing cases and with the flattened sides of tin cans; low of ceiling, the floor one huge brown discoloration of spring, creaking boards, knotted and split and worn into hollows, the unpretentious building offered its hospitality to all who might be tempted by the scrawled, sprawled lettering of its sign. The walls were smoke-blackened, pitted with numerous small and clear-cut holes, and decorated with initials carelessly cut by men who had come and gone.

Such was Cowan's, the best patronized place in many hot and dusty miles and the Mecca of the cowboys from the surrounding ranches. Often at night these riders of the range gathered in the humble building and told tales of exceeding interest; and on these occasions one might see a row of ponies standing before the building, heads down and quiet. It is strange how alike cow-ponies look in the dim light of the stars. On the south side of the saloon, weak, yellow lamp light filtered through the dirt on the window panes and fell in distorted patches on the plain, blotched in places by the shadows of the wooden substitutes for glass.

It was a moonlight night late in the fall, after the last beef round-up was over and the last drive outfit home again, that two cow-ponies stood in front of Cowan's while their owners lolled against the bar and talked over the latest sensation-the fencing in of the West Valley range, and the way Hopalong Cassidy and his trail outfit had opened up the old drive trail across it. The news was a month old, but it was the last event of any importance and was still good to laugh over.

"Boys," remarked the proprietor, "I want you to meet Mr. Elkins. He came down that trail last week, an' he didn't see no fence across it." The man at the table arose slowly. "Mr. Elkins, this is Sandy Lucas, an' Wood Wright, of the C-80. Mr. Elkins here has been a-looking over the country, sizing up what the beef prospects will be for next year; an' he knows all about wire fences. Here's how," he smiled, treating on the house.

Mr. Elkins touched the glass to his bearded lips and set it down untasted while he joked over the sharp rebuff so lately administered to wire fences in that part of the country. While he was an ex-cow-puncher he believed that he was above allowing prejudice to sway his judgment, and it was his opinion, after careful thought, that barb wire was harmful to the best interests of the range. He had ridden over a great part of the cattle country in the last few yeas, and after reviewing the existing conditions as he understood them, his verdict must go as stated, and emphatically. He launched gracefully into a slowly delivered and lengthy discourse upon the subject, which proved to be so entertaining that his companions were content to listen and nod with comprehension. They had never met any one who was so well qualified to discuss the pros and cons of the barb-wire fence question, and they learned many things which they had never heard before. This was very gratifying to Mr. Elkins, who drew largely upon hearsay, his own vivid imagination, and a healthy logic. He was very glad to talk to men who had the welfare of the range at heart, and he hoped soon to meet the man who had taken the initiative in giving barb wire its first serious setback on that rich and magnificent southern range.

"You shore ought to meet Cassidy-he's a fine man," remarked Lucas with enthusiasm. "You'll not find any better, no matter where you look. But you ain't touched yore liquor," he finished with surprise.

"You'll have to excuse me, gentlemen," replied Mr. Elkins, smiling deprecatingly. "When a man likes it as much as I do it ain't very easy to foller instructions an' let it alone. Sometimes I almost break loose an' indulge, regardless of whether it kills me or not. I reckon it'll get me yet." He struck the bar a resounding blow with his clenched hand. "But I ain't going to cave in till I has to!"

"That's purty tough," sympathized Wood Wright, reflectively. "I ain't so very much taken with it, but I know I would be if I knowed I couldn't have any."

"Yes, that's human nature, all right," laughed Lucas. "That reminds me of a little thing that happened to me once —"

"Listen!" exclaimed Cowan, holding up his hand for silence. "I reckon that's the Bar-20 now, or some of it-sounds like them when they're feeling frisky. There's allus something happening when them fellers are around."

The proprietor was right, as proved a moment later when Johnny Nelson, continuing his argument, pushed open the door and entered the room. "I didn't neither; an' you know it!" he flung over his shoulder.

"Then who did?" demanded Hopalong, chuckling. "Why, hullo, boys," he said, nodding to his friends at the bar. "Nobody else would do a fool thing like that; nobody but you, Kid," he added, turning to Johnny.

"I don't care a hang what you think; I say I didn't an' —"

"He shore did, all right; I seen him just afterward," laughed Billy Williams, pressing close upon Hopalong's heels. "Howdy, Lucas; an' there's that ol' coyote, Wood Wright. How's everybody feeling?"

"Where's the rest of you fellers?" inquired Cowan.

"Stayed home to-night," replied Hopalong.

"Got any loose money, you two?" asked Billy, grinning at Lucas and Wright.

"I reckon we have-an' our credit's good if we ain't. We're good for a dollar or two, ain't we, Cowan?" replied Lucas.

"Two dollars an' four bits," corrected Cowan. "I'll raise it to three dollars even when you pay me that 'leven cents you owe me."

"'Leven cents? What 'leven cents?"

"Postage stamps an' envelope for that love letter you writ."

"Go to blazes; that wasn't no love letter!" snorted Lucas, indignantly. "That was my quarterly report. I never did write no love letters, nohow."

"We'll trim you fellers to-night, if you've got the nerve to play us," grinned Johnny, expectantly.

"Yes; an' we've got that, too. Give us the cards, Cowan," requested Wood Wright, turning. "They won't give us no peace till we take all their money away from 'em."

"Open game," prompted Cowan, glancing meaningly at Elkins, who stood by idly looking on, and without showing much interest in the scene.

"Shore! Everybody can come in what wants to," replied Lucas, heartily, leading the others to the table. "I allus did like a six-handed game best-all the cards are out an' there's some excitement in it."

When the deal began Elkins was seated across the table from Hopalong, facing him for the first time since that day over in Muddy Wells, and studying him closely. He found no changes, for the few years had left no trace of their passing on the Bar-20 puncher. The sensation of facing the man he had come south expressly to kill did not interfere with Elkins' card-playing ability for he played a good game; and as if the Fates were with him it was Hopalong's night off as far as poker was concerned, for his customary good luck was not in evidence. That instinctive feeling which singles out two duellists in a card game was soon experienced by the others, who were careful, as became good players, to avoid being caught between them; in consequence, when the game broke up, Elkins had most of Hopalong's money. At one period of his life Elkins had lived on poker for five years, and lived well. But he gained more than money in this game, for he had made friends with the players and placed the first wire of his trap. Of those in the room Hopalong alone treated him with reserve, and this was cleverly swung so that it appeared to be caused by a temporary grouch due to the sting of defeat. As the Bar-20 man was known to be given to moods at times this was accepted as the true explanation and gave promise of hotly contested games for revenge later on. The banter which the defeated puncher had to endure stirred him and strengthened the reserve, although he was careful not to show it.

When the last man rode off, Elkins and the proprietor sought their bunks without delay, the former to lie awake a long time, thinking deeply. He was vexed at himself for failing to work out an acceptable plan of action, one that would show him to be in the right. He would gain nothing more than glory, and pay too dearly for it, if he killed Hopalong and was in turn killed by the dead man's friends-and he believed that he had become acquainted with the quality of the friendship which bound the units of the Bar-20 outfit into a smooth, firm whole. They were like brothers, like one man. Cassidy must do the forcing as far as appearances went, and be clearly in the wrong before the matter could be settled.

The next week was a busy one for Elkins, every day finding him in the saddle and riding over some one of the surrounding ranches with one or more of its punchers for company. In this way he became acquainted with the men who might be called on to act as his jury when the showdown came, and he proceeded to make friends of them in a manner that promised success. And some of his suggestions for the improvement of certain conditions on the range, while they might not work out right in the long run, compelled thought and showed his interest. His remarks on the condition and numbers of cattle were the same in substance in all cases and showed that he knew what he was talking about, for the punchers were all very optimistic about the next year's showing in cattle.

"If you fellers don't break all records for drive herds of quality next year I don't know nothing about cows; an' I shore don't know nothing else," he told the foreman of the Bar-20, as they rode homeward after an inspection of that ranch. "There'll be more dust hanging over the drive trails leading from this section next year when spring drops the barriers than ever before. You needn't fear for the market, neither-prices will stand. The north an' central ranges ain't doing what they ought to this year-it'll be up to you fellers down south, here, to make that up; an' you can do it." This was not a guess, but the result of thought and study based on the observations he had made on his ride south, and from what he had learned from others along the way. It paralleled Buck's own private opinion, especially in regard to the southern range; and the vague suspicions in the foreman's mind disappeared for good and all.

Needless to say Elkins was a welcome visitor at the ranch houses and was regarded as a good fellow. At the Bar-20 he found only two men who would not thaw to him, and he was possessed of too much tact to try any persuasive measures. One was Hopalong, whose original cold reserve seemed to be growing steadily, the Bar-20 puncher finding in Elkins a personality that charged the atmosphere with hostility and quietly rubbed him the wrong way. Whenever he was in the presence of the newcomer he felt the tugging of an irritating and insistent antagonism and he did not always fully conceal it. John Bartlett, Lucas, and one or two of the more observing had noticed it and they began to prophesy future trouble between the two. The other man who disliked Elkins was Red Connors; but what was more natural? Red, being Hopalong's closest companion, would be very apt to share his friend's antipathy. On the other hand, as if to prove Hopalong's dislike to be unwarranted, Johnny Nelson swung far to the other extreme and was frankly enthusiastic in his liking for the cattle scout. And Johnny did not pour oil on the waters when he laughingly twitted Hopalong for allowing "a licking at cards to make him sore." This was the idea that Elkins was quietly striving to have generally accepted.

The affair thus hung fire, Elkins chafing at the delay and cautiously working for an opening, which at last presented itself, to be promptly seized. By a sort of mutual, unspoken agreement, the men in Cowan's that night passed up the cards and sat swapping stories. Cowan, swearing at a smoking lamp, looked up with a grin and burned his fingers as a roar of laughter marked the point of a droll reminiscence told by Bartlett.

"That's a good story, Bartlett," Elkins remarked, slowing refilling his pipe. "Reminds me of the lame Greaser, Hippy Joe, an' the canned oysters. They was both bad, an' neither of 'em knew it till they came together. It was like this. . . ." The malicious side glance went unseen by all but Hopalong, who stiffened with the raging suspicion of being twitted on his own deformity. The humor of the tale failed to appeal to him, and when his full senses returned Lucas was in the midst of the story of the deadly game of tag played in a ten-acre lot of dense underbrush by two of his old-time friends. It was a tale of gripping interest and his auditors were leaning forward in their eagerness not to miss a word. "An' Pierce won," finished Lucas; "some shot up, but able to get about. He was all right in a couple of weeks. But he was bound to win; he could shoot all around Sam Hopkins."

"But the best shot won't allus win in that game," commented Elkins. "That's one of the minor factors."

"Yes, sir! It's *luck* that counts there," endorsed Bartlett, quickly. "Luck, nine times out of ten."

"Best shot ought to win," declared Skinny Thompson. "It ain't all luck, nohow. Where'd I be against Hoppy, there?"

"Won't neither!" cried Johnny, excitedly. "The man who sees the other first wins out. That's wood-craft, an' brains."

"Aw! What do you know about it, anyhow?" demanded Lucas. "If he can't shoot so good what chance has he got-if he misses the first try, what then?"

"What chance has he got! First chance, miss or no miss. If he can't see the other first, where the devil does his good shooting come in?"

"Huh!" snorted Wood Wright, belligerently. "Any fool can *see*, but he can't *shoot*! An' it's as much luck as wood-craft, too, an' don't you forget it!"

"The first shot don't win, Johnny; not in a game like that, with all the dodging an' ducking," remarked Red. "You can't put one where you want it when a feller's slipping around in the brush. It's the most that counts, an' the best shot gets in the most. I wouldn't want to have to stand up against Hoppy an' a short gun, not in that game; no, sir!" and Red shook his head with decision.

The argument waxed hot. With the exception of Hopalong, who sat silently watchful, every one spoke his opinion and repeated it without regard to the others. It appeared that in this game, the man with the strongest lungs would eventually win out, and each man tried to show his superiority in that line. Finally, above the uproar, Cowan's bellow was herd, and he kept it up until some notice was taken of it. "Shut up! *Shut up!* For God's sake, *quit!* Never saw such a bunch of tinder-let somebody drop a cold, burned-out match in this gang, an' hell's to pay. Here, *all* of you, play cards an' forget about cross-tag in the scrub. You'll be arguing about playing marbles in the dark purty soon!"

"All right," muttered Johnny, "but just the same, the man who —"

"Never mind about the man who! Did you hear *me?*" yelled Cowan, swiftly reaching for a bucket of water. "*This* is a game where *I* gets the most in, an' don't forget it!"

"Come on; play cards," growled Lucas, who did not relish having his decision questioned on his own story. Undoubtedly somewhere in the wide, wide world there was such a thing as common courtesy, but none of it had ever strayed onto that range.

The chairs scraped on the rough floor as the men pulled up to a table. "I don't care a hang," came Elkins' final comment as he shuffled the cards with careful attention. "I'm not any fancy Colt expert, but I'm damned if I won't take a chance in that game with any man as totes a gun. Leastawise, of *course*, I wouldn't take no such advantage of a lame man."

The effect would have been ludicrous but for its deadly significance. Cowan, stooping to go under the bar, remained in that hunched-up attitude, his every faculty concentrated in his ears; the match on its way to the cigarette between Red's lips was held until it burned his fingers, when it was dropped from mere reflex action, the hand still stiffly aloft; Lucas, half in and half out of his chair, seemed to have got just where he intended, making no effort to seat himself. Skinny Thompson, his hand on his gun, seemed paralyzed; his mouth was open to frame a reply that never was uttered and he stared through narrowed eyelids at the blunderer. The sole movement in the room was the slow rising of Hopalong and the markedly innocent shuffling of the cards by Elkins, who appeared to be entirely ignorant of the weight and effect of his words. He dropped the pack for the cut and then looked up and around as if surprised by the silence and the expressions he saw.

Hopalong stood facing him, leaning over with both hands on the table. His voice, when he spoke, rumbled up from his chest in a low growl. "You won't *have* no advantage, Elkins. Take it from me, you've had yore last fling. I'm glad you made it plain, this time, so it's something I can take hold of." He straightened slowly and walked to the door, and an audible sigh sounded through the room as it was realized that trouble was not immediately imminent. At the door he paused and turned back around, looking back over his shoulder. "At noon to-morrow I'm going to hoof it north through the brush between the river an' the river trail, starting at the old ford a mile down the river." He waited expectantly.

"Me too-only the other way," was the instant rejoinder. "Have it yore own way."

Hopalong nodded and the closing door shut him out into the night. Without a word the Bar-20 men arose and followed him, the only hesitant being Johnny, who was torn between loyalty and new-found friendship; but with a sorrowful shake of the head, he turned away and passed out, not far behind the others.

"Clannish, ain't they?" remarked Elkins, gravely.

Those remaining were regarding him sternly, questioningly, Cowan with a deep frown darkening his face. "You hadn't ought to 'a' said that, Elkins." The reproof was almost an accusation.

Elkins looked steadily at the speaker. "You hadn't ought to 'a' let me say it," he replied. "How did I know he was so touchy?" His gaze left Cowan and lingered in turn on each of the others. "Some of you ought to 'a' told me. I wouldn't 'a' said it only for what I said just before, an' I didn't want him to think I was challenging him to no duel in the brush. So I says so, an' then he goes an' takes it up that I *am* challenging him. I ain't got no call to fight with nobody. Ain't

I tried to keep out of trouble with him ever since I've been here? Ain't I kept out of the poker games on his account? Ain't I?" The grave, even tones were dispassionate, without a trace of animus and serenely sure of justice.

The faces around him cleared gradually and heads began to nod in comprehending consent.

"Yes, I reckon you have," agreed Cowan, slowly, but the frown was not entirely gone. "Yes, I reckon-mebby-you have."

Chapter XXIV
The Master

It was noon by the sun when Hopalong and Red shook hands south of the old ford and the former turned to enter the brush. Hopalong was cool and ominously calm while his companion was the opposite. Red was frankly suspicious of the whole affair and nursed the private opinion that Mr. Elkins would lay in ambush and shoot his enemy down like a dog. And Red had promised himself a dozen times that he would study the signs around the scene of action if Hopalong should not come back, and take a keen delight, if warranted, in shooting Mr. Elkins full of holes with no regard for an even break. He was thinking the matter over as his friend breasted the first line of brush and could not refrain from giving a slight warning. "Get him, Hoppy," he called, earnestly; "get him good. Let *him* do some of the moving about. I'll be here waiting for you."

Hopalong smiled in reply and sprang forward, the leaves and branches quickly shutting him from Red's sight. He had worked out his plan of action the night before when he was alone and the world was still, and as soon as he had it to his satisfaction he had dropped off to sleep as easily as a child-it took more than gun-play to disturb his nerves. He glanced about him to make sure of his bearings and then struck on a curving line for the river. The first hundred yards were covered with speed and then he began to move more slowly and with greater regard for caution, keeping close to the earth and showing a marked preference for low ground. Sky-lines were all right in times of peace, but under the present conditions they promised to become unhealthy. His eyes and ears told him nothing for a quarter of an hour, and then he suddenly stopped short and crouched as he saw the plain trail of a man crossing his own direction at a right angle. From the bottom of one of the heel prints a crushed leaf was slowly rising back towards its original position, telling him how new the trail was; and as if this were not enough for his trained mind he heard a twig snap sharply as he glanced along the line of prints. It sounded very close, and he dropped instantly to one knee and thought quickly. Why had the other left so plain a trail, why had he reached up and broken twigs that projected above his head as he passed? Why had he kicked aside a small stone, leaving a patch of moist, bleached grass to tell where it had lain? Elkins had stumbled here, but there were no toe marks to tell of it. Hopalong would not track, for he was no assassin; but he knew that he would do if he were, and careless. The answer leaped to his suspicious mind like a flash, and he did not care to waste any time in trying to determine whether or not Elkins was capable of such a trick. He acted on the presumption that the trail had been made plain for a good reason, and that not far ahead at some suitable place, —and there were any number of such within a hundred yards, —the maker of the plain trail lay in wait. Smiling savagely he worked backward and turning, struck off in a circle. He had no compunctions whatever now about shooting the other player of the game. It was not long before he came upon the same trail again and he started another circle. A bullet *zipped* past his ear and cut a twig not two inches from his head. He fired at the smoke as he dropped, and then wriggled rapidly backward, keeping as flat to the earth as he could. Elkins had taken up his position in a thicket which stood in the centre of a level patch of sand in the old bed of the river, —the bed it had used five years before and forsaken at the time of the big flood when it cut itself a new channel and made the U-bend which now surrounded this piece of land on three sides. Even now, during the rainy season, the thicket which sheltered Mr. Elkins was frequently an island in a sluggish, shallow overflow.

"Hole up, blast you!" jeered Hopalong, hugging the ground. The second bullet from Mr. Elkins' gun cut another twig, this one just over his head, and he laughed insolently. "I ain't ascared to do the moving, even if you are. Judging from the way you keep out o' sight the canned oysters are in the can again. *I* never did no ambushing, you coyote."

"You can't make remarks like that an' get away with 'em —I've knowed you too long," retorted Elkins, shifting quickly, and none too soon. "You went an' got Slim afore he was wide awake. I know *you*, all right."

Hopalong's surprise was but momentary, and his mind raced back over the years. Who was this man Elkins, that he knew Slim Travennes? "Yo're a liar, Elkins, an' so was the man who told you that!"

"Call me Ewalt," jeered the other, nastily. "Nobody'll hear it, an' you'll not live to tell it. Ewalt, Tex Ewalt; call me that."

"So you've come back after all this time to make me get you, have you? Well, I ain't a-going to shoot no buttons off you *this* time. I allus reckoned you learned something at Muddy Wells-but you'll learn it here," Hopalong rejoined, sliding into a depression, and working with great caution towards the dry river bed, where fallen trees and hillocks of sand provided good cover in plenty. Everything was clear now and despite the seriousness of the situation he could not repress a smile as he remembered vividly that day at the carnival when Tex Ewalt came to town with the determination to kill him and show him up as an imitation. His grievance against Elkins was petty when compared to that against Ewalt, and he began to force the issue. As he peered over a stranded log he caught sight of his enemy disappearing into another part of the thicket, and two of his three shots went home. Elkins groaned with pain and fear as he realized that his right knee-cap was broken and would make him slow in his movements. He was lamed for life, even if he did come out of the duel alive; lamed in the same way that Hopalong was-the affliction he had made cruel sport of had come to him. But he had plenty of courage and he returned the fire with remarkable quickness, his two shots sounding almost as one.

Hopalong wiped the blood from his cheek and wormed his way to a new place; when half way there he called out again, "How's yore health-Tex?" in mock sympathy.

Elkins lied manfully and when he looked to get in another shot his enemy was on the farther bank, moving up to get behind him. He did not know Hopalong's new position until he raised his head to glance down over the dried river bed, and was informed by a bullet that nicked his ear. As he ducked, another grazed his head, the third going wild. He hazarded a return shot, and heard Hopalong's laugh ring out again.

"Like the story Lucas told, the best shot is going to win out this time, too," the Bar-20 man remarked, grimly. "You thought a game like this would give you some chance against a better shot, didn't you? You are a fool."

"It ain't over yet, not by a damned sight!" came the retort.

"An' you thought you had a little the best of it if you stayed still an' let me do the moving, didn't you? You'll learn something before I get through with you: but it'll be too late to do you any good," Hopalong called, crouched below a hillock of sand so the other could not take advantage of the words and single him out for a shot.

"You can't learn me nothing, you assassin; I've got my eyes open, this time." He knew that he had had them open before, and that Hopalong was in no way an assassin; but if he could enrage his enemy and sting him into some reflex carelessness he might have the last laugh.

Elkins' retort was wasted, for the sudden and unusual, although a familiar sound, had caught Hopalong's ear and he was giving all his attention to it. While he weighed it, his incredulity holding back the decision his common sense was striving to give him, the noise grew louder rapidly and common sense won out in a cry of warning an instant before a five-foot wall of brown water burst upon his sight, sweeping swiftly down the old, dry river bed; and behind it towered another and greater wall. Tree trunks were dancing end over end in it as if they were straws.

"Cloud-burst!" he yelled. "Run, Tex! Run for yore life! Cloud-burst up the valley! Run, you fool; *Run!*"

Tex's sarcastic retort was cut short as he instinctively glanced north, and his agonized curse lashed Hopalong forward. "Can't run-knee cap's busted! Can't swim, can't do-ah, hell —!"

Hopalong saw him torn from his shelter and whisked down the raging torrent like an arrow from a bow. The Bar-20 puncher leaped from the bank, shot under the yellow flood and arose, gasping and choking many yards downstream, fighting madly to get the muddy water out of his throat and eyes. As he struck out with all his strength down the current, he caught sight of Tex being torn from a jutting tree limb, and he shouted encouragement and swam all the harder, if such a thing were possible. Tex's course was checked for a moment by a boiling back-current and as he again felt the pull of the rushing stream Hopalong's hand gripped his collar and the fight for safety began. Whirled against logs and stumps, drawn down by the weight of his clothes and the frantic efforts of Tex to grasp him-fighting the water and the man he was trying to save at the same time, his head under water as often as it was out of it, and Tex's vise-like fingers threatening him-he headed for the west shore against powerful cross-currents that made his efforts seem useless. He seemed to get the worst of every break. Once, when caught by a friendly current, they were swung under an overhanging branch, but as Hopalong's hand shot up to grasp it a submerged bush caught his feet and pulled him under, and Tex's steel-like arms around his throat almost suffocated him before he managed to beat the other into insensibility and break the hold.

"I'll let you go!" he threatened; but his hand grasped the other's collar all the tighter and his fighting jaw was set with greater determination than ever.

They shot out into the main stream, where the U-bend channel joined the short-cut, and it looked miles wide to the exhausted puncher. He was fighting only on his will now. He would not give up, though he scarce could lift an arm, and his lungs seemed on fire. He did not know whether Tex was dead or alive, but he would get the body ashore with him, or go down trying. He bumped into a log and instinctively grasped it. It turned, and when he came up again it was bobbing five feet ahead of him. Ages seemed to pass before he flung his numb arm over it and floated with it. He was not alone in the flood; a coyote was pushing steadily across his path towards the nearer bank, and on a gliding tree trunk crouched a frightened cougar, its ears flattened and its sharp claws dug solidly through the bark. Here and there were cattle and a snake wriggled smoothly past him, apparently as much at home in the water as out of it. The log turned again and he just managed to catch hold of it as he came up for the second time.

Things were growing black before his eyes and strange, weird ideas and images floated through his brain. When he regained some part of his senses he saw ahead of him a long, curling crest of yellow water and foam, and he knew, vaguely, that it was pouring over a bar. The next instant his feet struck bottom and he fought his way blindly and slowly, with the stubborn determination of his kind, towards the brush-covered point twenty feet away.

When he opened his eyes and looked around he became conscious of excruciating pains and he closed them again to rest. His outflung hand struck something that made him look around again, and he saw Tex Ewalt, face down at his side. He released his grasp on the other's collar and slowly the whole thing came to him, and then the necessity for action, unless he wished to lose what he had fought so hard to save.

Anything short of the iron man Tex had become would have been dead before this or have been finished by the mauling he now got from Hopalong. But Tex groaned, gurgled a curse, and finally opened his eyes upon his rescuer, who sank back with a grunt of satisfaction. Slowly his intelligence returned as he looked steadily into Hopalong's eyes, and with it came the realization of a strange truth: he did not hate this man at all. Months of right living, days and nights of honest labor shoulder to shoulder with men who respected him for his ability and accepted him as one of themselves, had made a new man of him, although the legacy of hatred from the old Tex had disguised him from himself until now; but the new Tex, battered, shot-up, nearly drowned, looked at his old enemy and saw him for the man he really was. He smiled faintly and reached out his hand.

"Cassidy, yo're the boss," he said. "Shake."

They shook.

The Bar-20 Three

Chapter I
"Put a 'T' in it"

Idaho Norton, laughing heartily, backed out of the barroom of Quayle's hotel and trod firmly on the foot of Ward Corwin, sheriff of the county, who was about to pass the door. Idaho wheeled, a casual apology trembling on his lips, to hear a biting, sarcastic flow of words, full of profanity, and out of all proportion to the careless injury. The sheriff's coppery face was a deeper color than usual and bore an expression not pleasant to see. The puncher stepped back a pace, alert, lithe, balanced, the apology forgotten, and gazed insolently into the peace officer's wrathful eyes.

"—an' why don't you look where yo're steppin'? Don't you know how to act when you come to town?" snarled the sheriff, finishing his remarks.

Idaho looked him over coolly. "I know how to act in any company, even yourn. Just now I ain't actin' I'm waitin'."

The sheriff's eyes glinted. "I got a good mind--"

"You ain't got nothin' of th' sort," cut in the puncher, contemptuously. "You ain't got nothin' good, except, mebby, yore reg'lar plea of self-defense. I'm sayin' out loud that that ain't no good, here an' now; an' I'm waitin' to take it away from you an' use it myself. You been trustin' too cussed much to that nickel badge."

Bill Trask, deputy, who had a reputation not to be over looked, now took a hand from the rear, eager to add to his list of victims from any of that outfit. The puncher was between him and the sheriff, and hardly could watch them both. Trask gently shook his belt and said three unprintable words which usually started a fight, and then glared over his shoulder at a sudden interruption, tense and angry.

"Shut up, you!" said the voice, and he saw a two-gun stranger slouching away from the hotel wall. The deputy took him in with one quick glance and then his eyes re turned to those of the stranger and rested there while a slight prickling sensation ran up his spine. He had looked into many angry eyes, and in many kinds of circumstances, but never before had his back given him a warning quite so plainly. He grew restless and wanted to look away, but dared not; and while he hung in the balance of hesitation the stranger spoke again. "Two to one ain't fair, 'specially with the lone man in th' middle; but I'll make th' odds even, for I'm honin' to claim self-defense, myself. It's right popular. I saw it all an' I'm sayin' you are three chumps to get all het up over a little thing like that. Mebby his toes are tender but what of it? He ain't no baby, leastawise he don't look like one. An' I'm tellin' you, an' yore badge-totin' friend, that I know how to act, too." A twinkle came into the hard, blue eyes. "But what's th' use of actin' like four strange dogs?"

Somewhere in the little crowd a man laughed, others joined in and pushed between the belligerents; and in a minute the peace officers had turned the corner, Idaho was slowly walking toward the two-gun stranger and the crowd was going about its business.

"Have a drink?" asked the puncher, grinning as he pushed back his hat.

"Didn't I just say that I knowed how to act?" chuckled the stranger, turning on his heel and following his companion through the door. "You must 'a' met them two before."

"Too cussed often. What'll you have? Make mine a cigar, too, Ed. No more liquor for me today Corwin—don't forget."

The bartender closed the box and slid it onto the back-bar again. "No, he don't," he said. "An' Trask is worse," he added, looking significantly at the stranger, whose cigar was now going to his satisfaction and who was smilingly regarding Idaho, and who seemed to be pleased by the frank return scrutiny.

"You ain't a stranger here no longer," said Idaho, blowing out a cloud of smoke. "You got two good enemies, an' a one-hoss friend. Stayin' long?"

"About half an hour. I got a little bunch of cows on th' drive west of here, an' they ought to be at Twitchell an' Carpenter's corrals about now. Havin' rid in to fix up bed an' board for my little outfit, I'm now on my way to finish deliverin' th' herd. See you later if yo're in town tonight."

"I don't aim to go back to th' ranch till tomorrow," replied Idaho, and he hesitated. "I'm sorry you horned in on that ruckus--there's mebby trouble bloomin' out of that for you. Don't you get careless till yo're a day's ride away from this town. Here, before you go, meet Ed Doane. He's one of th' few white men in this runt of a town."

The bartender shook hands across the bar. "Pleased to meet up with you, Mr.–Mr.?"

"Nelson," prompted the stranger. "How do you do, Mr. Doane?"

"Half an' half," answered the dispenser of liquids, and then waved a large hand at the smiling youth. "Shake han's with Idaho Norton, who was never closer to Idaho than Parsons Corners, thirty miles northwest of here. Idaho's a good boy, but shore impulsive. He's spent most of his life practicin' th' draw, et cetery; an' most of his money has went for ca'tridges. Some folks say it ain't been wasted. Will you gents smoke a cigar with me?"

After a little more careless conversation Johnny nodded his adieus, mounted and rode south. Not long thereafter he came within sight of the Question-Mark, Twitchell and Carpenter's local ranch.

Its valley sloped eastward, following the stream winding down its middle between tall cottonwoods, and the horizon was limited by the tops of the flanking hills, which dipped and climbed and zigzagged into the gray of the east, where great sand hills reared their glistening tops and the hopeful little creek sank out of sight into the dried, salty bed of a one-time lake. Near the trail were two buildings, a small stockaded corral and a wire-fenced pasture of twenty acres; and the Question-Mark brand, known wherever cattlemen congregated, even beyond the Canadian line, had been splashed with red paint on the wall of the larger building. The glaring, silent interrogation-mark challenged every passing eye and had started many curious, grim, and cynical trains of thought in the minds of tired and thirsty wayfarers along the trail. To the north of the twenty-acre pasture a herd of SV cattle grazed, spread out widely, too tired, too content with their feeding to need much attention.

Johnny saw the great, red question-mark and instantly drew rein, staring at it. "Why?" he muttered, and then grew silent for a moment. Shaking his head savagely he urged the horse on again, and again glanced at the crimson interrogation. "Damn you!" he growled. "There ain't no man livin' can answer."

He passed the herd at a distance and rode up to the larger building, where a figure suddenly appeared in the doorway, looked out from under a shielding hand and quickly stepped forward to meet him.

"Hello, Nelson!" came the cheery greeting.

"Hello, Ridley!" replied Johnny. "Glad to see you again. Thought I'd bring 'em down to you, an' save you goin' up th' trail after 'em. Why don't you paint out that glarin' question-mark on th' side of th' house?"

Ridley slapped his hands together and let out a roar of laughter. "Has it got you, too?" he demanded in unfeigned delight.

"Not as much as it would before I got married," replied Johnny. "I'm beginnin' to see a reason for livin'."

"Good!" exclaimed Ridley. "If I ever meet yore wife I'll tell her somethin' that'll make her dreams sweet." The expression of his face changed swiftly. "Do you know "he considered, and changed the form of his words. "You'd be surprised if you knew th' number of people hit by that painted question-mark. I've had 'em ride in here an' start all kinds of conservations with me; th' gospel sharps are th' worst. One man blew his brains out in Quayle's hotel because of what that sign started workin' in his mind. Go look at it: it's full of bullet holes!"

"I don't have to," replied Johnny, and quickly answered his companion's unspoken challenge. "An 1 I can sleep under it, an' smile, cuss you!" He glanced at the distant cattle. "Have you looked 'em over?"

Ridley nodded. "They're in good shape. Ready to count 'em now?"

"Be glad to, an' get 'em off my han's."

"Bring 'em up in front of th' pasture, an' I'll wait for you there," said Ridley.

Johnny wheeled and then checked his horse. "What kind of fellers are Corwin an' Trask?" he asked.

Ridley looked up at him, a curious expression on his face. "Why?"

"Oh, nothin'; I was just wonderin'."

"As long as you ain't aimin' to stop around these parts for long, th' less you know about 'em th' better. I'll be waitin' at th' pasture."

Johnny rode off and started the herd again, and when it stopped it was compacted into a long V, with the point facing the pasture gate, and it poured its units from this point in a steady stream between the two horsemen at the open gate, who faced each other across the hurrying pro cession and built up another herd on the other side, one which spread out and grazed without restraint, unless it be that of a wire fence. And with the shrinking of the first and the expanding of the second the SV ownership changed into that of the Question-Mark.

The shrewd, keen-eyed buyer for Twitchell and Carpenter looked up as the gate closed after the last steer and smiled across the gap at the SV foreman as he announced his count.

Johnny nodded. "My figgers, to a T," he said. "That 2-Star steer don't belong to us. Joined up with us some where along th' trail. You know 'em?"

"Belongs to Dawson, up on th' north fork of th' Bear. I'll drop him a check in a couple of days. This feller must 'a' wandered some to get in with yourn. Well, yourn is a good bunch of four-year-olds. You'll have to wait till I get to town, for I ain't got a blank check left, an' I shore ain't got no one thousand one hundred and forty-three dollars layin' around down here. Want cash or a check?"

"If I took a check I'd have to send somebody up to Sherman with it," replied Johnny. "I might take it at that, if I was goin' right back. Better make it cash, Ridley."

Ridley grinned. "I've swept up this part of th' country purty good."

Johnny shook his head. "I'm lookin' for weaners an' not in this part of th' country. I'll see you in town,"

"Before supper," said Ridley. "You puttin' up at Quayle's?"

"You called it," answered Johnny, wheeling. He rode off, picked up his small outfit and led the way to Mesquite, where he hoped to spend but one night. The little SV group cantered over the thin trail in the wake of their bobbing chuck wagon, several miles ahead of them, and reached the town well ahead of it, much to the cook's vexation. As they neared Quayle's hotel Johnny pulled up.

"This is our stable," he said. "Go easy, boys. We leave at daylight. See you at supper."

They answered him laughingly and swept on to Kane's place, which they seemed to sense, each for his favorite, drink and game.

The afternoon shadows were long when Ridley, just from the bank, left his rangy bay in front of the hotel and entered the office, nodding to several men he knew. He went on through and stopped at the bar.

"Howd'y, Ed," he grunted. "That SV foreman around? Nelson's his name."

Ed Doane mopped up the bar mechanically and bobbed his head toward the door. "Here he comes now. Make a deal?"

Ridley nodded as he turned. "Hello, Nelson! Read this over. If it's all right, sign it, an' we'll let Ed disfigure it as a witness. I allus like a witness."

Johnny signed it with the pen the bartender provided and then the bartender labored with it and blew on it to dry the ink.

"Disfigure it, hey?" chuckled Ed, pointing to his signature, which was beautifully written but very much over done. "That bill of sale's worth somethin' now."

Johnny admired it frankly and openly. "I allus did like shadin', an' them flourishes are plumb fetchin'. Me, now; I write like a cow."

"I'm worse," admitted Ridley, chuckling and giving Johnny a roll of bills. "Count 'em, Nelson. Folks usually turn my writin' upside down for th' first try. Speakin' of witnesses, there's another little thing I like. I allus seal documents, Ed. Take 'em out of that bottle you hide under th' bar. Three of 'em. Somehow, Ed, I allus like to see you stoop like that. Well, Nelson; does it count up right? Then, business bein' over, here's to th' end of th' drought."

It went the rounds, Ed accumulating three cigars as his favorite beverage, and as the glasses clicked down on the bar Ridley felt for the makings. "Sorry th' bank's closed, Nelson. It might be safer there over night."

"Mebby but it's safe enough, anyhow," smiled Johnny, shrugging his shoulders. "Anyhow th' bank wouldn't be open early enough in th' mornin' for us. Which reminds me that I better go out an' look around. My four-man outfit's got to leave at daylight."

"I'll go with you as far as th' street," said Ridley. As they neared the door Johnny hung back to let his companion pass through first and as he did so he heard a soft call from the bartender, and half turned.

"Come here a minute," said Doane, leaning over the bar. "It ain't none of my business, Nelson, but I'm sayin' *I* wouldn't go into Kane's with th' wad of money you got on you; an' if I did I shore wouldn't show it nor get in no game. You don't have to remember that I said anythin' about this."

"I never gamble with money that don't belong to me," replied Johnny, "nor not even while I've got it on me; an' already I've forgot you said anythin'. That place must be a sort of 'sink of iniquity,' as that sanctified parson called Abilene."

"Huh!" grunted Doane. "You can put a 'T' in that 'sink' an' there's only one place where a 'T' will fit. Th' money would be enough, but in yore case there's more. Idaho said it."

"He's only a kid," deprecated Johnny.

"'Out of th' mouths of babes'" replied Doane. "I'm tellin' you that's all."

Ridley stuck his head in at the door. "So-long, fellers," he said.

"Hey, Ridley!" called the bartender hurriedly. "Would you go into Kane's if you had Nelson's roll on you?"

"Not knowin' what I might do under th' infloonce of likker, I can't say," answered Ridley; "but if I did I wouldn't drink in there. So-long, an' I mean it, this time," and he did.

Johnny left soon afterward and wandered along the street toward the building on the northern outskirts of the town where Pecos Kane ran a gambling-house and hotel. Johnny ignored the hotel half and lolled against the door as he sized up the interior of the gambling-hall, and instantly became the center of well-disguised interest. While he paused inside the threshold a lean, tall man arose from a chair against the wall and sauntered carelessly out of sight through a narrow doorway leading to a passage in the rear. Kit Thorpe was not a man to loaf on his job when a two-gun stranger entered the place, especially when the stranger appeared to be looking for someone. Otherwise there was no change in the room, the bartender polishing his glasses without pause, the card players silently intent on their games and the man at the deserted roulette table who held a cloth against the ornate spinning wheel kept on polishing it. They seemed to draw reassurance from Thorpe's disappearance.

One slow look was enough to satisfy Johnny's curiosity. The room was about sixty feet long by half as wide and on his left-hand side lay the bar, built solidly from the floor by close-fitting planks running vertically, which appeared to be of hardwood and quite thick, and the top was of the same material. Several sand-box cuspidors lay before it. The backbar was a shelf backed by a narrow mirror running well past the middle half, and no higher than necessary to give the bartender a view of the room when he turned around, which he did but seldom. Round card-tables, heavy and crude, were scattered about the room and a row of chairs ran the full length along the other side wall. Several loungers sat at the tables, one of them an eastern tough, judging from his clothes, his peaked cap pulled well down over his eyes. At the farther end was a solid partition painted like a checkerboard and the few black squares which cunningly hid several peep holes were not to be singled out by casual observation. Those who knew said that they were closed on their inner side by black steel plates which hung on oiled pivots and were locked shut by a pin. At a table in front of the checkerboard were four men, one flung forward on it, his head resting on his crossed arms; another had slumped down on the edge of his chair, his chin on his chest, while the other two carried on a grunted, pessimistic conversation across their empty glasses.

Johnny's face flickered with a faint smile and he walked toward them, nodding carelessly at the man behind the bar.

Arch Wiggins looked up, a sickly grin on his flushed face. "Hullo," he grunted, foolishly.

"Not havin' nothin' else to do I reckoned I'd look you up," said Johnny. "Fed yet?"

Arch shrugged his shoulders and Sam Gardner sighed expressively, and then prodded the slumped individual into semblance of intelligence and erectness. This done he kicked the shins of the prostrate cook until that unfortunate raised an owlish, agonized, and protesting countenance to stare at his foreman.

"Nelson wants to know if yo're hungry," prompted Sam, grinning.

"Take it away!" mumbled the indignant cook. "I won't eat! Who's goin' to make me?" he demanded with a show of pugnacity. "I won't!"

Joe Reilly, painfully erect in his chair, blinked and focussed his eyes on the speaker. "Then don't!" he said. "Shut yore face others kin eat!" He turned his whole body, stiff as a ramrod, and looked at each of the others in turn. "Don't pay no 'tendon to him. I kin eat th' damned harness," he asserted, thereby proving that his stomach preserved family traditions.

Johnny laughed at them. "Yo're ah I of an outfit," he said without conviction. "What do you say about goin' up to th' hotel an' gettin' somethin' to eat? It's past grubtime, but let's see if they'll have th' nerve to try to tell us to get out. Broke?" he inquired, and as they silently arose to their feet, which seemed to take a great deal of concentration, he chuckled. Then his face hardened. "Where's yore guns?" he demanded.

Arch waved elaborately at the disinterested bartender. "That gent loaned us ten apiece on 'em," he said. "'Bligin' feller. Thank you, friend."

"Yo're a'right," said the cook, nodding at the dispenser of fluids.

"An' yo're a fine, locoed bunch, partin' with yore guns in a strange town," snapped Johnny. "You head for th' hotel, pronto! G'wan!"

The cook turned and waved a hand at the solemn bartender. "Goo'-bye!" he called. "I won't eat! Goo'bye."

Seeing them started in the right direction, Johnny went in and up to the bar. "Them infants don't need guns," he asserted, digging into a pocket, "but as long as they ain't shot themselves, yet, I'm takin' a chance. How much?"

The bartender, typical of his kind, looked wise when it was not necessary, finished polishing the glass in his hand and then slowly faced his inquisitor, bored and aloof. He had the condescending air of one who held himself to be mentally and physically superior to any man in town, and his air of preoccupation was so heavy that it was ludicrous. "Ten apiece," he answered nonchalantly, as behove the referee of drunken disputes, the adviser of sodden men, the student of humanity's dregs, whose philosophy of life was rotten to the core because it was based purely on the vicious and the weak, and whose knowledge, adjudged abysmal and cyclopedic by an admiring riffraff of stupefied mentality, was as shallow, warped, and perverted as the human derelicts upon which his observations were based. As Johnny's hand came up with the roll of bills the man of liquor kept his face passive by an act of will, but there crept into the ratlike eyes a strange gleam, which swiftly faded. "Put it way," he said heartily, a jovial, free-handed good fellow on the instant. "We got it back, an' more. It was worth th' money to have these where they wouldn't be too handy. We allus stake a good loser it's th' policy of th' house. Take these instead of th' stake." He slid the heavy weapons across the bar. "What'll you have?"

"Same as you," replied Johnny, and he slowly put the cigar into a pocket. "Purty quiet in here," he observed, laying two twenty-dollar bills on the bar.

"Yeah," said the bartender, pushing the money back again; "but it's a cheerful ol' beehive at night. Better put that in yore pocket an' drop in after dark, when things are movin'. I know a blonde that'll tickle you 'most to death. Come in an' meet her."

"Tell you what," said Johnny, grinning to conceal his feelings. "You keep them bills. If I keep 'em I'll have to let them fools have their guns back for nothin'. I'm aimin' to take ten apiece out of their pay. If you don't want it, give it to th' blonde, with Mr. Nelson's compliments. It won't be so hard for me to get acquainted with her, then."

The bartender chuckled and put the bills in the drawer. "Yo're no child, I'm admittin'. Reckon you been usin' yore head quite some since you was weaned."

One of the card players at the nearest table said some' thing to his two companions and one of them leaned back stretched and arose. "I'm tired. Get somebody to take my place."

The sagacious observer of the roll of bills started to object to the game being broken up, glanced at Johnny and smiled. "All right; mebby this gent will sit in an' kill a little time. How 'bout it, stranger?"

Johnny smiled at him. "My four-man outfit ain't leavin' me no time to kill," he answered. "I got to trail along behind 'em an' pick up th' strays."

The gambler grinned sympathetically. "Turn 'em loose tonight. What's th' use of herdin' with yearlin's, any how? If you get tired of their company an' feel like tryin' yore luck, come in an' join us."

"If I find that I got any heavy time on my han's I'll spend a couple of hours with you," replied Johnny. As he turned toward the door he glanced at the bartender. "Don't forget th' name when you give her th' forty," he laughed.

The bartender chuckled. "I got th' best mem'ry of any man in this section. See you later, mebby."

Johnny nodded and departed, his hands full of guns, and as he vanished through the front door Kit Thorpe reappeared from behind the partition, grinned cynically at the bartender and received a wise, very wise look in return.

Reaching the hotel Johnny entered it by the nearest door, that of the barroom, walked swiftly through with the redeemed guns dangling from his swinging hands and without pausing in his stride, flung a brief remark over his shoulder to the man behind the bar, who was the only person, besides himself, in the room: "You was shore right. It should ought to have a 'T' in it," and passed through the other door, across the office and into the dining-room, where his four men were having an argument with a sullen waiter and a wrathy cook.

Ed Doane straightened up, his ears preserving the words, his eyes retaining the picture of an angry, hurrying two-gun man from whose hands swung four more guns. He cogitated, and then the possible significance of the numerous weapons sprang into his mind. Ed did not go around the bar. He vaulted it and leaped to the door, out of which he hopefully gazed at the tranquil place of business of Pecos Kane. Slowly the look of hope faded and he returned to his place behind the bar, scratching his frowsy head in frank energy, his imagination busy with many things.

Chapter II
Well-known Strangers

The desert and a paling eastern sky. The penetrating cold of the dark hours was soon to die and give place to a punishing heat well above the hundred mark. Spectral agaves, flinging their tent-shaped crowns heavenward, seemed to spring bodily from the radiating circlet of spiny swords at their bases, their slender stems still lost in the weakening darkness. Pale spots near the ground showed where flower-massed yuccas thrust up, lancelike, from their slender, prickly leaves. Giant cacti, ghostly, bulky, indistinct, grotesque in their erect, parallel columns reached upward to a height seven times that of a tall man. They are the only growing things unmoved by winds. The sage, lost in the ground-hugging darkness, formed a dark carpet, mottled by lighter patches of sand. There were quick rustlings over the earth as swift lizards scurried hither and yon and a faint whirring told of some "side-winder "vibrating its rattles in emphatic warning against some encroachment. Tragedies were occurring in the sage, and the sudden squeak of a desert rat was its swan song.

In the east a silvery glow trembled above the horizon and to the magic of its touch silhouettes sprang suddenly from vague, blurred masses. The agave, known to most as the century plant, showed the delicate slenderness of its arrowy stem and marked its conical head with feathery detail. The flower-covered spikes of the Spanish bayonets became studies in ivory, with the black shadows on their thorny spikes deep as charcoal. The giant cacti, boldly thrown against the silver curtain, sprang from their joining bases like huge, thick telegraph poles of ebony, their thorns not yet clearly revealed. The squat sage, now resolved into tufted masses, might have been the purplish leaden hollows of a great sea. The swift rustlings became swift movements and the "side-winder" uncoiled his graceful length to round a nearby sage bush. The quaking of a small lump of sand grew violent and a long, round snoot pushed up inquiringly, the cold, beady eyes peering forth as the veined lids parted, and a Gila monster sluggishly emerged, eager for the promised warmth. To the northeast a rugged spur of mountains flashed suddenly white along its saw-toothed edge, where persistent snows crowned each thrusting peak. A moment more, and dazzling heliographic signals flashed from the snowy caps, the first of all earthly things to catch the rays of the rising sun, as yet below the far horizon. On all sides as far as eye could pierce through the morning twilight not a leaf stirred, not a stem moved, but everywhere was rigidity, unreal, uncanny, even terrifying to an imaginative mind. But wait! Was there movement in the fogging dark of the north? Rhythmic, swaying movement, rising and falling, vague and mystical? And the ghostly silence of this griddle-void was broken by strange, alien sounds, magnified by contrast with the terror-inspiring silence. A soft creaking, as of gently protesting saddle leather, interspersed with the frequent and not unmusical tinkle of metal, sounded timidly, almost hesitatingly out of the dark along the ground.

Silver turned into pink, pink into gold, and gold into crimson in almost a breath, and long crimson ribbons be came lavender high in the upper air, surely too beautiful to be a portent of evil and death. Yet the desert hush tightened, constricted, tensed as if waiting in rigid suspense for a lethal stroke. Almost without further warning a flaming, molten arc pushed up over the far horizon and grew with amazing bulk and swiftness, dispelling the chill of the night, destroying the beauty of the silhouettes, revealing the purple sage as a mangy, leaden coverlet, riddled and thin, squatting tightly against the tawny sand, across which had sprung with instant speed long, vague shadows from the base of every object which raised above the plain. The still air shuddered into a slow dance, waving and quivering, faster and faster like some mad dance of death, the rising heat waves distorting with their evil magic giant cacti until their fluted, thorny columns weaved like strange, slowly undulating snakes standing erect on curving tails. And in the distance but a few leagues off blazed the white mockery of the crystal snow, serene and secure on its lofty heights, a taunt far-flung to madden the heat-crazed brain of some swollen, clawing thing in distorted human form slowly dying on the baking sands.

The movement was there, for the sudden flare of light magically whisked it out of the void like a rabbit out of a conjurer's hat. Two men, browned, leather-skinned, erect, silent, and every line of them bespeaking reliance with a certainty not to be denied, were slowly riding south ward. Their horses, typical of their cow-herding type, were loaded down with large canteens, and suggested itinerant water peddlers. Two gallons each they held, and there were four to the horse. One could imagine these men counted on taking daily baths but they were only double-riveting a security against the hell-fires of thirst, which each of them had known intimately and too well. The first rider, as erect in his saddle as if he had just swung into it, had a face scored with a sorrow which only an iron will held back; his squinting eyes were cold and hard, and his hair, where it showed beneath the soiled, gray sombrero, was a sandy color, all of what was left of the flaming crimson of its youth. He rode doggedly with out a glance to right or left, silent, sullen, inscrutable. When the glorious happiness of a man's life has gone out there is but little left, often even to a man of strength. Behind him rode his companion, five paces to the rear and exactly in his trail, but his wandering glances flashed far afield, searching, appraising, never still. Younger in years than his friend, and so very much younger in spirit, there was an air of nonchalant recklessness about him, occasionally swiftly mellowed by pity as his eyes rested on the man ahead. Now, glancing at the sun-cowed east, his desert cunning prompted him and he pushed forward, silently took the lead and rode to a thicket of mesquite, whose sensitive leaves, hung on delicate stems, gave the most cooling shade of any desert plant. Dismounting, he picketed his horse and then added a side-line hobble as double security against being left on foot on the scorching sands. Not satisfied with that, he unfastened the three full canteens, swiftly examined them for leaks and placed them under the bush. Six gallons of water, but if need should arise he would fight to the death for it. Out of the corner of his eye he watched his companion, who mechanically was doing the same thing. Red Connors yawned, drank sparingly and then, hesitating, grinned foolishly and fastened one end of his lariat to his wrist.

"That dessicated hunk of meanness don't leave this hombre afoot, not nohow," said Red, looking at his friend; but Hopalong only stared into the bush and made no reply.

Nothing abashed at his companion's silence, Red stretched out at full length under the scant shade, his Colt at his hand in case some Gila monster should be curious as to what flavor these men would reveal to an inquisitive bite. Red's ideas of Gilas were romantic and had no scientific warrant whatever. And it was possible that a "side-winder" might blunder his way.

"It's better than a lava desert, anyhow," he remarked as he settled down, having in mind the softness of the loose sand. "One whole day of hell-to-leather fryin', an' one more shiverin' night, an' this stretch of misery will be behind, but it shore saves a lot of ridin', it does. I'll bet I'm honin' for a swim in th' Rio Placer an' I ain't carin' how much mud there is, neither. Ah, th' devil!" he growled in great disgust, slowly arising. "I done forgot to sprinkle them cayuses' insides. One apiece, they get, which is only insultin' 'em."

Hopalong tried to smile, arose and filled his hat, which his thirsty horse frantically emptied. When the canteen was also empty he went back to the sandy couch, to lay awake in the scorching heat, fighting back memories which tortured him near to madness, his mental torments making him apathetic to physical ones. And so dragged the weary, trying day until the cooling night let them go on again.

Three days later they rode into Gunsight, made care less inquiries and soon thereafter drew rein before the open door of the SV, unconscious of the excited conjectures rioting in the curious town.

Margaret Nelson went to the door, her brother trying to push past her, and looked wonderingly up at the two smiling strangers.

Red bowed and removed his hat with a flourish. "Mrs. Johnny?" he asked, and at the nodded assent smiled broadly. "My name's Red Connors, an' my friend is Hopalong Cassidy. He is th' very best friend yore fool husband ever had. We came down to make Johnny's life miserable for a little while, an' to give you a hand with his trainin', if you need it."

Margaret's breath came with a rush and she held out both hands with impulsive friendliness. "Oh!" she cried. "Come in. You must be tired and hungry let Charley turn your horses into the corral."

Charley wriggled past the barrier and jumped for Hopalong, his shrill whoop of delighted welcome bringing a smile to the stern face of the mounted man. A swoop of the rider's arm, a writhing twist of the boy's body, coming a little too late to avoid the grip of that iron hand, and Charley shot up and landed in front of the pommel, where he exchanged grins at close range with his captor.

"I knowed you first look," asserted the boy as the grip was released. "My, but I've heard a lot about you! Yo're goin' to stay here, ain't you? I know where there's some black bear, up on th' hills want to go huntin' with me?"

Hopalong's tense, wistful look broke into a smile, the first sincere, honest smile his face had known for a month. Gulping, he nodded, and turned to face his friend's wife. "Looks like I'm adopted," he said. "If you don't mind, Mrs. Johnny, Charley an' me will take care of th' cayuses while Red helps you fix up th' table." He reached out, grasped the bridle of Red's horse as its rider dismounted, and rode to the corral, Charley's excited chatter bringing an anxious smile to his sister, but a heartfelt, prayerful smile to Red Connors. He had great hopes.

Red paused just inside the door. "Mrs. Johnny," he said quietly, quickly, "I got to talk fast before Hoppy comes back. He lost his wife an' boy a month ago fever in four days. He's all broke up. Went loco a little, an' even came near shootin' me because I wouldn't let him go off by hisself. I've had one gosh-awful time with him, but finally managed to get him headed this way by talkin' about Johnny a-plenty. That got him, for th' kid allus was a sort of son to him. I'm figgerin' he'll be a lot better off down here on this south range for awhile. Even crossin' that blasted desert seemed to help he loosened up his talk considerable since then. An' from th' way he grabbed that kid, I'm say in' I'm right. Where is Johnny?"

"Oh!" Margaret's breathed exclamation did not need the sudden moisture in her eyes to interpret it, and in that instant Red Connors became her firm, unswerving friend. "We'll do our best and I think he should stay here, always. And Johnny will be delighted to have him with us, and you, too Red."

"Here he comes," warned her companion. "Where is Johnny? When will he get here?"

"Why, he took a herd down to Mesquite," she replied, smiling at Hopalong, who limped slowly into the room with Charley slung under his arm like a sack of flour. "He should be back any day now. And won't he be wild with delight when he finds you two boys here! You have no idea how he talks about you, even in his sleep--oh, if I were inclined to jealousy you might not be so welcome!"

"Ma'am," grinned Red, tickled as a boy with a new gun, "you don't never want to go an' get jealous of a couple of old horned toads like us--well, like Hoppy, anyhow. We'll sort of ride herd on him, too, every time he goes to town. Talk about revenge! Oh, you wait! So he went off an' left you all alone? Didn't he write about some trouble that was loose down here?"

"It was but it's cleaned up. He didn't leave me in any danger--every man down here is our friend," Margaret replied, quick to sense the carefully hidden thought which had prompted his words, and to defend her husband.

"Well, two more won't hurt, nohow," grunted Red. "You say he ought to get here any day?"

"I'm spending more time at the south windows every day," she smiled. "I don't know what will happen to the housework if it lasts much longer!"

"South windows?" queried Hopalong, standing Charley on his head before letting loose of him. "Th' trail is west, ain't it?" he demanded, which caused Red to chuckle inwardly at how his friend was becoming observant again.

"The idea!" retorted Margaret. "Do you think my boy will care anything about any trail that leads round about? He'll leave the trail at the Triangle and come straight for this house! What are hills and brush and a miserable little creek to him, when he's coming home? I thought you knew my boy."

"We did, an' we do," laughed Red. "I'm bettin' yore way--I hope he's got a good horse--it'll be a dead one if it ain't."

"He's saving Pepper for the homestretch if you know what that means!"

"Hey, Red," said Charley, slyly. "Yore gun works, don't it?"

"Shore thing. Why?"

"Well, mine don't," sighed the boy. "Wonder if yourn is too heavy, an' strong, for a boy like me to shoot? Bet it ain't."

Margaret's low reproof was lost in Red's burst of laughter, and again a smile crept to Hopalong's face, a smile full of heartache. This eager boy made his memories painfully alive.

"You an' me an' Hoppy will shore go out an' see," promised Red. "Mrs. Johnny will trust you with us, I bet. Hello! Here's somebody comin'," he announced, looking out of the door.

"That's my dad!" cried Charley, bolting from the house so as to be the first one to give his father the good news.

Arnold rode up laughing, dismounted and entered the house with an agility rare to him. And he was vastly relieved. "Well! Well! Well!" he shouted, shaking hands like a pump handle. "I saw you ride over the hill an' got here as fast as Lazy would bring me. Red an' Hopalong! Our household gods with us in the flesh! And that scalawag off seeing the sights of strange towns when his old friends come to visit him. I'm glad to see you boys! The place is yours. Red and Hopalong! I'm not a drinkin' man, but there are times when follow me while Peggy gets supper!"

"Can I go with you, Dad?" demanded Charley.

"You help Peggy set the table."

"Huh! *I* don't care! Me an' Hoppy an' Red are goin' after bear, an' I'm goin' to use Red's gun."

"Seems to me, Charley," reproved Arnold, "that you are pretty familiar, for a boy; and especially on such short acquaintance. You might begin practicing the use of the word 'Mister.'"

"Or say 'Uncle Red' and 'Uncle Hopalong,'" suggested Margaret.

"'Red' is my name, an' I'm shore 'Red' to him," defended that person.

"Which goes for me," spoke up his companion. "I'm Hopalong, or Hoppy to anybody in this family though 'Uncle' suits me fine."

"Then we'll have a fair exchange," retorted Margaret, smiling. "The family circle calls me 'Margaret' or 'Peggy.'"

"If you want to rile her, call her Maggie," said Charley. "She goes right on th' prod!"

"I'm plumb peaceful," laughed Red, turning to follow his host. "You help Mrs. Margaret, an' when I come back you an' me'll figger on goin' after bear as soon as we can."

Chapter III
A Question of Identity

Johnny sauntered into Quayle's barroom and leaned against the bar, talking to Ed Doane. An hour or two before he had finished his dinner, warned his outfit again about the early start on the morrow, advanced them some money, and watched them leave the hotel for one more look at the town, and now he was killing time.

"What do you think about Kane's?" asked Ed carelessly, and then looked up as a customer entered. When the man went out he repeated the question.

Johnny cogitated and shrugged his shoulders. "Same as you. Reg'lar cow-town gamblin'-hall, with th' same fixin's, wimmin', crooked games, an' wise bums hangin' 'round. Am I right?"

A group entered, and when they had been served they went into the hotel office, the bartender's eyes on them as long as they were in sight. He turned and frowned. "Purty near. You left a couple of things out. I'm not sayin' what they are, but I am sayin' this: Don't you ever pull no gun in there if you should have any trouble. Wait till you get yore man outside. Funny thing about that sort of a spell, I reckon but no stranger ever got a gun out an' workin' in Kane's place. They died too quick, or was put out of workin' order."

Johnny raised his eyebrows: "Mebby no good manever tried to get one out, an' workin'."

"You lose," retorted Ed emphatically. "Some of 'em was shore to be good. It's a cold deck with a sharp shooter. There I go again!" he snorted. "I'm certainly shootin' off my mouth today. I must be loco!"

"Then don't let that worry you. I ain't shootin' mine off," Johnny reassured him. "I'm tryin' to figger ':

A voice from the street interrupted him. "Hey, stranger! Yore outfit's in trouble down in Red Frank's!"

Johnny swung from the bar. "Where's his place?" he asked.

"One street back," nodded the bartender, indicating the rear of the room. "Turn to yore right third door. It's a Greaser dive look sharp!"

Johnny grunted and turned to obey the call. Walking out of the door, he went to the corner, turned it, and soon turned the second corner. As he rounded it he saw stars, reached for his guns by instinct, and dropped senseless. Two shadowy figures pounced upon him, rolled him over, and deftly searched him.

Back in the hotel Idaho stuck his head into the barroom. "Seen Nelson?" he asked.

"Just went to Red Frank's this minute his gang's in trouble there!" quickly replied Ed.

"I'll go 'round an' be handy, anyhow," said Idaho, loosening his gun as he went through, the door. Rounding the first corner, he saw a figure flit into the darkness across the street and disappear, and as he turned the second corner he tripped and fell over a prostrate man. One glance and his match went out. Jumping around the corner, he saw a second man run across an open space between two clumps of brush, and his quick hand chopped down, a finger of flame spitting into the night. A curse of pain answered it and he leaped forward, hot and vengeful; but his search was in vain, and he soon gave it up and hastened back to his prostrate friend, whom he found sitting up against the wall with an open jackknife in his hand.

"What happened?" demanded Idaho, stopping and bending down. "Where'd he get you?"

"Somethin' fell on my head an' my guns are gone," mumbled Johnny. "I bet I've been robbed!" His slow, fumbling search revealed the bitter truth, and he grunted. "Clean! Clean!"

"I shoved a hunk of lead under th' skin of somebody runnin' heard him yelp," Idaho said. "Lost him in th' dark. Here, grab hold of me. I'll take you to my room in th' hotel. Able to toddle?"

"Able to kill th' skunk with my bare han's," growled the unfortunate, staggering to his feet. "I'm goin' to Kane's!" he asserted, and Idaho's arguments were exhausted before he was able to have his own way.

"You come along with me I want to look at yore head. An', besides, you ought to have a gun before you go huntin'. Come, on. We'll go in through th' kitchen that's th' nearest way. It's empty now, but th' door's never locked."

"You gimme a gun, an' I'll know where to go!" blazed Johnny, trembling with weakness. "I showed my roll in there, like a fool. Eleven hundred h--l of a foreman *I* am!"

"You can't just walk into a place an' start shootin'!" retorted Idaho, angrily. "Will you listen to sense? Come on, now. After you get sensible you can do what you want, an' I'll go along an' help you do it. That's fair, ain't it? How do you know that feller belongs to Kane's crowd? May be a Greaser, an' a mile away by now. Come on be sensible!"

"Th' SV can't afford to lose that money oh, well," sighed Johnny, "yo're right. Go ahead. I'll wash off th' blood, anyhow. I must be a holy show."

They got to Idaho's room without arousing any unusual interest and Idaho examined the throbbing bump with clumsy fingers, receiving frank statements for his awkwardness.

"Shucks," he grinned, straightening up. "It's as big as an egg, but besides th' skin bein' broke an' a lot of blood, there ain't nothin' th' matter. I'll wash it off an' if you keep yore hat on, nobody '11 know it. I reckon that hat just about saved that thick skull of yourn."

"What did you see when you found me?" asked Johnny when his friend had finished the job.

Idaho told him and added: "Hoped I could tell him by th' yelp, but I can't, unless, mebby, I go around an' make everybody in this part of th' country yelp for me. But I don't reckon that's hardly reasonable."

"Yo're right," grinned Johnny. "Well," he said, after a moment's thought, "I don't go back home without eleven hundred dollars an' my guns; but I got to send th' boys back. They can't help me none, bein' known as my friends. Besides, we're all broke, an' they're needed on th' ranch. If I knowed that Kane had a hand in this, I'd cussed soon get that money back!"

"Yo're shore plumb set on that Kane dear."

"I showed that wad of bills in just two places: Ed's bar, an' Kane's joint."

"Ed's bar is out of it if nobody else was in there at th' time."

"Only Ridley, Ed, an' myself."

"Somebody could've looked in th' window," suggested Idaho.

"Nobody did, because I was lookin' around."

"If you go in Kane's an' make a gunplay, you'll never know how it happened or who done it; an' if you go in, without a gunplay, an' let 'em know what you think, some Greaser 'll hide a knife in you. Then you'll never get it 'back."

"Just th' same, that's th' place to start from," persisted Johnny doggedly. "An' from th' inside, too."

Idaho frowned. "That may be so, but startin' it from there means to end it there an' then. You can't buck Kane in his own place. It's been tried more'n once. I ain't shore you can buck him in this town, or part of th' country. Bigger people than you are suspected of payin' him money to let 'em alone. You'd be surprised if I named names. Look here: I better speak a little piece about this part of th' country. This county is unorganized an' ain't got no courts, nor nothin' else except a peace officer which we calls sheriff. It's big, but it ain't got many votes, an' what it has is one-third Greaser. Most Greasers don't amount to much in a stand-up fight, but their votes count. They are all for Kane. We've only had one election for sheriff, an' although Corwin is purty well known, he won easy. Kane did it, an' when anybody says 'Corwin,' they might as well say 'Kane.' He is boss of this section. His gamblin'-joint is his head quarters, an' it's guarded forty ways from th' jack. His gang is made up of all kinds, from th' near decent down to th' night killer. When Kane wants a man killed, that man don't live long. Corwin takes his orders before an' after a play like this one. Yo're expected to report it to him. Comin' down to cases, th' pack has got to be fed, an' they have got to make a killin' once in a while. Even if Kane ain't in on it direct, he'll get most of that money across his bar or tables. To wind up a long speech, you better go home with yore men, for that ain't enough money to get killed over."

"Mebby not if it was mine!" snapped Johnny. "An' I ain't shore about that, neither. An' there's more'n money in this, an' more than th' way I was handled. Somebody in this wart of a town has got Johnny Nelson's two guns an' nobody steals them an' keeps 'em! I got friends, lots of 'em, in Montanny, that would lend me th' money quick; but there ain't nobody can give me them six-guns but th' thief that's got 'em. I'm rooted solid.'"

"All right," said Idaho. "Yo're talkin' foolish, but cussed if I don't like to hear it. So me an' you are goin' to hog-tie that gang. If I get Corwin in th' ruckus, I'll be satisfied."

"Yo're th' one that's talkin' foolish," retorted Johnny, fighting back his grin. "An I'm cussed if *I* don't like to hear it. But there's this correction: Me an' you ain't goin' to bulldog that gang at all. *I* am. Yo're goin' to sprawl on yore saddle an' light out for wherever you belong, an' stay there. Yo're a marked man an' wouldn't last th' swish of a longhorn's tail. Yore brand is registered they got you in their brand books; but they ain't got mine. I'm not wearin' no brand. I ain't even earnotched, 'though I must 'a' been a 'sleeper' when I let 'em put this walnut on my head. I'm a plain, ornery maverick. Think I'm comin' out in th' open? I don't want no brass band playin' when I go to war. I'm a Injun."

"Yo're a little striped animal in this town one of them kind that's unpleasant up-wind from a feller," snorted Idaho. "How can you play Injun when they know yo're hangin' 'round here lookin' for yore money? Answer me that, maverick!"

"I'm comin' to that. Can you get me an old hat? One that's plumb wore out?"

"Reckon so," grunted Idaho, in surprise. "Th' clerk might be able to dig one up."

"No, not th' clerk; but Ed Doane," corrected Johnny. "Now you think hard before you answer this one: Could you see my face plain when you found me? Could they have seen it plain enough to be shore it was me?"

Idaho stared at him and a cheerful expression drifted across his face. "I'm gettin' th' drift of this Injun business," he muttered. "Mebby mebby cuss it, it will work! I couldn't see nothin' but a bump on th' ground along that wall till I lit a match. I'll get you a hat an' I'll plant it, too."

Johnny nodded. "Plant anythin' else you want that don't look like anythin' I own. Be shore that hat ain't like mine."

Idaho raised his hand as a sudden tramping sounded on the stairs. "That yore outfit?" he asked as a loud, querulous voice was heard.

Johnny went to the door and called, whereupon Arch waved his companions toward their quarters and answered the summons, following his foreman into the room. Johnny was about to close the door when Idaho arose and pushed past him.

"We been talkin' too loud," whispered the departing puncher. "You never can tell. I'm goin' out to sit on th' top step where there's more air," and he went on again, the door closing after him.

Johnny turned and smiled at Arch's expression. "You boys leave at daylight on th' jump. I got to stay here. You can say I'm waitin' for th' chance to pick up some money buyin' a herd of yearlin's cheap, or anythin' you can think of. Any thin' that'll stick. You'll have plenty of time to smooth it out before you get back home. I want you boys to scratch up every cent you've got an' turn it over to me. Any left of that I gave you after supper?"

"Shore quite some," grinned Arch. "We had better luck, down th' street. You must be aimin' to get a-plenty yearlin's, with that roll you got. What are we goin' to do, busted?"

"I want a couple of Colts, too," continued Johnny. "You won't need any money. Th' waggin is well stocked an' when you get back you can draw on Arnold."

"We was goin' to stop at Highbank for a good time," protested Arch.

"Have it in yore old man's hotel an' owe it to him," suggested Johnny.

"Have a good time in my old man's place!" exclaimed Arch. "Oh, h l!" He burst out laughing. "That'll tickle th' boys, that will!" The puncher looked searchingly at his foreman. "Hey, what's all th' trouble?"

Johnny thought it would be wiser to post his companion and crisply told what had happened.

Arch cleared his throat, hitched up his belt, and looked foolish but determined. "It's been comin' rapid, but I got it all. Yo're talkin' to th' wrong man. You want to fix up that story for th' ranch with some soft-belly that's ridin' that way. Better send a letter. We're all stayin' here. Fine bunch of - "

"You can help me more by goin' back like nothin's happened," interrupted Johnny. "Th' ranch won't be worry in' me then, an' if you stayed here it might give th' game away. Besides, one man can live longer on th' money we got than four can, only have a quarter of th' chance to drink too much, an' only talk a fourth as much. That's th' natural play, an' every thin' has got to be natural."

"That's th' worst of havin' a smooth face," grumbled Arch, ruefully rubbing his chin. "If I only had whiskers, I could shave 'em off an' be a total stranger; but I don't reckon I could grow a good enough bunch to get back here in time."

Johnny laughed, his heart warming to the puncher. "Take you a year or two; an' there's more'n whiskers needed to hide from a good man. There's little motions, gait, voice oh, lots of things. You can help me more if you go north. See Dave Green, tell him on th' quiet, an' ask him to send me down a couple hundred dollars. He can buy a check from th' Doc, payable to George Norton. There's a bank in this town. He's to send it to George Norton, general delivery."

"Dave will spread it far an' wide," objected Arch. "He tells all he knows."

"If he did," smiled Johnny, "it shore would be an eddication for th' man that heard it. He talks a lot an' says nothin'. If he told all he knew, hell would 'a' popped long ago on them ranges. I'm only wishin' he could get a job in Kane's!"

"Gosh!" exclaimed Arch. "Mebby he can. He's a bang-up bartender."

Johnny shook his head and laughed.

"Well, I reckon you know best," said Arch. "If you say so, we'll go home but it hurts bad as a toothache. An' as long as we're goin', we can start tonight this minute."

"You'll start at daylight, like honest folks," chuckled Johnny. "Think I want Kane to sit down an' figger why a lazy outfit got ambitious all at once? An' th' two boys that lend me their guns want to be ridin' close to th' waggin, on its left side, until they get out of town. I don't want anybody noticin' they ain't got their guns. Mebby their coats'll hide 'em, anyhow. But before you do anythin' else, get me a copy of that weekly newspaper down stairs. There's some layin' around th' office. Shore you got it all?"

Arch nodded, and his foreman opened the door. Idaho glanced around and then went down the stairs and through the office, stopping at the bar, where he held a low-voiced conversation with the man behind it. Ed looked a little surprised at the unusual request, but Idaho's earnestness and anxiety told him enough and he asked no questions. A few minutes later, after Idaho had disappeared into the kitchen, Ed told the clerk to watch the bar, and went up to his room, and dropped several articles out of the window before he left it again.

When Idaho had finished scouting and planting the sombrero, a broken spur, and a piece torn from a red kerchief, he went into the barroom and grinned at his friend Nelson, who leaned carelessly back against the wall; and then his eyes opened wide as he saw the size of the roll of bills from which Johnny was peeling the outer layer. For two hours they sat and played California Jack in plain sight of the street as though nothing unusual had occurred, Johnny's sombrero pushed back on his head, the walnut handle of one of his guns in plain sight, his boots not only guiltless of spurs, but showing that they never had borne them, and his faded, soiled, blue neckerchief was as it had been all day. His mood was cheerful and his laughter rang out from time to time as his friend's witticisms gave excuse. To test his roll, he pulled it out again under his friend's eyes and thumbed off a bill, changed his mind, rolled it back again, and carelessly shoved the handful into his pocket.

Idaho leaned forward. "Who th' devil did you slug?" he softly asked.

"Tell you later deal 'em up," grunted Johnny, a sigh of satisfaction slipping from him. It had been one of Tex Ewait's maxims never to be broke, even if carefully trimmed newspapers had to serve as padding, and in this instance, at least, Johnny believed his old friend to be right. The world finds bluff very useful, and opulence seldom receives a cold shoulder.

At daylight three horsemen and a wagon went slowly up the little street, two men sticking close to each other and the vehicle, and soon became lost to sight. Two or three nighthawks paused and watched the outfit, and one of them went swiftly into Kane's side door. Idaho drew back from the corner of the hotel where he had been watching, nodded wisely to himself, and went into the stable to look after his horse.

The little outfit of the SV stopped when a dozen miles had been put behind and prepared and ate a hurried break fast. As he gulped the last swallow of coffee, Arch arose and went to his horse.

"Thirty miles a day with a waggin takes too long," he said. "One of you boys ride in th' waggin an' gimme a lead hoss. Nelson's a good man, an' it's our job to help him all we can. I can do it that way between sleeps, if I can keep my eyes open to th' end of it. By gettin' a fresh cayuse from my old man at Highbank, I'll set a record for these parts."

Gardner nodded. "Take my cayuse, Arch. I'm crucify in' myself on th' cross of friendship. Cook, give him some grub."

Ten minutes later Arch left them in a cloud of dust, glad to get away from the wagon and keen to make a ride that would go down in local history.

After breakfast Johnny sauntered into the barroom, nodded carelessly to the few men there, and seated him self in his favorite chair.

"Thought mebby you might be among th' dear departed this mornin'," remarked Ed carelessly. "Heard a shot soon after you left last night, but they're so common 'round here that I didn't get none excited. Have any trouble in Red Frank's?"

"You better pinch yoreself ," retorted Johnny. "You saw me an' Idaho settin' right in this room, playin' cards long after that shot. I was upstairs when I heard it. Didn't go to Red Frank's. Changed my mind when I got around at th' side of th' hotel, an' went through th' kitchen, upstairs lookin' for Idaho. What business I got playin' nurse to four growed-up men? A lot they'd thank me for cuttin' in on their play."

"Did they have any trouble?"

"No; they wasn't in Red Frank's at all anyhow, that's what they said. Somebody playin' a joke, or seein' things, I reckon. Seen Idaho this mornin'?"

"No, I ain't," answered Ed sleepily. "Reckon he's still abed. Say, was that yore outfit under my winder before dawn? I come cussed near shootin' th' loud-mouthed fool that couldn't talk without shoutin'."

Johnny laughed. "I reckon it was. They was sore about havin' to go home. Know of any good yearlin's I can buy cheap?"

Ed yawned, rubbed his eyes, and slowly shook his head. "Too close to Ridley. Folks down here mostly let 'em grow up an' sell 'em to him. Prices would be too high, anyhow, I reckon. Better hunt for 'em nearer home."

"That's what I been doin'," growled Johnny. "Well, mebby yo're right about local prices an' conditions; but I'm goin' to poke around an' ask questions, anyhow. To tell you th' truth, a town looks good to me for a change, 'though I'm admittin' this ain't much of a town, at that. Sorta dead nothin' happens, at all."

"That's th' fault of th' visitor, then," retorted Ed, another yawn nearly disrupting his face. "Ho-hum! Some day I'm goin' out an' find me a cave, crawl in it, close it up behind me, an' sleep for a whole week. An' from th' looks of you, it wouldn't do you no harm to do th' same thing." He nodded heavily to the other customers as they went out.

"I'll have plenty of time for sleep when I get home," grinned Johnny. "I got to get some easy money out of this town before I think of sleepin'. Kane's don't get lively till dark, does it?"

Ed snorted. "Was you sayin' easy money?" he demanded with heavy sarcasm.

"I was."

"Oh, well; if you must, I reckon you must," grunted the bartender, shrugging his shoulders.

"A new man, playin' careful, allus wins in a place like Kane's, if he's got a wad of money as big as mine," chuckled Johnny, voicing another maxim of his friend Tex, and patting the bulging roll in his pocket.

Ed looked at the pocket, and frowned. "Huh! Lord help that wad!" he mourned.

"It's got all th' help it needs," countered Johnny. "I'm its guardian. I might change it for bigger bills, for it's purty prominent now. However, that can wait till it grows some more." He burst out laughing. "Big as it is, there's room for more."

"Better keep some real little ones on th' outside," suggested Ed wisely. "You show it too cussed much."

"Do you know there's allus a right an' a wrong way of doin' everythin'?" asked his companion. "A man that's got a lot of money will play safe an' stick a few little ones on th' outside; but a man that's got only little bills will try to get a big one for th' cover. One is tryin' to hide his money; th' other to run a bluff. Wise gamblers know that. I got little bills on th' outside of mine. You watch 'em welcome me."

Despite his boasts, he did not spend much time in Kane's, but slept late and hung around the hotel for a day or two, and then, one morning, he got a nibble on his bait. He was loafing on the hotel steps when he caught sight of the sheriff coming up the street. Corwin had been out of town and had returned only the night before. Seeing the lone man on the steps, the peace officer lengthened his rolling stride and headed straight for the hotel, his eyes fixed on the hat, guns, kerchief, and boots.

"Mornin'," he said, nodding and stopping.

"Mornin'," replied Johnny cheerily. "Bright an' cool, but a little mite too windy for this hour of th' day," he observed, watching a vicious little whirlwind of dust racing up the middle of the street. It suddenly swerved in its course, struck the sheriff, and broke, covering them with bits of paper and hurling dust and sand in their faces and mouths. Other furious little gusts sent the light debris of the street high in the air to be tossed about wildly before settling back to earth again.

"Yo're shore shoutin'," growled Corwin, spitting violently and rubbing his lips. "Don't like th' looks of it. Ain't got no love for a sand storm." He let his blinking eyes rest for a moment on his companion's boots, noted an entire absence of any signs of spur straps, glanced at the guns and at the opulent bump in one of the trouser pockets, noted the blue neckerchief, and gazed into the light blue eyes, which were twinkling at his expression of disgust. "D n th' sand," he grunted, spitting again. "How do you like this town of ourn, outside of th' dust, now that you've seen more of it?"

Johnny smiled broadly. "Leavin' out a few things besides th' dust such as bein' too quiet, dead, an' lackin' 'most everythin' a town should have I'd say it is a purty fair town for its kind. But, bad as it is, it ain't near as bad as that bed I've been sleepin' in. It reminds me of some of th' country I've rid over. It's full of mesas, ridges, canyons, an' valleys, an' all of 'em run th' wrong way. Cuss such a bed. I gave it up after awhile, th' first night, an' played Idaho cards till I was so sleepy I could 'a' slept on a cactus. After that, though, it ain't been so bad. It's all in gettin' used to it, I reckon."

The sheriff laughed politely. "Well, I reckon there ain't no bed like a feller's own. Speakin' of th' town bein' dead, that is yore fault; you shouldn't stay so close to th' hotel. Wander around a little an' you'll find it plumb lively. There's Red Frank's an' Kane's they are high-strung enough for 'most anybody." The momentary gleam in his eyes was not lost on his companion.

"Red Frank's," cogitated Johnny. Then he laughed. "I come near goin' in there, at that. Anyhow, I shore started."

"Why didn't you go on?" inquired the sheriff, speaking' as if from polite, idle curiosity. "You might 'a' seen some excitement in there."

"Somebody tried to play a joke on me," grinned Johnny, \" but I fooled 'em. My boys are shore growed up."

"How'd yore boys make out?"

"They said they wasn't in there at all. Reckon some body got excited or drunk if they wasn't try in' to make a fool out of me. But, come to think of it, I did hear a shot."

"They're not as rare as they're goin' to be," growled the sheriff. "But it's hard to stop th' shootin'. Takes time."

Johnny nodded. "Reckon so. You got a bad crowd of Greasers here, too, which makes it harder though they're generally strong on knifeplay. Mexicans, monte, an' mescal are a bad combination."

"Better tell yore boys to look sharp in Red Frank's. It's a bad place, 'specially if a man's got likker in him. An' they'll steal him blind."

"Don't have to tell 'em, for I sent 'em home," replied Johnny, and then he grinned. "An' there ain't no man livin' can rob 'em, neither, for I wouldn't let 'em draw any of their pay. Bein' broke, they didn't kick up as much of a fuss as they might have. I know how to handle my outfit. Say!" he exclaimed. "Yo're th' very man I been lookin' for, an' I didn't know it till just this minute. Do you know where I can pick up a herd of a couple or three hundred yearlin's at a fair figger?"

Corwin shook his head. "You might get a few here an' there, but they ain't worth botherin' about. Anyhow, prices are too high. Better look around on yore way back, up on some of them God- forsaken ranges north of here. But how'll you handle a herd with yore outfit gone?"

His companion grinned and winked knowingly. "I'll handle it by buy in' subject to delivery. Let somebody else have th' fun of drivin' a lot of crazy-headed yearlin's all that distance. Growed-up steers are bad enough, an' I've had all I want of them for awhile. Well," he chuckled, "not havin' no yearlin's to buy, I reckon I've got time to wander around nights. Six months in a ranchhouse is shore confinin'. I need a change. What do you say to a little drink?"

Corwin wiped more sand from his lips. "It's a little early in th' day for me, but I'm with you. This blasted wind looks like it's gettin' worse," he growled, scowling as he glanced about.

"It's only addin' to th' liveliness of yore little town," chuckled Johnny, leading the way.

"We ain't had a sand storm in three years," boasted the sheriff, hard on his companion's heels. "I see you know th' way," he commented.

Johnny set down his empty glass and brought up the roll of bills, peeled the outer from its companions, and tossed it on the bar. "You got to take somethin' with us, Ed," he reproved.

Ed shrugged his shoulders, slid the change across the counter, and became thoughtfully busy with the arrangement of the various articles on the backbar.

Corwin treated, talked a few moments, and then he parted, his busy brain asking many questions and becoming steadily more puzzled.

Ed mopped the bar without knowing he was doing it. and looked at his new friend. "Where'd you pick that up?" he asked.

"Meanin'?" queried Johnny, glancing at the windows, where sand was beating at the glass and pushing in through every crack in the woodwork.

"Corwin."

"Oh, he rambled up an' got talkin'. Reckon I'll go out, sand or no sand, an' see if I can get track of any yearlin's, just to prove that you don't know any thin' about th' cow business."

"Nobody but a fool would go out into that unless they shore had to," retorted Ed. "It's goin' to get worse, shore as shootin'. I know 'em. Lord help anybody that has to go very far through it!"

Johnny opened the door, stuck his head out and ducked back in again. Tying his neckerchief over his mouth and nose, he went to the rear door, closed his eyes, and plunged out into the storm, heading for the stable to look to the comfort of his horse. Pepper rubbed her nozzle against him, accepted the sugar with dignity, and followed his every move with her great, black eyes. He hung a sack over the window and, finding nails on a shelf, secured it against the assaults of the wind.

"There, Pepper Girl reckon you'll be right snug; but don't you go an' butt it out to see what's goin' on outside. I'm glad this ain't no common shed. Four walls are a heap better than three today."

"That you, Nelson?" came a voice from the door. Idaho slid in, closed the door behind him with a bang, and dropped his gun into the holster. "This is shore a reg'lar storm; an' that's shore a reg'lar hoss!" he exclaimed, spitting and blowing. He stepped toward the object of his admiration.

"Look out!" warned Johnny. "She's likely to brain a stranger. Trained her that way. She'll mebby kill any body that comes in here; but not hardly while I'm around, I reckon. Teeth an' hoofs she's a bad one if she don't know you. That's why I try to get her a stable of her own. What was you doin' with th' six-gun?"

"Keepin' th' sand out of it," lied Idaho. "Thiefproof, huh?" he chuckled. "I'm sayin' it's a good thing. Ever been tried?"

"Twice," answered Johnny. "She killed th' first one." He lowered his voice. "I'm figgerin' Corwin knows about that little fracas of th' other night. Did you tell anybody?"

"Not a word. What about yore outfit?"

"Tight as fresh-water clams, an', besides, they didn't have no chance to. They even left without their break fast. But I'm dead shore he knows. How did he find it out?"

"Looks like you might be right, after all," admitted Idaho. "I kept a lookout that mornin', like I told you, an' th' news of yore outfit leavin' was shore carried, which means that somebody in Kane's gang was plumb interested. How much do you think Corwin knows about it?"

"Don't know; but not as much now as he did before he saw me this mornin'," answered Johnny. "When he sized me up, his eyes gave him away just a little flash. But now he may be wonderin' who th' devil it was that got clubbed that night. An' he showed more signs when he saw my money. Say: How much does Ed know?"

"Not a thing," answered Idaho: "He's one of my best friends, an' none of my best friends ask me questions when I tell 'em not to. An' now I'm glad I told him not to, because, of course, you don't know any thin' about him. No, sir," he emphatically declared; "anythin' that Corwin knows come from th' other side. What you goin' to do?"

"I don't know," admitted Johnny. "I got to wrastle that out; but I do know that I ain't goin' out of th' hotel today. It looks like Californy Jack for us till this blows over. Yore cayuse fixed all right?"

"Shore; good as I can. Come on, if yo're ready."

"Hadn't you better carry yore gun in yore hand, so th' sand won't get in it?" asked Johnny gravely.

Idaho looked at him and laughed. "Come on I'm startin'," he said, and he dashed out of the building, Johnny close at his heels.

Chapter IV
A Journey Continued

Pounding into Highbank from the south, Arch turned the two fagged-out horses into his father's little corral, roped the better of the two he found there, saddled it, and rode around to the front of the hotel, where he called loudly.

Pete Wiggins went to the door and scowled at his son. "What you doin' with that hoss?" he demanded in no friendly tone.

"Breakin' records," impudently answered his young hopeful. "Left Big Creek, north of Mesquite, at sixtwenty this mornin', an' I'm due in Gunsight before dark. Left you two cayuses for this one but don't ride 'em too hard. So-long!" and he was off in a cloud of dust.

Pete Wiggins stepped forward galvanically and called, shaking his first. "Come back here! Don't you kill that hoss!"

His beloved son's reply was anything but filial, but as long as his wrathful father did not hear it, perhaps it may better be left out of the record.

The shadows were long when Arch drew up in front of the "Palace "in Gunsight, and dismounted almost in the door. He looked at his watch and proudly shouted the miles and the time of the ride before looking to see who was there to hear it. As he raised his head and saw Dave Green, Arnold, and two strangers staring at him, he called himself a fool, walked stiffly to a chair, and lowered himself gently into it.

"That's shore some ridin'," remarked Dave, surprised. "What's wrong? What's th' reason for killin' cayuses?"

"Wanted to paste somethin' up for others to shoot at," grinned Arch, making the best of the situation.

"How'd you come to leave ahead of Nelson?" demanded Arnold, his easy-going boss. "Where is he? An' where's th' rest of th' boys?" The SV owner was fast falling into the vernacular, which made him fit better into the country.

"Oh, he's tryin' to make a fortune buyin' up a herd of fine yearlin's," answered the record-maker with confident assurance. "It ain't nothin' to him that th' owner don't want to sell 'em. I near busted laughin' at 'em wranglin'. They was near fightin' when I left. You should 'a' heard 'em! Anybody'd think that man didn't own his own cattle. But I'm bettin' on Nelson, just th' same, for when I left they had got to wranglin' about th' price, an' that's allus a hopeful sign. He shore will tire that man out. I used a lead hoss as far as Highbank, changin' frequent', an' got a fresh off th' old man. Nelson told us all to go home, where we're needed but he'll be surprised when he knows how quick _I_ got there. Sam an' th' others are with th' waggin, comin' slower."

"I should hope so!" snorted Arnold. "An' you ain't home yet. What's th' real reason for all this speed, an' for headin' here instead of goin' to th' ranch? A man that's born truthful makes a poor liar; but I'll say this for you, Arch--with a little practice you'll be near as good as Dave, here. Come on; tell it!"

Arch looked wonderingly at his employer, grinned at Dave, and then considered the two strangers. "I've done told it already," he affirmed, stiffly.

"Shake hands with Red Connors an' Hopalong Cassidy," said Arnold. "You've heard of them, haven't you?"

"Holy cats! I have!" exclaimed Arch, gripping the hands of the two in turn. "I certainly have. Have you two ever been in Mesquite?" he demanded, eagerly. "Good! Now, wait a minute; I want to think," and he went into silent consultation with himself.

"Mebby he's aimin' to improve on me," said Dave. "Judgin' from th' studyin', I figger he's trying to bust in yore class, Arnold."

Arch grinned from one to the other. "Seein' as how we're all friends of Nelson, an' his wife ought to be kept calm, I reckon I ought to spit it out straight. Here, you listen," and he told the truth as fully and completely as he knew it.

Arnold shook his head at the end of the recital. The loss of the herd money was a hard blow, but he was too much of a man to make it his chief concern. "Arch," he said slowly, "yo're so fond of breakin' records that yo're goin' to sleep in town, get another horse at daylight, an' break yore own record gettin' back to Mesquite. Tell that son-in-law of mine to come home right away, before Peggy is left a widow. It's no fault of his that he lost it it's to his credit, goin' to the aid of his men. I wouldn't 'a' had it to lose if it wasn't for what he's done for th' SV. He earned it for me; an' if he's lost it, all right"

"Most generally th' East sends us purty poor specimens," observed Dave. "Once in awhile we get a thoroughbred. Gunsight's proud of th' one it got."

"Arnold," said Arch eagerly, "I'll get to Mesquite tomorrow if it's moved to th' other side of h--l!"

Hopalong took the cigar from his mouth. "Wait a minute," he said. He slowly knocked the ashes from it and looked around. "While I'm appreciatin' what you just said, Arnold, I don't agree with it." He thought for a moment and then continued. "You don't know that son-in-law of yourn like I do. Somebody knocked him on th' head, stole his money an' his guns. Don't forget th' guns. Bein' an easterner, that mebby don't mean anythin' to you; but bein' an old Bar-20 man, it means a heap to me. He won't leave till he's squared up, all around. I know it. Seein' how it is, we got to accept it; an' figger out some way to make his wife take it easy, an' not do no worryin'. Here!" he exclaimed, leaning for ward. "Arnold, you sit down an' write him a letter. Write it now. Tell him to stay down there until he gets a good herd of yearlin's. Then Arch has got to start back in th' mornin' an' join th' waggin, an' come home like he ought to. He stays here tonight, an' nobody has seen him, at all."

"An' Dave don't need to bother with any check," said Red. "Hoppy an' me has plenty of money. We'll start for Mesquite at daylight, Arch, here, ridin' with us till we meet th' waggin. Of course, Hoppy don't mean that yo're really goin' to write a letter, Arnold," he explained.

"That's just what I do mean," said Hopalong. "He's goin' to write th' letter, but he ain't goin' to send it. He'll give it to Arch, an' then it can be torn up. What's th' use of lyin' when it's so easy to tell th' truth? 'Though I'm admittin' I wasn't thinkin' of that so much as I was that a man can allus tell th' truth better'n he can lie. When he tells about th' letter, he's goin' to be talkin' about a real letter, what won't get to changin' around in a day or two, or when he gets rattled. Mrs. Johnny is mebby goin' to ask a lot of questions."

"I'll give odds that she does," chuckled Dave, looking under the backbar. "Here's pen an' ink," he said, pushing the articles across the counter. "There's paper an' envelopes around here some here it is. Go ahead, now:

' Dear Johnny: I take my ' "

"Shut up!" barked Arnold, glaring at him. "I guess I know how to write a letter! Besides, I don't take my pen in hand. It's your pen, you grinnin' chump! As long as we're ridin' on th' tail of Truth, let's stick to it, all th' way. Shut up, now, an' gimme a chance!" He glared around at the grinning faces, jabbed the pen in the ink, and went to work. When he had finished, he read it aloud, and handed it to Arch, who tore it up and threw the pieces on the floor.

Hopalong reached down, picked up the pieces, and gravely, silently put them on the bar. Dave raked them into his hand, dropped them into a tin dish, and put a match to them. Arnold looked around the little group and snorted.

"Huh! You an' Dave must 'a' gone to th' same school!"

Dave nodded. "We have, I reckon. Experience is a good school, too."

"Th' lessons stick," said Hopalong, looking at Dave with a new interest.

Arch chuckled. "Cuss it! I'll shore hate to stop at that waggin. I'm sayin' Mesquite is goin' to be terrible upset some day soon. Why ain't I got whiskers? I'd like to see his face when he sets eyes on you fellers. Bet he'll jump up an' down an' yell!"

"Mebby," said Hopalong, "for if there's any yellin', he'll shore have to start it. He sent you fellers away because you was known to be friends of his, didn't he?"

Dave slapped the bar and laughed outright. "If I wasn't so fat, I'd go with you! I'm beginnin' to see why he thought so much of you fellers. Here it's time for a drink."

"What are we goin' to tell Margaret?" asked Arnold. "She may get suspicious if you leave so suddenly."

"You just keep repeatin' that letter to yoreself," laughed Red, "an' leave th' rest to better liars. Yo're as bad a liar as Arch, here. Me an' Hoppy may 'a' been born truthful, but we was plumb spoiled in our bringin' up. Reckon we better be leavin' now. Arch, where'll we meet you about two hours after daylight tomorrow?"

Arch groaned. "Shucks! About daylight it'll take Fanning that long to get me out of bed oh, well," he sighed, resignedly. "I'll be at th' ford, waitin' for you to come along. Come easy, in case I'm asleep."

"South of here, on this trail?" asked Red. "Thought so. All right. So-long," and he followed his slightly limping friend out to the horses.

Dave hurried to the door. "Hey!" he shouted. "Hadn't I better send him that check, anyhow? He may need it before you get there."

A roar of laughter from behind answered him, and he wheeled to face Arch. "When does th' mail leave?" asked the puncher.

"Day after tomorrow," answered Dave, and swung around as a voice from the street rubbed it in.

"You must 'a' played hookey from that school, Dave," jeered Arnold.

"He's fat clean to th' bald spot," shouted Arch. "Come on in, Dave. We ain't got time to hold back for no mail to get there first." He stuck his head out of the window. "So-long, fellers! See you at th' ford."

Dave watched the three until they were well along the trail and then he turned slowly. "I never did really doubt th' stories Nelson told about that old outfit, but if I had any doubts I ain't got them no more. Did you see th' looks in their eyes when you was tellin' about Nelson?"

"I did!" snapped Arch. "Why in hell ain't I got whiskers?"

Reaching the SV, Arnold and his companions put up the horses and walked slowly toward the house, seeing a flurry of white through the kitchen door.

"Think it'll reach him in time?" asked Red, waiting outside the door for Arnold to enter first.

"Ought to. Slim said he would mail it at Highbank as soon as he got there," answered Arnold.

"I shore hope so," said Red. "I'd hate to have that ride for nothin' an' it would just be our luck to pass him somewhere on th' way, an' get there after he left."

"He'd likely foiler th' reg'lar trail up, anyhow," said Hopalong. "It ain't likely we'll miss him."

Margaret put down the dish and looked at them accusingly. "What are you boys talking about?" she demanded.

"Only wonderin' if yore father's letter will get to Johnny in time to catch him before he leaves," said Hopalong. "Dave says it will as long as that Slim feller is takin' it to Highbank with him. Slim live down there?" he asked his host.

"No; goin' down for th' Double X, I suppose," replied Arnold. "Supper ready, Peggy?"

"Not until I learn more about this," retorted Margaret, determinedly. "What letter are you talking about?"

"Oh, I told Johnny to look around and see if he could pick up a good herd of yearlings cheap," answered her father, going into the next room.

Margaret compressed her lips, but said nothing about it, whereupon Red silently swore a stronger oath of allegiance. "The table is waiting for you. I've had to keep the supper warm," she said.

Red nodded under standingly. "Men- folks are shore a trial an' tribulation," he said, passing through the door.

"Hadn't ought to take him very long, I suppose?" queried Arnold, passing the meat one way and the potatoes the other.

Red laughed. "You don't know him very well, yet," he replied. "Give him a chance to dicker over a herd an' he's happy for a week or more. He shore does like to dicker."

"I never saw anything in his nature which would indicate anything like that," said Margaret, tartly. "He always has impressed me with being quite direct Perhaps I did not understand you correctly?"

"Peggy! Peggy!" reproved her father. "It means bread and butter for us."

"I can eat my bread without butter," she retorted. "As a matter of fact I've seen very little butter out in this country."

Red screwed his face up a little and wriggled his foot. "I don't reckon you've ever seen him buyin' a herd, ma'am?"

"You are quite right, Mr. Connors. I never have."

Red did not take the trouble to inform her that he never had seen her husband buy a herd. "I reckon it's his love for gamblin'," he said, carelessly, and instantly regretted it.

"Gambling?" snapped Margaret, her eyes sparking. "Did you say gambling?"

Hopalong flashed one eloquent look at his friend, whose hair now was not the only red thing about him, and re moved the last of the peel from the potato. "Red is referrin', I reckon, to th' love of gamblin' that was born in yore husband, Margaret. It allus has been one of his, an' our, fears that it would get th' best of him. But," he said, proudly and firmly, "it never did. Johnny is gettin' past th' age, now, when a deck of cards acts strong on him. An' it's all due to Red. He used to whale him good every time he caught th' Kid playin'."

Red's sanctimonious expression made Hopalong itch to smear the hot potato over it, and the heel of his boot on Red's shin put a look of sorrow on that person's face which was not in the least simulated.

"We all had a hand in that, Margaret," generously re marked the man with the shuddering shin. "Tex Ewalt watched him closest. But, as I was sayin', out at th' corral, I don't believe he's got men enough to handle no herd of yearlin's. Them youngsters are plumb skittish, an' hard to keep on th' trail. Me an' Hoppy are aimin' to go down an' help him an' see him all th' sooner, to tell you th' truth."

"That will please him," smiled Margaret. She looked at her father, whose appetite seemed to be ravenous, judging by the attention he was giving to the meal. "What did you write, Dad?"

Arnold washed down a refractory mouthful of potato, which suffered from insufficient salivation, and looked up. He repeated the letter carelessly and reached for another swallow of coffee, silently thanking Hopalong for insisting that the letter actually be written.

The meal over they sat and chatted until after dark, Margaret doing up a bundle of things which she thought her husband might need. When morning came she had breakfast on the table at daylight for her departing friends, and she also had a fat letter for her husband, which she entrusted to Red, the sterling molder of her husband's manly character.

When they had ridden well beyond sight of the house Hopalong thoughtfully dropped the bundle to the ground, turned in the saddle and looked with scorn at his friend. "You shore are a hard-boiled jackass! For two bits I'd've choked you last night. How'd you like to have some body shoot off his mouth to yore wife about your gamblin'?"

"I've reformed, an' she knows it!"

"Yes, you've reformed! You've reformed a lot, you have!"

"You ain't got no business pickin' on th' man that taught th' Kid most all he knows about poker!" tartly retorted Red.

"Cussed little you ever taught him," rejoined Hopalong. "It was me an' Tex that eddicated his brain, an' fingers. He only used you to practice on."

And so they rode, both secretly pleased by this auspicious beginning of a new day, for the day that started without a squabble usually ended wrong, somehow. Picking up Arch, who yawningly met them at the ford, they pushed southward at a hard pace, relying on the relay which their guide promised to get at Highbank. Reaching this town Arch led them to his father's little corral, and exulted over the four fresh horses which he found there. Saddles were changed with celerity and they rolled on southward again.

Peter Wiggins in the hotel office held the jack of hearts over the ten of the same suit and cocked an ear to listen. Slowly making the play he drew another card from the deck in his hand, and listened again. Reluctant to bestir himself, but a little suspicious, he debated the matter while he played several cards mechanically. Then he arose and walked through the building, emerging from the kitchen door. Three swiftly moving riders, his son in the middle, were taking the long, gentle slope just south of town. Pete's laziness disappeared and he made good time to the corral. One look was enough and he shook a vengeful fist at his heir and pride.

"Twice!" he roared, kicking an inoffensive tomato can over the corral wall. "Twice! Mebby you'll try it again! All right; I'm willin'. I never heard of anybody around here thraskin' a twenty-three-year-old son, but as long as yo're bustin' records an' makin' th' Wigginses famous, I ought to do my share. Yo're bustin' ridin' records I'm aimin' to bust th' hidin' records, if you don't smash th' sprintin' records, you grinnin' monkey!"

Pete went into the hotel, soon returning with the cards and a box; and for the rest of the morning played solitaire with the steadily rising sun beating on his back, and swarms of flies exploring his perspiring person.

The three riders were going on, hour after hour, their speed entirely controlled by what they knew of horse flesh, and when they espied the wagon Arch suggested another change of mounts, which was instantly overruled by Hopalong.

"Some of them Mesquite hombres will be rememberin' them cayuses," he said. "We're doin' good enough as we are."

When they reached the wagon and drew rein to breathe their mounts, Joe Reilly grinned a welcome. "Thought you was goin' to Gunsight! "he jeered.

Arch laughed triumphantly. "I've done been there, but got afraid you fellers might get lost. Meet Hopalong assidy an' Red Conners, friends of th' foreman."

"Why'n h--l didn't you bring my hoss with you, you locoed cow?" blazed Sam Gardner from the wagon seat. "You never got to Gunsight. You must 'a' hit a cushion an' bounced back."

"Forgot all about yore piebald," retorted Arch. "But if you must have a cayuse you can ask my old man for one when you get to Highbank. I'd do it for you, only me an' him ain't on th' best of terms right now." He turned to his two new friends. "All you got to do now is foller th' wagon tracks to town."

"So-long," said the two, and whirled away.

They spent the night not many miles north of Big Creek and were riding again at dawn. As they drew nearer to their objective the frisking wind sent clouds of dust whirling around them to their discomfort.

"That must be th' town," grunted Red through his kerchief as his eyes, squinting between nearly closed lids, caught sight of Mesquite through a momentary opening in the dust-filled air to the southeast.

"Hope so," growled his companion. "Cussed glad of it. This is goin' to be a whizzer. Look at th' tops of them sand hills yonder streamin' into th' air like smoke from a roarin' prairie fire.

Here's where we separate. I'm takin' to th' first shack I find. Don't forget our names, an' that we're strangers, for awhile, anyhow."

Red nodded. "Bill Long an' Red Thompson," he muttered as they parted.

Not long thereafter Hopalong dismounted in the rear of Kane's and put his horse in the nearer of the two stables, doing what he could for the animal's comfort, and then stepped to the door. He paused, glanced back at the "P. W." brand on the horse and smiled. "Red's is a Horseshoe cayuse. That's what I call luck!" and plunged into the sand blasts. Bumping into the wall of Kane's big building he followed it, turned the corner, and groped his way through the front door.

At the sudden gust the bartender looked around and growled. "Close that door! Pronto!"

The newcomer slammed it shut and leaned against the wall, rubbing at his eyelids and face, and shed sand at every movement.

The bartender slid a glass of water across the bar. "Here; wash it out. You'll only make 'em worse, rubbin'," he said as the other began rubbing his lips and spit ting energetically.

Bill Long obeyed, nodded his thanks and glanced furtively at the door, and became less alert. "Much obliged. I didn't get all there was flyin', but I got a-plenty."

The dispenser of drinks smiled. "Lucky gettin' in out of it when you did."

"Yes," replied Bill, nervously. "Yes; plumb lucky. This will raise th' devil with th' scenery."

"Won't be a trail left," suggested the bartender, watching closely.

Bill glanced up quickly, sighed with satisfaction and then glanced hurriedly around the room. "Whose place is this?" he whispered out of the corner of his mouth.

"Pecos Kane's," grunted the bartender, greatly pleased about something. His pleasure was increased by the quick look of relief which flashed across the other's face, and he chuckled. "Yo're all right in here."

"Yes," said Bill, and motioned toward a bottle. Gulping the drink he paid for it and then leaned over the counter. "Say, friend," he whispered anxiously, "if any body conies around askin' for Bill Long, you ain't seen him, savvy?"

"Never even heard of th' gent," smiled the other.

"Here's where you should ought to lose yo're name," he suggested.

Bill winked at him and slouched away to become mixed up in the crowd. The checkerboard rear wall obtruded itself upon his vision and he went back and found a seat not far from it and from Kit Thorpe, bodyguard of the invisible proprietor, who sat against the door leading through the partition. Thorpe coldly acknowledged the stranger's nod and continued to keep keen watch over the crowd and the distant front door.

The day was very dull, the sun's rays baffled by the swirling sand, and the hanging kerosene lamps were lit, and as an occasional thundering gust struck the building and created air disturbances inside of it the lamps moved slightly to and fro and added a little more soot to the coating on their chimneys. Bill's natural glance at the unusual design of the rear wall caught something not usual about it and caused an unusual activity to arise in his mind. He knew that his eyes were sore and inflamed, but that did not entirely account for the persistent illusion which they saw when his roving glance, occasionally returning to the wall, swept quickly over it. There were several places where the black was a little blacker, and these spots moved on their edges, contracting and lengthening as the lamps swung gently. Pulling the brim of his hat over his eyes, he faced away from the wall and closed his burning eyelids, but his racing thoughts were keen to solve any riddle which would help to pass the monotonous time. Another veiled glance as he shifted to a more comfortable position gave him the explanation he sought. Those few black squares had been cut out, and the moving strips of black which had puzzled him were the shadows of the edges, moving across a black board which, set back the thickness of the partition, closed them.

"Peekholes," he thought, and then wondered anew. Why the lower row, then, so low that a man would have to kneel to look through the openings?" Peekholes," persisted hide-bound Experience, grabbing at the obvious. "Perhaps," doubted Suspicion; "but then, why that lower row?" Suddenly his gunman's mind exulted. "Peekholes above, an' loopholes below." A good gunman would not try to look through such small openings, nearly closed by the barrel of a rifle. But why a rifle, for a good gun man? "He'd need all of a hole to look through, an' a good gunman likes a hip shot. That's it: Eyes to th' upper, six-gun at th' lower, for a range too short to allow a miss."

He stirred, blinked at the gambling crowd and closed his eyes again. The sudden, gusty opening of the front door sent jets of soot spouting from the lamp chimneys and bits of rubbish skittering across the floor; and it also sent his hand to a gun-butt. He grunted as Red Thomp son entered, folded his arms anew and dozed again, as a cynical smile flickered to Thorpe's face and quickly died. Bill shifted slightly. "Any place as careful in thinkin' out things as this place is will stand a lot of lookin' over," he thought. "Th' Lord help anybody that pulls a gun in this room. An' I'll bet a man like Kane has got more'n loop holes. I'm shore goin' to like his place."

Kit Thorpe had not missed the stranger's alert interest and motion at the opening of the door, but for awhile he did not move. Finally, however, he yawned, stretched, moved restlessly on his chair and then noisily arose and disappeared behind the partition, closing the checkered door after him. It was not his intention to sit so close to anyone who gave signs which indicated that he might be engaged in a shooting match at any moment. It would be better to keep watch from the side, well out of the line of fire.

Bill Long did not make the mistake of looking at the holes again, but dozed fitfully, starting at each gust which was strong enough to suggest the opening of the door. "I got to find th' way, an' that's all there is to it," he muttered. "How am I goin' to be welcome around here?"

Chapter V
What the Storm Hid

The squeaking of the door wakened Johnny and his gun swung toward the sound as a familiar face emerged from the dusk of the hall and smiled a little.

"Reckon it ain't no shootin' matter," said the sheriff, slowly entering. He walked over to a chair and sat down. "Just a little call in th' line of duty," he explained.

"Sorry there wasn't a bell hangin' on th' door, or a club, or something' ' replied Johnny ironically. "Then you could 'a' waited till I asked you to come in."

"That wouldn't 'a' been in th' line of duty," chuckled Corwin, his eyes darting from one piece of wearing apparel to another. "I'm lookin' around for th' fellers that robbed th' bank last night. Yore clothes don't hardly look dusty enough, though. Where was you last night, up to about one o'clock?"

"Down in th' barroom, playin' cards. Why?"

"That's what Ed says, too. That accounts for you durin' an' after th' robbery. I've got to look around, any how, for them coyotes."

"You'd show more sense if you was lookin' around for hoss tracks instead of wastin' time in here," retorted Johnny, keeping his head turned so the peace officer could not see what was left of the bump.

"There ain't none," growled Corwin, arising. "She's still blowin' sand a-plenty a couple of shacks are buried to their chimneys. I'm tellin' you this is th' worst sand storm that ever hit this town, but it looks like it's easin' up now. There won't be a trail left, an' th' scenery has shifted enough by this time to look like some place else. Idaho turn in when you did?"

"He did. Here he is now," replied Johnny, for the first time really conscious of the sand blasts which rasped against the windows.

Idaho peered around the door, nodded at Corwin and looked curious, and suspicious. "If I ain't wanted, throw me out," he said, holding up his trousers with one hand, the other held behind his back. "Hearin' voices, I thought mebby somebody was openin' a private flask an', bein' thirsty, I come over to help. My throat is shore dusty. 'An' would you listen to that wind? It shore rocked this old hotel last night. Th' floor of my room is near ankle deep in places."

"Th' bank was robbed last night," blurted Corwin, watching keenly from under his hat brim. "Whoever done it is still in town, unless he was ad d fool!"

Idaho grunted his surprise. "That so? Gee, they shore couldn't 'a' picked a better time," he declared. "Gosh, there's sand in my hair, even!"

Johnny rubbed his scalp, looked mildly surprised and slammed his sombrero on his head. "It ain't polite," he grinned, "but I got enough of it now." He sat up, crossed his legs under the sand-covered blankets and faced his visitors. "Tell us about it, Sheriff," he suggested.

"Wait till I get a belt," said Idaho, backing out of the door. When he returned he carried the rest of his clothes and started getting into them as the sheriff began his recital.

"John Reddy, th' bank watchman, says he was a little careless last night, which nobody can hardly blame him for. He sat in his chair agin' the rear wall, th' whole place under his eyes, an' listened to th' storm. To kill time he got to makin' bets with hisself about how soon th' second crack in th' floor would be covered over, an' then th' third, an' so on. 'Long about a little after twelve he says he hears a moan at th' back door. He pulls his gun an' listens close, down at th' crack just above th' sand drift. Then he hears it again, an' a scratchin' an clawin'. There's only one thing he's thinkin' about then how he'd feel if he was th' poor devil out there, lost an' near dead. I allus said a watchman should ought to have no feelin's, an' a cussed strong imagination. John ain't fillin' th' bill either way. He cleared away th' drift on his side of th' door an' opens it an' beyond rememberin' somethin' sandy jumpin' for him, that's all he knows till he come to later on an' found hisself tied up, with a welt on th' head that felt big as a doorknob."

If the sheriff expected to detect any interchange of glances between his auditors at his reference to the watch man's bump on the head he was disappointed. Johnny was looking at him with a frank interest seconded by that of Idaho, and neither did anything else during the short pause.

"John got his senses back enough to know what had happened, an' one glance around told him that he was right," continued Corwin. "Finally he managed to get his legs loose enough to hobble, an' he butted out into th' flyin' sand with his eyes shut an' his nose buried agin' his shoulder so he could breathe; an' somehow he managed to hit a buildin' in his blind driftin'. It was McNeil's, an' by throwin' his weight agin' th' door an' buttin' it with his shoulders an' elbows, he woke up Sam, who let him in, untied his arms an' th' rest of him, fixed him up as well as he could in a hurry an' then left him there. Sam got Pete Jennings, next door, sent Pete an' a scatter-gun to watch over what was left in th' bank, an' then started out to find me. He had to give it up till it got light, so he waited in th' bank with Pete. Th' bank fellers are there now, checkin' up. Th' big, burglar-proof safe was blowed open neat as a whistle but they plumb ruined th' little one. They overlooked th' biggest of all, down in th' cellar. Well," he sighed, arising, "I got to go on with my callin' an' it's one fine day to be wanderin' all over town."

"If I was sheriff I wouldn't have to do much wanderin'," said Idaho. "But, anyhow, it can't last," he grinned.

Johnny nodded endorsement. "Th' harder, th' shorter. It's gettin' less all th' time," he said, pivoting and sitting on the edge of the bed. "But, just th' same," he yawned, stretching ecstatically, "I'm shore-e-e g-l-a-d *I* can stay indoors till she peters out. Yo're plumb right, Corwin; them fellers never left town last night. An' if I was you I'd be cussed suspicious of anybody that seemed anxious to leave any time today."

"They never did leave town last night," said Idaho, a strange glint showing in his eyes.

"An' nobody can leave today, neither." said Corwin.

"If they try it they will be stopped," he added, pointedly. "I've got a deputy coverin' every way out, sand or no sand. So-long," and he tramped down the bare stairs, grumbling at every step.

Johnny removed his hat to put on his shirt, and then replaced it. "You speakin' about sand in yore hair gave me what I needed," he grinned.

"That's why I said it," laughed his companion. "I saw that yore neck was stiff an' felt sorry for you. Now what th' devil do you think about that bank?"

"Kane," grunted Johnny, pouring sand from a boot.

"That name must 'a' been cut on th' butt of th' gun that hit you," chuckled Idaho. "It's been drove in solid. Get a rustle on; I'm hungry, an' my teeth are full of sand. I'm anxious to hear what Ed knows."

An unpleasant and gritty breakfast out of the way, they went in to visit with the bartender and to while away a few hours at California Jack.

"Hello," grunted Ed. "Sheriff come pokin' his face in yore room?" he asked.

"He did," answered Johnny; "an' he'll never know how close he come to pokin' it into h< 1."

"My boot just missed him," regretted Ed. "He sung out right prompt when he felt th' wind of it. D d fourflush."

"I'm among friends an' sympathizers," chuckled Idaho. "He says as how he's goin' wanderin' around in th' sand blasts doin' his duty. Duty nothin'! I'm bettin' he's settin' in Kane's, right now, takin' it easy."

"Then he can't get much closer to 'em," snorted Ed "He can near touch th' men that did it." He paused as Johnny laughed in Idaho's face and, shrugging his shoulders, turned and rearranged the glasses on the backbar: "All right; laugh an' be damned!" he snorted; "but would you look at that shelf an' them glasses? Cuss any country that moves around like that. I bet I got some of them Dry Arroyo sand hills in them glasses!"

"There was plenty in th' hash this mornin'," said Idaho; "but it didn't taste like that Dry Arroyo sand. It wasn't salty enough. Gimme a taste of that."

"Just because you'll make a han'some corpse ain't no reason why you should be in any hurry," retorted Ed. "Here! "he snorted, tossing a pack of cards on the bar. "Go over an' begin th' wranglin' agin 'though th' Lord knows I ain't got no thin' agin' Nelson." He glanced out of the window. "Purty near bio wed out. It'll be ca'm in another half-hour; an' then you get to blazes out of here, an' stay out till dark!"

"I wish I had yore happy disposition," said Idaho. "I'd shore blow my brains out."

"There wouldn't be anythin' to clean up, anyhow!" retorted Ed. "Lord help us, here comes Silent Lewis!"

"Hello, fellers!" cried the newcomer. "Gee but it's been some storm. Sand's all over every-thin'. Hear about th' bank robbery?"

"Bank robbery?" queried Ed, innocently. "What bank robbery? Sand bank?" he asked, sarcastically.

"Sand bank! Sand bank nothin'!" blurted Silent. "Ain't you heard it yet? Why, I live ten miles out of town, an' I know all about it."

"I believe every word you say," said Ed. "Tell us about it."

"Gee, where have you-all been?" demanded Silent "Why, John Reddy, settin' on his chair, watchin' th' safe, hears a moanin', so he opened th' door "

"Of th' safe?" asked Idaho, curiously.

"No, no; of th' bank. Th' bank door, th' rear one. He hears a moan "

"Which moan; first, or second?" queried Ed, anxiously.

"Th' first th' second didn't come till hey, I thought you didn't hear about it?" he accused.

"I didn't; but you mentions two moans, separate an' distinct," defended Ed.

"You shore did," said Idaho, firmly.

Johnny nodded emphatically. "Yessir; you shore did. Two moans, one at each end."

"But I didn't get to th' second moan at all!"

"Now, what's th' use of tellin' us that?" flared the bartender. "Don't you think we got ears?"

"If you can't tell it right, shut up," said Idaho.

"I can tell it right if you'll shut up!" retorted Silent. "As I said, he hears a moan, so he leaves th' safe an' goes to th' door. Then he hears a second moan, scratching an' "

"Hey I "growled Ed indignantly. "What you talkin' about? Who in h--l ever heard of a second moan scratchin' "

"It was th' first that scratched," corrected Idaho. "He said it plain. You must be listenin' with yore feet."

"If you'd gimme a chance to tell it "began Silent, bridling.

"Never mind my hearin' you," snapped Ed at Idaho.

"I know what I heard. An' lemme tell you, Silent, you can't cram nothin' like that down my throat. Before you go any further, just explain to me how a moan can scratch! I'm allus willin' to learn, but I want things explained careful an' full."

"He ain't quick-witted, like you an' me," said Johnny. "We understand how a scratch moans, but he's too dumb. Go on an' tell th' ignoramus."

"If yo're so cussed quick-witted, will you please tell me what'n blazes you are talkin' about?" demanded Silent, truculently. "What do you mean by a scratch moans?"

"That's what I want to know," growled Idaho. "You can't scratch moans. Cuss it, I reckon I ought to know, for I've tried to do it, more'n once, too."

"Yo're dumber than Nelson," jeered Ed. "It's all plain to me."

"What is?" snapped Idaho.

"Moanin' scratches, that's what!"

"Of a safe?" asked Johnny. "Then why didn't you say so? How'd *I* know that you meant that. Go on, Silent."

",You was at th' second moan," prompted Ed.

"He scratched that," said Idaho. "He got as far as leavin' th' safe, 'though what he was doin' in there with it, I'd like to know. Reddy let you in?"

"Look here, Idaho," scowled Silent. "I wasn't in there at all. You'll get me inter trouble, sayin' things like that. I was ten miles away when it happened."

"Then why didn't you say so, at th' beginnin'?" asked Ed.

"Ah!" triumphantly exclaimed Johnny. "Then you tell us how you could hear th' scratchin' an' moanin'; tell us that!"

"That's all right, Nelson," said Idaho, soothingly. "He can hear more things when he's ten miles away than any man you ever knowed. Go ahead, Silent."

"You go to h--l!" roared Silent, glaring. "You think yo're smart, don't you, all of you? I was goin' to tell you about th' robbery, but now you can cussed well find it out for yoreselves! An' don't let me hear about any of you sayin' I was in that bank last night, neither! D d fools!" and he stamped out, slamming the door behind him. "Blow an' be damned!" he growled at the storm. "I'd ruther eat sand than waste time with them ijuts. ' Scratch moans! ' Scratch."

Silent's departure left a more cheerful atmosphere in the barroom. The three men he had forsaken were grinning at each other, the petty annoyances of the storm for gotten, and the next hour passed quickly. At its expiration the wind had died down and the storm-bound town was free again. Ed finished cleaning the bar and the glassware about the time that his two friends had swept the last of the sand into the street and cleared away a drift which blocked the rear door. They were taking a congratulatory drink when Ridley, coming to town for the mail himself because he would not ask any of his men to face the discomforts of that ride, stamped in, and his face was like a thunder cloud.

"Gimme a drink!" he demanded, and when he had had it he swung around and glared at Idaho. "Lukins have any money in that bank? Yes? You better be off to let him know about it. H--l of a note: Thirty thousand stole! An' Jud Hill holdin' a gun on me when I rode into town, askin' fool questions! An' let me tell you somethin' judgin' from th' tools they forgot to take with 'em, it wasn't no amatachures that did that job. Diamond drills an' cow-country crooks don't know each other. An' that Jud Hill, a-stoppin' me!"

"Mebby he won't let you leave town," suggested Idaho. "Corwin's given orders like that."

Ridley crashed his fist on the bar, and then to better express his feelings he leaned over and stuck out his jaw. "Y-a-a-s? Then I'm invitin' you-all to Hill's funeral, an' Corwin's, too, if he cuts in! Thirty thousand! Great land of cows!"

"Corwin's out now, huntin' for 'em," said Ed.

"Is he?" sneered Ridley. "Then he wants to find 'em! Th' firm of Twitchell an' Carpenter owns near half of that bank every dollar th' Question-Mark has was in it. There's a change comin' to this part of th' country! "and he stamped out, mounted his horse and whirled down the trail. When he reached the sentry he rode so close to him that their legs rubbed and Hill's horse began to give ground.

"Do I go on?" snapped Ridley.

Jud Hill nodded pleasantly. "Shore. Seein' as how you come in this mornin' I reckon you do."

Ridley urged his horse forward without replying, reached the ranchhouse, wrote a letter which was a masterpiece of its kind and gave it to one of his men to post in Larkinville, twenty miles to the south. That done, all he could do was impatiently to await the reply.

After Ridley had left, Johnny went out to look after Pepper, found her all right, cleaned the sand out of the feed box and then went down to look at the bank. Four men with rifles were posted around it and waved him away. He could see several other men busy in the building, but beyond that there was nothing to claim his attention. Joining the small crowd of idlers across the street he listened to their conjectures, which were entirely vague and colorless, and then wandered back to look for Idaho in Quayle's. His friend was not to be seen and after exchanging a few words with the jovial proprietor he went in to talk with the bartender.

"No wind now, but my throat's dry. Gimme a drink, half water," and holding it untasted for the moment he jerked his head backward in the direction of the bank. "Nothin' to see, except some fellers inside lookin' for 'most anything an' four men with Winchesters on th' outside."

While he was speaking a man had entered and seated himself in the rear of the room. Johnny glanced carelessly at him, and the glass cracked sharply in his convulsive grip, the liquor squirting through his fingers and gathering a deeper color as it passed. A thin trickle of blood ran down his hand and wrist.

Ed had started at the sound and his head was bent forward, his unbelieving eyes staring at the dripping hand.

Johnny opened it slowly, shook the fragments from it and let it fall to his side, mechanically shaking off blood and liquor. "Cuss it, Ed," he gently reproved, looking calmly into the bartender's questioning face, "you should ought to pick out th' bad ones an' throw 'em away yes, an' bust 'em first."

Ed picked up the bottom of the glass and critically examined it, noting a discolored strip along one of the sharp edges, where dirt had accumulated from numberless washings. The largest fragment showed the greasy line to the rounded brim. "I usually do," he growled. "Thought I had this one, too. Must've got back somehow. Hurt bad?"

"Nothin' fatal, I reckon," answered Johnny, drawing the injured member up his trousers leg. "But I'm sayin' you owe me another drink; an' leave th' water out, this time. Water in whisky never does bring good luck, nohow."

Ed smiled, pushing out bottle and glass. "We might say that one was on th' house all that didn't get on you." He instinctively reached for and used the bar cloth as he looked over at the stranger. "I can promise you one that ain't cracked," he smiled.

"I'll take mine straight," said Bill Long. "I don't want no more hard luck."

"Wonder where Idaho is?" asked Johnny. "Well, if he comes in, tell him I'm exercisin' my cayuse. Reckon I'll go down an' chin with Ridley this afternoon. Th' south trail is less sandy than th' north one."

"An' give Corwin a chance to say things about you?" asked Ed, significantly. "He'll be lookin' for a peg to hang things on."

"Then mebby he won't never look for any more."

"That may be true; but what's th' use?"

"Reckon yo're right," reluctantly admitted Johnny. "Guess I'll go up to Kane's an' see what's happenin'. If Idaho comes in, or any more of my numerous friends," he grinned, "send 'em up there if they're askin' for me. I'll mebby be glad to see 'em," and he sauntered out.

Ed smiled pleasantly at the other customer. "Bad thing, a glass breakin' like that," he remarked.

Bill Long looked at him without interest. "Serves him right," he grunted, "for holdin' it so tight. Nobody was aimin' to take it away from him, was they?"

Johnny entered Kane's too busy thinking to give much notice to the room and the suppressed excitement occasioned by the robbery, and sat down at a table. As he leaned back in the chair he caught sight of a red-headed puncher talking to one of Kane's card-sharps and he got another shock. "Holy maverick!" he muttered, and looked carelessly around to see if any more of his Montana friends had dropped into town. Then he smiled as the card-sharp looking up, beckoned to him. As he passed down the room he noticed the quiet easterner hunched up in a corner, his cap well down over his eyes, and Johnny wondered if the man ever wore it any other way. He was out of place in his cow-town surroundings perhaps that was why he had not been seen outside of Kane's building. Ridley's remark about the tools came to him and he hesitated, considered, and then went on again. He had no reason to do Corwin's work for him. Dropping into a vacant chair at the gambler's table he grunted the customary greeting.

"Howd'y," replied the card-sharp, nodding pleasantly.

"No use bein' lonesome. Meet Red Thompson," he said, waving.

"Glad to meet you," said Johnny, truthfully, but hiding as well as he could the pleasure it gave him. "I once knowed a Thompson short, fat feller. Worked up on a mountain range in Colorado. Know him?"

Red shook his head. "Th' world's full of Thompsons," he explained. "You punchin'?"

"Got a job on th' SV, couple of days' ride north of here. Just come down with a little beef herd for Twitchell an' Carpenter. Ain't seen no good bunch of yearlin's that can be got cheap, have you?"

Red shook his head: "No, I ain't."

The gambler laughed and poked a lean thumb at the SV puncher. "Modest feller, he is," he said. "He's foreman, up there."

Red's mild interest grew a little. "That so? I passed yore ranch comin' down. Need another man?"

The SV foreman shook his head. "I could do with one less. Them bank fellers picked a good time for it, didn't they?"

"They shore did," agreed the gambler. "Couldn't've picked a better. Kane loses a lot by that, I reckon. Well, what do you gents say to a little game? Small enough not to cause no calamities; large enough to be interesting Nothin' else to do that I can see."

Red nodded and, the limit soon agreed upon, the game began. As the second hand was being dealt Bill Long wandered in, talked for a few moments with the bar tender and then went over to a chair. Tipping it back against the wall he pulled down his hat brim, let his chin sink on his chest and prepared to enjoy a nap. Naturally a man wishing to doze would choose the darkest corner, and if he was not successful who could tell that the narrow slit between his lids let his keen eyes watch everything worth seeing? His attention was centered mostly on the tenderfoot stranger with the low-pulled cap and the cut out squares in the great checkerboard partition at the rear of the room.

The poker game was largely a skirmish, a preliminary feeling out for a game which was among the strong probabilities of the future. Johnny and the gambler were about even with each other at the breaking up of the play, but Red Thompson had lost four really worth-while jack pots to the pleasant SV foreman. As they roughly pushed back their chairs Bill Long stirred, opened his eyes, blinked around, frowned slightly at being disturbed and settled back again. "Red couldn't 'a' got that money to him in no better way," he thought, contentedly.

The three players separated, Johnny going to the hotel, Red seeking a chair by the wall and the gambler loafing at the bar.

"An' how'd you find 'em?" softly asked the wise bar tender. "Coin' after that foreman's roll?"

The gambler grunted and shifted his weight to the other leg. "Thompson ain't very much; but I dunno about th' other feller. Sometimes I think one thing; sometimes, another. Either he's cussed innocent, or too slick for me to figger. Reckon mebby Fisher ought to go agin' him, an' find out, for shore."

"How'd you make out, last night, with Long?"

"There's a man th' boss ought to grab," replied the gambler. "He didn't win much from me but it's his first, an' last, chance with me. I don't play him no more. I'd like to see him an' Fisher go at it, with no limit. Fisher would have th' best of it on th' money end, havin' th' house behind him in case he had to weather a run of hard luck; but mebby he'd need it."

As the gambler walked away the easterner arose, slouched to the bar and held a short whispered conversation with the man behind it.

The bartender frowned. "You can't get away before night. Sandy Woods will take care of you before mornin', I reckon. Go upstairs an' quit fussin'. Yo're safe as h--l!"

The bartender's prophecy came true after dark, when Sandy Woods and the anxious stranger quietly left town together; but the stranger had good reason to be anxious, for at dawn he was careless for a moment and found him self looking into his escort's gun. He had more courage than good sense and refused to be robbed, and he died for it. Sandy dragged the body into a clump of bushes away from the trail and then rode on to kill the necessary time, leading the other's horse. He was five thousand dollars richer, and had proved wrong the old adage about honor among thieves.

Chapter VI
The Writing on the Wall

When the senior member of the firm of Twitchell and Carpenter read Ridley's letter things began to happen. It was the last straw, for besides being half-owners in the bank the firm had for several years been annoyed by depredations committed by Mesquite citizens on its herds. The depredations had ceased upon payment of "campaign funds" to the Mesquite political ring, but the blackmail levy had galled the senior member, who was not as prone as Carpenter was to buy peace. Orders flew from the firm's office and the little printing-plant at Sandy Bend broke all its hazy precedents, with the result that a hard-riding courier, relaying twice, carried the work of the job-print toward Mesquite. Reaching Ridley's domain he turned the package over to the local superintendent, who joyously mounted and carried it to town.

Tim Quayle welcomed his old friend, listened intently to what Ridley had to say and handed over an assortment of tacks and nails, and a chipped hammer. "'Tis time, Tom," he said, simply.

Ridley went out and selected a spot on the hotel wall, and the sound of the hammer and the sight of his unusual occupation caused a small crowd of curious idlers to gather around him. When the poster was unrolled there were sibilant whispers, soft curses, frank prophesies, and some commendations, which was entirely a matter of the personal viewpoint. Half an hour later, the last poster placed, Ridley took a short cut, entered the hotel through the kitchen and went into the barroom. What he had published for the enlightenment, edification, or disapprobation of his fellow-citizens was pointed and business-like, and read as follows:

$2,500.00 REWARD!

For Information Leading to the Capture and Conviction of the Men Who Robbed the Mesquite Bank.

TWITCHELL & CARPENTER

Sandy Bend TOM RIDLEY, Local Supt.

Quayle turned and smiled at the T & C man. "Ye've slapped their faces, Tom. Mind yore eye!"

"They've prodded th' old mosshead once too often," growled Ridley, looking around at Johnny, Idaho, and the others. "I reckon this stops th' blackmail to th' gang. When I wrote my letter I expected somethin' would hap pen, an' th' letter I got in return near curled my hair. Twitchell's fightin' mad."

"Th' reward's too big," criticized Idaho.

"I'm fearin' it ain't big enough," said Ed Doane, shaking his head.

Ridley laughed contentedly. "It's more than enough. There's men in this town, an' that gang, who would knife anybody for half of that. When they can get twenty-five hundred by simply openin' their mouths, without bein' known, they'll do it. Loyalty is fine to listen about, but there's few men in th' gang we're after that have any twenty-five hundred dollars' worth. This is th' beginnin' of th' end. Mark my words."

"A lot depends on how many were in on it," suggested Johnny, "an' how many of th' others know about it."

"He's throwin' money away," doggedly persisted Idaho. "A thousand would buy any of 'em, that an' secrecy."

"He ain't throwin' it away," retorted Ridley, "considerin' his letter. He's after results, amazin' results, an' he shore knows how to get 'em. It'll be sort of more pleasant if th' gang is sold out. He figgers a reward like that will save time an' be self-actin', for my orders are to stay in th' ranchhouse an' wait. That's what I'm goin' to do, too; an' I'll be settin' there with all guns loaded. No tellin' what'll happen now an', not bein' able to say how soon it will happen, I'm leavin' you boys. So-long."

He walked out to his horse and mounted. As he settled into the saddle there was a flat report, his hat flew from his head and he toppled from the horse, dead before he struck the ground.

Quayle swiftly reached over the desk and took a Winchester from its pegs, Irish tears in his eyes; and waited hopefully, Irish rage in his heart, watching the dirty windows and the open door. "It's to a finish, byes," he grated in a brogue thickened by his emotions, the veins of his forehead and neck swelling into serpentine ridges.

"They read th' writin' on th' wall, an' they read ut plain. D'ye mind what some of thim divils would be after doin' for all that money? They'd cut their own mither's throat an' Kane knows ut! An' I'm thinkin' they'll be careful now Kane has served his notice."

The idlers in the street stood as if frozen, gaping, not one of them daring to approach the body, nor even to stop the horse as it kicked up its heels and trotted down the street. Ed Doane was the third man through the door and he brought in the dead man's hat as Johnny and Idaho placed the warm body on the floor of the office. They hardly had stepped back when hurried footsteps neared the door and the sheriff, with two of his deputies, entered the office, paused instinctively at sight of the rifle in Quayle's hands, and then slowly, carefully bent over to examine the body. The sheriff reached forth a hand to turn it over, but stopped instantly and froze in his stooped position, his arm outstretched.

"Kape ut off him!" roared Quayle, his eyes blazing. "What more d'ye want to see?"

"From behind?" asked Corwin, slowly straightening up, but his eyes fixed on the proprietor.

"An' where'd ye be thinkin' 'twas from?" snarled Quayle, the veins standing out anew. "No dirty pup of that pack would dare try ut from th' front, an' ye know ut! An' need ye look twice to see where th' slug av a buffalo-gun came out? Don't touch him, anny av ye! Kape yore paws off Tom Ridley! An' I'm buryin' him, mesilf."

"But, as sheriff "began Corwin.

"Aye, but!" snapped Quayle. "We'll be after callin' things be their right names. Ye are no sheriff. Ye was choosed by th' majority av votes cast by th' citizens av an unorganized county, like byes choose a captain av their gangs. There's no laws to back ye up, an' ye took no oath. As long as th' majority will it, yore th' keeper av th' peace an' no longer. Sheriff?" he sneered. "An' 'tis a fine sheriff ye'll be makin', runnin' in circles like a locoed cow since th' robbery, questionin' every innocent man in town, an' hopin' 'twould blow over, an' die a natural death. But it's got th' breath av life in it now! What do ye think old Twitchell will be say in' to this" he thundered, his rigid arm pointing to the body on the floor. "Clear out, th' pack av ye! Ye've seen all ye need to!"

Corwin glanced at the body again, from it around the ring of set and angry faces, shrugged his shoulders and motioned to his deputies to leave. "We'll hold th' inquest here," he said, turning away.

"Ye'll hold no inquest!" roared Quayle. "Show me yore coroner! Inquest, is ut? I've held yore inquest already. There's plenty av us here an' we say, so help us God, Tom Ridley was murdered, an' by persons unknown. There's yer inquest, an' yer findin's. W r hat do ye say, byes?" he demanded. A low growl replied to him and he sneered again. "There! There's yer inquest! As long as yer playin' sheriff, go out an' do yer duty; but look out ye don't put yer han's on a friend! Clear out, an' run yer bluff!"

Corwin's eyes glinted as he looked at the fearless speaker, but with Idaho straining at a moral leash, Johnny's intent eagerness and the sight of the rifle in the proprietor's hands, he let discretion mold his course and slouched out to the street, where another quiet crowd opened silently to let him through.

Johnny passed close to Idaho. "Go to your ranch for a few days, or they'll couple you to me!" he whispered.

Bill Long, feeding his borrowed Highbank horse in the northernmost of the two stables at the rear of Kane's, heard the jarring crash of a heavy rifle so loud and near that he dropped instantly to hands and knees and crawled to a crack in the south wall. As he peered out he got a good, clear view of a pock-marked Mexican with a crescent-shaped scar over one eye and who, Sharp's in hand, wriggled out of the north window of the adjoining stable, dropped sprawling within five feet of the watcher's eyes, scrambled to his feet and fled close along the rear of Bill's stable. The watcher sprang erect, sped silently back to his horse and stirred the grain in the feed box with one hand, while the other rested on a six-gun in case the Mexican should be of an inquisitive and belligerent frame of mind. His view of the street had been shut off by the corner of the southern stable and he had not seen the result of the shot. Wishing to show no undue curiosity he did not go down the street, but returned to the gambling-hall. He had not been seated more than a few minutes when one of Kane's retainers ran in from the street with the news of Ridley's death. There was a flurry of excitement, which quickly died down, but under the rippling surface Bill sensed the deeper, more powerful currents.

"This man Kane, whoever an' wherever he is," he thought, "has shore trained this bunch of scourin's. I'm gettin' plumb curious for a look at him. Huh!" he muttered, as the window-wriggling, pock-marked Mexican emerged from behind the partition, bent swiftly over Kit Thorpe and betook his tense and nervous self to the roulette table. "I've got yore ugly face carved deep in my mem'ry, you Greaser snake!" he growled under his breath. "If it wasn't for loosin' bigger game I'd turn you over to Ridley's friends before night. You can wait."

Not long after the appearance of the Mexican, the sheriff came in by the front door, pushed through the crowd near the bar and walked swiftly toward the rear of the room. Speaking shortly to Kit Thorpe in a low voice he passed through the door of the checkerboard partition.

"I'm learnin'," muttered Bill. "I don't know who Kane is, but I'm dead shore I know where he is. An' I'm gettin' a better line on this killin'. I'll shore have to get a look behind that door, somehow."

Suddenly the doorkeeper arose and stuck his head around behind the partition and then, straightening up, closed the door, went up to the bar, spoke to several men there and led them to the rear. Opening the door again he let them through and resumed his vigil; and none of them reappeared before Bill went into the north building to eat his supper.

Chapter VII
The Third Man

Kane's gambling-hall was in full blast, reeking with the composite odor of liquor, kerosene lamps, rank tobacco, and human bodies, the tables well filled, the faro and roulette layouts crowded by eager devotees. The tenseness of the afternoon was forgotten and curses and laughter arose in all parts of the big room. The two-man Mexican orchestra strumming its guitars and the extra bartenders were earning their pay. Punchers, gamblers, storekeepers, two traveling men, a squad of cavalrymen on leave from the nearest post, Mexicans, and bums of several races made up the noisy crowd as Johnny Nelson pushed into the room and nodded to the head bartender.

"Well, well," smiled the busy barman without stopping his work. "Here's our SV foreman, out at night. Thought mebby you'd heard of some yearlin's an' hit th' trail after 'em."

"I don't reckon there was ever a yearlin' in this section," grinned Johnny.

"That so? There's several down at th' other end of th' bar," chuckled the man of liquor. "That blonde you left th' forty dollars for has shore been strainin' her eyes lookin' for you. Says she knows she's goin' to like you. Go back an' sooth her. Gin is her favorite."

"I ain't lookin' for her yet," replied Johnny. "That's somethin' you never want to do. It's th' wrong system. Don't pay no attention to 'em if you want 'em to pay attention to you. Let her wait a little longer. Where's that Thompson feller? I like th' way he plays draw, seein' as how I won some of his money. Seen him tonight?"

"Shore; he's around somewhere. Saw him a little while ago."

Johnny noticed a quiet, interested crowd in a far corner and joined it, working through until he saw two men playing poker in the middle. One was Bill Long and the other was Kane's best card-sharp, Mr. Fisher, and they were playing so intently as to be nearly oblivious of the crowd. On the other side of the ring, sitting on a table, was Red Thompson, his mouth partly open and his eyes riveted on the game.

The play was getting stiff and Fisher's eyes had a look in them that Johnny did not like. The gambler reached for the cards and began shuffling them with a speed and dexterity which bespoke weary hours of earnest practice. As he pushed them out for the cut his opponent leaned back, relaxed and smiled pleasantly.

"I allus like to play th' other fellow's game," Bill ob served. "If he plays fast *I* like to play fast; if he plays 'em close, *I* like to play 'em close; if he plays reckless, *I* like to play reckless; if he plays 'em with flourishes, *I* like to play 'em with flourishes. I'm not what you might call original. I'm a imitator." He slowly reached out his hand, held it poised over the deck, changed his mind and withdrew it. "Reckon I'll not cut this time. They're good as they are. I like yore dealin'."

Fisher yanked the deck to him and dealt swiftly. "I'm not very bright," he remarked as he glanced at his hand, "so I'm gropin' about yore meanin'. Or didn't it have none?"

"Nothin', only to show that I'm so polite I allus let th' other feller set th' pace," smiled Bill. "As he plays, I play." He picked up the cards, squared them into exact alignment and slid them from the table and close against his vest, where a deft touch spread them for a quick glance at the pips. "They look good; but, I wonder?" he muttered. "Reckon that's best, after all. Gimme two cards when you get time."

Fisher gave him two and took the same number.

"I find I'm gettin' tired," growled Bill, "an' it shore is hot an' stiflin' in here. As it stands I'm a little ahead not more'n fifty dollars. That bein' so, I quit after this hand and two more. There ain't much action, anyhow."

"If yo're lookin' for action mebby you feel like takin' off th' hobbles," suggested Fisher, carelessly.

"Hobbles, saddles an' anythin' else you can think of," nodded Bill. "Do we start now?"

Fisher nodded, saw the modest bet and doubled it.

Bill tossed his four queens and the ace of hearts face down in the discard and smiled. "Didn't get what I was lookin' for," he grinned into the set face across from him. "Got to have 'em before I can play 'em."

Fisher hid his surprise and carelessly 'tossed his four kings and the six of diamonds, also face down, into the discard, fumbled the deck as he went to pass it over and spilled it on top of the cards on the table. Cursing at his clumsiness, he scrambled the cards together and pushed them toward his opponent. "My fingers must be gettin' all thumbs," he growled as he raked in the money. What had happened? Had he bungled the deal, or wasn't four queens big enough for the talkative fool across from him?

Bill smilingly agreed. "They do get that way at times," he remarked, shuffling with a swift flourish which made Johnny hide a smile. He pushed the pack out, Fisher cut it, and the flying cards dropped swiftly into two neat piles almost flush on their edges, which seemed to merit a murmur of appreciation from the crowd. Johnny shifted his weight to the other leg and prepared to enjoy the game.

Fisher glanced at his hand and became instant prey to a turmoil of thoughts. Four queens, with an eight of clubs! He looked across at the calm, reflective dealer who was rubbing the disgraceful stubble on his chin while he drew two cards partly from his hand and considered them seriously. He seemed to be perplexed.

"I been playin' this game for more years than I feel like tellin'," Bill grumbled, whimsically; "but I ain't never been able really to decide one little thing." Becoming conscious that he might be delaying the game he looked up suddenly. "Have patience, friend. Oh, then it's all right! You ain't discarded yet," he finished cheerfully. Throwing away the two cards he waited.

"Gimme one," grunted Fisher, discarding, "an' I'm sayin' fifty dollars," he continued, shoving the money out without glancing at the card on the table. "How many you takin'?" he asked.

"Two," answered Bill, looking at him keenly. He glanced down at the single back showing on the table before him and grinned. "Th' other's under it," he explained needlessly. "Well, I'm still an imitator," he chuckled. "Here's yore fifty, and fifty more. I'm sorry I ain't playin' in my own town, so I could borrow when it all gets up."

Whatever Fisher's thoughts were he hid them well, and he was not to be the first one to weaken and look at the draw. He had a reputation to maintain, and he saw the raise and returned it Bill pushed out a hundred dollars and Fisher came back, but his tenseness was growing.

Bill considered, looked down at his unknown draw, shook his head and picked up one card. "I'm feelin' the strain," he growled, seeing the raise and repeating it. He glanced up at the crowd, which had grown considerably, and smiled grimly.

Fisher evened up and raised again, watching his worried opponent, who scowled, sucked his lips, shook his head and then, with swift decision, picked up the other card. "I can't afford to quit now," he muttered. "Here goes for another boost!"

His opponent having wilted first and saved the gambler's face, Fisher picked up his own draw and when he saw it he stiffened, his thoughts racing again. It was no coincidence, he decided. In all of his experience he had known but two men who could do that, and here was a third! But still there was a hope that there was no third, that it was a coincidence. And there was quite a sum of money on the table. The doubt must be removed and the truth known, and another fifty, sent after its brothers was not too big a price to pay for such knowledge. He pushed the money out onto the table. "I calls," he grunted.

Bill dropped his little block of cards and spread them with a sweep of one hand, while the other was ready to make the baffling draw which had made him famous in other parts of the country. Fisher glanced at the four kings and nodded, all doubts laid to rest the third man sat across from him.

He slowly pushed back as the crowd, not knowing just what to expect, scattered. "I'm tired. Shall we call it off for tonight?" he asked.

Without relaxing Bill nodded. "Suits me. I'm tired, too; an' near suffocated. See you to-morrow?"

Fisher grunted something as he arose and, turning abruptly, pushed through the thinning crowd to get a bracer at the bar, while the winner slowly hauled in the money. Gulping down the fiery liquor the gambler wheeled to go into the dark and deserted dining-room where he could sit in quiet and go over the problem again, and looked up to see the other gambler in his way.

"What did you find out?" asked the other in a low voice.

"I found th' devil has come up out of h--l!" growled Fisher. "Come along an' I'll tell you about it. He's th' third man! Old Parson Davies was th' first, but he's dead; Tex Ewalt was th' second, an' I ain't seen him in years cuss it! I wondered why this man's play seemed familiar! He's got some of Tex's tricks of handlin' th' cards."

"Shore he ain't Tex?"

"As shore as I am that you ain't," retorted Fisher; "but I'm willin' to bet he knows Tex. Come on let's get out of this hullabaloo. He's got a nerve, pickin' my cards, an' dealin' 'em alternate off th' top an' bottom, with me watchin' him!"

"We got to figger how to get it back," thoughtfully muttered the other, following closely. "Everythin's goin' wrong. They went after Nelson an' got somebody else; they stirred up th' T & C by robbin' th' bank, an' then had to go an' make it worse by gettin' Ridley! I'm admittin' I'm walkin' soft, an' ready to jump th' country right quick."

Fisher sank into a chair in the dining-room. "An' if Long hangs around here much longer Kane'll ditch me like a wore-out boot. A couple more losses like tonight an' he'll plumb forget my winnin's for th' past two years. An' me gettin' all cocked to strike him for a bigger per centage!"

Out in the reeking gambling-hall Bill put his empty glass on the bar and slid a gold piece at the smiling head man behind the counter. "Spend th' change on th' ladies in th' corner," he said. "It allus gives me luck; an' I had such luck tonight that I ain't aimin' to take no chances losin' it. Reckon I'll horn in on th' faro layout," and he did, where he managed to lose a part of his poker winnings before he turned in for the night.

Up late the next morning he hastened into the diningroom to beat the closing of the doors and saw the head bartender eating a lonely breakfast. The dispenser of liquors beckoned and pushed back a chair at his table.

Bill accepted the invitation and gave his order. "Well," he remarked, "yo're lookin' purty bright this mornin'."

"I'm gettin' so I don't need much sleep, I reckon," replied the bartender. "Did yore folks use a poker deck to cut yore teeth on?"

Bill laughed heartily. "My luck turned, an' Fisher happened to be th' one that got in th' way."

"He says you play a lot like a feller he used to know."

"That so? Who was he?"

"Tex Ewalt."

"Well, I ought to, for me an' Tex played a lot together, some years back. Wonder what ever happened to Tex? He ain't been down this way lately, has he?"

"No. I never saw him. Fisher knew him. He says Tex was th' greatest poker player that ever lived."

"I reckon he's right/' replied Bill. "I'm plumb grateful to Tex. It ain't his fault that I don't play a better game. But I got an idea playin' like his has got to be born in a man." He ate silently for a moment. "Now that I'm spotted I reckon my poker playin' is over in here. Oh, well, I ain't complainin'. I can eat an' sleep here, an' find enough around town to keep me goin' for a little while, anyhow. Then I'll drift."

"Unless, mebby, you play for th' house," suggested the bartender. "What kind of a game does that SV foreman play?"

"I never like to size a man up till I play with him," answered Bill. "I was sort of savin' him for myself, for he's got a fat roll. Now I reckon I'll have to let somebody else do th' brandin'." He sighed and went on with his breakfast.

"Get him into a little game an' see how good he is," suggested the other, arising. "Goin' to leave you now." He turned away and then stopped suddenly, facing around again. "Huh! I near forgot. Th' boss wants to see you."

"Who? Kane? What about?"

"He'll tell you that, I reckon."

"All right. Tell him I'm in here."

The other grinned. "I said th' boss wants to see you"

"Shore; I heard you."

"People he wants to see go to him."

"Oh, all right; why didn't you say so first off? Where is he?"

"Thorpe will show you th' way. Whatever th' boss says, don't you go on th' prod. If yore feelin's get hurt, don't relieve 'em till you get out of his sight."

"I've played poker too long to act sudden," grinned Bill, easily.

His breakfast over, he sauntered into the gambling room and stopped in front of Kit Thorpe, whose welcoming grin was quite a change from his attitude of the day before. "I've been told Kane wants to see me. Here I am."

Thorpe opened the door, followed his companion through it and paused to close and bolt it, after which he kept close to the other's heels and gave terse, grunted directions. "Straight ahead to th' left to th' right straight ahead. Don't make no false moves after you open that door. Go ahead push it open."

Bill obeyed and found himself in an oblong room which ran up to the opaque glass of a skylight fifteen feet above the floor, and five feet below the second skylight on the roof, in both of which the small panes were set in heavy metal bars. The room was cool and well ventilated.

Before him, seated at the far side of a flat-topped, walnut desk of ancient vintage sat a tall, lean, white-haired man of indeterminate age, who leaned slightly forward and whose hands were not in sight.

"Sit down," said Kane, in a voice of singular sweetness and penetrating timbre. For several minutes he looked at his visitor as a buyer might look at a horse, silent, thoughtful, his deeply-lined face devoid of any change in its austere expression.

"Why did you come here?" he suddenly snapped.

"To get out of th' storm," answered Bill.

"Why else?"

Bill looked around, up at the graven Thorpe and back again at his inquisitor, and shrugged his shoulders. "Mebby you can tell me," he answered before he remembered to be less independent.

"I think I can. Anyone who plays poker as well as you do has a very good reason for visiting strange towns. What is your name?"

"Bill Long."

"I know that. I asked, what is your name?"

Bill looked around again and then sat up stiffly. "That ain't interestin' us."

"Where are you from?"

Bill shrugged his shoulders and remained silent.

"You are not very talkative today. How did you get that Highbank horse?"

Bill acted a little surprised and anxious. "L I don't know," he answered foolishly.

"Very well. When you make up your mind to answer my questions I have a proposition to offer you which you may find to be mutually advantageous. In the mean while, do not play poker in this house. That's all."

Thorpe coughed and opened the door, and swiftly placed a hand on the shoulder of the visitor. "Time to go," he said.

Bill hesitated and then slowly turned and led the way, saying nothing until he was back in the gambling-hall and Thorpe again kept his faithful vigil over the checkered door.

"Cuss it," snorted Bill, remembering that in the part he was playing he had determined to be loquacious. "If I told him all he wanted to know I'd be puttin' a rope around my neck an' givin' him th' loose end! So he's got a proposition to make, has he? Th' devil with him an' his propositions. I don't have to play poker in his place there's plenty of it bein' played outside this buildin', I reckon. For two-bits I'd 'a' busted his neck then an' there!"

"You'd 'a' been spattered all over th' room if you'd made a play," replied Thorpe, a little contempt in his voice for such boasting words from a man who had acted far from them when in the presence of Kane. He had this stranger's measure. "An' you mind what he said about play in' in here, or I'll make you climb up th' wall, you'll be that eager to get out. You think over what he said, an' drift along. I'm busy."

Bill, his frown hiding inner smiles, slowly turned and walked defiantly away, his swagger increasing with the distance covered; and when he reached the street he was exhaling dignity, and chuckled with satisfaction he had seen behind the partition and met Kane. He passed the bank, once more normal, except for the armed guards, and bumped into Fisher, who frowned at him and kept on going.

"Hey!" called Bill. "I want to ask you somethin'."

Fisher stopped and turned. "Well?" he growled, truculently.

Bill went up close to him. "Just saw Kane. He says he has got somethin' to offer me. What is it?"

"My job, I reckon!" snapped the gambler.

"Yore job?" exclaimed his companion. "I don't want yore job. If I'd 'a' knowed that was it I'd 'a' told him so, flat. I'm playin' for myself. An' say: He orders me not to play no more poker in his place. Wouldn't that gall you?"

"Then I wouldn't do it," said the gambler, taking his arm. "Come in an' have a drink. What else did he say?"

Bill told him and wound up with a curse. "An' that Thorpe said he'd make me climb up th' wall! Wonder who he thinks he is Bill Hickok?"

Fisher laughed. "Oh, he don't mean nothin'. He's a lookin'-glass. When Kane laughs, he laughs; when Kane has a sore toe, he's plumb crippled. But, just th' same I'm tellin' you Thorpe's a bad man with a gun. Don't rile him too much. Say, was you ever paired up with Ewalt?"

Bill put down his glass with deliberate slowness. "Look here!" he growled. "I'm plumb tired of answerin' personal questions. Not meanin' to hurt yore feelin's none, I'm sayin' it's my own cussed business what my name is, where I come from, who my aunt was, an' how old I was when I was born. I never saw such an' oldwoman's town!"

Fisher laughed and slapped his shoulder. "Keep all four feet on th' ground, Long; but it is funny, now ain't it?"

Bill grinned sheepishly. "Mebby but for a little while I couldn't see it that way. Have one with me, after which I'm goin' up an' skin that SV man before you can get a crack at him. He's fair lopsided with money. If I can't play poker in Kane's, I shore can send a lot of folks to his place with nothin' left but their pants an' socks!"

"Don't overdo it," warned Fisher. "Come on I'm headin' back an' I'll leave you at Quayle's."

"How'd you ever come to let that yearlin'-mad fore man keep away from yore game?" asked Bill as they started up the street. "Strikes me you shore overlooked somethin'."

"Does look like it, from a distance," admitted Fisher, grinning. "Reckon we was goin' too easy with him; but we didn't know you was goin' to turn up an' horn in. We never like to stampede a good prospect by bein' hasty. We felt him out a little an' I was figgerin' on amusin' him right soon. There's somethin' cussed queer about him. We're all guessin', an' guessin' different"

"Yes?" inquired Bill carelessly. "I didn't notice nothin' queer about him. He acts a little too shore of hisself, which is how I like 'em. You ain't got a chance to get him now, for I'm goin' to set on his fool head an' burn a nice, big BL on his flank. So any little thing that you know shore will come in handy. I'd do th' same for you. I'm through spoilin' yore game in Kane's, an' I didn't take yore job. What's so queer about him?"

Fisher glanced at his companion and shook his head. "It ain't nothin' about cards. He figgered in a mistake that was made, an' don't know how lucky he was. Th' boss don't often slip up an' there's a white man an' some Greasers in this town that are cussed lucky too. They blundered, but they got what they went after. An' nobody's heard a word about th' gent that was unlucky, which makes me suspicious. I got a headache tryin' to figger it." He shook his head again and then exclaimed in sudden anger: "An' I've quit tryin'! Kane was all set to throw me into th' discard as soon as you come along. He can think what he wants to, for all I care. But let me tell you this: If you win a big roll in this town, an' th' one you got now is plenty big enough, be careful how you wander around after dark. I reckon I owe you that much, anyhow."

Bill stopped in front of the hotel. "I don't know what yo're talkin' about, but that don't make no difference. Th' last part was plain. Come in an' have somethin'.'"

Fisher looked at him and smiled. "Friend, I'd just as soon be seen goin' in there now as I would be seen rustlin' a herd; an' it might even be worse for me. Let it go till you come up to our place. Adios."

Chapter VIII
Notes Compared

Entering the barroom of the hotel Bill bought a cigar, talked aimlessly for a few minutes with Ed Doane and then wandered into the office, where Johnny was seated in a chair tipped back against the wall and talking to the proprietor. Bill nodded, took a seat and let himself into the conversation by easy stages, until Quayle was talking to him as much as he was to Johnny, and the burden of his words was Ridley's death.

Bill spat in disgust. "That ain't th' way to get a man!" he exclaimed. "Looks like some Greaser had a grudge agin' him somebody he's mebby fired off his payroll, or suspected of cattle-liftin'."

"You're a stranger here," replied the proprietor. "I can tell it."

"I am, an' glad of it," replied Bill, smiling; "but I'm learnin' th' ways of yore town rapid. I already know Fisher's poker game, Thorpe's nature, an' Pecos Kane's looks an' disposition. I cleaned Fisher at poker, Thorpe has threatened to make me climb up a wall, an' Kane told me, cold an' personal, to quit playin' poker in his place. I also learned that a white man an' some Greasers made a big mistake, but got what they went after; that Fisher riggers different from Kane an' th' others; an' that Kane won't slip up th' next time, after dark, 'specially if he don't use th' same fellers. All that I heard; but what it's about I don't know, or care."

Johnny was laughing at the humor of the newcomer, and waved from Bill to Quayle. "Tim, this is Bill Long, that we heard about, for I saw him clean out Fisher. Long, this is Quayle, an' my name's Nelson. Cuss it, man! I'd say you was gettin' acquainted fast. What was that you was sayin' about th' white man an' th' Greasers, an' some mistake? It was sort of riled up."

"It riled up," chuckled Bill, crossing his legs. "I gave it out just like I got it. As I says to Fisher last night, I'm a imitator. Any news about th' robbery?"

Quayle snorted. "Fine chance! An' d'ye think they'd be after tellin' on thimselves? That's th' only way for any news to be heard."

"I may be a stranger," replied Bill; "but I'm no stranger to human nature, which is about th' same in one place as it is in another. If that reward don't pan out some news, then I'm loco."

Quayle listened to a call from the kitchen. "It's th' only chance, then," he flung over his shoulder as he left them. "It's that damned Mick. I'll be back soon."

Johnny, with a glance at the barroom door, leaned slightly forward and whispered one word, his eyes moist: "Hoppy!"

Bill Long squirmed and grinned. "You flat-headed sage-hen!" he breathed. "*I* want to see you in secret."

Johnny nodded. "I reckon th' reward might start somethin' out in th' open, but I wouldn't want to be th' man that tried for it." His voice dropped to a whisper.

"We'll take a ride this afternoon from Kane's, plain an' open." In his natural voice he continued. "But, Twitchell an' Carpenter are shore powerful. An' they've got th' men an' th' money."

"Do you reckon anybody had a personal grudge?" asked Bill. "I'll fix it."

"I'm near as much a stranger here as you are," answered Johnny, "though I sold Ridley some cattle. I met him before, on th' range around Gunsight. Nice feller, he was. What time?

"He must 'a' been a good man, to work for th' T & C," replied Bill. "After dinner."

"He was."

"Oh, well; it ain't my funeral. Feel like a little game?"

"I used to think I could play poker," chuckled Johnny; "but I woke up last night. Seein' as how I still got them yearlin's to buy, I don't feel like playin'."

Quayle's voice boomed out suddenly from the kitchen. "If yer fingers was feet ye'd be as good! Hould it, now if ut slips this time I'll be after bustin' yer head. I've showed ye a dozen times how to put it back, an' still ye yell fer me. There, now hould it! Hand me th' wire annybody'd think blast th' blasted man that made ut! Some Dootchman, I'll wager."

"Shure an' we ought to get a new wan it's warped crooked, an' cracked "

"We should, should we?" roared the proprietor. "An' who are 'we'? Only tin years old, an' it's a new wan we'd be gettin', is ut? What we ought to be gettin' is a new cook, an' wan that's not cracked. Now, th' nixt time ye poke ut, poke gintly ye ain't makin' post holes with that poker. An' now look at me "A door slammed and a washbasin sounded like tin.

Ed Doane's laugh sounded from the barroom and he appeared in the doorway, where he grinned. "I hear it frequent, but it's allus funny. Sometimes they near come to blows."

"Stove?" queried Bill.

"Shore th' grate's buckled out of shape, an' it's a little short. Murphy gets mad at th' fire an' prods it good an' then th' show starts all over again. It's funnier than th' devil when th' old man gets a blister from it, for he talks so that nobody but Murphy can understand one word in ten. Easy! Here he comes."

"Buy a new wan, is ut?" muttered the proprietor, his red face bearing a diagonal streak of soot. "Shure for him to spile, like he spiled this wan. Ah, byes, I'm tellin' ye th' hotel business ain't what it used to be."

"Yore face looks funny," said Ed.

Quayle turned on him. "Oh, it does, does ut? Well, if my face don't suit ye now would ye look at that?" he demanded as he caught sight of his reflection in the dingy mirror over the desk. "But it ain't so bad, at that; th' black's above th' red!"

"Hey, Tim!" came from the kitchen. "Thought ye said ye fixed ut? Ut's down agin!"

"I--I--I!" sputtered Quayle wildly. He spread the soot over his face with a despairing sweep of his sleeve, leaped into the air and started on a lumbering run for the kitchen. "You--I--damn it!" he yelled, and the kitchen resounded to his bellowing demands for the cook.

Ed Doane wiped his eyes, looked around and shouted, his out-thrust hand pointing to a window, where a red face peered into the room.

"Shure," said the cook, apologetically, "he's the divvil himself. If I stay here wan more day me name ain't Murphy. Will wan av yez, that ain't go no interest in th' dommed stove, tell that Mick to buy a new grate? An' would ye listen to him, now?"

When he was able to Bill arose. "Well, I reckon I'll go up an' look in at Kane's. If I run this way, don't stop me."

Sauntering up the street he came to the south side of the gambling-hall and went along it, and when a certain number of paces beyond the fifth high window, the sill of which was above his head, he stumbled and fell. Swearing under his breath he picked up a Colt which had slipped from its holster and, arising to hands and knees, looked around and then stood up.

He could see under the entire building except at the point where he had fallen, and there he saw that under Kane's private room the walls went down into the earth. When he reached the stables he entered the one which sheltered his horse, closed the door behind him and made a hasty examination of the building, but found nothing which made him suspect a secret exit. He came to the opinion that the boards went down to the earth below Kane's quarters for the purpose of not allowing anyone to crawl under his rooms. In a few minutes he led his horse outside, mounted and rode around to the front of the gambling-hall, where he dismounted and went in for a drink, scowling slightly at the vigilant and militant Mr. Thorpe, who returned the look with interest.

"Got a cayuse?" he asked the bartender.

The other shook his head. "No, why?"

"Thought mebby you'd like to ride along with me. That one of mine will be better for a little exercise. What's east of here?"

"Sand hills, dried lakes, an' th' desert."

"Then I'll go west," grinned Bill. "But mebby it's th' same?"

"It ain't bad over that way; but why don't you ride south? There's real good country down in them valleys."

"Ain't that where th' T & C is?"

The bartender nodded.

"West is good enough for me. Better get a cayuse an' come along."

"Can't do it, an' I ain't set a saddle in two years. I'd be a cripple if I stuck to you. Why don't you hunt up that Nelson feller? He ain't got nothin' to do."

"Just left him. Don't reckon he'd care to go. Huh!" he muttered, looking at the clock. "I reckon I'll eat first, an' ride after."

Shortly after dinner Johnny strolled in and nodded to the bartender, who immediately called to Bill Long.

"Here's Nelson now; mebby he'll go with you," he said.

"Go where?" asked Johnny, pausing.

"Ridin'."

"What for?"

"Exercise. He wants to take th' devilishness out of his horse. You got one, too, ain't you?"

"Shore have," answered Johnny. "An' she's gettin' mean, too. It ain't a bad idea. Where are you goin', Long?"

"Anywhere, everywhere, or nowhere," answered Bill carelessly. "I'm aiming to ride him to a frazzle, an' I got to cut down his feed more."

"All right, if you says so," agreed Johnny, joining the group.

Red Thompson rode up to the door and came in. "Hey, anybody that's goin' down th' trail wants to ride easy. That T & C gang are so suspicious that they're insultin'. Got four men ridin' along their wire, with rifles across their pommels. Looks like they was goin' on th' prod."

Thorpe silently withdrew, to reappear in a few minutes and resume his watch.

Bill arose and nodded to Johnny as he went out. "Ready, Nelson?" he asked.

In a few minutes they met in front of the gambling-hall, and the SV foreman's black caused admiring and covetous looks to show on the faces of the idle group.

"Foller th' trail leadin' to Lukins' ranch, over west," suggested Fisher. "It's better than cross-country. You'll strike it half a mile above."

Long nodded and led the way, both animals prancing and bucking mildly to work off some of their accumulated energy. Reaching the cross trail they swung along it at a distance-eating lope.

"Tell me about everything" suggested Johnny. "How'd you come to ride south?"

"Kid," said Hopalong, "you got th' best cayuse ever raised in Montanny. That Englishman was shore right: it pays to cross 'em with thoroughbreds." Moodily silent for a moment, he slowly continued. "Kid, I've lost Mary, an' William, Junior. Fever took 'em in four days, an' never even touched me! I'm all alone. Either you move up north, or I stay with you till I die.

An' if I do that I'll miss Red an' th' others like th' devil. I'm goin' to have a good look at that Bar-H, that you chased them thieves off of. Montanny is too far north, an' I'm feelin' th' winters too hard. An' it's gettin' settled too fast, an' bein' ploughed up more every year. But all of this can wait: what's goin' on down here that I don't know?"

Johnny told him and when he had finished and listened to what his friend knew they spent the rest of the time discussing the situation from every angle and arranged a few simple signals, resurrected from the past, to serve in the press of any sudden need. They met two punchers riding in from Lukins' ranch, exchanged nods and then turned south into the cattle trail, crossed a crescent arroyo and turned again, when below the town, under the suspicious eyes of a Question-Mark sentry hidden in a thicket. Following the main trail north they entered the town and parted at Quayle's.

The evening passed uneventfully in Kane's and when the group began to break up Bill Long went up to his room. Gradually man after man deserted the gambling hall, until only Johnny and the head bartender were left, and after half an hour's dragging conversation the dispenser of liquids yawned and nodded decisively.

"Nelson, I'm goin' to lock up after you. See you tomorrow."

"Most sensible words said tonight," replied Johnny, and he stepped out, the door closing behind him. The lights went out, one by one, with a tardiness due to their height from the floor, and he stood quietly for a moment, scrutinizing the sky and enjoying the refreshing coolness.

Moving out into the middle of the street he sauntered toward the dark hotel, every sense alert as a previous experience came back to him. Suddenly a barely audible sound, like the cracking of a toe joint, caused him to leap aside. An indistinct figure plunged past him, so close that he felt the wind of it. His gun roared while he was in the air and when he alighted he was crouched, facing the rear, where another figure blundered into the second shot and dropped. Swiftly padding feet came nearer and he slipped further to the side, letting the sound pass without hindrance. Moving softly forward he turned and crept along the wall of a building, smiling grimly at the low Spanish curses behind him on the street Again the kitchen door served him well and the deeper blackness of the interior silently engulfed him.

Up at Kane's, Red Thompson, who was awake and waiting until the building should be wrapped in sleep, heard the shots and crept to the window. He could see nothing, but he heard whispers and heavy, slow and shuffling steps, which drew steadily nearer. The Mexican tongue was no puzzle to Red, whose years largely had been spent in a country where it was constantly used and his fears, instantly aroused, were soon followed by a savage grin.

"That Nelson, he is a devil," floated up to him, the words a low growl.

"Again he got away. I will not face the Big Boss. It is the second failure, and with Anton dead, an' Juan's arm broken, I shall leave this town. Put him here, at the door. May God forgive his sins! Adios!"

"Wait, Sanchez!" called a companion. "We will all go, even Juan, for he'd better ride than remain. There will be trouble."

"What's all th' hellabaloo?" came Thorpe's truculent voice in English from the corner of the building, where he stood, clad only in boots and underwear, a six-shooter in his upraised hand. At the sudden soft scurrying of feet he started forward, and then checked himself.

"If them Greasers bungled it this time, may th' Lord help 'em. They'll shore get a-plenty. I wouldn't be " he stopped and stared at the door, and then moved closer to it. "By G-d, they got him!" he whispered, and bent down, his hand passing over the indistinct figure. "Huh! I take it all back," he muttered in disgust. "That's a Greaser, by feel an' smell. They made more of a mess of it this time than they did before. Well, you ain't no fit ornament for th' front door. Might as well move you myself," and, grumbling, he grabbed hold of the collar and dragged the unresisting bulk around to the rear, where he carelessly dropped it and went back into the building. Soon two Mexicans, rubbing sleepy eyes, emerged with shovel and spade, that the dawn should find nothing more than a carefully hidden grave.

Red waited a little longer and then, knowing better than to go on his feet along the old floor of the hall, inched slowly over it on his stomach, careful to let each board take his weight gradually. Reaching the second door on his left he slowly pushed it open, chuckling with pride at his friend's forethought in oiling the one squeaking hinge. Closing it gently he scratched on the floor twice and then went on again toward the answering scratch. An hour passed in the softest of whispering and when he at last entered his own room again and carefully stood up, the darkness hid a rare smile on his tanned and leathery face, which an exultant thought had lighted.

"Th' Old Days: They're comin' back again!" he gloated. "Me, an' Hoppy, an' the Kid! Glory be!" and the smile persisted until he awakened at dawn, when it moved from the wrinkled face to the secrecy of his heart,

Chapter IX
Ways of Serving Notice

If Sandy Bend had been seized with a local spasm when the senior member of the T & C had learned of the robbery of the Mesquite bank, it now was having a very creditable fit. The little printing-shop was the scene of bustling activities and soon a small bundle of handbills was on its way to the office of the cattle king. McCullough, drive-boss par excellence and one of the surviving frontiersmen who not only had made history in several localities, but had helped to wear the ruts in the old Santa Fe Trail until the creeping roadbed of the railroad had put the trail with other interesting relics of the past, was rudely torn from his seven-up game with his cronies by one of the several couriers who lathered horses at the snapping behest of the senior partner. He hastened to the office, rumbled across the outer room and pushed open the door of the holy of holies without even the semblance of a knock. He was blunt, direct, and no respecter of persons.

"Hello, Charley!" he grunted. "What's loose now?"

"Hell's loose!" snapped Twitchell. "Ridley's been murdered by one of Kane's gang. Shot in th' back —head near blowed off. There's only four men up there now, an' they may be dead by this time. Take as many men as you need an' go up there we just bought a herd of SV cows, if there's any left. But I want th' man that killed Ridley. That's first. I want th' man who robbed th' bank that's second. An' I want Pecos Kane that's first, second, an' third. D n it! I growed up with Tom Ridley!"

"I'll take twenty men an' bring you th' whole gang but some of 'em will shore spoil before we can get 'em here, this kind of weather. Do I burn that end of th' town?"

"You'll burn nothin'," retorted Twitchell. "You'll not risk a man until you have to. You'll stay on th' ranch an' watch th' cattle. I've lost one good man now, an' I'm spendin' money before I risk losin' any more. There's a bundle of handbills. When they've been digested by that bunch of assassins you can sit in th' bunkhouse an' have yore game delivered to you, all tied up, an' tagged."

"Orders is orders," growled McCullough; "but some are damned fool orders. If you want somebody to set on th' front porch an' whittle, why'n h--l are you cuttin' me out of th' herd for th' job?"

"I'm cuttin' you out because I want my best man out there!" retorted the senior member heatedly. "You may find it lively settin',-an' have to do yore whittlin' with rifles an' six-guns. Look out that somebody don't whittle you at eight hundred while yo're settin' on th' front porch! You talk like you think yo're goin' to a prayer meetin'!"

"I'm hopin' they come that close," said McCullough, picking up the package of bills. "So Tom's gone, huh? Charley, there ain't many of us left no more. Remember how you an' Ridley an' me used to go off trappin' them winters, hundreds of miles into th' mountains, with only what we could easy carry on our backs? That was livin'."

"You get out of here, you old fraud!" roared Twitchell. "Ain't I got enough to bother me now? Take care of yoreself, Mac; an' my way's worth tryin', an' tryin' good. If it don't work, then we'll have to try yore way."

"All right; I'll give it a fair ride, Charley; but it will be time wasted," replied the trail-boss. "In that case I'm takin' a dozen men. We relay at th' Squaw Creek corrals, an' again at Sweetwater Bottoms. Send a wagon after us you'll know what we'll need. You send a new boss to th' Sweetwater, for I'm pickin' up Waffles. He's one of th' best men you got, an' he's been picketed at that twobits station long enough."

"Good luck, Mac. Take who you want. Yo're th' boss. Any play you make will be backed to th' limit by th' T&C."

When McCullough got outside he found a crowd of men which the hard-riding couriers had sent in from all parts of the town. They shouted questions and got terse answers as he picked his dozen, the twelve best out of a crowd of good men, all known to him in person and by deeds. The lucky dozen smiled exultantly at the scowling unfortunates and dashed up the street in a bunch after their grizzled pacemaker. One of the last, glancing be hind him, saw a stern- faced, sorrowful man in a black store suit standing in the office door looking wistfully after them; and the rider, gifted with understanding, raised his hand to his hat brim and faced around.

"Th' old man's sorry he's boss," he confided to his nearest companion.

"An' there's plenty up in Mesquite that will be th' same," came the reply.

Despite his years McCullough held his lead without crowding from the rear, for he was of the hard-riding breed and toughened to the work. When the first relay was obtained at Squaw Creek that evening there were several who felt the strain more than the leader. A hasty supper and they were gone again, pounding into the gathering dusk of the northwest. All night they rode along a fair trail, strung out behind a man who kept to it with uncanny certainty. Dawn found them changing mounts in Sweetwater Bottoms, but without the snap displayed at the Squaw. Waffles, one-time foreman of the O-Bar-O, needed all his habitual repression to keep from favoring them with a war dance when he heard his luck. Impatiently waiting for the surprised but enthusiastic cook to prepare their breakfasts, they made short work of the meal when it appeared and rolled on again, silent, grim, heavy-lidded, but cheerful. They gladly would do more than that for McCullough, Twitchell and Tom Ridley. The second evening found them riding up to the buildings of the Question-Mark, guns across their pommels, and they were thankfully received.

Mesquite awakened the next morning to a surprise, for handbills were scattered on its few streets and had been pushed under doors, one of them under the front door of Kane's gambling-hall. When Johnny came down to breakfast the proprietor handed him the sheet, pointing to its flaming headline.

"Read that, me bye!" cried Quayle.

Johnny obeyed:

$2,500.00 REWARD!

For Information Leading to the Capture and Conviction of the Murderer of Tom Ridley

STRICTLY CONFIDENTIAL

TWITCHELL & CARPENTER, Sandy Bend

JOHN McCULLOUGH, Gen'l. Supt., Mesquite

He thoughtlessly shoved it into his pocket and shrugged his shoulders. "That man Twitchell thinks a lot of his money," he said. "But, if it's his way, it's his way. I'm glad to say it ain't mine."

Quayle looked at him from under heavy brows and smiled faintly. "Mac's here, hisself," he said. "They've raised th' ante, an' if I was as young as you I'd have a try at th' game. An', me bye, it isn't only th' money; 'tis a duty, an' a pleasure. Go in an' eat, now, before that wild Mick av a cook scalps ye."

Hoofbeats pounded up the street from the south and a Mexican galloped past towards Kane's, followed on foot by several idlers.

"There ye go!" savagely growled the proprietor; "an' I hope ye saw a-plenty, ye Greaser dog!"

After a hurried breakfast Johnny went up to Kane's and found an air of tension and suspicion. Men were going in and out of the door through the partition and the half-friendly smiles which he had received the night before were everywhere missing. Feeling the chill of his reception did not blunt his powers of observation, for he saw that both Red Thompson and Bill Long, being unaccredited strangers, drew an occasional suspicious glance. The former was seated in a chair at the lower end of the bar, his back to the wall and only a step from the diningroom door. Bill Long was leaning against the upper end of the counter, where it turned at right angles to meet the wall behind it. At Bill's back and only two steps away was the front door. His chin was in his hand and his elbow rested on the bar, where he appeared to be moodily studying the floor behind the counter, but in reality his keen, narrowed eyes were watching Thorpe and the loopholes in the checkerboard. From his position he caught the light on them at just the right angle to see the backing plates. He let Johnny go past him without more than a casual glance and nod.

Thorpe moved forward, cleaving a straight path through the restless crowd and stopped in front of the newcomer. "Nelson," he said, tartly; "th' boss wants to see you, pronto!" As he spoke he let his swinging hand rest against the butt of his gun.

Johnny took plenty of time for his answer, his mind working at top speed. If Kane had caused inquiries to be made around Gunsight concerning him he knew that the report hardly would please any man who was against law and order; and he knew that Kane had had plenty of time to make the inquiries. The thinly veiled hostility and suspicions on the faces around him settled that question in his mind. He slouched sidewise until he had Thorpe in a better position between him and the partition.

"You shore made a mistake," he drawled. "Th' boss never even heard of me."

"I said pronto!" snapped Thorpe.

"Well, as long as yo're so pressin'," came the slow, acquiescent reply, "you can go to h--l!"

Thorpe's gun got halfway out, and stopped as a heavy Colt jabbed into his stomach with a force which knocked the breath out of him and doubled him up. Johnny's other gun, deftly balanced between his palm and the thumb on its hammer, freezing the expressions as it had found them on the faces of the crowd. "Stick up yore han's! All of you! You, in the chair! "he roared. "Stick 'em up!" and Red lost no time in making up for his delinquency. Bill Long, being out of the angry man's sight, raised his only halfway.

"I was welcome enough last night," snapped Johnny; "but somethin's wrong today. If Kane wants to see me, he can send somebody that can talk without insultin' me. An' as for this sick cow, I'm warnin' him fair that I shoot at th' first move, his move or anybody else's. Stand up, you!" he shouted; "an' foiler me outside. Keep close, an' plumb in front of me. I'll turn you loose when I get to cover. Come on!"

As he backed toward the door, Thorpe following, Bill Long, seeing that Johnny was master of the situation, got his hands all the way up, but the motion was observed and Johnny's gun left Thorpe long enough to swing aside and cover the tardy one. "You keep 'em there!" he gritted. "You can rest 'em later!" and he cautiously backed against the door, moved along it the few inches necessary to gain the opening, and felt his way to the street. "Don't you gamble, Thorpe!" he warned. "Stick closer!"

Being furthest from the front door and soonest out of Johnny's sight, Red Thompson let his hands fall to his hips and cautiously peered over the top of the bar, ready to cover the crowd until Bill Long could drop his upraised hands.

Bill was unfortunate, since he would have to be the last man to assume a more natural position; but he was growing tired and suddenly flung himself sidewise beyond the door opening. As he left the bar there came a heavy report from the street and the bullet, striking the edge of the counter where he had stood, glanced upward and entered the ceiling, a generous cloud of dust moving slowly downward.

"He's a mad dog," muttered Bill, shrinking against the wall. "An' he can shoot like h--l! I reckon he's itchin' to get me on sight, now. Somebody look out an' see where he is. But what'n blazes is it all about, anyhow?"

The chief bartender's head reappeared further down, the counter. "You fool!" he yelled. "Why didn't you let me know what you was goin' to do? Don't you never think of nobody but yourself? That parted my hair!"

Fisher swore disgustedly. "Look out, yourself, Long, if yo're curious! But why didn't you get him?" he demanded. "You was behind him!"

"I wasn't neither behind him; I was on th' side!" retorted Bill. "He was watchin' me out of th' corner of his eye, like th' damned rattler he is! I could see it plain, I tell you!"

"You can see lots of things when yo're scared stiff, can't you?" sneered a voice in the crowd.

"I wasn't scared," defended Bill. "But I wasn't takin' no chances for th' glory of it. He never done nothin' to me, an' I ain't on Kane's payroll yet."

"An' you ain't goin' to be, I reckon," laughed another.

Fisher's face proclaimed that he had solved whatever problem there might be in Bill's lack of action. "Ain't had a chance to get it from him yet, huh?" he asked. Sneering, he gave a warning as he turned away. "An' don't you try for it, neither. If he won't come back here no more, I can get him playin' somewhere else."

Red arose fully and stretched, hearing a slight grating hoise at a loophole in the partition behind him, where the slide dropped into place. "I'm dry; bone dry," he announced. "I never was so dry before. All in favor of a drink, step up. I'm payin' for this round."

All were in favor of it, and the bartender moved slowly behind the counter toward the front door, his head bent over far to the right. "Don't see him; but we better wait till Thorpe comes back. Great guns! Did you see it!" he marveled.

"I can see it better now than I could then," said Red, leaning against the bar. "Come on, boys; he's done gone. This means you, too, Long; 'though I ain't sayin' you hardly earned it. If he saw you before he backed up, I says he's got eyes in his ears. Why, cuss it, he was lookin' plumb at me all th' time. You got too hefty an imagination, Long."

Out in the street Johnny, backing swiftly from the building, saw Bill Long's sudden leap and fired, for moral effect, at the place vacated. Yanking his captive's gun from its holster, he was about to toss it aside when his fingers gripped the telltale butt and a colder look gleamed in his eyes. Slipping his right-hand gun into its holster he gripped the captured weapon affectionately, and then hazarded a quick glance around him. Someone was riding rapidly down the trail from the north, and a second sidewise glance told him that it was Idaho.

"Faster, you!" he growled to the doorkeeper. "Keep a-comin' keep a-comin'. One false move an' Kane'll need another sentry. You may be able to make Bill Long climb up a wall, but I ain't in his class."

Idaho, who was riding in to appease his burning curiosity, felt its flames lick instantly higher as he saw his friend back swiftly from Kane's front door, with Thorpe apparently hooked on the sight of the six-gun. Drawing rein instantly in his astonishment, he at once loosened them and whirled into the scanty and scrawny vegetation on the far side of the trail. Going at a dead run he sent the wiry little pony over piles of cans, around cacti and other larger obstructions until he reached the rear of Red Frank's, facing on the next street. Here he pulled up and drew the Winchester from its scabbard, feeling that Johnny was capable of taking care of Kane's if not interfered with from behind.

Johnny, reaching the rear of the building which he had sought the night before, leaped back and to one side as he came to the end of the wall, glanced along the rear end and then curtly ordered Thorpe back to his friends.

"There'll be more to this," snarled Thorpe, white from anger, his face working. His courage was not of the fineness necessary to let him yield to the mad impulse which surged over him and urged him to throw himself, hands, feet and teeth, in a blind and hopeless attack upon the certain death which balanced itself in the gun in Johnny's hand. His blazing eyes fixed full on his enemy's, he let discretion be his tutor and slowly, grudgingly stepped back, his dragging feet moving only inches at each shuffle, while their owner, poised and tense and ready to take advantage of any slip on Johnny's part, backed toward the sandy street and the scene of his discomfiture. At last reaching the front of the building he paused, stood slowly erect and then wheeled about and strode toward Kane's. At the door he glanced once more at his waiting adversary and then plunged into the room, striding straight for the partition door without a single sidewise glance.

Idaho's voice broke the spell. "I thought he was goin' to risk it," he muttered, a deep sigh of relief following the words. "He was near loco, but he just about had enough sense left to save his worthless life. You would 'a' bio wed him apart at that distance."

"I'd 'a' smashed his pointed jaw!" growled Johnny. "I ain't shootin' nobody that don't reach for a gun. An' if I'd had any sense I'd 'a' chucked th' guns to you an' let him have his beatin'. Next time, I will. Fine sort of a dog he is, tellin' me what I'm goin' to do, an' when I'm goin' to do it!"

"Wait till pay day, when I'll have more money," chuckled Idaho. "I can easy get three to two around here. He's th' champeen rough-an'-tumble fighter for near a hundred miles, but I'm sayin' any man with th' everlastin' nerve to pull Kit Thorpe out from his own kennel an' pack ain't got sense enough to know when he's licked. An' that bein' so, I'm bettin' on yore condition to win. He's gettin' fat an' shortwinded from doin' nothin'. Besides, I'm one of them fools that allus bets on a friend." He laughed as certain memories passed before him. "I've done had a treat come on, an' let me treat you. How many was in there when you pulled him out? An' why didn't th' partition work like it allus did before?"

"Because th' man that worked it was out in front," answered Johnny. "Things went too fast for anybody else to get behind it." A sudden grin slipped to his face. "Hey, I got one of my pet guns back! He was wearin' it. I knowed it as soon as my fingers closed around th' butt, for I shaped it to fit my hand several years ago. Did you see th' handbills? Twitchell's put up another reward, this one for Ridley; an' McCullough is down on th' Question-Mark. Things ought to step fast, now."

Chapter X
Twice in the Same Place

Thorpe reappeared through the partition door armed anew with the mate to the gun he had lost, too enraged to notice that it was better suited to a left than to a right hand. An ordinary man hardly would have noticed it, but a gunman of his years and experience should have sensed the ill-fitting grip at once. He glared over the room, suspiciously eager to catch some unfortunate indulging in a grin, for he had been so shamed and humiliated that it was almost necessary to his future safety that he redeem himself and put his shattered reputation back on its pedestal of fear. There were no grins, for however much any of his acquaintances might have enjoyed his discomfiture they had no lessened respect for his ability with either six-guns or fists; and there was a restlessness in the crowd, for no man knew what was coming.

Fisher conveyed the collective opinion and broke the tension. "Any man would 'a' been fooled," he said to the head bartender, but loud enough for all to hear it. His voice indicated vexation at the success of so shabby a trick. "When he answered Thorpe I shore thought he was goin' prompt an' peaceful why, he even started! Nobody reckoned he was aimin' to make a gunplay. How could they? An' I'm sayin' that it's cussed lucky for him that Thorpe didn't!"

"Anybody can be fooled th' first time," replied the man of liquor. He looked over at the partition door and nodded. "Come over an' have a drink, Thorpe, an' forget it. I got money that says there ain't no man alive can beat you on th' draw. He tricked you, actin' that way."

"He's th' first man on earth ever shoved a gun into me like that," growled Thorpe, slowly moving forward. "An' he's th' last! Seein' as there's some here that mebby ain't shore about it, I'll show 'em that I was tricked!" He stopped in front of Bill Long and regarded that surprised individual with a look as malevolent as it was sincere. "Any squaw dog can tote two guns," he said, his still raging anger putting a keener edge to the words. "When he does he tells everybody that he's shore bad. If he ain't, that's his fault. I tote one an' yo're not goin' to swagger around these parts with any more than I got. Which one are you goin' to throw away?"

Bill blinked at him with owlish stupidity. "What you say?" he asked, as though doubting the reliability of his ears.

"Oh," sneered Thorpe, his rage climbing anew; "you didn't hear me th' first time, huh? Well, you want to be listenin' this time! I asked, which gun are you goin' to throw away, you card-skinnin' four-flush?"

"Why," faltered Bill, doing his very best to play the part he had chosen. "I I dunno I ain't goin' to to throw any of 'em away. What you mean?"

"Throw one away!" snapped Thorpe, his animal cunning telling him that the obeyance of the order might possibly be accepted by the crowd as grounds for justification, if any should be needed.

Bill changed subtly as he reflected that the crowd had excused Thorpe's humiliation because he had been tricked, and determined that no such excuse should be used again. He looked the enraged man in the eyes and a contemptuous smile crept around his thin lips. "Thorpe," he drawled, "if yo're lookin' for props to hold up yore reputation, you got th' wrong timber. Better look for a sick cow, or "

The crowd gasped as it realized that its friend's fingers were again relaxing from the butt of his half-drawn gun and that three pounds of steel, concentrated on the small circumference of the barrel of a six-gun had been jabbed into the pit of his stomach with such speed that they had not seen it, and with such force that the victim of the blow was sick, racked with pain and scarcely able to stand, momentarily paralyzed by the second assault on the abused stomach, which caved, quivered, and retched from the impact. Again he had failed, this time after cold, calm warning; again the astonished crowd froze in ridiculous postures, with ludicrous expressions graven on their faces, their automatic arms leaping skyward as they gaped stupidly, unbelievingly at the second gun. Before they could collect their numbed senses the master of the situation had backed swiftly against the wall near the front door, thereby blasting the budding hopes of the bartender, whose wits and power of movement, re turning at equal pace, were well ahead of those of his friends. It also saved the man of liquor from being dropped behind his own bar by the gun of the alert Mr. Thompson, who felt relieved when the crisis had passed without calling forth any effort on his part which would couple him with the capable Mr. Long.

"Climb that wall!" said Bill Long, his voice vibrating with the sudden outpouring of accumulated repression. "I'm lookin' for a chance to kill you, so I ain't askin' you to throw away no gun. This is between you an' me anybody takin' cards will drop cold. You got it comin', an' comin' fair. Climb that wall!"

Thorpe, gasping and agonized, fought off the sickness which had held him rigid and stared open-eyed, openmouthed at glinting ferocity in the narrowed eyes of the two-gun man.

"Climb that wall!" came the order, this time almost a whisper, but sharp and cutting as the edge of a knife, and there was a certainty in the voice and eyes which was not to be disregarded. Thorpe straightened up a little, turned slowly and slowly made his way through the opening crowd to the wall, and leaned against it. He had no thought of using the gun at his hip, no idea of resistance, for the spirit of the bully within him had been utterly crushed. He was a broken man, groping for bearings in the fog of the shifting readjustments going on in his soul.

"Climb!" said Bill Long's voice like the cracking of a bull- whacker's whip, and Thorpe mechanically obeyed, his finger-nails and boot toes scraping over the smooth boards in senseless effort. He had not yet had time to realize what he had lost, to feel the worthlessness which would be his to the end of his days.

The two-gun man nodded. "I told you boys I was a imitator," he said, smiling; "an' I am. I imitated him in his play to kill me. I imitated that SV foreman, an' now I'm imitatin' Thorpe again. It's his own idea, climbin' walls."

Fisher, watching the still-climbing Thorpe, was using his nimble wits for a way out of a situation which easily might turn into anything, from a joke to a sudden shambles. He now had no doubts about the real quality of Bill Long, and he secretly congratulated himself that he had not yielded to certain temptations he had felt. Besides, his arms were growing heavy and numb. There came to his mind the further thought that this two-gun, card-playing wizard would be a very good partner for a tour of the country, a tour which should be lucrative and safe enough to satisfy anyone.

"Huh," he laughed. "We're imitatin', too; only we're imitatin' ourselves, an' we're gettin' tired of holdin' 'em up. I'm sayin', fair an' square, that I ain't aimin' to draw no cards in any game that is two-handed. I reckon th' rest of th' boys feel th' same as I do. How 'bout it, boys?"

Affirmation came slowly or explosively, according to the individual natures, and the two-gun man was confident enough in his ability to judge character to accept the words. He slowly dropped his guns back in the holsters and smiled broadly. Even the lower class of men is capable of feeling a real liking, when it is based on audacious courage, for anyone who deserves it; and he knew that the now shifting crowd had been caught in the momentum of such a feeling. There was also another consideration to which more than one man present gave grave heed: They scarcely had quit marveling at the wizardy of one two-gun man when the second had appeared and made them marvel anew.

"All right, boys," he said. "Thorpe, you can quit climbin', seein' that you ain't gettin' nowhere. Come over here an' gimme that gun. I'm still imitatin'. This ain't been no lucky day for you, an' just to show you that you can make it unluckier," he said as he took the Colt, "I'm goin' to impress somethin' on yore mind." He threw the barrel up and carelessly emptied the weapon into the checkerboard partition with a rapidity which left nothing to be desired. The distance was nearly sixty feet. "Reckon you can cover 'em all with th' palm of one hand," he remarked as he shifted the empty gun to his left hand, where he thought it would fit better. He looked at it and turned it over. Three small dots, driven into the side of the frame, made him repress a smile. His own guns had two, while Red Thompson's lone Colt had four. He opened the flange and shoved the gun down behind the backstrap of his trousers, where a left-handed man often finds it convenient to carry a weapon, since the butt points that way. Letting his coat fall back into place he walked slowly to the door and out onto the street, the conversation in the room buzzing high after he left.

He next appeared in Quayle's, where he grinned at Idaho, Quayle, Johnny, and Ed Doane.

"I just made Thorpe climb th' wall," he said. "He looked like a pinned toad. Do you ever like to split up a pair of aces, Nelson?"

Johnny considered a moment and then slowly shook his head.

"Neither do I," replied the newcomer. His left hand went slowly around under his coat and brought out the captured Colt. "An' I ain't goin' to begin doin' it now. Here," and he handed the weapon to Johnny.

Johnny took it mechanically and then quickly turned it over and glanced at the frame. Weighing it judicially he looked up. "Th' feel an' balance of this Colt just suits me," he said. "Want to sell it?"

"I don't hardly own it enough to sell it," answered Bill; "but I reckon I can give it away, seein' that Thorpe set th' fashion. I'm warnin' you that he might want it back. But you should 'a' seen him a-climbin' that wall!" and he burst into laughter.

"I'll gamble," grinned Johnny. "I'll get you a new one for it."

"No, you won't," replied Bill, still laughing. "I got more'n th' value of a wore-out six-gun watchin' yore show up there. Besides, if it was better'n mine I would 'a' kept it myself. I ain't expectin' you'll be there, tonight," he finished.

"Suits me right here," replied Johnny. "Much obliged for th' gun." He looked at Idaho and grinned. "I aim to clean out this sage-hen at Californy Jack, tonight."

"Which same you might do," admitted Idaho, slowly looking at the Colt in his friend's hand; "for you shore are a fool for luck."

Chapter XI
A Job Well Done

Pecos Kane looked up at the sound of shooting and signaled for the doorkeeper. Getting no response he pulled another cord and waited impatiently for the man who answered it.

"What was that shooting, and who did it?" demanded the boss. He cut the wordy recital short. "Tell Bill Trask to assume Thorpe's duties and send Thorpe to me."

Thorpe soon appeared, slowly closed the door behind him and faced the boss, who studied him for a silent interval, the object of the keen scrutiny squirming at the close of it.

"You are no longer suited for my doortender," said Kane's hard voice. "Report to the dining-room, or kitchen, or leave the hotel entirely. But first find Corwin and send him to me. That is all."

Thorpe gulped and shuffled out and in a few minutes the sheriff appeared.

"Sit down, Corwin," said Kane, pleasantly. "Trask has Thorpe's job now. Wait a moment until I think something out," and he sat back in his chair, his eyes closing. In a few moments he opened them and leaned forward. "I have come to a decision regarding some strangers in this town. I have reason to believe that Long and Thompson know each other a great deal better than they pretend. I want to know more about Nelson, so you will send a good man up to his country to get me a report on him. Do it as soon as you leave me, and tell him to waste no time. That clear?"

Corwin nodded.

"Very well," continued the boss. "I want you to arrest both Long and Thompson before tomorrow, and throw them into jail. Since Long's exhibition today it will be well to go about it in a manner calculated to avoid bloodshed. There is no use of throwing men away by sending them against such gunplay. You are to arrest them without a shot being fired on either side. It is only a matter of figuring it out, and I will give you this much to start on: Whatever suspicions may have been aroused in their minds about their welcome here not being cordial must be removed. Because of that there should be no ill-advised speed in carrying out the arrests. They could be shot down from behind, but I want them alive; and it suits my purpose better if they are taken right here in this building. They are worth money, and a great deal more than money to me, to you, and to all of us. Twitchell and Carpenter are very powerful and they must be placated if it can be done in such a way as not to jeopardize us. I think it may be done in a way which will strengthen us. You follow me closely?"

The sheriff nodded again.

"All right," said Kane. "Now then, tell me where each of the three men, Nelson, Long, and Thompson, were on the occasions of the robbery of the bank and the death of Ridley. Think carefully."

Corwin gazed at the floor thoughtfully. "When th' bank was robbed Nelson was playin' cards with Idaho Norton in Quayle's saloon. Quayle an' Doane were in there with 'em. Long an' Thompson were here, upstairs, asleep."

"Very good, so far," commented Kane; "go on."

"When Ridley was shot Nelson was with Idaho Norton in Quayle's hotel, for both of them rustled into th' street an' carried him indoors. Thompson was in th' front room, here, an' Long come in soon after the shot was fired."

"Excellent. Which way did he come?"

"Through th' front door."

"Before that?" demanded the boss impatiently.

"I don't know."

"Why don't you?" blazed Kane. "Have I got to do all th' thinking for this crowd of dumb-heads?"

"Why, why should I know?" Corwin asked in surprise.

"If you don't know the answer to your own question it is only wasting my time to tell it to you. Now, listen: You are to send four men in to me but not Mexicans, for the testimony of Mexicans in this country is not taken any too seriously by juries. The four are not all to come the same way nor at the same time. The dumbheads I have around me necessitate that each be instructed separate and apart from the others, else they wouldn't know, or keep separate their own part. Is this plain?"

"Yes," answered the arm of the law.

"Very well. Now you will go out and arrange to arrest and jail those two men. And after you have arranged it you will do it. Not a shot is to be fired. When they are in jail report to me. That is all."

Corwin departed and did not scratch his head until the door closed after him, and then he showed great signs of perplexity. As he went up the next corridor he caught sight of a friend leaning against the back of the partition, and just beyond was Bill Trask at his new post. He beckoned to them both.

"Sandy, you are to report to th' boss, right away," ordered the sheriff. "He wants four white men, an' yo're near white. Trask, send in three more white men, one at a time, after Woods comes out. An' let me impress this on yore mind: It is strict orders that you ain't to fire a shot tonight, when somethin' happens that's goin' to happen; you, nor nobody else. Got that good?"

"What do you mean?" asked the sentry, grinning.

"Good G-d!" snorted the sheriff. "Do I have to do all th' thinkin' for this crowd of dumb-heads?"

"Yo're a parrot," retorted Trask. "I know that by heart. You don't have to. You don't even do yore own. You may go!"

Corwin grunted and joined the crowd in the big room and when Bill Long wandered in and settled down to watch a game the sheriff in due time found a seat at his side. His conversation was natural, not too steady and not too friendly and neither did he tarry too long, for when he thought that he had remained long enough he wandered up to the bar, joked with the chief dispenser, and mixed with the crowd. After awhile he went out and strolled over to the jail, where a dozen men were waiting for him. His lecture to them was painfully simple, in the simplest words of his simple vocabulary, and when he at last returned to the gambling-hall he was certain that his pupils were letter-perfect.

Meanwhile Kane had been busy and when the first of the four appeared the clear-thinking boss drove straight to his point. He looked intently at the caller and asked: "Where were you on the night of the storm, at the time the bank was robbed?"

"Upstairs playin' cards with Harry."

"Do you know where Long and Thompson were at that time?"

"Shore; they was upstairs."

"I am going to surprise you," said Kane, smiling, and he did, for he told his listener where he had been on that night, what he had seen, and what he had found in the morning in front of the door of Bill Long's door. He did it so well that the listener began to believe that it was so, and said as much.

"That's just what you must believe," exclaimed Kane. "Go over it again and again. Picture it, with natural details, over and over again. Live every minute, every step of it. If you forget anything about it come to me and I'll refresh your memory. I'll do so anyway, when the time comes. You may go."

The second and third man came, learned their lessons and departed. The fourth, a grade higher in intelligence, was given a more difficult task and before he was dismissed Kane went to a safe, took out a bundle of large bills and handed two of them to his visitor, who nodded, pocketed them and departed. He was to plant them, find them again and return them so that the latter part of the operation would be clear in his memory.

Supper was over and the big room crowded. Jokes and laughter sounded over the quiet curses of the losers. Bill Long, straddling a chair, with his arms crossed on its back, watched a game and exchanged banter with the players during the deals. Red Thompson, playing in an other game not far away, was winning slowly but consistently. Somebody started a night-herding song and others joined in, making the ceiling ring. Busy bartenders were endeavoring to supply the demand. The song roared through the first verse and the second, and in the middle of the following chorus, at the first word of the second line there was a sudden, concerted movement, and chaos reigned.

Unexpectedly attacked by half a dozen men each Bill and Red fought valiantly but vainly. In Bill's group two men had been told off to go for his guns, one to each weapon, and they had dived head-first at the signal. Red's single gun had been obtained in the same way. Stamping feet, curses, grunts, groans, the soft sound of fist on flesh, the scraping of squirming masses of men going this way and that, the heavy breathing and other sounds of conflict filled the dusty, smoky air. Chairs crashed, tables toppled and were wrecked by the surging groups and then, suddenly, the turmoil ceased and the two bound, battered, and exhausted men swayed dizzily in the hands of their captors, their chests rising and falling convulsively beneath their ragged shirts as they gulped the foul air.

Two men rocked on the floor, slobbering over cracked shins, another lay face down across the wreck of a chair, his gory face torn from mouth to cheekbone; another held a limp and dangling arm, cursing with monotonous regularity; a fifth, blood pouring from his torn scalp and blinding him, groped aimlessly around the room.

Corwin glanced around, shook his head and looked at his two prisoners in frank admiration. "You fellers shore can lick h--l out of th' man that invented fightin'!"

Bill Long glared at him. "I didn't see you no where near!" he panted. "Turn us loose an' we'll dean out th' place. We was two-thirds licked before we -knew it was comin'."

"Don't waste yore breath" snarled Red. "There's a few I'm aimin' to kill when I get th' chance!"

"What's th' meanin' of this surprise party?" asked Bill Long.

"It means that you an' Thompson are under arrest for robbin' th' bank; an' you for th' murder of Ridley," answered the peace officer, frowning at the ripple of laughter which arose. A pock-marked Mexican, whose forehead bore a crescent-shaped scar, seemed to be unduly hilarious and vastly relieved about something.

Thorpe came swiftly across the room toward Bill Long, snarled a curse, and struck with vicious energy at the bruised face. Bill rolled his head and the blow missed. Before the assailant could recover his balance and strike again a brawny, red-haired giant, whose one good eye glared over a battered nose, lunged swiftly forward and knocked Thorpe backwards over a smashed chair and overturned table. The prostrate man groped and half arose, to look dazedly into the giant's gun and hear the holder of it give angry warning.

"Any more of that an' I'll blow you apart!" roared the giant. "An' that goes for any other skunk in th' room. Bear-baitin' is barred." He looked at Corwin. "You've got 'em now get 'em out of here an' into jail, before I has to kill somebody!"

Corwin called to his men and with the prisoners in the middle the little procession started for the old adobe jail on the next street, the pleased sheriff bringing up the rear, his Colt swinging in his hand. When the prisoners had been locked up behind its thick walls he sighed with relief, posted two guards, front and rear, and went back to report to Kane that a good job had been well done.

The boss nodded and bestowed one of his rare compliments. "That was well handled, Sheriff," he said. "I am sorry your work is not yet finished. A zealous peace officer like you should be proud enough of such a capture as to be anxious to inform those most interested. Also," he smiled, "you naturally would be anxious to put in a claim for the reward. Therefore you should go right down to McCullough and lay the entire matter before him, as I shall now instruct you," and the instructions were as brief as thoroughness would allow. "Is that clear?" asked the boss at the end of the lesson.

"It ain't only clear," enthused Corwin; "but it's giltedged; I'm on my way, now!"

"Report to me before morning," said Kane.

Hurrying from the room and the building the sheriff saddled his horse and rode briskly down the trail. Not far from town he began to whistle and he kept it up purposely as a notification of peaceful and honorable intentions, until the sharp challenge of a hidden sentry checked both it and his horse.

"Sheriff Corwin," he answered. "What you holdin' me up for?"

A man stepped out of the cover at the edge of the trail. "Got a match?" he pleasantly asked, the rifle hanging from the crook of his arm, both himself and the weapon hidden from the sheriff by the darkness. "Where you goin' so late? Thought everybody was asleep but me."

Corwin handed him the match. "Just ridin' down to see McCullough. Got important business with him, an' reckoned it shouldn't wait 'til mornin'."

The sentry rolled a cigarette and lit it with the borrowed match in such a way that the sheriff's face was well lighted for the moment, but he did not look up. "That's good," he said. "Reckon I'll go along with you. No use hangin' 'round up here, an' I'm shore sleepy. Wait till I get my cayuse," and he disappeared, soon returning in the saddle. His quiet friend in the brush settled back to resume the watch and to speculate on how long it would take his companion to return.

McCullough, half undressed, balanced himself as he heard approaching voices, growled profanely and put the freed leg in the trousers. He was ready for company when one of the night shift stuck his head in at the door.

"Sheriff Corwin wants to see you," said the puncher. "His business is so delicate it might die before mornin'."

"All right," grumbled the trail-boss. "If you get out of his way mebby he can come in."

Corwin stood in the vacated door, smiling, but too wise to offer his hand to the blunt, grim host. "Got good news," he said, "for you, me, an' th' T & C."

"Ya-as?" drawled McCullough, peering out beneath his bushy, gray eyebrows. "Pecos Kane shoot hisself?"

"We got th' fellers that robbed th' bank an' shot Ridley," said the sheriff.

"The h--l you say!" exclaimed McCullough. "Come in an' set down. Who are they? How'd you get 'em?"

"That reward stick?" asked Corwin anxiously.

"Tighter'n a tick to a cow!" emphatically replied the trail-boss. "Who are they?"

"I got a piece of paper here," said the sheriff, proving his words. He stepped inside and placed it on the table. "Read it over an' sign it. Then I'll fill in th' blanks with th' names of th' men. If they're guilty, I'm protected; if I've made a mistake, then there's no harm done."

McCullough slowly read it aloud:

"'Sheriff Corwin was the first man to tell me that and robbed the Mesqtiite bank, and that killed Tom Ridley. He will produce the prisoners, with the witnesses and other proof in Sandy Bend upon demand. If they are found guilty of the crime named the rewards belong to him.'"

The trail-boss considered it thoughtfully. "It looks fair; but there's one thing I don't like, Sheriff," he said, putting his finger on the objectionable words and looking up. "I don't like 'Sandy Bend.' I'm takin' no chances with them fellers. I'll just scratch that out, an' write in, 'to me' How 'bout it?"

"They've got to have a fair trial," replied Corwin. "I'm standin' for no lynchin'. I can't do it."

"Yo're shore right they're goin' to have a fair trial!" retorted the trail-boss. "Twitchell ain't just lookin' for two men he wants th' ones that robbed th' bank an' killed Ridley. You don't suppose he's payin' five thousan' out of his pocket for somebody that ain't guilty, do you? Why, they're goin' to have such a fair trial that you'll need all th' evidence you can get to convict 'em. Lynch 'em?" He laughed sarcastically. "They won't even be jailed in Sandy Bend, where they shore would be lynched. You take 'em to Sandy Bend an' you'll be lynched out of yore reward. You know how it reads."

Corwin scratched his head and a slow grin spread over his face. "Cuss it, I never saw it that way," he admitted. "I guess yo're shoutin' gospel, Mac; but, cuss it, it ain't reg'lar." "

"You know me; an' I know you," replied the trail-boss, smiling. "There's lots of little things done that ain't exactly reg'lar; but they're plumb sensible. Suppose I change this here paper like I said, an' sign it. Then you write in th' names an' let me read 'em. Then you let me know what proof you got, an' bring down th' prisoners, an' I'll sign a receipt for 'em."

"Yes!" exclaimed Corwin. "I'll deputize you, an' give 'em into yore custody, with orders to take 'em to Sandy Bend, or any other jail which you think best. That makes it more reg'lar, don't it?" he smiled.

McCullough laughed heartily and slapped his thigh. "That's shore more reg'lar. I'm beginnin' to learn why, they elected you sheriff. All right, then; I'm signin' my name." He took pen and ink from a shelf, made the change in the paper, sprawled his heavy-handed signature across the bottom and handed the pen to Corwin. "Now, d--n it: Who are they?"

The sheriff carefully filled in the three blanks, McCullough peering over his shoulder and noticing that the form had been made out by another hand.

"There," said Corwin. "I'm spendin' that five thou sand right now."

"'Bill Long' 'Red Thompson' 'Bill Long' again," growled the trail-boss. "Never heard of 'em. Live around here?"

Corwin shook his head. "No."

"All right," grunted McCullough. "Now, then; what proof you got? You'll never spend a cent of it if you ain't got 'em cold."

Corwin sat on the edge of the table, handed a cigar to his host and lit his own. "I got a man who was in th' north stable, behind Kane's, when th' shot that killed Ridley was fired from th' other stable. He was feedin' his hoss an' looked out through a crack, seem' Long sneak out of th' other buildin', Sharp's in hand, an' rustle for cover around to th' gamblin'-hall. Another man was standin' in th' kitchen, gazin' out of th' winder, an' saw Long turn th' corner of th' north stable an' dash for th' hotel buildin'. He says he laughed because Long's slight limp made him sort of bob sideways. An' we know why Long done it, but we're holdin' that back. That's for th' killin'.

"Now for th' robbery: I got th' man that saw Long an' Thompson sneak out of th' front door of th' dinin'room hall into that roarin' sand storm between eleven an' twelve o'clock on th' night of th' robbery. He says he remembers it plain because he was plumb surprised to see sane men do a fool thing like that. He didn't say nothin' to 'em because if they wanted to commit suicide it was their own business. Besides, they was strangers to him. After awhile he went up to bed, but couldn't sleep because of th' storm makin' such a racket. Kane's upstairs rocked a little that night. I know, because I was up there, tryin' to sleep."

"Go on," said the trail-boss, eagerly and impatiently, his squinting eyes not leaving the sheriff's face.

"Well, quite some time later he heard th' door next to his'n open cautious, but a draft caught it an' slammed it shut. Then Bill Long's voice said, angry an' sharp: 'What th' hell you doin', Red? Tellin' creation about it?' In th' mornin', th' cook, who gets up ahead of every body else, of course, was goin' along th' hall toward th' stairs an' he kicks somethin' close to Long's door. It rustles an' he gropes for it, curious-like, an' took it down stairs with him for a look at it, where it wasn't so dark. It was a strip of paper that th' bank puts around packages of bills, an' there was some figgers on it. He chucks it in a corner, where it fell down behind some stuff that had been there a long time, an' don't think no more about it till he hears about th' bank bein' robbed. Then he fishes it out an' brings it to me. I knowed what it was, first glance."

"Any more?" urged McCullough. "It's good; but, you got any more?"

"I shore have. What you think I'm sheriff for? I got two of th' bills, an' their numbers tally with th' bank's numbers of th' missin' money. You can compare 'em with yore own list later. I sent a deputy to their rooms as soon as I had 'em in jail, an' he found th' bills sewed up in their saddle pads. Reckon they was keepin' one apiece in case they needed money quick. An' when th' sand was swept off th' step in front of that hall door, a gold piece was picked up out of it."

"When were you told about all this by these fellers?" demanded the trail-boss.

"As soon as th' robbery was known, an' as soon as th' shootin' of Ridley was known!"

"When did you arrest them?"

"Last night; an' it was shore one big job. They can fight like a passel of cougars. Don't take no chances with 'em, Mac."

"Why did you wait till last night?" demanded McCullough. "Wasn't you scared they'd get away?"

"No. I had 'em trailed every place they went. They wasn't either of 'em out of our sight for a minute; an' when they slept there was men watchin' th' stairs an' their winders. You see, Kane lost a lot of money in that robbery, bein' a director; an' I was hopin' they'd try to sneak off to where they cached it an' give us a chance to locate it. They was too wise. I got more witnesses, too; but they're Greasers, an' I ain't puttin' no stock in 'em. A Greaser'd lie his own mother into her grave for ten dollars; anyhow, most juries down here think so, so it's all th' same."

"Yes; lyin' for pay is shore a Greaser trick," said McCullough, nodding. "Well, I reckon it's only a case of waitin' for th' reward, Sheriff. Tell you what I wish you'd do: Gimme everythin' they own when you send 'em down to me, or when I come up for 'em, whichever suits you best. Everythin' has got to be collected now before it gets lost, an' it's got to be ready for court in case it's needed."

"All right; I'll get back what I can use, after th' trial," replied Corwin. "I'll throw their saddles on their cayuses, an' let 'em ride 'em down. How soon do you want 'em? Right away?"

"First thing in th' mornin'!" snapped McCullough. "Th' sooner th' better. I'll send up some of th' boys to give you a hand with 'em, or I'll take 'em off yore hands entirely at th' jail. Which suits you?"

"Send up a couple of yore men, if you want to. It'll look better in town if I deliver 'em to you here. Why, you ain't smoked yore cigar!"

McCullough looked at him and then at his own hand, staring at the crushed mass of tobacco in it. "Shucks!" he grunted, apologetically, and forthwith lied a little him self. "Funny how a man forgets when he's excited. I bet that cigar thought it was in a vise my hand's tired from squeezin'."

"Sorry I ain't got another, Mac," said Corwin, grinning, as he paused in the door. "I'll be lookin' for yore boys early. Adios."

"Adios," replied McCullough from the door, listening to the dying hoof beats going rapidly toward town. Then he shut the door, hurled the remains of the cigar on the floor and stepped on them. "He's got 'em, huh? An' strangers, too! He's got 'em too d——d pat for me. It takes a good man to plaster a lie on me an' make it stick an' he ain't no good, at all. He was sweatin' before he got through!" Again the trousers came off, all the way this time, and the lamp was turned down. As he settled into his bunk he growled again. "Well, I'll have a look at 'em, anyhow, an' send 'em down for Twitchell to look at," and in another moment he was asleep.

Chapter XII
Friends on the Outside

While events were working out smoothly for the arrest of the two men in Kane's gambling-hall, four friends were passing a quiet evening in Quayle's barroom, but the quiet was not to endure.

With lagging interest in the game Idaho picked up his cards, ruffled them and listened. "Reckon that's singin'," he said in response to the noise floating down from the gambling-hall. "Sounds more like a bunch of cows bawlin' for their calves. Kane's comin' to life later'n usual. Wonder if Thorpe's joinin' in?" he asked, and burst out laughing. "Next to our hard-workin' sheriff there ain't nobody in town that I'd rather see eat dirt than him. Wish I could 'a' seen him a-climbin' that wall!"

"Anybody that works for Kane eats dirt," commented Quayle. "They has to. He'll learn how to eat it, too, th' blackguard."

"There goes somethin'" said Ed Doane as the distant roaring ceased abruptly. "Reckon Thorpe's makin' an other try at th' wall." He laughed softly. "They're startin' a fandango, by th' sound of it."

"'Tis nothin' to th' noise av a good Irish reel," deprecated the proprietor.

"I'm claimin' low this hand," grunted Idaho. "Look out for yore jack."

Johnny smiled, played and soon a new deal was begun.

"Th' dance is over, too," said Doane, mopping off the bar for the third time in ten minutes. "Must 'a' been a short one."

"Some of them hombres will dance shorter than that, an' harder," grunted Idaho, "th' next time they pay its a visit. They didn't get many head th' last time, an' I'm sayin' they'll get none at all th' next time. Where they take 'em to is more'n we can guess: th' tracks just die. Not bein' able to track 'em, we're aimin' to stop it at th' beginnin'. You fellers wait, an' you'll see."

Quayle grunted expressively. "I been waitin' too long now. Wonder why nobody ever set fire to Kane's. 'Twould be a fine sight."

"You'll mebby see that, too, one of these nights," growled the puncher.

"Then pick out wan when th' wind is blowin' up th' street," chuckled Quayle. "This buildin' is so dry it itches to burn. I'm surprised it ain't happened long ago, with that Mick in th' kitchen raisin' th' divvil with th' stove. If I didn't have a place av me own I'd be tempted to do it meself."

The bartender laughed shortly. "If McCullough hap pens to think of it I reckon it'll be done." He shook out the bar cloth and bunched it again. "Funny he ain't cut loose yet. That ain't like him, at all."

"Waitin' for th' rewards to start workin', I reckon," said Johnny.

Idaho scraped up the cards, shaped them into a sheersided deck and pushed it aside. "I'm tired of this game; it's too even. Reckon I'll go up an' take a look at Kane's." He arose and sauntered out, paused, and looked up the street. "Cussed if they ain't havin' a pe-rade," he called. "This ain't th' Fourth of July, is it? I'm goin' up an' sidle around for a closer look. Be back soon."

Johnny was vaguely perturbed. The sudden cessation of the song bothered him, and the uproar which instantly followed it only served to increase his uneasiness. Ordinarily he would not have been affected, but the day's events might have led to almost anything. Had a shot been fired he swiftly would have investigated, but the lack of all shooting quieted his unfounded suspicions. Idaho's remark about the parade renewed them and after a short, silent argument with himself he arose, went to the door and looked up the street, seeing the faint, yellow patch on the sand where Kane's lamps shown through the open door and struggled against the surrounding darkness, and hearing the faint rumble of voices above which rang out frequent laughter. He grimly told himself that there would be no laughter in Kane's if his two friends had come to any harm, and there would have been plenty of shooting.

"Anythin' to see?" asked Quayle, poking his head out of the door.

"No," answered Johnny, turning to reenter the building. "Just feelin' their oats, I reckon."

"'Tis feelin' their ropes they should be doin'," replied Quayle, stepping back to let his guest pass through. "An' 'twould be fine humor to swing 'em from their own. Hist!" he warned, listening to the immoderate laughter which came rapidly nearer. "Here's Idaho; he'll know it all."

Idaho popped in and in joyous abandon threw his sombrero against the ceiling. "Funniest thing you ever heard!" he panted. "Corwin's arrested that Bill Long an' Red Thompson. Took a full dozen to do it, an' half of 'em are cripples now. Th' pe-rade I saw was Corwin an' a bunch escortin' 'em over to th' jail. Ain't we got a rip-snortin' fool for a sheriff?" His levity died swiftly, to give way to slowly rising anger. "With this country fair crowded with crooks he can't find nobody to throw in jail except two friendless strangers! D n his hide, I got a notion to pry 'em out and turn 'em loose before mornin', just to make things right, an' take some of th' swellin' out of his flat head. It's a cussed shame."

The low-pulled brim of Johnny's sombrero hid the glint in his eyes and the narrowed lids. He relaxed and sat carelessly on the edge of a table, one leg swinging easily to and fro as conjecture after conjecture rioted through his mind.

"They must 'a' stepped on Kane's toes," said Ed, vigorously wiping off the backbar.

Idaho scooped up his hat and flung it on the table at Johnny's side. "You'd never guess it, Ed. Even th' rest of th' gang was laughin' about it, all but th' cripples. I been waitin' for them rewards to start workin,' but I never reckoned they'd work out like this. Long an' Thompson are holdin' th' sack. They're scapegoats for th' whole cussed gang. Corwin took 'em in for robbin' th' bank, an' gettin' Ridley!"

Ed Doane dropped the bar cloth and stared at the speaker and a red tide crept slowly up his throat and spread across his face. Johnny slid from the table and disappeared in the direction of his room. He came down again with the two extra Colts in his hands, slipped through the kitchen and ran toward the jail. Quayle's mouth slowly closed and then let out an explosive curse. The bartender brought his fist down on the bar with a smash.

"Scapegoats? Yo're right! It's a cold deck an' you bet Kane never would 'a' dealt from it if he wasn't dead shore he could make th' play stick. Every man in th' pack will swear accordin' to orders, an' who can swear th' other way? It'll be a strange jury, down in Sandy Bend, every man jack of it a friend of Ridley an' th' T & C. Well, I'm a peaceable man, but this is too much. I never saw them fellers before in my life; but on th' day when Corwin starts south with 'em I'll be peaceable no longer an' I've got friends! There's no tellin' who'll be next if he makes this stick. Who's with me?"

"/ am," said Quayle; "an' *I* got friends."

"Me, too," cried Idaho. "There's a dozen hickory knots out on th' ranch that hate Corwin near as much as I do. They'll be with us, mebby even Lukins, hisself. Hey! Where'd Nelson go?" he excitedly demanded. "Mebby he's out playin' a lone hand!" and he darted for the kitchen.

Johnny, hidden in the darkness not far from the jail, was waiting. The escort, judging from the talk and the glowing ends of cigarettes, was bunched near the front of the building, little dreaming how close they stood to a man who held four Colts and was fighting down a rage which urged their use. At last, thoroughly master of itself, Johnny's mind turned to craftiness rather than to blind action and formulated a sketchy plan. But while the plan was being carried through he would not allow his two old friends to be entirely helpless. Slipping off his boots he crept up behind the jail and with his kerchief lowered the two extra guns through the window, softly calling attention to them, which redoubled the prisoners' efforts to untie each other. Satisfied now that they were in no immediate danger he slipped back to his boots, put them on and waited to see what would happen, and to listen further.

"There ain't no use watchin' th' jail," said a voice, louder than the rest. "They're tied up proper, an' nobody ever got out of it before."

"Just th' same, you an' Harry will watch it," said Corwin. "Winder an' door. I ain't takin' no chances with this pair."

A thickening on the dark ground moved forward slowly and a low voice called Johnny's name. He replied cautiously and soon Idaho crawled to his side, whispering questions.

"Go back where there ain't no chance of anybody hearin' us, or stumblin' over us," said Johnny. "When that gang leaves there won't be so much noise, an' then they may hear us."

At last reaching an old wagon they stood up and leaned against it, and Johnny unburdened his heart to a man he knew he could trust.

"Idaho," he said, quietly, "them fellers are th' best friends I ever had. They cussed near raised me, an' they risked their lives more'n once to save mine. 'Most everythin' I know I got from them, an' they ain't goin' to stay in that mud hut till mornin', not if I die for it. They come down here to help me, an' I'm goin' to get 'em out. Did you ever hear of th' old Bar-20, over in th' Pecos Valley?"

"I shore did," answered Idaho. "Why?"

"I was near raised on it Bill Long is Hopalong Cassidy, an' Red Thompson is Red Connors, th' whitest men that ever set a saddle. Rob a bank, an' shoot a man from behind! Did Bill Long act like a man that had to shoot in th' back when he made Thorpe climb his own wall, with his own crowd lookin' on? Most of their lives has been spent fightin' Kane's kind; an' no breed of pups can hold 'em while I'm drawin' my breath. It's only how to do it th' best way that's botherin' me. I've slipped 'em a pair of guns, so I got a little time to think. Why, cuss it: Hoppy knows th' skunk that got Ridley! An' before we're through we'll know who robbed th' bank, an' hand 'em over to Mac. That's what's keepin' th' three of us here!"

"Bless my gran'mother's old gray cat!" breathed Idaho. "No wonder they pulled th' string! I'm sayin' Kane's got hard ridin' ahead. Say, can I tell th' boys at th' ranch?"

"Tell 'em nothin' that you wouldn't know except for me tellin' you," replied Johnny. "I know they're good boys; but they might let it slip. Me an' Hoppy an' Red are aimin' for them rewards an' we're goin' to get 'em both."

"It's a plumb lovely night," muttered Idaho. "Nicest night I think I ever saw. I don't want no rewards, but I just got to get my itchin' paws into what's goin' on around this town. An' it's a lovely town. Nicest town I think I ever was in. That 'dobe shack ain't what it once was. I know, because, not bein' friendly with th' sheriff, an' not bein' able to look all directions at once, I figgered I might be in it, myself, some day. So I've looked it over good, inside an' out. Th' walls are crumbly, an' th' bars in th' window are old. There's a waggin tongue in Pete Jarvis' freight waggin that's near twelve foot long, an' a-plenty thick. Ash, I think it is; that or oak. Either's good enough. If it was shoved between th' bars an' then pushed sideways that jail wouldn't be a jail no more. If Pete ain't taken th' waggin to bed with him, bein' so proud of it, we can crack that little hazelnut. I'm goin' back an' see how many are still hangin' around."

"I'm goin' back to th' hotel, so I'll be seen there," said Johnny.

"I'll do th' same, later," replied his friend as they separated.

Quayle was getting rid of some of his accumulated anger, which reflection had caused to soar up near the danger point. "Tom Ridley wasn't killed by no strangers!" he growled, banging the table with his fist. "I can name th' man that done it by callin' th' roll av Kane's litter; an' I'll be namin' th' bank robbers in th' same breath." He looked around as Johnny entered the room. "An' what did ye find, lad?"

"Idaho was right. They've got 'em in th' jail."

"An' if I was as young a man as you," said the proprietor, "they wouldn't kape 'em there. As ut is I'm timpted to go up an' bust in th' dommed door, before th' sheriff comes back from his ride. Tom Ridley's murderer? Bah!"

"Back from his ride?" questioned Johnny, quickly and eagerly.

"Shure. He just wint down th' trail. Tellin' Mac, I don't doubt that he's got th' men Twitchell wants. I was lookin' around when he wint past. This is th' time, lad. I'll help ye by settin' fire to Red Frank's corral if th' jail's watched. It'll take their attention. Or I'll lug me rifle up an' cover ye while ye work." He arose and went into the office for the weapon, Johnny following him. "There she is full to th' ind. An' I know her purty ways."

"Tim," said Johnny's low voice over his shoulder. "Yo're white, clean through. I don't need yore help, anyhow, not right now. An' because you are white I'm goin' to tell you somethin' that'll please you, an' give me one more good friend in this rotten town. Bill Long an' Red Thompson are friends of mine. They did not rob th' bank, nor shoot Ridley; but Bill knows who did shoot Ridley. He saw him climbin' out of Kane's south stable while th' smoke was still comin' from th' gun that shot yore friend. I can put my hand on th' coyote in five minutes. Th' three of us are stayin' here to get that man, th' man who robbed th' bank, an' Pecos Kane. I'm tellin' you this because I may need a good friend in Mesquite before we're through."

Quayle had wheeled and gripped his shoulder with convulsive force. "Ah!" he breathed. "Come on, lad; point him out! Point him out for Tim Quayle, like th' good lad ye are!"

"Do you want him so bad that yo're willin' to let th' real killer get away?" asked Johnny. "You only have to wait an' we'll get both."

"What d'ye mean?"

"You don't believe he shot Ridley without bein' told to do it, do you?"

"Kane told him; I know it as plain as I know my name."

"Knowin' ain't provin' it, an' provin' it is what we got to do."

"Tis th' curse av th' Irish, jumpin' first an' thinkin' after," growled Quayle. "Go wan!"

"Yo're friends with McCullough," said Johnny. "Mac knows a little; an' I'm near certain he's heard of Hopalong Cassidy an' Red Connors, of th' Bar-20. Don't forget th' names: Hopalong Cassidy an' Red Connors, of th' old Bar-20 in th' Pecos Valley. Buck Peters was foreman. I want you to go down an' pay him a friendly visit, and tell him this," and Quayle listened intently to the message.

"Bye," chuckled the proprietor, "ye leave Mac to me. We been friends for years, an' Tom Ridley was th' friend of us both. But, lad, ye may die; an' Bill Long may die life is uncertain anny where, an' more so in Mesquite, these days. If yer a friend av Tim Quayle, slip me th' name av th' man that murdered Ridley. I promise ye to kape han's off an' I want no reward. But it fair sickens me to think his name may be lost. Tom was like a brother."

"If you knew th' man you couldn't hold back," replied Johnny. "Here: I'll tell Idaho, an' Ed Doane. If Bill an' I go under they'll give you his description. I don't know his name."

"Th' offer is a good wan; but Tim Quayle never broke his word to anny man an' there's nothin' on earth or in hiven I want so much as to know who murdered Tom Ridley. I pass ye my word with th' sign av th' cross, on th' witness of th' Holy Virgin, an' on th' mem'ry av Tom Ridley I'll stay me hand accordin' to me promise."

Johnny looked deeply into the faded blue eyes through the tears which filmed them. He gripped the proprietor's hand and leaned closer. "A Greaser with a pock-marked face, an' a crescent-shaped scar over his right eye. He is about my height an' drags one foot slightly when he walks."

"Aye, from th' ball an' chain!" muttered Quayle. "I know th' scut! Thank ye, lad: I can sleep better nights. An' I can wait as no Irishman ever waited before. Annythin' Tim Quayle has is yourn; yourn an' yore friends. I'll see Mac tomorrow. Good night." He cuddled the rifle and went toward the stairs, but as he put his foot on the first step he stopped, turned, and went to a chair in a corner. "I'm forgettin'," he said, simply. "Ye may need me," and he leaned back against the wall, closing his eyes, an expression of peace on his wrinkled face.

Chapter XIII

Idaho slipped out of the darkness of the kitchen and appeared in the door. "All right, Nelson," he called. "There's two on guard an' th' rest have left. They ain't takin' their job any too serious, neither. Just one apiece," "he chuckled.

Johnny looked at the proprietor. "Got any rope, Tim?" he asked.

"Plenty," answered Quayle, arising hastily and leading the way toward the kitchen. Supplying their need he stood in the door and peered into the darkness after them. "Good luck, byes," he muttered.

Pete Jarvis was proud of his new sixteen-foot freighter and he must have turned in his sleep when two figures, masked to the eyes by handkerchiefs, stole into his yard and went off with the heavy wagon tongue. They carried it up to the old wagon near the jail, where they put it down, removed their boots, and went on without it, reaching the rear wall of the jail without incident, where they crouched, one at each corner, and smiled at the conversation going on.

"I'm hopin' for a look at yore faces," said Red's voice, "to see what they looked like before I get through with 'em, if I ever get my chance. Come in, an' be sociable."

"Yo're doin' a lot of talkin' now, you red-headed coyote," came the jeering reply. "But how are you goin' to talk to th' judge?"

"Bring some clean straw in th' mornin'," said Bill Long, "or we'll bust yore necks. Manure's all right for Greasers, an' you, but we're white men. Hear me chirp, you mangy pups?"

"It's good enough for you!" snapped a guard. "I was goin' to get you some, but now you can rot, for all I care!"

Johnny backed under the window, raised up and pressed his face against the rusty bars. "It's th' Kid," he whispered. "Are you untied yet?"

The soft answer pleased him and he went back to his corner of the wall, where he grudged every passing minute. He had decided to wait no longer, but to risk the noise of a shot if the unsuspecting guards could get a gun out quickly enough, and he was about to tell Idaho of the change in the plans when the words of a guard checked him.

"Guess I'll walk around again," said one of them, arising slowly. "Gettin' cramped, an' sleepy, settin' here."

"You spit in that window again an' I'll bust yore neck!" said Red's angry voice, whereupon Johnny found a new pleasure in doing his duty.

"You ain't bustin' nobody, or nothin'," jeered the guard, "'less it's th' rope yo're goin' to drop on." He yawned and stretched and sauntered along the side of the building, turned the corner and then raised his hands with a jerk as a Colt pushed into his stomach and a hard voice whispered terse instructions, which he instantly obeyed. "You fellers ain't so bad, at that," he said, with only a slight change in his voice; "but yo're shore playin' in hard luck."

"Keep yore sympathy to yoreself!" angrily retorted Bill Long.

Idaho, having unbuckled the gun-belt and laid it gently on the ground, swiftly pulled the victim's arms down be hind his back and tied the crossed wrists. Johnny now got busy with ropes for his feet, and a gag, and they soon laid him close to the base of the wall, and crept toward the front of the building, one to each wall. Johnny tensed himself as Idaho sauntered around the other corner.

"Makin' up with 'em?" asked the guard, ironically. "You don't want to let 'em throw a scare into you. They'll never harm nobody no more." He lazily arose to stretch his legs on a turn around the building. "You listen to what I'm goin' to tell 'em," he said. Then he squawked and went down with Johnny on his back, Idaho's dive coming a second later. A blow on his head caused him to lose any impertinent interest which he might have had in subsequent events and soon he, too, lay along the base of the rear wall, bound, gagged, and helpless.

"I near could feel th' jar of that in here," said Red's cheerful voice. "I'm hopin' it was th' coyote that spit through th' window. What's next?" he asked, on his feet and pulling at bars. He received no answer and commented upon that fact frankly and profusely.

"Shut yore face," growled Bill, working at his side. "He's hatchin' somethin' under his hat."

"Somethin' hatchin' all over me," grunted Red, stirring restlessly. "I'm a heap surprised this old mud hut ain't walkin' off some'ers."

Bill squirmed. ",You ain't got no call to put on no airs," he retorted. "Mine's been hatched a long time. I wouldn't let a dog lay on straw as rotten as that stuff. Oh!" he gloated. "Somebody's shore goin' to pay for this little party!"

"Wish th' sheriff would open that outside door about now," chuckled Red, balancing his six-chambered gift "I'd make him pop-eyed."

Hurrying feet, booted now, came rapidly nearer and soon the square-cornered end of a seasoned wagon tongue scraped on the adobe window ledge. Bill Long grabbed it and drew it between two of the bars.

"Go toward th' south," he said. "That's th' boy! Listen to 'em scrape!" he exulted. "Go ahead she's startin'. I can feel th' 'dobe crackin' between th' bars. Come back an' take th' next you'll have a little better swing because it's further from th' edge of th' window. Go ahead! It's bendin' an' pullin' out at both ends. Go on! Whoop! There goes th' 'dobe. Come back to th' middle an' use that pry as a batterin'-ram on this bar. Steady; we'll do th' guidin'. All ready? Then let her go! Fine! Try again. That's th' stuff she's gone! Take th' next Ready? Let her go! There goes more 'dobe, on this side. Once more: Ready? Let her go! Good enough: Here we come."

"Wait," said Johnny. "We'll pass one of these fellers in to you. If we leave 'em both together they'll mebby roll together an' untie each other."

"Like we did," chuckled Red.

"Give us th' first one you got," said Bill. "He's th' one that spit through th' window. I want him to lay on this straw, too. He's tied, an' can't scratch."

The guard was raised to the window, pushed and pulled through it and carelessly dumped on Red's bed, after which it did not take long for the two prisoners to gain their freedom.

"Good Kid!" said Bill, gripping his friend's hand. "An' you, too, whoever you are!"

"Don't mention no names," whispered Idaho. "We couldn't find no ear plugs," he chuckled, shaking hands with Red. "I'm too well known in this town. What'll we do with this coyote? Let him lay here?"

"No," answered Johnny. "He might roll over to Red Frank's an' get help. Picket him to a bush or cactus. Here, gimme a hand with him. I reckon he's come to, by th' way he's bracin' hisself. Little faster time's flyin'. All right, put him down." Johnny busied himself with the last piece of rope and stood up. "Come on Kane's stables, next."

As they crossed the street above the gambling-house, where in reality it was a trail, Bill Long took a hand in the evening's plans.

"Red," he said, "you go an' get our cayuses. Bring 'em right here, where we are now, an' wait for us. Idaho, you an' Johnny come with me an' stand under th' window of my room to take th' things I let down, an' free th' rope from 'em. I'm cussed shore we ain't goin' to leave all of our traps behind, not unless they been stole."

"I like yore cussed nerve!" chuckled Idaho. "Don't blame you, though. I'm ready."

"His nerve's just plain gall!" snapped Red, turning to Hopalong. "Think yo're sendin' me off to get a couple of cayuses, while yo're runnin' that risk in there? Get th' cayuses yoreself; I'll get th' fixin's!"

"Don't waste time like this!" growled Johnny. "Do as yo're told, you red-headed wart! Corwin will shore go to th' jail before he turns in. Come on, Hoppy."

"That name sounds good again," chuckled Hopalong, giving Red a shove toward the stables. "Get them cayuses, Carrot-Top!"

Red obeyed, but took it out in talking to himself as he went along, and as he entered the north stable he stepped on something large and soft, which instantly went into action. Red dropped to his knees and clinched, getting both wrists in his hands. Being in a hurry, and afraid of any outcry, he could not indulge in niceties, so he brought one knee up and planted it forcefully in his enemy's stomach, threw his weight on it and jumped up and down. Sliding his hands down the wrists, one at a time, he found the knife and took it from the relaxing fingers. Then he felt for the victim's jaw with one hand and hit it with the other. Arising, he hummed a tune and soon led out the two horses.

"Don't like to leave th' others for them fellers to use," he growled, and forthwith decided not to leave them. He drove them out of both stables, mounted his own, led Hopalong's, and slowly herded the other dozen ahead of him over the soft sand and away. When he finally reached the agreed-upon meeting place he reflected with pleasure that anyone wishing to use those horses for the purpose of pursuit, or any other purpose, would first have to find, and then catch them. They were going strong when he had last heard them.

Idaho had stopped under the window pointed out to him, and his two companions, leaving their boots in his tender care, were swallowed up in the darkness. They opened the squeaking front door, cautiously climbed the squeaking stairs and fairly oozed over the floor of the upper hall, which wanted to squeak, and did so a very little. Hopalong slowly opened the door of his room, thankful that he had oiled its one musical hinge, and felt cautiously over the bed. It was empty, and his sigh of relief was audible. And he was further relieved when his groping hand found his possessions where he had left them. He was stooping to loosen the coil of rope at the pommel of his saddle when he heard a sleepy, inquiring voice and a soft thud, and anxiously slipped to the door.

"Kid!" he whispered. "Kid!"

"Shut yore fool face," replied the object of his solicitude, striking a match for one quick glance around. The room was strange to him, since he never had been in it before, and he had to get his bearings. The inert man on the bed did not get a second glance, for the sound and weight of the blow had reassured Johnny. There were two saddles, two rifles, two of everything, which was distressing under the circumstances.

Hopalong had just lowered his own saddle to the waiting Idaho when the catlike Johnny entered the room with a saddle and a rifle. He placed them on the bed, where they would make no noise, and departed, catlike. Soon returning he placed another saddle and rifle on the bed and departed once more.

Hopalong, having sent down both of Johnny's first offerings, felt over the bed for the rest of Red's belongings, if there were any more, and became profanely indignant as his hand caressed another rifle and then bumped against another saddle.

"What'n hell is he doin'?" he demanded. "My G-d! There's more'n a dozen rooms on this floor, an' men in all of 'em! Hey, Kid!" he whispered as breathing sounded suddenly close to him.

"What?" asked Johnny, holding two slicker rolls, a sombrero, a pair of boots, and a suit of clothes. Two belts with their six-guns were slung around his neck, but the darkness mercifully hid the sight from his friend.

"D—n it! We ain't movin this hotel," said Hopalong with biting sarcasm. "It don't belong to us, you know. !An' what was that whack I heard when you first went in?"

"Somebody jumped Red's bed, an' wanted to know some fool thing, or somethin', an' I had to quiet him. An' what'n blazes are you kickin' about? I've moved twice as much as you have, more'n twice as far. Grab holt of some of this stuff an' send it down to Idaho. He'll think you've went to sleep."

"You locoed tumble-bug!" said Hopalong. "Aimin' to send down th' bed, with th' feller in it, too?"

A door creaked suddenly and they froze.

"Quit yore d——d noise an' go to sleep!" growled a sleepy, truculent voice, and the door creaked shut again.

After a short wait in silence Hopalong put out an inquiring hand. "Come on," he whispered. "What you got there?"

Johnny told him, and Hopalong dropped the articles out of the window, all but the hat, boots, and clothes. "Don't you know Red's wearin' his clothes, boots an' hat, you chump?" he said, gratis. "Leave them things here an' f oiler me," and he started for the head of the stairs.

They were halfway down when they heard a horse gal loping toward the hotel. It was coming from the direction of the jail and they nudged each other.

Sheriff Corwin, feeling like he was master of all he surveyed, had ridden to the jail before going to report to Kane for the purpose of cautioning the guards not to relax their vigil. Not being able to see them in the darkness meant nothing to him, for they should have challenged him, and had not. He swept up to the door, angrily calling them by name and, receiving no reply, dismounted in hot haste, shook the door and then went hurriedly around the building to feel of the bars. One sweep of his hand was enough and as he wheeled he tripped over the wagon tongue and fell sprawling, his gun flying out of his hand. Groping around he found it, jammed it back into the holster, darted back to his horse and dashed off at top speed for Kane's to spread the alarm and collect a posse.

There never had been any need for caution in opening the hotel door and his present frame of mind would not have heeded it if there had been. Flinging it back he dashed through and opened his mouth to emit a bellow calculated almost to raise the dead. The intended shout turned to a choking gasp as two lean, strong hands gripped his throat, and then his mental sky was filled with lightning as a gun-butt fell on his head. His limp body was carried out and dropped at the feet of the cheerful Idaho, who helped tear up portions of the sheriff's clothing for his friends to use on the officer's hands, feet, and mouth.

"Every time I hit a head I shore gloat," growled Johnny, his thoughts flashing back to his first night in town.

"Couldn't you send him down, too?" Idaho asked of Hopalong. "An' how many saddles do you an' Red use generally?"

"He wasn't up there," answered Hopalong. "We run into him as we was comin' out."

Johnny's match flashed up and out in one swift movement. "Corwin!" he exulted. "An' I'm glad it was me that hit him!"

Idaho rolled over on the ground and made strange noises. Sitting up he gasped: "Didn't I say it was a lovely night? Holy mavericks!"

"You fellers aim to claim squatter sovereignty?" whispered Red from the darkness. "If I'd 'a' knowed it I'd 'a' tied up somethin' I left layin' loose."

"We got to get a rustle on," said Hopalong. "Some cusses come to right quick. That gent in Red's bed is due to ask a lot of questions at th' top of his voice. Come on grab this stuff, pronto!"

"I left another in th' stable that's goin' to do some yellin' purty soon," said Red. "Reckon he's a Greaser."

They picked up the things and went off to find the horses and as they dropped the equipment Red felt for his saddle. "Hey! Where's mine?" he demanded.

"Here, at my feet," said Johnny.

Red passed his hand over it and swore heartily. "This ain't it, you blunderin' jackass! Why didn't you get mine?" he growled.

"Feel of this one," grunted Johnny, kicking the other saddle.

Red did so. "That's it. Who's th' other belong to?"

"*I* don't know," answered Johnny, growing peeved. "Yo're cussed particular, you are! Here's two rifles, two six-guns, an' two belts. Take 'em with you an' pick out yore own when it gets light. *I* don't want 'em."

Red finished cinching up and slipped a hand over the rifles. He dropped one of them into its scabbard. "Got mine. Chuck th' other away."

"Take it along an' chuck it in th' crick," said Idaho. "Now you fellers listen: If you ride up th' middle of Big Crick till you come to that rocky ground west of our place you can leave th' water there, an' yore trail will be lost. It runs southwest an' northeast for miles, an' is plenty wide an' wild. If you need any thin' ride in to our place any night after dark. I'll post th' boys."

"We ain't got a bit of grub," growled Red. "Well, it ain't th' first time," he added, cheerfully.

"We're not goin' up Big Crick," said Hopalong, decisively. "We're ridin' like we wanted to get plumb out of this country, which is just what Bill Long an' Red Thompson would do. When fur enough away we're circlin' back east of town, on th' edge of th' desert, where nobody will hardly think we'd go. They'll suspect that hard ground over yore way before they will th' desert. Where'll we meet you, Kid, if there's any thin' to be told; an' when?"

Johnny considered and appealed to Idaho, whose knowledge of the country qualified him to speak. In a few moments the place had been chosen and well described, and the two horsemen pulled their mounts around and faced northward.

"Get a-goin'," growled Johnny. "Anybody'd reckon you thought a night was a week long."

"Don't like to leave you two boys alone in this town, after tonight's plays," said Hopalong, uneasily. "Nobody is dumb enough to figger that we didn't have outside help. Keep yore eyes open!"

"Pull out!" snapped Johnny. "It'll be light in two hours more!"

"So-long, you piruts," softly called Idaho. "Yessir," he muttered, joyously; "it's been one plumb lovely night!"

Not long after the noise of galloping had died in the north a Mexican staggered from the stable, groping in the darkness as he made his erratic way toward the front of the gambling-hall, his dazed wits returning slowly. Leaning against the wall of the building for a short rest, he went on again, both hands gripping his jaw. Too dazed to be aware of the disappearance of the horses and attentive only to his own woes, he blundered against the bound and gagged sheriff, went down, crawled a few yards and then, arising again to his feet, groped around the corner of the building and sat down against it to collect his bewildering thoughts.

Upstairs in the room Red had used, the restless figure on the bed moved more and more, finally sitting up, moaning softly. Then, stiffening as memory brought some thing back to him, he groped about for matches, blundering against the walls and the scanty furniture, and called forth profane language from the room adjoining, whose occupant, again disturbed, arose and yanked open his door.

"What you think yo're doin', raisin' all this racket?" he demanded.

"Somebody near busted my head," moaned the other. "I been robbed!" he shouted as the lack of impedimenta at last sank into his mind.

"Say!" exclaimed his visitor, remembering an earlier nocturnal disturbance. "Wait here till I get some matches!"

He returned with a lighted lamp, instead, which revealed the truth, and its bearer swiftly led the way into the second room down the hall. A pair of boots which should not have been there and the absence of the equipment which should have been there confirmed their fears. The man with the lamp held it out of the window and swore under his breath as a bound figure below him gurgled and writhed.

"Looks like Corwin!" he muttered, and hastened down to make sure, taking no time to dress. The swearing Mexican received no attention until the sheriff staggered back with the investigator, and then the vague tale was listened to.

A bellowing voice awakened the sleepers in the big building and an impromptu conference of irate men, mostly undressed, was held in the hall. Sandy Woods returned from the stables, reporting them bare of horses; the investigator from the jail came back with the angry guards, one of whom was too shaky to walk with directness. Others came from a visit to Red Frank's corral, leading half a dozen borrowed horses, and, a hasty, cold breakfast eaten, the posse, led by a sick, vindictive sheriff, pounded northward along a plain trail.

Those who were not able to go along stood and peered through the paling darkness and two deputies left to take up positions in the front and rear of Quayle's hotel where they could see without being seen, while a third man crept into the stable to look for a Tincup horse. Had he been content with looking he would have been more fortunate, but thinking that the master would have no further use for the animal, he decided to take it for himself, trusting that possession would give him a better claim when the new ownership was finally decided by Kane. Reassured by the earliness of the hour and by the presence of the hidden deputy, he went ahead with his plans.

Pepper's flattened ears meant nothing to the exultant thief, for it had been his experience that all horses flattened their ears whenever he approached them, especially if they had reason to know him; so, with a wary eye on the trim, black hoofs, he slipped along the stable wall to gain her head. He had just untied the rope and started back with the end of it in his hand when there was a sud den, sidewise, curving swerve of the silky black body, a grunt of surprise and pain from the thief, pinned against the wall by the impact, and then, curving back again and wheeling almost as though on a pivot, Pepper's teeth crunched flesh and bone and the sickened thief, by a miracle escaping the outflung front hoofs, staggered outside the stable and fell as the whizzing hind feet took the half-open door from its flimsy hinges. Rolling around the corner, the thief crawled under a wagon and sank down unconscious, his crushed shoulder staining darkly through his torn shirt.

The watching deputy arose to go to his friend's assistance, but looked up and stopped as a growled question came from Ed Doane's window.

"Jim's hurt," he explained to the face behind the rifle. "Went in to see if his cayuse had wandered in there, an' th' black near killed him. Gimme a hand with him, will you?"

Quayle had nearly fallen off the chair he had spent the night on when the crash and the scream of the enraged horse awakened him. He ran to the kitchen door, rifle in hand, and looked out, hearing the deputy's words.

"I'll give ye a hand," he said; "but more cheerful if it's to dig a grave. Mother av G-d!" he breathed as he reached the wagon. "I'm thinkin' it's a priest ye want, an' there's none within twinty miles." He looked around at the forming crowd. "Get a plank," he ordered, "an' get Doc Sharpe."

Ed Doane, followed by Johnny and Idaho, ran from the kitchen and joined the group. One glance and Johnny went into the stable, calling as he entered. Patting the quivering nozzle of the black he looked at the rope and came out again.

"That man-killer has got to be shot," said the deputy to Ed Doane.

"I'll kill th' man that tries it," came a quiet reply, and "the deputy wheeled to look into a pair of frosty blue eyes. "Th' knot I tie in halter ropes don't come loose, for Pep per will untie any common knot an' go off huntin' for me. It was untied. If you want to back up a hoss thief, an' mebby prove yore part in it, say that again."

"Yo're plumb mistaken, Nelson," said the deputy. "Jim was huntin' his own cayuse, which Long an' Thompson stampeded out of th' stable last night. He was goin' over th' town first before he went out to look for it on th' plain."

"That's good!" sneered Johnny. "Long an' Thomp son are in jail. I'm standin' to what th' knot showed. Do you still reckon Pepper's got to be shot?"

"They broke out an' got away," retorted the deputy; "an' they shore as h--l had outside help." He looked knowingly into Johnny's eyes. "Nobody that belongs to this town would 'a' done it."

"That's a lie," said Quayle, his rifle swinging up carelessly. "I belong to this town, an' I'd 'a' done it, mesilf, if I'd thought av it. Seein' that I didn't, I'm cussed glad that somewan had better wits than me own."

"I was aimin' to do it," said Idaho, smiling. "I was goin' out to get th' boys, an' bust th' jail tonight. I was holdin' back a little, though, because I was scared th' boys might get a little rough an' lynch a few deputies. They're on set triggers these days."

The cook started to roll up his sleeves. "I'll lick th' daylight out av anny man that goes to harm that horse, or me name's not Murphy," he declared, spitting. "I feed her near every mornin', an' she's gintle as a baby lamb. But she's got a keen nose for blackguards!"

Dr. Sharpe arrived, gave his orders and followed the bearers of the improvised stretcher toward his house. As the crowd started to break up Johnny looked coldly at the deputy. "You heard me," he said. "Pass th' word along. An' if she don't kill th' next one, *I* will!"

North of town the posse reached Big Creek and exulted as it saw the plain prints going on from the further bank. Corwin, sitting his saddle with a false ease, stifled a moan at every rise and fall, his head seeming about to split under the pulsing hammer blows. When he caught sight of the trail leading from the creek he nodded dully and spoke to his nearest companion.

"Leavin' th' country by th' straightest way," he growled. "It'll mebby be a long chase, damn 'em!"

"They ain't got much of a start," came the hopeful reply. "We ought to catch sight of 'em from th' top of th' divide beyond Sand Creek. It's fair level plain for miles north of that. Their cayuses ain't no better than ourn, an' some of ourn will run theirs off their feet."

Sand Creek came into sight before noon and when it was reached there were no tracks on the further side. The posse was prepared for this and split without hesitation, Corwin leading half of it west along the bank and the other half going east. Five minutes later an exclamation caused the sheriff to pull up and look where one of his men was pointing. A rifle barrel projected a scant two inches from the water and the man who rode over to it laughed as he leaned down from the saddle.

"It lit on a ridge of gravel an' didn't slide down quite fur enough," he called. "An' it shore is busted proper."

"Bring it here," ordered Corwin. He took it, examined it and handed it to the next man, whose head ached as much as his own and who would not have been along except that his wish for revenge over-rode his good sense.

"That yourn?" asked the sheriff.

The owner of the broken weapon growled. "They've plumb ruined it. It's one more score they'll pay. Come on!" and he whirled westward. Corwin drew his Colt and fired into the air three times at counted intervals, and galloped after his companions when faint, answering shots sounded from the east.

"They're makin' for that rocky stretch," he muttered; "an' if they get there in time they're purty safe."

Not long after he had rejoined his friends the second part of the posse whirled along the bank, following the trail of the first, eager to overtake it and learn what had been discovered.

Well to the east Hopalong and Red rode at the best pace possible in the water of the creek, now and then turning in the saddle to look searchingly behind them. Fol lowing the great bend of the stream they went more and more to the south and when the shadows were long they rode around a ridge and drew rein. Red dismounted and climbed it, peering over its rocky backbone for minutes. Returning to his companion he grinned cheerfully.

"No coyotes in sight," he said. "Some went west, I reckon, an' found that busted rifle where we planted it. No coyotes, at all; but there's a black bear down in that little strip of timber."

"I can eat near all of it, myself," chuckled Hopalong. "Let's camp where we drop it. A dry wood fire won't show up strong till dark. Come on!"

Chapter XIV
The Staked Plain

Pecos Kane sat behind his old desk in the inner room and listened to the reports of the night's activities, his anger steadily mounting until ghostly flames seemed to be licking their thin tongues back in his eyes. The jail guards had come and departed, speaking simply and truthfully, suggesting various reasons to excuse the laxity of their watch. The Mexican told with painful effort about the loss of the horses, growing steadily more incoherent from the condition of his jaw and from his own rising rage. Men came, and went out again on various duties, one of them closely interrogating the owner of the freight wagon, whose anger had died swiftly by the recovery of the great tongue, which was none the worse for its usage except for certain indentations of no moment. A friend of Quayle and hostile to Kane and for what Kane stood for, the wagon owner allowed his replies to be short, and yet express a proper indignation, which did not exist, about the whole affair. When again alone in the sanctity of his home he allowed himself the luxury of low-voiced laughter and determined to put his crowbar where any needy individual of the future could readily find it.

Bill Trask, because of his short-gun expertness temporarily relieved of guarding the partition door, led three companions toward Quayle's hotel, his face and the faces of the others tense and determined. Two went around to the stable, via Red Frank's and the rear street and one of them stopped near it while the other slipped along the kitchen wall and crouched at the edge of the kitchen door. The third man went silently into the hotel office as Trask sauntered carelessly into the barroom and nodded at its inmates.

"Them fellers shore raised hell," he announced to Ed Doane as he motioned for a drink.

"They did," replied Doane, spinning a glass after the sliding bottle, after which he flung the coin into the old cigar box and assiduously polished the bar, wondering why Trask patronized him instead of Kane's.

"They shore had nerve," persisted the newcomer, looking at Johnny.

"They shore did," acquiesced the man at the table, who then returned to his idle occupation of trying to decipher the pattern of the faded-out wall paper. Wall paper was a rarity in the town and deserved some attention.

"Them guards was plumb careless," said Kane's hired man. Not knowing to whom he was speaking there was no reply, and he tried again, addressing the bartender.

"They was careless," replied Doane, without interest.

Johnny was alert now, the persistent remarks awakening suspicion in his mind, and a slight sound from the wall at his back caused him to push his chair from the table and assume a more relaxed posture. His glance at the lower and nearer corner of the window let him memorize its exact position and he waited, expectant, for whatever might happen. The surprise and capture of his two friends had worked, but that had been the first time; there would be no second, he told himself, especially as far as he was concerned.

"Is th' boss in?" asked the visitor.

"Th' boss ain't in," answered Ed Doane as Johnny glanced at the front door, the front window and the door of the office, which the bartender noticed. "Too dusty," said Doane, going around the bar to the front wall and closing the window.

"When will he be in?"

"Dunno," grunted the bartender, once more in his accustomed place.

"I got to see him."

"I handle things when he ain't here," said Doane. "See me," he suggested, looking through the door leading to the office, where he fancied he had heard a creak.

"Got to see him, an' pronto," replied the visitor. "He made some remarks this mornin' about gettin' them fellers out. We know it was done by somebody on th' outside, an' we got a purty good idea of who it was since Quayle shot off his mouth. He's been gettin' too swelled up lately. If he don't come in purty quick I'm aimin' to 'dig him out, myself."

Johnny was waiting for him to utter the cue word and knew that there would be a slight change in facial expression, enunciation, or body posture just before it came. He was not swallowing the suggestions that it was Quayle who was wanted.

"You shore picked out a real job to handle all alone," said Doane, not letting his attention wander from the hotel office. "Any dog can dig out a badger, but that's only th' beginnin'," he said pleasantly, his hand on the gun which always lay under the bar. He expected a retort to his insult, and when none came it put a keener edge to his growing suspicions.

"I'm diggin' him out, just th' same," said Trask. "There's law in this town, an' everybody's on one side or th' other. Bein' a deputy it's my job to see about them that's on th' other side. Gettin' arrested men out of jail is serious an' I got to ask questions about it. Of course, Quayle don't allus say what he means we none of us do. We all like to have our jokes; but I got to do my duty, even if it's only askin' questions. Is he out, or layin' " low?"

"He's out," grunted Doane, "but he'll be back any; minute, I reckon."

"All right; I'll wait," said Trask, carelessly, but he tensed himself. "How's business?" and at the words he flashed into action.

A chair crashed and a figure leaped back from it, two guns belching at its hips. The face and hand which popped up into the rear window disappeared again as the smoking Colt swung past the opening and across Johnny's body to send its second through the office doorway, and curses answered both shots. Trask, bent over, held his right arm with his left hand, his gun against the wall near the front door. The first shot of Johnny's righthand Colt had torn it from Trask's hand as it left the holster and the second had rendered the arm useless for the moment. A shot from the corner of the stable sang through the window and barely missed its mark as Johnny leaned forward, but his instant reply ended all danger from that point.

"Trask," he said, "I'm leavin' town. I ain't got a chance among buildin's again' pot-shooters. I'm leavin' ' but th' Lord help Kane an' his gang when I come back. You can tell him I'm comin' a-shootin'. An' you can tell him this: I'm goin' to get him, Pecos Kane, if I has to pull him out of his hell-hole like I pulled Thorpe. Go ahead of me to th' stable I'll blow you apart if any pot-shooter tries at me. G'wan!"

Trask obeyed, the gun against his spine too eloquent a persuader to be ignored. He knew that there were no pot-shooters yet, and he was glad of it, for if there had been one, and his captor was killed, the relaxation of the tense thumb holding back the hammer of a gun whose trigger was tied back would fire the weapon. The man who held it would fire one shot after his own death, how ever instantaneous it might be.

Passing through the kitchen Johnny picked up his saddle and ordered his captive to carry the rifle and slicker roll. They disappeared into the stable and when they came out again Johnny ordered Trask into the saddle, mounted behind him and rode for the arroyo which lay not far from the hotel. At last away from the buildings he made Trask dismount, climbed over the cantle and settled himself in the vacated saddle.

"I'm goin' down to offer myself to McCullough," he said. "You can tell Kane that, too. They'll need men down there, an' I'll be th' maddest man they got. An' th' next time me an' you have any gun talk, I'm shootin' to kill. Adios!"

He left the cursing deputy and went straight for the trail, where the rising wind played with the dust, and along it until stopped by a voice in a barranca.

"I'm puttin' 'em up," he called. "My name's Nelson an' I'm mad clean through. Get a rustle on; I want to see Mac."

"Go ahead, Bar-20," drawled the voice. "I wasn't dead shore. There's a good friend of yourn down there."

"Quayle?" asked Johnny.

"There's another: Waffles, of th' O-Bar-O," came the reply, and a verse of a nearly forgotten song arose on the breeze.

I've swum th' Colorado where she runs down dost to hell, I've braced th' faro layouts in Cheyenne;

I've fought for muddy water with a howlin' bunch of Sioux, An' swallered hot tamales, an' cayenne.

"There's more, but I've done forgot most of it," apolo gized the singer.

Johnny laughed with delight. "Why, that's Lefty Allen's old song. Here's th' second verse:"

I've rid a pitchin' broncho till th' sky was underneath,

I've tackled every desert in th' land;

I've sampled Four-X whisky till I couldn't hardly see,

An' dallied with th' quicksands of th' Grande.

"That's shore O-Bar-O. Lefty made it up hisself, an' that boy could sing it. It all comes back to me now," he called it 'Th' Insult.' Why here, you!" he chuckled. "I said I was mad an' in a hurry. I ain't mad no more, but I am in a hurry. See you tonight, mebby. So-long."

Riding on again he soon reached the Question-Mark bunkhouse and dismounted as a puncher turned the corner of the house. They grinned at each other, these good, old-time friends.

"You son-of-a-gun!" chuckled Johnny, holding out his hand.

"You son-of-a-gun!" echoed Waffles, gripping it, and so they stood, silent, exchanging grins. It had been a long time since they last had seen each other.

McCullough loomed up in the doorway and grinned at them both.

"Hear yo're married," said Waffles.

"Shore!" bragged Johnny.

"It ain't spoiled you, yet. How's Hoppy an' Red?"

"Fine, now they're out of jail."

Waffles threw his head back and laughed heartily. "I near laughed till I busted when Quayle told us who they was. Hoppy an' Red in jail! It was funny!"

"Hello, Nelson," said McCullough. "What are you doin' down here?"

"Had to leave town; too many corners, an' too much cover. I'm lookin' for a job, if it don't cut me out of th' rewards."

"She's yourn."

"Wait a minute," said Johnny. "I can't take it. I got to be free to do what I want; but I'll hang out here for awhile."

"You've got th' job instanter," said the appreciative trail-boss smiling broadly. "It's steady work of bossin' yoreself. I've heard of yore work, up Gunsight way. Feed yet? Then come on."

"Shore will. Where's Quayle?"

"Rode back, roundabout; him not courtin' bein' seen; but I reckon everybody in town knows he's been here. He swears by you."

Despite Idaho's boasts to the contrary his ranch again had nocturnal visitors, and there was no lead-flying welcome accorded them. Having spied out the distribution of Lukins' riders the visitors chose a locality free from guards and with the coming of night drifted a sizable herd of Diamond L cattle across an outlying section of the range and with practiced art and uncanny instinct drove the compacted herd onto and over the rocky plateau, where the chief of the raiders obtained a speed with the cattle which always bordered upon a panicky flight, but never quite reached it. All that night they rumbled over the rocky stretch and as dawn brightened the eastern sky the running herd passed down a gentle slope, picked up the waiting caviya and not long thereafter moved over the hard bottom of a steep-walled ravine which could have been called a canyon without unduly stretching the meaning of the word.

The chief of the raiding party cared nothing for the fatness of the animals, or other conditions which might operate against the possibilities of a lucrative sale. There later would be time for improving their condition, plenty of time in a valley rich with grass. All he cared for now was to put miles speedily behind him, and this he was accomplishing like the master cattleman he was. After a mid-day breathing space they went on again, alternately walking and running, and well into the second night, stop ping at a water-hole known only to a few men other than these. Some miles north of this water-hole was another, and very much smaller one, being only a few feet across, and there also was a difference between the waters of the two. The larger was of a nature to be expected in such a locality, but much better than most such holes, for the water was only slightly alkaline and the cattle drank it eagerly. The other was sweet and pure and cold, but rather than to cover the distance to it and back again, it was ignored by all but one man, for the other stayed with the herd. There was grass around both; not enough to feed a herd thoroughly, but enough to keep it busy hunting over the scanty growth. With more than characteristic thought these holes had been named in a manner to couple and yet to keep them separate, and to Kane's drive crew they were known as "Sweet "and "Bitter."

Again on the trail before the sun had risen above the horizon, the herd was sent forth on another day's hard drive, which carried it, with the constantly growing tail herd of stragglers, far into the following night, despite all dumb remonstrances. No mercy was shown to it, but only a canny urging, and if no mercy was shown the cattle none was accepted by the drivers, who rode and worked, swore and panted on wiry ponies which, despite frequent changing, began to show the marks of their efforts under the pitiless sun and through the yielding sands. Both cattle and horses had about reached their limits when the late afternoon of the next day brought them to a rocky ledge sticking up out of the desert's floor, which now was hard and stony; and upon turning the south end of the ridge an emerald valley suddenly lay before their eyes, from whence the scent of water had put a new spirit into cattle and horses for the last few miles; and now it nearly caused a fatal stampede at the entrance to the narrow ledge which slanted down the steep, rock walls.

To a stranger such a sight would have awakened amazed incredulity, and strong suspicion that his sanity had been undermined by the heat-cursed, horror-laden desert miles; or he might have sneered wisely at so palpable a mirage, scorned to be tricked by it in any attempt to prove it other wise and staggered on with contemptuous curses. But Miguel and the men he so autocratically bossed knew it to be no vision, no trick of air or mind, and sighed with relief when it finally lay before them. While they all knew it was there and had visited it before, none of them, except Miguel, had ever learned the way, try as they might, for until the high ledge of rock, hidden on the west by a great, upslanting billow of sand, came into sight there were no landmarks to show them the way. Each new journey across the simmering, shimmering plateau found fears in every heart but the guide's that he would lose his way. That their fears may be justified and to show them blame less in everything but their lack of confidence in him, it may be well to have a better understanding of this desert and what it meant; and to show why men should hold as preposterous any claim that a cattle herd could safely cross it. Some went even further and said no man, mounted or not, could make that journey, and confessed to themselves a superstitious fear and horror for it and everything pertaining to it.

Before the deep ruts had been cut in the old Santa Fe Trail in that year of excessive rains; before the first wheel had rolled over the prairie soil to prove that wagons could safely make the long and tiresome trip; before even the first pack trains of heavily laden mules plodded to or from the Missouri frontier, and even before the peltloaded mules of the great fur companies crossed Kansas soil to the trading posts of the East, Mexican hunters rode from the valley of Taos and Santa Fe to procure their winter meat from the vast brown herds of buffalo migrating over their curious, crescent-shaped course to and from the regions of the Arkansas, Canadian, and Cimarron. They dried the strips of succulent meat in the sun or over fires, the fuel for the latter having been supplied by the buffalo themselves on previous migrations; they stripped the hides from the prostrate bodies and cured them, and trafficked with the bands of Indians which followed the herds as persistently as did the great, gray wolves. Of these ciboleros, swarthy-skinned hunters of Mexico, some more hardy and courageous than their fellows, or by avarice turned trader, ventured further afield and were not balked by the high, beetling cliffs which bordered a great, forbidding plateau lying along and below the capricious Cimarron, in places a river of hide-and-seek in the sands, wet one day and dry the next.

From the mesa-like northern edge, along the warning arroyos of the Cimarron, where erosion, Nature's patient sculptor, carved miracles of artistry in the towering clays, shales, and sandstones, to the great sand hills billowing along its far-flung other edges, this barren waste of dreary sand and grisly alkali was a vast, simmering playground for dancing heat waves and fantastic mirage, and its treacherous pools of nauseous, alkaline waters shrunk daily from their encrusted edges and gleamed malignantly under a glowering, molten sun. Arroyos, level plain, shifting sand, and imponderable dust, with a scrawny, scanty, hopeless vegetation which the whimsical winds buried and then dug up again, this high desert plateau lay like a thing of death, cursing and accursed. It sloped imperceptibly southward, its dusty soil gradually breaking into billowy ridges constantly more marked and with deeper troughs, by insensible gradations becoming low sand hills, ever growing more separate and higher until at last they were beaten down and strewn broadcast by more persistent winds, and limited by the firmer soils which were blessed with more frequent rains to coax forth a thin cover of protecting, anchoring vegetation.

To the west they intruded nearly to the Rio Pecos, a stream which in almost any other part of the country would have been regarded as insignificant, but here was given greatness because its liquid treasure was beyond price and because it was permanent, though timid.

Of the first of the Mexicans to push out over this great desolation perhaps none returned, except by happy chance, to tell of its tortures and of the few serviceable waterholes leagues apart, the permanency of which none could foretell. But return some eventually did, and perhaps deprecated the miseries suffered, in view of the saving in miles; but their experience had been such as to impel them to drive a line of stakes along the happily chosen course to mark in this manner the way from each more trustworthy water-hole to the next, be they reservoirs or furtive streams which bubbled up and crept along to die not far from their hopeful springs, sucked up by palpitant air and swallowed by greedy sands, their burial places marked by a shroud of encrusted salts. In the winter and spring an occasional rain filled hollows, ofttimes coming as a cloudburst and making a brave showing as it tumultuously deepened some arroyo and roared valiantly down it toward swift effacement The trail was staked, if not by the swarthy traders, then by their red-skinned brothers, and from this line of stakes the tableland derived its name, and became known to men as the Lano Estacada, or Staked Plain.

Of this accursed desert no one man had full knowledge, nor thirsted for it if it were to be had only through his own efforts. There were great stretches unknown to any man, and there were other regions known to men who had not brought their knowledge out again; and what knowledge there was of its south-central portions was not to be found in men with white skins, but in certain marauding redmen fitted by survival to cope with problems such as it presented, and to live despite them. One other class knew something of its mysteries, for among the Mexicans there were some who had learned by bitter pilgrimages, but mostly from the mouths of men long dead who had passed the knowledge down successive generations, each increment a little larger when it left than when it came, who had a more comprehensive, embracing knowledge of the baking tableland; and these few, because what they knew could best be used in furtive, secretive pursuits bearing a swift penalty for those caught in them, hugged that knowledge closely and kept it to themselves. A man who has that which another badly needs can drive shrewd bargains. 'And of the few Mexicans who were enriched by the possession of this knowledge, those who knew most about it had mixed blood flowing through their veins, for the vast grisly plateau had been a short cut and place of refuge for marauding bands of Apaches, Utes, and Comanches while civilization crawled wonderingly in swaddling clothes.

Of the knowing few Pecos Kane owned two, owned them body and soul, and to make his title firmer than even proof of murder could assure, he threw golden sops to the wise ones' avarice and allowed them seats in the sun and privileges denied to their fellows. One of them, by name Miguel, a small part Spaniard and the rest Mescalero Apache, was a privileged man, for he knew not only the main trails across the plain but certain devious ways twisting in from the edges, one of which wandered for accursed miles, first across rock, then over sand and again over rock and unexpectedly turned a high, sharp ridge to look upon his Valle de Sorprendido, deep and green, whose crystal spring wandered musically along its gravelly bed from the graying western end of the canyon-like ravine to sink silently into the thirsty sands to the east and be seen no more. Manuel, also, knew this way.

Surprise Valley was no terminal, but a place for tonguelolling, wild-eyed cattle to pause and rest, drink and eat before the fearful journey called anew. No need for corral, fence, or herders here to keep them from straying, but an urgent need for pressing riders to throw the herd back on the trail again, to start the dumbly protesting animals on the thirty-six-hour drive to the next unfailing water, against the instinct which bade them stay. A valley of delight it was, a jewel, verdant and peaceful, forced by man to serve a vicious purpose; but as if in punishment for its perversion the glistening sand hills crept slowly nearer, each receding tide of their slow advance encroaching more and more each year until now the valley had shrunk by half and a stealthy grayness crept insiduously into its velvety freshness like the mark of sin across a harlot's cheek.

Near the fenced-in spring was an adobe building, deserted except when a drive crew sought its shelter, and it served principally as a storehouse should a place of refuge suddenly be needed. It lay not far from the sloping banks of detritus which now ran halfway up the sheer, smooth stone walls enclosing the valley. Across from it on the southern side of the depressed pasture a broad trail slanted up the rock cliffs to the desert above. The cabin, the trail, and the valley itself long ago would have been obliterated by sand but for the miles of rocks, large and small, which lay around it like a great, flat collar. Should some terrific sand storm sweep over it with a momentum great enough to bridge the rocky floor the valley would cease to be; and smaller storms raging far out on the encircling desert carried their sands farther and farther across the stubborn rock, until now its outer edge was closer by miles. Already each rushing wind retained sand enough to drop it into the valley and powder everything.

The pock-marked guide, disdaining the precarious labors of getting the herd down the ledge with no fatalities among the maddened beasts, lolled in his saddle on the brink of the precipice and watched the struggle on the plain behind him, where hard-riding, loudly yelling herders were dashing across the front of the weaving, shifting, stubborn mass of tortured animals, letting them through the frantic restraining barrier in small groups, which constantly grew larger. Here and there a more determined animal slipped through and galloped to the descending ledge, head down and tail up. The cracking of revolvers fired across the noses of the front rank grew steadily and Miguel deemed it safer to leave the brim of the cliff. It was possible that the maddened herd might break through the desperate riders and plunge to its destruction. Had the trail been a few hours longer nothing could have held them.

"Give a hand here!" shouted the trail-boss as the guide rode complacently out of danger. "Ride in there an' help split 'em!"

"I weel be needed w'en we leeve again," replied Miguel. "To run a reesk eet ees foolish. I tol' you to stop 'em a mile away an' spleet 'em there. Eet ees no beesness of Miguel's, theese. You deed not wan' to tak' the time? Then tak' w'at you call the consequence."

Eventually the last of the herd which mercifully was composed of stragglers whose lack of strength made them more tractable, were successfully led to the ledge and stumbled down it to join their brothers standing or lying in the little brook as if to appease their thirst by absorption before drinking deeply. The frantic, angry bawling of an hour ago was heard no more, for now a contented lowing sounded along the stream, where the quiet animals often waited half an hour before attempting to drink. They stood thus for hours, reluctant to leave even to graze and after leaving, left the grass and returned time after time to drink. There were a few half-blinded animals among the weaklings, but water, grass, and rest would restore their sight. Here they would stay until fit for the second and lesser ordeal, and the others in turn.

The weary riders, turning their mounts loose to join the rest of the horse herd, piled their saddles against the wall of the hut and waited for the cook to call them to fill their tin plates and cups. One of them, more energetic and perhaps hungrier than the rest, unpacked the load of firewood from a spiritless horse and carried it to the hut

The perspiring Thorpe looked his thanks and went on with his labors and in due time a well-fed, lazy group sprawled near the hut, swapping tales or smoking in satisfied silence. At the other side of the building Miguel sat with those of his own kind, boasting of his desert achievements and in reply to a sneering remark from the other group he showed his teeth in a mocking smile, raised his eyebrows until the crescent scar reached his sombrero and shrugged his shoulders.

"Eet ees not good to say sooch theengs to Miguel," he complacently observed. "Eef he should get ver' angree an' leeve een the night eet would be ver' onluckie for Greengos. Quien sabe?"

"He got you there, Jud," growled a low voice. "He shore hurts me worse'n a blister, but I'm totin' my grudge silent."

"Huh," muttered another thoughtfully. "A man can travel fast without no cattle to set th' pace. He shore can 'leeve' an' be damned, for all *I* care. An' I'm sayin' that if he does there'll be a d d dead Greaser in Mesquite right soon after I get back. Th' place for him to ' leeve ' us is at Three Ponds for then we shore would be in one bad fix."

"I ain't shore I'd try to get away," said Sandy Woods slowly. "There's good grass an' water here, no herdin', no strayin', nobody to bother a feller. A man can live a long time on one steer out here, jerkin' th' meat. Th' herd would grow, an' when it came time to turn 'em into money he'd only have to drive plumb west. It wouldn't be like tryin' to find a little place like this. Just aim at th' sunset an' keep goin'."

"How long would this valley feed a herd like th' one here now?" ironically demanded the trail-boss. "You can tell th' difference in th' grass plain at th' end of a week. Yo're full of loco weed."

"Eef you say sooch things to me I may leeve in the night," chuckled the other. "Wish they'd stampeded an' knocked him over th' eege! One of these days some of us may be quittin' Kane, an' then there'll be one struttin' half-breed less in Mesquite. Tell you one thing: I won't make this drive many more times before I know th' way as well as he does; an' from here on we could stake it out."

Soft, derisive laughter replied to him and the trail-boss thoughtfully repacked his pipe. "It ain't in you," he said. "You got to be born with it."

"You holdin' that a white man ain't got as much brains as a mongrel with nobody knows how many different kinds of blood in him?" indignantly demanded Sandy.

"'He's got generations behind him, like a setter or a pointer, an' it ain't a question of brains. It's instinct, an' th' lower down yore stock runs th' better it'll be. There ain't no human brains can equal an animal's in things like that. I doubt if you could leave here an' get off this desert, plumb west or not. You got a big target, for it's all around you behind th' horizon; but I don't think you'd live till you hit it at th' right place. Don't forget that th' horizon moves with you. If there wasn't no tracks showin' you th' way you'd die out on this fryin' pan."

"An' th' wind'll wipe them out before mornin'," said one of the others.

The doubter laughed outright. "Wait till we come back. I'll give you a chance to back up yore convictions. Don't forget that I ain't sayin' that I'd try it afoot I'd ride an' give th' horse it's head. There ain't nothin' to be gained arguin' about it now. An' I'm free to admit that I'm cussed glad to be settin' here lookin' out instead of out there some'ers try in' to get here to look in. Gimme a match, Jud."

The trail-boss snorted. "Now yo're takin' my end," he asserted. "If you ride a cayuse an' give it its head it ain't a white man's brains that yo're dependin' on. That ain't yore argument, a-tall. I'll bet you, cayuse or no cayuse, you can't leave Three Ponds an' make it. A cayuse has to drink once in awhile or he'll drop under you an' you'll lose yore instinct-compass."

"I'll take that when we start back," retorted Sandy, "if you'll give me a fair number of canteens. I'm figgerin' on outfittin' right."

"Take all you want at Cimarron corrals," rejoined the trail-boss. "After we leave there I'm bettin' no body will part with any of theirs." He looked keenly at the boaster and took no further part in the conversation, his mind busy with a new problem; the grudge he already had

Chapter XV
Discoveries

Hopalong and Red liked their camp and were pleased that they could stay in it another day and night. They jerked the bear meat in the sun and smoke and took a much-needed bath in the creek, where the gentle application of sand freed them from the unwelcome guests which the jail had given them. Clothing washed and inspected quickly dried in the sun and wind. Neither of them had anything on but a sombrero and the effect was somewhat startling. Red picked up his saddle pad to fling it over a rock for a sun bath and was about to let go of it when he looked closer.

"Hey, did you rip open this pad?" he asked, eying his friend speculatively.

Hopalong added his armful of fuel to the pile near the fire and eyed his friend. "For a growed man you shore do ask some childish questions," he retorted. "Of course I did. I allus rip open saddle pads. All my life I been rippin' open every saddle pad I saw. Many a time I got mad when I found a folded blanket instead of a pad. I've got up nights an' gone wanderin' around looking for pads to rip open. You look like you had sense, but looks shore is deceivin'. Why'n blazes would I rip open yore saddle pad? I reckon it's plumb wore out an' just nat'rally come apart. You've had it since Adam made th' sun stand still."

"You must've listened to some sky pilot with yore feet!" retorted Red. "Adam didn't make th' sun stand still. That was Moses, so they'd have longer light for to hunt for him in. An' you needn't get steamed up, neither. Somebody ripped this pad, with a knife, too. Seein' that it was in th' same camp all night with you, I nat'rally asked. I'm shore *I* didn't do it. Then who did?" He swaggered off to get his friend's pad and picked it up. "Of course you wouldn't rip yore own. That--" he held it closer to his eyes and stared at it. "Cussed if you didn't, though! It's ripped just like mine. I reckon you'll be startin' on th' saddles, next!"

Hopalong's amusement at the ripping of his companion's pad faded out as he grabbed his own and looked at it. "Well, I'm cussed!" he muttered. "It shore was ripped, all right. It never come apart by itself. Both of 'em, huh?" He pondered as he turned the pad over and over.

"They didn't play no favorites, anyhow," growled Red. "Wonder what they thought they'd find? Jewels?"

Hopalong pushed back his hat and gently scratched a scalp somewhat tender from the sand treatment. "Things like that don't just happen," he said, reflectively. "There's allus a reason for things." He grew thoughtful again and studied the pad. "Mebby they wasn't lookin' for anythin'," he muttered, suspiciously.

Red snorted. "Just doin' it for practice, mebby?" he asked, sarcastically. "Not havin' nothin' else to do, somebody went up to our rooms an' amused themselves by rippin' open our pads. You got a head like a calf, only it's a hull lot smaller."

"We was accused of robbin' th' bank, Reddie," said Hopalong in patient explanation. "They knowed we didn't do it so they must 'a' wanted us to be blamed for it. Th' best proof they could have, not seein' us do it, was to plant somethin' to be found on us. This is past yore ABC eddication, but I'll try to hammer it into you. If it makes you dizzy, hold up yore hand. What does a bank have that everybody wants? Money! Why do people rob banks? To get money, you sage-hen! What would bank robbers have after they robbed a bank? Money, you locoed cow! Now, Reddie, there's two kinds of money. One is hard, an' th' other is soft like yore head. Th' soft has pretty pictures on it an' smells powerful. It also has numbers. Th' numbers are different, Reddie, on each bill. Some banks keep a list of th' numbers of the biggest bills. Reckon I better wait an' let you rest up."

"Too bad they got us out of jail both of us," said Red. "I should 'a' stayed behind. It wouldn't 'a' been half as bad as hangin' 'round with you."

"Now," continued his companion, looking into the pad, "if some of them numbered bills was found on us they'd have us, wouldn't they? We wasn't supposed to have no friends. An' where would a couple of robbers be likely to carry dangerous money? On their hats? No, Reddie; not on their hats. In their pockets, where they might get dragged out at th' wrong time? Mebby; but not hardly. Saddle pads, says th' little boy in th' rear of the room. Right you are, sonny. Saddle pads, Reddie, is a real good place. While you go all over it again so you can get th' drift of it I'll put on some clothes. I'm near baked."

"It started some time ago," said Red innocently.

"What did?"

"Th' bakin'. You didn't get that hat on quick enough," his friend jeered. "I've heard of people eatin' cooked calves' brains, but they'd get little nourishment an' only a moldy flavor out of yourn. An' you'd shore look better with all yore clothes on. I can see th' places where you've stopped washin' yore hands, feet, an' neck all these years."

Hopalong mumbled something and slid into his under wear. "Gee!" he exulted. "These clean clothes shore do feel good!"

"You'd nat'rally notice it a whole lot more than I would," said Red, following suit. As his head came into sight again he let his eyes wander along the eastern and southeastern horizon. "You know, them bluffs off yonder remind me a hull lot of parts of th' Staked Plain," he observed. "We hadn't ought to be very far away from it, down here."

"They're its edge," grunted Hopalong, rearranging the strips of meat over the fire. Both became silent, going back in their memories to the events of years before, when the Staked Plain had been very real and threatening to them.

At daylight the following morning they arose and not much later were riding slowly southward and as near the creek as the nature of its banks would allow. When the noon sun blazed down on them they found the creek dwindling rapidly and, glancing ahead down the sandy valley they could make out the dark, moist place where the last of it disappeared in the sands. They watered their horses, drank their fill and went on again toward the place where they were to meet Johnny, riding on a curving course which led them closer and closer to the forbidding hills. In mid-afternoon they came to a salt pond and instead of arguing about the matter with their thirsty mounts, let them go up to it and smell it. The animals turned away and went on again without protest. A little later Red squinted eastward and nodded in answer to his own unspoken question.

"Shore it is," he muttered.

Hopalong followed his gaze and grunted. "Shore." He regarded the distant bulk thoughtfully. "Strikes me no sane cow ever would go out there, unless it was drove. It's our business to look into everythin'. Comin'?"

"I shore am. Nobody can buffalo me an' chuck me into jail without a comeback. I'm lookin' for things to fatten it."

"It can't get too fat for me," replied his friend. "Helpin' th' Kid get his money back was enough to set me after some of that reward money; but when I sized up Kane an' his gang it promised to be a pleasure; now, after that jailin', it's a yelpin' joy. If there's no other way I'm aimin' to ride into Mesquite an' smoke up with both guns."

As they neared the carcass Red glanced at his cheerful friend. "Head's swelled up like a keg," he said. "Struck by a rattler."

"Reckon so; but cows dead from snakebite ain't common."

They pulled up and looked at it at close range.

"Shot," grunted Hopalong.

"Then somebody was out here with it," said Red swinging down. "He was tender-hearted, he was. Gimme a hand. We'll turn it over an' look at th' brand."

Hopalong complied, and then they looked at each other and back to the carcass, where a large piece of hide had been neatly trimmed around and skinned off.

"Didn't dare let it wander, an' they plugged it after it got struck," said Red.

"Careful, they was," commented his companion. "They was too careful. If they'd let it wander it wouldn't 'a' told nothin', 'specially if it wandered toward home. But shootin' it, an' then doin' this I reckon our come back is takin' on weight"

"It shore is," emphatically said Red. "Cuss this hard ground! It don't tell nothin'. They went north or south an' not long ago, neither. Which way are you ridin'?"

Hopalong considered. "If they went either way they'd be seen. I got a feelin' they went right across. Greasers an' Injuns know that desert, an' there's both kinds workin' 1 for Kane. It allus has been a shore-thing way for 'em. Remember what Idaho said?"

"It can't be done," said Red.

"Slippery Trendly an' Deacon Rankin did it."

"But they only crossed one corner," argued Red.

"McLeod's Texans did it!"

"They didn't cross much more'n a corner," retorted Red. "An' look what it did to 'em!"

"It's a straight drive for them valleys along th' Cimarron," mused Hopalong. "Nobody to see 'em come or go, good grass to fatten 'em up after they got there, an' plenty of time for blottin' th' brands. I'll bet Kane's got men that knows how to get 'em over. There's waterholes if you only know where to look, an' how to head for 'em; an' some of these half-breeds down here know all of that. If they went north or south on a course far enough east to keep many folks from seein' 'ehi they'd find it near as dry. Well, we better go down an' meet th' Kid before we do anythin' else. We got our bearin's an' can find th' way back again. What you say?"

Red mounted and led the way. "If I'm goin' to ride around out here I'm goin' to have plenty of water, an' that means canteens. I'm near chokin' for a drink; an' this cayuse is gettin' mean. Come on."

"We might pick up some tracks if we hunt right now," said Hopalong. "If we wait longer this wind'll blot 'em out. I ain't thirsty," he lied. "You go down an' meet th' Kid an' I'll look around east of here. We can't gamble with this: if I find tracks they'll save us a lot of ridin' an' guessin'. Go ahead."

"If you stay I stay," growled Red.

"Listen, you chump," retorted Hopalong. "It's only a few hours more if I stay out here than if I go with you. Get canteens an' supplies. Th' Kid can bring us more tomorrow. I'm backin' my guess: get a-goin'."

Red saw the wisdom of the suggestion and wheeled, riding at good speed to the southwest while his friend went eastward, his eyes searching the desert plain. It was night when Red returned, picking his way with a plainsman's instinct to the carcass of the cow, and he softly replied to a low call which came from behind a billow of sand.

Hopalong arose. "You made good time," he said.

"Reckon so," replied Red, riding toward him. "I only got two canteens an' not much grub. Th' Kid'll be ready; for us tomorrow. What about yore cayuse?"

"Don't worry," chuckled Hopalong. "It's th' cayuses that's been botherin' me most. They're all right now. I found a little hole with cold, sweet water, an' there's grass around it for th' cayuses. There ain't much, but enough for these two goats. Th' water-hole ain't more'n three feet across an' a foot deep, but it fills up good an' has wet quite a spot around it. An' Red, I found somethin' else!"

"Good; what is it?"

"There's clay around it an' a thin layer of sand over th' clay," replied Hopalong. "I found th' prints of a cayuse an' a man, an' they was fresh not more'n twenty- four hours old if I'm any judge. I cast around on widenin' circles, but couldn't pick up th' trail any distance from th' hole. Th' wind that's been blowin' all day wiped 'em out; but it didn't wipe out much at th' edge of th' water. I could even make it out where he knelt to drink. There you are: a dead cow, with th' brand skinned off; tracks of a man an' a cayuse at that water-hole; no herd tracks, no other cayuse tracks just them two, an' our suspicions. What you think?"

Red chuckled. "I think we're gettin' somewhere, cussed slow an' I don't know where; but I'm playin' up that skinned cow. If it was all skinned I'd say a hide hunter might 'a' done it, an' that he made th' tracks you saw; but it wasn't. You should 'a' looked better near th' carcass instead of huntin' up th' water-hole. You might 'a' seen th' tracks of a herd, or what th' wind left of 'em, 'though I reckon they drove that cow off quite a ways before they dropped it."

"Did you cross any herd tracks after you left me?" asked Hopalong.

"No; why?"

"An' we didn't cross any before you left," said Hopalong. "If there's been any to see runnin' east an' west we'd 'a' found 'em. That was all hard ground; an' there was th' wind. There wasn't none to find."

"Huh!" snorted Red, and after a moment's thought he looked up. "Mebby that feller found th' cow all swelled up with snakebite, away off from water as he thought, an' just put an end to its misery?"

"Then why did he cut out th' brand?" snapped Hopalong.

"What are you askin' me for?" demanded Red, truculently. "How'd I know? You shore can ask some !d n fool questions!"

"Yo're half-baked," growled his companion. "I will be, too, before I get any answer to what I'm askin' myself. I'm aimin' to squat behind a rise north of that water-hole an' wait for my answer if it takes a month. I can get a good view from up there."

Red, whose hatred for deserts was whole-hearted, looked through the darkness in disgust at his friend. "You've picked out a fine job for us!" he retorted. "If yo're right an' they did drive a herd across to th' other side it'll shore be a wait. Be more'n a week, an' mebby two."

"They've got to drive hard between waters," replied Hopalong. "They'll waste no time; an' they won't waste time comin' back again, when they won't have th' cows to hold 'em down. There's one thing shore: They won't be back tomorrow or th' next day, an' we both can ride down an' see th' Kid, an' mebby McCullough. It's too good a lead to throw away. But before we meet Johnny we're goin' to have a better look around, 'specially south an' east."

"All right," agreed Red. "How'd you come to find th' hole?"

"Rode up on a ridge an' saw somethin' green, an' knowin' it wasn't you I went for it," answered his friend. "If it had been made for us it couldn't be better. With water, an' grass enough for night grazin', an a good ridge to look from, it's a fine place for us. We'll take turns at it, for it won't feed two cayuses steady. Th' off man can ride west to grass, mebby back to our camp, an' by takin' shifts at it we can mebby save most of th' grass at th' hole."

"An' mebby get spotted while we're ridin' back an' forth?"

"Th' ridge will take care of that, an' I reckon when it peters out there'll be others to hide us. I'm dead set on this: I'm so set that I'll stick it out all alone rather than pass it by. I tell you I got a feelin'"

"I ain't quittin'," growled Red; "I ain't got sense enough to quit. Desert or no desert I'm aimin' to do my little gilt-edged damndest; but I'm admittin' I'll be plumb happy when it's my time off. We'll get supplies an' more canteens from th' Kid tomorrow, an' be fixed so we can foller any other lead that sticks up its head. I shore can stand more than ridin' over a desert if it'll give us any thin' on them fellers."

"Here we are," grunted his companion, swinging from the saddle. "Finest, coldest water you ever drunk. I'm puttin' double hobbles on my cayuse tonight, just to make shore."

"Me, too," said Red, dismounting.

In the morning they rode up for a look along the ledge, found that it would answer their requirements and then went southeast, curving further into the desert, and it was not long before Red's roving glance caught something which aroused his interest and he silently rode off to investigate, his companion going slowly ahead. When he returned it was by another way and he rode with his eager eyes searching the desert beneath and ahead of him. Reaching his friend, who had stopped and also was scanning the desert floor with great intentness, he nodded in quiet satisfaction.

"Think you see 'em, too?" he smilingly inquired. "They're so faint they can't hardly be seen, not till you look ahead, an' then it's only th' difference between this strip of sand that we're on an' th' rest of th' desert. It's a cattle trail, Hoppy; I just found another water-hole, a big one. Th' bank was crowded with hoof marks, cattle an' cayuses. Looks like they come from th' west, bearin' a little north. Th' only reason we didn't see 'em when we rode down was because they was on hard ground. That shore explains th' dead cow."

"An' in a few hours more," said his companion, "this powdery dust will blot 'em out. If they was clearer I'd risk follerin' them, even if we only had a canteen apiece.

We can ride as far between waters as they can drive a herd, an' a whole lot farther. It's only fearin' that th' trail will disappear that holds me back."

"We don't have to risk it yet," said Red, grimly. "We've found out where they cut in an' how they start across; an' all we got to do is to lay low up there an' wait for 'em to come back, or start another herd across, to learn who they are."

"If we wait for their next drive we can foiler 'em on a fresh, plain trail, an' be a lot better prepared," supplemented Hopalong. "I reckon we're shore goin' to fatten our comeback!"

"It's pickin' up fast," gloated his friend. "All we got to do is watch that big water-hole' an' we got 'em. There ain't so many water-holes out on this skillet that they can drive any way they like. We'll camp at th' little one, of course, but we can lay closer to th' big one nights."

"An' from th' ridge up yonder th' man on day watch can see for miles."

"Yes; an' fry, an' broil, an' sizzle, an' melt!" muttered Red. "D n'em!"

Hopalong had wheeled and was leading the way into the southwest as straight as he could go for the meeting with Johnny, and Red pushed up past him and bore a little more to the west. They had seen all they needed to see for the day, and they had made up their minds.

At last after a long, hot ride they reached the bluffs marking the side of the plateau and soon were winding down a steep-walled arroyo which led to the plain below, and the country began to change with such insensible gradations that they hardly noticed it. Sage and greasewood became more plentiful and after an hour had passed an occasional low bush was to be seen and the ground sloped more and more in front of them. A low fringe of greenery lay along the distant bottom, where Sand Creek or some other hidden stream came close to the top of the soil, later to issue forth and become the stream into which the Question-Mark's creek later emptied. They crossed this and breasted an opposing slope, followed around the base of a low ridge of hills and at last stopped under a clump of live-oak and cotton woods in the extreme east end of the Question-Mark valley.

While the two friends were riding toward the little clump of trees west of the Question-Mark ranch visitors rode slowly up to the door of the ranchhouse and one of them dismounted. The shield he wore on his open vest shone in the sun with nickel brightness, but his face was anything but bright. The job which had been cut out for him was not to his liking and had destroyed his peace of mind, and the peace of mind of the two deputies, who needed no reflection upon their subordinate positions to keep them in the sheriff's rear. What little assurance they might have started with received a jolt soon after they had left town, when a gruff and unmistakably unfriendly voice had asked, with inconsiderate harshness and profanity, their intended destination and their business. At last allowed to pass on after quite some humiliation from the hidden sentries, they now were entering upon the dangerous part of their mission.

Corwin stepped up to the door and knocked, a formality which he never dispensed with on the Question-Mark. Other visitors usually walked right in and found a chair or sat on the table, but it never should be said to Corwin's discredit that an officer of the law was rude and ignorant in such a well-known and long-established form of etiquette. So Sheriff Corwin knocked.

"Come in!" impatiently bawled a loud and rude voice.

The sheriff obeyed and looked around the door casing. "Ah, hello, Mac," he said in cheery greeting.

"Mac who?" roared the man at the table.

"McCullough," said the man at the door, correcting himself. "How are you?"

"Yo're one full-blooded d--n fool of a sheriff," sneered the trail-boss. "Where's them two prisoners I been waitin' for?"

"They got away. Somebody helped 'em bust th' jail. I sent word back to you by yore own men."

"Shore, I got, it; I know that. That's no excuse a-tall!" retorted the trail-boss. "I went an' sent word down to Twitchell on th' jump that his fool way worked an' that I was goin' to send him th' men he wanted. Then you let 'em bust out of jail! Fine sort of a fool you made of me! Where's yore reward now, that you was spendin' so fast? An' what'll Twitchell say, an' do? He wants th' bank robbers, not excuses; an' more'n all he wanted th' man that shot Ridley. It ain't only a question of pertectin' th' men workin' for him, but it's personal, too. Ridley was an old friend of his'n an' he'll raise h--l till he gets th' man that killed him. What about it? What have you done since they got away?"

"We trailed 'em, but they lost us," growled Corwin. "Reckon they got up on that hard ground an' then lit out, jumpin' th' country as fast as they could. Kane had it on 'em, cold an' proper but I had my doubts, somehow. I ain't quittin'; I'm watchin' an' layin' back, an' I'm figgerin' on deliverin' th' man that got Ridley."

"(You mean Long an' Thompson are innocent?" demanded McCullough with a throaty growl. "Yo're sayin' it yoreself! What was you tryin' to run on me, then?"

"They must 'a' robbed th' bank," replied the sheriff; "but I got my own ideas about who killed yore friend. This is between us. I'm waitin' till I get th' proof; an' after I get it, an' th' man, I'll mebby have to leave th' country between sunset an' dawn. I ain't no dog, an' I'm gettin' riled."

"Then it was Kane who cold-decked them two fellers?" demanded McCullough.

"I ain't sayin' a word, now," replied the sheriff. "Not yet, I ain't, but I'm aimin' to get th' killer. Where's that Nelson?"

"What you want with him?" asked the trail-boss. "Reckon he done it?"

"No; he didn't," answered Corwin. "He only helped them fellers out of jail, an' I'm goin' to take him in."

"What?" shouted McCullough, and then burst out laughing. "I'm repeatin' what I said about you bein' full-blooded! Say, if you can turn that trick I won't raise a hand not till he's in jail; an' then I'll get him out cussed quick. He's workin' for me, an' he didn't do no crime, gettin' a couple of innocent men out of that mud hut; an', besides, I don't know that he did get 'em out. Go after him, Corwin; go right out after him." He glanced out of the window again and chuckled. "I see you brought some of yore official fam'ly along.

Shucks! That ain't no way to do, three agin' one. An' I heard you was a bad hombre with a short gun!"

"It ain't no question of how bad I am!" retorted the sheriff. "We want him alive."

"Oh, I see; aim to scare him, bein' three to one. All right; go ahead but there ain't goin' to be no pot-shootin'. Tell yore fam'bly that. I mean it, an' I cut in sudden th' minute any of it starts."

"There won't be no pot-shootin'," growled the sheriff, and to make sure that there wouldn't be any he stepped out and gave explicit instructions to his companions before going toward the smaller corral. When part way there he heard whistling, wheeled in his tracks and went back to the bunkhouse, hugging the wall as he slipped along it, his gun raised and ready for action.

Johnny turned the corner, caught sight of the two deputies, who held his suspicious attention, and had gone too far to leap back when he saw Corwin flattened against the wall and the sheriff's gun covering him. Presumably safe on a friendly ranch, he had given no thought to any imminent danger, and now he stood and stared at the unexpected menace, the whistling almost dying on his pursed lips.

"Nelson!" snapped the sheriff, "yo're under arrest for helpin' in that jail delivery. I'll shoot at th' first hostile move! Put up yore hands an' turn 'round!"

Johnny glanced from him to the deputies and thought swiftly. Three to one, and he was covered. He leaned against the wall and laughed until he was limp. When he regained control of himself he blinked at the sheriff and drew a long breath, which nearly caused Corwin to pull the trigger; but the sheriff found it to be a false alarm.

"What th' devil makes you think *I* was mixed up in that?" he asked, laughing again. He drew another long breath with unexpected suddenness, and again the nervous sheriff and the two deputies nearly pulled trigger; and again it was a false alarm.

"I've done my thinkin'!" snapped Corwin. "Watch him, boys!" he said out of the corner of his mouth. "An' if you wasn't mixed up in it you won't come to no harm."

"No; not in a decent town," rejoined Johnny, leaning against the wall again, where Corwin's body somewhat sheltered him from the deputies. The sheriff tensed again at the movement. "But Mesquite's plumb full of liars," drawled Johnny, "trained by Kane. How do I know I'll get a square deal?"

"You'll get it! Put 'em up!" snapped Corwin, raising his gun to give the command emphasis, and it now pointed at the other's head.

"Long an' Thompson "began Johnny, and like a flash he twisted sidewise and jerked his head out of the line of fire, the bullet passing his ear and the powder scorching his hair. As he twisted he slipped in close, his left hand flashing to Corwin's gun-wrist and the right, across his body, tore the weapon from its owner's hand. The movement had been done so quickly that the sheriff did not realize what had occurred until he found himself disarmed and pressing against his own weapon, which was jammed into his groin. Johnny's left-hand gun had leaped into the surprised deputies' sight at the sheriff's hip and they lost no time in letting their own guns drop to the ground in instant answer to the snapped command. Corwin's momentary surprise died out nearly as quickly as it was born and, scorning the menace of the muzzle of his own gun, he grabbed Johnny. As he shifted his foot Johnny's leg slipped behind it and a sudden heave turned the sheriff over it, almost end over end, and he struck the ground with a resounding thump. Johnny sprang back, one gun on the sheriff, the other on the deputies.

"Get off them cayuses," he ordered and the two men slowly complied. "Go over near th' corral, an' stay there." In a moment he gave all his attention to the slowly arising officer.

"All this was unnecessary," he said. "You put us all in danger of bein' killed. Don't you never again try to take me in till you know why yo're doin' it! My head might 'a' been blowed off, an' all for nothin'! You don't know who busted that jail, judgin' by yore fool actions, an' you cussed well know it. You got plenty of gall, comin' down here an' throwin' a gun on me, for that! I'm sayin', frank, that whoever done that trick did th' right thing; but that ain't sayin' that I did it. Hope I didn't hurt you, Corwin; but I had to act sudden when you grabbed me."

"Don't you do no worryin' on my account!" snapped the sheriff.

"I ain't blamin' you for doin' yore duty, if you was doin' it honest," said Johnny; "but you ain't got no business jumpin' before yo're shore. I ain't holdin' th' sack for nobody, Corwin; Kane or nobody else. Now then: you can tell what proof you got that it was me that busted th' jail."

Corwin was watching the smiling face and the accusing eyes and he saw no enmity in either. "Then who did?" he demanded.

Johnny shrugged his shoulders. "Quien sdbef" he asked. "There's a lot of people down here that would have more reason to do a thing like that, even for strangers, than I would. You ain't loved very much, from what I've heard. I don't want any more enemies than I got; but I'm tellin' you, flat, that I ain't goin' back with you; an' neither would you, if you was in my place, in a strange town. Here," he said, letting the hammer down and tossing the gun at the sheriff's feet, "take your gun. I'm glad you ain't hurt; an' I'm cussed glad I ain't. But somebody's shore goin' to be th' next time you pull a gun on me on a guess. You want to be dead shore, Corwin. We've had enough of this. Did you get any trace of them two?"

The sheriff watched his opponent's gun go back into its holster and slowly picked up his own. "No; I ain't," he admitted, and considered a moment as he sheathed the weapon with great care. "I ain't got nothin' flat agin' you," he said; "but I still think you had a hand in it. That's a good trick you worked, Nelson; I'm rememberin' it. All right; th' next time I come for you I'll have it cold; an' I'm shore expectin' to come for you, an' Idaho, too."

"That's fair enough," replied Johnny, smiling; "but I don't see why you want to drag Idaho in it for. He didn't have no more to do with it than I did."

"I'm believin' that, too," retorted the sheriff; "since you put it just that way. I haven't heard you say that you didn't do it. Before I go I want to ask you a question: Where was you th' night th' Diamond L lost them cows?"

"Right here with Mac an' th' boys."

"He was," said McCullough. "Yo're ridin' wide of th' trail, Cor win."

"Mebby," grunted the sheriff. "There's two trails. I mebby am plumb off of one of 'em, as long as you know he was down here that night; but I'm ridin' right down th' middle of th' other. When did you meet Long an' Thompson first?" he asked, wheeling suddenly and facing Johnny.

"Thinkin' what you do about me," replied Johnny, "I'd be a fool to tell you anythin', no matter what. So, as long as yo're ridin' down th' middle you'll have to read th' signs yoreself.

Some of 'em must be plumb faint, th' way yo're guessin', an' castin' 'round. Get any news about them rustlers?"

"What's th' use of makin' trouble for yoreself by bein' stubborn?" asked McCullough. He looked at Corwin. "Sheriff, I know for shore that he never knowed any Bill Long or Red Thompson until after he come to Mesquite. What news did you get about th' rustlers?"

"Huh!" muttered Corwin, searching the face of the trail-boss, whose reputation for veracity was unquestioned. "I ain't got any news about 'em. Once they got on th' hard stretch they could go for miles an' not leave no trail. I'm figgerin' on spendin' quite some time north of where Lukins' boys quit an' turned back. There's three cows missin' that are marked so different from any I've ever seen that I'll know 'em in a herd of ten thousan' head; an' when they're cut out for me to look at there's some marks on horns an' hoofs that'll prove whose cows they are. I'm takin' a couple of his boys with me when I go, to make shore. Of course, I don't know that we'll ever see 'em, at all. Well," he said, turning toward his horse, "reckon I'll be goin'." He waved to the deputies, who approached, picked up their guns under Johnny's alert and suspicious scrutiny, and mounted. "As for you, Nelson, next time I'll be dead shore; an' I'll mebby shoot first, on a gamble, an' talk afterward. So-long."

Watching the three arms of the law ride away and out of sight, Johnny swung around and faced the grinning trail-boss. "You told th' truth, Mac; but I wonder if Corwin heard it like I did?"

McCullough shrugged his shoulders. "Who cares? I'm thankin' you for an interestin' lesson in how to beat th' drop; but I reckon I'm gettin' too old to be quick enough to use it. I reckon Waffles has been tellin' th' truth about yore Bar-20 outfit. Where you goin' now?"

"Off to see a couple of better men from that same outfit," grinned Johnny.

He went on with his preparations and soon rode Pepper toward a gap in the southern chain of hills, leading a loaded pack horse behind him. Emerging on the other side of the pass he followed the chain westward and in due time rounded the last hill and headed for the little clump of trees where he saw his two friends waiting. They waved to him and he replied, chuckling with pleasure.

Red looked critically at the pack animal. "Huh! From th' looks of that cayuse I reckon he figgers we're goin' to be gone some months, like a prospector holin' up for th' winter."

"He never underplays a hand," grunted Hopalong, a warm light coming into his eyes. "Desert or no desert, it's shore good to be with him again. He never should 'a' left Montanny,"

Johnny soon joined them, dismounted, picketed the pack horse, pushed back his sombrero and rolled a cigarette, grinning cheerfully. "If you want any more can teens you can have th' pair on my cayuse," he said. "Find anythin'?"

They told him and he nodded in quiet satisfaction. "You shore ain't been asleep," he chuckled. "You've just about found out somethin' that's been puzzlin' a lot of folks down here for some years. I wonder how close they ever come to them water-holes when they was scoutin' around? But mebby they never scouted over that way much everybody was bankin' on 'em stayin' on th' hard stretch over Lukins' way, instead of crossin' it so close to town. You'd never thought of lookin' for 'em over east if you hadn't remembered Slippery Trendly, now would you?"

"We wasn't lookin' for nothin' nor nobody except you," admitted Hopalong. "But when Red saw a dead cow is far out on th' desert as it was, we just had to take a look at it. An' when we saw it had been shot we couldn't do nothin' else but look for th' brand. That bein' cut out made us plumb suspicious. One thing just nat'rally led to th' next, as th' mule said when its tail was pulled."

"What you bet that missin' brand wasn't a Diamond "w?" Johnny asked.

"Ain't that th' ranch Idaho works for?" queried Red.

Johnny nodded. "They raided Lukins th' night of th' day you an' Hoppy left town. That outfit put in two days ridin' along th' hard ground, half of 'em up an' half of 'em down. They lost over a hundred head."

His friends exchanged looks, each trying to visualize the all but obliterated trail, and both nodded.

"Mebby it was a Diamond L," said Hopalong, and he explained their plans to some length.

"That's goin' to win if you can stick it out," said Johnny. "McCullough's steamin' a little, but he's still carryin' out Twitchell's wishes; an' I been arguin' with him, too, to give you fellers a chance. Hey!" he ex claimed, grinning. "I allus knowed I'd get a bad name for hangin' out with you two coyotes; an' I done got it. I'm suspected strong of bein' a criminal, like you fellers, an' I'll mebby be an outlaw, too. Sheriff Corwin just said so, an' he ought to know if anybody does. He arrested me for helpin' to get you fellers out of jail, but he didn't say how he aimed to keep me in it, busted like it is."

"How'd you get away?" asked Red. "Wouldn't you go with him?"

"Mebby he didn't have th' rest of th' dozen," suggested Hopalong.

"Oh, he wasn't real shore about it really bein' me he wanted, so he turned me loose," replied Johnny. "Any how, I couldn't 'a' gone with him: I had to get this stuff out to you fellers. An' besides, I knowed if I got in that 'dobe hut you wouldn't have th' nerve to bust me out again."

"I'm honin' to bust Corwin's 'dobe head," growled Red.

"There's four canteens an' plenty of grub, with Mac's compliments," said Johnny, waving at the pack horse. "When am I to meet you again?"

Hopalong considered a moment. "There's too much ridin', comin' down here unless we has to," he said. "Tell you what: We'll find a hill, or a ridge up on th' plateau where a fire can be lit that won't show to nobody north of them hills you just come around. Take that white patch up yonder: we can see it plain for miles. You ride up to it every day about two hours after sun-up; an' every night just after dark. If you see smoke puffs in daylight, or a winkin' fire at night, ride toward that split bluff be hind us. We'll meet you there. If you get news for us, do th' same thing on th' other slope, so it can't be seen from across this valley. As long as it can be seen on a line with th' split bluff we won't miss it."

Johnny scratched his head. "Strings of six puffs or six winks means trouble: come a-latherin'," he suggested. "Strings of three means news, an' take yore time. Better have a signal for grub an' supplies: it'll mebby save ridin'. Say groups of two an' five, alternate?"

Hopalong nodded and repeated the signals to make certain that he had them right. "Two an' five, alternate, for supplies; strings of six, come a-runnin'; strings of three, news, an' take our time. Couple of hours after sun-up an' just after dark. All right, Kid."

"Mac's got an old spyglass. Want it, if I can get it?" asked Johnny.

"Shore!" grunted Red.

"Bring it next time you come," said Hopalong.

"All right. Where you goin' now?"

"Up on Sand Creek, where we're camped," answered Red. "We got a couple of days before we move out on th' fryin' pan, an' we're aimin' to make th' most of it"

"Wait till I get th' glass, an' I'll go along," suggested Johnny, eagerly.

"Get a rustle on an' take this pack animal back with you," smiled Hopalong as Johnny started without it. "We'll empty out th' canteens, an' we can tote th' sup plies without it."

Chapter XVI
A Vigil Rewarded

The days passed quietly for the two watchers after Johnny had gone back to the Question-Mark, the hours dragging in monotonous succession. In the Sand Creek camp time passed pleasantly enough, but out on the great, up-slanting billow of sand north of Sweet Spring, devoid of shelter from the blazing sun and from the reflected glare of the gray-white desert around it, was another matter. Prone on his stomach lay Hopalong on the northward slope, his face barely level with the crest of the ridge. Down in the hollow behind him was his horse, picketed and hobbled as well, and at his side on his blanket to keep the cutting sand and clogging dust from barrels and actions lay his rifle and his six-guns, so hot that their metal parts could not be touched without a grimace of discomfort coming to his face. The telescope at intervals swung around the shimmering horizon, magnifying the dancing heat waves until the distortion of their wavering, streaming currents at times rendered the view chaotic and baffling. Strange sights were to be seen in the air and knowing what they were he watched them as his only source of amusement. A tree-bordered lake appeared, its waters sparkling, arose into the air, became vague and slowly dissolved from view, calling from him caustic comment. Inverted mountains reached down from the heavens, standing on snow-covered tops, writhed more and more from their outer edges and melted down from the up-flung bases, slowly fading from view. They were followed by a silvery, winding river, certain features which caused him to think that he recognized it and while he studied it a herd of cattle upside down, and greatly magnified, pushed through into sight as the river scene faded away. Another hour passed and then a steepwalled, green valley inverted itself before his gaze. He could make out a hut and a few trees and then as mounted men began to ride up its slanting bluff trail his attention became riveted on it and he reached for the hot telescope. One look through the instrument made him grunt with disgust, for the figures danced and shrunk and expanded, weaved and became like shadows, through which he looked as though through a rare, discolored vapor. He was mildly excited and tried in vain to search his visual image of the sight for the faces of the men; but it was in vain, and he opened his eyes as the image faded and then closed them again to better search the memory picture. This, too, availed him nothing and he realized that he had not really seen the faces. He was perplexed and vexed, for there was something familiar about some of those riders. About to move for a look around through the telescope, he yielded to a humorous warning and lay quiet for awhile. Was it possible that the mirage had been double-acting, and had revealed each to the other?

"Mebby they won't put as much stock in theirs as I did in mine," he said, and slowly picked up the telescope for a final look all around the horizon before Red should relieve him. East, south, west he looked and saw nothing, Swinging it toward the Sand Creek camp he grunted in satisfaction as a figure very much like Red wavered and danced as it emerged over a ridge of sand. Further north he swung it and slowly swept the northern horizon. Swearing suddenly he stopped its slow progress and brought it back searchingly over ground it had just covered. Rigid he held it and looked with unbelieving eyes.

"Mirage?" he growled, questioningly. "It's too solid for that I'm goin' up to see."

Getting his horse he gingerly slipped the hot rifle into its scabbard, hastily dropped the six-guns into their holsters and, mounting, rode to meet his nearing friend.

"Cooked?" queried Red, grinning. "You shore didn't lose no time gettin' started after you saw me! Ain't it h lout here?"

"H--l is right," answered Hopalong, handing over the telescope. "But we got cayuses, full canteens, an' know where we are. Swing that blisterin' tube over yonder," pointing, "an' tell me what you see?"

Red obeyed and the moving glass suddenly stopped and swung back a little. After long scrutiny he raised his head and gazed steadily over the rigid tube as though along a rifle barrel. "I see him, now, without it," he said. "A-foot, he is, staggerin' every-which way. Comin'?"

His companion replied by pushing into the lead and setting a stiff pace through the soft sand and alkali dust. As they drew near they both shivered at the sight which steadily was being better revealed.

The figure of a man. and scarcely more than figure, stumbled crazily across the sand, hatless, his bare feet covered with dust which had become pasty with the blood exuding through the deepening clefts in the skin and flesh. Progress on such feet would have made him mad from pain if he had not already become so from other causes. His trousers were ripped and frayed to the swollen, dustplastered knees, the crimson fissures running up and down his swollen legs. Shirt he had none, save the strip which hung stiff and crimson from his belt. His upper body was a thing of horror, swollen, matted with crusts of dried blood, from beneath which more oozed out to in turn coagulate. His burning eyes peered through slits in the puffed face and his tongue, blackened and purplish, stuck out of his mouth.

"G-d!" muttered Red, glancing awesomely at the tense face of his companion.

"He's gone," said Hopalong, softly. "Nothing can save him. It would be a mercy "but he checked the words, searching Red's acquiescent eyes.

"Can't do it," said Red. "Can you?"

Hopalong drew in a deep breath and shook his head. "We got to try th' other first," he said. "It's wrong but there's nothin' else. We ain't doctors, an' there may be a fightin' chance. Hobble th' cayuses. We'll both tackle him one alone might have to be too rough, for he'll mebby fight."

"He's down," said Red as he swung from his saddle. "Lookin' right at us, too, an' don't see us."

The figure groveled in the sand, digging with blundering fingers worn to the bone by previous digging, and choked sounds came from the swollen throat. Red talked to himself as he hobbled his horse and pushed down the picket pin.

"Lost his cayuse, somehow, or went crazy an' chased it away. Used up his last water an' then threw away everythin' he had. Tore off his shirt because th' neck band got too tight, an' th' cloth stuck to th' blood clots an' pulled at 'em. I've seen others, but they warn't none of 'em as bad as him," growled Red more to himself than to his companion.

Hopalong pushed home his own picket pin and stood up. "Comin'?" he asked, starting slowly for the groveling, digging thing on the sand.

They stepped up to him and lifted the unfortunate from the ground. Dazed and without understanding, the pitiful object of their assistance suddenly snarled and reached its bleeding fingers for Red's throat, and for the next few minutes two rational, strong men had as hard a fight on their hands as they ever had experienced; and when it was over and the enraged unfortunate became docile from exhaustion they were covered with blood. Letting a few drops of water trickle down the side of the protruding tongue, which they forced to one side when the drops were stopped by it, they worked over the dying man as long as they dared in the sun and then, carrying him to Hopalong's horse they put him across the saddle, lashing him securely, and covered him with a doubled blanket to cheat the leering sun.

"Go ahead to th' water-hole," said Hopalong, straightening up from tying the last knot. "I'll take him to camp an' do what I can. There won't be no trouble handlin' him, tied like he is. Got to try to save him--'though I hope somebody puts a bullet through my head if I ever get like him."

"Bein' crazy, he mebby ain't feelin' it as much as he might," replied Red. "Seems to me he's the one they called Sandy Woods; but he's so plumb changed I ain't shore."

Hopalong thought of the last mirage he had seen, was about to speak of it, but abruptly changed his mind. He conveyed his warning in another way. "Keep a-lookin' sharp, Red," he said. "Th' poor devil shore was one of them rustlers; an' they mebby ain't far behind him. It's gettin' nearer an' nearer th' time they ought to come back. I'll stay with him in camp an' let th' Kid's signal go, if he makes one. This feller ain't got long to live, I'm figgerin'."

"It's a wonder he lived this long," said Red, riding off to take up the vigil.

Hopalong swung his belts and guns over the pommel of the saddle to lighten him, drank sparingly from a canteen and started on foot for the camp, leading his dispirited horse. After a walk through the hot, yielding sand which became a punishment during the last mile he sighed with relief as he stopped the horse on the bank of Sand Creek and tenderly placed its burden on the ground in the shade of a tree. More water, in judicious quantities, and at increasingly frequent intervals brought no apparent relief to the sufferer, and in mid-afternoon Sandy Woods lost all need of earthly care. Kane's thieving trail-boss had won his bet.

Hopalong looked down at the body freed of its suffering and slowly shook his head. "Th' other way would've been th' best," he said. "I knowed it; Red knowed it yet, both plumb shore, an' knowin' it was better, we just couldn't do it. A man's trainin' is a funny thing."

He looked around the little depression and walked toward a patch of sand lying near a mass of stones which had rolled down the slope; and before the evening shadows had reached across the little creek, a heaped-up pile of rocks marked the place of rest of one more weary traveler. At the head, lying on the ground, was a cross made of stones. Why he had placed it there Hopalong could hardly have told, but something within him had stirred through the sleep of busy and heedless years, and he had unthinkingly obeyed it.

He looked up at the sun and found it was time to go on watch again. He had been given no opportunity to sleep, but did not complain, carelessly accepting it as one of the breaks in the game. When he reached his friend, ready to go on duty again, Red looked up at him and scrutinized his face.

"Lots of sleep you must 'a' got," said Red. "How's our patient?"

"Gettin' all th' sleep there is," came the reply. "We was right both ways."

"Spread yore blanket here," said Red. "I'm stickin' to th' job till you have a snooze. Anyhow, somethin' tells me that two won't be more'n we need out here at night, from now on."

"It's my trick," replied Hopalong, decisively. "Spread yore own blanket."

"Him turnin' up like he did was an accident," retorted Red, "an' accidents are shared between us both. Anyhow, I ain't sleepy an' th' next few hours are pleasant. Get some sleep, you chump!"

"Well, as long as we're both handy, it don't make much difference," replied Hopalong, spreading the blanket. "We can spell each other any time we need to. Hope th' Kid ain't tryin' to signal nothin'."

"We got more to signal than he has," growled Red. "Shut up, now; an' go to sleep," and his companion, blessed by one of the prized acquirements of the plains man, promptly obeyed; but it seemed to him that he scarcely had dozed off when he felt his friend's thrusting hand, and he opened his eyes in the darkness, staring up at the blazing stars, in surprise.

"Yes?" whispered Hopalong, without moving or making any other sound, again true to his training.

His companion's whisper, a whisper by force of habit rather than for any good reason, reached him: "Turn over, an' look over th' ridge."

Hopalong obeyed, threw off the blanket which Red had spread over him when the chill of the desert night descended, and became all eyes as he saw the faint glow of a distant fire, which rapidly grew and became brighter. "It's them, down at th' other water-hole," he said, arising and feeling to see if his Colts had slid out of their holsters while he slept. "I'm goin' down for a better look," and he glanced at the northern sky just above the horizon, memorized a group of stars and disappeared noiselessly into the night.

Nearing the larger water-hole he went more slowly and finished by wriggling up to the crest of a sand billow, his head behind a lone sage bush, and his eyelids closed to a thin crack, lest the light of the fire should reflect from his eyes and reveal him to some keen, roving glance.

The grease wood fire blazed under a pair of skillets, while a coffeepot imitated the Tower of Pisa on the glowing coals at one edge. Around it, reclining on the powdery clay, or squatting in the more characteristic attitude of men of the saddle, were a half-dozen of Kane's pets, Miguel and his cronies well to one side. The hidden watcher knew them all by sight and saw several men who had helped the sheriff trick him and Red. In the darkness behind the group he heard their horses moving about as they grazed.

"Do you reckon he made it, Miguel?" asked the trailboss, apropos of the conversation around the fire.

Miguel turned his face to the light, the scar over his eye glistening against the duller skin around it. "I say no," he drawled. "He change hees horrse at the corrals, no? The-e horrse he took was born at the-e Cimarron corral an' foaled eet's firrst colt there. I would not lak' sooch a horrse eef I did not know my way. But, quien sabef' '

The trail-boss looked at him searchingly, wondering how much the half-breed knew about Sandy's reasons for making the change. Kane would not allow fighting in the ranks, and grudges live long in some men. Besides, to lose the bet was to lose his share of the drive profits to a man he secretly hated, and this did not suit the trailboss.

Miguel smiled grimly into the cold, searching eyes and shrugged his shoulders, his soft laugh turning the cold stare into something warmer. "Eef he deed, then eet ees ver' good," he said; "eef he deed not, then eet hees own fault. But he should not change hees horrse."

"We'll know tomorrow night, anyhow," said a voice well back from the fire. "Get a rustle on you, Thorpe," it growled. "You move around like an old woman."

"Ain't no walls to climb," said another, laughing.

The red- faced cook did not raise his head or retort, but in his memory another name was deeply carved, to replace the one he was certain would be erased when they reached Mesquite. Sandy Woods' dislike for the horse given to him at the corrals had been overcome by the smooth words of the unforgiving cook, who also had a score to pay.

"When do we rustle next?" asked a squatting figure. "We been layin' low too long, an' my pile has done faded; I wasn't lucky, like you, Trask, an' the sheriff," he said, looking at the trail-boss. "Next time a bank is busted / aim to be in on it. You fellers can't hog all th' good things."

"Don't do no good to talk about it," snapped the trailboss. "Kane names them he wants. Trask an' me was robbed of half of our share I ain't forgettin' it, neither. An' as for th' next raid, that's settled. As long as all of us are in it, you might as well know. We're cleanin' up on McCullough's west range, an' there won't be much of a wait." Neither the speaker, his companions, nor the man behind the sage brush knew that Kane already had changed his mind, and because of Lukins' activity had decided to raid McCullough's east range.

"How soon?" demanded the questioner.

"Some night this week, I reckon," came the answer. "If we get a good bunch we'll sit back an' take things easy for awhile. Too many drives may cut a trail that'll show, an' we can't risk that"

"Too bad we have to drive west an' north before we hit for the plain," said Jud Hill. "Takes two days more, that way."

The trail-boss smiled. "I know a way that would suit you, Jud," he said. "So does Miguel but we've been savin' it till th' old route gets too risky. It joins th' regular trail right here. Well, at last th' cook has really cooked pass it this way, Thorpe. I'm eatin' fast an' I'm turnin' in faster. Th' more we beat th' sun gettin' away from here, th' less it'll beat on us. We're leavin' an hour ahead of it."

Not waiting until the camp should become silent, when any noise he might make would be more likely to be heard, Hopalong crept away while the rustlers ate and returned to his friend, who waited under a certain group of stars.

Red cocked his head at the soft sound, his Colt swinging to cover it, when he heard his name called in his friend's voice, and he replied.

Hopalong sat down on the blanket and related what he had seen and heard without comment from his listener until the end of the narrative.

"Huh!" said Red. "You learned a-plenty. An' I'm glad they reached that water-hole after dark, an' are goin' to go on again before it gets light. They missed our tracks. I call that luck," he said in great satisfaction. "We wasn't doin' much guessin'. That's shore their drive trail, an' th' best thing about it is that it's th' bottom of th' Y. They've got two ways of leavin' th' ranges without showin' tracks, but they both come together down yonder. I reckon mebby we'll have a piece to speak when they come this way again. Coin' to tell McCullough what's bein' hatched?"

"We ought to," answered his companion, slowly. "We'll tell th' Kid an' leave it to him. They must be purty shore of themselves to rustle Question-Mark cattle at this time. If th' Kid tells Mac, an' they try it, Mesquite shore is goin' to be a busy little town. I think I know his breed."

"They ain't takin' much of a chance, at that, if they try it," said Red. "They don't know that we know anythin' about it an' that McCullough will know it, if th' Kid tells him. Mebby they rigger that by springin' it right now when th' feelin' is so strong agin' 'em, that it would make folks think they didn't do it, because they oughten't to oh, pshaw! You know what I'm gettin' at!"

"Shore," grunted Hopalong. He was silent a moment and then stirred. "We ain't got no reason to stay out here for a day or two. Let's pull out an' go down where we can signal th' Kid after sun-up. We'll ride well to th' east past their camp. What wind is stirrin' is comin' from th' other way, an' there's no use makin' any fresh tracks in front of 'em."

An hour or so after daylight a small fire sent a column of smoke straight up, the explanation of its smoking qualities suggested by the canteen lying near it. Hopalong and Red slid a blanket over the fire and drew it suddenly aside, performing this operation three times in succession before letting the column mount unmolested for brief intervals. In the west, above and behind a bare spot on a ridge of hills an answering column climbed upward, and then a series of triple puffs took its place. Scattering the fire over the ground the two friends absent-mindedly kicked sand over the embers, and suddenly grinned at each other at the foolishness of their precautions.

When they reached the little grove they found Johnny waiting for them, his horse well loaded with more pro visions. As they transferred the supplies to their own mounts they told him what had occurred and he decided that McCullough should be informed of the forthcoming raid, whether or not it would in any way jeopardize the winning of the rewards.

"It's a toss-up whether Mac will wait for them to run it off," he said, "when I tell him. He's gettin' more riled every minute, but he seemed to calm down a little after Corwin visited him. Somethin' sort of pulls him back when he gets to climbin' onto his hind legs, an' he ends up by leanin' agin' th' wall an' swearin'. I'm not tellin' him nothin' about anythin' but th' raid. You aimin' to go back to that water-hole?"

Hopalong shook his head. "No, sir," he answered. "There ain't no reason to till th' raid happens. We're campin' on Sand Creek till you signal that it's been run off. Time enough then for us to watch on that cussed griddle."

"Have special signal for that?" suggested Red. "Say two, two an' three, repeated. Mebby won't have time to hear what th' news is. When you get our answer don't bother ridin' down here to tell us anythin' we'll be makin' tracks pronto."

Johnny nodded. "Two, two an' three is O. K. I'll be ridin' back to tell Mac there's goin' to be a party on his west range some night soon. I'm bettin' it'll be a bloody party, too. Say," he exclaimed, pulling up, "Lukins an 5 Idaho was down last night. They're mad as h--l, an' they're throwin' a cordon of riders plumb across th' hard stretch every night. Lukins an' Mac are joinin' forces, an' from now on th' two ranches are workin' together as one. With us scoutin' around east of town somethin' shore ought to drop." He pressed Pepper's sleek sides and started back to the sheltering hills.

"Somethin's goin' to drop," growled Red, the memory of the jailing burning strongly within him. "Don't for get, Kid two, two an' three."

Johnny turned in his saddle, waved a hand and kept on going. Rounding the westernmost hill he rode steadily until opposite the white patch of sand on the northern slope and then, dismounting, collected firewood, and built it up on the dead ashes of his signal fire, ready for the match. Going on again he rode steadily until he reached the place in the arroyo which lay directly behind the ranchhouse.

McCullough returned from a ride over the range to find his cheerful friend smoking some of his tobacco.

"Want a job, Nelson?" asked the trail-boss, swinging from the saddle with an easy agility belying his age and weight.

Johnny smiled at him. "A'nythin', that don't take me away from th' ranch too far or too long. Call it."

"One of th' boys, ridin' south of th' hills on a fool's errand, this mornin', thought he saw smoke signals back of White Face," said McCullough. "He says he reckons he's loco. I ain't goin' that far. Think you could find out any thin' about 'em?"

Johnny considered, and chuckled. "Huh!" he snorted. "He's plumb late. *I* saw them before he did, an' know all about 'em. You stuck a couple of jabs into me about bein' lazy, an' likin' to set around all day doin' nothin'. Any chump can wear out cayuses ridin' around discoverin' things, but th' wise man is th' feller that can set around all day, lazy an' no-account, an' figger things out. I don't have to go prowlin' around to find out things. I just set in th' shade of th' house, roll cigarettes an' hold pow wows with my medicine bag. [You'd be surprised if you knowed what I got in that bag, an' what I can get out of it. You shore would."

McCullough looked at him with an expression which tried to express so many uncomplimentary things at once that the composite was almost neutral; at least, it was somewhat blank.

"Ye-ah?" he drawled, his inflection in no way suggesting anything to Johnny's credit.

"Ye-ah," repeated the medicine man somewhat belligerently.

"Oh," said the trail-boss, eyeing his victim speculatively. "You know all about 'em, huh?"

"Everythin'," placidly replied Johnny, rolling another cigarette.

"I wish to heaven you'd quit smokin' them cussed things around here," said McCullough plaintively. "Yo're growed up now, purty near; an' you ain't no Greaser. I'll buy you a pipe if you'll promise to smoke it."

"Pipes, judgin' from yourn," sweetly replied Johnny, calmly lighting the cigarette, "are dangerous, unless a man hangs around th' house all th' time. When I used to go off scoutin', I allus wished th' other fellers smoked pipes, corncob pipes, like Mister McCullough carries around. Why, cuss it, I could smell 'em out, if they did. It would 'a' saved me a lot of crawlin' an' worryin'. I knowed you was comin' back ten minutes before I saw you. Now, you can't blame a skunk he was born that way, an' he's got good reasons for keepin' on th' way he was born. But a human, goin' out of his way, to smell like some I knows of," he broke off, shrugging his shoulders expressively.

McCullough slowly produced the corncob, blew through the stem with unnecessary violence, gravely filled and lit it, his eyes twinkling. "Takes a man, I reckon, to enjoy it's aromer," he observed. "Goin' back to yore medicine bag, let's see what you can get out of it," he challenged.

Johnny drew out his buckskin tobacco pouch, placed it on the floor, covered it with his sombrero and chanted softly, his eyes fixed on the hat. "I smell a trail-boss an' his pipe. They went to th' bend of th' crick, an' they says to Pete Holbrook, who rides that section, that he ought to ride on th' other side of th' crick after dark." He was repeating information which he had chanced to overhear near the small corral the night before; when he had passed unobserved in the darkness.

McCullough favored the hat with a glance of surprise and. Johnny with a keen, prolonged stare.

K Pete, he said that wouldn't do no good unless he went far enough north to leave his section unprotected. He borrowed a chew of tobacco before th' man an' th' pipe went away an' let th' air get pure again." The medicine man knew Pete's thrifty nature by experience.

"Yo're shore a good guesser," grunted McCullough. "What about them smoke signals, that you know all about?"

Johnny readjusted the hat a hair's breadth, passed his hands over it and closed his eyes. "I see smoke signals," he chanted. "There's palefaces in 'em, ridin' cautious at night over a hard plain. They're driftin' cows into a herd. Th' herd is growin' fast, an' it drifts toward th' hard ground. Now it's goin' faster. Th' brands are Diamond L. I see more smoke signals an' more ridin' in th' dark. Another herd, bigger this time, is runnin' hard over that same plain. Th' brands are SV, vented; an' plain Question-Mark. It seems near within a week an' it's on yore west range." He opened his eyes, kicked the hat across the room and pocketed the tobacco pouch.

"Mac," he said, gravely. "That's a shore-enough prophecy. Leavin' out all jokin', it's true. Hoppy an' Red told me, a little while ago, that they overheard some of Kane's gang talkin'. They're goin' to raid you like I said. Th' smoke signals was me answerin' theirs. They say Sandy Woods is dead. They ought to know because they buried him. They know three of th' men that robbed th' bank an' they've knowed ever since Ridley was shot, who killed him. They've seen Kane's drive trail crew an' they know a whole lot that I ain't goin' to tell you now; mebby I'll not tell you till we get th' rewards; but if it'll make you feel any better, I'm saying' that we're goin' to get them rewards right soon. When Kane raids you he springs th' trap that'll clear a lot of vermin off this range."

"How much of all that do you mean?" demanded the trail-boss, his odorous pipe out and reeking more than ever. He was looking into his companion's eyes with a searching, appraising directness which many men would have found uncomfortable.

"All of it," complacently answered the medicine man, rolling a new cigarette. "There's only one thing I'm doubtful about, 'though it was what Hoppy overheard, so I gave it to you that way. They said yore west range. If Kane learns how th' Diamond L riders are spread out, an' I'm bettin' he knew it near as soon as Lukins did, he'll be a fool to drive that way. If it was me, I'd split my outfit an' put half of 'em on th' east end! but I'm a gambler."

McCullough considered the matter. "They'll leave a plain trail if they raid th' east section," he muttered; "an' th' desert'll hold 'em to a narrow strip north or south. There's water up th' north way, but there's people scattered all around, an' they're nat'rally near th' water. South, there's less water, an' more people th' further they go. They might tackle th' desert, but Lukins an' me figger they go west from th' hard ground. I ain't agin' gamblin', but I don't gamble with anythin' *I* don't own. If yore friends heard them coyotes say 'west,' I'm playin' my cards accordin' to their case-rack. I may call it wrong, I may get a split, or I may win but I'm backin' the' case-keepers, 'specially when they're keepin' th' rack for me. West it is an' west is where h--l will pop when they pay their visit. An' lemme tell you this, Nelson: Win, lose, or split on th' raid, if it comes off within a week, I'll be dead shore who's behind it, an' there's a cyclone due in Mesquite right soon after. Twitchell had his chance. His game's no good I'm playin' th' cards I've drawn in my own way when they show their hand in this raid. I'm bein' cold-decked by Corwin but I'll warm it a-plenty. You hang around an' see th' fire works!"

Johnny stretched, relaxed, and grinned. "I'm aimin' to touch some off, myself," he replied, "an' I reckon Hoppy an' Red will send up a couple of rockets on their own account. Rockets?" He grinned. "No; not rockets there's allus burned sticks comin' down from rockets. Besides, they're too smooth an' easy. Reckon they'll touch off some pinwheels. Whizzin', tail-chasin' pinwheels; or mebby nigger-chasers. Most likely they'll be nigger-chasers, th' way some folks'll be steppin' lively to get out of th' way. Don't you bank on this bein' yore, celebration you'll only own th' lot an' make th' noise. Th' grand display, th' glorious finish is Bar-20. Just plain, old-fashioned Bar-20. Gee, Mac, it makes me a kid again!"

"It's got an easy job, then!" snorted the trail-boss.

Chapter XVII
A Well-Planned Raid

On night shift again Pete Holbrook reached the end of his beat, waited until his fellow-watcher on the east bulked suddenly out of the darkness, exchanged a few words with him and turned back under the starfilled sky, his horse having no difficulty in avoiding obstructions, but picking its way with ease around scattered thickets, grass-tufted hummocks, and across shallow ravines and hollows. Objects close at hand were discernible to eyes accustomed to the darkness and Pete's range of vision attained the enviable limits enjoyed by those who live out-of-doors and look over long distances. An occasional patch of sand moved slowly into his circumscribed horizon as he rode on; vague, squatting bulks gradually revealed their vegetative nature and an occasional more regular bulk told him where a cow was lying. These latter more often were catalogued by his ears before his eyes defined them and from the contentment in the sounds he nodded in satisfaction. Soon he felt the gentle rise which swept up to the breeze-caressed ridge which projected northward and forced the little creek to follow it for nearly a mile before the rocky obstruction could be passed.

There had been a time when the ridge had forced the creek again as far out of its course, but on quiet nights a fanciful listener could hear the petulant grumblings of the stream and its constant boast. Placid and slow above the ridge, the waters narrowed and deepened when they reached the insolent bulk as in concentrating for the never-ending assault. They had cut through softer resistance along the edges and now gnawed noisily at the stone itself. Narrower grew the stream and deeper, the pools clear and with clean rock bottoms and sides where the hurrying water, now free from the last vestige of color imposed by the banks further up, became crystal in the light of day. Hurrying from pool to pool, singing around bowlders it ran faster and faster as if eager for the final attempt against its bulky enemy, and hissed and growled as it sped along the abrupt rock face. Loath to leave the fight, it followed tenaciously along the other side of the ridge and at last gave up the struggle to turn sharply south again and flow placidly down the valley on a continuation of the line it had followed above.

This forced detour made the U-Bend, so called by Question-Mark riders, and the sloping ground of the ridge was as much a favorite with the cattle as were its bordering pools with the men. Here could be felt every vagrant breeze, and while the grass was scantier than that found on the more level pastures round about, and cropped closer, the cattle turned toward it when darkness came. It was the best bed-ground on the ranch.

The grunting, cud-chewing, or blowing blots grew more numerous as Holbrook went on and when he had reached the crest of the ridge his horse began to pick its way more and more to avoid them, the rider chanting a mournful lay and then followed it with a song which, had it been rightfully expurged, would have had little left to sing about. Like another serenade it had been composed in a barroom, but the barroom atmosphere was strongly in evidence. It suddenly ceased.

Holbrook stopped the song and his horse at the same instant and his roving glances roved no more, but settled into a fixed stare which drew upon itself his earnest concentration, as if the darkness could better be pierced by an act of will.

"Did I, or didn't I?" he growled, and looked around to see if his eyes would show him other lights. Deciding that they were normal he focussed them again in the direction of the sight which had stopped the song. "Bronch, I shore saw it," he muttered. "It was plain as it was short." He glanced down at the horse, saw its ears thrust rigidly forward and nodded his head emphatically. "An' so did you, or I'm a liar!"

He was no liar, for a second flash appeared, and it acted on him like a spur. The horse obeyed the sudden order and leaped forward, careening on its erratic course as it avoided swiftly appearing obstacles.

"Seems to me like it was further west th' last time," muttered Holbrook. "What th' devil it is, I don't know; but I'm goin' to show th' fambly curiosity. Can't be Kane's coyotes folks don't usually show lights when they're stealin' cows. An' it's on Charley's section, but we'll have a look anyhow. Cuss th' wind."

The light proved to be of will-o'-the-wisp nature, but he pursued doggedly and after a time he heard sounds which suggested that he was not alone on the range. He drew his six-gun in case his welcome should take that course and swung a little to the left to investigate the sounds.

"Must be Charley," he soliloquized, but raised the Colt to a better position. One would have thought Charley to be no friend of his. The Colt went up a little higher, the horse stopped suddenly and its rider gave the night's hailing signal, so well imitated that it might easily have fooled the little animal to whom Nature had given it. It came back like a double echo and soon Charley bulked out of the dark.

"You follerin' that, too?" he asked, entirely reassured now that his eyes were all right, for he had had the same doubts as his friend.

"Yes; what you reckon it is?"

"Dunno," growled Charley. "Thought mebby it was some fool puncher lightin' a cigarette. It wasn't very bright, an' it didn't last long."

"Reckon you called it," replied Holbrook. "Well, th' only animal that lights them is humans; an' no human workin' for this ranch is lightin' cigarettes at night, these nights. Bein' a strange human where strange humans shouldn't ought to be, I'm plumb curious. All of which means I'm goin' to have a closer look."

"I'm with you," said Charley. "We better stick to gether or we'll mebby get to shootin' each other; an' I'm frank in sayin' I'm shootin' quick tonight, an' by ear. There ain't no honest human ridin' around out here, day or night, that don't belong here; an' them that does be long ain't over there, lightin' cigarettes nor nothin' else. That lightnin' bug don't belong, but he may stay here. Look! There she is again this side of where I saw it last!"

"Same place," contradicted Holbrook, pushing on.

"Same place yore hat!"

"Bet you five it is."

"Yo're on; make it ten?"

"It is. Shut yore face an' Keep goin'. Somethin's happenin' over there."

Minute after minute passed and then they swore in the same breath.

"It's south!" exulted Charley. "You lose."

"He crossed in front of us, cuss him," said Holbrook.

As he spoke an answering light flashed where the first ones had been seen and Holbrook grunted with satisfaction. "You lose; there's two of 'em. We was bettin' on th' other."

"They're signalin', an' there's mebby more'n two. What's th' difference? Come on, Pete! We'll bust up this little party before it starts. But what are they lightin' lights for if they're rustlin'? An' if they ain't rustlin' what'n blazes are they doin'?"

"Head over a little," said his companion, forcing his horse against his friend's. "We'll ride between th' flashes first, an' if there's a herd bein' collected we'll mebby hit it. Don't ask no questions; just shoot an' jump yore cay use sideways."

South of them another puncher was riding at reckless speed along the chord of a great arc and although his section lay beyond Holbrook's, he was now even with them. When they changed their course they drew closer to him and some minutes later, stopping for a moment's silence so they could listen for sounds of the enemy, they heard his faint, far-off signal and answered it. He announced his arrival with a curse and a question and the answer did not answer much. They went on together, eager and alert.

"Heard you drummin' down th' ridge you know that rocky ground rolls 'em out," the newcomer explained. "Knowed somethin' was wrong th' way you was poundin', an' follered on a gamble till I saw th' lights. Reckon Walt ain't far behind me. I'm tellin' you so you'll signal before you shoot. He's loose out here somewhere."

When the light came again it was much further west and the answering flash was north. The three pulled up and looked at each other.

"There ain't no cayuse livin' can cover ground like that second feller," growled Holbrook. "He was plumb south only a few minutes ago, an' now will you look where he is!"

"Mebby they're ghostes, Bob," suggested Charley, who harbored a tingling belief in things supernatural.

"'Ghostes'!" chuckled Holbrook. "Ghosts, you means! Th' same as ' posts! ' Th' ' es ' is silent, like in 'cows.' I never believed in 'em; but I shore don't claim to know it all. There's plenty of things *I* don't under stand an' this is shore one of 'em. My hair's gettin' stiff!"

"Yo're a couple of old wimmin!" snorted Bob. "There's only one kind of a ghost that'll slow me up . that's th' kind that packs hardware. Seein' as they ain't supposed to tote guns, I'm goin' for that coyote west of here. He don't swap ends so fast. Mebby I can turn him into a real ghost. Look out where you shoot. So-long!"

"We'll assay his jumpin' friend," called Charley.

Again the flashes showed, one to the south, the other to the north, and while the punchers marveled, the third appeared in the southwest.

"One apiece!" shouted Holbrook. "I'll take th' last. Go to 'em!" and drumming hoofbeats rolled into silence in three directions.

Soon spitting flashes in the north were answered in kind, the reports announcing six-guns in action; in the west a thinner tongue of flame and a different kind of report was answered by rapid bursts of fire and the jarring crashes of a Colt. Far to the south three stabbing flashes went upward, Walt's signal that he was coming. From beyond the U-Bend, far to the east, the triple signal came twice, flat and low. Beyond them a yellow glow sprang from the black void and marked the ranchhouse, where six sleeping men piled from their bunks and, finishing their dressing as they ran, chased the cursing trail-boss to the saddled, waiting horses, their tingling blood in an instant sweeping the cobwebs of sleep from their conjecturing brains. There was a creaking of leather, a soft, musical jingling of metal and a sudden thunderous rolling of hoofbeats as seven bunched horses leaped at breakneck speed into the darkness, the tight-lipped riders eager, grim, and tense.

Through a bushy arroyo leading to Mesquite three Mexicans rode as rapidly as they dared, laughing and carrying on a jerky, exultant conversation. A mile be hind them came a fourth, his horse running like a frightened jack rabbit as it avoided the obstructions which seemed to leap at them. A bandage around the rider's head perhaps accounted for his sullenness. The four were racing to get to Red Frank's, and safety. Out on the plain the fifth, and as Fate willed it, the only one of the group openly allied to Kane, lay under his dead horse, his career of thieving and murder at an end. Close to him was a dead Question-Mark horse, and the wounded rider, wounded again by his sudden pitch from the saddle as the horse dropped under him, lay huddled on the ground. Slowly recovering his senses he stirred, groped and sat up, his strained, good arm throbbing as he shakily drew his Colt, reloaded it and fired into the air twice, and then twice more. A burst of firing answered him and he smiled grimly and settled back as the low rumbling grew rapidly louder. It threatened to pass by him, but his single shot caused a quick turn and soon his friends drew up and stopped.

"Who is it?" demanded McCullough, dismounting at his side.

"Holbrook," came the answer, shaky and faint. "They got me twice, an' my cayuse, too. Reckon I busted my leg when he went down I shore sailed a-plenty afore I lit."

"You got one!" called an exultant voice. A match flared and in a moment the cheerful discoverer called again. "Sanchez, that Greaser monte dealer of Kane's. Plumb through th' mouth an' neck, Pete! I call that shootin', with th' dark an' all "his voice trailed off in profane envy of the accomplishment.

But Pete, hardy soul that he was, had fainted, a fractured leg, the impact from his flying fall and three bullet holes excuse enough for any man.

The flaring of the match brought a distant report and a bullet whined above the discoverer's head. Someone hurriedly fired into the air and a little later the group heard hoofbeats, which stopped abruptly when still some distance away. A signal reassured the cautious rider and soon Walt joined the group, Bob and Charley coming up later. Two of the men started back to the ranchhouse with Holbrook, the rest of the group riding off to search the plain for the two riders who had not put in an appearance, and to see what devilment they might discover. Both of the missing men were found on the remote part of the western range, one plodding stolidly toward the ranchhouse, his saddle and equipment on his shoulders; the other lay pinned under his dead horse, not much the worse, as it luckily happened, for his experience.

While the outfit concentrated on the western part of the ranch, events of another concentration were working smoothly and swiftly east of the ranchhouse, where mounted men, now free from interference, thanks to their Mexican friends, rode unerringly in the darkness, and drifted cattle into a herd with a certainty and dispatch born of long experience. Steadily the restless nucleus grew in size and numbers, the few riders who held it together chanting in low tones to keep the nervous cattle within bounds. The efficiency of these night raiders merited praise, nefarious as their occupation was, and the director of the harmonious efforts showed an uncanny understanding of the cattle, the men, and the whole affair which belongs to genius. Not a step was taken in uncertainty, not an effort wasted. Speed was obtained which in less experienced hands would have resulted in panic and a stampede. Steadily the circle of riders grew shorter and shorter; steadily, surprisingly, the shadowy herd grew, and as it grew, became more and more compact. Further down the creek a second and smaller herd was built up at the same time and with nearly the same smoothness, and waited for the larger aggregate to drift down upon it and swallow it up. The augmented trail herd kept going faster and faster, the guarding and directing riders in their alloted places and, crossing the creek, it swung northeast at a steadily increasing pace. The cattle had fed heavily and drunk their fill and to this could be ascribed the evenness of their tempers. Almost without realizing it they passed from the Question-Mark range and streamed across the guarding hills, flowing rapidly along the northern side. Gradually their speed was in creased and they accepted it obediently, and with a docility which in itself was a compliment to the brains of the trailboss. Compacted within the close cordon of the alert riders it maintained a speed on the very edge of panic, but went no further. Shortly before dawn two hardriding rustlers pounded up from the rear, reported all clear, and fell back again, to renew their watch far back on the trail. For three hours the herd had crossed hard ground and as it passed over a high, dividing ridge and down the eastern slope the trail-boss sighed with relief, for now dawn held no terrors for him. He had passed the eastern horizon of any keen-eyed watchers of the pillaged range. On went cattle and riders, and the paling dawn saw them following the hard bottom of a valley which led to others ahead, and kept them from dangerous sky lines. When the last hard-floored valley lay behind and sloping hollows of sand lay ahead, the trail-boss dropped back, uncorked his canteen of black coffee tempered with brandy, and drank long and deep. It was interpreted by his men to mean that the danger zone had been left in the rear, and they smilingly followed his example, and then leisurely t and more critically looked over the herd to see what they had gained. The entire SV trail herd was there, a large number of Question-Mark cattle and a score or more miscellaneous brands, which Ridley from time to time had purchased at bargain prices from needy owners. The trail-boss grinned broadly and waved his hand. It was a raid which would go down the annals of rustler history and challenge strongly for first honors. At noon the waiting caviya was picked up, and Miguel and his three friends added four more riders to the ranks. He took his place well ahead of the hurrying cattle, and remained there until the first, and seldom visited, water-hole was reached, where a short rest was taken. Then he led the way again, abruptly changing the direction of the herd's course and, following depressions in the desert floor, struck for Bitter Spring, which would be reached in the early morning hours. By now the raid was a successful, accomplished fact, according to all experience, and the matter of speed was now decided purely upon the questions of water and food, which, however, did not let it diminish much.

The trail-boss dropped back to his segundo and smiled. "Old Twitchell's got somethin' to put up a holler over now."

The other grinned expansively. "He'll mebby ante up another reward he shore is fond of 'em."

Back on the Question-Mark a sleepy rider jogged along the creek, idly looking here and there. Suddenly he stiffened in the saddle, looked searchingly along the banks of the little stream, glanced over a strangely deserted range and ripped out an oath as he wheeled to race back to the ranchhouse. His vociferous arrival caused a flurry, out of which emerged Johnny Nelson, who ran to the corral, caught and saddled his restive black, and scorning such a thing as a signal fire, especially when he feared that he could not start it within the limits of the time specified, raced across the valley, climbed the hills at a more sedate pace, dropped down the further slopes like a stone, and raced on again for the little camp on Sand Creek.

Chapter XVIII
The Trail-Boss Tries His Way

McCullough watched the racing horseman for a moment, a gleam of envious appreciation in his eyes at the beautiful action of the black horse, nodded in understanding of the rider's journey and wheeled abruptly to give terse orders.

Charley swung into the saddle and started in a cloud of dust for the Diamond L, to carry important news to Lukins and his outfit; two men sullenly received their orders to stay behind for the protection of the ranch and the care of Pete Holbrook, their feelings in no way relieved by the remark of the trail-boss, prophesying that Kane and his gang would be too busy in town to disturb the serenity of the Question-Mark. The rest of the outfit, procuring certain necessaries for the visit to Kane's head quarters, climbed into their saddles and followed their grim and taciturn leader over the shortest way to town.

Far back on the west end of the northern chain of hills a Mexican collapsed his telescope, hazarded a long-range shot at the hard-riding Charley and, mounting in haste, sped to carry disturbing news to his employer. The courier looked around as the singing lead raised a puff of dust in front of him, snarled in the direction from whence he thought it had come and, having no time for personal grievances, leaned forward and quirted the horse to greater speed. Whirring across the Diamond L range Charley caused another Mexican, watching from a ridge overlooking the ranch buildings, to run to the waiting horse and mount it, after which he delayed his departure until he saw the Diamond L outfit string out into a race for town, whereupon he set a pace which promised to hold him his generous lead.

In Mesquite a Mexican quirted a lathered horse for a final burst of speed up the quiet street, flung himself through Kane's front door, shouted a warning as he scrambled to his feet and dashed through the partition door to make his report direct to his boss. As he bolted out of sight behind the partition, other men popped from the building like weasel-pursued rabbits from a warren and scurried over the town to spread the alarm to those who were most vitally concerned by it. Two streams forthwith flowed over their trails, the first and larger heading for Kane's; the other, composed entirely of Mexicans, flowed toward Red Frank's, which had been allotted the role of outlying redoubt, to help keep harmless the broken ground between it and Kane's front wall, and was now being put in shape to withstand a siege.

Around Kane's was the noisy activity of a beehive. Hurrying men pulled thick planks from the piles under the floor and hauled them, on the jump, to windows and doors, feeding them into eager hands inside the building. Numbers of empty sacks grew amazingly bulky from the efforts of sand shovelers and were carried, shoulder high, in an unending line into the building. Great shutters were unfastened and swung away from the outer walls, their cobwebbed loopholes soon to play their ordained parts. A feverish squad emptied the stables of horses and food, taking both into the dining-room, and returned, posthaste, to remove doors and certain planks which turned the stables into sieves of small use to an attacking force, even if they were won. That the need for haste was pressing was proved by the sound of a handbell on the roof, where a selected group of riflemen lay behind the double-planked parapet to give warning, and exhibitions of long-range shooting. The shovelers hurled their tools through open windows, the plank carriers shoved the last board into the building and leaped to the shutters, slamming them shut as they hastened along the side of the building, and poured hastily through the front door, which now was protected by a great, outer door of planks, mortised, bolted, and braced in workman-like manner. From the roof sounded two heavy reports, and grim iron tubes slid into loopholes along the walls. The bartenders carried boxes of ammunition and spare weapons, leaving their offerings below every oblong hole. To threaten Kane was one thing; to carry it to a successful end, another.

Puffs of gray-white smoke broke unexpectedly from points around the building, to thin out as they spread and drifted into oblivion. The cracking of rifles and the echo-awakening, jarring reports of heavy six-guns, were punctuated at intervals by the booming roar of old-time buffalo guns, of caliber prodigious. Punchers, guns in their hands, made the rounds of the town, going from building to building to pick up any of Kane's men who might have loitered, or who planned to hide out and open fire from the rear. Their efforts were not entirely wasted, for although Kane's brood had flocked to its nest, there were certain of the town's inhabitants who were neither flesh nor fish and might become one or the other as expediency urged. These doubtful ones were weeded out, disarmed, and escorted to their horses with stern injunctions as to the speed of their departure and their continued absence. Some of the neutrals, seeing that the mastery of the town at present lay with the ranchmen, trimmed their sails for this wind and numbered themselves with the offense in spirit if not in deeds. Of these human pendulums Quayle had a fair mental list and the owners of certain names were well watched.

The first day passed in perfecting plans, assigning men to strategic stations, several of these vantage-points remaining tenantless during the daylight hours because of the alertness and straight shooting of the squad on Kane's roof, who speedily made themselves obnoxious to the attackers. The owner of the freight wagon, remembering a smooth-bore iron cannon of more than an inch caliber, a relic of the prairie caravans which had followed the old Santa Fe and other trails a generation past, exulted as he dragged it from its obscurity and spent a busy hour scaling the rust from bore and touch-hole. Here was the key to the situation, he boasted, and rammed home a generous charge of rifle powder. To find a suitable missile was another question, but he solved it by falling upon bar-lead with ax and hammer. Wheeled into position, its rusty length protruding beyond the corner of an adobe building, it was sighted by spasmodic glances, an occupation not without danger, for which blame could be given to the argus-eyed riflemen on the roof of the target. Consternation seized the defenders, who had not allowed for artillery, and they awaited its thundering debut with palpitant interest.

The discoverer and groom of the relic was unanimously elected gunner, not a dissenting voice denying his right to the honor, a right which he failed either to mention or press. The powder heaped over the touch-hole was jarred off by the impact of a Sharp's bullet and to replace it required a kitchen spoon fastened to a stick, which was an alluring if small target to the anxious aerial riflemen. At last heaped up again, the gunner declined methods in vogue for the firing of such ancient muzzle-loaders and used a bundle of kerosene-soaked paper swinging by a wire from the end of the spoon. A few practice swings were held to be fitting preliminaries to an event of such importance, and then the nervous cannoneer, screwing his courage to the sticking-point, swept the blazing mass across the scaly breach and shrunk behind the sheltering corner. He escaped thunderous destruction by an eyelash, for what he afterward found was a third of the doughty weapon whizzed past his corner, taking a large chunk of sun-dried brick with it. From the besiegers arose guffaws; from the defenders, howls of derision; and from the owner of the adobe hut, imprecation and denouncement in fluent Spanish. The wall of his habitation closest to the fieldpiece justified all he said and even all he thought.

"You should ought 'a run it under Kane's before you touched her off," bawled a hilarious voice from cover. "Got another?" he demanded. "Tie it together an' try again."

The cannoneer without a job affected gaiety, drew inspiration from the taunts and hastened home to fashion bombs out of anything he could which would answer his purpose, finally deciding upon a tomato can and baling wire, and soon had a task to occupy the flaming fires of his genius.

Red Frank's, being the weaker of the two defenses and only point-blank range from the old adobe jail whose walls, poor as they were, could be relied upon to stop bullets, formed the favorite point of attack while the offense settled down into better-ordered channels. Idaho and others of his exuberent youth decided that it was their "pudding" and favored it with attentions which were as barren of results as they were full of enthusiasm. Discovering that their bullets passed entirely through the frame second-story and whirred, slobbered, and screamed into the air, they wasted ammunition lavishly, ignorant that for three feet above the second-story floor the walls were reinforced with double planking of hard wood, each layer two inches thick. They might turn the upper two-thirds of walls into a bird cage and do no one any material damage. And so passed the first day, McCullough's efforts unavailing in face of the careless enthusiasm of his men, caused by the novelty of the situation; and not until one man had died and several others received serious wounds did the larking punchers come fully to realize that the game was deadly, and due to become more so.

Chapter XIX
A Desert Secret

While McCullough argued and swore and waited for sanity to return to his frisking men, three punchers lay on the desert sands north of Sweet Spring, and baked. The telescope occasionally swept the southern horizon and went back between the folds of the blanket, which also hid the guns from the rays of the molten sun. The situation and most of the possible variations had been gone over from every angle and a course of action yet had to be agreed upon. Knowing that a fight in town was imminent, each feared he would miss it and that the reward would be lost to them. From their knowledge of deserts in general they did not wish to assume the labors of driving a herd back across it, even if they were able to capture it; but neither did they wish to let it get entirely away and be lost to McCullough. And so they continued to discuss the problem, jerkily and without enthusiasm, writhing under the sun like frogs on a gridiron. The afternoon dragged into evening and with the coming of twilight came quick relief from the heat, soon to be fol lowed by a cold undreamed of by the inexperienced. The stars appeared swiftly and blazed with glittering brilliance through the chill air and the three watchers sought their blanket rolls for relief.

Hopalong unrolled from his covering and arose. "Dark enough, now," he said. "I'm goin' down to th' other water-hole to wait for 'em. May learn somethin' worth while." He rolled his rifle in the blanket to protect it from sand and stretched gratefully.

"I'm goin' with you," said Johnny, covering his own rifle.

"I reckon I'll have to lay up here an' hold th' sack, like a fool," growled Red, who longed for action, even if it were no more than a tramp through the sand.

"You shore called it, Reddie," chuckled Johnny. "Somebody has got to stay with th' cayuses; an' I don't know anybody as reliable as you. Don't forget, an' build a camp fire while we're gone," and with this parting insult Johnny melted into the darkness after his leader and plodded silently behind him until Hopalong stopped and muttered a command.

"We're not far away now," he said. "Reckon we oughtn't get too close till they come to th' hole an' get settled down. Some of 'em may have to ride far an' wide if th' herd's ornery, an' run onto us. We've got th' trumps, an' they're worth twice as much if they don't know we got 'em. They shoot off their mouths regardless out here."

Johnny grunted his acquiescence and squatted comfort ably on his haunches, the tips of the fingers of one hand in the sand. "Never felt more like smokin' than I do now," he chuckled. "Got any chewin'?"

His friend passed over the desired article and Johnny worried off a generous mouthful. "It's got too many stems in it; but bein' th' first chew I've had since I got married I ain't kickin'," he complacently remarked. "Margaret says it sticks to me for hours."

Hopalong grunted. "Gettin' to be real lady-like, ain't you?" he jeered. "Put perfumery on yore shirt bosom?"

"I would if she wanted me to," retorted his companion. "I don't just know what I wouldn't do if she wanted me to."

Hopalong snorted. "That so?" he demanded, pugnaciously. "Reckon she might like to know what yo're doin' down here, how much longer you aim to stay, an' if yo're still alive an' other little foolish things like that. Let me tell you, Kid, you don't know how big a woman fills up yore life till you've lost her."

"I can imagine what it would be without her," said Johnny, slowly and reverently, his heart aching for his friend's loss. "She knows all about it; nearly all, anyhow. I've writ to her every third day, when I could, an' some times oftener. She may be worryin', but I'm bettin' every cent I'll ever have that she ain't doin' no cryin'! There ain't many wimmen like her, even in this kind of country."

"Then she's shore got Red an' me figgered for a fine pair of liars," murmured Hopalong; "but just th' same I'm feelin' warmer toward you than I have for a week," he announced. "When did you tell her all about this scrambled mess?"

"When I found that I couldn't tell how much longer I'd have to stay here," confessed Johnny. "I couldn't write letters an' lie good enough to fool her; an' I had to write letters, didn't I?"

"I'll take everythin' back, Kid," said his companion, grinning in the dark.

Johnny grunted and the silence began again, a silence which endured for several hours, such a silence that can exist between two real friends and be full of under standing. It endured between them and was not even broken by the distant, dim flare of a match, nor when low sounds floated up to them and gradually grew into the clicking and rattle of horns against horns, and the low rumble of many hurrying hoofs hoofs hurrying toward the water which bovine nostrils had long since scented. The rumble grew rapidly as the thirst-tortured herd stampeded for Bitter Spring. A revolver flashed here and there on the edges of the animated avalanche and then a sweet silence came to the desert, soon to be tune fully and pleasantly broken by the soft lowing of cattle leg deep in the saving water.

Let th' air blow in up-on m-e-e,
Let me see th' mid-night s-k-y;
Stand back, Sisters, from a-round m-e-e:
God, it i-s s-o-o h-a-r-d to d-i-e, wailed a cracked voice, the owner relieving his feelings. "Thorpe, if you don't wrastle a hot snack damned quick, I'll eat yore ears!"

"Give him anythin' to stop that yowlin'," bellowed another. "Can't he learn nothin' but ' Th' Dyin' Nun '? Thank heaven he never learned no more of it. A sick calf ain't no cheerfuller than him."

"You'll have to eat lively, boys," sang out the trail-boss. "Everythin' is on th' move in an hour. If yo're in such a cussed hurry, Jud, get some wood for him. Take it from that lame pack horse. Reckon we'll have to shoot him if he don't get better in a hurry."

Up to my knees in mud I go
An' water to my middle;
Whenever firewood's to be got
I'm Cookie's sec-ond fid-die, chanted Jud, splashing out to where the lame pack horse conducted an experiment in saturation. "Hot, cussed hot," he enlightened the cheerful, but tired group on the bank. "Hot an' oozy. Hello, hoss," he greeted, slapping the shrinking shoulder. "You heard what th' boss said about you? Pick up, Ol' Timer; pick up or you'll get shot. What? Don't blame you a bit, not a cussed bit. I'd ruther be shot, too, than tote wood over this part of h--l. Oh, well; life's plumb funny. You'll fry if you do, an' you'll die if you don't. What's th' difference, anyhow, Ol' Timer?"

"Hey, Jud," called a voice. "Got a new bunkie?"

"I could have worse than a cayuse," replied Jud. "A cussed sight worse."

"There's mocassins, rattlers, copperheads, tarantulas, an' scorpions in that pond! "warned another.

"You done forgot Gila monsters, tigers an' an' Injuns," retorted Jud. "Now comes a job. With both arms full of slippin', criss-crossin' firewood, th' rest slidin' from th' pack, I got to hang on to what I got, put th' rest back like it ought to go an' make every thin' tight. Come out here, some damned fool, an' gimme a hand. Better move lively only got four arms an' six hands.

"There!" he exploded. "There goes th' shootin'-match off th' hoss. Th' wind'll blow 'em ashore an' we can pick up th' whole caboodle."

"Wind?" jeered the snake-enumerator. "Where's th' wind? Yo're a fool!"

"On th' bank, where yo're settin', you thick-headed ass!" yelled Jud. "You got so cussed much to say, suppose you muddy yore lily-white pants an' do somethin' besides bray!"

"Did you spill any of 'em, Jud?" anxiously asked a voice. "I heard a splash."

Jud's reply was such that the trail-boss snapped a warning which checked some of the conversation, and promised his help. "Wait for me, Jud; I'm comin'," he said.

"Why don't you send that white-washed idol?" asked Jud. "I'll show him who's th' fool; an' what a splash sounds like!"

Hopalong nudged his companion and they crept for ward, feeling before them for anything which might make a sound if stepped on. A vibrant whirl made them spring back and go around the warning snake, and soon they reached the little, sandy ridge which had sheltered Hopalong on his other visit.

"I'm glad you hung on to what you had, Jud," came Thorpe's thankful voice as his match caught the sun baked wood and sent a tiny flame licking upward among the shavings whittled by his knife. "What you do you allus do right. It's dry as a bone."

"An' so am I," grunted the horse wrangler. "Who's got their canteen?"

"He's askin' for a canteen, with th' whole pond in front of him!" laughed a squatting rustler. "Here; take mine."

The fire grew quickly and a coffeepot, staunch friend of weary travelers, was placed in the flame, no one caring what it looked like or how hot the handle got. Time passed swiftly in talking of the raid and in consuming the light, hurried meal and soon the wrangler argued to his charges from the bank, and then waded in for his own horse, after which the matter was much simplified. He had them bunched, the next change of horses had been cut out by the men and they were ready to resume the drive when a distant voice hailed them. Soon a lathered horse glistened in the outer circle of light, and the hardriding courier dashed up to the fire.

"They've hit th' town, boys!" he shouted. "Th f Question-Mark an' th' Diamond L have joined hands agin' us. Their friends in town are backin' 'em. Kane says to drive this herd hell-to-leather to th' valley, leave it there an' burn th' trail back. Where's Hugh Roberts?"

"Here," answered the trail-boss, stepping forward. "Hello, Vic."

"Got strict orders from th' boss," said Vic, leaning over and whispering in the ear of the trail-boss.

Roberts stiffened and swore angrily. "Is that all he says for us to do?" he sneered. "I got a notion to tell him to go to h--l!"

Eager questions assailed him from the pressing group and he pushed himself free. "He says we are to take Quayle's hotel, their headquarters, from th' rear at dawn of th' day we get back an' hold it! That's all!"

An angry chorus greeted the announcement and the shouting courier had a hard time to make himself heard, "That's wins for us!" he yelled. "You get their leaders, you split 'em in two an' Kane'll turn his boys loose to hit 'em during th' confusion. He's got a wise head, I'm shoutin'. Red Frank's gang smashes from th' west end, an' they'll never know what happened. We'll have 'em split three ways, leaderless, not knowin' what's happened. It'll be a stampede an' a slaughter. Cuss it, I'll be with you! That shows what I think of it!"

"Throw th' herd back on th' trail," ordered the boss. "We'll drive hard, an' turn th' rest of it over in our minds as we go. So we can have yore valuable assistance yo're goin' with us. Get a fresh cayuse from th' caviya. I say, yo're goin' with us, savvy?"

Covered by the noise of the renewed drive Hopalong and Johnny wriggled back until they could with safety arise to their feet, when they hastened back to Red and tersely reported what they had learned. Red's reply was instant.

"One of us has got to learn where that herd is kept; th' others light out for McCullough. Th' herd trailer can go to town when he gets it located. We can't lose them cattle, now."

"Right!" said Hopalong. "I'm puttin' cartridges in my hand. Th' worst guesser goes after th' herd. Odd or even. Red, you first," and he placed his clenched fist in Red's hand.

"Even," said Red, and then he opened the fist, felt of the cylinders and chuckled. There were two.

Hopalong fumbled at his belt and placed his fist in Johnny's hand. "Call it, Kid," he said.

"Even," said Johnny, carelessly. He felt the closed hand slowly open and cast his fingers over its palm, rinding two cartridges, and he grunted. "Better take th' extra canteens, Hoppy; an' that spyglass. It'll mebby come in handy. Want Pepper?"

"Just 'cause she's a good cayuse for you don't say that she is for me," chuckled the loser. "She knows you; I'm a stranger," and he led the way to the picketed and hobbled horses. In a few minutes he swung into the saddle, the telescope under his arm, cheerily said his good-byes and melted into the darkness, bound further into the desert, where or how far he did not know. Passing the southern water-hole he drew two cartridges from his belt, placed one in the palm of his right hand and held the other between his fingers. Slowly opening the clenched fist he relaxed the fingers and the second cartridge dropped onto its mate with a little click. There was no need to cough now and hide that slight, metallic noise, so he grinned instead and slowly pushed them back into the vacant loops.

"Fine job, lettin' th' Kid go out on this skillet," he snorted, indignant at the thought. "Me, now it don't matter a whole lot what happens to me these days; but th' Kid's got a wife, an' a darned fine one, too. Go on, you lazy cow yo're work's just startin'."

It was not long before he caught the noise of the harddriven herd well off to his right and he followed by sound until dawn threatened. Then, slowing his horse, he rode off at an angle and hunted for low places in the desert floor, where he went along a course parallel to that followed by the herd. Persistently keeping from sky lines, although added miles of twisting detours was the price, and keeping so far from his quarry that he barely could pick out the small, dark mass with the aid of the glass, he feared no discovery. So he rode hour after weary hour under the pitiless sun, stopping only once to turn his sombrero into a bucket, from which his horse eagerly drank the contents of one huge canteen, its two gallons of water filling the hat several times.

"Got to go easy with it for awhile, bronch," he told it. "Water can't be so terrible far ahead, judgin' from that herd pushin' boldlike across this strip of h--l but cows can go a long time without it when they has to; an' out here they shore has to. I'm not cheatin' you there's four for you an' one for me, an' we won't change it."

Mile upon burning mile passed in endless procession as they plodded through hard sand, soft sand, powdery dust, and over stretches of rocky floor blasted smooth and slippery by the cutting sands driven against it by every wind for centuries. An occasional polished bowlder loomed up, its coat of "desert-varnish "glistening brown under the pale, molten sun. He knew what the varnish was, how it had been drawn from the rock and the mineral contents left behind on the surface as its moisture evaporated into the air. An occasional "side-winder," diminutive when compared to the rattlesnakes of other localities, slid curiously across the sand, its beady, glittering eyes cold and vicious as it watched this strange invader of its desert fastness.

Warned at last by the fading light after what had seemed an eternity of glare, he gave the dejected horse another canteen of water and then urged it into brisker pace, to be within earshot of the fleeing herd when darkness should make safe a nearer approach.

With the coming of twilight came a falling of temperature and when the afterglow bathed the desert with magic light and then faded as swiftly as though a great curtain had been dropped the creeping chill took bold, sudden possession of the desert air to a degree unbelievable. So passed the night, weary hour after cold, weary hour; but the change was priceless to man and beast. The magic metamorphosis emphasized the many-sided nature of the desert, at one time a blazing, glaring thing of sinister aspect and death-dealing heat; at another cold, almost freezing, its considerable altitude being good reason for the night's penetrating chill. The expanse of dim gray carpet, broken by occasional dark blots where the scrawny, scattered vegetation arose from the sands, stretched away into the veiling dark, allowing keen eyes to distinguish objects at surprising distances. Overhead blazed the brilliant stars, blazed as only stars in desert heavens can, seeming magnified and brought nearer by the dry, clear air. His eyes at last free from the blinding glare of quivering air and glittering crystals of salts in the sand; his dry, parched, burning skin free from the baking heat, which sucked moisture from the pores before perspiration could form on the surface; he sucked in great gulps of the vitalizing, cold air and found the night so refreshing, so restful as to almost compensate for the loss of sleep.

The increased pace of his mount at last brought reward, for there now came from ahead and from the right the low, confused noise of hurrying cattle, as continuous, unobtrusive, and restful as the soft roar of distant surf. So passed the dark hours, and then a warning, silver glow on the eastern horizon caused him to pull up and find a sandy depression, there to wait until the proper distance was put behind it by the thirsty herd, still reeling off the miles as though it were immune to fatigue. The silver band widened swiftly, changed to warmer tints, became suffused with crimson and cast long, thin, vague, warning shadows from sage bush and greasewood and then a molten, quivering orb pushed up over the prostrate horizon and bathed the shrinking sands with its light.

The cold, heavy-lidded rider glowered at it and removed the blanket which had been wrapped around him, rolling it tightly with stiff fingers and fumblingly made it secure in the straps behind the cantle of his saddle.

"There it is again, bronch," he growled. "We'll soon wonder if th' cold was all a dream."

He stood up in the stirrups and peered cautiously over the bank of the depression, making out the herd with unaided eyes.

"They can't go on another day," he muttered. "This ain't just dry trail it's a chunk out of hell. They can't stand much more of it without goin' blind, an' that's th' beginnin' of th' end on a place like this. I'm bettin' they get to water by noon an' then we got to wait till th' coast is clear." He shook the canteen he had allotted himself and growled again. "About a quart, an' I could drink a gallon! All right, bronch; get a-goin'," and on they plodded, keeping to the hollows and again avoiding all elevations, to face the torments of another murderous day. Again the accursed hours dragged, again the horse had a canteen of water, a sop which hardly dulled the edge of its raging thirst. Earth, air, and sky quivered, writhed and danced under the jelly-like sun and the few, soft night noises of the desert were heard no more. The leveled telescope kept the herd in sight as mile followed mile across the scorched and scorching sand.

The sun had passed the meridian only half an hour when the sweeping spyglass revealed no herd, but only a distant ridge of rock, like a tiny island on a stilled sea.

"It shore is time," muttered the rider, dismounting. "Seein' as how we're nearly there, I reckon you can have th' last canteen. You shore deserve it, you game old plodder. An' I'm shore glad them rustlin' snakes have their orders to get back pronto; but it would just be our luck if that bull-headed trail-boss held a powpow in that valley of theirs. His name's Roberts, bronch; Hugh Roberts, it is. We'll remember his name an' face if he makes us stay out here till night. You an' me have got to get to that water before another sunrise if all th' thieves in th' country are campin' on it we got to, that's all."

An hour passed and then the busy telescope showed a diminutive something moving out past the far end of the distant ridge. Despite the dancing of the heat-distorted image on the object-glass the grim watcher knew it for what it was. Another and another followed it and soon the moving spots strung out against the horizon like a crawling line of grotesque, fantastic insects, silhouetted against the sky.

"There they go back to Mesquite to capture Quayle's hotel an' win th' fight," sneered Hopalong. "I could tell 'em somethin' that would send them th' other way but we'll let 'em ride with Fate; an' get to that water as quick as yore weary legs can take us. Th' herd is there, bronch; all alone, waitin' for us. It's our herd now, if we want it, which we don't. Huh! Mebby they left a guard! All right, then; he's got a big job on his hands. Come on; get a-goin'!"

Swinging more and more to the south he soon forsook the windings of the hollows and struck boldly for the eastern end of the valley, and when he reached it he hobbled and picketed the horse, frantic with the heavy scent of water in its crimson, flaring nostrils, and went ahead on foot, the hot Sharp's in his hands full cocked and poised for instant action. Crawling to the edge of the valley he inched forward on his stomach and peered over the rim. An exclamation of surprise and incredulity died in his throat as the valley lay under his eyes, for it was the valley he had seen in the mirage only a few days before.

The stolen herd filled the small creek, standing like statues, soaking in the life-giving fluid and nosing it gently. One or two, moving restlessly, blundered against those nearest them and the watcher knew that they had gone blind. The sharpest scrutiny failed to discover any guard, and he knew that his uncertain count of the kaleidoscopic riders had been correct. Hastening back to the restless horse he soon found that it had in reserve a strength which sent it flashing to the trail's edge and down the dangerous ledge at reckless speed. At last in the creek it, too, stood as though dazed and nosed the water a little before drinking.

Hopalong swung into the stream, removed saddle and bridle and then splashed across to the hut, dumping his load, canteens, and all against the front wall. To make assurance doubly sure he scouted hurriedly down one side of the little valley, crossed the creek and went back along the other wall.

Thorpe's carefully stacked firewood provided fuel for a cunningly built-up fire; one of Thorpe's discarded tomato cans, washed and filled in the spring near the hut's walls sizzled and sputtered in the blazing fire and soon boiled madly. Picking it out of the blaze with the aid of two longer sticks the hungry cook set it to one side, threw in a double handful of Thorpe's coffee, covered it with another washed can and then placed Thorpe's extra frying pan on the coals, filling it with some of Thorpe's bacon. A large can of Thorpe's beans landed close to the fire and rolled a few feet, and the cheerful explorer emerged from the hut with a sack of sour-dough biscuits which the careless Thorpe had forgotten.

"Bless Thorpe," chuckled Hopalong. "I'll never make him climb no more walls. I wouldn't 'a' made him climb that one, mebby, if I'd knowed about this."

Looking around as a matter of caution, his glance embracing the stolid herd and his own horse grazing with the jaded animals left behind by the rustlers, he fell to work turning the bacon and soon feasted until he could eat no more. Rolling a cigarette he inhaled a few puffs and then, picking up telescope and rifle, he grunted his lazy way up the steep trail and mounted the ridge, sweeping the western horizon first with the glass and then completed the circle. Satisfied and drowsy he returned to the valley, spread his folded blanket behind the hut, placed the saddle on one end of it for a pillow and lay down to fall asleep in an instant.

When he awakened he stretched out the kinks and looked around in the dim light. He felt unaccountably cold and he looked at the blanket which he had pulled over him some time during his sleep, wondering why he had felt the need for it during the daylight hours in such a place as this.

"Well, I'll cook me some more bacon before it gets dark, an' then set up with a nice little fire, with a 'dobe wall at my back. It'll be a treat just to set an' smoke an' plan, th' night chill licked by th' fire an' my happy stomach full of bacon, beans, an' biscuits an' coffee, cans an' cans of coffee."

It suddenly came to him that the light was growing stronger instead of weaker, that it was not the afterglow, and that the chill was dying instead of increasing. Shocked by a sudden suspicion he glanced into the eastern sky and stared stupidly, surprised that he had not noticed it before.

"I was so dumb with sleep that I didn't savvy east from west," he muttered. "It's daylight, 'stead of evenin' I've slept all afternoon an' night! Well, I don't see how that changes th' eatin' part, anyhow. No wonder I pulled th' blanket over me, an' no wonder I was stiff."

With the coming of the sun a disagreeable journey loomed nearer and nearer but, as he told the horse when cinching the saddle on its back, the return trip would not be one of uncertainty; nor would they be held down to such a slow pace by any clumsy herd. A further thought hastened his movements: there was a big fight going on in Mesquite, and his two friends were in it without him. Looking around he saw that he had cleaned up and effaced all signs of his visit and, filling the canteens and fastening them into place, he mounted and rode up the steep slope, turned his back to the threatening sun and loped westward along a plain and straight trail, a grim smile on his face.

Chapter XX

After Hopalong had ridden off on his desert trailing, Johnny and Red rode to the Question-Mark, reaching it a little after daylight and were promptly challenged when near the smaller corral. The sharp voice changed to a friendly tone when the sentry had a better look at the pair.

"Thought you'd be up with th' circus," said the Question-Mark puncher.

"On our way now," replied Johnny. "Come down here to learn what was happenin'. Meet Red Connors, an old friend of Waffles."

"Howd'y," grunted the puncher, looking at Red with a keener interest. "You fellers are lucky we got to stay here an' miss it all. Walt come down last night an' said Kane's goin' to be a hard nut to crack. He's fixed up like a fort."

"Reckon we'll take a look at it," said Johnny, wheeling.

"Hey! If you want to find Mac, he's hangin' out at Quayle's."

Johnny waved his thanks and rode on with his cheerful companion. In due time they heard the distant firing and not much later rode up to Quayle's back door and went in. McCullough was raging at the effectiveness of the sharpshooters on Kane's roof who had succeeded in keeping the fight at long range and who dominated certain strategic positions which the trail-boss earnestly desired to make use of; all of which made him irritable and unusually gruff.

"Where you been?" he demanded as Johnny entered.

"Locatin' a missin' herd of yore cattle," retorted Johnny, nettled by the tone. "They're waitin' for you when you get time to go after 'em. Now we'll locate them sharpshooters. Anythin' else you can't do, let us know. Come on, Red," and he went out again, his grinning friend at his heels. At the door Red checked him.

"Looks like a long-range job, Kid. My gun's all right for closer work, but I ought to have a Sharp's for this game."

Johnny wheeled and went back. "Gimme a Sharp's," he demanded.

"Take Wilson's they got him yesterday," growled the trail-boss, pointing.

Johnny took the gun and the cartridge belt hanging on it, joined Red and led the way to a place he had in mind. Reaching the selected spot, an adobe hut on the remote outskirts of the sprawled town, he stopped. "This is good enough for me," he grunted, "except th' range is too cussed long. Well, we'll try it from here, anyhow."

"I'm goin' to th' next shack," replied Red, moving on. "We'll use our old follow-shootin' an' make 'em sick. Ready? I'm goin' to cross th' open." At his friend's affirmative grunt Red leaned over and dashed for the other adobe. A bullet whined in front of him, barely heard above the roar of Johnny's rifle. He settled down, adjusted the sights and proceeded to prove title to his widely known reputation on other ranges of being the best rifle-shot of many square miles. "Make a hit, Kid?" he called. "It's mebby further than you figger."

"It is," answered Johnny. "Like old times, huh? Lord help 'em when you get started! Are you all set? I'm ready to draw 'em."

"Wind gentle, from th' east," mumbled Red. "Dirty gun got to shoot higher. All right," he called, nestling the heavy stock.

Johnny pushed his rifle around the corner of the building, aimed quickly and fired. A hatted head arose above Kane's roof and a puff of smoke spurted into the air above it as Red's Sharp's roared. The hat flew back ward and the head ducked down again, its owner surprised by the luck of the shot.

Johnny laughed outright. "For a trial shot I'm admittin' that was a whizzer. I ain't no slouch with a Sharp's but how th' devil you can make one behave like you do is a puzzle to me."

"I'm still starin'," said a humorous, envious voice behind them and they looked around to see Waffles hugging the end of the building. "If I can get over on Red's right I'll help make targets for him."

"Walk right over to that other shack," called Johnny. "Yo're safe as if you was home in yore bunk. Cover him, Red."

Waffles' mind flashed back into the past and what it presented to him greatly reassured him, but to walk was tempting Providence; he ran across the open and again Red's rifle roared.

"Got him!" yelled Johnny, staring at the body lying over the distant parapet. It was swiftly pulled back out of sight. The rest of Johnny's words were profanely eulogistic.

"Shut yore face," growled Red. "It was plumb luck."

"Shore it was," laughed his friend in joyous irony; "but yo're allus makin' 'em. That's what counts."

Waffles, having gained the shelter he coveted, looked around. "Heads was plentiful up there yesterday. There was allus one or two bobbin' up. I'm bettin' they'll be scarcer today."

"They'll be scarcer tomorrow, when we are behind them other shacks," replied Red. "They're easy three hundred paces nearer, an' that's a lot sometimes."

"An' twice as much to them," rejoined Johnny. "Th' nearer you get th' more you make it even terms. You stay where you are me an' Waffles'll go out there tonight."

When the afternoon dragged to an end Red had another sharpshooter to his credit, and the dominating group on the roof were much less dominant. They cursed the long-range genius who shot hats off of heads, clipped ears, and had killed two men. The shooting, with a rest and plenty of time to aim, would have been creditable enough; but to hit a bobbing head meant quick handling. They were properly indignant, for it was a toss-up with Death to show enough of their heads to sight a slanting rifle. One of their number, whose mangled ear was bound up with a generous amount of bandage, savagely hammered the chisel with which he was cutting a loophole through four inches of seasoned wood, vowing vengeance on the man who had ruined his looks.

The light failing for close shooting, the three friends left their positions and went to the hotel for a late supper, Red receiving envious, grinning looks as he entered the dining-room. Idaho promptly forsook his bosom friends and went over to finish his meal at the table of the new comers.

"We got Red Frank's place plumb full of holes you can see daylight through th' second floor," he announced; "but it don't seem to do no good. If I could get close enough to use a bomb I got, we might clean 'em up."

"Crawl up in th' dark," suggested Waffles.

"Can't; they spread flour all around th' place, an' th' minute a man crosses it he shows up plain. Two of us found out all about that!"

"Go through or over th' buildin's this side of th' place," said Johnny, visualizing the street. "They lead up close to Red Frank's."

Idaho stared, and slapped his thigh in enthusiastic endorsement. "I reckon you called it!" he gloated. "Wait till I tell th' boys," and he hastened back to his friends. Judging from the sudden noise coming from the table, his friends were of the same opinion and, bolting the rest of the meal, they hastened away to forthwith try the plan.

McCullough entered the dining-room and strode straight to Johnny. "Did I hear you say you know where my cattle are?" he asked, sitting down.

Johnny nodded, chewed hurriedly and replied. "I didn't finish it. *I* don't know where they are, but Hopalong is trailin' 'em, an' he'll know when he comes back. Pay us them rewards now, instead of later, an' I'll do some high an' mighty guessin' about yore head an' bet you th' rewards that I guess right."

The trail-boss laughed. "You've shore got plenty o nerve," he retorted. "When this fight is over there won't be no rewards paid. We got th' whole gang in them two buildin's, an' we got 'em good. You've had yore trouble for nothin', Nelson."

"How 'bout th' gang that are with th' herd?" asked Johnny, a note of anger edging his words.

McCullough shrugged his shoulders. "I ain't worryin' about them they'll never come back to Mesquite."

"That so?" queried Johnny, sarcastically. "I ought to keep my mouth shut, th' way yo're talkin', but I hate to see good men killed. I'll bet you they'll come back just at dawn, some time in th' next five days. An' I'll bet you they'll sneak up on this hotel an' raise th' devil, while Kane starts a bunch from his place and Red Frank's, to help 'em. Th' minute they start shootin' in here their friends '11 sortie out an' carry th' fight to you. Want to bet on it?"

McCullough regarded the speaker through narrowed lids. "How do you figger that?" he demanded suspiciously. "You gettin' that out of yore medicine bag, too?" and then he eagerly drank in every word of the explanation. After a moment's thought he looked around the room and then back to the smiling Johnny. "Much obliged, Nelson. I'm beginnin' to see that I owe you fellers somethin', after all. If them fellers we want were loose an' you got 'em, then of course th' reward would stand; but you can't win it very well when we've got 'em corraled. Who-all is in that bunch with th' herd?"

Johnny smiled but shook his head.

"Didn't you say you knowed who killed Ridley?" persisted the trail-boss.

"I know him, an' how he did it. Hopalong saw him while his gun was smokin', but didn't know what he had shot at till later."

"Why didn't you tell me, an' earn that reward right away?"

"That's only half of th' rewards," replied Johnny. "There's money up for th' fellers that robbed th' bank. If we got Ridley's murderer th' others might 'a' smelled out what we was after. You see, I was robbed of more than eleven hundred dollars th' first night I was in town. Th' money belonged to th' ranch. Th' only chance I had of gettin' it back was to make th' rewards big enough to stand three splits that would be large enough to cover it. An' I'm still goin' to do that, Mac. Pay it now an' we'll stick with you till you get th' men an' yore herd. Of course, yo're going to get th' herd, anyhow, as far as we are concerned. I ain't holdin' that over yore head; I'm only tryin' to show you why I can't be open an' free with you."

"I couldn't pay th' rewards now even if I wanted to," said the trail-boss.

"I know that, an' I didn't think you would. I was only showin' you how things are with us."

McCullough nodded, placed a hand on the speaker's shoulder and arose, turning to Red. "Connors," he said, "yo're a howlin' wonder with a Sharp's. Much obliged for holdin' down that roof. If you can clean 'em up there this fight'll go on a cussed sight faster. Th' cover on th' north side of Kane's is so poor that we can't do much out there, but we can do a little better when them sharp shooters are driven down. From what I know of you two, yore friend Cassidy is shore able to trail that herd. I've quit worryin' about everythin' but th' fight here in town. An' lemme make a long speech a little longer: If you fellers can earn them rewards I won't waste no time in payin' up; but there ain't a chance for you. We got 'em under our guns."

"Who was right about where that raid on you was goin' to take place?" asked Johnny. "You was purty shore about that, too, wasn't you?"

The trail-boss smiled and shook his head. "Yo're a good guesser," he admitted, and went out to consult with Lukins.

The next day found the line a little tighter around the stronghold, thanks to Red's shooting, which increased in accuracy after he had decided to use closer cover and cut three hundred paces out of the range. Better positions had been gained by the attackers during the night, some of the more daring men now being not far from pointblank range, which enabled them to make the use of Kane's loopholes hazardous. To the north another rifle man lay in a hollow of the sandy plain, but too far away to do much damage. The north parapet of the building was hidden from Red by the one on the south and the aerial marksmen made free use of it.

Red Frank's place was in jeopardy, for Idaho and his enthusiastic companions were in the building next on the south, separated from the Mexican's house by less than twenty feet. There was an open window facing the gambling-house and Idaho, chancing quick glances through it, noticed that one of the heavy, board shutters of a window of the upper floor sagged out a little from the top. Signaling the men behind the jail to increase their fire, he coiled his rope and cast it through the window. It struck the upper edge of the shutter, dropped behind it and grew swiftly taut Two of his companions added their strength to his, while the other two covered them by pouring a heavy revolver fire at the two threatening loopholes. The shutter creaked, twisted, and then slowly gave way, finally breaking the lower hinge and sailing over against the other house to a cheer from the jail. Heavy firing came through the uncovered window, the bullets passing through the opposing wall and driving the Diamond L men to other shelter. Here they waited until it died down and then, picking up the bomb made by the owner of the new freight wagon, Idaho lit the jumpy, uncertain fuse, waited as long as he dared and hurled it across the intervening space and through the shutterless window as the opening was being boarded up. There was a roar, jets of smoke spurt from windows and holes and the wild cursing of injured men rang out loudly. A tongue of flame leaped through a trapdoor on the roof and grew rapidly brighter. At intervals the smoke pouring up be came suddenly heavy and thick, but cleared quickly be tween the onslaughts of the water buckets. Fire now crept through the side of the frame structure and mounted rapidly, and such a hail of lead poured through the smokespurting, upper loopholes that it became impossible for the buckets to be properly used. It was only a matter of time before the blazing roof and floor would fall on the defenders in the adobe- walled structure below, and through a loophole Red Frank suddenly shoved out a soiled towel fastened on the end of a rifle barrel.

"Come ahead, with yore hands up! "shouted a stentorian voice from the jail. "Quit firin', boys; they're surrenderin'." Almost on the tail of his words a hurrying line of choking Mexicans, bearing their wounded, streamed from the front door. They were promptly and proudly escorted by the hilarious attackers to safe quarters on the southern outskirts of the town.

Chapter XXI
All Wrapped Up

McCullough and Lukins drew men from the cordon around the gambling-hall until the line was thinned and stretched as much as prudence allowed, covering only the more strategic positions, while the men taken from it were placed in an ambuscade at the rear of Quayle's hotel. Both leaders would have preferred to have placed their reception committee nearer the outskirts of the rambling town but, not knowing from which direction the attack would come and not being able to spare men enough for outposts around the town, they were forced to concentrate at the object of the attack. When night fell and darkness hid the movement they set the trap, gave strict orders for no one to approach the rear of the hotel during the dark hours, and waited expectantly.

The first night passed in quiet and the following day found the cordonreen forced until it contained its original numbers. By nightfall of the second day Red, Johnny, and Waffles had cleared the parapet and made it useless during daylight, and as the moon increased in size and brightness the parapet steadily became a more perilous position at night for the defenders. All three marksmen, now ensconced within three hundred yards of the gambling-house and out of the line of sight of every lower loophole, had the range worked out to a foot. Red and Waffles had discarded their borrowed Sharp's and were now using their own familiar Winchesters, and it was certain death to any man who tried to shoot from Kane's roof on any side but the north one.

Evening came and with it came a hair-brained attempt by Idaho and his irrepressibles to capture and use the stables. Despite McCullough's orders to the contrary the group of young-sters, elated by their success against Red Frank's, made the attempt as soon as darkness fell; and learned with cost that the stables were stacked decks. One man was killed and all the others wounded, most of them so badly as to remove them from the role of combatants; but one dogged, persistent, and vindictive unit of the foolish attack managed to set fire to the sun-dried structures before crawling away.

The baked wood burned like tinder and became a mass of flames almost in an instant, and for a few minutes it looked as though they would take the gambling-hall with them. It was a narrow squeak and missed only because of a slight shift of the wind. The scattered line of punchers to the north of the building, not expecting the sudden conflagration, had crawled nearer to the gambling-hall in the encroaching darkness, only to find themselves suddenly revealed to their enemies by the towering sheets of flame. They got off with minor injuries only because the north side of the building was not well manned and be cause the stables were holding the attention of most of the besieged. When the flames died down almost as swiftly as they had grown, the smouldering ashes gave a longer and less obstructed view to the guards of Kane's east wall and rendered useless certain positions cherished by McCullough.

The trail-boss, seething with anger, stamped up to Lukins and roared his demands, with the result that Idaho and the less injured of his companions were sent to take the places of cooler heads in the ambush party and were ordered to stay in Quayle's stable until after the expected attack.

In Quayle's kitchen four men waited through the drag ging hours, breaking the silence by occasional whispers as they watched the faintly lighted open spaces and the walls of certain buildings newly powdered with flour so as to serve as backgrounds and to silhouette any man passing in front of them. Only the north walls had been dusted and there was nothing to reveal their freshly acquired whiteness to unsuspecting strangers coming up from the south. In the stable Idaho and his restless friends grumbled in low tones and cursed their inactivity. Three men at the darkened office windows, and two more on the floor above watched silently. Outside an occasional shot called forth distant comment, and laughter arose here and there along the alert line.

On the east end of the line a Diamond L puncher, stretched out on his stomach in a little depression he had scooped in the sand during the darker hours of the second night, stuck the end of his little finger in a bullet hole in his canteen and rimmed the hole abstractedly, the water soaking his clothes making him squirm.

"Cuss his hide," he growled. "Now I got to stay thirsty." He slid a hand down his body and lifted the dinging clothing from the small of his back. "If it was only as cold as that when I drink it, I wouldn't grumble. An' I wasn't thirsty till he spilled it," he added in petulant afterthought.

To his right two friends crouched behind the aged ruins of an adobe house, paired off because one of them shot left-handed, which fitted each to his own corner. "Got any chewin'?" asked Righthand. "Chuck it over. Seems to me that they "he set his teeth into the tobacco, tore off a generous quantity and tossed the plug back to its owner "ain't answerin' as strong as they was this after noon."

"No?" grunted Lefthand, brushing sand from the plug. He shoved it back into a pocket and reflected a moment. "It was good shootin' while th' stable burned." Another pause, and then: "Did you hear Billy yell when them fools started th' fire?"

Righthand laughed, stiffened, fired, and pumped the lever of the gun. "I'm gettin' so I can put every one through that loophole. Hear him squawk?" He dropped to his knees to rest his back, and chuckled. "Shore did. Billy, he was boastin' how near he could crawl to them stables. I reckon he done crawled too close. Lukins ought to send them kids home."

In a sloping, shallow arroyo to their right Walt and Bob of the Question-Mark lay side by side. Behind them two shots roared in quick succession. Walt lazily turned his head from the direction of the sounds and peeped over the edge of the bank.

"I reckon some coyote took a look over th' edge of th' roof," he remarked.

"Uh-huh," replied Bob without interest and without relaxing his vigil.

"I don't lay out here one little minute after Connors leaves that 'dobe," said Walt. He spat noisily and turned the cud. "I'm savin' shootin' like his is a gift. I'm some shot, myself, but h--l"

"You'd shore a thought so," replied Bob, grinning as he reviewed something, "if you'd seen that sharpshooter flop over th' edge of th' roof th' other day. I'd guess it was close to fifteen hundred." He changed his position, grunted in complacent satisfaction and continued. "Some folks can't see a man's forehead at that distance, let alone hit it. Of course, th' sky was behind it."

"Which made it plainer, but harder to figger right," observed Walt. "Waffles says Connors can drive a dime into a plank with th' first, an' push it through with th' second, as far away as he can see th' dime. When it's too far away to be seen, he puts it in th' middle of a black circle, an' aims for th' middle of th' circle. But I put plenty of salt on th' tails of his stories."

"Which holds 'em down," grunted Bob. "Who's that over there, movin' around that shack?"

Walt looked and cogitated. "Charley was there when I came out," he answered. "Cussed fool showin' hisself like that." He swore at a thin pencil of flame which stabbed out from a loophole, and fired. "Told you so!" he growled. "Charley is down!"

Both fired at the loophole and hazarded a quick look at the foolish unfortunate, who had dragged himself behind a hummock of sand. Rapid firing broke out behind them and, sensing what it meant, they joined in. A crouched figure darted from a building, sprinted to the hummock, swung the wounded man on its back, and staggered and zigzagged to cover.

"That was Waffles," said Walt, reloading the magazine of his rifle. "It's a cussed shame to make a man take chances like that by bein' a fool."

Behind the building Waffles lowered his burden to the ground, ripped off the wet shirt and became busy. He fastened the end of the bandage and stood up. "Fools are lucky sometimes," he growled; "an' I says you are lucky to only have a smashed collar bone. You try a fool trick like that again an' I'll bust yore head. Ain't you got no sense?"

"Don't you go to put on no airs, Waffles," said Red Connors. "I can tell a few things on you. I know you."

Johnny chuckled. "Tread easy," he warned. "We both know you."

"Go to h--l!" grunted the ex- foreman of the O-Bar-O, grinning. "Fine pair of sage-hens you are to tell tales on me! I got you thro wed and hog-tied before you even start." He wheeled at a noise behind him, and glared at the wounded man. "Where'n h--l are you goin'?" he demanded, truculently.

"Without admittin' yore right to ask fool questions," groaned Charley, still moving, "I'll say I'm goin' to join th' ambush party at Quayle's, an' relieve somebody else." He gritted his teeth and stood erect. "I can use a Colt, can't I?" he demanded.

"Yo're so shaky you can't hit a house," retorted Waffles.

"Which I ain't aimin' to do," rejoined the white-faced man. "You'll show more sense if you'll tie my left arm like it ought to be, instead of standin' with yore mouth open. You'll shore catch a cold if you don't shut it purty soon."

"You stubborn fool!" growled Waffles, but he fixed the arm to its owner's satisfaction.

"If he gets smart, Charley," suggested Johnny, "pull his nose. He allus was an old woman, anyhow."

With the coming of midnight the cordon became doubled in numbers as growling men rubbed the sleep from their eyes and took up positions for the meeting of Kane's sortie in case the hotel was attacked by his expected drive outfit.

The hours dragged on, the silence of the night infrequently broken by bits of querulous cursing by some wounded puncher, an occasional taunt from besieger or besieged and sporadic bursts of firing which served more for notifications of defiance and watchfulness than for any grimmer purpose. Patches of clouds now and then drifted before the moon and sailed slowly on. Nature's denizens of the dark were in active swing and filled the night with their soft orchestration. The besiegers, paired for night work, which let one man doze while his companion watched, hummed, grumbled, or snored; in the gamblinghall fortress weary men slept beside the loopholes, the disheartened for a few hours relieved of their fears or carrying them across the borderland of sleep to make their slumbers restless and broken, while scowling, disheartened sentries kept a keener watch, alert for the rush hourly expected.

South of town a group of horsemen pulled up, dismounted, tied their mounts to convenient brush and slipped like shadows toward the nearest house, approaching it round-about and with animal wariness. From house to house, corral to corral, cover to cover they crept, spread out in a fan-shaped line, silent, grim, vindictive and desperate. Not a shadow passed unsearched and unused, not a bowlder or thicket was above suspicion nor below being utilized. Nearer and nearer they worked their way, eyes straining, ears tuned for every sound, high-strung with nerves quivering, keyed to swift reflex and instant decision. The scattered, infrequent firing grew steadily nearer, every flat report was searched for secret meanings and the sharp squeak of a gyrating bat overhead sent every man flat to the earth. The last in the group became cannily slower as opportunity offered and soon managed to be so far behind that his quick, furtive desertion was un-noticed in the tenseness of conjecture as to what lay immediately ahead.

Kane's trail-boss slanted his watch under the moon's rays and gave a low, natural signal, whereupon to right and left a man detached himself and left the waiting group. Minutes passed, their passing marked on nervous foreheads by the thin trickle of cold sweat. Any instant might a challenge, a shot, a volley ring out on any side; hostile eyes might be watching every movement, hostile guns waiting for the right moment, like ravenous hounds in leash. The scouts returned as silently as they had departed and breathed their reassuring words in Roberts' ear. The town lay unsuspecting, every waking eye bent on the bulking gambling-hall. Not a hidden outpost, not a pacing sentry to watch the harmless rear. To the right showed the roof of a two-story building, bulking above the low, thick roofs of scattered, helter-skelter adobes, in any one of which Death might be poised.

Again the slow advance, and breathed maledictions on the head of any unfortunate who trod carelessly or let his swinging six-gun click against buckle or button. Roberts, peering around the end of an adobe wall, held his elbows from his sides, and progress ceased while a softly whistling figure strode across the street and became lost to sight. This was the jumping-off place, the edge of a black precipice of fate, unknown as to depth or what lay below. The savage, thankful elation which had possessed every man at his success in making this border line of life and death faded swiftly as his mind projected itself into the unknown on the other side of the house. Roberts knew what might follow if hesitation were allowed here, and that the conjecturing minds might have scant time to waver he nerved himself and snapped his fingers, leaping around the corner for Quayle's kitchen door, his men piling after him, still silent and much more tense, yet tortured to shout and to shoot. Ten steps more and the goal would have been reached, but even as the leaping group exulted there came a shredded sheet of flame and the deafening crash of spurting six-guns worked at top speed at point-blank range. The charging line crumpled in mid-stride, plunged headlong to the silvered sands and rolled or flopped or lay instantly still. At the head of his men the rustler trail-boss offered a target beyond the waiting punchers' fondest hopes, yet he bounded on unscathed, flashed around the hotel corner, turned again, doubling back behind the smoke-filled stable and scurried like a panic-stricken rabbit for the brush-filled arroyo, while hot and savage hunters searched the street for him until a hail of lead from Kane's drove them to any shelter which might serve.

When the sheltering arroyo led him from his chosen course Roberts forsook it and ran with undiminished speed toward where the horses waited. At last he reached them and as he stretched out his arm his last measure of energy left him and he plunged forward, rolling across the sand. But a will like his was not to be baffled and in a few moments he stirred, crawled forward, clawed him self into a saddle, jerked loose the restraining rope and rode for safety, hunched over and but half conscious. Gradually his pounding heart caught up with the demand, his burning lungs and spasmodic breathing became more normal, his head steadied and became a little clearer and he looked around to find out just where he was. When sure of his location he turned the horse's head toward, Bitter Spring, and beyond it, to follow the tracks he knew were still there to the only safe place left for him in all the country.

He seemed to have been riding for days when he caught sight of something moving over a ridge far ahead of him and he closed his eyes in hope that the momentary rest would clear his vision. After awhile he saw it push up over another low ridge and he knew it to be a horseman riding in the same direction as himself. Again he closed his eyes and unmercifully quirted the tired and unwilling horse into a pace it could not hold for long. Another look ahead showed him that the horseman was a Mexican, which meant that he was hardly a foe even if not a friend.

And he sneered as he thought how little it mattered whether the Mexican was an enemy or not, for one enemy ahead and a Greaser at that was greatly to be preferred to those who might be following him. Soon he frowned in slowly dawning recognition. It was Miguel and he had obtained quite a start. Conjecturing about how he had managed to be so far in the lead stirred up again the vague suspicions which had been intruding themselves upon him while he had been unable to think clearly; but he was thinking clearly now, he told himself, and his eyes glinted the sudden anger.

He thought he now knew why the town had been entered so easily, why they had been allowed to penetrate unopposed to its center. It was plain enough why they had been permitted to get within a few feet of Quayle's back door, and then be stopped with a volley at a murderously short range. As he reviewed it he almost was stunned by the thought of his own escape and he tried to puzzle it out. It might be that every waiting puncher thought that others were covering him and in this he was right. The compact group behind him had drawn every eye. It had been one of those freakish tricks of fate which might not occur again in a hundred fights; and it turned cold, practical Hugh Roberts into a slave of superstition.

On the way to town he had sneered when Miguel had pointed out a chaparral cock which raced with them for several miles and claimed that it was an omen of good luck; but from this time on no "roadrunner" ever would hear the angry whine of his bullets. Thinking of Miguel brought him back to his suspicions and he looked at the distant rider with an expression on his face which would have caused chills to race up and down the Mexican's back, could he have seen them. Miguel, unhurt, riding leisurely back to the herd, with a head-start great enough to be in itself incriminating. And then the Mexican turned in his saddle and looked back, and Roberts let his horse fall into a saner pace.

The effect upon Miguel was galvanic. He reined in, flung himself off on the far side of his horse and cautiously slid the rifle from its scabbard while he pretended to be tightening the cinch. His swarthy face became a pasty yellow and then resumed its natural color, a little darker, perhaps, by the sudden inrush of blood. After what he had done in town Hugh Roberts would be on his trail for only one thing. Miguel's racing imagination and his sudden feeling of guilt for his deliberate, planned desertion found a sufficient reason for the pursuing horse man. Sliding the rifle under his arm he waited until the man came nearer, where a hit would be less of a gamble. The Mexican knew what had happened, for he had delayed until he heard that crashing volley, and knew it to be a volley. Knowing this he knew what it meant and had fled for Surprise Valley and the big herd waiting there. That Roberts should have escaped was a puzzle and he wrestled with it while the range was steadily shortened, and the more he wrestled the more undecided he be came. Finally he slipped the gun back, mounted, and waited for the other to come up. He had a plausible answer for every question.

Roberts slowed to a walk and searched the Mexican's eyes as he pulled up at his side. "How'd you get out here so far ahead of me?" he demanded, his eyes cold and threatening.

Miguel shrugged his shoulders, but did not take his hand from his belt. "Ah, eet ees a miracle," he breathed. "The good Virgin, she watch over Miguel. An' paisano, the roadrunner deed I not tell you eet was good luck? An' you, too, was saved! How deed eet happen, that you are save?"

"They none of them looked at me, I reckon," replied Roberts. "They got everybody but me an' you. How is it that yo're out here, so far ahead of me?"

"Jus' before the firs' shootin' the what you call volley I stoomble as I try not to step on Thorpe. I go down the volley, eet come I roll away they do not see me an' here I am, like you, save."

"Is that so?" snapped Roberts.

"Eet ees jus' so, so much as eet ees that somewan tell we are comin' to Quayle's," answered Miguel. "For why they do not see us, in the town, when we come in? For why that volley, lak one shot? Sometheeng there ees that Miguel he don' understan'. An' theese, please: Why ees there no sortie wen we come in? We was on the ver' minute eet ees so?"

"Right on th' dot!" snarled Roberts, his thoughts racing along other trails. "Huh!" he growled. "Our shares of th' herd money comes to quite a sizable pile, mebby that's it. Take th' shares of all of us, an' it's more'n half. Well, I don't know, an' I ain't carin' a whole lot now. Think we can swing that herd, Miguel, an' split all th' money, even shares?"

The Mexican showed his teeth in a sudden, expansive smile. "For why not? Theese hor-rses are ver' tired; but the others they are res' now. We can wait at Bitter Spring tonight, an' go on tomorrow. There ees no hurry now."

"We don't hang out at Bitter Spring all night," contradicted Roberts flatly. "We'll water 'em an' breath 'em a spell, an' push right on. Th' further I get away from Mesquite th' better I'm goin' to like it. Come on, let's get goin'."

"There ees no hurry from Bitter Spring," murmured the Mexican. "They ees only one who know beyond; an' Manuel, he ees weeth Kane."

"I don't care a d--n!" growled his companion, stubbornly. "I'm not layin' around Bitter Spring any longer than I has to."

Neither believed the other's story, but neither cared, only each determined to be alert when the drive across the desert was completed. Before that there was hardly need to let their mutual suspicions have full play. Each was necessary to the success of the drive but after? That would be another matter. Fate was again kind to them both, for as they hurried east Hopalong Cassidy hastened west along his favorite trail, the rolling sand between hiding them from him.

Back in the town the elated ambushers buried the bodies, marveled at the escape of Roberts and drifted away to take places on the firing line, which soon showed increased activity. Here and there a more daring puncher took chances, some regretting it and others gaining better positions. Red, Johnny, and Waffles attended strictly to the roof, which now had been abandoned on all sides but the north, where lack of cover prohibited McCullough's men from getting close enough to do any considerable damage. The few punchers lying far off on the north were there principally to stop a sortie or an attempt at escape. As the day passed the defenders' fire grew a little less and the Question-Mark foreman was content to wait it out rather than risk unnecessary casualties in pushing the fighting any more briskly.

Evening came, and with it came Hopalong, tired, hungry, thirsty, and hot, which did not add sweetness to his disposition. Eager to get the men he wanted and to return for the herd, he listened impatiently to his friends' account of the fight, his mind busy on his own account. When the tale had been told and McCullough's changing attitude touched upon he shoved his hat back on his head, spread his feet and ripped out an oath.

"!" he growled. "All these men, all this time, to clean up a shack like that?"

"Mac's playin' safe it's only a matter of time, now," apologized Waffles, glaring at his two companions, who already had worn his nerves ragged by the same kind of remarks.

"Hell!" snorted Hopalong impatiently. "We'll all grow whiskers at this rate, before it's over!" He turned to Johnny and regarded him speculatively. "Kid, let Red an' Waffles handle that roof an' come along with me. I'm goin' to start things movin'."

"You'll find Mac plumb set on goin' easy," warned Waffles.

"Th' hell with Mac, an' Lukins, an' you, an' everybody else," retorted Hopalong. "We're not workin' for nobody but ourselves. All I got to do is keep my mouth shut an' Mac loses a plumb fine herd. Let me hear him talk to me! Come on, Kid."

Johnny deserted his companions as though they were lepers and showed his delight in every swaggering movement. A whining bullet over his head sent his fingers to his nose in contemptuous reply, but nevertheless he went on more carefully thereafter. As they reached the rear of a deserted adobe Hopalong pulled him to a stop.

"I'm tired of this blasted country, an' you ought to be, for you've got a wife that's havin' dull days an' sleepless nights. I'm goin' to touch somethin' off that'll put an end to this fool quiltin' party, an' let us get our money an' go home. By that I'm meanin' th' SV, for it's goin' to be home for me. Besides, it's our best chance of gettin' them rewards. So he's aimin' on cuttin' us out of 'em, huh? All right; I'm goin' to Quayle's, an' while I'm holdin' their interest you fill a canteen with kerosene an' smuggle it into th' stable."

"What you goin' to do?" demanded his companion with poorly repressed eagerness.

"I'm goin' to set fire to that gamblin'-joint an' drive 'em out, that's what!"

"Th' moon won't let you," objected Johnny, but as he looked up at the drifting clouds he hesitated and qualified his remark. "You'll have times when it won't be so light, but it'll be too light for that."

"When I start for th' hotel gamblin'-joint I go agin' th' northeast corner, where there ain't but one loophole that covers that angle. I got it figgered out. When I start, you an' Red won't be loafin' back there where I found you, target-practicin' at th' roof."

Reaching the hotel they found a self-satisfied group complacently discussing the fight. Quayle looked up at their entry, sprang to his feet and heartily shook hands with both.

"Welcome to Mesquite, Cassidy," he beamed. "'Tis different now than whin ye left, an' it won't be long be fore honest men have their say-so in this town,"

"Couple of weeks, I reckon, th' way things are driftin'," replied Hopalong, smiling as Johnny left the office to invade the kitchen, where Murphy gave a grinning welcome and looked curiously at the huge canteen held out to him.

"Couple of days," corrected Quayle.

McCullough arose and shook hands with the new comer. "Hear you been trailin' my herd," he said. "Locate 'em?"

"They're hobbled, and' waitin' for yore boys to drive 'em home. Wish you'd tell yore outfit an' th' others not to shoot at th' feller that heads for Kane's northeast corner tonight, but to cut loose at th' loopholes instead. I'm honin' to get back home, an' so I'm aimin' to bust up this little party tonight. To do that I got to get close."

"That's plumb reckless," replied the trail-boss. "We got this all wrapped up now, an' it'll tie its own knots in a day or two. What's th' use of takin' a chance like that?"

"To show that bunch just who they throwed in jail! Somebody else might feel like tryin' it some day, an' I'm aimin' to make that ' some day ' a long way off."

"Can't say I'm blamin' you for that. Whereabouts did you leave th' herd?"

"Where nobody but me an' my friends, on this side of th' fence, knows about," answered Hopalong. "I'll tell you when I see you! again ain't got time now." He nodded to the others, went out the way he had come in and walked off with Johnny, who carried the innocent canteen instead of putting it into the stable.

As they started for the place where Hopalong had left his horse, not daring to ride it into town, they chose a short-cut and after a few minutes' brisk walking Hopalong pointed to a bunch of horses tied to some bushes.

"Th' fellers that owned them played safer than I did," he said, "leavin' 'em out here. I reckon they're all Question-Mark. "

Johnny put a hand on his friend's arm and stopped him. "I got a better guess," he said. "I know where all their cayuses are. Hoppy, that rustlin' drive crew must 'a' come in this way. What you bet?"

"I ain't bettin'," grunted his companion, starting toward the little herd, "I'm lookin'. I don't hanker to lose that cayuse of mine, an' they'll mebby get th' hoss I ride after I start for their buildin' tonight. He's so mean I sort of cotton to him. An' he's got some thoroughbred blood in his carcass, judgin' from what Arch said. In a case like this it's only fair to use theirs. Be sides, they're fresh; mine ain't."

Johnny pushed ahead, stopped at the tethered group and laughed. "Good thing you didn't bet," he called over his shoulder.

Hopalong untied a wicked-looking animal. "He looks like he'd buffi 1 th' ground over a short distance, an' that's what I'm interested in. I'm goin' down an' turn mine loose. If things break like I figger they will there's no tellin' when I'll see him again, an' I don't want him to starve tied up to a tree. He's so thirsty about now that he'll head for McCullough's crick on a bee line."

Johnny nodded, considered a moment and went toward the tie ropes. "Shore, an' not stray far from that grass, neither." He released the horses except the one he mounted and then rode up so close to his friend that their knees rubbed. "No tellin' when anybody will be comin' this way or when they'll get a drink. You look like you been hit by an idea. That's so rare, suppose you uncork it?"

"It's one I've been turnin' over," replied his friend, "an' it looks th' same on both sides, too."

"Turn it over for me an' lemme look."

"Kid, I'm lookin' for somethin' to happen that shore will bother Mr. McCullough a whole lot if he happens to think of it. When that buildin' starts burnin' it's shore goin' to burn fast They can't fight th' fire like they should with them punchers pourin' lead into them lighted loopholes. Once it starts nothin' can stop it; an' I'm tellin' you it's shore goin' to start right. Th' south side is goin' first. They know there's only a few men watchin' th' north side, an' them few are layin' too far back. It won't take a man like Kane very long to learn that he's got to jump, an' jump quick; an' when he does he'll jump right. Right for him an' right for us. He can't do nothin' else. You said they got their cayuses in there with 'em?"

Johnny nodded. "So I was told. I'm seem' yore drift, Hoppy; an' when Kane an' his friends jump me an' Red shore will have jammed guns an' not be able to shoot at 'em."

"Marriage ain't spoiled yore head," chuckled his com panion. "Kane havin' us jailed that way riled me; an' McCullough tryin' to slip out of payin' them rewards has riled me some more. I'm washin' one hand with th' other. Do you think you an' Red could get yore cayuses an' an extra one for me, in case they get this one, around west somewhere back of where yo're goin'?"

"How'll this one do for you?" asked his companion, slapping the horse he was on.

"Plenty good enough."

"Then he'll be there, ready to foller th' jumpers," laughed Johnny.

"Good for you, Kid. You shore have got th' drift. Now, seem' that I may get into trouble an' be too late to go after 'em when they jump, you listen close while I tell you where to ride, an' all about it," and the description of the desert trail and the valley was as meaty as it was terse. He told his friend where to take the horses and where to look for him before the night's work began, and then went back to Kane and his men. "They're bound to head for that valley. There ain't no place else for 'em to go. I'll bet they've had that figgered for a refuge ever since they learned about it."

Johnny laughed contentedly. "An' Mac tellin' me that he's got 'em all tied up an' ain't aimin' to pay no rewards! But," he said, becoming instantly grave, "there's one thin' I don't like. I'm admittin' it's yore scheme, but we ought to draw lots to see who's goin' to use that kerosene. After all, yo're down here to help me out of a hole. Dig up some more cartridges, you maverick!"

"Don't you reckon I got brains enough to run it off? " demanded his friend.

"An' some to spare," replied Johnny; "but I ain't no idjut, myself. Here; call yore choice," and he reached for his belt.

"Yo're slow, Kid," chuckled Hopalong, holding out his hand. "Call it yourself."

Johnny hesitated, pushed back the cartridges and placed his hand on those of his friend. "You went at that like you was pullin' a gun: an' I can't say nothin' that means anythin' faster. Why th' hurry?"

"Habit, I reckon," gravely replied his friend. "Savin' time, mebby; I dunno why, you chump!"

"It's a good habit; an' I'm shore you saved considerable time, which same I'm aimin' to waste," replied Johnny. He thought swiftly. Last time he had called "even," and lost. He was certain that Hopalong wanted the task. How would his friend figure? The natural impulse of a slow-witted man would be to change the number. Hopalong was not slow-witted; on the contrary so far from slow-witted that he very likely would be suspicious of the next step in reasoning and go a step further, which would take him back to the act of the slow-witted, for he knew that the cogitating man in front of him was no simpleton. Odd or even: a simple choice; but in this instance it was a battle of keen wits. Johnny raised his own hand and looked down at his friend's, the upper one clasping and covering the lower; and then into the night-hidden eyes, which were squinting between narrowed lids to make their reading hopeless. Being something of a gambler Johnny had the gambler's way of figuring, and this endorsed the other line of reasoning: he believed the chances were not in favor of a repetition.

"Cuss yore grinnin' face," he growled. "I said ' even ' last time, an' was wrong. Now I'm say in' ' odd.' Open up!"

Hopalong opened the closed hands and his squinting eyes at the same instant and laughed heartily. "Kid, I cussed near raised you, an' I know yore ways. Mebby it ain't fair, but you was tryin' hard to outguess me. There they are pair of aces. Count 'em, sonny; count 'em."

"Count 'em yourself," growled Johnny; "if you can count that far!" He peered into the laughing eyes and thrust out his jaw. "You know my ways, do you? Well, when we get back to th' SV, me an' you are goin' in to Dave's, get a big stack of two-bit pieces an' go at it. I'll cussed soon show you how much you know my ways! G'wan! Get out of here before I get rough!"

"He's too old to spank," mused Hopalong, kneeing the horse, "an' too young to fight with reckon I'll have to pull my stakes an' move along." Chuckling, he looked around. "Ain't forgot nothin' about tonight, have you, child?"

"No!" thundered Johnny. "But for two-bits I would!" Hopalong's laugh came back to him and sent a smile over his face. "There ain't many like you, you old son-of-a-gun!" he muttered, and wheeled to return to the town and to Red.

His departing friend grinned at the horse. "Bronch." he said, confidently, "he shore had me again. I'm gettin' so cheatin's second nature; an' worse'n that, I'm cheatin' my best friends, an' likin' it. Yessir, likin' it! Ain't you ashamed of me? You nod that ugly head of yourn again an' I'll knock it off you! G'wan: This ain't no funeral yet!"

Chapter XXII
The Bonfire

Johnny rode up to the hotel, got a Winchester and ammunition for it from the stack of guns in the kitchen and then went to the stable for Red's horse and Pepper. As he led them out he stopped to answer a pertinent question from the upper window of the hotel and rode off again, leading the extra mounts.

Ed Doane lowered the rifle and scratched his head. "Coin' for a moonlight ride," he repeated in disgust as he drew back from the window. "Cussed if punchers ain't gettin' more locoed every day. Moonlight ride! Shore go out an' look at th' scenery. Looks different in th' moonlight bah! To me a pancake looks like a pancake by kerosene, daylight, wood fire or or moonlight. I suppose th' moonlight'll get into 'em an' they'll be singin' love-songs an' harmonizin'; but thank th' Lord I don't have to go along!" He glanced around at a sudden thap! grinned in the darkness at the double planking on that side wall and sat down again. "Shoot!" he growled. "Shoot twice! Shoot an' be damned! Waste 'em! Reckon th' moonlight's got into you, you cow-stealin', murderin' pup." Filling his pipe he packed and lit it, blew several clouds through nose and mouth and scratched his head again. "Coin' for a moonlight ride, huh? Well, mebby you are, Johnny, my lad; but Ed Doane's bettin' there's more'n a ride in it. You didn't go for no moonlight rides before that missin' friend of yourn turned up; an' then, right away, you ride up on one hoss, collect two more an' go gallivantin' off under th' moon. I'm guessin' close. Eddie Doane, I'll bet you a tenspot them three grizzlies are out for to put their ropes on them rewards. An' I hope they collect, cussed if I don't. That Scotch trail-boss is puttin' on too many airs for me an' he's rilin' Nelson slow but shore. Go get it, Bar-20: I'm bettin' on you."

There came steps to his door. "Ar-re ye there, Ed? " called a voice.

"Shore; come in, Murphy."

The door opened and closed as the cook entered. "Have ye a pipeful? Mine's all gone."

"Help yourself," answered Doane, tossing the sack. "There it is, by yore County Cork feet."

"I have ut," grunted Murphy. "An' who was th' lad ye was talkin' to from th' windy just now?"

"Nelson. He's goin' ridin' in th' moonlight. Must aim to go far, for he's got three horses."

"Has he, now?" Murphy puffed in quiet satisfaction for a moment. "He's a good la-ad, Ed. Goin' ridin', is he? Well, ridin' is fine for them as likes it. But I'm wonderin' what he's doin' with th' kerosene I gave him?"

"Kerosene? When?"

"Whin he come in with his friend Cassidy an' a fine bye that man is, too. Shure: a hull canteen av it. Two gallons. He says for me to kape it quiet: as if I'd be tellin'! Quayle would have me scalp if he knowed it givin' away his ile like that. Now where ye goin' so fast?"

"For a walk, under th' moonlight!" answered Doane. "Yo're goin', too an' we're goin' with our mouths shut. Not a word about th' hosses or th' kerosene. You remember what Cassidy said about goin' agin' Kane's northeast corner? Come on an' see th' bonfire!"

"Shure, an' who's fool enough to have anny bonfires now?"

"Murphy, I said with our mouths shut. Come on, up near th' jail!"

The cook scratched his head and favored his companion with a sidewise glance, which revealed nothing because of the darkness of the room. "Th' jail?" he muttered. "He's crazy, he is. Th' jail won't make no bonfire. It's mud. But as long as he has th' 'baccy, I'll go wid him. Whist!" he exclaimed as another thap! sounded on the wall. "An' what's that?"

"This room's haunted," explained Ed.

"Lead th' way, thin; or let me," said Murphy in great haste. "I'll watch yore mud bonfire."

After leaving the hotel Johnny kept it between himself and Kane's building, rode to the arroyo which Roberts had found so useful and followed it until out of sight of anyone in town. When he left it he turned east, crossed the main trail and dismounted east of the place where he and Red had kept watch on the gambling-house roof. Working his way on foot to his sharpshooting friends he lay down at Red's side and commented casually on several subjects, finally nudging the Bar-20 rifleman.

"I'm growin' tired of this spot an' this game," he grumbled. "They know where we are now, an' that roof's plumb tame."

Red stirred restlessly. "You must 'a' read my mind," he observed. "You've had a spell off stay here while I take a rest."

"Stay nothin'!" retorted Johnny. "This ain't our fight, anyhow."

"Somebody's got to stay," objected Red.

"Let Waffles, then," rejoined Johnny. "You don't care if we look around?"

"I'd just as soon stay here as go any place else," said the ex- foreman of the O-Bar-O. "Where you fellers aimin' to go?"

"Over west to cover Hoppy," answered Johnny, remembering that this much was generally known. "He aims to make a dash for th' hotel, an' he's so stubborn nobody can stop him. He says th' fight's been goin' on too long; an' you know how he can use six-guns. To use 'em right he'll have to get plumb close."

"Cussed fool!" snorted Red, arising to his knees. "How can he end it by makin' a dash, an' usin' his short guns? Mebby he's aimin' to put his rope on it an' pull it over, shootin' as they pop out from under!" he sarcastically suggested.

"Mebby; better ask him," replied Johnny. "I did. Mebby you can get it out of him. When he wants to keep his mouth shut, he shore can keep it shut tight. There's no use wastin' our breath on it. He's got some fool scheme in his head an' he's set solid. All we can do is to try to save his fool skin. Waffles can hold down this place till we come back. Come on, Red."

Red grumbled and stretched. "All right. See you later mebby, Waffles."

Johnny turned. "Don't forget an' shoot at th' feller runnin' for th' east end of th' buildin'," he warned.

"Mac sent th' word along a couple of hours ago," re plied Waffles, settling down in the place vacated by Red to resume the watch on the hotel roof, which was fairly well revealed at times by the moon. He seemed to be turning something over in his mind, but finally shrugged his shoulders and gave his attention to the roof. "They've got somethin' better'n six-guns at close range," he muttered. "Well, a man owes his friends somethin', so I'm holdin' my tongue."

Reaching the horses Johnny and his companion mounted and rode northward, leading the spare mount.

"What's he up to?" demanded Red.

"Goin' to set fire to th' shack," answered Johnny, and he forthwith explained the whole affair.

"Huh!" grunted Red. "There ain't no doubt in my mind that it'll work if he can get there an' get th' fire started." He was silent for a moment and then pulled his hat more firmly down on his head. "If he don't get there, I'll give it a whirl. Anyhow, I'd have to leave cover to get to him if he went down so it ain't much worse goin' th' rest of th' way. An' I'm tellin' you this: That lone loophole is shore goin' to be bad medicine for any body try in' to use it after he starts. I'll put 'em through it so fast they'll be crowdin' each other."

"An' while yo're reloadin' I'll keep 'em goin'," said Johnny, patting his borrowed Winchester. "They'll shore think somebody's squirtin' 'em out of a hose."

Some time later he stopped his horse and peered around in the faint light.

Red stopped, also. "This th' place?"

"Looks like it we ought to get some sign of Hoppy purty soon. Anyhow, we'll wait awhile. Glad that moon ain't very bright."

"An' cussed glad for th' clouds," added Red. "Clouds like them ain't th' rule in this part of the country." He leaned over and looked down at the sand. "Tracks, Kid," he said. "Follow 'em?"

"No," answered his companion slowly. "I'm bettin' they're Hoppy's. Stay with th' cayuses I'm goin' to look around," and as he dismounted they heard a hail. Red swung to the ground as their friend appeared.

"You made good time," said Hopalong, advancing. "I been off lookin' things over. We can leave th' cayuses in a little hollow about long rifle-shot from th' buildin'. From there you two can get real close by travelin' on yore bellies from bush to bush. Th' cover's no good in day light, but on a night like this, by waitin' for th' clouds, it'll be plenty good enough."

"How close did you get?" asked Johnny.

"Close enough to send every shot through that loop hole, if I wanted to."

"Did they see you? Did you draw a shot?"

"No. They ain't watchin' that loophole very close. Ain't had no reason to since th' stables burned. There ain't nobody been layin' off in this direction. Th' cover wasn't good enough to risk it, with only a blank wall to watch, an' with them fellers on th' roof to shoot down. Red couldn't cover th' north part of it from where he was. I been wonderin' if I ought to use a cay use at all."

"There's argument agin' usin' one," mused Johnny.

"Th' noise, an' a bigger object to catch attention," re marked Red. "If you walked th' cayuse to soften its steps, it still looms up purty big; an' if you cut loose an' dash in, th' noise shore will bring a shot. Me an' th' Kid would have to start shootin' early an' keep it up a long while an' we're near certain to leave gaps in th' string."

"What moonlight there is shines on this end of th' buildin'," observed Johnny. "That loop-hole show up plain?" he asked.

"You can't see nothin' else," chuckled Hopalong. "It's so black it fair hollers."

Red drew the Winchester from its sheath and turned the front sight on its pivot, which then showed a thin white line. He never had regretted having it made, for since it had been put on he had not suffered the annoyance of losing sight of it against a dark target in poor light. "Bein' bull-headed," he remarked, "you chumps has to guess; but little Reddie ain't doin' none of it. I told you long ago to have one put on."

"Shut up!" growled Johnny, turning his own Win chester over in his hands.

"I reckon I'm travelin' flat on my stomach," said Hopalong, slinging the big canteen over his head. "I'll go with you till we has to stop, let you get set an' then make a run for it. Seein' that th' Kid has got a repeater, too, you'll be able to keep lead flyin' most of th' time I'm in th' open if you don't pull too fast; an' when you run out of cartridges I'll start with my Colts. I'll be close enough, then, to use 'em right. When you see that I'm under th' buildin' go back quite a ways so th' fire won't show you xip too plain, an' watch th' roof. I'll start a fire under that loophole before I leave, an' that'll spoil their view through it; an' I ain't leavin' before I've fixed things so them fellers will have so much to do they won't have much time for sharpshootin'. That buildin' will burn like a pine knot"

"Then yo're comin' back th' way you go in?" asked Red.

"Shore," answered Hopalong. "Everythin' plain?"

"Watch me," ordered Red, his hand rising and falling. J 'If we space our shots like this we ought to be able to reload while th' other is emptyin' his gun. Is it too slow?"

"No," said Johnny, considering.

"No," said the man with the canteen, watching closely. "It'll take that long to throw a gun into th' loophole an' line it up, in this light."

"Not bein' used to a repeater like Red is," suggested Johnny, "I'd better shoot th' second string that'll give us three of 'em before it's my time to reload. Red can slide 'em in as fast as I can shoot 'ern out, timin' 'em like that."

"You can put 'em through that hole as good as I can," said Red. "It's near point-blank shootin'. You do th' shootin' an' I'll take care of loadin' both guns. We can't make no blunders, with Hoppy out there runnin' for his life."

"That's why I ought to do th' runnin'," growled Johnny. "I can make three feet to his two."

"It's all settled," said Hopalong, decisively. "I got th' kerosene, an' I'm keepin' it. Come on. No more talkin'."

They followed him over the course he had picked out and with a caution which steadily increased as they advanced until at length they went ahead only when the crescent moon was obscured by drifting clouds. Ahead loomed the two-story gambling-hall, its windowless rear wall of bleached lumber leaden in the faint light. An occasional finger of fire stabbed from its south wall to be answered by fainter stabs from the open, the reports flat and echoless. A distant voice sang a fragment of song and a softened laugh replied to a ribald jest. A horse neighed and out of the north came quaveringly the faint howl of a moon-worshiping coyote.

The three friends, face down on the sand, now each behind a squat bush, wriggled forward silently but swiftly, and gained new and nearer cover. Again a cloud passed before the moon and again they wriggled forward, their eyes fixed on the top of the roof ahead, two of them heading for the same bush and the other for a shallow gully. The pair met and settled themselves to their satisfaction, heads close together as they consulted about the proper setting of the rear sights. One of them knelt, the rifle at his shoulder reaching out over the top of the bush, his companion sitting cross-legged at his side, a pile of dull brass cartridges in the sombrero on the ground be tween his knees to keep the grease on the bullets free from sand.

The kneeling man bent his head and let his cheek press against the stock of the heavy weapon, whispered a single word and waited. Twice there came the squeak of a frightened rat from his companion and instantly from the right came an answering squeak as the figure of a man leaped up from the gully and sprinted for the lead-colored wall, the heavy, jarring crash of a Winchester roaring from the bush, to be repeated at close intervals which were as regular as the swing of a pendulum. A round, dark object popped up over the flat roof line and the cross-legged man on the ground threw a gun to his shoulder and fired, almost in one motion. The head dropped from sight as the marksman slid another cartridge into the magazine and waited, ready to shoot again or to ex change weapons with his kneeling friend.

The runner leaped on at top speed, but he automatically counted the reports behind him and a smile flashed over his face when the count told him that the second rifle was being used. He would have known it in no other way, for the spacing of the shots had not varied. Again the count told of the second change and a moment later an other extra report confirmed his belief that the roof was being closely watched by his friends. A muffled shout came from the building and a spurt of fire flashed from the loophole, but toward the sky and he fancied he heard the sound of a falling body. Far to his left jets of flame winked along a straggling line, the reports at times bunched until they sounded like a short tattoo, while be hind him the regular crashing of an unceasing Winchester grew steadily more distant and flatter.

His breath was coming in gulps now for he had set himself a pace out of keeping with the habits of years and the treacherous sand made running a punishment. During the last hundred feet it was indeed well for him that Johnny shot fast and true, that the five-hundred grain bullets which now sang over his aching head were going straight to the mark. He suddenly, vaguely realized that he heard wrangling voices and then he threw himself down onto the sand and rolled and clawed under the building, safe for the time.

Gradually the jumble of footsteps over his head impressed themselves upon him and he mechanically drew a Colt as he raised his head from the earth. Suddenly the roaring steps all went one way, which instantly aroused his suspicions, and he crawled hurriedly to the black darkness of a pile of sand near the bottom of the south wall, which he reached as the steps ceased. No longer silhouetted against the faint light of the open ground around the building, a light which was bright by contrast with the darkness under the floor, he placed the canteen on the ground and felt for chips and odds and ends of wood with one hand while the other held a ready gun.

There came the sharp, plaintive squeaking of seldom-used hinges, which continued for nearly a minute and then a few unclassified noises. They were followed by the head of a brave man, plainly silhouetted against the open sand. It turned slowly this way and that and then became still.

"See anythin'?" came a hoarse whisper through the open trap.

There was no reply from the hanging head, but if thoughts could have killed, the curious whisperer would have astonished St. Peter by his jack-in-the-box appearance before the Gates.

"If he did, we'd know by now, you fool," whispered another, who instantly would have furnished St. Peter with another shock.

"He'd more likely feel somethin', rather than see it," snickered a third, who thereupon had a thrashing coming his way, but did not know it as yet.

The head popped back into the darkness above it, the trapdoor fell with a bang, and sudden stamping was followed by the fall of a heavy body. Furious, high-pitched cursing roared in the room above until lost in a bedlam of stamping feet and shouting voices.

"He ought to kill them three fools," growled Hopalong, indignant for the moment; and then he shook with silent laughter. Wiping his eyes, he fell to gathering more wood for his fire, careless as to noise in view of the free-for-all going on over his head. Removing the plug from the canteen he poured part of the oil over the piled-up wood, on posts, along beams and then, saturating his neckerchief, he rubbed it over the floor boards. Wriggling around the pile of sand he wet the outer wall as far up as his arm would reach, soaked two more posts and another pile of shavings and chips and then, corking the nearly empty vessel, he felt for a match with his left hand, which was comparatively free from the kerosene, struck it on his heel and touched it here and there, and a rattling volley from the besiegers answered the flaming signal. Backing under the floor he touched the other pile and wriggled to the wall directly under the loophole. Again and again the canteen soaked the kerchief and the kerchief spread the oil, again a pile of shavings leaned against a wetted post, and another match leaped from a mere spot of fire into a climbing sheet of flame, which swept up over the loop hole and made it useless. As he turned to watch the now well-lighted trapdoor, there came from the east, barely audible above the sudden roaring of the flame, the reports of the rifles of his two friends, the irregular timing of the shots leading him to think that they were shooting at animated targets, perhaps on the roof.

The trapdoor went up swiftly and he fired at the head of a man who looked through it. The toppling body was grabbed and pulled back and the door fell with a slam which shook the building. Hopalong's position was now too hot for comfort and getting more dangerous every second and with a final glance at the closed trapdoor he scrambled from under the building, slapped sparks from his neck and shoulders and sprinted toward his waiting, anxious friends, where a rifle automatically began the timed firing again, although there now was no need for it. Slowing as he left the building further and further behind he soon dropped into a walk and the rifle grew silent.

"Here we are," called Johnny's cheery voice. "I'm admittin' you did a good job!"

"An' *I'm* sayin' you did a good one," replied Hopalong. "Them shots came as reg'lar as th' tickin' of a clock."

"Quite some slower," said Red. "That gang can't stay in there much longer. Notice how Mac's firin' has died down?"

"They're waitin' for 'em to come out an' surrender," chuckled Hopalong. "Keep a sharp watch an' you'll see 'em come out an' make a run for it."

"Better get back to th' cayuses, an' be ready to foller," suggested Red.

"No," said Johnny. "Let 'em get a good start If we stop 'em here Mac may get a chance to cut in."

"An' we'll mebby have to kill some of th' men we want alive," said Hopalong. "Let 'em get to that valley an' think they're safe. We can catch 'em asleep th' first night"

The gambling-hall was a towering mass of flames on the south and east walls and they were eating rapidly along the other two sides. Suddenly a hurrying line of men emerged from the north door of the doomed structure, carrying wounded companions to places of safety from the flames. Dumping these unfortunates on the ground, the line charged back into the building again and soon appeared leading blind-folded horses, which bit and kicked and struggled, and turned the line into a fighting turmoil. The few shots coming from the front of the building increased suddenly as McCullough led a running group of his men to cover the north wall. A few horses and a man or two dropped under the leaden hail, the ac curacy of which suffered severely from the shortness of breath of the marksmen. The group expanded, grew close at one place and with quirts rising and falling, dashed from the building, pressing closely upon the four leaders, and became rapidly smaller before the steadying rifles of its enemies took much heavier toll. Before it had passed beyond the space lighted by the great fire only four men remained mounted, and these were swiftly swallowed up by the dim light on the outer plain.

McCullough and most of his constantly growing force left cover and charged toward the building to make certain that no more of their enemies escaped, while the rest of his men hurried back to get horses and form a pursuing party.

Chapter XXXIII
Surprise Valley

Hopalong turned and crawled away from the lurid scene, his friends following him closely. As soon as they dared they arose to their feet and jogged toward where their horses waited, and soon rode slowly northeastward, heading on a roundabout course for Sweet Spring.

"Take it easy," cautioned Hopalong. "We don't want to get ahead of 'em yet. If my eyes are any good th' four that got away are Kane, Corwin, Trask, an' a Greaser. What you say?"

Reaching the arid valley through which Sand Creek would have flowed had it not been swallowed up by the sands, they drew on their knowledge of it and crossed on hard ground, riding at a walk and cutting northeastward so as to be well above the course of the fleeing four, after which they turned to the southeast and approached the spring from the north. Reaching the place of their former vigil they dismounted, picketed the horses in the sandy hollow and lay down behind the crest of the ridge. Half an hour passed and then Johnny's roving eyes caught sight of a small group of horsemen as it popped up over a rise in the desert floor. A moment later and the group strung out in single file to round a cactus chaparral and revealed four horsemen, riding hard. The fugitives raced up to Bitter Spring, tarried a few moments, and went on again, slowly growing smaller and smaller, and then a great slope of sand hid them from sight.

Hopalong grunted and arose, scanning their back trail. "They've been so long gettin' out here that I'm bettin' they did a god job hidin' their trail. I can see Mac an' his gang ridin' circles an' gettin' madder every minute. Well, we can go on, now. By goin' th' way I went before we won't be seen."

"How long will it take us?" asked Red, brushing sand from his clothes as he stood up.

"Followin' th' pace they're settin' we ought to be there tonight," answered Hopalong. "Give th' cayuses all they can drink. If them fellers hold us off out there we'll have to run big risks gettin' our water from that crick. Well, let's get started."

The hot, monotonous ride over the desert need not be detailed. They simply followed the tracks made by Hopalong on his previous visit and paid scanty attention to the main trail south of them, contenting themselves by keeping to the lowest levels mile after burning mile. It was evening when they stopped where their guide had stopped before and after waiting for nightfall they went on again in the moonlight, circling as Hopalong had circled and when they stopped again it was to dismount where he had dismounted behind a ridge. They picketed and hobbled the weary, thirsty horses and went ahead on foot. Following instructions Red left them and circled to the south to scout around the great ridge of rock before taking up his position at the head of the slanting trail from the valley. His companions kept on and soon crawled to the rim of the valley, removed their sombreros and peered cautiously over the edge. The faint glow of the fire behind the adobe hut in the west end of the sink shone in the shadows of the great rock walls and reflected its light from bowlders and brush. Below them cattle and the horses of the caviya grazed over the well-cropped pasture and a strip of silver told where the little creek wandered toward its effacement. Moving back from the rim they went on again, looking over from time to time and eventually reached the point nearly over the fire, where they could hear part of the conversation going on around it, when the voices raised above the ordinary tones.

"You haven't a word to say!" declared Kane, his out stretched hand leveled at Trask, the once- favored deputy sheriff. "If it wasn't for your personal spite, and your d d avarice, we wouldn't be in this mess tonight! You had no orders to do that."

Trask's reply was inaudible, but Corwin's voice reached them.

"I told him to let Nelson alone," said the sheriff. "He was dead set to get square for him cuttin' into th' argument with Idaho. But as far as avarice is concerned, you got yore part of th' eleven hundred."

"Might as well, seeing that the hand had been played!" retorted Kane. "What's more, I'm going to keep it. Any body here think he's big enough to get any part of it?"

"Nobody here wants it," said Roberts. "Th' boys I had with me, an' Miguel, an' myself have reasons to turn this camp fire into a slaughter, but we're sinkin' our grievances because this ain't no time to air 'em. I'm votin' for less squabblin'. We ain't out of this yet, an' we got four hundred head to get across th' desert. Time enough, later, to start fightin'. I'm goin' off to turn in where there ain't so much fool noise. I've near slept on my feet an' in th' saddle. Fight an' be damned!" and he strode from the fire, keen eyes above watching his progress and where it ended.

The hum around the fire suffered no diminution by his departure, but the words were not audible to the listeners above. Soon Corwin angrily arose and left the circle, his blankets under his arm. His course also was marked. Then the two Mexicans went off, and the eager watchers chuckled softly as they saw the precious pair take lariats from the saddles of two picketed horses and slip noiselessly toward the feeding caviya. Roping fresh mounts, and the pick of the lot, they made the ropes fast and went back to the other horses. Soon they returned with their riding equipment and blankets, saddled the fresh mounts and, spreading the blankets a few feet beyond the radius of the picket ropes, they rolled up and soon were asleep.

"Sensitive to danger as hounds," muttered Johnny.

"Cunnin' as coyotes," growled Hopalong, glancing at the clear-cut, rocky rim across the valley, where Red by this time lay ensconced. "I hope he remembers to drop their cayuses first Miguel's worth more to us alive."

"An' easier to take back," whispered Johnny. "We want 'em all alive an' we'd never get 'em that way if they wasn't so played out. They'll sleep like they are dead luck is with us."

Down at the dying camp fire Kane, his back to the hut, talked with Trask in tones which seemed more friendly, but the deputy was in no way lulled by the change. He sensed a flaming animosity in the fallen boss, who blamed him for the wreck of his plans and the organization. Muttering a careless good night, Trask picked up his blankets and went off, leaving the bitter man alone with his bitterness.

Tired to the marrow of his bones, so sleepy that to remain awake was a torture, the boss dared not sleep. In the company of five men who were no longer loyal, whose greed exceeded his own, and each of whom nursed a real or fancied grudge against him and who searched into the past, into the days of his contemptuous treatment of them for fuel and yet more fuel to feed the fires of their resentment, he dared not close his eyes. On his person was a modest fortune compacted by the size of the bills and so well distributed that unknowing eyes would not suspect its presence; but these men knew that he would not leave his wealth behind him, to be perhaps salvaged from a hot and warped safe in the smoking ruins of his gambling-house.

He stirred and gazed at the glowing embers and an up-shooting tongue of flame lighted up the small space so vividly that its portent shocked through to his dulled brain and sent him to his feet with the speed and silence of a frightened cat. He was too plain a target and too defenseless in the lighted open, and like a ghost he crept away into the darker shadows under the great stone cliff, to pace to and fro in an agonizing struggle against sleep. Back and forth he strode, his course at times erratic as his enemy gained a momentary victory; but his indomitable will shook him free again and again; and such a will it was that when sleep finally mastered him it did not master his legs, for he kept walking in a circular course like a blind horse at a ginny.

When he had leaped to his feet and left the hut the watchers above kept him in sight and after the first few moments of his pacing they worked back from the valley's rim and slipped eastward.

"Here's th' best place," said Hopalong, turning toward the rim again. They looked over and down a furrow in the rock wall. "We'll need two ropes. It'll take one, nearly, to reach from here to that knob of rock an' go around it. Red's got a new hemp rope bring that, too. If he squawks about us cuttin' it, I'll buy him a new one. Got to have tie ropes."

Johnny hastened away and when he returned he threw Red's lariat on the ground, and joined the other two. Fastening one end around the knob of rock he dropped the other over the wall and shook it until he could see that it reached the steep pile of detritus. Picking up the hemp rope he was about to drop it, too, when caution told him it would make less noise if carried down. Slinging it over his shoulder he crept to the edge, slid over, grasped the rope and let himself down. Seeing he was down his companion was about to follow when Johnny's whisper checked him.

"Canteens better fill 'em while it's easy."

Hopalong drew his head back and disappeared and it was not much of a wait before the rope was jerking up the wall and returned with a canteen. To send down more than one at a time would be to risk them banging together. When they all were down Johnny took them and slipped among the bowlders, Hopalong watching his progress. For caution's sake the water carrier took two trips from the creek and sent them up again one at a time. Soon his friend slid down, glanced around, took the hemp rope and cut it into suitable lengths, giving half of the pieces to Johnny and then without a word started for the west end of the valley, treading carefully, Johnny at his heels.

Roberts, sleeping the sleep of the exhausted, awoke in a panic, a great weight on his legs, arms, and body, and a pair of sinewy thumbs pressing into his throat. His struggles were as brief as they were violent and when they ceased Hopalong arose from the quiet legs and re leased the limp arms while his companion released the throat hold and took his knees from the prostrate chest. In a few minutes a quiet figure lay under the side of a rock, its mouth gagged with a soiled neckerchief and the new hemp rope gleaming from ankles, knees, and wrists.

Corwin, his open mouth sonorously announcing the quality of his fatigue, lay peacefully on his back, tightly rolled up in his blankets. Two faint shadows fell across him and then as Johnny landed on his chest and sunk the capable thumbs deep into the bronzed throat on each side of the windpipe, Hopalong dropped onto the blanketswathed legs and gripped the encumbered arms. This task was easy and in a few minutes the sheriff, wrapped in his own blankets like a mummy, also wore a gag and several pieces of new hemp rope, two strands of which passed around his body to keep the blanket rolled.

The two punchers carried him between two bowlders, chuckled as they put him down and stood up to grin at each other. The blanket-rolled figure amused them and Johnny could not help but wish Idaho was there to enjoy the sight He moved over against his companion and whispered.

"Shore," answered Hopalong, smiling. "Go ahead. It's only fair. He knocked you on th' head. I'll go up an' spot Kane. Did it strike you that he must have a lot of money on him to be so h--l-bent to stay awake? I don't like him pacin' back an' forth like that. It may mean a lot of trouble for us; an' them Greasers are too nervous to suit me. When yo're through with Trask slip off an' watch them Mexicans. Don't pay no attention to me no matter what happens. Stick close to them two. I'll give you a hand with 'em as soon as I can get back. If you have to shoot, don't kill 'em," and the speaker went cautiously toward the hut.

Johnny removed his boots and, carrying them, went toward the place where he had seen the deputy bed down; but when he reached the spot Trask was not there. Thanking his ever-working bump of caution for his silent and slow approach he drew back from the little opening among the rocks and tackled the problem in savage haste. There was no time to be lost, for Hopalong was not aware that any of the gang was roaming around and might not be as cautious as he knew how to be. Why had Trask forsaken his bed-ground, and when? Where had he gone and what was he doing? Cursing under his breath Johnny wriggled toward the creek where he could get a good view of the horses. Besides the two picketed near the sleeping Mexicans none were saddled nor appeared to be doing anything but grazing. Going back again Johnny searched among the bowlders in frantic haste and then decided that there was only one thing to do, and that was to head for the hut and get within sight of his friend. Furious because of the time he had lost he started for the new point and finally reached the hut. If Trask was inside he had to know it and he crept along the wall, pausing only to put his ear against it, turned the corner and leaped silently through the door, his arms going out like those of a swimmer. The hut was empty. Relieved for the moment he slipped out again and started to go toward Kane.

"I'll bet a month's pay "he muttered and then stopped, his mind racing along the trail pointed out by the word. Pay! That was money. Money? As Hopalong had said, Kane must have plenty of it on him money? Like a flash a possible solution sprang into his mind. Kane's money! Trask was a thief, and what would a thief do if he suspected that the life savings of a man like Kane might easily be stolen? And especially when he had been so angered by the possessor of the wealth?

"I got to move pronto!" he growled. "I'm no friend of Kane's but I ain't goin' to have him killed not by a coyote like Trask, anyhow. We got to have him alive, too. An' Hoppy?" His reflections were such that by the time he came in sight of Kane his feelings were a cross between a mad mountain lion and an active volcano. He stopped again and looked, his mind slowly forsaking rage in favor of suspicion. Kane was walking around in a circle, his eyes closed; his feet were rising and falling mechanically and with an exaggerated motion.

"War dancin'?" thought Johnny. "What would he do that for? He ain't no Injun. I'm sayin' he's loco. Kane loco? Like hell! Fellers like him don't get loco. Makin' medicine? I just said he ain't no Injun. Prancin' around in th' moonlight, liftin' his feet like they had ropes to 'em to jerk 'em. An' with his eyes close shut! I'm gettin' a headache an' I'm settin' tight till I get th' hang of this walkin' Willy. Mebby he thinks he's workin' a charm; but if he is he ain't goin' to run it on me!"

He pressed closer against the bowler which sheltered him and searched the surroundings again, slowly, painstakingly. Then there came a low rustling sound, as though a body were being dragged across dried grass. It was to his left and not far away. If it is possible to endow one sense with the total strength of all the others, then his ears were so endowed. Whether or not they were strengthened to an unusual degree they nevertheless heard the rubbing of soft leather on the bowlder he lay against, and he held his breath as he reversed his grip on the Colt.

"Hoppy, or Trask?" he wondered, glad that his head did not project beyond the rock. A quick glance at the milling Kane showed no change in that person's antics and he felt certain that he had not been detected by the boss. He froze tighter if it is possible to improve on perfection, for his ears caught a renewal of the sounds. Then his eyes detected a slow movement and focussed on a shadowy hand which fairly seemed to ooze out beyond the rock. When he discerned a ring on one of the fingers he knew it was not Hopalong, for his friend wore no ring. That being so, it only could be Trask who was creeping along the other side of the rock. Johnny glanced again at the peripatetic gang leader and back to the creeping hand, and wondered how high in the air its owner would jump if it were suddenly grabbed. Then he men tally cursed himself, for his independent imagination threatened to make him laugh. He could feel the tickle of mirth slyly pervading him and he bit his lip with an earnestness which cut short the mirth. The hand stopped and the heel of it went down tightly against the earth as though bearing a gradual strain. Johnny was reassured again, for Trask never would be stalking Kane if he had the slightest suspicion that enemies, or strangers, were in the valley, and he hazarded another glance at Kane.

The mechanical walker was drawing near the rock again and in a few steps more would turn his back to it and start away. By this time Johnny had solved the riddle, for although such a thing was beyond any experience of his, his wild guess began to be accepted by him: Kane was walking in his sleep. Where was Hopalong? He hoped his friend would not try to capture the boss until he, himself, had taken care of Trask. This must be his first duty, and knowing what Trask would do very shortly he prepared to do it.

He got into position to act, moving only when the slight sound of Kane's footfalls would cover the barely audible noise of his own movements. Kane's rounding course brought him nearer and then several things happened at once. The owner of the hand leaped from behind the rock and as his head popped out into sight a Colt struck it, and then Johnny started for Kane; but as he reached his feet something hurtled out of the shadows to his right and bore the boss to the ground. Then came the sound of another gun-butt meeting another head and the swiftly moving figure seemed to rebound from the boss and sail toward Johnny, who had started to meet it. He swerved suddenly and muttered one word, just as Hopalong swerved from his own course. They both had turned in the same direction and came together with a force which nearly knocked them out. Holding to each other to keep their feet, they recovered their breath and without a word separated at a run, Hopalong going to Kane and Johnny to Trask. Less dazed by the collision than his friend was, Johnny finished his work first and then helped Hopalong carry Kane to the shelter of the rock.

"Good thing you forgot what I said about watchin' them Greasers," grunted Hopalong. "It's them next, if "his words were cut short by two quick shots, which reverberated throughout the valley, and without another word he followed his running companion, and scorned cover for the first few hundred yards.

When they got close to the trail they saw two bulks on it, which the moonlight showed to be prostrate horses.

"Where are they, Red?" shouted Johnny. "They're th' only ones free!"

"Down near you somewhere," answered the man above, and his words were proved true by a bullet which hummed past Johnny's ear. He dropped to his stomach and began to wriggle toward the flash of the gun, Hopalong already on the way.

Cut off from escape up the trail the two Mexicans tried to work toward the hut, from which they could put up a good fight; but their enemies had guessed their purpose and strove to drive them off at a tangent.

Red, watching from the top of the cliff, noticed that the occasional gun flashes were moving steadily northwestward and believed it safe to leave his position and take an active hand in the events below. After their experience on the up-slanting trail the Mexicans would hardly attempt it again, even though they managed to get back to the foot of it, which seemed very improbable. The thought became action and the trail guard started to wriggle down the declivity, keeping close to the bottom of the wall, where the shadows were darkest. Because of the necessity for not being seen his progress was slow and quite some time elapsed before he reached the bottom and obtained cover among the scattered rocks. The infrequent reports were further away now, and they seemed to be getting further eastward. This meant that they were nearer to the hut, and his decision was made in a flash. The hut must not be won by the fugitives, and he arose and ran for it, bent over and risking safety for speed. After what seemed to be a long time he reached the little cleared space among the rocks, bounded across it, and leaped into the black interior of the hut. Wheeling, he leaned against the rear wall to recover his breath, watching the open door, a grim smile on his face. While keeping his weary watch up on the rim he had craved action, and congratulated himself that he now was a great deal nearer to it than he was before.

Meanwhile the two fugitives, not stomaching a real stand against the men whom they had seen exhibit their abilities in Kane's gambling-hall, had managed to work on a circular course until they were northwest of the hut and not far from it. This they were enabled to do because they were not held to a slow and cautious advance by enemies ahead of them, as were the old Bar-20 pair. They were moving toward the hut, not far from the north wall of the valley, when they blundered upon Trask. In a moment he was released and began a frantic search for his gun, which he found among the rocks not far away. Losing no time he hurried off to release the man he would have robbed, glad to have his assistance. Kane went into action like a spring released and began a hot search for his Colt. When he found it, the cylinder was missing and suspicious noises not far away from him forced him to abandon the search and seek better cover, armed only with a deadly and efficient steel club.

Hopalong and Johnny, guided entirely by hearing, fol lowed the infrequent low sounds in front of them, thinking that they were made by the Mexicans, and drew steadily away from the hut. The Mexicans, motionless in their cover, exulted as their scheme worked out and finally went on again with no one to oppose them. Reaching the last of the rocky cover they arose and ran across the open, leaped into the hut and turned, chuckling, to close the door, leaving Trask to his fate.

Warned by instinct they faced about as Red leaped. Miguel dropped under a clubbed gun, but Manuel, writhing sidewise, raised his Colt only to have it wrenched from his hand by his shifty opponent. Clinching, he drew a knife and strove desperately to use it as he wrestled with his sinewy enemy. At last he managed to force the tip of it against Red's side, barely cutting the flesh; and turned Red into a raging fury. With one hand around Manuel's neck and the other gripping the wrist of the knife-hand, Red smashed his head again and again into the Mexican's face, his knee pressing against the knifeman's stomach.

Suddenly releasing his neck hold Red twisted, got the knife-arm under his armpit, gripped the elbow with his other hand and exerted his strength in a twisting heave. The Mexican screamed with pain, sobbed as Red's knee smashed into his stomach and dropped senseless, his arm broken and useless. Red dropped with him and hastily bound him as well as possible in the poor light from the partly opened door.

He had just finished the knot in the neckerchief when a soft, swift rustling appraised him of danger and he moved just in time. Miguel's knife passed through his vest and shirt and pinned him to the hard-packed floor. Before either could make another move the door crashed back against the wall and Kane hurtled into the hut, landing feet first on the wriggling Mexican. He put the knife user out of the fight and pitched sprawling. His exclamation of surprise told Red that he was no friend and now, free from the pinning knife, Red pounced on the scrambling boss.

The other struggles of the crowded night paled into in significance when compared to this one. Red's superior strength and weight was offset by the fatigue of previous efforts, and Kane's catlike speed. They rolled from one wall to another, pounding and strangling, Kane as innocent of the ethics of civilized combat as a maddened bob cat, and he began to fight in much the same way, using his finger-nails and teeth as fast as he could find a place for them. Red wanted excitement and was getting it. Torn and bleeding from nails and teeth, his blows lacking power because of the closeness of the target and his own fatigue, Red shed his veneer of civilization and fought like a gorilla.

Planting his useful and well-trained knee in the pit of his adversary's stomach, he gripped the lean throat with both hands and hammered Kane's head ceaselessly against the hard earth floor, while his thumbs sank deeply on each side of the gang leader's windpipe. Too enraged to sense the weakening opposition, he choked and hammered until Kane was limp and, writhing from his victim's body, he knelt, grabbed Kane in his brawny arms, staggered to his feet and with one last surge of energy, hurled him across the hut. Kane struck the wall and dropped like a bag of meal, his fighting over for the rest of the night.

Red stumbled over the Mexicans, fell, picked himself up, and reeled outside, fighting for breath, his vision blurred and kaleidoscopic, staring directly at two men among the rocks but seeing nothing. "Come one, come all damned you!" he gasped.

Trask, thrice wounded, hunted, desperate, fleeing from a man who seemed to be the devil himself with a six-gun, froze instantly as Red appeared. Enraged by this unexpected enemy and sudden opposition where he fondly expected to find none, Trask threw caution to the winds and raised the muzzle of the Colt. As he pulled the trigger a soaring bulk landed on his shoulders, knocking the exploding weapon from his hand and sending him sprawling. Snarling like an animal he twisted around, wriggled from under and grabbed Johnny's other Colt from its holster. Before he could use it Johnny's knee pinned it and the hand holding it to the ground. A clubbed six-gun did the rest and Johnny, calling to Red to watch Trask, hurried away to see if Roberts and Corwin were loose. The latter was helpless in the blanket, but Roberts had freed his feet and was doing well with the knots on his wrists when Johnny's appearance and growled command put an end to his efforts. He put the rope back on the kicking feet and arose as Hopalong limped up.

"Phew!" exclaimed Johnny. "This has been a reg'lar night! Here, you stay with Corwin while I tote this coyote to th' hut." He got Roberts onto his back and staggered away, soon returning for the sheriff.

Dawn found six bound men in varying physical condition sitting with their backs to the hut, their wounds crudely dressed and their bounds readjusted and calculated to stay fixed. Kane was vindictive, his eyes snapping, and he seethed with futile energy, notwithstanding the mauling he had received. His lean face, puffed, discolored and wolfishly cruel, worked with a steadily mounting rage, which found vent at intervals in scathing vituperative comments about Trask, whom he still blamed for the predicament in which he found himself. Corwin, sullen and fearful, kept silent, his fingers picking nervously at the buckle and strap on the back of his vest. Roberts was angry and defiant and sneered at his erstwhile boss, sending occasional verbal shafts into him in justification of Trask. The two Mexicans had sunk into the black depths of despair and acted as though they were stunned. Trask, a bitter sneer on his face, glared unflinchingly at the storming boss and showed his teeth in grim, ironical smiles.

"Th' crossbreed shows th' cur dog when th' wolf is licked," he sneered in reply to a particularly vicious attack of Kane's. "What you blamin' me for? You took yore share of Nelson's money, an' took it eager. You heard me!" he snarled. "I don't care who knows it I got it, an' you took yore part of it. It was all right then, wasn't it? An' you didn't know it was his you let him make a fool of you an' wouldn't listen to me. But as long as you got yourn you didn't care a whole lot who lost it. Serves you right."

"Shut up!" muttered Roberts.

"Shut up nothin'," jeered Trask. "Think I'm goin' to swing to save a mad dog like him? Look at him! Look at th' dog breakin' through th' wolf! Wolf! Huh! Coyote would be more like it. Don't talk to me!" He looked at the camp fire and at the man busy over it. "I can eat some of that, Nelson," he said.

Johnny nodded and went on with the cooking.

Sounds of horses clattering down the steep trail suddenly were heard and not much later Red rode up on a horse he had captured from the rustlers' caviya and dismounted near the fire. His face was a sight, but the grin which tried to struggle through the bruises was sincere. He dropped two saddles to the ground, the saddles belonging to the Mexicans, which he had stopped to strip from the dead horses on the trail up the wall.

"Our cayuses went loco near th' crick," he said. "I left Hoppy to take off th' saddles an' let 'em soak themselves," referring to the three animals they had left up on the desert the evening before. "I'm all ready to eat, Kid. How's it shapin' up?"

"Grab yore holt," grunted Johnny. He stood up to rest his back. "Mebby it would be more polite to feed our guests first," he grinned.

Red looked at the line-up. "We'll have to feed 'em, I reckon. I ain't aimin' to untie no hands. Who's first?"

"Don't play no favorites," answered Johnny. "Go up an' down th' line an' give 'em all a chance." He faced the prisoners. ",You fellers like yore coffee smokin'?" Only two men answered, Roberts and Trask, and they did not like it smoking hot. "Let it cool a little, Red; no use scaldin' anybody."

The prisoners had all been fed when Hopalong appeared on another horse from the rustlers' caviya and swung down. "Smells good, Kid! an' looks good," he said. "I got all th' saddles on fresh cayuses, waitin' all but these here. We'll lead our own cayuses. That Pepper-hoss of yourn acts lonesome. She ain't lookin' at th' grass, at all." He sat down, arose part way and felt in his hip pocket, bringing out the cylinder of a six-gun. Glancing at Kane, to whom it belonged, he tossed it into the brush and resumed his seat.

Johnny's face broke into a smile and he whistled shrilly. Quick hoof beats replied and Pepper, her neck arched, stepped daintily across the little level patch of ground and nosed her master.

"Ha!" grunted Trask. "That's a hoss!" A malignant grin spread over his face and he turned his head to look at Kane. "Kane, how much money, that money you got on you now, would you give to be on that black back, up on th' edge of th' valley? All of it, I bet!"

"Shut up!" snapped Roberts, angrily.

"Go to h--l," sneered Trask, and he laughed nastily. "You wait till I speak my little piece before you tell me to shut up! No dog is goin' to ride me to a frazzle, blamin' me for this wind-up, without me havin' somethin' to say about it!" He looked at Red. "What was them two shots I heard, up there on top? They was th' first fired last night."

"That was me droppin' th' Greasers' cayuses from under 'em on th' ledge," Red answered. "They was pullin' stakes for th' desert."

"Leavin' us to do th' dancin', huh?" snapped Trask. "All right; I know another little piece to speak. Where you fellers takin' us?"

Red shrugged his shoulders and went off to get horses for the crowd.

A straggling line of mounted men climbed the cliff trail, the horses of the inner six fastened by lariats to each other, and three saddleless animals brought up the rear. They pushed up against the sky line in successive bumps and started westward across the desert.

Chapter XXIV
Squared Up All Around

Mesquite, still humming from the tension of the past week felt its excitement grow as Bill Trask, bound securely and guarded by Hopalong, rode down the street and stopped in front of Quayle's, where the noise made by the gathering crowd brought Idaho to the door.

"Hey!" he shouted over his shoulder. "Look at this!" Then he ran out and helped Hopalong with the prisoner.

Quayle, Lukins, Waffles, McCullough, and Ed Doane fell back from the door and let the newcomers enter, Idaho slamming it shut in the face of the crowd. Then Ed Doane had his hands full as the crowd surged into the bar room.

"Upstairs!" said Hopalong, steering the prisoner ahead of him. In a few minutes they all were in Johnny's old room, where Trask, his ropes eased, began a talk which held the interest of his auditors. At its conclusion McCullough nodded and turned to Hopalong.

"All this may be true," he said; "but what does it all amount to without th' fellers he names? If you'd kept out of th' fight an' hadn't set fire to that buildin' we would 'a' got every one of them he names. Gimme Kane an' th' others an' better proof than his story an' you got a claim to that reward that's double sewed."

Hopalong seemed contrite and downcast. He looked around the group and let his eyes return to those of the trail-boss. "I reckon so," he growled. "But have you got th' numbers of th' missin' bills?" he asked, skeptically.

"Yes, I have; an' a lot of good it'll do me, now!" snapped McCullough. "We was countin' on them for th' real proof, but that fool play of yourn threw 'em into th' discard! What'n h--l made you set that place afire?"

Hopalong shrugged his shoulders. "I dunno," he muttered. "Waz you aimin' to find th' missin' bills on them fellers?" he asked. "Would that 'a' satisfied you?"

"Of course!" snorted the trail-boss. "An' with Trask, here, turnin' agin' 'em like he has it would be more than enough. Any fool knows that!"

Hopalong arose. "I'm glad to hear you come right out an' say that, for that's what I wanted to know. I've been bothered a heap about what you might ask in th' line of proof. You shore relieve my mind, Mac. If you fellers will straddle leather we'll ride out where Kane an' th' others Trask named are waitin' for visitors. I don't reckon they none of them got away from Johnny an' Red."

"What are you talkin' about?" demanded McCullough, his mouth open from surprise.

"I mean we've got Kane, Roberts, Corwin, Miguel, an' another Greaser all tied up, waitin' to turn 'em over to you an' collect them rewards. As long as we know just what you want, an' can give it to you, I don't see no use of waitin'. I'm invitin' Lukins an' th' rest along to see th' finish. What you goin' to do with Trask?"

McCullough was looking at him through squinting eyes, his face a more ruddy color. Glancing around the group he let his eyes rest on Trask. Shrugging his shoulders he faced Hopalong. "Take him south, I reckon, with th' others. If he talks before a jury like he's talked up here I reckon he won't be sorry for it." He walked to a window and looked down into the street. "Hey!" He called. "Walt, get a couple of th' boys an' come up here right away. We got somebody for you to stay with," and in a few minutes he and the others left Walt and his companions to guard and protect the prisoner.

The sun was at the meridian when Hopalong led his companions into the Sand Creek camp and dismounted in front of Red, who was watching the [missing].

"Where's th' Kid?" he asked curiously.

"Don't you do any worryin'" answered. He lowered ms voice and put his mouth close to his friend's ear. "Th' Greaser on th' end is goin' to pieces. Pound him hard an' he'll show his cards."

The information was conveyed to McCullough, who stood looking at the downcast group. He strode over to Miguel, grabbed his shoulders and jerked him to his feet. Running his hands into the Mexican's pockets he brought out a roll of bills. Swiftly running through them he drew out a bill, compared it with a slip which he produced from his own pocket, whirled the bound man around and glared into the frightened eyes.

"Where'd you get this?" he shouted, shaking his captive.

"Kane geeve eet to me--he owe me money," answered the Mexican.

"What for?" demanded McCullough, shaking him again.

"I lend heem eet."

"You loaned him money?" roared the trail-boss. "That's likely! Why did he give it to you?"

Miguel shrugged his shoulders and did not answer. McCullough jerked him half around and pointed to Hopalong. "This man here saw you sneakin' from Kane's south stable with a smokin' Sharp's in yore hand after you shot Ridley. Trask says you did it. Is this all Kane gave you for that killin'?"

"I could no help," protested Miguel, squirming in the trail-boss' grip. "Wen Kane he say do theese or that theeng, I mus' do eet. I no want to but I mus'."

McCullough whirled around and faced Corwin. "That story you told me down in th' bunkhouse that night about how Bill Long shot Ridley is near word for word what Bill says about th' Greaser, an' Trask's story backs him up. How did you come to know so much about it? Come on, you coyote; spit it out! Who told you what to say?"

Corwin's silence angered him and he showed his teeth.

"There's a lynchin' waitin' for you in town, Corwin, if you don't stop it by speakin' up. Who told you that?"

Corwin looked away. "Miguel," he muttered. "I told you I was hopin' to get th' real one."

"He lie! I never say to heem one word!" shouted the Mexican. "He lie! Kane, he was the only one who know like that--beside me!"

"Stand up, Sheriff!" snapped McCullough. He searched the sullen prisoner and found two rolls of bills. Going quickly over them he removed and grouped certain of them, and then compared them with his list. "There's five here that tally with th' bank's numbers." he said, looking up. "Where'd you get 'em?"

"Won 'em at faro-bank."

"Won five five-hundred-dollar bills at faro, when everybody knows yo're a two-bit gambler?" shouted the trail-boss. "I'm no damned fool! Don't you forget what I said about th' lynchin', Corwin. I'm all that stands between you an' it. Where'd you get 'em? Like Trask said?"

Corwin's hunted look flashed despairingly around the group. "No," he said. "Kane gave 'em to me, to get changed into smaller bills!"

"Reckon Kane must 'a' robbed that bank all by hisself," sneered McCullough. "I never knowed he had diamond drills an' could bust safes. Didn't you go along to protect an' keep an eye on that eastern safe-blower that Kane had come to do th' job? Pronto! Didn't you?"

"I had to," growled Corwin, in a voice so low that the answer was lost to all but the man to whom he was talking.

McCullough gave him a contemptuous shove and wheeled to question Roberts. "Get up," he ordered, and searched the rustler trail-boss. "By G-d!" he exclaimed when he saw the size of the roll. "You coyotes was makin' money fast! There's near three thousand here! Let's see how they compare with my list." In a few moments he nodded. "How'd you get these five hundred-dollar bills? Kane give 'em to you, too?"

"No, Kane didn't give 'em to me!" snapped Roberts in angry contempt. "I earned 'em as my share of th' bank robbery, along with Corwin, th' white-livered snake! Kane didn't give in to either of us." He glared at the one-time sheriff. "I'm sayin' plain that if I ever get a chance I'm aimin' to shoot this skunk, along with Trask. You hear me?"

"If you ain't got a gun, hunt me up an' I'll lend you one," offered Idaho.

"Shut up!" snapped McCullough, glaring at the puncher. Whirling he pushed Roberts away. "It'll be a long time before you shoot anybody or anythin'. Now, then," he said, stepping up in front of Kane: "Get up!"

Kane arose slowly, his eyes burning with rage. He submitted to the exploring fingers of the trail-boss and maintained a contemptuous silence as his shirt was whipped right out of his trousers and the two money belts removed from around his waist.

McCullough opened the belts and his eyes at the same time. Neatly folded bunches of greenbacks followed each other in swift succession from the pockets of the belts and, scattering as they were tossed into a pile, made quite an imposing sight. Staring eyes regarded them and more than one observer's mouth gaped widely.

"Seven thousand," announced McCullough, reaching for another handful. "I'm sayin' you wasn't leavin' nothin' behind." He looked up again after a moment. "Eighteen thousand five hundred," he growled and picked up another handful. "Holy mavericks!" he breathed as the last bill was counted and placed on the new pile. "Forty-nine thousand eight hundred and seventy! You was takin' chances, totin' all that with this gang of thieves! Fifty thousand dollars, U. S.!"

Handing his written list to Quayle, he selected the five-hundred-dollar bills and called off the numbers laboriously, Quayle as laboriously hunting through the list. It took considerable time before they were checked off and put to one side, and then he looked up.

"There's still a-plenty of them bills missin'," he announced. "Where did they get to?"

Hopalong stepped forward and drew a roll from his pocket. "Here's what I found on Sandy Woods when he died in this camp," he said, offering it to the astonished trail-boss.

McCullough took it, opened and counted it and called the numbers off to the excited holder of the list.

"They're all on th' list th' Lord be praised!" said Quayle.

"Where'd Sandy Woods come in this?" demanded' McCullough, looking around from face to face.

Roberts sneered. "Huh! He was th' man that took th' safe-blower out of th' country. He didn't have no hand in th' bank job. I'm glad th' skunk died, an' I'm glad it was me that planned his finish. He shore must 'a' held up that feller. How much is there, in th' bank's bills?"

"Five thousand," answered the trail-boss.

"He got it all, cuss him!" snorted Roberts.

McCullough looked at Kane. "I never hoped to meet you like this," he said. "I ain't goin' to ask you no questions--you can talk in court, an' explain how you came to have so many of th' registered bills; an' there's other little things you can tell about, if somebody don't tell it all first." He turned to Hopalong. "We'll be takin' these fellers to th' ranch now."

"Better take th' reward money out of that bundle," replied Hopalong, nodding at the money in the hands of the trail-boss. "We've dealt 'em like you asked, an' gave you th' cards you want. Our part is finished."

McCullough looked from him to the prisoners and then at his friends. "How can I hand it to you?" he asked. "Where's Nelson? He's settin' in this."

"He'll show up after th' money's paid," said Red innocently as he arose.

McCullough hesitated and looked around again. As he did so Idaho carelessly walked over to Red, smoothing out a cigarette paper, and took hold of a paper tag hanging out of Red's pocket and pulled it. Carelessly rolling a cigarette he shoved the tobacco sack back where he had found it, but he did not leave Red's side. Blowing a lungful of smoke into the air he smiled at McCullough.

"Shucks, Mac," he said. "You shouldn't ought to have no trouble findin' them rewards in that unholy wad. An' mebby you could find Nelson's missin' eleven hundred on Trask, if you looked real hard. I like a man that goes through with his play."

"I'm not lookin' for no eleven hundred at all!" snapped McCullough. "An' I ain't shore that they've earned th' reward, burnin' that buildin' like they did! They let these fellers get away, first!"

"I just handed you th' money I found on Sandy Woods," said Hopalong. "That's like givin' it to you to pay us with. H--l! You act like you hated to make good Twitchell's bargain. Well, of course, you don't have to take this bunch, nor th' money, neither; but I'm sayin' they don't go separate. Suits us, Mac we'll keep th' whole show money an' all, if you say so."

"Fine chance you got!" retorted the trail-boss, bridling. "They're here an' I'm takin' 'em, with th' money."

"There ain't nobody takin' nothin'," rejoined Hopalong calmly, "until th' bargain's finished. Don't rile Johnny, off there in th' brush; he's plumb touchy." His drawling voice changed swiftly. "Come on--a bargain's a bargain. Five thousand, now!"

"Mac!" said Quayle's accusing voice.

The trail-boss looked at the money in his hand and slowly counted out the reward amount, careful not to include any of the registered bills. "Here," he said, handing them to Hopalong. "You give us a hand gettin' 'em to th' ranch?"

"If three of us could catch 'em, an' bring 'em here," said Hopalong, coldly, "I reckon you got enough help to take 'em th' rest of th' way if you steer clear of town."

"Don't worry, Mac," said Idaho, cheerfully. "I'll go along with you."

The trail-boss growled in his throat and began, with Lukins, Waffles, and Quayle, to get the prisoners on the horses. This soon was accomplished and he headed them south, Lukins on the other side, Quayle and Waffles and Idaho bringing up the rear.

"Better come to town for a celebration," called the proprietor, disappointment in his voice. "Ye can leave at dawn."

Johnny shook his head. "There's a celebration waitin' at th' ranch," he shouted, and turned to find his two companions mounted and his black horse waiting impatiently for him. Mounting, he wheeled to face northward, but checked the horse and turned to look back in answer to a faint hail from Idaho, and grinned at the insulting gesture of the distant puncher.

He replied in kind, chuckled, and dashed forward to overtake his moving friends.

"Home!" he exulted. "Home an' Peggy!"

www.ingramcontent.com/pod-product-compliance
Lightning Source LLC
Chambersburg PA
CBHW070514310726

48976CB00002BA/429